Unreal Estate written by Stefan Gagne
(copyright 2002-2014)
Artwork by Amanda Kilburn

Thanks to J. Norburn, the Franklin W.
Quackenbush Home for Displaced Rainforest
Monkeys, and all of my awesome Kickstarter
backers for making this possible.

Keep supporting free web novels!
Read more at: stefangagne.com

It was 13 o'clock on a typical day when the sky turned blue.

Mallory didn't even have to open his eyes to know something was wrong. When the sky turns blue, you can feel it down to your core... the air feels thick around you, harder to breathe than usual. Sounds are muffled and dull, and your stereo hearing gets slapped back down to mono. In short, it feels unreal.

For some reason, it had been happening around 13 o'clock more often than not. He wasn't sure why; maybe it was because he was on break during those hours. A full morning in classes, a full afternoon of plowing fields... he needed this little lunchtime break. It was his time to flop down on the nearest grassy hill, put on his headphones, and listen to the streams over the integrated (but quite low bandwidth and tinny sounding) RealNet audio receiver. He could tune out his world, and tune into others...

He turned down the volume, because he knew what was coming next.

"MALLORY HEISENBERG!" a loud voice almost echoed through the acoustic cotton wads in the air.

"Over here, Dad!" Mallory called back, sitting up. He quickly packed away his headphones into his school sack, before his father could spot them. "We're running in safety mode again, huh?"

The man in peasant farmer's clothes (you can tell from the amount of dirt and color tones ranging the spectrum from brown and green) jogged to a halt, glancing up at the sky with a frown of displeasure. "Blue Sky of Death. Third time this week," he reminded him. "Third time, Mallory. We really should call in a technician tonight to fix the blasted thing once and for all. Something can't be right if it's crashing this often..."

"C'mon, Dad! They charge an arm and a leg, why should we pay 'em through the nose? I can handle it just fine," Mallory said, smiling to try to cheer his father up. "Although, if you'd like to cut down on my chores a bit in payment...?"

The elder farmer crossed his arms, giving his boy a flat look. No words.

"Yeah, yeah, but it was worth a try," Mallory said, hiking his sack up over one shoulder.

The windmill was quite a ways away, but there wasn't a rush. Safety mode would last at least a day before anything else went wrong; the glossy brochures had said so, complete with language like 'Money Back Guarantee!'. Mallory knew the way, and walked on past the planting fields, past the farmers and his classmates at work in the fields. Past the classroom building, past the church, even past his own house... to the tallest structure in the land.

Not that he needed to climb to the top of the windmill. The engine was, in fact, kept in the basement.

Mallory studied the instrument panel. All the blinking red warning lights, the pop-up images projected on the cheap liquid display pane above the machine. He read the complicated error code. He scratched his chin.

"This may take a while," he said.

"A while?" his father asked. "You're usually done with it pretty quickly..."

Mallory shrugged, trying to look noncommittal. "It varies, Dad. Six of one, half a dozen of another. You should probably go tell the Council this can be fixed... they're likely running around like chickens with their heads cut off as usual. I'll join you when I finish, I promise!"

With a nod, the elder Heisenberg walked up the stairs, closing the basement door behind him.

The boy looked up, and listened for the departing footsteps. Thud, thud, thud... thud.... quiet.

He sat down and waited a few minutes. Picked at some wax that had been building in his ear lately.

Once enough time had passed, he walked up to the complicated piece of reality technology, and repaired it via a good swift kick to the metal casing.

The lights on the machine went out.

The lights on the machine clicked back on.

Reality asserted itself. Faint, stereoscopic sounds could be heard. Colors felt less muted. The air was musty and old, but he was technically in the basement of a windmill.

Better this cheap trick than to worry him with how I REALLY fix the engine each time it crashes, Mallory thought to himself for the dozenth time. He shut down the engine's display panel to reduce load on the windmill's power generators, walked back up the stairs, and headed back to his favorite grassy hillside. Back to the old grind.

Things were shaping up to be another typical day in Mallory's life... classes, relaxation, reality crashes, reality reboots, chores, watching the network, bed. Nineteen years to date in this loop. Day in, day out, same old same old, the usual, the tried and true, staying the course...

He'd read once on the network about how people sailed across worlds with oceans, in vehicles built to harness the power of the wind. There would be spots in the middle of an ocean where no wind blew and the waves were calm... doldrums, they were called. Places where everything just sort of sits there until you die of boredom and/or hunger, with no wind to aid your escape.

To carry the metaphor too far (which he had an uncanny habit of doing even in his own mind) he was hungry for something other than the boredom of this world, and even the perpetual wind which drove the windmill wasn't enough to blow him to new ports of call. He'd need tornado-like winds, winds that tore up trees by the root and dumped them in parts unknown. Unfortunately, tornadoes never popped up on Grünwald, metaphorical or literal —it had been specifically designed to avoid dangerous weather, cultured to avoid dangerous situations. Even the rain was scheduled. This reality, this world, his home had been specifically designed to tick along at a nice and predictable pace. Nothing out of the ordinary could happen here.

As he pondered such tornados, walking along to rejoin his life already in progress, a house fell on him.

01: Boy Meets Worlds

For most people, that would be the end of their life story. Humorous obituaries on tabloid video streams would follow: "Boy With Hideous Luck Hit By Falling House!", right next to "Bizarre Creatures From Nullspace Impregnated Me!".

Fortunately for Mallory's continued existence, three factors other than his bad luck came into play:

1. **Survival Instincts**, the sort that are coded in the genes and kick in despite having a soft life where the nastiest surprise you have to worry about is whether or not you passed your exam in Baking and Bread Goods 101. These allowed Mallory to hit the ground nice and fast when he noticed a very rectangular, non-cloud shaped shadow surrounding him.

2. **Geographical Layout**, specifically the two lumpy hills to his left and right which formed a nice valley just deep enough for a human to flop face-first into, and were firm enough to support the house's weight without crushing him.

In short: Mallory hit the deck and miraculously survived.

It did take a few moments for his non-death to register in his brain, of course. Once he had the nerve to open his eyes, he saw brown. Once he had the nerve to wipe the dust kicked up from the impact off his glasses, he saw light in the narrow crack between the lumpy underside of the house and the ground.

Some part of him which was too stunned to be stunned pondered how new and interesting this situation was.

Because you can never have too much bewildering confusion, next Mallory observed a pair of legs stepping down to the ground from what was presumably the front door of the house. One foot after the other; sandal-like shoes of some sort, although not the dirt- and animal-dung-covered sort he was used to. They looked like something that might very well be "fashion," to his untrained farmer's boy eye. The stunned/nonstunned part of him also recognized the faint brown tinge of pantyhose, which he had never seen in person, but plenty of times on video streams...

As if the legs weren't enough new stimulus to make his brain go *pop*, the woman who leaned down to peer into the narrow space at him had enough details to make his brain go *WHUMPH* and trickle out his ears in twin gray streams of liquid. Metaphorically, of course. Long brown hair, and—

"Hello?" she called to him, staring at him funny.

"Hello?" Mallory replied, since it was polite to greet strangers.

"Hello," she said back, waving her hand, a bit puzzled at this.

"Hello!" Mallory spat back cheerfully, since it was nice to be cheerful and have a good outlook on life.

"Haven't I seen you somewhere?" she asked, because... well, she thought she had seen him somewhere before.

"Uh..." Mallory said, his mind racing to cope with all this. "I don't think so, I've never left this reality. Sorry."

"Ah. You're not dead, right? Or paralyzed from the waist down or something like that?"

Mallory wiggled his toes in his hand-me-down shoes.

"I don't think so," he said.

"So what are you still doing down there? You pinned?"

The dirt really did a number on his favorite battered gray hooded sweatshirt, but he wriggled his way out and was standing on his own two feet next to her in a matter of moments. (Which made him feel a bit silly for lying there under the house the whole time.)

Now that the two of them were upright, Mallory managed more than a narrowly defined view of her. She was about his age, but dressed in more business-y attire than he'd ever seen someone wearing... at least, someone who wasn't on a video stream. It'd make sense, considering the mobile home implied she was from outside Grünwald, and was...

...and was glaring at him slightly, arms crossed. "You sure you didn't get a concussion? You've got this blank, glassy stare thing going on..."

"Uh... sorry, sorry," Mallory apologized, meeting her eyes. "It's just... there aren't a lot of pretty girls in Grünwald."

"Λh," she said, emphasizing the 'Ah'. "That statement would make you either charmingly innocent or a skirt chaser, then..."

"Huh? I'm not... uh, what's a 'skirt chaser'?"

"Charmingly innocent it is," she said, without technically being charmed by it. "You got a name, impressionable youth? Does this reality have a name? Can I please get a little information now that we've established you're of sound mind and body and capable of answering questions?"

"Oh, sorry! You're in Grünwald. So, uh... is this your house?" Mallory asked, looking at the brick-and-aluminum-siding structure with well painted window shutters and a brass knocker on the door. "Why'd you park it here? The Dock is a few kilos that way."

"Grunwald?"

"No, Grünwald."

"What's the difference?"

"Two dots, I think," Mallory replied.

"Right. Grünwald. Grünwald, Grünwald..." she thought aloud, trying to recall a few details. "Ah. That would explain the pastoral acres of green and corn as high as an elephant's eye. Returning to your questions: yes, this is my house, and if I had stolen it I probably wouldn't fess up to you. And finally, I didn't PARK here, I quite obviously crashed here—who're those people?"

Now would be a good time to pause and reflect in further detail upon Mallory's frame of mind.

Many things of a dangerously interesting nature had happened to Mallory in the last two minutes. Ordinary people would be very unsettled by this; for someone who lived a sheltered life for nearly two decades, it was enough to throw his crossbeam askew on the treadle and then some.

He had heard of Transients, of course. That's how he knew what the house truly was: a mobile home that doesn't take root anywhere, but moves from reality to reality like a tractor. (The only vehicles he had handy to make the analogy were tractors. If his brain were operating at full speed he'd recall ground cars and other sorts of ships from his daily video stream viewing of other realities.) Transients were uncommon in Grünwald, which rarely interacted with other realities beyond basic trade of goods, but he had seen trade buildings come and go from the Docks before.

This is also why he knew to ask "Why didn't you park at the Dock," since typically houses, cargo huts, small businesses and other mobile buildings would 'land' at the specially zoned Dock area on the other side of the village. This house had not parked at the Dock; it had parked on top of him. He was able to register this fact quickly. So, you have to give him some credit; despite all that had gone completely wrong in this situation, his brain zeroed in on relevant details. Unfortunately for him, the information would prove to be completely useless at that time—and also unfortunately, his distraction caused him to lose track of who was approaching.

"Huh?" he said, his mind moving in six directions at once (two of which were only theoretical under conventional reality) as the group approached. "Uh, dunno—"

"You are trespassing!!" the leader of the small group accused, pointing the Finger of Accusation firmly at the woman, despite trembling with rage. "You did not contact us ahead of time to consult on your arrival in Grünwald and your presence is illegal! You could be bringing in foreign diseases and contaminating our crops, or worse! We demand you leave immediately, woman!"

"Oh, uh, this is the Council," Mallory introduced well after the fact. "Um. Some of them, at any rate. Uh, hi, Dad."

The woman stepped forward, blocking Mallory (who would likely only befuddle matters more than they were befuddled) and attempted to be cool and charming. "I'd love to leave, but I have a problem," she said, in more even and measured tones than she had used with him. "I didn't land here on purpose. My Reality Engine for Mobiles crashed while I was trying to get to another reality. We're all very lucky Safety Mode kicked in and I didn't phase into existence through something else or suffer structural damage on landing. A close call, but everything's fine, yes?"

"Uh, but it nearly crushed me—"

"So if you could just let me borrow your resident Reality Engineer or can give me the address to one that's local to Grünwald, I'll get repaired and be on my way," she concluded.

The Council member frowned at her. Not that he had stopped frowning since his arrival, but he made a point to frown just a little more. "We haven't got a Reality Engineer. What do you think this is, Urbana? Where you can snap your fingers and get anything you want? We're a farming and cooking community. And your presence is disrupting the harmony of the—"

"Then it's going to have to keep disrupting until I can call in an Engineer from RealWare," she interrupted, losing a bit of her cool and dropping into 'curt' levels of attitude. "That's the way it is. I'll warn, they've been known to take days to service Class C contracts like mine—but I assure you I have proper passport data and I'm not carrying anything that'll cause trouble here—"

"We can have you Deported!" the Councilmember threatened, shaking a fist with rage! or at least trying to be threatening and fist-shaking but ending up somewhere between 'unimpressive' and 'a complete joke.' "We may be backwoods to you 'city folk' but we've got a Deporter and can kick your ugly house out of here in an instan... in a few minutes or so!"

"...ugly house?" she asked, her eyebrows tightening. "Now, listen up, Farmer John—"

"I can fix it!"

This time, she didn't interrupt him. In fact, all attention turned to him directly.

"Uh... I mean, I think I can," Mallory clarified. "Reality Engines for Realities and Reality Engines for Mobiles are based on the same... err... stuff. Technology! The same technology. And Dad, you know I can fix Reality Engines! I could get her up and running and nobody would have to do anything, okay? It'll be fine!"

Because he was being a complete pain in the ass, the Council leader looked aghast at this proposal. "What, allow you to enter that... that monstrosity?" he asked, nodding towards the house. "I won't allow it! Outsiders are not to be trusted. She could kidnap you, or worse things I can't even think of at the moment! If—"

Since Mallory had played the peacekeeper role once already, his father stepped up to the plate. "He can fix it," he said, calm and reasonable about it. "Then the problem will be solved. I'm in favor of it."

"Your voice isn't as great on our Council as you think, Josef!" one of the generic old guys who hadn't spoken up spoke up with. "If you seriously think —"

"I have no problems with my boy entering the house," Josef Heisenberg said. "Let's clear this up and get back to work. You're not in favor of a delay of work, yes?"

"Terrific!" Mallory cheered, resisting the urge to jump for joy. "Okay! I'll be done in a minute! Let's go, miss!"

"Wha?" she asked, before being dragged into her own front door by the excited youth.

With that, Mallory stepped into another world. Or at least a piece of a world he had never seen in person before which had been dumped on his front lawn, which was just as exciting to him...

It's not like homes in Grünwald were crude mud huts or anything of the sort.

They were well constructed, with good firm wood harvested from the local forests and nails custom made by the town blacksmith. The fireplaces were built of stout brick, the furniture crafted of quality joinery, and generally speaking the standard of housing was nice and high. Plumbing and electricity, absolute musts for modern cooking, were also available.

But aluminum siding? Weather stripping around windows? Drywall, plaster, wallpaper, carpeting, central air conditioning... these were all things Mallory had only seen on a tiny Video Network Player over a low-bandwidth video stream. To have this house—this icon of all things non-Grünwaldian— drop in his lap (and on his back) was an opportunity he couldn't pass up!

So naturally, upon entering the house, he started gawking like a tourist, soaking up the sights like a sponge, and rubbernecking like only a redneck can rubberneck.

The walls weren't made of wood! They were solid, flat shapes. Was that plaster? Or maybe concrete? And there were things plastered all over them, little funny shapes and things in eye-pleasing symmetric patterns! That table there, in the kitchen to his left (because even in an alien environment like this, Mallory damn well knew a kitchen when he saw one)... was it metal? A whole table made of metal! True, there were metal cook surfaces in the Grünwald schools, but those were a luxury! And—

"Hello?"

—in the room to his right, that was a sofa, yes, although unlike any one he'd ever seen... it was huge! Sort of L-shaped and pressed up against the wall surrounding a low table, who could sit at a table that low and why were there huge books on it with names like 'Cheeses of Pia Pia' and 'Urbana Tower: Modern Wonder Of The Multiverse'—

"Yoo hoo, farm boy?"

—but the one thing, the one thing that drew him like a fly to a bug zapper, was the Video Network Set.

If there were a God (and like all good multiversal folk, Mallory was an Agnostic Atheist) this would be His Video Network Set.

"It's almost as big as I am but not quite but BOY is that a big screen!!" he exclaimed, nearly floating over to the hulking monolith of electronic might and majesty. "This is a RealWare Video Network Set 3.11, isn't it, I've seen ads for it how many subscriber streams do you get boy oh boy I can't get anything but the free streams on my cheesy little Video Network Player and man how much did this cost how could you afford all this where'd you get it and what's that place like 'cause I've never left Grünwald and—"

"HEY!!"

"Yes?" Mallory asked, turning to face the irate woman.

"Reality Engine?" she prompted, while tapping her foot and folding her arms and giving off universal vibes of impatience. "Fix it? Like you said you would? I'm not paying you to watch video streams, farm boy."

"You're paying me?"

"It's a figure of speech. There. Right there," she said, pointing... sort of next to and around the corner from the video set. "In that niche there, that's where we keep the engine."

"Oh, right, right," Mallory said, and made a very big mistake as he walked right over to the machine and gave it a sharp blow with his fist. The metal of the box echoed nicely...

...and the wobbly liquid readout, which was showing a blue Safety Mode screen, wobbled itself back to the familiar purple RealWare logo as it rebooted. The subsequent quiet hum was proof positive of normal operations.

"There, fixed," he said, dusting off his hands even though they weren't dirty. "Hey, do you live in this house alone? It's HUGE! You're a Transient, right? Why do you bring such a huge house around with you? It's two stories, right? What's on... the.... second floor...?"

Even someone as dense as Mallory was could pick up on that kind of evil energy radiating off the woman.

"You... PUNCHED... my Reality Engine!!?" she shouted with sound and fury. "YOU HIT MY REALITY ENGINE??"

"Uh... well..." Mallory backpedaled in more ways than one, as she stomped up to confront him (and pin him against one of those nicely wallpapered surfaces). "It's funny, but I've found generally all these things need is a good whack to get 'em going again—"

"Are you insane?!" she shouted, grabbing him by his comfy sweatshirt and throttling him ever so gently. "You MORON, you could've crashed the thing completely and sent my house careening into Nullspace!!"

"I-I could have?" Mallory asked, curiosity perking up at exactly the wrong time, as usual. "Really? I didn't know that. It's funny what you learn when—"

She let go of him, began a silent count from five to one backwards to control her murderous rage, then pointed firmly to the open door.

"OUT," was her edict.

"But—"

Dirt doesn't taste very good, Mallory decided, after landing face first in it.

He staggered back to his feet, spitting out clods of grass and topsoil that were jammed in his mouth from the impact. Before he could say a word, the door of the Transient house slammed shut, the whole building started to glow purple... and in a soundless flash, it was gone.

The Head Councilman helped Mallory dust off his clothes, while scowling with an 'I told you so' look. "Foreigners! Rude bastards, all of 'em," he reaffirmed. "We're better off without them. You all right, Mallory? She didn't give you drugs or show you improper things?"

"Uh, I don't think so," Mallory said, bending his neck left and right to work out the kinks.

"Right. Well then, situation averted. Good work, boy. You may resume your duties now," the Councilman spoke, as the group started to disband and return to normality. "Lads, let's get back to work. Josef, I'll see you at the meeting hall."

The elder Heisenberg nodded, and turned to follow—before being tugged back by his sleeve.

"She had a video set, Dad! A 3.11 model!" Mallory hiss-whispered, at least until the others had distanced themselves enough. "It was HUGE! I've never seen one that expensive before!"

"Yes, son. Offworlders can be very rich," his father confirmed.

"But, I mean, it took a year's savings just to buy my used Video Network Player 1.0!"

Josef looked around, uncertain. "Son... keep your voice down. You know we're not supposed to have ANY video sets. It's not the law, but if the Council knew... "

"Why is that, Dad? Why is it bad to have one?"

"It's our way, son. You know that. We try to lead a simple life... away from the politics and the chaos of other realities, away from RealWare's interests," Josef emphasized. "Life can be hard enough without taking on the problems of the multiverse at the same time."

"But... but Dad, there's so much STUFF out there!" Mallory insisted, waving his arms around wildly to mime the nature of 'Much Stuff'. "Things I can barely believe! Houses that move from reality to reality, just like that one... it was a big house, too. Bigger than any one in the village! I can't even imagine living in a place like that!"

"I can, and you wouldn't like it. A wandering rogue's lifestyle? Transients can't really say they're home, no matter where they happen to be. Mallory... you've got a good life here, son. An honest one and a stable one. I don't mind you watching network shows... but you know what I say, right?"

"That the grass is always greener on the other side?" Mallory quoted.

"No."

"That a fool can have infinite riches, but only a wise man knows what truly holds value?"

"Not that, I meant—"

"Is it the one about the dog and the bone and the bridge and his reflection?"

"I meant to say it's time for your chores. Get back to work."

"...nuts."

The sun passed along its arc in the sky and the moon rose, because that's how Grünwald wanted things to be, and that's how the Reality Engine told things to be.

Mallory fell in his arc and landed flat on his back, back in his bed. His 1.0 player was pulled out from under his pillow and turned on in one smooth motion.

The end of another typical day. Classes, relaxation, reality crashes, reality reboots, mysterious house falls on him, chores, watching the network, bed. Nineteen years to date in this loop. Day in, day out, same old same old, the usual, the tried and true, staying the course...

Mysterious houses.

It all reminded him of the tornado. A tornado carrying a house away... something about that had a curious echo deep in his brain. The dream of being swept away, carried away to a distant land where everything was colorful and new and wonderful and...

And it felt distinctly like he had missed the tornado. Weather report said chances of it returning were slim, because every day in Grünwald was nice and sunny.

He thumbed the rocker dial on the side of the small handheld device, scrolling up the list of free video streams. One caught his eye; RealWare Travel & Weather. He clicked the rocker dial once to load it, waited the requisite one minute for the buffer to fill, then let the grainy images of dream worlds filter through his head...

"The streets of Urbana! The waterslides of Aquarius!" an announcer with a precisely spoken voice declared, while the photos blurred and faded into each other. "The harsh jungles of Tribal Alpha! The neon paradise of Nippon! Even the private corporate retreats of Reality Prime! When you're a certified RealWare Reality Engineer, the multiverse is at your disposal to dispose of as you please!"

Reality Engineer. She'd mentioned something about that, about how she needed one. But he helped her out instead. And he never even learned her name...

"Enjoy a wide variety of experiences as you support our vast customer base with the kind of quality service and customer care they've come to expect from RealWare," he continued, the spinning RealWare logo filling his small screen. The RealWare Sound, the official audio intellectual property of RealWare, played gently across his ears as their familiar slogan followed the notes. "For quality reality products and technical support, there's only one true choice: RealWare!"

And then it was on to a weather report about the oceanic temperatures of Aquarius, and what sorts of swimwear were trendy there this time of year.

Mallory had never learned how to swim. The only bodies of water on Grünwald were in artificial reservoirs. He'd never own a swimsuit in his lifetime...

Unless he left, of course. Went somewhere with pools, or even real oceans.

It wasn't swimming that drew him... that was simply one of his many desires. Something much stronger, and less definable, tugged at him. He felt a need to go elsewhere—to be somewhere else.

This was something he never mentioned to anyone, not even his father, but he never felt like he truly fit in Grünwald. He could farm, he could cook, he was a good Grünwaldian in every aspect a Grünwaldian must be good... but he didn't have many friends. Something about him seemed to put them off, like he was an outsider in any circle, even the one he was born into. There wasn't any proof of it; nobody was rude to him. Things just never seemed to click properly.

Mallory sat up in his bed, watching the cute weather girl point out where rain would be falling in Nippon today. She had on a skirt a lot like the girl who he met today...

He didn't have to leave forever. That would be silly. But maybe, just maybe, he could leave for a little while. 'Vacation' was an alien concept to the locals, but on the video streams Mallory had learned it inside and out.

But the crops were coming in. He had chores to do, classes to attend. It was silly to think he could leave, even for a short time—and how would he leave, anyway? He hadn't a clue how one actually left their home reality, not unless they had a mobile building of some sort...

It was futile. He clicked off his video player, not wanting to watch the sights anymore tonight. Sleep, however, was not going to smack him upside the head anytime soon... and a glass of milk sounded good to wash his worries away about now.

The wooden steps creaked as he made his way down them; familiar creaks, ones he had memorized. The third step from the bottom would always be loudest... and tonight was no different.

What was different was his father enjoying the glass of milk he had descended that staircase to find. Not the same exact glass, of course, but A glass, and likely the same fluid ounces he would have ingested had his father not gotten there first. Which was not actually on his mind, but it's (probably not) worth pointing out anyway.

"Dad?" Mallory asked, surprised at this new development. "S'matter, can't sleep? You've got the seasonal rotation tomorrow, you know... you should get some rest."

"I'll be fine," Josef Heisenberg dismissed, as he set down his glass. "Mallory... come on, have a seat. You and your old man need to have a little talk. Not a bad one, though. You want some milk too?"

"Uh, yeah, thanks," Mallory thanked, pulling out a wooden chair and sitting at the wooden table while his dad poured the not-so-hard stuff. "What sort of a talk?"

"Mmm... how best to approach this..." Josef pondered aloud. "Been thinking about what you were saying before. About other realities, and such. You've got a bit of wanderlust, don't you, boy?"

"C'mon, Dad, you know I couldn't leave. Not with my classes and my chores, and the new crops being planted tomorrow. You'd need my—"

"But you do wish you weren't here, yes?"

"Dad... this is my home," Mallory reminded him. "Maybe... I have daydreams about other places, yes. But I'm not gonna leave because of a daydream."

"Why not? I did once."

The second surprise of the evening.

"You what?" Mallory asked.

"I left Grünwald, many years ago," Josef explained, leaning on the table and looking off through the kitchen window as he called up the memories. "I was actually a year younger than you are now. And I was really not interested in farming and cooking and all that, not when there were so many fascinating things just out of reach... in other realities. So, against my father's wishes, I left."

"You... against you... you... YOU left? You?"

"What, is there an echo in here?" Josef mocked, in a non-mean sort of way. "Yeah. Your old man wasn't always this calm and patient with things, I was a bit of a hotheaded fool then... but in the end, it was the right decision. I wouldn't have met your mother, rest her soul, if not for my travel. She was from Nippon. It's not widely talked about, but it's the honest truth."

"That's... I mean, that's... wow! It's... wow!" Mallory said, almost but not quite able to finish his own sentences. "I'm half Nipponese? It's funny, I don't look it..."

"Anyway... it's a hard life out there. I was being honest with you earlier about it. Here, we don't have many economic worries, no real politics to speak of... well, no, we have both, but they're on a much smaller scale. Out there it can be harsh. I learned the hard way; I went out with no plan, nowhere to live, and no job to make a living from. Shortly after we were married we came back to Grünwald. It was simply the best place we knew of to raise a family... and shortly after that, you arrived, and the rest is history."

"How come you didn't mention any of this before?" Mallory asked, curious. "I mean, the adventures... or at least, um, the experiences you must have had!"

"I guess... I didn't want you following in your foolhardy father's footsteps," Josef said, with a sigh. "I didn't want you making the same mistakes, so I didn't fill your head with nonsense about the glories of the outside world. Heh. And I still let you own a video player... go figure, eh?"

"Dad, Dad, it's okay. I'm not leaving. I—"

"I said I didn't want you to make the same mistakes, Mallory."

"I know, and—"

"That's why I want you to prepare ahead of time for your trip. I'll help you find a job and a place to live, give you some points to spend, and THEN you can go," Josef announced calmly. "That way you'll be prepared for what lies ahead. Is it a deal?"

"................wha?" Mallory asked, jaw having trouble returning to its full upright position.

"I said I made mistakes, but I didn't say I regretted it," Josef said, with a wry little grin. "Be honest, Mallory... you don't really want to live here all your life. You don't want to be a farmer, or a chef. You don't have to be; I just want you to approach reality in a realistic way."

"B-But... my chores, and the Council, and—"

"Eh, they'll grow to accept it in time," his father predicted. "Just as they accepted my leave, and my return. I'm on the Council now. That should say something about their standards and how much they REALLY adhere to them."

There wasn't a draft in the room, but Mallory could almost feel that tornado looming over the horizon again...

"You're serious about this, aren't you?" he asked. "You'd really help me and let me leave?"

"Would I lie to you? You're my only son. I want to help you get it right. Mallory... this is your future. You have to set out to find your own future; maybe my future isn't for you. Only way you can tell is if you go out there and look for it."

Despite sitting still in his chair, Mallory took the metaphoric first step forward without hesitation.

"Where do we start?" he asked.

The whirlwind day that kicked this wacky madcap adventure off with both feet running when they hit the ground... piffled out very quickly.

The process of preparing for his stage left exit took time. They had to work quietly; while the Council wouldn't stop them, exactly, they could get very cross if they knew. Josef smuggled in a very rudimentary RealNet Workstation —an economy model four hundred years obsolete, but it accessed the network all the same.

"Technically, your video player is the same sort of thing," his father had explained as he set up the battered workstation, a strange thing that looked like a video set attached to a rack of buttons with letters on them. "It's all RealNet in the end, the only communication medium people have that spans realities. RealNet carries streams; good for your video-only units, or sound-only units like your headphones... but it also has fully interactive things like this."

"Uh-huh," Mallory had said without totally understanding. "How do you know all this, Dad?"

"Your mother was a Reality Engineer. Worked for RealWare itself, before she quit to come to Grünwald with me. Now, this RealNet Node is a 'search node', which can find you job placement nodes, and this applet here can edit your résumé and this one here can blah blah blah blah blah blah..."

Two days of extreme hunt and peck typing later, some fibbing about his job experiences, some blatant lying about his job skills and he had a résumé ready.

The problem then became finding a job his dad would approve of.

Mallory could certainly cook, and there were plenty of jobs for chefs in Urbana. "Forget it," Josef said, vetoing it instantly. "Urbana is not fit for anybody but businessmen. Cooks, janitors, lower jobs like that... they have to LIVE there, and it's not a good place to live."

Mallory also was able to do some farming, and Aquarius was looking for people to take part in an experimental sea kelp farming operation. "Can you swim?" Josef asked, and that was the end of that.

There was an opening for a trainee chef in SubUrbana, but the rent cost for below-average housing there had an above-average price tag. "Have pity on your poor old man's pocketbook, he doesn't have many points left," Josef begged.

"Points?" Mallory had asked.

"Money, son. Not everybody in the multiverse barters like we do. You'll learn in time."

And of course, there was the esteemed role of the Reality Engineer.

"Mom was one, right?" Mallory argued. "And you know I've got the knack. Maybe I got it from her!"

"You'd have to take the Reality Engineer Certification Test, the REC," Josef explained. "According to your mother may she rest in peace, it's the most hideous educational experience ever devised by man and only 25% of the students who apply actually pass it. You'd have nowhere to live while you were studying and you can't study from here—"

"All right, all right, I get the point."

The point was that nothing was popping up that met every need he had. The whirlwind adventure was stalled out.

Five nights after they had made the secret pact to get Mallory off this plane of existence, he was no farther along than when he started.

Staring at the ceiling of his bedroom, with the glow of the cheap workstation monitor the only light that touched the walls, Mallory pondered his future. And his present.

At present, he was nothing to the multiverse at large. A half-trained chef, a newbie farmer. Nobody really needed farmers; chefs got paid peanuts. (Sometimes literally, on some of the more obscure realities.) He didn't have the cred to be a Reality Engineer. He had no skills anybody wanted. He wasn't wanted...

All he wanted was to get his foot in the door. Why was that so hard? He could adapt, he could learn; he was good at adapting to new situations! (Well, not really, but he thought he was. Very tragic.) Why not bite off just a LITTLE more than he could chew? Surely he could get to the chewing in quick time, be ready to go even if it was a rocky start, as the mixed metaphors almost but not entirely spoke to his internal grammar.

Of course, Pop wouldn't be happy about it. But what he didn't know...

Mallory swung his legs over and got back to his feet, walking across his room to the RealNet Workstation. He poked a random key to disable the colorful RealWare logo 'screen saver' (a term that even his dad didn't quite understand), accessed the job search node, and started bending reality to his liking.

First, he stated he had ten year's experience as a chef. This was true, even if the first year was spent learning how to boil water and how to make peanut butter and jelly sandwiches. Next he specified that he had overseen the tilling and crop rotation on 6000 acres of farmland—which made sense if you had handled the same two hundred acres or so over and over during your life. And finally, while crossing his fingers (which made it very hard to type) he stated he was a certified Reality Engineer.

Praying that he wasn't breaking some sort of obscure multiversal law, he keyed SEARCH and waited for the node to respond to his request.

Moments passed. Grünwald wasn't real high on the RealNet totem pole, and streams took a while to get there...

78 results found. Master chefs, agricultural experts, resident engineers... jobs spanning an insane amount of salaries and locales. He only recognized maybe 4.33333% of the realities represented...

He couldn't exactly go running to Daddy to help him sort through the list. He would have asked God to lend him a hand, but he wasn't quite sure if there were a God, which was the proper way to view things as he was raised. There was always blind luck, but with his sort of luck...

A story bubbled to the forefront of his brain.

"Ancestors," the trader had explained, when he traded some turnips for his precious (and now battered and hole-riddled) hooded sweatshirt. "In Nippon, they worship their ancestors or something. I don't see how it works, since once you're dead you're out of hearing range, and too buried in the ground to do anything worth note. But you see that symbol on the front of your finely crafted 100% cotton exquisite exotic sweatshirt thingy?"

"What, this?" Mallory had asked, poking at the embroidered symbol. Sort of a squiggly white thing meshed up against a squiggly black thing...

"That's a Yang Ying. Or a Ying Yang. Or somethin'. Anyway, it's spiritual," the trader explained. "It represents harmony. Everything in the multiverse in tune with everything else. Which I don't see, given how crazy the multiverse can be, but supposedly there's harmony out there somewhere. 'That which is separate becoming whole once more' and all that."

"So... what does that have to do with ancestors?"

"Dunno, you got me. So do you want it or not? One bag of turnips."

I'm half Nipponese, Mallory reasoned. That means I should be worshipping my ancestors.

Not quite sure if he was going about it the right way, he clasped his hands together in prayer like he saw in really old movies on the video network.

"Ohm... um... ooooohm," he tried chanting. "Ohm. ...Mom, if you're listening, help me find a job. Please? ...right, okay. Here I go."

Covering his eyes with one hand, making a pointy-finger with the other, he waved his finger around randomly, reaching forward... and eventually poking the glass of the workstation screen.

Peeking between two fingers, he read the entry he had hopefully selected via mystical spiritual powers beyond his comprehension.

```
Live-in REALITY ENGINEER wanted to maintain and
repair Reality Engine for Mobiles. 10k points
annually, room and board provided. See the
multiverse, meet interesting people, be a team player
in the hottest troubleshooting firm on the market. No
fixed address, please send resumes to nodebox
'JOBS@MIRAI'.
```

Granted, the amount of knowledge Mallory had of the multiversal job market could make an optimist declare the glass to be half empty. A shotglass. But even he knew that ten thousand points, compared to some of the other jobs he had looked at, was small potatoes. (It's easy to think in food metaphors when you tend to the soil for a living.) What's more, it was for his least strong suit: reality engineering. He barely understood the concept beyond giving funny machines a serious beating until they hummed 'ahh' instead of 'aagh'.

With a classic sigh of disappointment, he reached for the power switch on the workstation...

But this was the job his mother had selected, wasn't it?

See the multiverse. Meet interesting people... exactly what he was hoping for.

And so, on a whim, Mallory keyed in the commands to send his résumé along. They probably wouldn't reply tonight, so once again, his hand reached for the power swi—

A little blinking picture distracted him. Sort of a funny flower thing with a mail envelope superimposed on it. It was flashing and beeping and spinning and animating and generally doing everything except whipping out a megaphone and yelling "CLICK ON ME, STUPID!"

It took Mallory a minute to figure out what to do with it, since his dad hadn't shown him what the 'mouse' did. ("Your mother said real engineers only use keyboards," was his justification.)

The envelope flew away from the flower, opened, and a new box appeared.

```
           : Hello, received resume. Reading now.
```

Mallory froze, as if he were caught with his hand in the cookie jar. It was his first time communicating with anybody outside of shouting distance, and his first time communicating only by text...

```
: Looks good. We're in a tight fix here, the stupid
thing keeps crashing and we need to be on the move a
lot. You're certified, and that's all that matters,
                                        Mallory-san.
```

Nervously, his hands reached for the keys. He was supposed to reply, that much he could figure out...

```
> my family name is heisenberg, not san
    : Sorry, old Nipponese habit. When can you start?
> tomorrow i think
    : Good. I'm glad you understand we can't pay very
much, we haven't had any takers yet. We're currently
    at Urbana, Victor Suezo's Economy Dock, Row 12,
Column 3. Show at thirteen o'clock, UST. Listen, I'd
like to meet f2f before I officially hire you, okay?
> whatsf2f
        : Face to face? Is something wrong with your
  Workstation? All I'm getting is lowercase letters.
> No, Everything is fine
                             : See you tomorrow.
```

The on-screen box closed itself.

With that, Mallory was unofficially gainfully employed.

Almost there. Just a few more steps.

Step one, doctor the job offer to read 'Entry Level Chef' and present it as the truth while feeling mild guilt.

"It doesn't pay much, but I get room and board," Mallory explained, pointing to the piece of paper like a showroom piece. "I'll be the personal gourmet chef of a Transient home! I can't think of a better way to see the multiverse! Look, it even says 'See the multiverse!' So, um, that means I'm going to see the multiverse, and that's what I want. So. Uh. It's okay, right?"

Josef sat back in his kitchen chair, frowning very mildly. "I don't know, Mallory... the pay is a bit low..."

"Daaaad!" Mallory 3/4ths-whined. "C'mon, we haven't had anything pop up. This is a great offer! And... if it doesn't work out, I can always come back.

Pleaaase?"

1/4th of a whine later and the job was a lock.

Step two, pack.

This step proved to be the hardest of the three.

Mallory had always been a bit of a packrat; buying whatever trinkets and baubles and consumer cultural collectables the traders brought with them. There was his sweatshirt, his video player, his headphones... and of course, his nearly-complete run of Angst Boy holographic comics, his six of seven limited edition Love & Hate Glasses (available at a Joe's near you, at least, fifty years ago)... and his prized 8-Bit Commandos card collection.

Collecting things felt good to him in a way he couldn't quite put his finger on; the act of bringing together a complete set, scrounging, bartering, trading, searching as far and wide as he could from the comfort of his own home... it was as close as he could get to an adventure. All of his collections were incomplete, unfortunately. There's only so much hunting you can do while rooted to the fields.

Stuffing all of that valuable junk into a suitcase was not an option, so Josef quietly purchased a travel trunk from an old friend in the village. That could store all his goodies, all his clothes, and still have a little room left over. It was also over one hundred pounds and could only be rolled along on dinky little wooden wheels, but beggars couldn't be choosers and Mallory saw it as making a silk purse out of a square pig in a round hole.

Step three, hop a taxi and start his new life!

At least, try to hop a taxi before the Council got wind of what was going on and met them at the Grünwald Dock with intent of halting the entire adventure. Which, of course, is what happened.

The act of blocking them wasn't as dramatic as the Council Leader wanted. Instead of stepping boldly forward in great surprise just as they reached the gate leading to the docking slots, they had to stand at the gate and wait for the Heisenbergs to approach. Mallory took a long time getting to the dock despite being in plain sight, since he was lugging around three figures' worth of weight in luggage.

"We are not in favor of this!" the Councilman warned, shaking a mighty fist while the two were a hundred feet away.

"There's no law against it," Josef defended. "This is a private family matter, not a matter of Council."

"He is a valuable member of our community, and his presence in the fields will be missed! It will mean more work for the community at large to cover the gap he leaves behind! We won't allow it! Unmutual! UNMUTUAL!"

Josef groaned in mild irritation, and put a hand up to stop his boy's slow lugging progress. "I'll handle this," he said. "Wait here."

The elder Heisenberg approached the Council, as Mallory watched in befuddlement.

Arms were waved around, hand gestures were made. Voices were raised and lowered. Minutes went by. Arguments were repeated ad nauseam, and they went like this:

Council: "A!"
Josef: "B."
Council: "A!"
Josef: "C?"
Council: "A!"
Josef: "D...?"
Council: "A!!"
Josef: "E."
Council: "A. A, A, A! A—"
Josef: "$."
Council: "...OK."

"What was that all about?" Mallory asked, as the group and Josef went their separate ways.

"I paid them to ignore this," Josef admitted. "That's how I got out of this reality in the first place, ironically. I should have realized they'd accept nothing other than a bribe... I'm sorry, son. You'll have to start out with considerably fewer points than I wanted you to have... take this."

Mallory accepted the odd plastic card, studying the glowing number '0025' on it, as he stepped over the transition from the grassy fields of Grünwald and onto the concrete base of the Dock. "What's this thing?" he asked, turning the card over and over.

"It's a scorecard. Standard money transfer device; I put my savings on there for you, but they just drained nearly all of the funds. See, you remember what I said about points, right? Points get stored on that card. ...no, not ON it, Mallory, in it. No, don't try to open it. It's digital."

"Oh. What's 'digital' mean?"

"Unless inflation's been on the rise since I last took a taxi, I don't think you have enough money for a Transreality Taxi Company cab," Josef said, stopping in front of the only docking slot this dock had. He opened the door to the public RealNet terminal's booth, and keyed up a transportation search node.

"Darn. What if inflation is on the rise, though?"

"Then you absolutely can't afford a taxi."

"Oh. I was hoping that'd mean something good," Mallory said, looking around. "What're you doing now?"

"You've seen the Council using this workstation when the traders arrive, right? It's a special purpose workstation just for calling out to transportation companies. I'm trying to find you one with a low fare, so I have a search running at a transport node with a crosscheck on your asking price..."

Mallory smiled and nodded his head.

"You have no idea what I'm doing, do you?" Josef asked, looking up.

"No, not really," he replied, peering over Josef's shoulder at the search list. "But I'm expecting I'll pick this stuff up real quick. Eventually. ...hey, what about that one? There's a big zero in the fare column! I can sure afford a free cab! Or am I not supposed to kick a gift horse in the mouth or something?"

Scratching his chin, Josef furrowed his brow and twisted his lips into a frown. "I don't know, Mallory..."

"It's the only one under twenty-five on the list, Dad. We don't have a choice," the boy said, reaching around his father to select the company and click 'Hail Taxi'. "There. How long will it take for—"

The same flash, Mallory recalled. The same purple flash that that woman's house made when it vanished... although in reverse, with a building appearing flush against the edge of the dock slot before him...

...although 'building' was used in the loosest sense of the word possible.

To call it a ramshackle shantytown hut would be an affront to proud ramshackle shantytown huts everywhere.

Whoever built the thing seemed to have thrown it together from whatever materials were handy. One wall was a dented metal sheet; another was half-constructed of amateurishly laid bricks, half-constructed of a large, hardened wad of glue. The door was stolen from an abandoned refrigerator, and the window was only a window in the sense that it was a square-ish gap in the front of the hut. A smokestack made of cheap oven pipes jaunted merrily from the roof... right next to a big, blinking neon green sign.

In friendly letters, next to a grinning cartoon face of a guy with sunglasses, it read *MELLOW FELLOW'S SMILING TAXI SERVICE!!* with two exclamation marks. Some sort of strange music floated out of the window and the various cracks in the building... something mild but with a steady beat.

"..................what's that thing?" Mallory asked, after the utterly alien sight had set into his retinas.

"I'm not sure, but I suspect it's a taxi," his father replied, unable to take his eyes off the eyesore. "Transients can move around any kind of building, after all..."

The fridge door slammed open hard enough to nearly knock the building into component parts. Mallory jumped three feet backwards and thankfully landed on his feet.

"YO!" a scruffy looking guy who almost but not entirely didn't resemble the neon sign's cartoon said, leaning out of the doorway. "One of you two call for a cab? I's here! Let's get movin', time is money, and money is nothin'."

Josef took a few steps back as well, to join his son and whisper to him. "Maybe we should wait until another day, after I've earned some more points?" he suggested. "I don't like the looks of this..."

Shaking his head, Mallory grasped the handle of his rolling luggage once more. "No choice, Dad. My job interview is today. I gotta go today. Don't worry! Sure, this is... bizarre... but I have to learn how to deal with the bizarre, right? I'm officially a multiversal person! We fear nothing but fear itself and some other things!"

"Send me RealNet messages once you're settled in," Josef suggested, adjusting Mallory's jacket and other last minute nervous parent type actions. "And if you need to come home, I can try to arrange something. I'll send you some more points as soon as I can—"

"YO YO, c'mon!" the cabbie called out to them. "We on this trip or not?"

"Coming!" Mallory called back, stepping up to the edge of the dock, suitcase squeakily tugged along behind him. "'bye, Dad! I'll contact you soon, I promise! I love you!"

If only his mother could see him now, Josef thought. How proud she'd be...

After some tricky maneuvering to get the luggage over the door jam, the cabbie shut the entrance closed, and the adventure was finally underway!

Almost.

Mallory adjusted his eyes to the darkness inside the taxi hut. The inside was just as ratty as the outside... a few candles here and there, melted down to nearly nothing, were the only light source beyond the window. A portable iron oven kept the hut warm, and somehow generated steam to power the Reality Engine...

It didn't look a thing like the one in the woman's house. Hers was clean, metal, professional-grade. A true RealNet product. This one... it was lumpy, with bits taped in place or sottered cheaply. The liquid display was nowhere to be found, with a simple video screen much like his portable Video Network Player only less impressive.

"Can that thing really move this thing around?" Mallory had to ask, as Reality Engines were always a bit of a fascination to him.

"What, my Open Engine? This tub gets here and there on mighty wings of freedom, mon!" the guy who presumably was named Mellow Fellow exclaimed, giving the Reality Engine a few love taps not unlike Mallory's fix-it taps. "She'll get us where you wanna go. And speaking of which, let's be talkin' about where you wanna go. You saw my price, yah?"

"Zero, yah."

"Not quite zero," Mellow Fellow explained, having a seat on a beanbag chair and turning down the volume on his RealNet Audio Player, positioned helpfully at his side. "Have a seat on I's passenger beanbag. See, I's a businessman. I's barter. I's apprecatin' points, yah, but I's also accept other things. So, what you got?"

Mallory eased himself carefully into what he presumed was a seat (having never seen a beanbag chair before in his life). "Errr... I've got this scorecard thing, but it only has twenty-five points..."

"Your last pennies 'n coppers, eh?" the sunglasses-sportin' guy replied. "I's don't wanna be busting your piggy bank, Mon. You dig?"

"Yes, actually, I dig quite often to plant seeds and pull up crops when they're ripe! Why do you ask?"

"...uh-huh," he replied, looking a bit flatly at Mallory. "I's be thinkin' this is your first time away from this reality. I's right?"

"Gosh, how could you tell?"

"Magic. Okay, so that be your only nest egg. Like I's said, I's not gonna be deprivin' you of all you got in the way of the monies of the Babylonians. So, we barter. What you got to barter with? You DO know how to barter, yah?"

"Definitely! We barter all the time," Mallory said, finally feeling like he had a toehold on this conversation. He cracked open his luggage in a way that thankfully did not spill his life's possessions on the floor. "Umm, I have a lot of collectibles... although I'd hate to part with any, they were so hard to get... beyond that it's just clothes—"

The cabbie lunged forward, making Mallory fear for his life... although all he really was going for was Mallory's commemorative whistle-tube celebrating the 200th year of Aquarius's Aquazone Theme Park.

"All right!" Mellow proclaimed, studying it from all angles. "Now, THIS'll make a damn good bong!"

"A what?"

"I's taking this, and that be all I's taking," the cabbie replied, setting it aside for now. "So, payment's settled. Now, I's repeat from before: where you wanna go today?"

Mallory pulled the crumpled piece of paper from his pocket. "I wrote the address on this. It's in some place called Urbana. Can you get me there?"

The cabbie studied Mallory's crappy handwriting a moment. "Mmmm... I's can get you there. Real close to that address in Urbana, too. Gimmie a minute to 'figure the Engine and handle the Dockin' procs."

"You're doing what to the what?"

Rolling his eyes behind the sunglasses, the cabbie switched to a voice he'd use explaining things to a small child. "I's... makin' sure... we have a place to dock. Can't travel less we got a place to land, yeah?"

Mallory had a brief horrific flashback to a house landing on his head.

"Yes yes," he replied quickly, eyes wide. "Let's make sure we have somewhere to land this time. I think that's a very good idea. How long will this take?"

"Time be time, Mon."

"Okay. Uh. So how long is time?"

The hut shook slightly, and purple light flashed across Mallory's eyes.

"Time be nothin'," Mellow Fellow said, with a sly grin. "You're off world for the first time, Mon. Say hello to Urbana."

Mallory stepped onto the sidewalk, eyes bright and open to the new world!

"Hel-LO, UrbAAAAAAAAAAAAAAAAAAHHH!!!"

"Eh? What?" Mellow Fellow asked, peering around the flash-frozen-in-fear boy. "Somethin' wrong, man?"

TALL! TALL!

Everything was so TALL!...

Of course, Mallory had seen pictures of Urbana. It was featured quite often in the video stream news; most of the business deals in the multiverse went down here. He'd seen Urbana Tower. He'd seen the Square. None of this was new to him.

What was new to him was seeing those two-hundred-story skyscrapers on a screen more than two and a half inches tall.

For a brief moment, his inner caveman felt the urge to run and hide from the gods who were towering over him lest they crush him in a unit of time so small that it wasn't measurable with little rocks and pebbles and shadows. Then the modern guy in him forced his eyes to the pavement. Nice, sweet pavement. Concrete. Stable. Solid...

"I'm... I'm okay," Mallory spoke, breathing in the polluted air with lungs that were used to pristine, freshly flora-recycled oxygen. "Just a bit of a shock..."

"You sure you gonna be okay, mon?" Mellow asked, with genuine concern in his voice. "Look, you wanna get home, I-and-I's okay with that. Give you back your bong too. I's seen the effect Urbana has on folks who just steppin' out into the lands of Babylonia—"

"I'll be okay, honest," he insisted, stepping out of the taxi hut completely and onto the rock-hard ground of the dock sidewalk. "I can't go back now. I've got my whole future ahead of me!"

"Time be time, Mon."

"And time be nothin'," Mallory finished, adding the saying to his internal database of metaphors and wisdoms, to be scrambled until rendered meaningless for future use. "Yeah, I know. But I don't think my future employer sees things that way. We have a saying in Grünwald: the early bird gets wormed!"

"...I's agreein' on that," Mellow said, leaning back into his hut. "Okay. That address, that be in a dock three blocks from here. Right now, we be at Abel's Fifteen Minute Stopover Dock... you be seein' the gate there with the dock management office next to it?"

Mallory tried to look in that direction without letting his brain acknowledge the frighteningly tiny amount of sky he could see between the skyscrapers. Indeed, a squat brick building sat next to the main gate of the docking area. "I see it, yeah..."

"Okay, I-and-I's gonna clue your ass in. Docks, they usually be in a grid pattern," he explained. "Empty slots for buildings to land in, yah? Sidewalks to run between 'em. Okay, so walk down this here sidewalk, straight through that gate. You make a right. The STABLE buildings be in the same kinda grid, Urbana's real into grids, very Babylonian... so turn right and you walk down three blocks. You know what a block be?"

"Umm... it's like... wait, don't tell me, I know," Mallory insisted, trying to recall his video stream knowledge. "It's...a square clump of buildings separated by a paved street for ground traffic?"

"Hey, you got it! Okay. So you cross three streets. You see a sign, Victor Suezo's Economy Dock. That be what you want. You go through the gate, you go twelve rows deep and three rows to your right and that's where you be goin'. You got it all?"

"Hey, I'm an educated, modern lifestyle kinda guy," Mallory noted, with a bit of pride in his voice as he lugged his ridiculously large trunk on the ridiculously small wheels onto the sidewalk. "I can handle it, no problem! Thanks for the ride, Mister Fellow."

"Yo, that's Mellow," Mellow reminded him. "And I's likin' you, Mon. You need a ride anytime you message me on the RealNet, dig? Can't promise I-and-I come runnin' right away, but I's come eventually."

"Uh, thanks! Okay. Anything else I should know?"

"Yeah, try to avoid gettin' in trouble. You be new at this, and—"

"Ahh, don't worry! I'm not looking for trouble," Mallory spoke, grinning goofily. "I'm sure everything will be just fine! What could possibly go wrong?"

"Give me your scorecard!"

"Huh?"

"NOW!!"

"Well, okay," Mallory replied, puzzled as he pulled the small plastic card from his pocket and handed it to the strange young man. "But why do you want my— HEY! Where are you going?"

And off the stranger went, running along the sidewalk, shoving people aside as he went.

Mallory stood in place, waiting for him to come back, still not quite sure why the fellow was so insistent on having his scorecard.

It was good to take a break from walking. Now that he was getting used to the height of the buildings (or at least shoving them into a tar pit of denial deep within his brain) he was rather enjoying the sights of Urbana. The buildings had such colorful decorations on them; "Advertisements," just like the ones he saw in his video streams. Some of them were actually animated, showing people enjoying prepackaged food or helpfully informing him about why the Cougar traffic vehicle was the finest traffic vehicle in all of Urbana because of its 'Smart-Stick Tires'. If Mallory was ever in the market for a traffic vehicle, he would be certain to make the right choice and insist on Smart-Stick Tires! If...

Wait.

Something wrong. Something tugging at the back of his mind, something from one of the many news video streams he had absorbed over the years. Something about... coffee?

Which was odd, because he wasn't very thirsty. And besides, he forgot bring his favorite mug with him from—

Mug?

Mugged!

"I've been mugged!" Mallory realized, the realization coming as a very, very delayed shock to him.

Only twenty-five points, all the money he had in this life, and it was gone. Only a few minutes into his first trip outside Grünwald, and he'd completely screwed things up! The only way things could be worse was if the mugger took his luggage as w...

Where was his luggage?

The tar pit of denial threatened to upheave all his panic and paranoia. Alone in an alien place with no money to his name and no worldly possessions other than the shirt on his back and the pants on his legs and his underwear with his name sewn into them... a horrifying thought indeed. In a single moment of absolute rage at the multiverse and the horrors it had inflicted on his person, Mallory whimpered pathetically...

And found his scorecard pressed into his limp hand.

"Take it," she said. "It's yours, right? And this is your ratty old luggage, right?"

The '0025' on his scorecard flickered back at him, as if it was happy to see him. His other hand, guided by some dazed, wobbly muscular control grasped for the familiar feel of the wooden trunk handle...

"Y'know, when they do that, you've got three options," she instructed him. "You either kick their ass in righteous fury, or you run away screaming like a little girl."

"...and the third?" Mallory found himself asking.

"You fork over your stuff like you did just there and run home crying to mommy. Certainly not what I'd pick, but then again, not everybody can be as madskilled as I am... you okay? You have this sort of glassy look in your eyes."

It wasn't her, of course. The chances of running into HER in this wide multiverse were slim to none... but she was just as wild and strange in Mallory's eyes. Curly orange hair, heavy eye makeup, figure-hugging clothing that would get her in serious trouble with the Council if she were to wear it in public or private or locked inside her own closet...

"Helloooo?"

"Th-thank you for getting my stuff back!!" Mallory praised. "I'm—"

"Yeah, yeah, whatever," she dismissed, fading back into the crowd before any further words could be exchanged.

"...I'm Mallory," he finished lamely as the pedestrians sucked her up and yanked her from sight. One would think that a girl that outstandingly strange would be easy to find in a crowd of folks in business suits, and one would be wrong for reasons one was not aware of. And Mallory was one.

With his belongings belonging to him once more, he decided to quit stalling and finish walking the three blocks already. He paused at the crosswalk, having thankfully observed how people react to the colored lights at each intersection and thus avoiding a fatal roadkill incident. When the light went green, he joined the mob and crossed...

He was relatively prepared for Urbana. He knew about the size of the buildings, and knew that a lot of them were shops not unlike the Store in his village. As he passed by windows holding wonders he could only wonder about, he started to hear the siren song of the impulse buyer... and in a rare display of competence, opted not to buy anything. He only had a lousy twenty-five points, and some of these price tags were pretty extreme...

Although... there WAS the 'Snack Vendor' he saw at the corner of the next intersection. The inner gourmet of his soul demanded that he at least drop a few points and sample the fine cuisine of these strange new lands. Figuring it couldn't hurt, he strolled up to the umbrella-covered cart, and read the menu...

His jaw dropped.

"You guys cook dogs?!" he exclaimed. "That's disgusting!"

"They're just CALLED Hot Dogs," spoke the bored-looking vendor in the paper hat who was obviously used to tourists from across the multiverse freaking out over such things. "They're 15% compressed pig meat filler 50% various animal byproducts 25% soy and other synthetic additives with 10% Krap Foods Multiversal Yum-Yum Juices.™And they cost four points. You buying or not?"

"What are 'synthetic additives'?"

"Yummy. You buying or not?"

"You know, I do some cooking myself," he said with a small hint of pride. "How do you prepare these Dogs of Heat?"

"Ah. A fellow chef," the bored man said boredly. "Okay. You see the metal box there with the glass door?"

"Uh-huh."

"I put these frozen packages in there and I push the button and wait for the light to turn green then I sell them for four points. You buying or not?"

"I wanna FreezieFreak!"

Funny, Mallory thought, I don't recall saying that. And I could swear my voice was lower than that while coming from higher up in the air...

He glanced to his side, where an adorable young girl in pigtails and overalls was trying to peer over the top of the cart. "You have FreezieFreaks, right? I want one, I want one! I haven't had one in days!"

"Five points," the vendor indicated, pointing to the menu with his tongs after dumping another load of frozen compressed animal parts into the big metal box.

The little girl pouted, clearly unhappy with this price. "Fiiiive? But I could get a doll for five! I'll pay three," she responded, holding up three fingers.

"What does this look like, a peddler's cart? Push off, kid."

The kid's pout turned to a full-blown frown, as she got off her tippy-toes to give this serious thought... before settling eyes on Mallory. "Hey, mister!" she addressed. "Loan me two points!"

Now's my chance, the boy thought. I can make a good impression on these strangers AND do it without breaking the bank!

"Awww, no need for that!" he said in his kindest and sweetest voice possible as he flashed his scorecard in Financial Triumph of Generosity. "I'll pay for the whole price! Five points for one FreakyFreeze, my good man, here is my card—"

"Hoooold it!" the girl warned, holding up one hand to stop him... and holding out a contract paper that had been folded six times to fit in the pocket of her overalls (with tiny pencil). "Sign this loan form, please, under standardized terms of multiversal personal loan and barter as accepted by the

Financial Authority of Urbana for the amount of five points (adapted under clause 2.3 of the Common Exchange Act) so that this is above board and registered with the tax authority."

Gooberdom settled onto Mallory like fresh snowfall. "...whaaa?"

"Sign on the bottom line," she insisted, waggling the paper.

Dumbfounded (ie, 'Founded on Dumbness'), Mallory took the tiny stub of a pencil and signed his name.

"One FreezieFreak," the vendor replied 0.01 seconds after the little girl jumped in the air, grabbed the frosty beverage snacky thing and pocketed the signed contract in one smooth and practiced motion.

"Thanks, mister!" she thanked. "I'll be in touch about repaying the 0.5 credits plus interest we have mutually agreed to later! BYEEE!"

"Byeee!" Mallory said while waving and smiling stupidly, being unaware of the finer points of economics which just stiffed him out of 4.5 credits.

Of course, he'd have to pass on the 'Hot Dog'. He wanted to save his money, after all. He strolled into the intersection, stepped back quickly before he could be hit by a truck, waited for the light to turn green and crossed onto block number three of his Long March Towards Destiny.

Because good things come in threes (other than world wars), Mallory was fortunate enough to have another unusual encounter while traversing the third city block.

He was just getting used to the idea of people walking back and forth along a narrow strip of pavement after years of randomly organized dirt paths; the idea of people walking out of nearby buildings on a perpendicular path to his was new. Which is why he walked directly into someone leaving a nearby military surplus outlet.

A brown paper bag of lumpy objects went spilling onto the sidewalk, as did Mallory, landing firmly on his ass. (The relative hardness of sidewalk compared to dirt roads was also a new concept.) His victim didn't fall over or even get knocked off balance; she immediately crouched down (voluntarily) to start gathering her items.

And Mallory, being polite, helped her. "I'm so sorry!" he apologized, stuffing a few boxes marked EXPLOSIVE roughly into the bag. "I'm not from around here, and I forgot about people walking out of stores and here let me help you with that.... is this a pineapple? It looks kinda rotten and green, and it's really hard, why's it got this pin in it—"

Before Mallory could lose an appendage, a gloved hand yanked the grenade back, WITH its pin.

Looking up, he realized he'd bumped into another girl. Easily taller than him, with long black hair and some sort of fancy green military uniform and cape like he'd see in really old war movie video streams— and glaring at him with a look that lowered his body temperature at least five degrees Celsius.

Unlike the last two chance encounters, this one had nothing to say beyond a 'Hmph' and a curt turn on one boot heel to march away.

O-kay, he thought. And decided not to let anything else distract him; the three block progression was complete! There was no fanfare except inside his mind, however.

Twelve rows deep, three rows to the right.

Wait. First things first.

One, two, three, four... row after row of houses, huts, office buildings, warehouses, oddly shaped structures he couldn't identify. He'd always heard of Transients as shady characters, always on the move, never to be trusted even if they had a romantic and adventurous lifestyle packed with excitement and intrigue—most of these buildings he passed looked dreadfully ordinary. Much like the cottages the traders would move into Grünwald; functional, rather than thrilling.

Seven rows, eight, nine, then... empty slots, this deep into the docking lot. Indentations in the ground with unused water and gas hookups. Grünwald didn't have a fancy dock with these features, but he knew the basics of how they worked from countless advertisements in the video streams; houses land in a slot, and their internal toilets and sinks and things hook up to the water supply. It was all part of the docking service. It was also hideously expensive, even in thrifty places like this...

Twelve! He turned sharply and marched three rows to the right. Getting closer. Closer... so close to his bright and promising future!

Head in the clouds and feet on the ground and ear to the grindstone, he paid little attention to his surroundings as he boldly stepped forward to knock on the door of House 12/3 loudly, ignoring the doorbell because he didn't know what it was!

Four moments later, she opened the door, and Mallory's jaw didn't literally hit the sidewalk. But if you dropped another house on him much like this one had dropped on him, he might not have noticed...

"Y-You?!" he exclaimed.

"You again?" the woman in the stylish business clothes who had talked to him many days ago asked. "What're you doing out of the sticks? If you're looking for a job, Mr. Faker Reality Engineer, I already have an applicant to interview today. Push off."

"Crash!" shouted the fragile dream of Mallory's exciting and adventurous future.

His voice was nice and small after that. "...you already hired someone?" he asked. "But... But I came all this way and—"

"Right, right. How sad for you," she said with el zippo compassion. "Now quit cluttering my doorstep, I'm waiting for Ms. Heisenberg to show up."

"But I don't have a sister," Mallory found himself saying.

To say that there was an awkward pause would give deadly silence a bad name.

She stood rock still in the doorway, after her brain put the two pieces of the two-piece puzzle together and found it not liking the photograph of the lion. "...what?" she replied, for lack of anything better to say.

"Uh... I... don't know a Ms. Heisenberg?" Mallory supplied. "Unless you mean my mother, but she's been gone for a long time. Or my dad, but he's back at home and he's not a Ms. Or you mean me, because... I, uh... applied for the job and you told me to come to this address. My name's Mallory Heisenberg, it sounds like a girl's name but I'm actually a guy, I know I didn't get a chance to tell you before but you were in a rush to leave, and—"

The door was closing on his future! LITERALLY, this time!

Mallory jammed himself into the doorway, despite the rib-crunching pain it caused as the woman tried to close the doorway. There was a brief struggle, while he frantically tried to justify his presence to her. Something like: "No no wait please hear me out please okay?!" while she was going: "OUT! Out of my house! Beat it! I didn't hire you! There was a mistake!" and so on. It would be comical if not for the bandages he'd have to wear around his midsection for the next four days...

Fortunately for him, he was saved by three beautiful visions of loveliness. One had curly orange hair. Another had a shopping bag. The youngest had a 66% empty cup of FreezieFreak.

"What's that guy doing here?" the one with the largest breasts and no bag full of munitions asked. "And haven't I seen him before?"

"He's trespassing, that's what!" the woman Mallory was struggling with yelled. "Out! Out of my—"

One sharp blow to the back of the neck by the orange haired woman and Mallory crumpled to the ground like the sacks of potatoes he was hauling around not two days ago. Which means he fell in a lumpy and awkward sort of way. Everything got really distant and quiet really fast to him...

"...you didn't have to knock him out," the woman spoke, stepping away from the pile of country boy. "Terrific. Well, we can't just dump him on the sidewalk. Kisei, you grab his feet; Lorelei, you get his head..."

Less than blissful unconsciousness overtook him like a blanket of lumpy hard objects.

No fear. Green grass beneath his feet. Blue sky above...

"I can't believe you hired this guy sight unseen. We're not THAT desperate for an Engineer..."

Water trickling down a creek. Birds chirping from the trees...

"Actually, oneechan was right to hire him! No real Engineer would accept that pay scale even with room and board due to the projected cost of living release issued by RealWare a month ago during the Q1 financial report. Umm, but I didn't think we'd get a fake boy-engineer. Oneechan, why'd you hire a boy?"

Her smile...

"The name on the resume was MALLORY, okay? If that's not a girl's name, I don't know what is—"

"Y'know, 'Mirai Meiko', for someone many years removed from Nippon, you still haven't gotten the hang of gaijin names..."

"Stuff it, okay? Is he alive? Can he walk? Can he walk out of here, specifically?"

Was she smiling?

No, actually, she was frowning.

"Hello?" Mallory asked, sitting up despite the million throbbing hammers of unrelenting pain attacking his frontal lobes. "Where... oh, wait, I know where I am..."

It was the same living room. The same funny L-shaped couch area, the same huge Video Network Set 3.11... the wallpaper with patterns all over it. Although the girls were new additions... new additions he had the luck to meet prior to his arrival as he traversed Urbana.

The one who he'd met first, however... the one who dropped the house on him to begin with... she was leaning against the end of the couch, arms crossed, expressing extreme annoyance and disappointment. "You're not hired, obviously," she spoke. "Which means you can go now. I'd say sorry to trouble you, but you've been more trouble for me than—"

"He fixed the engine, didn't he?" the orange-haired girl pointed out. "Albeit in a pretty funky way, but it counts."

Feeling the need to speak up in his defense before he was booted forcibly from the house for a second time, Mallory nodded along and then stopped nodding when the pain was too intense. "R-Right! I mean... I can fix engines! I swear I can, I fixed the one in my home reality like that for years. I don't know why it works, it just does, and... and I can cook and I can farm! Does that count?"

"You see any fertile topsoil around here, except maybe in Meiko's underwear drawer?" Orange Hair joked.

'Meiko,' who was clearly the girl Mallory had gotten to know in the first place given her fuming reaction, fumed quite a bit. "Lorelei, c'mon! We don't need a farmer, we need an engineer! And—"

The younger girl popped up in front of Mallory. "You can cook? Really?" she asked. "Oneechan's cooking is awful! She can burn water! And my toast is always black and my hamburgers leak this red stuff and it's all icky!"

Mallory latched onto this like a starving man latches onto whatever it is starving men crave. "Hamburgers? I can cook those!" he exclaimed, starting to go into Self Justification Overdrive. "As well as french fries and steak and pork chops and soups and salads and fish filet and pasta and meatballs and riceballs and various types of sauces and sushi that's from Nippon isn't it and I can do cakes and if I have the right ingredients I can even make ice cream although it usually ends up all runny but I can improve I SWEAR!"

"Deal!" the little girl agreed, grabbing Mallory's hand and shaking it. "I'll draw up the contract and—"

"Mirai Eikooo! Don't YOU start on this—no deal! Deal, no! No!" Meiko objected, waving her arms frantically. "We don't NEED a chef!"

"I dunno about that," Lorelei aka The One With Orange Hair replied smoothly. "If I have to deal with another Meiko Mystery Meat Surprise for dinner, I might encourage House mutiny... unless Kisei wants to share her hidden supply of hard rations? It could be preferable. How about it, Kiss?"

True to form, the quiet one in the green military uniform who had been staying out of this completely despite watching over the situation like a hawk silently ignored the taunt.

"Let's run down the basics of our needs, shall we?" Lorelei suggested, getting up from her seat on the couch to assume an authoritative speaking position. "The money is running low, and we can only live on instant ramen so long before we start using each other as alternative food sources. If we could get someone to cook for us from ingredients we'd be saving money. And saving money is good, isn't it, Eiko-chan?"

"Haaaaai!" the little girl agreed, giving a big 'ol thumbs up.

"So, he can cook for us. And being a farmer, you're no doubt used to hard work, yes?" Lorelei continued. "How does housecleaning and laundry and running errands sound to you? Assuming you won't hand over our money to a mugger like a dumbass, of course."

Mallory nearly wept with joy at the newfound acceptance. "Yes yes, I can clean!" he insisted. "I tidied up around my dad's house all the time. I'm a hard worker and I can do anything you need me to!"

"Mmmm... anything?" Lorelei asked, with a suggestive wink and a bump of the hips and a pursing of the lips.

"Well... I can't do complex math," Mallory noted, completely missing the point. "But... Eiko here can, right?"

Beaming with joy, Eiko jumped up to give Mallory a big hug, which stunned him for 1d6 rounds. "I like him!" Eiko announced. "Can we keep him, oneechan? He can be my oniichan!"

"Ah, Eiko agrees with me. I'd call it an open and shut case," Lorelei recommended. "Okay, so he's male. I have no problems with that. Can he sleep in my room? We were going to have the new recruit bunk with me back when we assumed we were hiring a girl—"

Meiko stamped her foot, which didn't make as much noise as she wished it would have. "He can sleep on the sidewalk for all I care!" she declared. "We are NOT hiring him, and—"

"Democracy," Lorelei reminded her. "We vote on decisions regarding the House and our direction. You said so yourself."

"Who's signing your paychecks, 'Bodyguard'?" Meiko asked her, narrowing her eyes to Evil Slits. "Fine. Let's be democratic. I vote NO."

"I wanna keep him!" Eiko replied, thankfully letting go of him as well. "I vote HAI!"

Mallory waved politely to the little girl. "Err, hello? Hi?"

"She means 'Yes'. It's Nihongo," Lorelei informed Mallory... while evaluating him with hungry eyes. "As for me, having my own personal man-servant tickles my fancy. I vote YES. You got a vote, Kiss? Or do you abstain in morbid silence?"

Kisei, AKA The One In The Military Uniform Who Hadn't Taken Her Eyes Off Mallory In The Last Ten Minutes, paused almost dramatically. "I vote no," she spoke softly.

"...ummm..." Mallory almost spoke up with in an assertive way. "That's two to two, isn't it? Uh. What do you guys do in the case of a tie?"

...for a change, Meiko was wearing a smile. It wasn't a very nice one.

The field of combat was simple.

One surface. Rectangular. Bisected.

A netting of string stretched across the center. A few inches tall. Imposing in its simplicity.

Two weapons of war... circular wooden boards with rubberized surfaces. Wooden handles. Paddles designed only for the violent striking of the ball in such a way as to punish one's enemies...

"We settle ties," Meiko spoke as she spun the tiny plastic ball on the tip of one finger, "With Ping Pong."

Mallory held his game paddle like it was a three week dead fish, standing at his end of the kitchen table. "Uh... Ping Pong? What's Ping Pong?"

From the spectator pit (AKA, 'standing in front of the fridge and the oven') Lorelei smacked her forehead, mumbled something, and explained. "Don't you watch sports video streams? It's only the most popular sport in the multiverse for the last, oh, SEVEN HUNDRED YEARS! Honestly, are you that much of a rube?"

"I'm afraid so," Mallory apologized lamely.

"Fine. Okay. You knock the little ball back and forth with the paddles," Lorelei explained. "First person to miss the ball and have it get knocked past them loses. That's the basics."

Meiko chuckled, the first laugh Mallory had heard out of her... ever. "And I just happen to be the undefeated Ping Pong Champion of Seven Lucky Gods Street Orphanage in Edo, Nippon," she warned him. "Which means I generally get my way whenever we have a vote split. And it means you have no chance. You want to back out, hick boy?"

Mallory trembled with something that was three parts fear and two parts mild mannered rage. "I... I won't back down!" he declared. "And my name is Mallory Heisenberg; don't call me hick boy! If you don't mind 'cause it's kind of mean and I don't mean to be such a bother because I don't know anything, umm, okay?"

"So you do have at least a few vertebrae, if not a whole spine," Meiko commented, absently bouncing the ball up and down on her paddle with practiced ease. "Okay, MALLORY... taste my RISING SUN DEATH SWAN POWER SERVE!!"

In a blurring motion of the arm, Meiko snapped the ball into the air, twisted her arm back, and pounded a power serve over the net. It bounced off the kitchen table so hard the noise echoed throughout the House...

Panicking, Mallory raised his paddle to protect his delicate face, and ended up deflecting the ball in an accidentally perfect defensive maneuver that squeaked it over the net, off the table and right past Meiko.

The ball landed in the kitchen sink next to the dirty dishes, making a 'plop' in the soapy water.

Meiko's paddle had a satisfying rubbery wooden clatter when it hit the floor, her fingers limp with shock.

"VICTOLY!!" Eiko cheered, tossing a handful of pink confetti in the air.

"...I won?" Mallory asked, just as shocked. "I won...? I won! Hey, I won! Wow! I mean... wow! I got the job, right? This means I'm employed?"

Meiko took a moment to reply, her neurons firing a little too fast to stay in the present frame of mind. "...one second," she spoke quietly... turning her back to the others, and fishing something from her pocket.

It looked like some sort of pocket video set or something, from Mallory's poor point of view. A little red plastic thing with an antenna and a keyboard, just like his dad's RealNet Workstation...

"Feh. Checking with F.P. again?" Lorelei asked. "Honestly, Mei, can't you make a decision without—"

Meiko snapped the folding device closed again quickly, as if shocked by something she saw there. She took a good moment to turn around again... and tried not to blush any.

"Okay, fine, you're hired," she spoke quickly. "But as owner of the House I'm putting some conditions on you you'd DAMN well better follow if you know what's good for you, and one of those is that you don't look at this as some way to 'pick up chicks,' got that?"

"Oh, that's okay, I didn't handle the poultry back on the farm," Mallory said, trying to give her a reassuring smile.

"Right And you're gonna start studying immediately for your REC Test," she continued. "We need an Engineer more than a cook and I'm not gonna let an untrained maniac fix our engine. If you pass the test, you can stay. If not—"

"I can do it!" Mallory insisted. "My mother was a Reality Engineer. Dad said the test is hard, but... if I have to pass it to stay here, I'll do it, I swear!"

"Fine. It's settled, he's hired. Eiko, draw up a contract. Lorelei, he's sleeping on the couch, deal with it."

"Damn," Lorelei cursed, snapping her fingers.

"I'm going to my room," Meiko announced, pocketing her F.P., whatever that was. "I'm closing my door, too. Do not enter under penalty of severe personal discomfort. Especially you... Houseboy."

Speaking up for the second time in as many hours, Kisei stepped away from the kitchen counter. "I'll be upstairs as well," she commented, stepping around the group and heading quickly (but quietly) to the stairs. Meiko wasn't real far behind her.

"Wonder what got up her ass, anyway?" Lorelei wondered, watching said ass retreat upstairs. "Looks like you're hired, kid. Congrads. You sure you want to sleep on the couch?"

Mallory waved his hands and shook his head and tried to look unassuming. "No no, it's okay. A couch is just fine. Um... what's an F.P.? Meiko looked kind of surprised by something it said..."

"It's her personal organizer. Little pocket workstation thing. And it can sorta predict the future so it can fill in your daily timetable for you. Neat gizmo, huh?"

A tugging on his arm drew his attention to the younger Mirai sister. "C'mon, Mallory-oniichan! Let's go draw up your contract! And I promise to be nice and fair to you this time, okay?"

"Uh... okay! Um. One more question?"

"Hai?"

"What does 'oniichan' mean?"

Dear dad

I got the job!! I am writing to you from the House Workstation, which Meiko told me if I break I have to pay for but I remember how to use the one you bought for me, so I do not think I will break it.

It was a close call but I got the job!! I have been here a few hours now. There are some very interesting people here in the 'House'. Eiko says I am her Oniichan, which I'm told means 'big brother' in Nihongo. I'm going to learn more Nihongo since it's the language mom spoke and I want to learn more about Nippon and stuff. Lorelei keeps asking if I want to move into her room but I don't think that is a good idea because Meiko keeps looking at me in a very nasty way when it's suggested and I do not want to rock the boat when leading a yak to water. Kisei does not say a whole lot and I don't think she likes me but I have time to make friends with her and Meiko (who does not like me either) and I know I will get along with all them.

Enclosed is no money but once I get my first paycheck I will send some home I promise. I have to go make dinner for the others now I promised them something really good but all they have are bags of candy and snacks marked 'Krap' which I am told is a very popular brand of food but it does not look very good. I will do what I can with what I have and do some shopping tomorrow unless we have to leave Urbana, Meiko said we move around a lot doing 'jobs'. I wonder what those jobs are? I will find out!

I am very excited to be here. Everything is new to me. Everything feels so strange, but it's weird. I feel like I fit here. More than I ever felt I fit back home, it's like being a Transient makes sense. I'm still very confused and things are a little scary but I feel oddly good about it all.

remind me to tell you about the tornado. I think it took me somwhere very special.

your son Mallory. will write soon.

It was 7 o'clock on an *a*typical day when his alarm clock went off. It went off because he programmed it to go off at 7 o'clock, and thus was typical in its own right on this atypical day. Time to wake up.

Most farmers could pop right to their feet and hit the fields within minutes of waking, but Mallory was the sort to take a minimum of ten minutes to groan, roll around a bit, and ponder the idea of going back to sleep. This would have worked fine except that he was used to his bed, which was considerably wider than the couch, and on his first roll he rolled right off the cushions. Thankfully he missed the coffee table, but the floor was more than happy to rush up to greet him in a painful manner.

Dragging himself back onto the couch (which he sat on for a change, as opposed to the less traditional use of overnight sleep) he rubbed his head a few times, which only made the pain worse. It was probably for the best that he had a rude awakening, though; it meant no chance of dropping back to sleep. He had to make a good impression on his first day, after all, and Meiko wouldn't appreciate it if he slept in!

Mallory Heisenberg had a saying: "The early bird never gets a second chance to have first dibs on the worm." This saying mutated every time he thought of it, of course, but the basic idea remained the same.

Shaking his head a bit to clear out the sleepy cobwebs and multiply his mounting headache by 1.3, he walked over to the back closet. Not the large one where they stored winter coats and unused furniture, but the tiny closet that Meiko had emptied out so Mallory would have some privacy for changing clothes and somewhere to store his material possessions. It was a bit cramped and he kept bumping his head on the light bulb as he hopped up and down to get his pants on, but he didn't mind. After all, they only had enough bedrooms for the girls, and he didn't want to raise a fuss about his Living Room Couch + Broom Closet combined living space. It wouldn't make the right impression if he complained.

Properly dressed, the next step was to take care of personal hygiene. Mallory came out of the closet (in a literal sense) and turned the corner into the downstairs hallway, making a left into the only bathroom in the house. He brought a small cup with him that had a tiny bottle of mouthwash, a single serving tube of toothpaste, and his special RealWare Dental Products issue toothbrush that had the extra bristles for cleaning those hard-to-reach places. Five minutes later he was fresh and ready to face the day!

Next step was to begin his official House duties. This was the part he was actually quite looking forward to. Although the House didn't have a whole lot to work with ingredient-wise, he had thought up an excellent variation on pancake batter that would truly impress his new employers.

And so, with batter in his heart (but not his arteries) and good intentions in mind, he stepped into his new domain—The Kitchen. Feeling the innate country home need to enjoy the fresh air and sunlight of a new day, he unlocked the kitchen window, swung it open, and was knocked unconscious by the coconut that slammed into his forehead.

The sound the coconut made when it bounced once or twice on the floor was not entirely unlike the sound his head made when he hit the linoleum floor.

02: EULA, I-and-I

While unconscious, Mallory had a highly prophetic dream of foreshadowing images and metaphors which, once properly decoded, would have revealed the mystery of the multiverse if not for the fact that Lorelei was shaking him awake.

"Oi, oi!" she shouted in his ear at a volume suitable for stunning an elephant. (Fortunately her bathrobe was tightly closed, or Mallory might have been stunned for other reasons.) "Mal! You alive in there? If you're dead, who am I gonna get to clean my room?!"

"I think I'm alive," Mallory replied with much uncertainty as one eye slid open. "Where am I— ah! Window! Big tree! Urbana's overgrown with big, funny-looking trees—"

"Relax, kiddo, we're not in Urbana anymore," Lorelei said, stepping back to let Mallory pick his own self off the floor without any help whatsoever from her. "We're in I's Land now. Meiko moved us last night while you were asleep; we've got a job to do here. Good thing too, the house fund was running low..."

Mallory pulled himself up by the window sill... careful not to bump his head against the huge green palm leaf that had swung into the open window when he had opened it earlier. His eyes adjusted to the light—it was brighter than the dull sunlight that trickled down through the towers of Urbana. The sky was actually a bright cyan (a generic relative to blue in the 'groovy' phylum) with a golden yellow sun that didn't hurt to look at, despite being so bright. There wasn't a cloud in sight... and rather than pavement and buildings, all Mallory saw as far as his eyes could reach through his glasses was sand, surf, and wooden buildings.

"A... a beach!" he recognized from the grainy streaming videos he'd see on RealNet's Travel Video Network. "We're parked on a beach!"

"Yeah, I's Land doesn't have much in the way of docks," Lorelei complained, as she took a seat at the kitchen table (which had been converted back to an eating surface after yesterday's fateful Ping Pong match). "You just pick a spot of sand, negotiate with 'em to clear away from it, and WHAM. No power or water hookups. I hate it, the toilets revert to using the internal tanks and end up smelling awful... Mal?"

"What? Yes?" Mallory asked, wrenching his eyes away from the sights of paradise.

"Food?" Lorelei suggested. "C'mon, houseboy. I know it's early but let's get up to speed, mmm?"

"Foo—aah! Breakfast! I forgot!"

"No, you were unconscious. There's a difference."

"Pancakes, pancakes..." Mallory chanted to himself, scrounging through the meager food stocks of the House. "I think I have enough here to make pancakes for five—"

"Three."

"Three?"

"Meiko already left, and Kisei doesn't eat with the rest of us except at dinner time," Lorelei explained, drumming her fingers on the table. "So that means you're feeding yourself, myself, and—"

"Eiiiko-chaaan!" a musical voice piped in with, as the young girl popped in from the hallway filled with pep. She skipped over to a seat and hopped up, while simultaneously pulling a pink plastic pocket wireless workstation from her overalls, keying up the morning stock quotes, and ordering her meal. "I want Chocolate Frosted Chocolate Choco-Chunks Cereal! And a bagel and orange juice."

"And I'll just take toast, I'm in a hurry," Lorelei spoke, her fingers drumming a bit faster. "Light, not dark, with just a bit of butter."

Mallory reoriented his Gears of Customer Service, sliding the drawer with the batter spoon shut. Bread was plucked from another cabinet and plopped into the toaster with precision and skill while his other hand hunted through the cabinets for a bowl. "Chocolate... err... one bowl of cereal comin' up! And a bagel and orange juice and toast. Have it for you in a minute!" he announced... before pausing. "Err... Meiko and Kisei are gone, then?"

"Kisei doesn't eat with us except at dinner, like I said. She's not really the type for light social banter over eggs and bacon. She's not really the type for any banter whatsoever with any of us. Or any contact of any kind whatsoever unless it's needed for a job..."

Eiko shrugged, while performing six stock transactions at the tap of a fingernail. "Kisei doesn't mind me," she commented. "She just doesn't like you because you're mean to her. And she respects oneesama even if they aren't bestest friends..."

Mallory sighed, as he set the completed Cereal + Bowl + Milk + Spoon in front of Eiko. "I don't think she likes me very much, though," he noted. "She really gave me the cold shoulder nose in the air with the silent treatment yesterday..."

"The wha?" Lorelei spoke, raising an eyebrow 'o confusion. "Anyway... I'm not surprised. You're goofy. She hates goofy. I don't mind goofy guys as long as they've got a good... ...err..."

"Hey! Are you making another sex joke like Meiko-oneesama told you not to make in front of me?" Eiko asked, perking up adorably at the possibility of getting Lorelei in trouble.

"I like guys with good... hair," Lorelei lamely finished. "Hey, hair boy, toast?"

"Toast!" Mallory announced, placing a plate of fine china topped by four precisely sliced triangular pieces of golden brown toast with rich, creamy butter which had been spread evenly with a skilled sweeping wrist motion.

Lorelei sat in speechless silence as what could be described as the Purest Ideal of Toast glistened in the sunlight of I's Land before her. She prodded it lightly with one finger... a perfect number of crumbs falling off, just enough to give it a tasty texture, without being messy. "...you cook other stuff as good as you make toast?" she asked, curiously.

"No, I'm actually ahead of my class a little in soups and stews and behind the others in breakfasts," Mallory admitted. "I got a C-minus when I made Triple-Layer Syrup-in-the-Middle Waffle Surprise for my final exam last year. It was stickier than it was supposed to be—"

"WHOA!" Lorelei exclaimed after swallowing the last bite of her toast. "I say DAMN that was good!! Thanks for the grub, Mal, gotta go now."

"—smoother than that," Mallory finished, staring in horror at the living food vacuum. "Err. Teacher also said we should enjoy our food with even, slow bites—"

"Teacher didn't have surfing and sunbathing to do, did he?" Lorelei asked, pushing in her chair. "I do. By the way, I was supposed to look after Eiko today but I'm going to be far too busy so I leave her in your capable hands. If she's missing an eye or caught on fire when Meiko gets back she'll be pretty angry."

"Really?" Eiko asked, looking up. "I'm going to play with Mallory-oniichan today? Great! We can go to the beach and make sand castles and stuff!"

"—huh?" Mallory intelligently inquired. "But... but I have to clean the house today! And couldn't she go to the beach with you if she wants to make sand castles?"

"I'm going to a nude beach on the other side of this island," Lorelei explained. "I actually haven't a thing on under this bathrobe, and— Mallory? You okay? You look a little pale."

"Let's go make sand castles, Eiko!!" Mallory happily and enthusiastically demanded. "I've never been to a beach before, it'll be fun! Ha ha!"

"Wai! I'll go get my bathing suit on, and I'll meet you in four minutes!" Eiko chirped.

"Right! You do that! And I'll go.... um... bathing suit...?"

Lorelei grinned at the hapless boy. "You don't have one, do you? Not a lot of beachfront property in Grünwald? You could always come with me to my beach, then, nobody would mind there..."

"I... errr... um... I have to look after Eiko!" he reminded her in a not-so-clever twist of logic. "Sorry, can't go. Um. But... can you tell me where can I buy a bathing suit in I's Land?"

"Mmmm... you could borrow mine, houseboy. I'm not needing it today. You might look cute in it..."

"Oh, okay! That would be very helpful!" Mallory said, with genuine relief. "I don't think we're exactly the same size, but... err... what? Is there something on my nose?"

"You really know NOTHING about the worlds beyond your crops, do you?" Lorelei asked, while giving him That Look.

"...no, I don't," Mallory admitted, hanging his head. "I'm trying, really... I'm sorry to disappoint—"

And to his surprise, she laughed out loud.

"Skip it, skip it," Lorelei suggested, turning off the vamp act. "And you can buy a pair of MEN'S trunks at the tailor's shop around the corner. Take heart, okay? You'll pick up on this stuff eventually. Doe-eyed innocent determination like this doesn't grow on trees... take it from an expert."

After stumbling wildly through Urbana in a stupor of confusion, Mallory had decided he required a new approach to new realities. Instead of simply reacting to things around him as he bumped into them, he would study his surroundings intensely, trying to figure out the Hows and Whys of the worlds he walked in a logical manner of observation and analysis.

This is to say that instead of staring straight ahead, he rubbernecked and gawked at everything with a 'Gee whiz' expression. Not too far separated from his previous methodology.

There certainly was a lot to gawk at in I's Land. The climate and the sky, those he had already gawked at; the layout of the place he had not. It reminded him a lot of Grünwald, with a variety of buildings of a variety of styles scattered here and there, loosely connected by sidewalks and roads and paths. There wasn't much rhyme or reason to the town map... as if structures were placed by randomly lobbing a rock into the sand and saying "Okay, there." Sidewalks connected to dirt paths connected to sandy dunes connected to asphalt roads like in Urbana... and none of them had helpful green signs with street names, unlike Urbana.

This became a problem when Lorelei's "Around The Corner" actually turned out to be "Down That Path On Your Left And Around A Corner And In The Alley Between Two Buildings You'll Find A Small Unmarked Door." He had to inquire about the tailor shop's location from the occasional street musician... or rather, the FREQUENT street musician, as it wasn't uncommon to spot someone sitting/standing next to a building drumming on some bongos or playing a guitar. Music floated from every corner of the town, and despite each musician playing a different song... it all flowed together in a steady, harmonic way.

"That's Lander Dub," Eiko had explained (in between complaining about the delay in getting to the beach). "It's a really cool kind of music that they make here! And it all kinda sounds the same but you never really get tired of it..."

With all these distractions, it would have been easy to forget the original quest: Obtain swimwear. Mallory eventually got back on track, found the shop, and walked right in expecting to see the polished department store feel he'd seen in Urbana and on various video streams...

The tiny building had clothes in it, yes. On some scattered racks, draped over tables and chairs, hanging on the walls, hanging from the ceiling fan which rotated slowly to circulate warm air around the room. But beyond that, Mallory would have never guessed it for a commercial enterprise.

He had to call out "Erm, hello?" two or three times before the shopkeeper appeared.

"Ey mon?" a woman in her thirties replied, leaning in from a door to the back room. "Finishin' my brunch, be with you, yeah? Time be time."

"I wanna go to the beeeaach," Eiko whined, stomping one sandal'd foot, which caused the plastic shovel in her sand bucket to rattle around. "Mallory-oniichan, this isn't any fun!"

"Ah, I'm sure we'll be ready to go any minute now," Mallory replied, putting aside the fact that he wasn't sure how to get back to the beach after wandering this far.

Twelve minutes later the shopkeep emerged, finishing up a sandwich. After taking the last bite, she did not stroll to the counter as there was none, but walked right up to Mallory with a big smile. "Okay, mon, what you be wantin'? I-and-I's got a little of everything, and I's can be makin' it for you custom if you need something I's not havin'."

"Err... men's bathing suit?" Mallory asked. "I was told you'd have one..."

The shopkeep snatched up a pair of shorts Mallory had been looking at for the last ten minutes without realizing they were intended for swimming.

"Trunks, here you go," she said. "So, what're you offering?"

"Pardon?"

"In trade. For the trunks. Don' need much, so don' worry if you don' got much... you know, that's a nice sweatshirt."

"Eh? What, this?" Mallory asked, tugging on it by one of the many holes in the fabric. "It's kind of old..."

"The yin-yang," she said, invading Mallory's personal space and tapping it with a finger. "Righteous symbol. Far enough to the left of Babylonia, good Shinto, that. We've got it in Iism too, upside down, but we got it... all things have a balance, find it to find what you need in life, yeah? You want to trade the shirt? Don't need a shirt to go swimming, right?"

"This is... er, kinda personal to me," Mallory replied. "I'd rather not trade it, it's got sentimental value. Besides, it's probably not worth much money, since it's so old and has so many holes—"

"How about if I sew 'em up for you?" she suggested, studying the frayed thread up close in a way that made Mallory uneasy. "Patch it up nice, make it look like new. Don't have to give it to me, but I's enjoyin' a good challenge, so that'd be a good trade in itself. Deal?"

In a blatantly obvious way, it reminded Mallory of his experience with Mellow Fellow the taxi cab pilot... a casual sort of capitalism, a trade, and an effort to keep everybody happy. Something about this clicked with the simple farm boy side of him, as he tugged off the sweatshirt (which was too hot to wear in this climate anyway) and handed it over.

"This isn't a very stable negotiation," Eiko warned, putting in her two credits. "Transactions for goods are best handled via legal tender and contract agreement such as receipts, in order to be smoothly handled in a court of law at a later time in the event of negotiation breakdown—"

"It's a deal," he agreed. "Don't worry, Eiko! I'm sure it'll be fine. I'll be back in... uh... a few hours for the shirt, ma'am. I'm not sure exactly how long, though—"

"Don't worry, mon," she said, folding the shirt over one arm.

"Time be time?" Mallory guessed.

"That it be," she said with a cheerful smile.

Much to Eiko's disappointment, the shaky deal was quite solid. Mallory used a changing room in the back to put on his snazzy new purple swim trunks, and one stroll with a few mistakenly taken forks in the road later, they had reached The Beach.

Even the half-concept of a beach that Mallory held from seeing them on the tiny view window of his Video Network Player didn't match the real thing. There weren't any garishly colored sun umbrellas or bouncy women in small bathing suits that made him feel nervous. There weren't any beach chairs or towels or boxes streaming pop music or food vendors or boardwalks or shops selling local curios and huge, tacky plastic sunglasses... instead there was:

1. Sand.

2. Surf.

3. People.

Which was in his original idea of a beach, but not quite like this. The sand wasn't immaculately groomed into dunes and such; it was natural beach, patchy in spots, quite nice in others. The surf he was expecting even if he didn't understand what force kept pushing the water onto the shore, nor why it kept receding. But the people...

These weren't tourists; he had enough analytical prowess to figure that out. These were simply local folks who lived here and happened to be out enjoying the beach that day. Occupying a spot of sand a ways away was a Lander Dub band; a guitar, three or four types of drums and a guy strumming something that made low, bassy tones. They didn't seem to be playing songs that start and end like Mallory would hear on the music-oriented streams—it was one continuous jam that somehow pulled itself along in a group harmony, like flocking birds with unspoken mutual understanding...

In a way, this new arrangement of elements made for a better beach than Mallory was expecting. He had nowhere to sit except on his butt in his new trunks on the sand, but that didn't matter. Everything felt quite relaxed without being forcibly fun. He could "dig" it, as his ten-minute-friend Mellow Fellow would say.

Eiko certainly could dig it in the literal sense, as she skillfully mixed parts of sand with parts of water to make a rudimentary form of building cement suitable for temporary beach-bound structures.

"Oneechan doesn't take me to the beach very often," Eiko was explaining, as she used her shovel to carve a nice 45° slope off the top of her sand-house. "We don't have enough time or money, because every time we move the house, it costs us. We usually only move around when we have a job somewhere... Mallory-oniisan, are you listening to me?"

"What? Err, what?" Mallory replied, taking his eyes off the oddly hypnotic way the water kept rolling in and out near their spot on the wet sand. "Ah, yes... my dad mentioned Transients have to spend a lot of money to move around."

"Oneechan doesn't like that word," Eiko warned, waving her plastic shovel at him. "She says 'transients' usually is a bad word and people say it when they want to make fun of us. Just because our house moves around doesn't mean we're bad people!"

"Oh, no, of course not!" Mallory protested, waving his arms in panic. "I didn't mean it that way, honest! Cross my heart and hope to stick a needle in my eye—"

"ONIISAN!"

"Er, yes?"

Eiko cocked her head cutely as she studied him. "You're really hyperactive. Meiko-oneechan says I can't have a lot of sugar in one day or I get hyper. Do you eat a lot of sugar?"

"Err... no, not usually," Mallory said, settling down a bit. "Sorry, I'm just trying to adjust to all this..."

"You also apologize a whole bunch. I don't think oneechan likes that. She likes people who stand up for themselves."

"I... guess I'm not making a great impression on her, am I?" Mallory asked, shoulder sagging in defeat.

Eiko shrugged a bit, trying to smile more to perk him up as she refilled her sand bucket. "Don't worry! Lorelei-san was right, you'll get used to it in time. Ne! Do you like my sand-House?"

"Ah... it's very lovely, Eiko-kun!"

"-chan!"

"Eiko-chan," Mallory corrected, recalling Eiko's quickie lesson in Adorable Adapted Nihongo she gave him on the way over here. "I thought people built sand castles, though? Like you see in storybooks with round towers and princesses sleeping on mattresses with pee on them and stuff?"

"I like building sand-Houses," Eiko replied, packing the next 'brick' for the house with her hands. "Like ours, but bigger and it stays in one place. Meiko-oneechan says one day we'll live in a house like that... we'll just stay in one place and not have to move around all the time. Then when we go all over the multiverse it'll be for fun, not because we have to..."

Forgetting the brick in her hands for the moment, she turned her eyes up to study Mallory intently.

"Er, yes? Do I have something on my nose?" he asked, brushing his nose as a preemptive measure. He glanced to the side, wondering why the Lander Dub band had picked up all their instruments and moved about twenty feet towards land...

"Are you going to marry oneechan?" Eiko asked simply, interrupting every single train of thought he had.

If it were possible for the human jaw to distend so far as to hit the ground, Mallory's would have. As it is simply hung open in a less impressive manner.

"Wh... what?!" he exclaimed, barely heard as the waves rolled in closer, tide coming in. "No, no, I'm... what? I'm just your houseboy and Reality Engineer, not her boyfriend, I mean, I don't quite see how those things would relate or how you could get that idea and anyway I don't think she likes me very much although I'm doing my best and I hope I get in her good graces sometime but you can't rush things and the early bird gets the silk purse out of the—waagh!"

"I was just wondering because of what I saw in her Future Perfect," Eiko replied, placing the brick onto the sand-House roof. "I snuck a peek at it this morning before she left for work, and... ano? Oniichan? Oniichan, doko wa?"

Look left, look right... and Eiko didn't spot him. Look behind herself and she saw Mallory washing out to sea.

It's stated in Twoday's Guidebook (a fine travel compendium for the discerning tourist who wants to only visit realities approved by RealWare) that the seas of I's Land are remarkable in two aspects. One, they're always a comfortable warm temperature that's not too hot and not too cold, but always refreshing after a hot day on the beach. Two, to make surfing easier, the midday tide rolls in quite swiftly rather than tapering in and out. Say, ten seconds swiftly.

While this is very handy for folks doing wakeboarding, surfing and jetski riding, it's not very good for farmboys who have never been fully immersed in water outside of slipping in the bathtub.

Fortunately for Mallory, while Eiko didn't have the manpower needed to drag his sorry ass out of the deadly, vicious one-foot-deep surf, someone else did.

Coughing up salt water and sputtering and remembering to thank the spirits he was supposed to be believing in, Mallory clung to that arm like a drowning man clings to the arm of a rescuer. He shook water and sand out of his hair, fumbled down in the muck for his glasses, rinsed them off a bit, put them on, and...

"YO!" Mellow Fellow greeted, grabbing Mallory and crushing him in a friendly hug. "Didn'expect to see you here, mon! How it is, yo? I's wonderin' if I's ever seein' you again! S'matter, you look pale and stuff..."

"Gah," Mallory greeted in return.

"ONIICHAN!" Eiko wailed, running up to join them—and beat cutely on Mellow Fellow's back with her fists... "Wah! Let go of my oniichan, strange man!"

The taxi cab pilot set Mallory down, backing off. "Easy, easy!" he said. "I-and-I's cool, don' worry! Mallory's a righteous friend of Mellow Fellow's so you don' be worryin' none, okay? You Eiko Mirai, yeah?"

"What's it to you?" Eiko asked, still suspicious as she gave Mellow the Evaluating Eye she'd learned from her sister.

"Your sis sent me, dig? Needs you at the negotiatin' table. Go get changed, right, I'll take you there."

"Only if Mallory-oniichan is coming!" Eiko warned.

Mallory fumbled with his grasp on things as one would fumble with the soap in the bath after being laminated with a thin layer of oiled plastic. "Er, I'll come along," he agreed. "No problem. Don't worry, Eiko, ah... I-and-I's cool too?"

"Righteous!" Mellow exclaimed, slapping Mallory's hand in some bizarre bonding gesture he knew nothing of.

"Well... okay," Eiko agreed, tentatively."Keep an eye on my bucket and don't let anybody knock over my house! I'm going back to the house to change, I'll wave when I'm ready."

"Right, right. Have fun! Err, not that you're specifically off to do anything fun, I mean, uh... so!" Mallory said, switching chat-subjects back to Mellow Fellow. "Mellow! Ah... it's good to see you again! You're from around here, right?"

"I's from I's Land, yeah. Actually... I's hirin' your boss for this job. I's and the Elders," Mellow explained, walking back to their sand-House encampment area. "We got some truly unrighteous trouble here in I's Land right now, Mon. The vibes of Babylonia comin' down to hamper us..."

"Really? Trouble?" Mallory asked, looking around. "I haven't seen any trouble today. I mean, nobody seems worried about anything, either... everybody I've talked to has been really friendly. This is a great place to live, Mellow-chan!"

"...chan?"

"Err... anyway, I'll have to tell you about my home sometime. It's a lot like this; small community, people who know each other, err, not quite as friendly to outsiders, but—"

"This... this place is righteous, I's agreein'," Mellow said, losing some of the jovial tone in his voice. "I's travellin' far and wide, reality to reality, and I's never findin' a place that fits in my heart like I's Land. It's home. But we's got troubles, definitely... I's doin' my best to help, but the cab, it only brings in a small amount of the monies of Babylonia. We don't get some more of the monies soon, man, we're... hrm. How to explain..."

"I think it's gonna have to wait," Mallory spoke, shielding his eyes from the sun with one hand as he peered House-wards. "Eiko's ready to go. Err I have to change out of my trunks and dry off too, don't I?"

"Meiko didn't say to bring you, mon, jus' Eiko. But if you wanna come..."

"I think I do. I mean... maybe I can help?" Mallory offered. "I'll only take a minute, I swear!"

"Eh... time be time," his friend said without the usual vigor. "And I guess it be nothin'. 'cept to some people..."

"You're late," Meiko admonished without looking up from her reading. "I'll be with you guys in a minute."

Mallory had no idea if he was in fact late or not; he wasn't wearing a watch, and he hadn't seen any clocks on any walls anywhere in the tiny sample of I's Land he'd been exposed to. And this new chunk of I's Land that Mellow Fellow had led their fellowship of three to didn't look any different.

Like most buildings, it was unmarked, and had some sort of domestic feel to it. There were open windows to allow fresh air and sunlight to pour in, a large table that made the House kitchen table look like a lunch counter, and a variety of comfortable-looking padded wicker chairs of varying designs.

At one end of the table sat Meiko, perusing some sort of complicated-looking document displayed on a nearly paper-thin electronic widget. Now and then she'd tap a button on the side of the thing and a fresh load of text would scroll into view. She hadn't even noticed Mallory's likely-to-be-a-surprise presence, that's how engrossed she was in her work.

At the opposite end of the table... sat a man Mallory didn't recognize, beyond recognizing the archetype. He wore a serious dark gray business suit much like you'd see in a video stream news profile, and was 80% bald on top. He adjusted his tie slightly as Mallory entered the room, to maintain a perfect presence in front of strangers.

Finally, sitting sort of off to the side but close to Meiko was someone who could possibly have been Mellow Fellow's grandfather. He wore the same style of loud and colorful I's Lander wear, but had a knotted, gnarly beard of silver along with wild dreadlocks flowing out from beneath a strange yellow hat. Combined with the yellow sash he wore over his shoulders, Mallory (correctly) guessed this would be one of the "Elders" that Mellow had mentioned...

Meiko set the info-pad down, shaking her head. "No. Tanner-san, it doesn't matter where you put it in the document or what number of 'resources' are involved... I's Land can't accept membership in the PPP. I thought I made that clear to you when we started negotiation..."

"Yes, but there are a number of other concessions in there which I hoped would balance out your dislike of the Preferred Partners Program," the balding man spoke, quite calm and friendly about it. "This package should represent a good compromise that will allow I's Land to continue their lease even with their limited means—"

The Elder cleared his throat. Mellow Fellow turned his head sharply, ready to listen intently to his words...

"I-and-I's not meaning to be rude, Mister Tanner," the man spoke in a softer voice than Mallory would have figured him for. "But this plan... I-and-I's not seeing how it's preferable to be a partner in this plan. The Elders, we've been looking over your proposal some time now. This is not an uninformed decision; it's simply not the direction we want to go with our community. RealWare may be a fine and profitable company, and no doubt you see yourself as having good intentions... but in the eyes of Iism, RealWare is the true heart of Babylonia. To do this, to send our most loved into that heart... no.

We cannot. I-and-I's apologizing for any undue troubles this is causing, but we cannot go along with this. That's why we hired Mirai Consulting to negotiate on our behalf, so we could be finding a deal to make all happy."

"And that's what's on the table now," Tanner insisted. "I understand not wanting to part with a large amount of your human resources, but the RealWare Preferred Partners Program pays you in the end. The training programs teach valuable skills and trades which can then be directed back to your own economy, which frankly could use a boost given how much barter and charity you seem to utilize, which is what led you to this crisis in the first place—"

"You're saying you want their children," Meiko clarified... with a small amount of ice in her voice.

"In many realities, persons over the age of thirteen are legal adults," Tanner noted.

"And if they let you take a dozen of their children—or let's say legal adults for the sake of argument, as you're asking for those in the range of thirteen to eighteen years of age—"

"Which we've scientifically determined to be the optimal age to begin the learning process for skilled work," Tanner noted. "This program has been available for nearly four hundred years now with many satisfied participants —"

"—and then in return for keeping them for five years at Reality Prime to clean your wastebaskets and cook your food, you'll lower the lease fee on the I's Land Reality Engine to something I's Land can actually afford. Barely. Then five years later you'll give them their 'adults' back."

"After we help them learn valuable job skills which will be beneficial to I's Land," Tanner reminded. "This isn't slave labor, Miss Mirai. We train for worthwhile careers. Training for the janitorial and hospitality industries could later be plied to development of reality tourism for I's Land. There's even potential for training as construction workers or even reality engineers if they prove to be bright enough, although with the education standard here so much lower than the RealWare norm—"

Meiko slid the pad back across the table, with practiced skill—it scraped to a halt on the wooden table right in front of Tanner, perfectly aligned with his seat.

"No deal," Meiko also reminded. "My apologies, Tanner-san, but I's Land does not want to be a member of your Preferred Partners Program. That's not something you're going to change my mind on—I've been hired to find an alternative. I've never failed in my contracts before and I don't plan to begin today."

"Oh?" Tanner asked, tapping a finger on the data pad. "What about—"

"Eiko, I think I need your skills now," Meiko smoothly spoke, cutting him off and turning to face her sister. "We're starting to get down to the financial brass tacks. To keep this thing under budget, we... ...what're you doing here, Mallory?"

Mallory's intense focus on the conversation shattered like a collectable limited edition Love & Hate Glass (available at a Joe's near you fifty years ago). "Err, yes? Meiko-san?"

She started to speak, but paused to raise an eyebrow at the '-san'... before continuing. "I don't know what you're doing here, but go home," she commanded. "The house is a mess. Tidy up downstairs and upstairs. Eiko and I will be back shortly before dinnertime."

"Erm—"

"Don't worry, Mallory-oniichan!" Eiko declared, rolling up her sleeves cutely after hopping into an offered chair. "With me at the negotiations, we'll have this deal signed, sealed and delivered in time to have a yummy dinner! Okay, Tanner-san, let's get down to business!"

Because this was I's Land, where even the rains were polite and pleasant, the weather was quite invigorating. There was nothing Mallory liked better than good weather when cleaning the house; even when you're indoors, knowing it's sunny and warm outside keeps you in good spirits!

He ran the self-propelled FloorCleen™ combination soap / scrub / dry / vacuum cleaner across the living room carpet as he hummed a happy tune... while trying to keep the thing from running away without him, as he wasn't strong enough to truly wrest the self-propelled demonic thing under his control. But he had just enough control not to make more of a mess than he was cleaning up, so it was all good...

"It be a very unrighteous mess," Mellow explained, as he and Mallory walked back to the beach. "I-and-I's lovin' this land with all my heart, but I's been around the multiverse... I's knowin' the score, and the score be money, and money be time and time not be nothin' to anyone outside I's Land. And that means we don't got a lot of the monies of Babylonia. And that means we's in unrighteous trouble."

Getting the machine to scrub under the coffee table in the conversation pit was some trouble, but Mallory was quickly learning how to tame the beast. A few passes that put a few hopefully unnoticeable dents in the wood finish later, and he could power the machine down and store it away. Next up was picking up Eiko's stray toys from the family room floor, and putting them back in her room.

"Eiko's on the job, so I'm sure you'll be okay," Mallory tried to assure him. "I mean, she's a whiz with numbers!"

"This be more than numbers, though. The Elders, they don't be seein' that. They think, we give RealWare the monies they wantin', we can go back to our

peaceful life here. And it is peaceful here, but that means they don't see that it ain't peaceful anywhere else like I's seen... out there, on the shores of Babylonia, they be steppin' with a mean razor, Mal. They want blood. And I-and-I's thinkin' RealWare won't stop until they got our blood and bone. 'til they get into us and turn us into them."

Carrying an armload of toys up the stairs without tripping and falling and breaking his neck was Mallory's primary goal at that point, as he tried to ignore the various voice box speeches and squeaky sounds from Eiko's dolls, concentrating on one foot in front of the other. He'd have to get better at this if he was going to carry laundry up and down the narrow, spiraling stairwell.

Opening a door with an armload of toys was the next task. The problem was, he wasn't sure which room was Eiko's... truth be told, he hadn't even seen the second floor of the house before. Figuring nobody was home, a little trial and error couldn't hurt...

The first door was an error. The room just felt too grown up to be Eiko's... it was sparsely furnished, done in tasteful grays and browns. A gray futon in one corner, a brown low table in the center with some sort of blanket around the edges... it seemed a bit odd to put the mattress on the floor to someone who was used to beds with four legs keeping them up. And the table was so low the only way you could use it was to kneel down or lie down or something... but there was also a desk with a RealNet Workstation (expensive-looking) and a framed picture of Eiko and Meiko, much younger than they were now.

Probably Meiko's room, Mallory decided, closing the door behind himself and looking around the upstairs hallway for the next option.

"But... it's not like you guys have any options, right?" Mallory had asked. "RealWare makes Reality Engines. So you have to come to some kind of terms with them..."

"Well... yes and no," Mellow explained. "See, you know the engine in I's taxi, right? It be powered by wings of freedom, like I's tellin' you before. 'Open Engine.' Righteously smart guys, they copy the Reality Engine, make their own. Give it away for free, try to spread the cause... I's Land, we could be goin' that way instead of the way of Babylonia, but... Babylonia, she be a jealous mother, you know? Be a harsh way. Maybe too harsh..."

The next room was also not likely Eiko's, unless she had skipped a few years straight into puberty and really liked posters of half-naked men all over her walls.

Even more sparsely be-furnitur'd than Meiko's room, this room was obviously Lorelei's. The posters were Mallory's first clue, and discarded underwear lying around formed clue number two. Just to increase his level of nervousness, a weapons rack with various curvy, dangerous-looking bladed things greeted him to his right just as he entered the door. (Lorelei said she was Meiko's bodyguard. Maybe she was some sort of martial artist ninja thing like he'd see on video streams?) There was a bed (covered in discarded clothing) and a table (covered in discarded clothing) and a large exercise mat that had been thickly padded in some parts and stamped flat in others.

Praying that Lorelei would pick up her own laundry and hand it to him in a nice safe hamper when the time came to clean clothes, Mallory closed the door and went for the next one. It didn't open at first, but as he was a man on a mission, a bit of a bump with the shoulder and it magically gave way...

"So... you can get a real, honest-to-goodness Reality Engine for free?" Mallory asked, confused. *"No kidding? I didn't think something like that was possible! But... why would anybody pay RealWare for one when they could just get it for free? You should do that—then you wouldn't have to give them anything! I mean, it's just business—it's not like they can kill you, right?"*

"Not directly," Mellow Fellow conceded, as they reached the door to the House. *"But... aah. I's hatin' to be worried, Mallory. Not my groove. You know my cab? Mellow Fellow's Smiling Taxi Service? Named that 'cause I's be smilin', it be my way. My way in life, I-and-righteous-I's smilin'. But this, this is takin' away my smile. Curse of Babylonia like a creepin' shadow... and until I's seein' the knife pulled away from the throat of I's Land, I's not thinkin' I's gonna be doin' much smilin'..."*

Peering into the dark depths of the third bedroom, Mallory felt around the wall for the light switch. Until he felt a knife blade pressed to his neck.

Perhaps the girly little whimper he squeaked out was enough to let the knife bearer know he wasn't much of a threat.

"...I was under the impression they had told you my rule," a voice whispered in his ear. "No one enters my room. Ever. What are you doing here, Mallory Heisenberg?"

"Ki... Kisei?" Mallory whispered, careful not to let his body twitch in the slightest. "Just... room... Eiko... looking for... toys?" he added, holding up the armload of plush animals carefully.

With an audible whoosh and a flash of her cloak, Kisei stepped around from behind the houseboy. Whatever blade she wielded was no longer in her hands. Where it had gone to would be a matter of conjecture.

"Eiko Mirai's quarters are at the other end of the hall," Kisei informed him. "Now that you know this, you may exit my quarters immediately and not return. I will handle my own laundry and room cleaning; those services are not required. When is dinner time?"

Backing out of the room slowly to avoid any bodily harm, Mallory made a guesstimate. "Err... about one hour—"

After nodding once in acknowledgment, Kisei shut the door. Firmly. And then, from the sounds of it, activated about five or six complicated-sounding locking mechanisms. (What, was it unlocked before? he thought briefly.)

Now pointed the right way, he opened the door to Eiko's room. Exactly what he was expecting, this time; bright and colorful wallpaper, lots of stuffed dolls all over the place on her bed and on shelves and on the floor. A video set, a workstation, lots of expensive toys... even more than her sister had.

He dumped his armload (lovingly and carefully) on her bed for now. Mission completed, Mallory strolled down the stairs with a lighter burden to bear...

Meiko, on the other hand, looked like she had just held up all of I's Land for at least three days. She slumped in through the floor door with Eiko just as Mallory was coming around the bend... Eiko, who also looked a bit upset as she slumped past Mallory without a word, heading upstairs.

"Errrr..." Mallory opened with, not sure what to say. "I take it negotiations didn't go real well?"

"What negotiations?" Meiko asked... getting a bit more snarl in her voice, a bit more energy to her exhaustion. "'Negotiation' implies variance on an issue with an overall goal of a common ground. There isn't one here. Tanner didn't budge an inch. RealWare isn't leaving until they've made this place pay their tithe. He wants money or fresh bodies, and since they don't have the money and won't give the fresh bodies... we got nowhere. Even Eiko couldn't wring enough money out of I's Land's economy to meet RealWare's demands... dammit. When's dinner, houseboy?"

"Why don't they just use an Engine Opened?" Mallory asked, determined to show he had some smarts on the subject. "Mellow-san mentioned them, although he said that even though they were free, they might cause problems..."

"Huh? Engine Op—Open Engine, you mean?" Meiko asked, raising an eyebrow. "Are you studying for your REC Test already, Mr. Reality Engineer?"

"My wha—oh, uh, no. I just heard it in conversation..."

"Sure, they could go open source. Get in league with the grassroots upstarts trying to overthrow RealWare, save a lot of money in the process, and I's Land would never be bothered by RealWare again," Meiko explained, leaning heavily on a wall. "But RealWare wouldn't like it. I brought it up as a solution today... and Tanner explained as polite as can be exactly what would happen. They'd de-list I's Land from Twoday's Guidebook, cut off of all RealNet communication feeds, and blacklist I's Land from doing business with their allied partners across the multiverse. I's Land would have to go rogue and probably sell their native Weeds through the illegal drug market to stay alive, which would just make their black mark on the multiverse bigger..."

"And... all of that sounds bad," Mallory concluded. "So, uh... what are we gonna do?"

"'We' aren't going to do anything. 'I' am going back to war tomorrow with that bastard Tanner," Meiko spoke, tugging herself upright again, trying to maintain some dignity. "Meanwhile, 'You' are going to cook dinner. I'm tired, I'm hungry and I'm expecting nothing less than that five-star cuisine you supposedly can produc... what's that smell? Are you cooking already?"

"Smell?" Mallory asked, sniffing the air... and catching it for the first time. Something vaguely rotten... "Uh, no... I'm not sure what that is. I—"

"Tell me you're not using the local coconuts in your cooking. PLEASE tell me that. I don't think I could take this on top of everything else..."

Mallory smacked his forehead. "OH! I know, I know what it is! When I opened the window this morning, a coconut hit me in the head. It must still be on the kitchen floor..."

"Well, throw it out," Meiko said, as she walked past him. "They're technically called 'Rectalnuts' and they taste as good as that sounds. They grow wild in I's Land, but nobody cooks with them. It's gonna stink worse after ripening on the kitchen floor all day, so toss it outside, not in the garbage. Got it?"

"Ah, got it, boss!" Mallory chirped off, trying to give her a comforting smile and a thumbs up. "You can count on me!"

"Eeh," she offered in response as she slogged past him, taking the spiral stairwell one foot at a time.

Five star. Five-star cuisine...

He'd heard of the star rating system, of course. Half of the video feeds he got on his cheap video network player were oriented around tourism, business travel, things like that... the restaurant business, that much he knew about. Five-star was the best of the best...

Of course, he had jumped ship from Grünwald without completing his training. His marks in school were decent, especially in stews and soups, but otherwise he wouldn't consider himself a five-star chef. Still, he was a firm believer that making a good effort and believing in yourself would achieve anything! Even if "Humiliating Failure" was technically part of the "Anything" set of outcomes...

In all the activity today, he hadn't actually gotten around to shopping. This meant he had the limited, fairly junk-food-oriented stocks of the House to work with. This meant that he had to use his three-star skills plus two-star ingredients to make five stars, and since two and three made five, he hadn't a worry in the world.

Until he actually tried to put some things together in a nice stew and ended up with one star at best. He rinsed his mouth out with water to cleanse the palette and prevent from choking to death on the broccoli-and-melted-cheese-and-ground-spice-he-could-not-identify soup experiment. A quick glance at the clock showed he had wasted thirty minutes on what amounted to food that would be superior coming up than it would be going down...

But it was workable. He could work this. The core ingredients were okay, but they didn't mix well. He needed something strong to mask the mixture in a different flavor entirely...

Four samples of spices and additives went into the pot next, with mild effect. Not strong enough.

This was his chance to make a first impression with his cooking. He couldn't afford to screw it up; Meiko might even kick him out, jobless and alone, if he didn't live up to the tasks they hired him for...

But more importantly, Meiko was in a depressed mood, and Mallory wanted to try to turn that frown upside down with a good meal. He couldn't help them negotiate a deal. He didn't know enough about anything at all to be useful to them, but the one thing he COULD do was cook... and after seeing Mellow Fellow so unhappy, "Losing his smile," he had frankly had enough of people being depressed today. Meiko didn't deserve to be depressed after working so hard to help out these people. If he could do something about it with his cooking, he would. And maybe he could, if he took a risk...

His eyes glanced at the floor under the kitchen table.

Then they glanced at the clock.

An unworkable ingredient...

"We'll see about that," Mallory spoke to himself, grabbing the Rectalnut from the floor with one hand. And holding his nose shut with the other.

"Dinnertime!" Mallory called out, banging a pot lid with a wooden spoon. "Ah, come on! It's hot and ready and waiting! And, um, tasty! Dinnertime! Din —"

"I heard you just fine," Kisei spoke, already seated at the table after somehow sneaking downstairs and evading Mallory's sight in a stealthy manner which sent cold chills up and down his central nervous system.

"Ah... right," he said, setting the lid down and fetching a stack of bowls. "Are the others—"

Eiko bounced into her chair, showing none of her ill mood from before. "Dinner! Wai!" she cheered, eagerly anticipating the edible delights to come. "Nothing's better after my favorite cartoons than a good dinner! Oniichan, do we have dessert? Can I have cake?"

"No cake, Eiko, you get hyperactive," Meiko warned, entering the kitchen and taking her seat in a more dignified way. "Just serve for four, Mallory. Lorelei called to say she met someone at the beach today and won't be back until tomorrow."

"Oh," Mallory said, disappointment clear in his voice. "Well... uh... we'll have plenty of leftovers, so... I can put some in the fridge for her! Ah, this is a new recipe of mine, currently untitled but I'm leaning towards 'I'Stew'. It's a dish which utilizes only vegetables, since Mellow-san told me today about how Iism follows vegan diets—"

"Skip the speech and serve the chow," Meiko suggested/commanded.

And thus, four bowls worth of the thick and mysterious stew were spooned out with four dinner rolls. (Technically 'Hot Dog Buns', from what Mallory recalled, but they would work in a pinch.) Mallory took his place at the table, but didn't start into his food right away... eagerly watching for the reactions of his servees.

Eiko took a spoonful first... and the reaction Mallory sought, he received. She smiled brightly, nodding to him vigorously. "It's really good, oniichan!" she spoke up. "It's kind of sweet and sour and stuff and... it's just really different! Ooh, kinda strong, though... can I have some milk?"

Kisei was next... and took much longer to evaluate her tasting. She concentrated as if studying some complex thing which required great focus to comprehend, before finally swallowing... and nodding slowly. "It has an adequate taste," was the sum total of her critique as she went for a second spoonful.

Finally, there was Meiko. Who didn't really WANT to like it, especially not with Mallory looking at her with puppy dog eyes that beg for praise, but she couldn't get around the simple facts. "It's good," she decided. "I guess you live up to the hype, houseboy. It's really good. I mean... really, REALLY good, and I've eaten at a few four- and five-star restaurants when I could afford to... so, it's original? Or some Grünwald recipe?"

"WOOHOO! Ah, heh, not really," Mallory laughed off, glowing from the praise. "I started out with a little of everything I could find in here, plus some seasoning mixes I learned in second year Condiments but that wasn't enough and it didn't feel right so I added some Rectalnut chunks—"

The temperature in the room dropped six degrees. Meiko's spoon clattered against her bowl after it fell from her limp fingers.

"WAAAAH?!" Eiko gagged (literally), clutching at her throat. "Oneesama, I ate a Rectalnut? I'm gonna die! I'm too young to die!! It's not fair!"

"I... TOLD... you to get rid of that thing!" Meiko barked out, standing up in a way that knocked her chair aside for maximum dramatic effect. "I told you to throw it out, and instead, you put it in my food?! What are you THINKING?! You could have—"

"Could have what?" Kisei asked calmly, after her fifth spoonful. "From my limited knowledge of local foods, Rectalnut is not fatal if ingested. You are not dying, Eiko. You will know death when you see it."

"Well... of course not," Meiko admitted, "But for Kami's sake, Kisei—!"

"I do not believe I should have to remind you that you were enjoying your dinner a moment ago," Kisei spoke... locking her eyes on Meiko's unbelieving gaze. "I appreciate consistency of behavior, which you are certainly not exhibiting at the moment, Meiko-san. I mean no disrespect by this, mind you. I point out that simply because others have failed to implement an ingredient in the past does not mean Mallory has failed in his task now. As I said before... it has an adequate taste. I would like seconds to take to my room tonight, Mallory, if you believe this stew will suffice when cold as well."

All eyes then turned to Mallory. Even Eiko had stopped gagging, watching curiously as the boy's silent look of Absolute Bliss radiated outward like the sun over I's Land.

"S... sure!" he finally said. "I think it'll be okay cold. See, the taste of the Rectalnut by itself isn't very good, but the stew wasn't very good either, and three lefts make a right and birds of a feather stew together so I figured it'd work out! And, uh... yes, you can have... seconds. Meiko? Err, what's wrong? Ah, if you really don't like it, I can make you something else..."

"You said... that this is made from common stuff we had lying around, and Rectalnut?" she asked... a spark of an idea gathering behind her eyes.

Mallory scratched his head. "Well... yeah—"

"And there's no meat in it, so it works fine with Iism?"

"Oh, definitely, see, I believe that when working with local cuisine you have to adopt an understanding of—"

"How hard was it to cook? Some crazy technique which can only be learned by Grünwaldians?"

"Err, no, I just sort of tossed it all together, um, I think I could recall the exact amounts if I sit down and think about—"

"You can sit down later," she decided, glancing around the kitchen quickly... spotting a rubber ReSeel container. "Fill that with as much as you can and bring a spoon. We could still catch him before he calls it a night."

"Err, what?" Mallory said with his usual flair for the oblivious. "Huh? Him? Who? Wha—"

"Come ON!" Meiko urged, grabbing the container and scooping a liberal amount of stew into it herself, as Mallory remained jammed in a state of confusion. She tucked it carefully under one arm as not to mess up her blouse, and grabbed his wrist with the spare hand. In moments, the front door had shut behind them.

Kisei resumed patiently enjoying her meal. Not that she showed facial expressions of enjoyment.

As I's Land lacked a formal dock, they had to jog across the island to another beach.

Parked there on a tall dune was a portable RealWare office. Mallory saw the glow of the tasteful neon sign before he even saw the whole building; it was like a miniature complex, with windows of offices up top, a hotel-room like door at the base, and even a garage to park a land vehicle in.

It made perfect sense to drag as much of the home office with you as possible on business trips, but Mallory didn't have time to ponder the many technical wonders of the multiverse; Meiko was on a mission and dragged him along at a high rate of speed. She marched right up to the hotel room door, knocking on it sharply after stopping to catch her breath...

After a few moments, Mr. Tanner opened the door. Mallory peeked over his shoulder at the five-star hotel suite behind him, superior to any residential room he'd ever seen, even those in the House.

"Miss Mirai," he acknowledged. "It's very late, so I trust you have a good reason for this interruption? I'd really prefer to conduct our negotiations during business hours, and I do have dinner being prepared by our chef—"

Seconds later, the reality executive found himself holding an open ReSeel container in one hand and a spoon in the other

"Try some of that," Meiko ordered him... with a bit of a smile on her lips. "Trust me on this. You might not want your dinner after you taste it."

With a Suspicious Look, he carefully spooned a bit of the stew, and tipped it in his mouth. A familiar look to Mallory swept across his face; eating satisfaction.

"Best local cuisine I've had since I got here," he noted. "Whenever I could find a restaurant with actual marked opening and closing times... so, what is it?"

"Rectalnut Stew," Meiko said with pride. "We're calling it I'Stew."

"...I'm going to assume poisoning me isn't your new negotiating tactic. Besides, this can't actually be—"

"It is."

"If it is, then you're apparently as skilled in the kitchen as you are at the negotiation table. And I don't mean that sarcastically, Miss Mirai. If you don't mind, I suppose I will have this for dinner. Thank you for—"

"I didn't come just to feed you. I have a proposal. And it can't wait until business hours. How would you like to have the rights to produce that stew?" Meiko asked. "I's Land can give you all the Rectalnuts you want—they grow like ragweed here, and aren't suitable for anything else. In return, you lower the lease on the Reality Engine to the level we discussed earlier today, without the Preferred Partners Plan. Deal?"

"You're joking, right?" Tanner asked, setting the ReSeel down on a nearby table inside the suite. "I work for RealWare, Miss Mirai, not an eatery—"

"But RealWare owns the multiversal chain of Joe's Fast Food restaurants," Meiko interrupted. "It's common knowledge in the business world, Tanner-san, even if most of the folks who eat there aren't aware. Joe's would be a perfect outlet for this recipe; it can be made fast, and is good served cold or reheated."

Tanner frowned, caught in a spot. "Perhaps... this would make a good token to add to our negotiations, yes. We're always looking for new consumer food products to introduce through... certain channels such as Joe's. But this alone is not enough to—"

"If you don't accept this proposal, I's Land is going Open Engine," Meiko continued. "They'll produce I'Stew in mass quantities and using Open Engine-driven cabs like Mellow Fellow's, become the premiere hot food delivery service. Executives working long hours won't even have to go down to Joe's, they can simply order it from here—and I know how to get them cloned, open source RealNet workstations even if you decide to revoke their rights to the official ones. They'll compete against you and even if they can't possibly topple you... they could probably eat a nice amount out of your share of the food industry. All the while, they'll build a reputation as an Open Reality Movement-aligned world with a successful enterprise that's standing up to RealWare. Classic little guy versus the unstoppable giant... the media loves that sort of thing, at least the parts of the media that you don't directly own. And I somehow doubt that your CEO, Gillian Bates, would be happy to hear that you personally allowed this mess to get to that point...... correct?"

Mallory's head span from the effort of following the rapid fire series of financial threats... but somehow, he comprehended it all. Which is why he wasn't surprised to see Tanner's cheeks go a bit pale.

"They'd never succeed against us," he defended weakly. "Joe's controls the majority of the multiversal restaurant industry and we control Joe's. All I's Land could ever be is a tick on our backside—"

"That's all they'd have to be to show that RealWare has another chink in the armor," Meiko retorted. "Another chink for the Open Reality Movement to exploit as they love to do... But you're not going to anyone see the flaw, are you? You're going to buy rights to the recipe, allow I's Land to grow Rectalnuts at whatever pace they're comfortable with, then you're going to leave them alone. You won't jack their rates up or try to turn them into a satellite tourist reality again. There's a lot of realities out there, Tanner-san; you don't want this one as an enemy, or as a close friend. All they want is to live in peace. Surely there are more lucrative places to find your close friends, yes...?"

An uneasy silence hung in the air as thick as a bowl of I'Stew.

"I think your proposal is bordering on lunacy," Tanner spoke quietly.

Meiko egged him on, nodding. "And...?"

"I'll contact my superiors in the morning for guidance," he added. "Good night, Miss Mirai."

The suite door closed, with Tanner and his stew on one side, Meiko and Mallory on the other.

For the first time since his arrival at the House, Meiko gave Mallory a nice, happy smile.

"We got 'em," she declared. "We got 'em. Eiko can take it from there and haggle them down even further. This time tomorrow, I's Land won't have a thing to worry about. ...thanks, Mallory."

Happiness grabbed Mallory by the neck and throttled him so hard he couldn't even say "You're welcome."

"Gaarghble," he replied instead.

But it's the sentimental thought that counts the eggs before they hatch, he thought silently, smiling to himself.

The stroll back across the island played out nice and slow. Meiko took her time, in no great rush; her smile had faded a little until it was a more reasonable level, but never quite vanished. It simply went from ecstatic to quietly smug.

Mallory strolled along behind her, wishing he had stopped off to pick up his sweatshirt from the tailor; it wasn't cold, exactly, but it wasn't warm out tonight by any thermometer either. He walked in silence as well... Meiko seemed happy and he didn't want to shatter that by babbling out the wrong thing at the wrong time. Compared to her earlier mood of hopelessness, seeing her content and pleased was like a refreshing drink given to a man who really wanted a refreshing drink as opposed to a punch in the face or something to that extent.

Plus, the starry night sky simply made for a quiet, peaceful evening. It would be a shame to shatter that. Other than some light folk-guitar variant Lander Dub floating in from some zone of the city, which fit the mood perfectly, there was no need for sound...

Mallory accidentally broke that peace when he glanced up and to the left.

"...whoa," he said quietly.

"'Whoa'?" Meiko asked, pausing in her walk to turn and look at him curiously. "What whoa?"

"Uh... nothing, really," Mallory said, keeping his eyes on the sight high above the waves of the I's Land oceans. A brilliant white circle, notches and patterns on it that almost made it seem to smile down upon them... he smiled back. "Up there. Look at that... it's a beautiful moon out tonight."

"It's artificial," Meiko replied, unimpressed as she didn't bother to look out across the waters. "Just a funny circular thing that's fashionable to put in the sky. Reality decoration. I don't see what the big deal is."

"But the way it's over the water like that, and... and the reflection, and..."

"So?"

"So... we never had oceans on Grünwald," he explained. "And the moon was just... a thing, like you say. It really wasn't a big deal. But this, it feels... uh... it's sort of... ...ehh. Hard to say, sorry. I'm really new at all this, I haven't seen all the things you've probably seen... I guess it feels special to me."

Looking a bit annoyed at him for a fraction of a second, Meiko turned to look... and her expression softened a bit as she looked at the I's Land moon for the first time. "...well... I guess it can be special. Especially if it's the first new one you've seen. I've seen plenty of moons myself: sometimes in pairs, sometimes they're company logos... it's different in every reality."

"Right! I mean, you've seen things I've only dreamed about! This is half of the reward, you know, of me working with you guys. I can see the multiverse, just like... like my mom used to. She was a Reality Engineer. I bet she saw this moon once..."

"Oh, that reminds me..." Meiko said, reaching inside her vest pocket... and pulling out a small data pad, similar to the one she used at the negotiation table. "Take it."

"Huh?" Mallory standardly stated, accepting the object and poking at it a bit. Text started to pour down the screen in a syntax so complex it felt alien without actually being outside the realm of his language base...

"That's your preparation material for the REC Test," Meiko explained. "Remember, I'm giving you a month to pass the Reality Engineering Certification Test. That's the condition I've hired you under. You should start studying toni... tomorrow. Whenever you get free time around your other duties."

"Ah... right, right! I'll study very hard!" he promised, pocketing the data pad.

"Good. It's important. ...the future is very important, Mallory," Meiko spoke, her voice quiet, her voice serious. "Too important to laugh off like these people..."

"Huh?"

"I's Land," she said, looking back across the water. "They don't worry about the future. 'Time be time, and—'"

"'Time be nothin'.'"

"Right. And that's why they're in this situation. They didn't think about their future, they didn't plan for it. They lived happy and innocent for years, coasting along on just enough to survive without making any coordinated effort to prosper..."

"I don't know... I kind of like it here. It's beautiful, and the people are so nice... and I'd say they do prosper. It's just not money kinda prospering..."

"That's true. And I... kind of like it here too. It's a good place to live... safe, and quiet. This is the kind of place I'd want to settle down in one day... but we need to plan our future if we want to live like this realistically, Mallory," she said, sharpening her tone a bit to bring the point home. "I's Land didn't plan ahead, didn't accept some of the unpleasant facts about reality, and RealWare almost caught them. You can't just hope for the best, you have to make it happen. You have to be vigilant. Like me. I want to provide a good home for my sister, to make sure we're secure in the days to come..."

Turning away from the view, she faced Mallory... and looked him squarely in the eyes.

"Mallory, don't just pass that test because I said so," she said. "Pass it for yourself. Reality Engineering is a good, solid thing to build a lifetime on. Sure, you're a thick-headed farmboy who's hopeless at comprehending anything outside his sealed bubble of a life, but... everybody deserves a good future. Understand?"

"I... I guess so," Mallory replied, hearing the echo of his father's words. Plan ahead, seek your future, make it happen...

The smile Meiko offered him felt brighter than the one before, outside Tanner's door.

"Good," she said simply. "Now, let's go home."

MONDAY

So, you have decided to enter the rewarding career of Reality Engineering!

Reality Engineers are in demand in today's reality-based economy. While various realities have various industries, specializations, and cultural standards, they have one common need: trained, professional reality engineers working to find efficient reality solutions to their reality issues. A Reality Engineer's intense Reality Engineering Certification training guarantees realistically real results for reality issues pertaining to reality...

If it were possible for mild-mannered Mallory Heisenberg to become intensely annoyed, he would have become intensely annoyed at the unnecessary, overdone redundant repetition of the word reality in such a way as to go overboard without a paddle.

And that was just the first paragraph.

It went on and on like this for a few screens of the Introduction to the Reality Engineering Certification Preparatory Material, Copyright RealWare, Incorporated. Sitting on the living room couch, Mallory flicked the jog dial on the side of the data pad a few times trying to find a page without the word 'reality', and failed miserably.

Still, the advertising had soaked into his brain; even if he knew it was overcooked material it made him feel excited—anxious—on edge—and READY to face the challenges of a brave new tomorrow with nothing but his... his... whatever it was Reality Engineers used as their primary, culturally-identifying tool! Which was probably not a steel-toed boot used for kicking engines until they worked properly. True, he did thumb his way past most of the fluff material in the introduction, but it was only to get at the meat of the lessons much faster in a bold demonstration of his enthusiasm!

Lesson 1: Reality Engine Basics

Basics. You can't go wrong with the basics, his farming tutors had tutored into him from an early age of tutoring...

The phase shift harmonics generated by the distilled water core of the engine, when tuned using an advanced reality sequencing system operating on RealWare proprietary code, induce a field of reality definition upon launch of a fresh engine. This field is supported in longevity using power feed and dispersal units which assure the flux metric stays within six standard deviations from acceptable norms

as established in Core Directive 34.0134. But odds
are you knew that already...

...it read, while the glaze settled over Mallory's eyes like so many freshly baked, honey-dipped doughnuts.

A few flicks of the thumb verified his second worst fears, as it continued on and on like this, complete with incomprehensible diagrams and flow charts using words that had more syllables than nature should allow.

"Houseboy!"

Mallory's eyes gratefully peeled away from the textual nightmare, sliding instead on the welcome vision of Meiko Mirai.

"House meeting," Meiko explained, nodding towards the kitchen table in the other room. "C'mon. You'll have plenty of time to study for the REC later this week..."

"Six days?!" Lorelei groaned, slumping back in her chair.

"Six days," Meiko confirmed, snapping her Future Perfect shut. "The next job offer is going to be farther away than we'd hoped, and we knew going into it that the I's Land job wouldn't pay a whole lot. That means we have to stretch the budget a little until the next client calls... we'll have to make sacrifices. Lorelei, no more beer. Eiko, you're going to have to wait before buying that new doll house..."

Eiko crossed her arms and pouted. "We wouldn't have this problem if you'd let me invest my allowance in the Urbana day trading markets," she noted. "There's a 37.8% chance of a high-yield return, you know!"

"And you, fearless leader?" Lorelei asked, raising an eyebrow. "Planning any sacrifices of your own while I'm on the wagon? What about your... 'quarterly'?"

"...that's a business expense," the businesswoman vaguely explained, before quickly moving on to the newcomer. "Mallory... for you, that means no running out and buying lots of expensive ingredients. And no bartering anything we own for them from the locals, either! We're going to be stuck at I's Land for the duration since they're giving us docking space for free."

"Ahh, that's okay," Mallory added, trying to play cheerleader for the dour girls. "I'm sure I can make do with what we've got and, er, any Rectalnuts I can find for my stew—"

"RealWare owns the intellectual property to your stew, Mallory. You're not legally allowed to make it anymore, or we'll be in breach of contract and subject to suit under the EMCA (Edible Millennium Copyright Act) Section 8a."

Lorelei snickered. "All the better. I doubt lightning strikes twice, and I'd hate to be at ground zero when Mallory launches into a second round of

Rectalnut experiments—"

A loud scrape of chair on cheap linoleum floor cut Lorelei off in mid quip.

Kisei placed both hands on the table as she stood. "...I will be going now," she announced. "Miss Mirai, I hereby request two days of unpaid leave for purposes of training. I will handle said expenses from of my own pocket out of respect to the house fund situation."

"Bowing and scraping like a salaryman, are we?" Lorelei mocked, leaning forward and looking up at Kisei with a grin. "Or are you issuing a formal request to your commanding officer? What, are we no fun to hang around with on the off days, Kiss?"

Quasi-glaring down at the other woman, Kisei's tongue added the tiniest taste of acid to her words. "Unlike Some," she noted, "I do not allow my combat skills to go rusty from prolonged periods of disuse, nor do I water them down with bottled toxins on a regular basis."

"You could do with a few bottled toxins, Kiss. They might help you relax enough that we can finally pull the stick out of your—"

Meiko cleared her throat while glancing at the young, innocent picturesque icon of little sisterly childhood purity to her left.

"—ear," Lorelei finished lamely.

"Hey... hey, I think it's a good idea," Mallory interjected, trying to cool things down. "I mean, we have a lot of days off, so we should all do our best to use them wisely! I'm going to study for the REC Test, and if Kisei's training, and Meiko's doing her... quarterlies, those sounded important, and Eiko can, er, do whatever it is she does which I don't know because I've only known you a few days but I think ninety percent of a week will be perfect for me to get to know you all better and the money won't be a problem it seems so let's all make the best of things and have fun! Right?"

Waving her arms in the air, Eiko bounced in her seat with delight. "Wai!" was her statement of confidence in Mallory's plan of attack. "Let's all do our best, minna-san!"

"...eh, Mal's right," Lorelei agreed, cooling down a bit. "Hell, I could probably train a bit this week. And get some nude bodyboarding in at that beach! Downtime sounds fine here, Mei... Kiss, you go and shoot stuff and blow shi—"

The clearing of the throat repeated itself.

"—blow stuff up and have fun," Lorelei corrected. "Save me some shrapnel as a souvenir and say hi to Duke for me."

"Then it's settled!" Mallory spoke up, rising to his seat and pumping a fist in the air with dramatic intensity! "Let's all do our best! House team, GAHM BATTLE KNEE! YOOOOSH!"

It took him half a minute to realize they were staring at him.

"...err, that means 'good luck,' right?" Mallory whispered to Eiko, confused. "Did I pronounce it wrong, or something...?"

"Oniichan no baka," Eiko giggled.

Good, Mallory thought, quite proud of himself. After all, 'baka' means idiot, so that must mean 'Big brother is NO idiot.'

03: Daze of the Weak

TUESDAY

Cooking, cleaning, laundry, cooking, cleaning, laundry...

With Kisei out of the house / Lorelei at the beach / Meiko out shopping, things were nice and quiet around the House. Mallory had hoped he could get some REC studying in during this quiet time, but with each attempt he made at the material, he invariably went cross-eyed trying to parse the thick, creamy nuggets of technobabble. Compared to that, the daily chores related to upkeep of the House were preferable.

He cooked with intensity, cleaned with fury, and did laundry like a man possessed by an ancient dead laundry master. Breakfast quality had risen so dramatically that Lorelei had started dragging herself out of bed before 10:00 AM to grab some leftovers, no matter what the state of her hangover was. The house was as spotless as he could manage without invading the privacy of his housemates—after the incident with Kisei the prior week, he tried to only enter their rooms when he absolutely had to.

'Absolutely had to' including putting away laundry, unfortunately. He walked up the stairs carrying two baskets of freshly washed/cleaned/pressed/dried clothing, with the datapad of REC study information balanced on top. He could read it after he put away the clothes. And after he straightened out the stock room. And after he vacuumed the upstairs hallway. And after...

For now, after he put away Eiko's clothes. She certainly did have a lot of them, as she liked to wear a new outfit every day, much like her sister. He fumbled for the doorknob to her room, hand brushing by a cardboard door hanger sign before opening up and walking in...

"ONIICHAN!"

For a little girl, she managed to sack Mallory like an expert linebacker. Clothes went flying hither, tither, yon, and on the floor as well.

"Wagh!" Mallory protested, shaking his head to clear it. "Eiko...! Agh, now I gotta pick all this up... you should be careful when you run up to hug people! I mean, it's not polite to do otherwise, and... err, why are you looking at me like I'm your favorite flavor of ice cream and you're starving? It's making me very nervous..."

"It's time to play with Eiko-chan now!" Eiko spoke, with a decidedly predatory grin. "You can pick up the clothes after you finish your contractually accepted period of playtime!"

"My what of what of what?" Mallory asked, sitting up on the floor to be eye level with her.

With pride, Eiko pointed to the tiny sign hanging on her door knob. "Didn't you read the End User Licensing Agreement I posted? All those who enter agree to the following terms: Will play with Eiko for a minimum of one (1) hour!"

"Ah... er, that's very clever!" Mallory said, laughing nervously. "Ha ha... um, but I really don't have time to play, I want to get the laundry done so I can study for my test—what's this?"

"A subpoena for failure to meet contractual terms, of course," Eiko said, holding out the prepared document in question. "You'll hear from my lawyers for failure to play with me if you walk out that door!"

"...you're just kidding, right?"

Eiko pointed to her adorable face with both hands. "Do these eyes lie?" she asked, staring with big, wide, only slightly frightening optic orbs.

"I... guess I can play an hour," Mallory decided, determined to turn this into a positive. "It'll be a lot of fun, and I can still study for my test after dinner, I guess... okay! Um, what are we playing? Do you have a video game or something? I've never played one before, so—"

"Bah! Video games are for little kids," Eiko spoke, nose in the air. "They're just pattern memorization and button mashing. There's no talent to them at all!"

"Really? They looked kind of fun to me... so, uh, what are we playing with, then?"

"DOLLS!" she announced, holding up a Kensuke™ doll and a Biiko™ doll. "We're gonna play House!"

"...House? Err... how do you play?"

"Just make believe, silly," she instructed, shoving her Kensuke™ doll into his hands as she dragged over her old, beat up doll house. "C'mon, it's not that hard! Okay, you start by coming home after work..."

The front door latch clicked open, as Kensuke™ strolled in after a long day of work. He hung his coat on the pink plastic coat rack next to the door, and called out to his loving wife.

"Biiko™ honey, I'm home!" he spoke loudly, with a proud smile. "It was a long day at the restaurant where I am a top chef, respected by all my fellow workers and customers alike!"

"No you're not, you work as a golf course caretaker!" Biiko™

corrected, leaning out of the kitchen and waving a plastic spoon at him... before handing it to him. "Now make me dinner! I had a long day at the office buying, selling, trading, and crushing smaller corporations with hostile takeovers so I could put bread on our table, you good-for-nothing ingrate!"

"Eh?" Kensuke™ asked, studying the spoon, confused. "Wait, you mean I'm not a good husband, Eiko?"

"It's Biiko,™ and no! You never attend to my needs. With you, it's always me, me, me!" Biiko™ scolded. "That's why I'm cheating on you with the mailman."

Kensuke's™ plastic jaw sagged. "Err... cheating on me? You know about that stuff?"

"Well, of course! In soap operas, whenever the wife wants revenge on her deadbeat husband, she cheats," Biiko™ explained, smoothing out her felt apron. "I don't know what game she cheats at, but they always say she cheats. And I'm cheating! I sold all of your stuff for a modest sum and you're sleeping on the couch tonight."

"Well, of course I am. I don't have a room. But the couch is very comfortable," Kensuke™ commented, smiling. "I don't mind at all!"

Biiko™ groaned. "No, no! Not you, Mallory-oniichan, Kensuke,™ Kensuke!™ He's on the couch!"

"Oh. Well, I don't think Kensuke™ would mind either. After all, clearly Biiko™ is angry at him and it's best to back off a bit and talk to her later to try and smooth things out, right?"

Pouting, Biiko™ sagged a bit in disappointment. "Mallory, that's no fun! Couples on the soap operas are always fighting and plotting and stuff. C'mon, play along!"

"Right, right," Kensuke™ agreed, shaking his arms loose and trying to get back into character. "Well, okay... hey! I work hard for this family too, honey! And I'm doing the best I can! And... and I'm a better husband than any mailman could be!"

The door flew off its hinges, as a burly, muscle-bound guy in camouflage and bandoliers loaded with ammo suitable for his heavy machine gun burst onto the scene.

"GRRRR!! I'm the MAILMAN!" Muscles Manslaughter™ shouted. "And I'm gonna kick your butt!"

A Kensuke™-shaped hole in the air formed as he zipped behind his wife to hide, pointing at the massive action figure in shock. "THAT'S the mailman!?"

"I don't have a mailman action figure, they don't make them," Biiko™ noted while her husband was promptly manhandled by the man who cuckolded him. "Anyway, we're leaving you! And here are legal papers entitling me to 50% of everything that you make in future years to support me, along with appropriate tax forms to include the nondeductible amounts on your annual return. Okay, honey?"

Kensuke's™ eyes rolled around funny after Muscles Manslaughter™ bounced his head off the floor for the sixth time. "Okay, honey, whatever you say," he groggily replied.

The earth began to shake, as plastic furniture toppled over. Muscles Manslaughter™ fell on his side in mid-heroic lantern-jawed action pose.

"Wh-what's that?!" Kensuke™ asked, scrabbling against a wall in fear.

Biiko™ stared in horror at the giant yellow eye staring in at her through the window. "Oh no! Very bad! Most terrible Mecha-Lizard King™ is attacking the city! We're done for! I'll use my emergency ejector seat. Goodbye forever, husband!"

"ROAR! ROAR!" Mecha-Lizard King™ roared in a very young girlish voice.

"W-wait! Take me with you! I don't want to die!" Kensuke™ shouted, waving his arms in protest.

Biiko™ buckled her pretty pink seat belt, pulling a lever to open the house's skylight. "You should have thought of that before you kept leaving the toilet seat up. Bye!"

With a sound of roaring rockets, she was gone. The walls crumbled and shook, and Kensuke™ screamed in absolute terror as the giant green scaled foot came crushing down on him...

"But since Biiko™ got Kensuke™ to take out monster accident insurance the prior fiscal year, the premiums paid out with double indemnity and she lived happily ever after!" Eiko declared, hugging her Biiko™ dolly while Kensuke's™ legs stuck out under the ruined doll house. "The end. Wai! I love a happy ending."

"......." Mallory spoke, staring at the gruesome fate his poor avatar met.

"Don't worry, oniichan! I'm gonna be getting a new dollhouse next week anyway. That was a lot of fun! Don't you think so?"

"............." Mallory continued.

Eiko cocked her head, peering at him curiously. "Oniichan?"

"Huh—? Oh, ah, yes?"

"I want you to make Eiko-chan a promise," she said, suddenly serious. "You'll do that, right?"

"Err... I think it depends on what the promise is," he replied, recalling the

EULA and even the hot dog incident. Fool me once, shame on you, fool me twice, shame on me, fool me three times—

"You'll be a better husband than that to Meiko-oneechan, right?"

—he fell over.

"Ha ha ha! Oh, Eiko, you're so cute when you're joking around!!!" he exclaimed after popping to his feet and gathering up the strewn laundry at subsonic speeds. "Well, it was very fun but I have to go study for the REC test now! So much to do, so much to do!"

"Hey, our hour isn't done yet!" Eiko complained.

"I had a lot of fun! Put it on my tab, I'll play with you another time!" Mallory replied 0.3 seconds before he was out the door.

The young Mirai sister pouted. He hadn't said if he promised or not...

WEDNESDAY

Cooking, cleaning, laundry, cooking, cleaning, laundry... studying? Cooking.

Cooking was simpler with only the Mirai sisters in the house; Lorelei was missing again, presumably off somewhere having more fun than Mallory was. Not that he didn't enjoy cooking, but the tedium of daily chores was really bringing him down. Mind you, the tedium meant he wasn't able to study for the REC, which was a bad thing considering he was only on page six. The tedium also meant he wasn't able to study for the REC, which was a relief because every time he looked at the datapad, he felt too woefully inadequate to use big words like 'woefully inadequate'...

Perhaps it was the sigh of boredom that sent him off on his journey that evening.

"S'matter, having breathing problems?" Meiko asked, between spoonfuls of the new soup concoction Mallory had whipped up.

"Ah, no, I'm quite well," Mallory replied, halting his sigh so fast it came out as 'sig'. "In fact, the air around here is much nicer than it was at Urbana. It's more like home, really!"

"Eiko-chan thinks oniichan's bored," Eiko said, kicking her feet a bit under the table for fun, while she listlessly played with her soup spoon. "I'm bored too. I's Land is nice but I want a cheeseburger and they're all vegetarians here! I wish this stupid week was over so we could go..."

"For starters, his name is not 'oniichan,'" Meiko corrected, trying to sound firm rather than angry at this... while giving Mallory the Evil Eye. "He's named Heisenberg, not Mirai. So he's not your big brother. Second... if you're good and eat... drink? Mallory, do you drink soup or eat it? You're the food expert."

"What? Uh, Dad usually said 'finish your soup'. So, um, I don't know."

"Finish your soup, Eiko... and I'll take you out for ice cream," Meiko completed, adding a smile that melted her earlier flare of anger. "It's not a cheeseburger, but it'll be fun, right?"

"Ice cream! Ice cream!" Eiko cheered. "I'd eat five bowls of soup for some ice cream! I want a cone of rocky road and a sundae with hot sauce and some popsicles to put in the freezer for later. We can afford it, right?"

"I'll find some room in the budget, imouto. Now finish up your soup, then we—"

Empty spoon clattered into empty bowl, and feet hit the floor running while "I'll go get my shoes on!" echoed in the space that Eiko Mirai previously occupied. Due to lack of high speed time lapse photography equipment, the exact process which led to this end result would be lost to the sands of time.

"Wow, I guess she really liked my soup," Mallory incorrectly guessed, with a bright smile. "She's really great, isn't she? I... err... Meiko?"

"You're NOT her big brother," Meiko warned, standing upright in order to tower over the boy as best as her height would allow. "So don't go getting chummy. You're our houseboy, and in a month, you'd better be our Reality Engineer or you're out on your ear. You've been studying your datapad, right?"

"Yes ma'am," Mallory lied, tapping the flat techie widget lying on the table by his spoon.

Meiko pulled her F.P. pocket organizer from her, well, pocket. "Good. I'm beaming an address into your datapad... while I'm getting ice cream with MY sister, I want you to take Mellow Fellow's taxi to this reality and fetch Kisei. She's due back tonight, and it'd save us some money if Mellow handles the transport."

"Mellow's...? You mean you want me to leave I's Land?"

"You're bored, aren't you?" Meiko asked, pocketing her, well, pocket organizer. "Get some fresh air and enjoy the trip. But don't get sidetracked, I want you back here before we return. Got it?"

"Got it!" Mallory declared, rising to his feet. "You can count on me, Miss Mirai! As your, err, houseboy, it's my duty to complete this task with efficiency and valor and determination and... and stuff! I—"

"Yes, whatever."

Mallory studied the digital (watermarked, copy protected, digital rights managed) business card that had been transferred to his datapad. One word stuck out like a green thumb. "It's a reality called Arboria?" he asked, after looking up. "That word means nature and plants and trees and stuff, right?"

"...more or less," Meiko decided after a moment's hesitation. "But bring a scarf to keep wrapped around your mouth, too. Makes it easier to breathe there..."

If any gods watched over this land, they either abandoned it in disgust or died in shame hundreds of years ago.

Blasted pockmarks were the only decoration on the rocky landscape... craters and holes torn from the bleeding landscape, red clay kicked up in explosions, pulverized dust settling like a layer of choking filth on top of every surface. No mountains. No trees. No rivers. Only holes, and the ground which wore the holes like still-open wounds.

The sky itself was as red as blood, poisoned clouds from an ecosystem gone horribly awry hovering dangerously overhead with threats of acidic rains made every minute. This was a world which had been kicked, beaten, torn limb from limb and left for dead... only not to be allowed to die, only to suffer through eternity. And it loathed all who walked on its mangled form, those who kept it from the still silence of a peaceful final rest...

"Daaaaaaaamn," was Mellow Fellow's professional assessment, as he peered out the window of his taxi. "Yo, man, you SURE this be the right place? Looks like the armpit 'o Bablyonia..."

Mallory tugged the thick scarf down a bit, so he could at least see over the top of it. "I... THINF thif iff tha plaffe," he spoke without absolute determination. "If Aforia, riff?"

"Arboria, yeah... uh, Mallory, don't be thinkin' I'm any less of a buddy, but I think I be takin' off, yah?" Mellow Fellow said, shivering slightly as a cold wind blew into his hut. "This place eats at me. You ready to go, you call me back, kay?"

Shrugging into the coat he had pulled on before leaving the House, Mallory stepped out of the hut. "If okay," he called over his shoulder. "Fo, fo. I'll call."

Without a thank you, Mellow Fellow's Smiling Taxi Service departed in a brief purple flash, leaving Mallory standing in front of the only structure in this world... a large building, with a flickering green neon sign reading DUKE'S MUNITIONS. The name matched the address Meiko gave him... even if he couldn't say he cared for the sights.

He quickly jogged over to the building, and pushed open the rusted double doors...

Into a fairly nice lobby, all things considered. The floor was a dusty and battered iron grating, but there was a couch, a coffee table loaded with magazines that appealed to warlords and assassins and mercenaries alike, and even a RealNet audio receiver tuned into some easy listening music.

More importantly, there was someone Mallory presumed to be Duke, sitting behind the counter leafing through a copy of Modern Massacre Monthly, in camo fatigues that were far too large for his wiry thin frame.

"Hey, welcome to Duke's Munitions," he greeted with a friendly little nod. "Usually we ask that folks call ahead and schedule a meeting... but hey, beggars can't be choosers. How can I help you? Looking for a weapon?

Ammunition? Access to our training grounds? We have excellent corporate rates for weekend survival seminars. ...hey, haven't I seen you somewhere before?"

"I don't think so... ah, I'm looking for someone named Kisei," Mallory spoke, after tugging down the scarf enough to talk without inserting the letter F into every word he spoke. "She's here training, and her boss sent me to pick her up... although, um, I'm going to need to use your RealNet terminal to call for my ride, he didn't want to hang around... what's WITH this place? I wouldn't expect anybody to run a business here..."

"The real estate is cheap and needs no upkeep," Duke said with a grin, sliding his magazine aside on the counter. It was a topic he liked to talk about, since it made him look particularly clever. "I bought the license off some settlers who were leaving in a hurry after a wartime biological disaster. They were just gonna shut the engine down, but engines aren't cheap, and it'd cost a bundle to have a whole new world coded into it or get the existing one repaired... and for what I do, it's actually better to leave it as is."

"Ah, I see! That's very clever of you!" Mallory agreed, as he was easily impressed. "Uh... so what DO you do, exactly? Sell guns and stuff?"

"Yep! Buy, sell, trade... and provide training grounds, like I said. They're... well, here, take a look..."

Duke turned a nearby RealNet Workstation monitor around so Mallory could see. A few keyboard clicks later, and a window appeared with a streaming video feed of Kisei at work.

She was lying flat on the rocky ground, a breathing mask pulled up over her face... leaving only her eyes exposed. One was squeezed shut tightly, the other staring through the scope of an ordinary-looking sniper rifle with a wooden stock and a steel scope. It took Mallory a moment to notice the video artifacts that proved this was a moving image... Kisei made no noticeable motion whatsoever, not even visibly breathing.

"Kisei knows how to shoot a gun?" Mallory asked, puzzled.

"How long have you been living with her not to know that?" Duke asked, peering at the boy incredulously. "Of course she does. She's a professional sniper and military tactician. Here, lemme... there. See that other video window? The four targets lined up? She's practicing on them. Check this— been lying there about twenty minutes now, just like that. Best pro I've ever seen walk through my doors. Cold. Intense. Precise. Patient. DAMN, she's impressive—"

A tiny hole appeared dead in the center of the first target. Mallory hadn't noticed a single flicker of movement in the window that showed Kisei.

"Gosh," he said. "She hit that thing right in the center! That's good, right?"

"...yes, that's good. She—"

The next target sprouted a tiny dart, pegged exactly in the center of the interlocking red and white circles.

"Tranquilizer shot," Duke explained. "She told me your boss doesn't take missions that involve killing people, so she buys a lot of different types of ammo like that—"

The third target glowed brightly, before melting to red hot slag. The camera image washed out temporarily, the light overpowering it momentarily.

"Compressed heat pulse," the man answered before Mallory could ask.

The fourth target vanished, along with the first two and the remains of the third. As did the camera that was tracking them, the video image going to static.

Of course, far more noticeable than that was the muffled explosion sound and the way the entire building shook. Dust eddies whirled up from the floor briefly, before settling back down.

"Err" Mallory said, glancing around nervously. "And that last one...?"

"Miniaturized tactical nuclear explosive," Duke answered calmly.

"Wha...?! But those are really really really big explosions!" Mallory exclaimed, his limited knowledge of the world proving to be just enough to make do. "She'd be killed!"

"Of course not. The targets were five miles away from her," Duke responded. "My standard issue 86a miniature tactical nuclear explosive sniper shells have a blast radius of one mile only with a clean, accelerated radioactive half life. Only the finest from Duke's Munitions!"

"...five.... miles," Mallory repeated, realizing for the first time that the targets and Kisei were (in reality) not two inches of workstation video screen apart. "That far away, and she still managed to... ... uh. Wow. I mean... wow!"

"Like I said... damn, she's impressive," Duke said, with no small amount of reverence in his tone. "It's a shame she's working for a podunk troubleshooting consultant outfit like yours—no offense, 'course. But man, she used to take higher profile jobs where she could really FLEX that skill! She'd be in and out of here every week picking up supplies for all sorts of missions, from assassinations to covert ops to amphibious squad-based night raids! Hardcore paramilitary work for hire at its finest, man! When he was still alive, I'm tellin' you, she was like death incarnate, pale horse riding—"

By this point, Kisei was no longer visible on the camera feed. She was instead visible directly in front of Duke, glaring down at the smaller man with a look blazingly fierce enough to put the 34c Compressed Heat Pulse Round's melting point to shame.

For a change, Mallory realized it was in his best interests to stay quiet and did so.

"... uh... you want those four ammo types, right?" Duke asked, squirming under that gaze and trying to deflect it into safer territory. "I can get you bulk boxes at discount—"

"We have discussed improper disclosure of information, yes?" Kisei asked, adding a subtle touch of acid to her calm words. "I was understanding that your establishment took pride in its customer privacy..."

"I got carried away. Mistakes were made," Duke readily admitted, stepping back once to retain some personal space as Kisei leaned closer. "But... I mean, uh, really..."

"Yes?" Kisei asked, trying to sound politely inquisitive. "You mean, really?"

"Look, you're wasted on that woman, okay?" Duke finally spoke, deciding to let it out. "I KNOW you. You KNOW me. We could get something going without her! Or hell, do some work on the side, I know you're usually sitting around doing nothing around that house. If you'd let me arrange you some work, act as a middleman, I could get you MUCH higher profile stuff, just like the good old—"

The sound of Kisei's scorecard smacking down on the counter was like a crack shot from a gun.

"I am Meiko Mirai's retainer," Kisei explained, smooth and calm once more. "The way says that fealty to one's master is all. Her requests are my duty to obey. She does not wish me to freelance, therefore I do not seek any freelance work. She does not wish me to kill, therefore I do not kill. Yes, I will take ten boxes of each ammo type I have tested today, along with ten extra of the tranq rounds. And to assure that our working relationship stays fruitful, please do not dishonor me ever again by suggesting I break my oaths. Of course, I mean no disrespect by this. Do you understand, Lawrence?"

"Yes'm," 'Duke' spoke quickly, running the scorecard through a reader next to his workstation. "I'll go in the back and fetch your ammo right away. Mallory, you can call for your ride from this workstation. Be back right away. Right away."

He disappeared like a shot. (Lots of things in this place worked best with military metaphors.)

Not able to deal well with awkward silence, Mallory cleared his throat of some of Arboria's dust, and spoke up. "Err... for the record, I wasn't really asking him about you," he said. "I wouldn't want to invade your privacy, Miss Kisei..."

"I know," Kisei spoke, turning to face him... without the evil glare. "You have many faults, Mallory Heisenberg, but impolite behavior is not one of them. Aside from entering my room without permission the other day, of course."

"Eh, ah, right. Sorry about—"

"You have apologized once already. There is no need for a second apology. You go farther out of your way to be polite than is required for one in your position."

"Err... but we're both sort of in the same position," Mallory reasoned. "We're both hired by Meiko to do a job. Right? So I should do my best to be polite and impress her, and—"

Kisei almost rolled her eyes. Almost.

"Believe me... our positions are not the same. But as you please, Mallory Heisenberg. Don't you have a call to be making?"

"Call? Call! Right, right..."

The call was placed, ammo was packaged up, the pair returned to I's Land, Kisei went to her room, Mallory went to his couch, and that was the end of that. No important words were exchanged.

THURSDAY

The HARMONIC SYNC parameter, which must be present, contains a textual definition of the textual convention, which provides all semantic definitions necessary for cross-induction generator implementation, and should embody any information which would otherwise be communicated in any RNS.1 commentary annotations associated with the object.

Note that, in order to conform to the RNS.1 syntax, the entire flow sequence of this reality generation wave must be prefixed / suffixed by double ACK pulses, and therefore cannot itself contain double ACK pulses, although the value may be multi-wave.

The ASYNCRONOUS SYNC parameter, which must be present in cases when HARMONIC SYNC is DISHARMONIC across the third pylon, defines abstract data structures corresponding to the textual convention. The data structure must be one of the alternatives defined in the ObjectSyntax PHYSICS or the METAPHYSICS construct (see section 7.1 in [2]).

The remainder of the tertiary reality wave harmonic pylon interface codec is trivial and left as an exercise to the reader.

"Progress, Professor Bates?"

Mallory's brain was too soaked in novocaine-esque reality engineering trivia to panic at the surprise voice. Instead he slowly looked up, eyes slightly glazed over.

"Hellllo?" Mallory greeted slowly. "Oh, Meiko. Professor who?"

"You're making progress, yes?" she asked, looking down at the boy who was lying on the couch. "I haven't seen you reading from that thing too often, you know... I had assumed after our little chat that night—"

"No no, I'm reading," he replied quickly, skipping past four screens of data with a jitter of the thumb. "It's really amazing stuff! I mean... harmonic... wave pool... pylon... things. Really amazing stuff!"

"Oh? So you know the basics of reality generation, then?" Meiko asked, sitting on the coffee table for lack of a better place to sit. "Prove it."

"Prove...? Well. The... okay. The engines act like this thing that generates reality," Mallory tried to explain, disconnected bits of technobabble floating around his brainpan as he wildly grasped at straws with the clock ticking and the fat lady singing. "They do it by creating pulses through absolutely pure water using these complex math thingys, which somehow set up, err, these waves that radiate outward and, um... reality! There."

"...you aren't studying at all, are you."

"Wha—? No no, I am! See? Here's me pushing this little button and making text go by! Pushpushpushpush..."

"Get real. Water waves that make reality? What, so Reality Engines are just kiddie swimming pools?" Meiko mocked, looking more than slightly annoyed. "You aren't studying at all! If you think you're gonna get by in MY house just cooking and clean—"

Meiko found her world view occupied by a large diagram of a water molecule.

"WATER!" Mallory exclaimed at last, out of breath from the frantic button pushing. "See? I knew I remembered that! Professor Archimedes Bates the First discovered that absolutely pure water, when set up with resonating waves in a special machine he invented loaded with a really complex computer program he also invented... it makes a reality bubble. If you control the program that defines the contents and behaviors of the bubble, you get... you get a Reality! And even if it was such a simple idea, because nobody had ever thought to apply it in this way nor had they figured out the math behind it, Reality Engineering went undiscovered until that day. Ha! See? I studied!"

"No, you're reading off the screen," Meiko noted, glancing over her shoulder to where Mallory had snuck around behind her to better see the screen.

"Err, well, I still got the water part right," Mallory said, trying to find some scrap of victory. "So you can't say I haven't been studying! ...um. Maybe not as much as I SHOULD, but I have been studying, and I WILL be a Reality Engineer like my mother before me and be of invaluable help to your home and family! RIGHT!"

"...your excitement over this is scaring me. I'm leaving now," Meiko noted, getting up. "Just as soon as I find Lorelei. Which is why I bugged you in the first place, actually. Where is she? I checked her room and the onsen, no go..."

"On-scene?" Mallory asked, confused.

"Onsen. Sort of an indoor hot spring and bath, Nipponese concept, very popular among corporate success types. We've got one. You didn't know? It's the green door next to the stairs."

"Uh... I thought it was just for decoration, since it's just sort of propped up against the wall..."

"No, it's... wait, I'm getting sidetracked," Meiko realized. "I'll explain about the Onsen-of-the-Month later. Lorelei. Where? Do you know? Are you of any use at all, Houseboy?"

"Lore—oh! Yeah, she told me she was going deep sea diving with some guy named... suhven? Seven? Sven? Someone visiting I's Land from a place that she tells me has a great deal of cakes made of beef! Although I've never heard of a recipe for 'beefcake'. Hmm. Maybe I should try to make some for dinner tonight..."

Meiko grumbled under her breath, but not at Mallory's ignorance. "Dammit. I TOLD her that my appointment was for today... count me out of dinner, houseboy. I'll be eating out. I've got to take care of my quarterly... Lorelei usually comes with me, but I'm not putting on a scuba tank just to fetch her. And for a change, I won't make you do it, either."

"'Quarterly'?" he asked, memory pulling a tidbit from multiple days previous. "Uh, is it anything I can help with, then? Since she's not here, I mean..."

"No. No, no. No. No no NO," Meiko affirmed, stepping back and away from him. "You have to study, and this is NOT the sort of thing that you should be—"

"I can study later!" he promised, getting to his feet and pressing the issue (by advancing on her with hands reaching for her in a scary way.) "Take me with you! I'm dying of boredom! I'll do whatever it takes! I learn fast! I can help you with the 'quarterly'—"

The young woman put up a hand in Mallory's face, to block him from getting any closer. This worked as the two were about equal height, but her arms were a wee bit longer.

"If you promise to obey every word I say and not freak out and make a scene and embarrass me with your hick boy roots," she said quickly without pausing for breath or dramatic purpose in order to speak quickly without pause, "Then...... okay. I need someone to carry the stuff, anyway."

"Okay! I'd be happy to help, Miss Mirai! What stuff will I be carrying?"

"Women's underwear?!"

It's a certain law in the universe that two statements which connect at an abstract level will not connect at a concrete level.

This means that between the question and the answer, there was a period of time in which the following events transpired:

1. Calling Mellow Fellow for a taxi ride,

2. Trying to find Meiko's purse, which had been misplaced,

3. Taking the taxi to Urbana,

4. Navigating the sidewalk crowds,

5. Entering the ConsuTopia MegaShopping PlazaComplex,

6. Navigating the shopping crowds,

7. Arriving at Sylvie's Silks,

8. Meiko mentioning that she had to buy some underwear.

"Of course," Meiko replied, digging her scorecard out of her purse as they stood in front of the shop. "The new spring season just launched today, and if I want to get in on this quarter's fashion trends, I have to buy before anyone else. We're going to be getting underwear, skirts, blouses, jackets, shoes, and other items today so I can update my wardrobe. It's a cost of doing business in the modern age, everybody knows that—if you're not wearing the latest power ensemble for women in business, others will notice and you lose leverage at the negotiating table. Therefore, it's always smart to look your best. ...Mallory, you're staring at that plastic mannequin's breasts."

"No I'm not," Mallory lied, glancing aside. "Uhm. So. We'll be going in, then?"

He found a purse roughly shoved into his limp hands.

"No, **I** am going in," Meiko corrected. "**You** are waiting out here. I have this feeling that the polite farmboy in you who's never touched a girl before would freak out and cause a huge scene if you stepped into that place. For your sake and my sanity, you will stay out here while I will shop."

"H-Hey, I would not cause a scene," Mallory defended. "I mean, I handle your underwear all the time when I do laundry! ...of course that's strictly business and I don't think of it as clothes that have touched any particular places on your body that I wouldn't mention in specific—"

Meiko pressed a finger to his lips.

"Stop. Just... stop right there. Before you dig yourself any deeper," she warned, not QUITE angry, but clearly indicating that she could get very angry if need be.

Mallory stepped back a bit to avoid the finger. "Uh, right. —and I have too touched a girl before. So you're wrong there."

"Really? When?"

"Uh... just now, when you did that thing with your finger. And you did pick me up and throw me out of your house way back when! Plus I think there was this girl in my Bakery II class who gave me a pencil once and I touched her finger. And Lorelei was, er, touching me at one point too, so actually it's a lot of girls, and... I think I'll be quiet now."

"Good," Meiko spoke with a capital G and a look that could K. She pointed to a nearby wall. "Go stand there. I won't be too long, I have a tailor's appointment to make in twenty minutes."

"Gotcha! I'll be right over here!" he replied, holding her purse and waving as she entered the store of feminine unmentionables.

Then he glanced at the wall, where four other guys holding purses were also waiting.

"You too, huh?" one asked him, with a knowing look.

In the 15.7 minutes that followed, Mallory steeled himself to the concept of carrying around Meiko's new underwear. Of course, the steel willpower proved useless when Meiko emerged carrying a perfectly harmless shopping bag loaded with tissue paper wrapped bundles that did nothing to set off Mallory's Nervousness Nerve.

He also spent a lot of time being heckled by the other men waiting in line, who knew an easy target when they saw one, and felt the need to assert their manliness to balance out standing around holding a purse.

"Man, what are you, her boyfriend or her slave?"

"Ah, I'm not her boyfriend—"

"Slave, then."

"I'm not that either! I'm... I'm her HOUSEBOY!"

Needless to say, he didn't come off looking like Muscles Manslaughter™ after that.

Fortunately, Meiko's tailor proved not to be an assault on his manhood, as he was a she. A she who was so horrified at Mallory's ripped-up jeans and his battered gray sweatshirt that she decided to pretend he didn't exist from that point onward. (Except when she had to rub anything with a cloth that Mallory touched in case it became contaminated.) In return, Mallory got to experience the joy of sitting around holding the purse again, but at least this time he could enter the store and watch as Meiko modeled various snappy-looking business ensembles in front of various shiny-looking mirrors.

And model she did, taking her time to turn this way and that, study each article of clothing from various acute angles, all while the tailor sat back quietly and watched.

"I don't know..." Meiko spoke, uncertain as she tugged on a black vest that was nearly identical to her last-seasonly one. "What do you think, Mallory? Should I go with the vest in the jet, the onyx, or black?"

"Uh... I like the dark one," he wisely answered.

"And the skirt, does this work? I mean, I know that white is very *in* this season, but I feel like I should be adding a little bit of color. Red, maybe? Or is that too strong? What says 'I'm a modern girl with an eye on the future and I'm going to crush your soul at the negotiating table and take you for everything you have while you kiss my feet and beg me for more?'"

"Clothing can SAY that?"

"Well, of course!" Meiko exclaimed, turning to face him. "Appearances are the first criteria others judge you by! That's when you have to establish your position. So, what color?"

His glance flickered to Meiko's dark blue skirt she walked in there with.

"Blue," he decided. "Blue works. I mean, it's... an intimidating, color, right? I don't know why, but it intimidates me quite a bit..."

Equally intimidating: the common hot dog.

When he bumped into the cart-pushing chef at Urbana on his first day away from home, he wanted to sample these 'hot dogs' the man had mentioned. Of course, Eiko distracted him and grifted him for five credits instead, causing him to miss his shot at some genuine non-Grünwaldian cuisine.

Now that he'd had a bite of it, he wasn't sure he ever wanted to stray from his home menu again.

"I mean, it's... it's just STUFF! I can't even tell what stuff it is, and I usually get good marks in Taste Appreciation!" he exclaimed, still perplexed by the 'delicacy', while Meiko sipped a lemonade and gave him a 'duh' sort of look.

"Of course it's stuff," she said, setting down her lemonade. "It's not exactly a five-star dinner, it's one of those greasy, fatty, tasty things you grab when you're in a hurry or don't have a knife and fork or chopsticks..."

"But... but how could anyone stand to eat this, even in a casual sense?" he insisted. "It might not actually be meat! I can't tell! That's very frightening, you know! If I didn't know any better, I'd guess this was, like... compressed pig snouts and tails and things..."

"This is reality, houseboy," Meiko reminded him, vaguely annoyed. "Here, people don't cook that often. They get takeout, they buy prepackaged stuff, they stick to things you can warm up and eat fast. We don't set up feasts three times a day to savor the delicate tastes and fortify our bodies with vitamins and minerals. Before you came along we were living off cup ramen, instant beefbowl, microwaved french fries, hamburgers, and sandwiches..."

Mallory nudged his remaining uneaten hot dog away, in favor of his side salad. "It's a good thing I came along, then," he said, spearing a forkful of salad. "You guys would waste away without proper nutrition! Um, does that mean you like my cooking? I'm doing a good job?"

"Uh... well... yeah, of course," Meiko spoke, shifting from uneasiness to false gruffness. "Sheesh, isn't it obvious? But I forget, it's Houseboy I'm talking to here... do you constantly need positive reinforcement? Are you that desperate to make us all happy?"

"I... wouldn't say I'm desperate," he replied, in his own meek defense, salad thusly forgotten. "I'm just trying to make sure you guys are happy with my work..."

"The house is clean and we're well fed. In a month we'll have an engine repairman on board. Beyond that, I shouldn't care... I'm your boss, after all. And you're doing a job. And that's all there is! Honestly, it's so annoying... quit bugging me about it!"

"Okay, okay," Mallory agreed, despite not being exactly sure what he was agreeing to. "I'm only trying to help..."

"'I'm only trying to help,'" she replied in a whiny mocking voice. "Honestly! If I didn't know any better, I'd assume Mallory WAS a girl's name! You act just like girls do back in Nippon. Always so meek and apologetic and desperate to please... and I can't stand that!"

"I'm trying to stop apologizing so much, I swear! I know it's sort of annoying you guys—"

"Oh, of COURSE Lorelei doesn't mind, since she likes having a slave around the house," Meiko continued to rant. "And Kisei doesn't care one way or another about anybody beyond her duty. And Eiko... Eiko...! Argh! ...forget it. Just forget it. I have one more errand to run and then we're leaving. Wait here with the bags."

Mallory fought a panic attack, under that sort of assault. "Wait? Uh, here? Why? I can—"

"Because I want some time alone, that's why! I hate it when I get this angry about something!" Meiko replied, rising to her feet fast enough to knock her chair 2.6 feet away. "I'm supposed to be businesslike and always in control of a situation while OTHERS are getting emotional, and... forget it! Forget it! Sit. Stay. Good boy."

Before he could manage a 'but' or an 'erm' or an 'uh', she was gone, marching off and into a store three mall slots down the hallway.

He slumped in his chair, grabbed his hot dog, and took a bite in some sort penance ritual.

Why? Why was it going so wrong? He didn't WANT to make any of them angry. He always prided himself on being friendly to everybody... to the people in his village, to the elders, even to the offworlders who traded with them. Even when few of his peers wanted anything to do with offworlders... Mallory treated everybody the same way. With respect, and with a desire to make them happy...

And he wasn't making Meiko happy.

She doesn't like people without a spine, Lorelei had told him. Kisei had told him he apologized too much for someone of his station... and that his relation to Meiko was not appropriate for that.

Ever since he left home, he was so desperate to please... always with the fear of rejection, especially since Meiko tried once to physically boot him from the premises, leave him stranded and alone in this crazy outside world... was he really going overboard from that fear? Was it possible to be TOO nice to people? A good houseboy would...

She kept calling him 'Houseboy'. Because someone in that station WOULD be a slavish, devoted lackey, maid, butler, servant. Kisei said as much that he wasn't a servant... or maybe Meiko didn't want Mallory to be a servant...

Needless to say, conflicting ideas jousted with big double-ended padded sticks like cheaply televised gladiator combat inside Mallory's brain. Tugging at his hair, he stewed in the frustration, trying to figure out what he should be, what they wanted him to be.

What did HE want to be? What did HE want to do? Not just in relation to what others wanted...

He really wanted to follow her.

If he didn't, she'd finish her shopping, and it'd be a quiet, awkward ride home and then she probably wouldn't speak to him again for a long time. Unless she had a houseboy sort of order, since that's all she thought he could be. She told him not to follow, but rather than struggle to please her...

Mallory scooped up the various bags, several per arm, and hurried off after her. Something rare clicked in his head, burning with the desire to make things right with Meiko, and he knew exactly what he wanted to do... and what he had to do.

"Hey!" Skreee.

The first a rather forceful greeting, the second the sound of Mallory's sneakers squeaking to a halt against the tiny toy store's tile floor.

Meiko's head turned quickly towards the sound, her hands almost dropping the boxed doll that she was examining. Her frown deepened like a strip mine on seeing who had 'Hey'd her.

"I thought I told you to stay put, Houseboy," she barked off. "I said I'd be back in a minute, so—"

In terms of expected / projected behavior, Meiko was figuring on one of two reactions from her Houseboy.

1. Begging apology for interrupting and backing slowly out of the store while mumbling.

2. A slim chance of an angry reaction for how she yelled at him, which would lead to more yelling, which she really wanted to do despite not wanting to lose control.

Instead, she got

3. A friendly smile, and a slow approach as Mallory studied the toy she held in her hands.

"You're buying a toy for Eiko, right?" he asked, tone upbeat but not overly so. In control of himself, unlike others present. "Isn't that an Aquarius Waterslide Biiko?™"

It took Meiko multiple moments to come to grips with option 3, but her business sense took control: when your opponent in negotiation was calm and you were emotional, he had leverage. And she wouldn't allow that. She had to try...

"...yes, it's a Biiko™ doll," she replied, holding the box up to study the swimsuit-wearing 1/6th size woman inside. "How do you know that?"

"Because she already has one," Mallory replied smoothly. "So you should probably pick something else... ah, no no, not that one, she already has that Kensuke™ err, Meiko? What's wrong?"

The second box she had picked up crumpled slightly in her grip. And she gave up on keeping her control.

"...I should have known that," she replied, quietly. Half angry, half... other. "I should know what dolls she has. I give her the allowance to buy them. I've played dollhouse with her before... I'm her sister and I should know these things. I have to spend a lot of money to keep up my business wardrobe, so much I can't even get her a new dollhouse, but the least I can do is buy her a doll... and even if I haven't played with her lately, I should certainly know things that even my Houseboy knows..."

"Well, uh, she DOES have a lot of dolls," he replied, taking the box from her hands to put back on the shelf. "I doubt even she could list them all from memory. So we just pick one that we don't THINK she has, and cross our fingers and throw salt over our shoulder while looking for a tea stem turned upright. Right?"

"You're not her big brother, you know. I don't like her calling you that."

"Huh?"

"I'm the only family she has," Meiko spoke, turning to face Mallory... a serious expression, but no longer with anger. "I've done my best to raise her, to nurture her interests and encourage her towards her future... because nobody else would. You remember what I told you the day we had the Ping Pong match, right?"

"The match...? I... uh, I think I... ah! Right! You're a Ping Pong champion! Of... of an... oh. Oh, right..."

"Seven Lucky Gods Street Orphanage, in Nippon," she recited. "I'm the only family she has, because Mother and Father are gone... a traffic accident, when I was little and she was barely a toddler. We don't really have any distant family, aunts and uncles... I guess the only thing lucky about the Mirai family is the name of the street we ended up on... look. Look, my point is, you're not a Mirai. And I don't want you... I don't know if I'm happy with how close you are to Eiko. And I didn't even know she had that doll already..."

"Uh... it's okay, it's okay. I understand! Really. I don't understand much, but people? I understand people," Mallory spoke, trying to be reassuring. "I really like Eiko. She's a bright girl, and very friendly! But I know I'm not her real brother. I'm not trying to be one—I'm just friendly to everybody. It's guess it's my nature. I can even be friendly to people nobody else wants to be friendly to. Sometimes it looks kind of silly, since I like people to be happy... so I apologize too much, I try too hard to please them... but in the end I'm just trying to be a good person, like my father raised me to be. And like my mother would want me to be, I think."

"Your mother's dead, isn't she?" Meiko guessed.

"Yeah, she died a little after I was born," Mallory replied, not losing his light tone. "I never got to know her. But it's okay... because I know I'm doing my best to make her happy. I know she's gone and she can't see what I'm doing since she's buried on Sleep Hill, but she was Shinto, so... if she was right about that religious stuff, maybe she can see me!"

"Golly. That's so annoyingly upbeat of you," Meiko said, without any real annoyance in her voice... and a little bit of a smile. "You're really like this, aren't you? It's not just some big act to impress people and make them like you..."

"Umm, not that I know of. I'm not much of an actor; you should have seen me in my school play years ago. I was playing the carrot in our Salad Comedy and I knocked the bowl over... the guy playing thousand island dressing got mad and gave me a black eye!"

"Salad... Com.... noo, on second thought, I don't think I want to solidify my mental image of that. It's already going to be nightmare-inducing."

"Uh, sorry..."

Meiko did the eye-rolling thing. "Jeez, forget it. All right... we gotta get home soon. Time to pick a doll. Which do you think Eiko would like?"

"Me? I don't know anything about dolls. I just collect trading cards, comics, magazines, action figures, model kits, novelty goods and stuff like that from all around the multiverse...! But no dolls. Or do action figures count...? "

"Collect...? Is that what all the junk is that's in your closet? I was wondering... all right, all right..."

With a swift arm motion, she grabbed the nearest long cardboard box off the shelf, and showed it to Mallory.

"These, then," she replied. "Current season Love & Hate dolls of Alex Gunthar and Tia Liason. She likes that soap opera, but I know for a FACT she has no toys from it. And they're on sale, so we can easily buy the two-in-one box set, and... what now? She doesn't have these, Mallory, you can quit staring at them..."

"No no, it's that, that," he replied, poking at the clear plastic between the manly Alex and the feminine Tia. "It comes with a cardboard moonlit beach backdrop!"

"Pretty cheap of them. The higher grade toys have plastic playsets—"

"It looks a lot like the sky over I's Land," Mallory continued. "Remember, when you gave me the datapad and we talked while looking at the waves and the moon? That's really neat! It's a place with a great memory, so that makes this the perfect toy buy for Eiko! Right? I mean, I could be wrong... maybe you should consult your F-P thing—?"

Meiko tucked the box under one arm quickly, to obscure the plastic viewing window.

"It's fine," she said sharply. "Let's pay up and get moving."

She stepped ahead of the confused Mallory, striding right up to the sales counter. And stayed ahead of him the whole way back to the house, because she was in control, she had control, and she absolutely would not let him see her blush.

FRIDAY

By aligning the constant echo feedback loop, we...

Not happening. Not even attempting to be happening. Barely possibly getting out of the gate in such a way as to suggest the starting of the thing which was happening which was not, in fact, happening.

Some distractions are simply too great to allow one to focus their thoughts, and Lorelei sitting around on Mallory's beloved couch in a nearly nonexistent pair of panties and a tight tank top ranks up there with big lizards stepping on your hometown.

In righteous fury and indignation, Mallory summoned up all his RAGE and exclaimed, "errr..."

"Can't talk. Watching TV," Lorelei indicated, while picking at her left ear, eyes half drooped in boredom as she watched a cheesy martial arts flick.

"But can't you watch somewhere else?" Mallory asked, trying to look at the screen instead. "I sort of have to study for this, and this is my couch, and stuff..."

"First, I can't watch somewhere else; the only other video set in the house is in Eiko's room and she's watching cartoons. Second, this is Meiko's couch, if you wanna get technical. Finally, I could say the same of you: can't you study elsewhere? Oooh!—how about the onsen? Perfect for weary students! Go right on in and soak your cares away!"

"I can't, Meiko's in there," Mallory said.

"Darn. I almost had you..."

"Eh?"

"This movie's boring," Lorelei stated, changing tracks in a way that would derail most trains. She flicked the air in front of her, triggering the RealNet Video Set's sensors to toggle the default clock-and-light-show mode back on. Hopping to her feet with parts of her body bouncing more than others, she stretched her arms over her head while arching her back, unkinking muscles in a highly kinky way.

"errrr," Mallory repeated, turning as red as the tomatoes he harvested a little over a week ago. "Does... that mean you're leaving?"

"This house is too boring. I'm outta here," she confirmed... before grabbing the hand not holding the REC test datapad. "And you're coming with me, Houseboy. Flying solo bores me as well. I seek anti-boredom tonight!"

Mallory never before felt the urge to study quite as intensely as he did at that moment, clinging to the datapad despite Lorelei's attempts to drag him to the door. And given that the pad wasn't nailed down to a load-bearing structure, this meant being quite easily dragged around. "H-Hey! I can't leave! I have to study—and you're not even dressed!!"

"...yeah, I guess you got a good point there," Lorelei said, releasing his wrist with a sigh. "Bummer."

"I have a good point?—I mean, of course! Now if you'll excuse me..."

And thus, Lorelei left him alone.

That is, for three minutes while she changed into something that only marginally differed from her underwear. It was red and it was tight and it was only a one-piece dress if the straps and buckles that held it together counted.

Minutes later after that, and Mallory was no longer in I's Land, and instead in a world of light and sound and color and bodies pressed together and an intense clawing fear that chilled his flesh to the bones.

All it took was a command of 'The usual, please' to Mellow Fellow, and they were off to a reality called Nocturn. According to Lorelei's explanations, which Mallory could only half-hear over the slamming beat of a musical style that seemed optimized for maximum ear damage, Nocturn was a night club. An entire reality devoted to one night club, albeit a night club with approximately 34,000 specialized miniclubs. She had dragged his body, operating on a sort of shock-induced autopilot, up to an information kiosk.

"Two nights ago I tried 'Ultimate Party'," Lorelei explained, somehow able to pitch her voice to be audible despite the clashing music echoing around the kiosk chamber. She poked various lights on the monolithic information system, trying to call up a map. "Ultimate Party proved to be anything but. All the guys wanted to do was impress me with the pickup lines that they couldn't even deliver properly. So I tried the 'Manhole' next, since I heard it was filled with really hunky guys, and it was. Problem was, they weren't interested in girls. I'm figuring that tonight, since I'm coming WITH a date, I'd head to the 'Swing Thing'... Mallory, are you paying attention?"

"errr," Mallory repeated from earlier, clinging Lorelei's hand for fear of being sucked into the crowd of sweaty hot twentysomethings. "Aaah. Errr. I... oooaoaah. Uhhh..."

"I see you are practicing your vowels! Very good," Lorelei said, with a wry little grin. "Wow, this is really blowing your mind, ain't it? I can't believe you've never been to a party before. What did you farmboys do for kicks on your Saturday nights, country line dancing after raising a barn?"

"Party? Saturday? There were parties and festivals and things," Mallory spoke, trying to wrangle a grip on things and not look too panicky. "I didn't go to many of them. Uh. I didn't have many friends back home, really. It never really felt like I fit in..."

"I hear you, I hear you. Same way back at my home, after a while," she replied, half paying attention as she poked at the map image. "So no girlfriends, either? Not one beyond five-fingered Mary?"

"I never met anybody named Mary. And, uh, no girlfriends. Although I've read about them! I mean, I know what you mean. I just never had one. Uh. Is it normal to be really freaked out by this place?"

"Actually... yes. I can see it being hella intense for someone like you. But deep breaths, Mal. Relax! Everybody's here to have fun, that's all it is. Roll with it, okay?—THERE it is! Damn, 'Swing Thing' is a mile away. Not worth it. How does the 'Technobabble' work for you? It's a pretty low-impact place, good to ease you into things. They only play remixed video game music or somethin'. Kinda appeals to techie nerds, but hey, I can adjust..."

"I think I'd really appreciate low-impact," Mallory admitted. "I should learn how offworlders party, so that I will be able to party too! But, err, one step at a time. Right?"

"Now THAT'S more like it!" she spoke through a big grin, slapping him on the back several times. "Let's go! ...give me your arm."

"But I like it still attached to my body," Mallory spoke, feeling vaguely threatened.

Showing infinite patience, Lorelei hooked her arm around Mallory's. "Like THIS. Proper way to show your date around, right?"

"Wha—date? Date? I'm on a DATE?!"

"That is generally what this is called, yes. Never had one, I take it? No, of course not... hey! Breathe slower! Deep and even. Sheesh, Mal... why in the blue hell did you take a job in a house with four other women if you can barely handle this?"

"I didn't know there were four other women when I took the job! I didn't know! I don't know anything! I have no idea what I'm doing right now, even! I don't know! I DON'T—"

He found his lips pinched shut.

"I think," Lorelei decided, "That we need to get a very stiff drink into you before you suffer from a fatal bowel obstruction due to your tight ass."

It didn't make sense calling it a stiff drink.

If he were naming it, he'd call it a loose drink. That would make more sense, seeing how he felt so incredibly loose that he was in immediate danger of falling off his barstool. Nor did it make any sense to call it a 'Screwdriver', since screwdrivers... well, why not share?

"A screwdriver," he announced, "Tightens something. But I don't feel so tight now. Although... hey, if you twist it counterclockwise... clockwise? Righty tighty, lefty loosey... one of those two. If you do that, it loosens. So I guess that works! Wow, I wonder what chef came up with this recipe? Do you think I could ask him for a copy? I might want to experiment on the process a bit and see if I can make it better... isn't it cool the way it swirls around in the glass, though? I mean, it's like a spiral, which makes sense, since it's called a screwdriver. It works on so many levels! And—"

"Mallory?"

"Yeah?"

"Correct me if I'm wrong, but you've only had half of the first glass I gave you. Right?"

"Right."

"I think that you just hit your legal limit," Lorelei announced, grabbing the drink away and swallowing the remainder. "I need a designated taxi caller tonight, and if you actually finished that, you might be too blind to push the buttons on the callbox. Bartender! Two more of the same. For me. Not him."

Mallory rotated his stool (also a rotational motion, like a screwdriver, which pleased him even more) to face the crowd. The Technobabble was a fairly low-impact club—most of the people on the dance floor had apparently been taught to dance by one-legged, one-eyed, three-armed men with epilepsy. While they thankfully didn't actually cause injury to each other, they never quite managed to agree on a tempo to bop around to. Plus, for every person on the dance floor, two more were plastered up against the walls bobbing their heads and trying to look like they were participating.

"I hope you appreciate the sacrifices I'm making for you, farmboy," Lorelei noted, before downing an entire glass of orange concoction. "Mmm. This is SO not my scene. But if I'm gonna condition you to the point where we can have some REAL fun, I guess I gotta take baby steps..."

"You know what's interesting? The audio streams coming out of the speakers there have a regular pattern to them," Mallory babbled. "It seems to have four thumps per part, and four parts per larger part. So it's all like mathematics in the end. I'm not very good at math but I think that's important for some reason. Am I right?"

"Make that three screwdrivers for me," Lorelei corrected to the bartender, wincing inside.

"It's funny, but I can almost FEEL the music," Mallory continued. "Maybe just because it's really loud and I'm getting this funny feeling in my rear each time it goes 'thump' but I think I mean beyond that. Like the way it moves through the room. And like the ripples in your glass! Like water moving, you know? If you vibrate water in a particular way it makes reality. I know that much even if I don't understand anything else about that stupid test. Do you think Meiko will kick me out if I don't pass it? I have a bad feeling I'm not going to pass it."

Lorelei paid more attention to the liquid ripples going down her throat than to their theoretical significance. "What? Uh... I dunno. I don't think she likesh you that much, man. That's half why I dragged you out here, you deserve SOME fun. Can't shtudy all the time, it's boring. Gotta LIVE! Not enough people live, I say. Too busy dyin' or avoidin' it..."

"Oh, I think she's starting to like me more. I helped her buy Eiko some dolls yesterday and we talked a bit and I think I helped her understand that I really do want to be friends with her."

"Uh-huh. Shyeah. I know how it ish... friends or FRIENDS?"

"Err... friends?" Mallory guessed. "Aren't they the same?"

"Baby steps, baby steps..." she reminded herself. "Jusht friends, huh? I thought as much wash goin' on... well, if SHE don't appreciate you, I do. Finally gettin' some proper food and someone to clean my room. Good to have a man around the houshe. Little variety to life, you know? And for a clueless wonder boy, you're irritatingly cute. Like a lost puppy."

The flush on his cheeks was probably just from the 50% of a stiff drink pumping through his veins. "Err... thanks. I think. I've never been called cute before. No, wait, I think Eiko said that once. But kids are kids. And you're...

errrrr... err..."

"Like that! Just like that!" Lorelei said, pointing to Mallory, misjudging distance and ending up poking him on the nose. He wobbled slightly, as did she. "That's what I'm talking about! God, the guysh you meet in clubs, they're all hey baby hey baby hey, I've got a great big tonker, I ain't never seen a guy actually BLUSH when I flirt unless they were so pathetically nice I wouldn't give them time of day, like all 'I could get dates but I'm too nice' and smug about it, and I guess you're not that way, and that's cool with me. Right."

"Right?" Mallory repeated, not following what she was yammering on about.

"RIGHT!"

"Left!"

"Wha?

"I'm sorry, I thought we were playing a game. Is there something strange in this screwdriver? I feel really bizarre. Although Dad said that liquor would do that to you. That's why he said I shouldn't have any. ....uhoh. I think I just did something he wouldn't approve of..."

"Oh, live a little! It's a party!" Lorelei exclaimed, spinning in place and waving her arms. "WHO WANTS TO PARTY?! I feel damned alive right now! I... oh, hey."

The last two words decidedly deflated, as two fairly preppy guys approached, with monogrammed sweater vests tied around their necks and artificially induced skin tans and million-dollar orthodontically corrected smiles. (Mallory felt an instant disliking of them, as they radiated the same smug bastard vibe that boys from prominent Grünwaldian farms did.)

"Hey, baby, hey!" the larger of the two greeted Lorelei. "What's a nice girl like you doing in a square place like this?"

"What're rich kids like you two doing in a square place like this?" Lorelei asked, leaning on the bar and assuming an aura of cool annoyance. "And what kind of l4m3r uses the word 'square'?"

"What's an elfourmthreer?" Mallory asked, trying to parse the unusual spurt of alien dialect.

Since Lorelei hadn't followed the script and the guy didn't know how to reply wittily, he moved on to his second prescribed line. "Why don't you ditch the loser there and hang with us a bit?" he suggested. "Name's Mitch, baby. Chad and I are buying a round of drinks for that table over there, and it's got an empty seat that I just KNOW would fit that nice bod of yours..."

Chad and Mitch's script derailed completely when Lorelei laughed out loud, hanging onto the bar for support so she didn't immediately proceed to roll on the floor laughing her ass off.

"ROTFLMAO!!" she exclaimed, sending all three boys scrambling for their internal dictionaries. "You have GOTTA be kidding me! Push off, guysh. Mal's with me and he's all the man I need. You two wouldn't last a minute with me, anyway..."

Their sacred manhood threatened, both boys turned fiery looks to the scruffy farmboy. Looks that would kill if not for the overly high-priced lawyers they'd need to beat the rap.

"Erm," Mallory replied, feeling very sober for some strange reason.

"You know, why don't we just work over the geek here a bit and show you he's not gonna be enough for you, baby?" Mitch suggested, cracking his knuckles as a musical prelude to cracking Mallory's femurs. "From the looks of him, it won't take a minute..."

"Oooh, a fight?" Lorelei asked, perking up even more than her perky state. She unstrapped her purse from her shoulder (which had blended into her nearly bondage-fetish costume so well Mallory was unaware she HAD a purse) and shoved it into Mallory's hands. "Hold my purse, pleashe," she requested politely, while sneaking something tubelike out of it...

Mallory would have replied in the affirmative, if not for being lifted off his stool by a meaty fist clenched around the neck of his favorite sweatshirt.

"You look poor," Mitch noted. "I kinda like mauling lesser... wait, haven't I seen you b—"

ZWOOM.

That would be the sound of a curved, wicked-looking blade appearing between the faces of Mitch and Mallory. A metal blade would be scary enough... a blade made of glowing blue plasma that crackled with raw power was enough to make anybody wet their pants. Fortunately for Mallory, he was feeling dehydrated.

To make matters worse, there wasn't just one blade to deal with—there were twin plasma blades at opposite ends of the handle, one at Mitch's throat, the other neatly pointing at Chad's nose. It was the kind of weapon that does half its job via sheer intimidation, and the other half in what would most likely be an expertly choreographed Nipponese film action sequence. The kind of weapon that you can make extremely long lists about that start with 'the kind of weapon'.

"A fight," Lorelei repeated, with a tight two-handed grip on the central handle of the double saber, an instinctive control over the horrific thing that trumped any level of drunken stupor. "I haven't had a good fight shince two missions ago. And I LIKE a good fight. HYAH!!"

A brief flick of the wrist, and Mitch was transformed into a living example of Newtonian physics. The parabolic arc of objects in motion within a gravitational field was adequately demonstrated as he screamed like a little girl, soaring neatly over the heads of the dancing crowd, and crashing into a small horde of wallflowers on the opposite end of the room. One spin on her barstool later, another twist of the wrist, and the other end of the blade had sent Chad flying to land on top of Mitch in a vaguely suggestive position.

The audience, of course, applauded in appreciation.

"Inertial acceleration fields," Lorelei explained to the farmboy whose jaw was scraping the bar. "Non-lethal. Meiko doeshn't let me use the cooler modes against folks. HA! That was great! Bartender, gimmie a Suburbanan Iced Tea!"

The crowd of dancers parted like hair, as five more preppies advanced on the pair. They were cracking their knuckles and squaring their jaws and one was phoning a family attorney. They meant business, or at least semi-official activity.

"Err... I think Chad and Mitch's friends aren't happy," Mallory said, because he felt that in Lorelei's state, pointing out the obvious would be advisable. "I think we should be going now. I REALLY think we should be going now. We're going now, right?"

"'course not!" Lorelei replied, hopping off her barstool swiftly, despite the risk of her 'dress' snagging and being yanked off in the process. (Which did not happen, much to the disappointment of the males in the room.) She whirled her double saber in a circle before her, before positioning it behind her back, preparing an attack stance. "I haven't had a good fight since... fifteen sheconds ago! Let's danshe, farmboy! Mallory, you cover my back!"

"I don't have a blanket!" Mallory exclaimed, getting his wires crossed. "And I don't know how to fight! We should really, really be leaving—"

"You two are SO gonna get it now!" Mitch shouted, dashing up to join his group and make the posse of five into five plus one. He shook with mighty rage, pointing the finger of accusation at Lorelei. "You're DEAD, BITCH!"

"Oh, really?" she replied, as the group surrounded her, not a one of them willing to jump in saber range just yet. She sized them up, glancing from fratboy to fratboy. "You think that scares me? Nothing scares me. You know how many times I've died, boys? Do you? Ninety-nine times. *Ninety-nine times.* And you n00bs are NOT gonna be the magic one hundred—"

"QUICK!" a voice called from across the room. "Someone's condo is on fire at the docking yard!"

All six sweatervesters turned their heads towards the voice.

When they turned back, their targets had fled, leaving only a swinging double door to mark their passing.

Mallory shoved through the second set of kitchen doors, running on adrenaline as he dragged Lorelei along by the wrist. His arm was sending signals of Intense Agony as she tried to pull away, and he did his best to ignore them in favor of the I Want To Live, Don't Stop Running signals from the rest of his body.

"L3ggo!" Lorelei demanded, skidding along the tile floor as Mallory darted down an aisle of ovens and storage cabinets. "Those guys have a righteoush asskicking comin' to them—"

"Meiko would kill me if anything happened to you! And I would kill me if anything happened to me! Or something!" he replied, focusing more on escape than coherency.

Grumbling, Lorelei fell into step/sprint beside him, her short attention span having lost interest in the boys. "Fine, fine! Take all the fun outta my evening. How'd you throw your voice like that, anyway?"

"How'd I what?"

"You know, the 'Fire!' thing. Neat trick, I—"

"HEY!"

"DON'TKILLME!" Mallory begged, dropping to his knees and skidding to a stop in front of the imposing figure before him, assuming the jig was up and the fat lady had sung. "Don't...! errr..."

The head chef waved a meat cleaver at the pair, but not in a threatening way; plus, he seemed too busy regulating the burner temperature on his stove to start actively cleaving them. "You're not supposed to be back here. Kitchen staff only!" he protested. "Get out of here! The staff of Nocturn will not be liable for accidents due to being out of bounds—"

Mallory sprung back to his feet like the season between Winter and Summer back at Grünwald. "You need to add a bit more paprika to that while it's simmering. That's why it's not thick enough," he noted quickly, instincts kicking in. "Keep it at that temperature, add it, then stir for two minutes."

"...I was wondering about that," the chef spoke, staring at Mallory in surprise. "Mrs. Henderson's Soups, midterm exam? Aren't you Josef's boy?"

"Yeah! I got an A on that exam, too!" Mallory replied, recognizing a fellow Grünwaldian. "Man, that was a rough one!"

"How about I go back there and trash those guysh while you talk shop?" Lorelei suggested, getting impatient.

"Uh, look, we really gotta get out of here," Mallory replied, keeping his grip tight, and hoping that Lorelei didn't start dragging his own weak ass off. "Someone's sort of hot on our heels—can you direct us to the taxi stop? That way I can hail a friend of mine and get out of here..."

The chef pointed with the cleaver to a door behind him. "Down that hall. Third door on the left, cut through the Rat Trap, around the Blue Oyster Bar, and the taxi stop's right there. Someone's following you? I'll call security. Get moving."

"You've a lifesaver!" Mallory replied over his shoulder while running for it.

He didn't stop to take a breath until the door to the House was safely locked behind him.

"Honestly, Mal, it wash going just fine," Lorelei replied, leaning heavily on the coat rack for support. "I had it in hand, you didn't have to bail out like that..."

"Better safe than sorry," Mallory replied, using a wizened saying properly and without gross additions for a change. "Hope I didn't wreck your evening, I just figured, you know... I'd hate for you to get hurt..."

"Awwww, it's sweet you were thinking about me," Lorelei spoke, grinning at the boy. "Even if you jumped the gun a bit. Eh, room for improvement, but we gotsh time, yeah? Thanks for the lovely evening..."

Then, she

kissed

him on the cheek.

Mallory's internal thermometer multiplied by a factor of four.

"Shame we're gettin' a job shoon," Lorelei spoke, adjusting her purse strap and starting to walk away. "I'd love to try again tomorr... oh, hey, Meiko. Whassup?"

Mallory's internal thermometer divided by a factor of six. Mostly due to the icy glare of Meiko Mirai, who stood arms crossed and foot tapping...

"Hello," she spoke, making sure to keep it as unfriendly of a greeting as possible.

"Oooooh, bus-ted!" Lorelei giggled. "Hey, Meiko, if this is about his test, shorry I dragged him away from his shtudies, I figured he could use a—"

"Why should I care?" Meiko asked, shrugging her shoulders in a very precise manner. "It's none of my business what he does with his time... or who he does it with. I'm expecting breakfast hot and ready when I get up tomorrow, Houseboy. Good evening."

With a 180° turn on one heel, she marched her way through the family room, intent on getting upstairs and to her room and locking the door behind her for a minimum of eight hours. Which she did.

"Sheesh, what a stick in the mud," Lorelei grumbled. "Feh. I'm goin' to bed, Mal. Seeya at breakfast. Go figure, I'm acshually gonna be here for breakfast! Huh? Seeyah."

Quiet, once more.

With Mallory standing perfectly still in front of the door for a good six minutes while his brain tried to figure out exactly what the hell just happened.

SATURDAY

And on the sixth day, he rested.

If he knew anything about the various branches of the Christian religion, he'd know you're supposed to rest on the seventh day. Not that he would have cared, since the REC material was fitting into his brain like a dodecahedral peg in a round hole. And the house was so tense that only a back rub to the roof would ease things.

Which is why he decided to spend some time in the one room of the house he had yet to visit: the Onsen-of-the-Month Club.

The way Lorelei had explained it to him almost made some semblance of a notion of something coherent, especially after random bits of reality trivia had been floating in his head all week. In order to move from Reality to Reality, you needed an engine that bridged the gap for an instant and moved a predetermined amount of space from one location to another. A Reality Engine for Mobiles, typically attached to a hut, house, condo, split-level home, office building, and so on.

The Onsen-of-the-Month Club didn't work exactly like that. It was an experimental new technology that allowed you to step through a transitional space which was continually generated, and literally 'link' a door to another reality. Thus, the green door with the funny squiggly-lined symbol which propped up at the base of the stairwell actually would go somewhere if you opened it... it'd go to an onsen, which was a sort of natural hot spring with rocks and warm water and steam and acted like a nonmedical muscle/brain relaxant.

Since the technology was very new, very experimental, and very much sought after by RealWare from the privately owned Nipponese company that developed it, it was also hideously expensive. Lorelei explained that simply as Meiko knowing the inventor and left it there.

However it worked technically, Mallory couldn't deny that it worked figuratively. He'd taken baths before, in ordinary bathtubs... not like this, though. Here, you scrubbed up first so the water would stay clean, then you just... soaked. It didn't seem to serve any functional purpose, but the way his woes melted away the moment he stepped in the water said he liked its nonfunctional uses very much big time.

There was one very visible reminder of his troubles, though... a makeshift screened-away section of the hot spring, off in the upper right corner, with a sign on it reading "MALLORY ONLY!". Meiko had apparently put it there the day he arrived, just in case he felt like taking a dip. She didn't want him peeping on the girls if they wanted to soak at the same time, after all.

And after the previous night... she'd probably give him the boot if he did peep. (Not that he wanted to.)

He still wasn't sure what happened. Not because he was too drunk, but because it didn't make sense. He was getting along much better with Meiko after their shopping trip... they'd shared a bit, talked, and things went okay. Except that she was very quiet on the ride home, but... she was talkative enough the rest of the day, so that couldn't be it.

After he came home with Lorelei, though, she got as cold as the three-week Winter season on Grünwald. He got the feeling she didn't want him dating Lorelei, after the strange exchanges the two had the day he was hired... but it wasn't HIS idea to have a date! (And having no prior examples to compare it against, he had to take Lorelei's word that the previous night was in fact a 'date'.) Maybe if he explained to Meiko...

That is, if Meiko would talk to him. Other than 'Pass the salt, Houseboy' and 'The living room needs to be vacuumed, Houseboy' she hadn't said a thing to him today.

Times like these made Mallory wish he'd focused a little less on his chores and a little more on other girls back home. Or even other guys. He didn't have many friends back at Grünwald—this week had been a crash course in girls and friends and all sorts of things. A crash course he was failing miserably. All he needed was to fail the REC Test miserably and he'd be limping home with his tail between his legs and salt over his shoulder while hanging his head low and kissing his head goodbye with his butt between his—

The scrape of wood on stone was heard, as the door to Onsen-of-the-Month opened. Mallory started to lean around to peek around his "MALLORY ONLY!" screen, before he heard the Voices.

"...don't see what the big deal is, anyway," Lorelei's voice echoed off the rocks and the water. "All you care about is his job performance, right, boss lady? So he missed a few hours last night. He works his ass off trying to impress you, I'm sure he can make up for a few hours..."

Mallory sank down into the water, trying to make himself small. Some part of him had to laugh at the predicament, the guy secretly overhearing while two naked girls chat in the bath... but the voting majority of him (97%) was just panicking at being caught and trying not to utter a peep...

"I told you when he got here to keep your hands off him," Meiko 'Boss Lady' Mirai spoke. (The distinct splash of someone climbing into the water... a towel hitting the ground, fluffy-like...) "This House has enough personality conflicts without a workplace romance added on top of it. I won't have it, Lorelei. And it doesn't establish a good atmosphere for Eiko to be raised in! I —"

"She seems to get along fine with him. And didn't you tell me you two talked about that? He's just a nice guy, Mei. Absurdly nice. We meet a lot of scumbuckets in this biz, it's no doubt you've forgotten what a nice guy is like..."

"That's besides the point! I'm saying... it's just not good. And I won't stand for it!"

"Oh? You're going to fire me, then? I doubt it; I've pulled you out of the fire more times than I can count when a job gets dangerous. Fire him, then? We need someone to keep the engine fixed. Sure, it hasn't broken down since he got here, but how long do you expect THAT to last? Plus he cooks and cleans, two things we were in desperate need of—"

"This isn't about his skill set, or yours!"

"Then what could it be about, huh? I thought you were the boss lady. What else would you care about, hmmmm?"

An awkward pause. Mallory actually found himself straining to hear, in case they were whispering, and while the voting majority demanded he mind his business the curious minority dark horse candidate won the election.

"...I don't have to explain myself," Meiko decided.

"Oh, get off it," Lorelei spoke... but with a friendly laugh, not a mean tone. "Everybody KNOWS what's going on. It's no big secret, that look on your face when you checked Future Perfect to see if you should hire him..."

"What—how would you know? Have you been going through my organizer —?!"

"Naw, Eiko did. She was worried, okay? She's used to her big sister 'staying in control', right? And she told me it said you'd 'hire your true love' at 3pm on that day."

The " " that followed was the sound Mallory's heart made when it stopped.

"...said nothing of the sort," Meiko lied blatantly. "And... F.P.'s been wrong before..."

"Oh, very convenient. Whenever we're doubting what it says, like a job not rolling in for a week, it's 'never wrong'. When it says something that spooks you, it's 'been wrong before'. You want me to drag Kisei in here to rag on you for being inconsistent?"

Mallory pressed his ear to the screen, resisting the urge to peer around it a little to see her reaction...

"It's been wrong before," Meiko repeated, trying to stay calm. "And... and I don't believe in fate. Even if I believe F.P. is reliabl... I mean... ...what do you WANT me to say, Lorelei?! Yes, it said that! I couldn't believe my eyes, but what was I supposed to do, kick him out after I saw that? I had to hire him, if just to make sure—"

"Make sure it was right, or make sure it was wrong?"

"You're putting your boss in a very uncomfortable position," Meiko complained, voice a bit shaky. "You know I hate losing my composure. But...

I've been having the hardest time keeping it lately! I don't know how to deal with that guy. Sometimes he pisses me off, sometimes he's annoying, sometimes he's... so naively nice... do you know what he said to me the first time he saw me and I caught him staring at my legs? 'Sorry, there aren't a lot of pretty girls in Grünwald.' And he was being HONEST, wasn't an attempt at a witty pick-up line..."

"Yeah, isn't it wild? Kinda cute, too—WHOA, Meiko, I think that's the first time I've ever seen you blush!"

"You think I WANT to be blushing?" Meiko bit off, harshly. "I hate this! It's stupid, it's like a soap opera, you just don't end up fated to fall in love with some guy you barely met and barely know! That's not... *reality* doesn't work like that. F.P. has to be wrong here. I wish I could just fire him and not have to deal with this, but... we do need an Engineer, and... and I'll admit, I'm glad the food's improved, and... and..."

"Say no more. But... you really wanna avoid the issue? Would that make life easier on you?"

"I don't know. For the first time in my life, I'm totally stumped. I've always had this plan, you know that... pull myself and my sister out of the gutter, out of the orphanage, run a business, get rich, settle down and live a comfortable future... I never really planned on having a boyfriend in the mix. It seemed like it'd just be a distraction to my life plan..."

"Right, right. Well! I have the answer to your woes, Mei!"

"Namely?" Meiko asked, suspicious.

"I'll take him off your hands."

(Mallory turned pale and red at the same time for two different reasons, leaning on the screen more to listen as Lorelei made her offer...)

"He's kinda cute and he's easy to mold, two great tastes that go great together," Lorelei continued. "So, consider him taken care of! That way you don't have to have a forced storybook romance with him and you can go about your busin... what? Not to your liking?"

Meiko's tone got angry all over again. "Now we're back where we started! I SAID I didn't want you dating him for a reason!"

"A reason you never stated. At least, not truthfully. Do you have a good reason? If not, that means he's a free man and I can stake my claim, yes? He's a hell of a lot more interesting than the one-night stands I've had lately—"

"NO. No, no—"

"Why no? C'mon, Mei, one good reason. And not 'it promotes a bad atmosphere for Eiko' or nonsense like that. Give me the truth. You're the cool customer, right? How hard is—"

"LORELEI—"

"One good reason! ALL I ask! C'mon! Lay it on me! Do it! L—what was that?"

'That' was the sound of the "MALLORY ONLY!" screen tipping over and splashing into the water of the onsen. With Mallory floating on top of it, looking surprised. Then looking at the two naked girls.

Oh well, it's been a good life, he decided, squeezing his eyes shut and awaiting death...

Since death was taking its sweet time, he decided to crack one eye open and see what was going on.

Meiko stood in the bath, holding her towel up defensively... with an all-over body blush. Trembling with rage and something else. And glaring at Mallory hard enough to burrow twin holes in his back and carve his liver up for dinner...

"You... you were LISTENING IN...?!" she asked, giving up all semblance of control as the last two words came out through grinding teeth.

"Only for a little while!" Mallory exclaimed, waving his arms and splashing in a panic. "It was an accident! I didn't mean it! I'd never do it if I could avoid it! I didn't want to embarrass you! I wasn't sure what to do! I'll do my best to forget what I heard! Even the bit about true love—"

The Onsen-of-the-Month Club door slammed shut behind Meiko before the 'o' in that word could be intoned.

"Oooh, that's not good," Lorelei decided, relaxing away in the water without bothering with her towel. "But hey, it means you're free! Let's hit the town tonight, Mal! I feel like partying!... Mal? Hey, mmmgblblblrlrlrll..."

Which was the sound Mallory heard as he blacked out and sank to the bottom of the two-foot-deep onsen.

---

dear dad.

This week has been bad and good. I am having troubles with girls and I have no idea what to do, so I may be asking for your advice in the days to come assuming I am not kicked out because I think I am in trouble for something. Currently I am writing this late at night as I had to fake having a cold in order to avoid going on a date, how is that for a strange thing!! I felt bad about lying because you always say lying is bad and gets you in the end when the piper is paid and the check bounces under the ladder across the black cat, but I have this bad feeling that things will get worse with Meiko if I did not lie and went out for the evening.

I do not think you have had these kinds of troubles since you just met mom and that was that but I will explain more in my next letter assuming I am not homeless soon. oddly I do not think I am as worried about that as I am about making Meiko upset, because she seems to not like being upset, she likes to be very calm and feeling like things are going her way and lately I do not think they have been. I have been trying to avoid upsetting her because I don't like her to be upset, especially not when it is my fault and I could have done something but I don't always know what that thing is.

Tomorrow we will have a job to do, and hopefully that will distract! will write again asap. Wish me luck please, lots and lots of it.

"UNREAL ESTATE"
EPISODE #104: STAR CROSS'D
FINAL COPY - FOR INTERNAL STUDIO USE ONLY

PROLOGUE - EXT. BEACH @ SUNSET

In this world, the sunset is beyond golden.

It skirts the edges of ordinary golden, but goes beyond with brilliant streaks of red and orange. Bright red and orange, dark red and orange... it all depends on the clouds, which are only there for dramatic effect, hazy things for the light to strike and illuminate. The sun is the director of the lighting, with the clouds as assistants, never totally obscuring the grand performance.

As the sunset sank slowly below the horizon, he placed the edge of his hand to his forehead, cutting down on the glare. He would have worn his usual sunglasses, but they would only shield his eyes, which he wanted as honest and true as possible on this last day.

"It's funny... but from here, it looks like it goes on forever," he spoke, eyes never straying from the horizon... raising one hand to reach out towards that sun. "Just on and on, without end. Not some predefined Reality with hard-set limits... but it has to end eventually, doesn't it? I knew that when I started this. You can only explore so far, and then you get stopped cold by the reality of it all..."

His hand closed around the sun before his eyes, making a fist. A smirk played over his lips.

"It's been real, and it's been good, but it ain't been REAL good," he decided, turning his back on the sunset. "And I'm outta here."

ACT I, SCENE I - EXT. BEACH @ SUNSET [TRANSIT]

Sorrowful music swelled as the sun set in the distance, the atmospheric haze obscuring the golden light, tinted with streaks of red and orange.

"It's funny... but from here, it looks like it just goes on and on, like a symphony that never ends in its beauty," Tia Liason semipoetically spoke, her sundress flapping in the light breeze coming up from the sea. "But all symphonies end, even the unfinished ones, as they reach their requiem... then, it is over."

The man behind her stood, arms folded, sunglasses on to shield his eyes. "Yeah," he spoke, noncommittally.

Tia turned in place, her beautiful and very expensive dress flowing with her motions.

"Will I ever see you again, Alex?" she asked, clasping her hands to her bosom. "Please, be honest, even if it hurts me..."

Alex Gunthar gave a shrug of his shoulders, unimpressed.

"It's been real, and it's been good," he recited. "But it ain't been REAL good. And I'm outta here."

The music swelled to a tragic crescendo as Alex walked away... Tia sinking to her knees, and starting to cry...

"Boy, that guy's a jerk," Mallory decided.

"What do you expect him to do? He doesn't love her," Lorelei explained, tugging Mallory closer to herself on the couch, by force if necessary (it was necessary). "A real man breaks it to a woman honestly, even if it hurts. It's better than stringing them along. Alex hasn't really fallen in TRUE love with any of the women of Love & Hate... not Tia Liason, not Shelly Regina, not even her long-lost twin sister Princess Natasha Regina... Eiko, pass the popcorn."

Eiko dabbed at her eyes with a hanky, despite not actually crying. "It's so tragically beautiful!" she announced, as the credits for today's episode rolled. "Love & Hate is the bestest video stream program ever! Do you think Alex will ever truly find someone he loves, Lorelei-san? I thought that he and Nurse Chapel were destined for love, but then she was lost in that Nullspace accident last season..."

"That's because Nurse Chapel was stolen by hackers, then leaked to the Hot Chixx Network for their production of 'Night Nurses XXVI'."

"Yeah, but I prefer to see it as a tragic love which could never be," Eiko corrected. "That's funner... oneesama, you missed the show! You shoulda seen it—Alex finally told Tia that.... err..."

The looming specter of Meiko crossed through the living room, from one side to the other without a word as she tapped at the keyboard of her Future Perfect. Soon she was walking up the stairs, and out of earshot.

"Feeh, she doesn't have to act all mopey about it," Lorelei complained, putting her arm around Mallory's shoulders, despite the whimpering noise this pulled from him. "She's been like that since yesterday... honestly, it's a bit juvenile. Just because I'm dating you she's giving everybody the cold shoulder..."

"Ah... maybe if you... didn't... sit so close?" Mallory suggested, hopeful. "Then she'd be less annoympghghpmh..."

"Oooh, don't you turn cold shoulder on me too, Mallory!" Lorelei mock-pleaded, smothering his face in her cleavage despite his wildly gesticulating arms of protest. "I just couldn't bear it if you were to break up with me, so soon after we've discovered our love for each other! It's so tragic! ...Eiko, don't watch this, you're too young."

Eiko crossed her arms, putting on a cute little pout. "I'm not a little kid, and I'm old enough to watch soap operas, so I can watch you suffocating Mallory-oniichan. ...why are you doing that, anyway?"

"No reason," Lorelei said, releasing the boy so he could flop backwards and gasp for air. "Man, now I'm all p5ych3d to see tomorrow's episode! I wish it wasn't off the net last week when we were all bored and waiting for work..."

Trying to get back into the conversation, Mallory coughed a few times before resuming his seat... at least a foot away from Lorelei. "Wh... why wasn't it on the net?" he asked, catching his breath. "Actor's strike or something?"

Eiko giggled with 2.3x adorable cuteness. "No, silly! The actors on Love & Hate can't strike. They don't even get paid! They don't even EXIST!"

"...huh?"

"It's all generated by powerful Workstations!" Eiko explained. "Computing machines designed and programmed just to produce soap operas. All the sets, characters, dialogue, and plot twists are done by complicated and very expensive software named LHART, programmed by the late Art Pasadina! That's why they can do a new one every single day, ensuring a ratings bonanza for first run episodes and re-runs on demand for discerning soap fans. With a low overhead, they make an incredible profit off the advertising, making Love & Hate the most successful RealNet video stream program for four hundred years running!"

While most of that tirade went over Mallory's head or just around it to the side or in one ear and out the other, he did catch on to the important bit. "They're not real people?" he asked, trying to confirm that he got it right. "They're... they're just faked by software...?"

"Eh, it's no big deal," Lorelei said, leaning back on the couch and stretching her arms over her head, which stretched her t-shirt against her chest, which stretched Mallory's comfort zone out a few more inches. "So what if they're fake? All acting is fake. It's still an awesome show. And ever since they introduced Alex Gunthar two seasons ago, it's been better than ever. He's just so... so non-soap-operaey. He fights in bars, he cracks dirty jokes, he only hooks up with the girls for brief, wild flings... my kind of guy! Not that I don't adore you with every fiber of my being, Mal."

"Uhhh..."

"You should try to be more like him! You know, actually funny instead of unintentionally funny. Alex Gunthar is a laugh riot! He's always pulling witty stuff out of his a... err... ear."

"You were about to say a bad word, weren't you?" Eiko asked, peering at her.

"No," she lied. "I... hey, Meiko! Long time no see..."

The ghost of Meiko Mirai drifted into the room, settling into the chair at the Reality Engine Control Workstation on the opposite side of the room. Without looking over her shoulder at anyone, she started keying up various passport processing programs.

"Our job finally came in, just as F.P. predicted," she spoke in an average tone without any implied intent of any sort whatsoever at all. "We'll be meeting our new client once I arrange for a docking at Drome. Lorelei, put on something less revealing, I don't want us looking bad in front of the client. Mallory, make yourself useful and go clean something."

Since cleaning something meant being out of Lorelei's reach (and doing something that might make Meiko happy), Mallory was off and sweeping up in the kitchen in 2.3 seconds.

Ignoring his departure, Lorelei instead stared at Meiko in abject surprise (a rare event for her). "Drome? We're going to Drome? Home of the hottest video stream studios? Is our client a rich stream star? Is he single?"

"Autographs!" Eiko cheered. "I can get some autographs for my collection! Wai!"

"I'll definitely go get changed!" Lorelei decided, springing to her feet. "Gotta look my best to match up to the glamorous standards of today's stream actors!"

ACT I, SCENE II – INT. HOUSE [KITCHEN]

It should be illegal to be that ugly, Lorelei thought.

It wasn't just the pimples. Plenty of people have zits. Maybe they don't have that many, to the point where it looks like a nest of angry wasps decided to kamikaze his face. Maybe theirs didn't ooze that much pus, either... but it wasn't just the pimples. It was the pimples, the uneven stubble complete with bloody bits of toilet paper stuck to spots on his face, the oily and clumpy hair, and the pink sweater-vest tied around his neck that clashed with the striped shirt. The cigarette he smoked was simply icing on the cake after that point.

For this, Lorelei had dressed up in her finest 'classy' yet sultry threads. She pondered sneaking away from the house meeting with their new client, so she could put on something very, very covering and unsexy. After all, the first thing he had done on entering the house was leer at her...

To her right, Mallory wasn't paying the same kind of attention to the client. He was too busy staring in fascination through the kitchen window, to the video stream windows playing across the sky of Drome...

"Oi, pay attention," Lorelei whispered, nudging the boy with a pointy yet shapely elbow. "There might be a test."

"Eh?" Mallory asked, glancing away from the video sky. "What?"

"It really is a disaster," the man was saying, as he ground out his cigarette on Meiko's kitchen table (while she barely restrained her irritation). "We had to go offline all last week just to rebuild enough code for today's 'farewell' scene. If the character was missing that long, our hardcore viewers would've noticed, and the shit would've hit the fa—"

"Mr. Cox, I would appreciate you not swearing in front of my sister," Meiko spoke, each phoneme turning into ice as it was spoken. (Eiko meanwhile quietly grinned, as she learned a new word.)

"My point is, I need your help. And money is ... not much of an object," he said, catching himself before he made a promise Eiko could latch to.

Meiko drummed her fingernails on the table, pushing down her irritation. "Let me summarize, just so we're all on the level," she said, eyes locked on the nebbishly producer in such a way as to make him squirm in his seat. "Alex Gunthar, anti-hero star of Love & Hate, has been kidnapped. Or rather, his data module was stolen from your studio by his programmer."

"We haven't gotten a single ransom note, either," Mr. Cox added. "We have no idea where the bitch might have taken our data—"

"What I want to know, Cox," Meiko interrupted with a deliberate stripping of the Mr. title, "Is why you need our help with this. Your studio is owned in part by RealWare, and they have mandated that intellectual property legislation be set up in every single customer reality. It's part of the EULA attached to a Reality Engine. RealWare IP Police are trained for just such an incident as this; they could track down your renegade programmer and retrieve your data. We're troubleshooting consultants, and yes, occasionally bounty hunters... but we're not experts in this type of crime compared to them. Why us?"

"... paperwork issues," the producer decided. "It's a hassle. Red tape up the wazoo, my hands are tied really, this is the best way to get things done, and I can offer a terrific fee on return of my data so I don't see why—"

"His masters would punish him if it became public knowledge that a theft had occurred."

Everybody turned to look at Kisei—who had been forgotten until then, as she stood silently in the corner of the kitchen.

"The reason is obvious," she continued. "After the earlier kidnapping of Nurse Chapel by hackers, another incident would cause him to lose face with his superiors. In an effort to skate around the consequences of his slovenly attitude towards security, he seeks private assistance that can deal with the affair quietly."

Cox frowned at the woman. "Hey, I'll have you know we do NOT have a slov... sloven... we're not lazy bastards. This was a fluke, and I don't much like your implication, missy. Meiko, are you gonna let her talk to me that way?"

"Yes," Meiko replied, rising from her chair. "Cox-san, normally I would suggest you deal with the problem you have caused on your own, but I'm feeling generous today. I am interested in taking your case. Eiko, draw up a contract with him... standard retrieval contract. Half payment now, and on successful return of the stolen data, we get the rest plus any incidental expenses incurred during the manhunt."

"Right, oneechan!" Eiko chimed in with, her light tone a stark contrast to the tension in the room. "Don't worry, Cox-san! We'll get that bitch for you!"

"Eiko, don't use that word."

"...sorry, oneechan."

ACT I, SCENE III - EXT. JOE'S

The second date...

Perhaps sensing that Mallory would not survive an experience as intense as the first date, Lorelei suggested a lunch date. Mallory was actually excited about the prospect before realizing he wasn't going to be preparing lunch.

Instead, they went to a local Joe's, located only two blocks away from the Drome Docking Station. It was populated mostly with video studio types on lunch break, who paid them no attention—they were here to obtain edible items, eat them, and leave. They were not here for lovely romantic date adventures...

Although for Mallory, the adventure came in the form of the food. This 'hamburger' before him may have been revered by food-on-the-go fans around the multiverse, but Mallory didn't quite see what was praiseworthy. The meat was nearly paper thin. Toppings looked old and nasty, mashed together in such a way as to blend weakly colored bits together to the point of unrecognizability. The bread? The bread could only be considered bread in that it was soft and thus mashed up with the rest into a pastelike material in your mouth...

"And you said there's HOW many places like this?" Mallory asked, opting to grab his soft drink and rinse the nasty taste of that first bite away.

"Millions," Lorelei replied, crumpling up the foil wrapper of her own burger after devouring it (the burger). "Joe's is the most popular fast food franchise in the multiverse. It's not about how good it tastes, or how well it's cooked... it's about how fast you can eat it and how cheap it is. Not every meal can be a six-course feast crafted by a loving chef, you know."

"I know, I know... Meiko gave me the same speech when I had hot dogs with her in Urbana—"

"Are you cheating on me behind my back, Mal...?"

"Wah? Err, no no no, this was the day before the night we went out..."

Lorelei waved a finger at him, grinning. "Watch it, farmboy. Anyway, out here in the REAL world, we eat what we can afford, quality or not. Even with the half-payment, we gotta cut corners... and those corners are getting smaller the longer it takes to find this chick. I don't get it, usually Meiko can track them in two days, and it's been three since we took the assignment..."

"I know, I know," Mallory said, nudging his soda cup back and forth listlessly. "She's spending all her time in her room on her Workstation... I tried bringing her dinner yesterday, but she ignored me completely. Not that she noticed me any other time since we..."

"Since what, hmm?"

Nudging the unholy corpse of his hamburger away, Mallory leaned with his elbows on the plastic table. "Uh... look, Lorelei... about, er... 'us'?"

"Yes, Mallory my sweet?" Lorelei asked, batting her eyebrows at him.

"I, uh... err... workplace romances... and... things that kind of... not quite sure how... I mean to say... uh... look, this is going to sound odd but can I close my eyes and say this instead? I was practicing it earlier by myself and it was coming out so well but I hadn't counted on being able to see right down your errrrr... ...it's very distracting..."

His date folded her arms over her chest. "Better?" she asked, with a smirk. "I knew there was a libido somewhere inside you, Mal!"

"I'm not like that! I just... I... okay. Right..." He glanced aside, which worked better. "I... Idontreallythink we should be dating! There. I said it."

"Awwwww... why not?" she asked... reaching out and taking his hand, which multiplied the distraction factor. Her fingers started slowly walking up his arm, as she scooted around the plastic table, closer and closer, inch by inch... "I'm single, you're single. I have an incredible amount of fun with you, too! Maybe you're not a wild untamed animal in the sack (although I haven't got official proof one way or another yet) but you're sweet and you grow on me like mold. So what's the problem?"

On the last word, her hips bumped his, and he nearly jumped out of his skin.

"L-Love!" he blurted, without the rest of the words to go in the sentence alongside the Power Word.

Lorelei cocked her head at him, puzzled. "Love?"

Jerking his arm away, Mallory scooted away from his date, looking away as he scooted away so that he could get away. "I mean to say... I mean, we don't... okay, I may not know a lot but I do know what 'love' means, and kind of like my dad and my mom may she rest in peace I kind of assumed that two people had to be in love in order to date, because that's just how it works and I don't really think that you love me so why the heck are you dating me?! ...if you don't mind me asking."

Against even his admittedly weak predictions, Lorelei slapped one thigh and doubled over laughing.

"ROTFL!" she exclaimed. "Oh, Mal, you are a prize, I tell you! You really think all dating is based on heart-swelling romantic love like in the soaps? C'mon, farmboy, we're talking reality here, okay? Hey, you're a swell guy and you'll be a great pick for the one who eventually gets ya, but I can't honestly say I'm in love with you, no. I'm dating you for another reason entirely."

Twice as confused now, Mallory stared at her helplessly. "Another... reason? What rea—"

"*ahem*."

Confusion jumped to Fear, as he turned and saw Meiko standing there with her hands on her hips. (Fear leads to Anger which leads to Hate which leads to Suffering, but Mallory stopped at Fear. He wasn't the sort to get Angry easily.)

Lorelei didn't lose her grin. "I swear, Meiko, you always have picture perfect timing!" she exclaimed. "Got a reason to be interrupting Mallory and I's lovely date, though...?"

"I found her," Meiko spoke evenly. "Get back to the House. We're leaving Drome."

With that, Meiko Mirai turned sharply on one heel and marched House-ward.

"Wow, she's really sticking it out," Lorelei commented to herself. "I assumed she'd crack by now... Mallory? Hey, reality to Mal, come in Mal...?"

Mallory Heisenberg was too busy watching Meiko walk away to even hear his "girlfriend's" voice.

ACT II, SCENE I – EXT. PRINCESS MOTEL

The best motels in the mulitverse come with all the trimmings... Video Network Sets, daily housekeeping to turn down the sheets and add fresh towels, and room service that can deliver everything from pancakes to porterhouse steaks. There's always a swimming pool (with jacuzzi), a game room, and sometimes even a tennis court. Even if a motel didn't fully measure up to a regal hotel, it could still be within inches of luxury's lap.

The Princess Motel, if you traveled at the speed of sound, could reach the lap of luxury in about three days. The joint was so seedy that a flock of ravenous birds would peck it up in minutes if that was not simply a metaphor. The best you got was a dinky, obsolete RealNet Messaging terminal in every room, housekeeping that would add some delousing powder to your sheets if you bribed them heavily enough, and the potholes in the nearby public lot would make excellent swimming pools if filled with heavy rain. And yes, it rained quite often in the hotel- and motel-loaded reality named Restless.

Restless specialized in being a transitional point for people who needed somewhere to stay for a short period of time. They had higher-end hotels and even condos for rent, but most folks who needed to "get away from it all" ("it all" usually being the local law enforcement back home) would stick to the run-down sidebar dives like the Princess Motel. There you'd find the sort of people with shifty eyes, seven o'clock shadows, and one hand on the trigger of a gun at all times...

Beautiful young women with flowing red hair and pretty white dresses were not usually found there, unless they only rented motel rooms by the hour.

This one had been staying there for three days now. And every day, she'd emerge around noon, a heavy bag slung over one shoulder and an empty aching in her tummy.

"Our runaway programmer is staying here, at the Princess Motel, under the name 'Marlena,'" Meiko explained during the pre-strike meeting. Her F.P. organizer projected a helpful slide presentation on the refrigerator, and a laser pointer touched on the various maps, diagrams, bullets, and textual labels. "It took a lot of tracking from my leads on RealNet, but I'm certain that's the woman we want. She matches the physical description."

"I sure hope so," Lorelei said, slumped in her seat at the kitchen table. "Nobody wants a repeat of the time we grabbed that guy who turned out to be the evil twin of the guy we were really gunning for..."

Mallory glanced over. "Err, don't you mean the good twin?"

"I know what I said, Mal. See, there was this saxophone and a bottle of scented oil—"

"We don't have time to wax nostalgic about past missions with the Houseboy," Meiko interrupted. "We've just docked at Restless, and she's going to be on the move soon. We have a good chance at nabbing her today and recovering the data. The suspect's obviously new at the whole hiding-out thing, since she walks into the open with regular frequency... at noon every day, Urbana Standard Time, to get some soup at a corner deli."

Keeping one arm through the strap on her heavy burlap bookbag, the woman signaled a waitress with her spare arm. "Chicken soup please," she ordered. "And a peanut butter and jelly sandwich, and some tea—"

"Same as last time, then," the waitress spoke with Ultimate Boredom.

"Ah, yes. Thank you."

She resumed nervously fingering at the bookbag strap, glancing around the room... and completely missing the fact that someone was indeed tracking her.

"I'll take a booth in the deli ten minutes before she gets there and order a bottomless cup of coffee with Lorelei," Meiko continued. "Once I get a good up-close look at her, if it matches the profile we've been given, I'll signal the go-ahead. Lorelei, you follow her out of the deli. Light tailing, but—"

"I know the drill," Lorelei spoke dryly. "We've done other bounty jobs before. She's really an amateur? I won't have to brawl a bit and take her down with m4dsk1llz?"

"No. Now, the forecast calls for rain, so she'll probably have an umbrella. Kisei...?"

The quiet one at the end of the table gave a simple nod in reply.

"Don't act all smug just 'cause this is your plan," Lorelei commented to Kisei, peering at her. "It's worked dozens of times before, but you never know when something unexpected will go down..."

Kisei stood, fetching her wooden stocked sniper rifle from underneath the table. "I am being paid to expect the unexpected, therefore I will be prepared," she noted simply.

"Good. You all know the drill. We don't technically have jurisdiction here since there isn't a RealWare authorized bounty on her, so act fast and act quietly. Mallory, stay here with Eiko. Lorelei, Kisei, with me..."

With her favorite lunch in her tummy, the woman strolled along the cracked sidewalks back to her motel. It had started to rain, unfortunately... she wondered quietly why it had to rain all the time here, as she opened a bright red umbrella that marked her as a blatantly obvious target to anybody who could be stalking her, like the blonde who was studying a shop window ten paces behind her...

Blonde? Wasn't that the same one who had left the deli before she finished—

The tiny dart pierced her umbrella's nylon fabric, and stuck neatly at the side of her neck. The blonde moved in quickly, putting an arm around her shoulders before she could fall into that unconscious void...

On a high rooftop one block away, the sniper closed up the scope on her rifle, and jumped off a fire escape, darting into the rain-soaked streets.

ACT II, SCENE II - INT. STORAGE ROOM @ THE HOUSE

There are two rooms on the first floor of the House which are unfinished. The walls are little more than insulation and wooden beams; the floors are concrete. The ceilings are only there to provide floors to the rooms above.

Both are lit with one or two lightbulbs hanging from the ceiling, the kind with the little pull-chains to get them going. Not nearly as impressive as a gesture-sensitive light emitting bio-organic lumination generator, but replacing the bulbs is much cheaper.

One room houses the backup power generator that gives the House its lifeline when not docked in a feed-enabled docking yard, such as the recent visit to I's Land. There are also valves and pipes and things that push water around the house, and a backup storage tank for a likewise feedless situation.

The other room is used for storage, with shelves to hold various dry goods and objects that have no home anywhere else in the House. It also makes a handy prison cell / interrogation chamber of horrors, even if the scariest things in there are dried prunes in old cardboard boxes.

"Hey, Meiko, do we have any prunes?" Mallory called out, as he leaned into the open doorway. "I was thinking of an old recipe I know that'd make a great dinn... err...? Kisei? Meiko? What're you doing in here, anyway?"

"Reviving her," Meiko said, pointing with her thumb to the young woman handcuffed to a kitchen chair in the center of the storage room. "Beat it, Houseboy. This is dangerous—"

"No it's not," a cheerful Eiko-esque voice chirped in with, popping up from behind Mallory. "It's really cool, oniichan! Kisei uses a special chemical thing that paralyzes them so they're totally harmless, even the really nasty ones that use words I'm not supposed to know!"

Sure enough, Kisei was busying herself with a small military-grade medical kit, pouring a measure of fluid into a spray bottle. "It will be quite safe," she repeated. "You have no need for concern, Meiko Mirai. One moment..."

"It's still official mission business, and none of your concern," Meiko spoke gruffly, looking away from the two at the doorway. "Don't you have dinner to be making, Houseboy? And... don't you have that new dollhouse to play with, Eiko?"

"This is funner," Eiko protested. "C'moooon! I'll be quiet..."

"Either way, I must administer this now," Kisei informed, pressing the spray against the woman's neck, and thumbing the control button. "This will counter the tranquilizer, but render her quite safe for interrogation as well..."

The effect was instant. Her head, previously sagging downward, snapped to attention—eyes darting around the storage room in fright, looking for something to be legitimately afraid of. Unfortunately, Mallory and Eiko were offering friendly smiles directly across from her, and Kisei and Meiko looked at best neutral rather than menacing. (But that box of prunes was looking like it was quite past the expiration date...)

"Wh... where am I?" she asked. And after a moment, added, "Why can't I move?!"

"You'll be released soon, as long as you cooperate," Meiko spoke, knowing the routine, establishing control of the situation with a cool but indifferent tone of assurance. "You won't be harmed. We're independent troubleshooting consultants acting as bounty hunters for SudsNet Soap Opera Productions, Inc. We don't have authorization to hold you, but we do have authorization to retrieve some stolen data currently in your possession. Do you understand?"

"Y-Yes, but—"

"Where have you put the data?" Meiko asked. "The sooner we retrieve it, the sooner you can go. You won't be unparalyzed until we've escorted you back to your motel room and administered a time-release countermedicine, so don't plan on trying to steal the data again by force."

"Then... then I won't tell you," she decided, trying to find a logical hole through Meiko's explanation of How Things Were Going To Be. "I'll never give him up. I've come too far to give him up now!"

Mallory scratched his head, puzzled. "Err... him? Oh! I get it, you stole one of the characters from Love & Hate!"

"Of course she did! Keep up, Houseboy!" Meiko barked... before turning the cool voice back on, and facing the programmer. "What's your real name, 'Marlena'?"

"B... Belle Pasadina," she explained. "I'm the great-great-great-granddaughter of Art Pasadina, original programmer of Love & Hate. And you're not getting him back! I don't care what that slimeball Cox says, he's... he deserves better than to be a puppet for that stupid show! I'll never tell you where he—"

"Found it," Kisei announced, pulling a cubelike object out of Belle's bookbag.

"—ahh! Leave him alone!" Belle blurted out, before catching herself. "...I mean... that's not him. That's just... it's..."

"I was not sure, as the data store is unmarked," Kisei spoke, passing the cube to Meiko. "Which is why we revived you, to have you confirm my suspicion. Mission complete. Thank you for your cooperation, and my apology for the disrespect in retaining you in such a manner. Meiko, shall I sedate and return her to the motel now?"

"NO!" Belle wailed, eyes wide as she tried desperately to pull away from the chair... doing little more than crane her neck forward a bit. "Please, don't! You don't understand!"

"I'm sorry, but theft of intellectual property is a crime under RealWare's EULA charters," Meiko spoke. "The law is the law, and it's out of our hands. You're very lucky that we're the ones handling this quietly instead of having the IP Police after you, Ms. Pasadina—"

"BUT WE'RE IN LOVE!"

Blank stares bounced off the unfinished walls of the storage room, as Meiko looked to Kisei who looked to Belle who looked to Mallory who looked to Eiko and then to Meiko.

"Huh?" Mallory summarized for all of them.

"W-We're in love!" Belle continued, desperate to avoid the fate of sedation, which would effectively end the game for good. "We're in love, and... and we're eloping! I stole his data module since I couldn't copy the files, they were encrypted heavily with DRM after the Nurse Chapel incident. And I was trying to find someone who could... I don't know, make a robot form for him, or grow a clone, I know not many RealWare realities have that kind of technology, but I thought a private one, if I could find someone who could help me, I just... we're in love and if you take him from me, he'll be a slave again and I'll never be able to rescue him! Please don't do this!!"

Meiko stared at the cube a bit. "This is just an AI," she noted, too puzzled to keep her cool control. "What're you talking about? You're a programmer, it's your program, it's not a lover—"

"He... he was always better at explaining it," Belle spoke, keeping her eyes on the cube. "The lock panel... key in 351. It'll start the holographic projector. He can explain it for you himself! Then you'll understand..."

Meiko frowned, turning the cube around to the control buttons. "Kisei...?"

"I've already scanned her bag for explosives or chemical agents," Kisei spoke, also keeping her eyes on the cube... voice a bit less indifferent, but very guarded. "I am... familiar with that sort of data store unit. It would be safe to activate. I would not endanger you or Eiko Mirai if I was not absolutely sure of this."

Mallory spoke u—

"You are collateral," Kisei told him before he could even ask.

"...oh," he said, deciding to interpret that as a good thing.

"Just to inform you, this won't change anything," Meiko told Belle, shifting back to her coldness. "The data is still coming with us. But..."

She keyed in the three-digit sequence... and a tiny hologram of Alex Gunthar, the most popular character of Love & Hate, hovered over the cube.

Alex wore the same sunglasses that shielded his eyes from view as he kicked Tia Liason to the curb. He wore his beloved 'Wildcats' leather jacket from his days as a rough-and-tumble biker thug. A fake dramatic wind even brushed through his scruffy locks, drama added to his folded arms, his equally cold expression pointed at Meiko...

"Heard the whole thing," he commented. "External microphone. Won't change anything, huh? I'm used to unchanging worlds. Nothing ever really changes on a soap. It just shuffles around periodically... that didn't stop me from escaping, and I'm gonna escape here, too. Belle and I are destined to be together; nothing you do can stop that... just to inform you, of course."

"...COOOOL!" Eiko exclaimed, clasping her hands and stepping into the room to study his image up close. "That's the same determination and proud heart that makes Alex Gunthar so great! Wow, Meiko, can I get his autograph?"

Meiko ignored the program, looking up to the programmer. "You actually coded him to love you?" she asked. "That's more than a little strange, Ms. Pasadina. You can't love a bunch of ones and zeroes. We could be doing you a public service by—"

"I'm down here, you know," Alex spoke in a warning tone, as his 1/6th size hologram glared up at Meiko. "Leave her alone. She's had enough abuse for my sake; you want to deal with this, you deal with me, bit......" A glance to Eiko. "Miss."

"HEY! You were gonna call my sister a bad word!" Eiko recognized instantly.

Alex shrugged... but put on his trademarked charming smile. "Yeah, but I'd hate to corrupt a nice young lady like you with coarse dialect. Wouldn't be right, huh?"

...a little blush passed over Eiko's cheeks. "Young lady...?"

"And for your information, I'm not like the other cheeseball AIs in that glorified puppet show," Alex continued. "Belle wasn't content to let the show run like it had for hundreds of years, when she took the job of lead director. She decided to try to innovate a bit, since RealWare hadn't bothered to update Art Pasadina's original code in the slightest. 'If it ain't broke, just patch it,' right?"

Belle spoke up, a bit of fire back in her voice. "Exactly! My ancestor was a good programmer, but... but there was so much room for improvement that even if RealWare doesn't approve of new code development, I had to try. And I decided I'd make this one self-aware by teaching him that he was a soap opera AI, and then one night, ... uh..."

"I started flirting with her," Alex finished, with a wry grin. "And nature took its course. Pretty soon, we both decided we had to get away from there and find me a real body... it was either that or break up. I couldn't live in that prison anymore once I realized my love; do you have any idea what it's like, living in a soap opera? I'd rather die than go back to that... and if I could erase myself or knock out my own sentience, I would. I'm dead serious about this, Belle is dead serious about this... for us, it's true love or bust."

Eiko almost floated in the air with little hearts in her eyes, except that was not biologically possible. "Oh, true love or bust...! It's so romantic! Oneechan, we just HAVE to help these two! Escaping into the night, with evil people at their heels, with only their love to give them wings—"

"This is... it's flat-out ridiculous," Meiko spoke, glancing around nervously. "He's a PROGRAM. You can't love a program—"

"I don't care what I am," Alex stated flatly. "I don't even care if I can't truly love someone, I don't care if it's all a simulation. All that matters is what I feel. Even if it doesn't work, we have to try, or we'll never have known for sure. Maybe it's just my defined character trait table speaking, but I am not gonna let anybody tell me what I supposedly can and can't do. I'm gonna find out for myself. Belle and I know what we're doing, even if we don't know how it'll end... but that's wild, young love for you, isn't it?"

Meiko's frustration seeped to the surface, much as it had in the onsen only a few days whence. "You're the intellectual property of your company, which is owned in turn by RealWare," she stated, trying to put down some concrete facts to leverage from. "Even if you're... in love, you're still stolen property, and... we have to return you. Otherwise we'd be HELPING her break the law, landing us in deep, deep trouble. I'm not going to jeopardize my family over a program that claims it's sentient—"

"There are precedents."

Meiko looked up sharply at her military tactician... who cleared her throat, and glanced aside before continuing.

"There are precedents," Kisei spoke quietly. "In private realities established for corporate research, sentient AI has been made. Some have even leaked to the mainstream press; surely you have not forgotten the articles published about Oscar some years previous? In addition... work on artificial intelligence with bio-logic interfaces is quite advanced in private study, with entire people capable of being grown and implanted with a preprogrammed neural layout... so such things are possible. There is a chance that this AI is capable of the emotions he professes. ...I am merely stating matters of fact as are in my knowledge from work before your employ, Miss Mirai. I mean no disrespect."

"Right! RightrightrightRIIIGHT!" Eiko agreed, bouncing up and down and pointing to Kisei. "She's right! I remember reading about that. So he's a person! Even if he's a little glowy thingy in a cube he's a person and he's in love, and love is a beautiful thing! And—"

"And it's illegal to steal computer data!" Meiko reiterated, stomping her foot... and realizing how silly she looked doing it. Shaking her head, she set the cube down on the floor. "None of this matters! We have to... there's not... HOUSEBOY! You've been staring for the last five minutes —do you have ANYTHING of interest to add to this discussion? Huh?!"

Mallory stepped back from the doorframe, taken by surprise (which was remarkably easy to do). "Wh—?! Uh, um, err, uh, um—"

"Spit it out!" Meiko ordered.

"I—I think we should help!" Mallory spoke quickly. "I know it's risky and we'd be better off just giving Alex back to the guy from Drome but I don't think I'd feel right about doing it since I think he's telling the truth and even if we don't have a choice I mean there has to be some kind of choice since you guys are so smart and know so much more about this than I do and surely you could think of something since you're so smart about troubleshooting stuff and I really just think we have to think about this and I don't know, it just feels WRONG!"

The looks of Relief (Belle), Smirking Approval (Alex), Bouncy Approval (Eiko), Reserved Unreadableness (Kisei) and Utter Confusion (Meiko) were enough to make Mallory want to crawl under a rock somewhere and hide.

" ....that's all I'm saying, it feels wrong," he said, slowing down as best he could. "You guys don't take missions where you kill people or do anything that's wrong, right? Isn't kidnapping wrong? There's gotta be something we could do to make everybody happy... it's always better if you can make everybody happy. What's the worst RealWare could do if we just, uh, sort of let them get away and say we couldn't find them...?"

Meiko snapped to attention at that, frowning. "Spoken by someone who still doesn't get what RealWare is," she stated, with a roll of the eyes. "You saw how they almost enslaved the kids of I's Land. And that was one of their more common, up-front, legitimate business deals. No, they wouldn't hunt us down and kill us. But they'd find out eventually we let these two go... and there are other ways to punish someone. We use a RealWare engine; we could get it revoked, be grounded, have no way of getting a job since RealWare has their finger in nearly every pie of the multiversal economy, be... no. I'm not going to rant. You are NOT going to make me lose my control. And we are NOT going to defy RealWare on this over a matter of tr... true love. By tomorrow... Alex Gunthar is going to be back on our Video Network Set screen, and likely back with Tia Liason. We'll deal with this in the morning. Kisei, sedate her for now and turn off the cube."

Before Belle could protest, Kisei had pressed a loaded spray to her neck. A second later and the hologram winked out in the middle of Alex giving Meiko the finger.

One person was definitely not sedate, however, as Eiko balled up her fists in anger. "But ONEECHAN—"

"We can't always follow the flowery path of so-called true love, Eiko," Meiko replied coldly... although she couldn't look Eiko in the eyes when she did so. "You'll learn when you grow up... sometimes you just have to do what has to be done. Everybody out. Belle will stay here for the night."

Kisei cocked her head, in a rare show of confusion. "You don't want me to deliver her to the motel—?"

"We'll deal with this in the morning," Meiko iterated, rubbing her temple. "I have a headache. I have... arrangements to make. Mallory, Eiko, I'm locking the door to this room, please don't do anything foolish..."

"ONEECHAN—!"

Eiko paused, as Mallory rested a hand on her shoulder.

"Come on, Eiko," he said... with a slightly sad smile. "It's almost dinnertime. We better go..."

"I'm not hungry!" she declared, casting a last glare at her sister before pulling away, running off to her room.

Mallory sighed... and reached around Meiko, to fetch the box of prunes he came for. "I'll... I'll just go make dinner for the rest of us, then," he said. "It'll be ready in about a half-hour, Meiko—"

"Yeah, whatever," she said, looking away so she couldn't see him leave.

Quiet.

Meiko glanced at the only conscious person in the room. "Do you have an opinion on this?" she asked, trying not to sound annoyed.

After a pause, Kisei gave a noncommittal shrug. "It is my duty as your retainer to carry out your orders," she spoke. "How I feel on any given issue is not a component of my duty. Your words are pragmatic; we do not need RealWare's wrath upon this home. I would have advised you similarly."

Meiko nodded along... while seeing straight through the words. "Of course. I just took the initiative, knowing you'd advise me to that end. Although... would HE accept that advice in this situation, Kisei?"

"...absolutely not," Kisei spoke. "I will be returning to my quarters now, Miss Mirai. Please summon me if you have further need of my services."

Alone in the room, aside from the sleeping woman, her deactivated lover and a few hundred pounds of dry goods, Meiko's thoughts were the only noise she paid attention to.

After ten minutes of standing in place, she withdrew Future Perfect from her pocket, and started keying in an address.

ACT II, SCENE III – THE HOUSE @ NIGHT

Of course, he really had no say in this.

Meiko was right. If RealWare was really that bad... and the job at I's Land hinted in that direction... then they didn't want to run afoul of them over some young couple who they'd just met that day. If you could call them a couple, with one being nothing more than a program...

So why didn't it click?

Maybe love had just been soaking into his brain lately. There was the whole problem with Lorelei and Meiko... how he really felt about either of them, or if he had any right to feel any way in particular about either one of them, or what exactly Lorelei was up to when she really didn't seem to love him or the dire warning Future Perfect had given Meiko about her True Love or...

The boy closed his eyes and told his racing thoughts to please come to a full stop. He had to put them out of his head; no matter how he felt, he needed sleep, and catching a half-hour here and there tonight on his living room couch wasn't helping. Briefly, he had the idea of quietly firing up the house's primary RealNet Workstation and messaging some all night video stream talkshow, like he'd seen others do on his secret video player back in Grünwald... people with all manners of questions about love, relationships, and other subjects that made his ears turn red. Many an evening was spent in the glow of that tiny, cracked screen watching people work out their problems with thirty-second psychiatric nuggets from the show hosts...

Maybe he could call himself 'Restless in Restless', or something...

He drifted off for another hour, having a strange dream about Meiko throwing a chair at him on a talk show while Lorelei egged on the crowd in a 'Lor-e-lei! Lor-e-lei!' chant and a yellow-shirt-wearing Kisei tried to break up the brawl. For some reason, the audience was entirely filled with copies of him, and this worried him much more than being bludgeoned by furniture...

Not enjoying the stress of the dream, Mallory's body woke itself up for the third time that night. With a groan of giving-upness, he swung his legs off the couch, and stood. It was milk time—Heisenbergs were big fans of having a glass of milk when you couldn't sleep.

All that kept him from cool, frosty white relief was the fact that the closet door was hanging open by a crack. The same closet Belle and Alex were kept in...

Very, very, very, very, very, very, very, very quietly, he tiptoed over to the door and peeked in.

No Belle and Alex.

He considered turning right around and going to bed. They'd escaped... good for them. Maybe it'd solve the problem for Meiko... no matter what her words were saying, Mallory had a sense that she wished there was another way. An escape would work for everybody...

The second thing he noticed was how the door to the Onsen-of-the-Month Club was slightly ajar. He frowned as much as Mallory Heisenberg was capable of frowning. If they'd tried to escape into THERE, it was a dead end; the onsen was walled in, with only one door.

He could just go back to bed. Belle could find her own way out. Unless Kisei or someone had heard, and would be coming downstairs any second while the couple was trying to find a back door out of the Onsen... it couldn't hurt to warn them. Then he could zip back to the couch and pretend he was asleep. But if Meiko caught him, she'd hate him even more than she did now...

Just go with it, his guts told him while his brain spun its wheels. *Quit thinking it and just do what you have to.*

He opened the Onsen-of-the-Month Club door, and stepped through the reality interface layer, ready for anything except what he actually saw.

ACT II, SCENE IV - ONSEN-OF-THE-MONTH CLUB

Belle was there.

So was Meiko.

And Kisei.

And... some guy he didn't recognize.

And apparently there WAS a secret back door to the onsen, as it was hanging open, leading to another rippling reality interface similar to the one he had just stepped through.

Rather than panic, he quickly ducked behind the soggy 'MALLORY ONLY!' screen which had been propped up against a wall to dry out a few days ago. The second time he was spying behind the thing, but maybe this time he wouldn't be caught—

"Mallory is spying on us," Kisei commented casually.

The spy's blood froze. That does it. If Meiko didn't clobber him last time, she'd surely do it now...

"Come on out of there, Mallory," Meiko spoke, voice soft. "Unless I can convince you to go back to bed and forget what you're seeing...?"

Mallory stepped out from behind the screen, hands over his eyes. "Ha ha, I didn't see anything! I was just looking for a glass of milk from the fridge and opened the wrong door. Silly me! I'lljustbegoingnow—"

"I don't see any problem with him being here," a voice spoke that could only belong to the stranger... not menacing at all, a simple friendly tone. "You're not doing anything shameful, Meiko... hmm, almost there... honestly, if RealWare would have changed their encryption systems at least once in the last thousand years they wouldn't be so simple to crack... there! All done. Say, you're Mallory, right? Meiko's told me all about you—"

"I don't want Eiko knowing I'm breaking the law," Meiko replied, trying to ignore the houseboy peeking between cracks in his fingers. "It's not the right example to set for her..."

"Errr... you're going to help them escape?" Mallory asked, letting his hands dip a bit and creeping closer. "I thought you said..."

"I'm fulfilling the letter of my contract, Houseboy," Meiko snapped. "I was told to retrieve the data, so I am. What happens to Belle... and what happens to a COPY of Alex doesn't matter."

The stranger smiled to him, tossing the copy-cube up and down lightly in his hand. Now that Mallory COULD take a good look, he did... and the man wasn't anything much to look at, an average Nipponese guy maybe five years older than him, with an average haircut, and average looks. He wore a white lab coat and a bow tie, which was a little odd, but he'd blend into a crowd perfectly if not for that.

"Of course, I'll alter the copy a bit..." he said, taking out a pocket device that resembled a blue version of Future Perfect, and plugging the cube into a side socket. "Belle, which blocks do I knock out to remove your sentience code? I don't think this copy of Alex would want to wake up back in Love & Hate with his expanded understanding of the world and full memories..."

Belle took back her original cube, cradling it in her arms with a smile that could light up a thousand video network sets. "If you delete everything past the thirty-seventh gigabyte mark, where I started a file named BHART, it should remove the expansion code. He'll revert to being an ordinary soap character under Art Pasadina's LHART system. I don't think Mr. Cox would even notice the data was stripped; he doesn't pay attention to the fine details as long as the show goes on..."

"And even if he did notice, his hands are tied," Meiko added. "If he told his superiors about a crippled copy of the code they'd know he also tried to cover things up. This is the best solution... thank you, Noyori-san..."

'Noyori' laughed, and ruffled a hand through Meiko's hair... causing a rare blush to rise on her cheeks. (One which Mallory eyed with shock.) The copy cube was dropped into Meiko's hands, although she nearly fumbled it in surprise...

"Come on now, Mei-chan... I tell you every time: just call me Ryo!" Noyori mock-begged. "And I'm happy to help whenever you need it; like I always say, anything for a fellow orphan. It was good thinking, messaging me... there's no way RealWare could trace Belle's escape through my Onsen-of-the-Month system. They haven't even begun to understand the interface technology. I swear, if they'd actually try innovating instead of just patching what they made years ago... but I'll go into a techie geek political rant if I don't stop now..."

Belle stepped forward, taking the spotlight away from the embarrassed Meiko. "And you can help me find a way to make Alex real?" she asked. "Really real...?"

"Hmmm... it might take some time," Ryo Noyori said, scratching at an itch behind his head. "Bioprogrammed clone would be the safest bet, although I haven't totally figured out Tachi's system... but hey, now I have some incentive to try harder! I like a challenge. You can stay in Nippon until we get him squared away."

Kisei cleared her throat. "Now that all matters are settled, I would recommend a hasty parting of ways," she spoke. "If one as simple as Mallory could discover this rendezvous, then I don't like the chances of a second witness..."

"Hai, hai..." Ryo said, stretching a bit. "S'getting late, too. I really should square things away and get to bed... and Mei-chan, don't worry about Future Perfect, okay? You KNOW I haven't ironed out all the bugs yet..."

"R-Right," Meiko stammered, before grabbing her composure and pulling it on tightly. "I will stay in contact to monitor your progress... over F.P.'s secured lines, of course. Belle, please try to avoid running afoul of RealWare again; I suggest going to Grep or another Open Engine world once you're finished in Nippon. You'll be outside their jurisdiction there. And I trust we don't have to suggest you forget we ever met you..."

"I understand, I understand," Belle spoke, smiling and holding onto her lover's temporary container tightly. "Thank you so much for everything... thank you...!"

She turned, and hurried off around the onsen, departing via the hidden door. Ryo gave a little grin and mock-salute to Kisei, before strolling through the portal himself. In seconds, it faded away, replaced by smooth and seamless onsen wall.

"I will maintain secrecy as well, although at the speed rumors spread in this house, I doubt it will last," Kisei noted. "Do not worry if your sister hears of this, Miss Mirai. I believe she will understand your motivations, even if they are not wholly in compliance with RealWare's edicts. Tachi always taught me that honor and law are often separate concepts. Good evening."

As the sniper left through the main portal, three became two.

"...quit looking at me like that," Meiko ordered softly.

Mallory quickly averted his eyes... before glancing back to her. "I, uh... I was just wondering..."

"Why I went against my word?"

"Kinda. ...kinda, I guess. You seemed so determined..."

"If I believed that returning Alex was the right thing to do," Meiko spoke, "Then I'd also have recommended I's Land turn over their children to RealWare. ...I don't always agree with RealWare's politics. Even if I try to avoid trouble, and especially try to avoid trouble for my family... sometimes you have to do things that are questionable in order to do what's right."

"Oh. So, uh, it was more of an ethnics kind of thing?"

"Ethics."

"Right, ethics. It makes sense. Really! I just... I was figuring maybe you also felt kind of sympathetic since they were in I—"

"Ethics and my own sense of integrity are important concepts to me. Simple as that. Go to bed, Mallory," Meiko suggested firmly, looking at the copy cube in her hands. "It's been a very long night, and we're all tired. And I'm expecting a good breakfast before I try to swindle Mr. Cox. I'll need to be sharp to avoid raining corporate antagonism upon this house."

"I'll make pancakes," Mallory promised. "And bacon. I've been saving the ingredients for a good occasion. And we get the rest of the pay for the job tomorrow, right? I can finally stock the kitchen properly!"

"Yes yes, good," she dismissed, walking away quickly.

ACT II, SCENE V - UPSTAIRS HALLWAY @ THE HOUSE

A good night's rest awaited Meiko. But it would have to continue to wait, since someone was standing in front of her bedroom door. Waiting.

Meiko groaned internally, but tried to put up her cold front. "Lorelei, what are you doing awake?" she asked. "It's late, and we have a meeting with the client in the—"

"You helped 'em escape, didn't you?" Lorelei asked... one foot propped against the closed door, arms crossed, and a smug smirk on her lips. A pose she had been holding for minutes, waiting for Meiko's return. "I had a feeling you would, so I stayed up to find out how it'd go down. Letting an IP pirate go... business as usual. See a conflict?"

"I'm too tired to deal with this," Meiko grumbled. "Just—"

"Why'd you do it? I simply must know. And if you say something silly like 'justice' or 'ethics' you know I'll stay put. Because while that's probably true, that's not the only reason why you did it..."

"You want me to say 'true love'," Meiko guessed, dryly glaring at her.

"It's true, isn't it? Been on the brain lately. It's been on Mallory's, too," Lorelei said, almost gleeful. "Love is in the air. And who can deny love? Even back when I was carving up the n00bs I had that yearning for something more than I had. It has to happen eventually, Mei. You just put off puberty by a few years so you could build your business acumen—"

"Are you going to taunt me all night? If so, I'll go to your room and sleep there instead. Or I'll go sleep with Mallory on the couch. That's what you want to see me do, isn't it? That's why you're flaunting dating him, showing how you're supposedly keeping my 'true love' from me..."

"I just want you to admit the truth. That's all. Not such a big thing to ask, is it? I'm your guardian. I *saves* your ass. And the way I see it, that includes saving you from yourself, sometimes... I've always said there's nothing sadder than passing on a great near-life experience out of pure fear. Belle understood that; don't think I wasn't listening in. She's going to try, and even if things fail in the end, at least she didn't turn away from her heart to opt for the safe bet instead..."

"Yes, yes. Ha ha. Now if you'll excuse me—"

"Meiko, I'm serious here! I'm not just doing this to make fun of you. Just because all four of us had to grow up fast doesn't mean you should be acting like an old spinster—"

"FINE. I was sympathetic because they were in love," Meiko spoke in even tones. "Yes. That's true. It was the right thing to do because they had the right to find out if it was love or not. They had the right to be happy, and RealWare was stomping on that. Yes, I believe in love. And I don't believe I have time for it. This isn't fear, it's... it's not part of the PLAN. I will lead my family to prosperity and a bright future... and I'm tired of you waving Mallory under my nose. I... I have no feelings for the Houseboy whatsoever, and—"

Lorelei stepped away from the door, clearing the path.

"If you don't have any feelings, then I'm gonna keep on dating him," Lorelei said. "Makes sense to me. If you're telling the truth, then it's just like I told you back in the onsen. You go and be prosperous and have fun, and I'll have my fun on my own. I think we're going to get serious soon. I might have to show the farmboy how to plow my field properly, too..."

Meiko's teeth ground together. "You are SUCH a bitch, Lorelei," she hissed.

"Then why do you keep me on the payroll?" Lorelei asked, with a smirk. "Sleep well, boss."

In this world, the sunrise is always the traditional bright red rising sun of Nippon.

A perfect circle, inching over the horizon... all the effects of normal sunlight, with all the symbolism of eternal glory. It casts brilliant streaks of red and orange across the morning sky. Bright red and orange, dark red and orange... it all depends on the clouds.

She stood at the edge of the water, holding her cube... looking out across the waves.

"Soon," she spoke. "Soon we'll be together, in a world that does go on forever. On and on, without end. Not some predefined Reality with hard-set limits... it's only a matter of time now. We're free..."

With a smile, she turned and began the long walk back to Noyori Labs.

And inside his memory cube shell, he thought...

Now that you've helped me escape... well, babes, it's been real, and it's been good...

...well, no, he thought nothing of the sort. But it would be ironic.

The night sky. The only sky Antiparadisia had ever known.

"It's funny, you'd think they would change that," he said, gazing out the window in wonder, teacup in his hands long since forgotten. "A featureless black sky... that's just apathy. They could make this world anything they want to. They own this patch of reality, but what do they do with it? They turn it into a breeding hive for the baser instincts. Antiparadisia, née Paradisia, anarchic core of black market trade and questionable deals... although why not form a breeding hive? It's their reality. It's their kingdom. That's not my problem. My problem is that it could be so much more than that..."

He turned away from the window, away from the ants running ant errands, away from everything that was trivial and unimportant. He turned to something equally trivial and unimportant, but at least it held more interest for him. With his spare hand, he pushed up his purple sunglasses, and gave the nice lady a smile.

"It makes you think, doesn't it? In man's wildest dreams, is this really all they can imagine?" he asked. "This is the peak they choose to soar to? There's so much more they could be doing... but I don't think they can handle the power. They have the power, certainly, but they choose not to use it because it scares them. I don't look afraid, do I? That's because my eyes stay open to the wonder of the multiverse. Nothing jades me. Nothing jades any of us, that's our calling card—no matter where we end up, we never belong there, so our eyes never truly close... I hope I'm not boring you, ma'am."

The old lady rocked in her chair, knitting needles clacking away. "Oh, quite all right, young man," she said, with a smile. "My ear's always open to someone who wants to talk. Is the tea good? Would you like a biscuit?"

"Yes, it's very good, thank you," he said, with a soft smile. "I like tea. It's very real. But at the same time... well, look at this."

The boy let go of his teacup, folding his hands in his lap. The saucer and cup did not break, nor spill. Nor drop.

"Isn't that a wonder?" he asked her. "And it's something in your hands. All of you. It's not exclusive to me. Reality belongs to everybody... but they let it go to waste, they never use it to the full potential—"

Gravity resumed normal operational status. The sound of the shattering teacup against the floor didn't even cause him to flinch.

"That's what happens when you're given that power over your own reality. You let things break. You waste it," he said in the kindest, gentlest tones possible. "It's a shame, I know. But you don't have to feel sad. Those whose hands are too weak will simply be guided by one who has a firmer hand. That's how it always works; that's how RealWare got to where it was, for instance. That's where it's going now. Eventually everybody will be able to see the wonder and glory of reality... after all, the mundane will simply be abolished. Um. I guess I'm getting ahead of myself... we do tend to ramble a bit. I've done my best to curtail my tendencies, but... uh, frankly, it helps to let loose and just get that weight off my chest. Like I'm doing now. With your open ear. Do you understand me, ma'am?"

The elderly woman paused in her knitting. "Mmmm... not all of it, I suppose..." she said, trying to recall what he had been talking about. "But I've still got my open ear, yes I do. Plenty of folks around these parts have troubles they like to tell an open ear, and I don't minds listenin' to them, even if I don't understand. It does folks a world of good to sit down a bit, have some tea, and speak their mind. Sometimes that's all they need to go out there and face the day again, and I don't mind one bit to help 'em out like that. Would you like another cup of tea, mister...?"

The young man smiled gratefully, rising to his feet. "Then you do understand, in some simple way. Thank you. You're not who I was hoping to find here, but perhaps it's for the best that I met you. I've only found one other person who understands... which makes it a shame that I have to do this..."

With great kindness, he made it as painless as possible for her.

05: You Are I Am We Will

The cute couple cuddled on the couch while kung fu killers cracked spines.

Of course, 'couple' was a nebulous term; despite the arm around the shoulder and the closeness, it was more like two separate people in two separate worlds. One sat back with her feet on the coffee table, grinning and enjoying the sights of martial arts masters kicking butt, living vicariously through the images on the video network set. The other fidgeted nervously against the plush couch cushions, looking at anything other than his alleged lover. There was very little actual cuddling going on, as well... but despite these flaws, seeing the couple in this position had become a common sight over the last few days.

Then Meiko entered the room.

Her gaze locked on Lorelei's. Waves of rage crashed behind both, electricity arcing between the two lightning rods of feminine aggression. The flames of their opposing wills roared like geothermal furnaces hooked into the cores of negative religious afterlives... white-hot light that burned the eyes merely to look at it, and melted flesh within five thousand feet. If given a weight of its own, such willpowers would cause great dips in the fabric of space and time, collapsing into a pair of singularities spiraling about each other in a dance of oblivion, and so on, and so on...

All Mallory saw was the girls glare at each other a moment before Meiko smoothly walked between his eyes and the video network set, taking her usual seat at the house's RealNet Workstation.

"Yo, Mei-chan," Lorelei greeted, grinning the grin of one who made it clear by the grin that it was a grin which had a meaning which was not usually attached to grins in a conventional or at least positive emotional connotation. "Whazzup?"

"If you must know, we have new potential clients," the homeowner replied, pulling up various Passport Processing Programs. "A high-paying consortium for a basic bounty job. I'm moving the House so I can meet with them. Don't let me interrupt your lovely loving fun, of course."

"Seen this movie five thousand times," Lorelei spoke, with a shrug of the shoulder of the arm that was not ensnaring Mallory in her black widow's web. "Heck, it was on just last night when Mal-chan and I were making out on the couch. Isn't that right, Mal?"

"I do not recall making anything!!" he blurted, tense enough to snap when addressed like that.

Meiko's fingers banged on the keyboard a little harder. "...doesn't matter to me. I won't be needing your bodyguarding services today; I'm taking Kisei with me to the meeting. You two can do whatever you feel like..."

Purple light flared in the windows for a flash-moment, as the house settled into its new dock. The familiar mechanical clunks and whirs of feed lines connecting beneath the floors echoed, as Lorelei turned the movie off for now with a flick of the wrist.

"Where are we, anyw....... Antiparadisia?!" she exclaimed, glancing at the ramshackle buildings that had appeared outside the window. "We're taking a bounty job in Antiparadisia?"

"It shouldn't matter to you two where we are," Meiko spoke, rising from her chair. "You can watch movies and cuddle up all the same—"

Mallory breathed a sigh of relief as Lorelei apparently forgot about him, rising to her feet as well... and taking a more serious tone. "I'm coming with you to the meeting," Lorelei announced. "You've never been here before. You don't know what it's like—"

"Antiparadisia, formerly known as Paradisia before the locals got tired of the irony," Meiko recited from memory. "No governmental body, operating under pure anarchy as a center for lawless black market trade. Only three businesses have stood for more than a year before being burned down or blown up or taken over by rival gangs. Not recommended by Twoday's Guidebook for Discerning Reality Tourists despite the zero percent crime rate... because by having no laws to speak of, there can be no crime rate. Muggings, murders and kidnappings occur on a minute-by-minute basis regardless. Yes, Lorelei, I know what Antiparadisia is like."

"Which is why you need me with you, as your bodyguard. I'm not joking around, Mei, put the cold war aside for a moment and—"

"Kisei will do just fine."

"She's a long-range weapons and strategy expert. She doesn't improvise and she doesn't do hand-to-hand—"

This is where Lorelei would've noticed Kisei standing next to her, if the sniper weren't so (un)noticeable in her entrances and exits from rooms.

"I fulfill my duty, instead of intentionally aggravating my employer," Kisei spoke calmly. "Meiko, I will wait for you outside."

This is where Lorelei would've noticed Kisei leaving the house, if the sniper weren't so (un)noticeable in her entrances and exits from rooms.

Meiko adjusted her business jacket, before walking towards the door. "You and the Houseboy stay here and have fun. Stay. Here," she reiterated, pointing to the floor for emphasis. "And don't let Eiko out, either. Lock the door and initiate level one security."

"MEI—"

The door slammed shut, since simply closing it wouldn't be loud enough.

It got quiet after that.

"...is Antiparadisia anything like antipasta?" Mallory asked, trying to say something to break the silence even if it was a stupid thing to say. His eyes stayed on the door Meiko had just exited... while his worry spiked.

Nobody wants to live in Antiparadisia.

For some, there's no option. Maybe their line of work involves activities that other realities don't enjoy being a party to. Perhaps they don't have enough money for a business in a respectable reality. Or likely they came here on business, found themselves lying penniless and battered in an alley somewhere, and were trying to work up the money to get the hell out.

For others, maybe they liked it here on some masochistic level. Day-to-day life became an ongoing fight for survival and prosperity; take your eye off the ball for a minute and you get clocked in the jaw with the Ping Pong paddle of real life. That kind of lifestyle can get your adrenaline pumping, keep your feet moving, keep your life going forward for fear of looking back at what's chasing you...

You can feel it in the streets. Quiet, high-speed desperation. Despite her outward shell of ice, something inside Meiko was feeling it. The part that kept her eyes darting nervously from bystander to bystander as she walked the streets, despite not wanting to make eye contact with anyone.

"You have nothing to worry about," Kisei spoke, as she had true and sincere calm. "I am familiar with Antiparadisia. I would not let any harm come to you."

"If we didn't need the money, I wouldn't take this job," Meiko admitted through gritted teeth. "Give me a familiar board room or negotiation table any day..."

"It is your goal, yes? To prosper and never have to touch upon a street life again. Which likely includes not living in a place like this. I believe you are working towards your goal admirably, even if the results have not been delivered at a rate you seek... although..."

"Yes?"

"It is of no importance," Kisei replied smoothly, hand resting on the stock of her rifle as she glared at someone who was about to mug them (resulting in the would-be thief having second thoughts).

"Spit it out, Kisei. I know you don't like criticizing me, but I can tell when you're holding back."

"...I mean no disrespect, of course," she disclaimed as usual. "But I believe at the least Lorelei should have come with us. My skills will suffice in your protection, yes... but perhaps you could have used the time away from Mallory Heisenberg—"

"Feh!"

"—to soothe over various issues you and she have developed. House morale has been low and tension has been high. While I have no problem with this atmosphere, since they do not matter to me... it would make your work easier if Lorelei's relations with you normalized."

"They'll NORMALIZE when she quits being a teasing, mean-spirited...! Can you believe she's flaunting her 'relationship' with Mallory around just to force me to say that... that I...! Oooh!"

Kisei shook her head (without taking her eyes off the street predators). "As you wish, Meiko."

"I don't care about him," she quickly added. "Not one bit. I'm not going to fall madly in love with someone just because my pocket organizer told me to. I won't do it. Besides, Ryo said it had bugs. It's just a bug. There's absolutely no reason for me to feel one way or another about him whatsoever."

"As you wish."

"So don't you be thinking that I love him, because that's just stupid. I'm a sensible, modern woman and I don't believe in fairy tales. Besides, he's... he's too nice and I don't like that. Nice guys like him aren't anything special, they're just... really nice. Kind of in a sweet way instead of an irritatingly empty way once you actually get to know them. I don't care if he is a genuinely compassionate person rather than the typical fakers, or that he really cares about me and Eiko and wants us to be happy, or that he helped me buy her a toy when he could've just sat outside the store like I ordered him to—that stuff doesn't change anything between us! And furthermor—"

The sniper rifle made a light 'Pff' sound, and the heavily armed man in front of her crumpled to the ground, twitching with little sparks of electricity playing over his body.

Kisei ejected the used cartridge, and loaded a new stun round. "Do go on," she prompted.

"....I think we should move a little faster," Meiko decided, once her heart resumed standard operations.

"As you wish."

The coffee wasn't as good as the tea.

He wasn't expecting it to be any better, really. Not even AS good. Tea like that was real like a rock was real. It had a heavy sense about it, a tangible sort of feel...

There was no regret, of course. He'd filled her open ear with things she wasn't supposed to know, things nobody knew. He had to close the ear in order to keep such words from leaking out to other ears. Not that it would have mattered, but his employer always stressed that he should be neat in his work. Elegance was the key.

He barely glanced up when a man was shot point blank range by a sniper rifle. He didn't know who did the shooting, but more importantly he knew that the one being guarded was the prospective hunter. The torn wanted poster on the cafe table before him was retrieved before the Antiparadisia Chamber of Commerce decided to seek professional help rather than open the case to any simpleton who might see his face. Their face. Our face...

Probably for the best, he reasoned as he drained his coffee. Despite his cause, he was never really much of a bounty hunter. A casual investigator from time to time, when he had the time to spend for the time-to-time hobby. But never a hardcore bounty hunter... he let others do the hunting for him, when he could. Such as today.

The one in the fashionable attire would do the hunting, and he would take the trophy from her. Ears would have to be closed afterward, of course. That went without saying.

Common sense would have Mallory tucked safely away inside the House, behind locked doors and electrified windows. That was the reasonable thing to do when squatting in the middle of a world defined by its anarchic chaos. That was the course of action as suggested by Meiko Mirai, his boss, his supposed true love...

And because Meiko told them to stay put, they were on the streets twelve minutes later for their Third Date.

"Would you relax already? They smell fear around here," Lorelei spoke, completely failing to soothe Mallory's nerves. "You don't wanna look like the naive farmboy waiting to be skeletonized by vicious flesh-eating piranhas. You should walk like me."

"You mean swaying my hips and strutting and stuff?" Mallory asked, too scared to avoid being honest.

"Okay, maybe not exactly like me. But don't worry! I won't let anyone hurt you too much. I'm a professional bodyguard, remember? And if Meiko doesn't want me guarding her, I can earn my keep guarding your ass. Admittedly I painted this place as a netherworld of greed and pain from which no one emerges unscathed, but that was just me tryin' to spook Meiko into seeing reason. It's not so bad, really—"

She paused to cut down a nearby lamp post with her double saber, sending a pack of street punks scattering.

"If you know how to handle it, eking out a living here's not so bad," she continued, without missing a beat. "I had to work here for a few months doing odd jobs before Meiko hired me on full-time, for instance. All you really need to know is how to keep your eyes on everybody that needs watching, and of course where the three sanctuaries are."

"Sanctuary is sounding very very good right now," Mallory spoke, glancing at the ramshackle buildings with unease, as if they would collapse on him at a moment's notice. "Hopefully sanctuary that's up to fire codes..."

"There aren't any fire codes here, except the code that says anyone can light your shop on fire if they feel like it. The landscape changes all the time; this street wasn't even here months ago. No, there are only three places that have gone undemolished for years... one's the South Side Docks, where we're parked. The other docks are always being fought over by rival gangs and are typically out of order, but South Side is always spared."

"Err, why? Does the owner have a bigger stick to hit people with than anyone else?"

"No, it's just that if it blew up, there would be no way to LEAVE Antiparadisia," Lorelei explained. "And nobody here wants that. So it's an unspoken rule not to hassle the place. Second sanctuary is the Joe's on the east side of town... it's the only place you can get a hamburger that's guaranteed not to be laced with nanite weaponry or chemical exfoliants. Since even crooks need to eat, there's another unspoken law not to mess with Joe's. And finally, the third sanctuary is—"

"A church?" Mallory guessed, trying to look smart.

"You think anybody here fears a big man with a white beard who tells them that naughty people are destined to spend eternity in a lake of fire?" Lorelei asked, looking flatly at him.

"Err... no. No, I guess not... so what's the third sanctuary, then?"

"Auntie Mae's Flower Shop, of course."

Even in the depths of his limited brain, that did not compute.

"Wait... wait, wait. Being able to leave and being able to eat, okay, I can see that. But what's so important about buying flowers—"

He was stopped by bumping into Lorelei's cleavage since the cleavage had stopped when Lorelei stopped in front of a recently built shop. She failed to notice Mallory's mumbling apology, eyes too busy reading and rereading the sign over her head...

"You've gotta be kidding me," she spoke quietly. "QwikSlvr's Exotic Blades...?"

Mallory ceased his apology immediately, lest Lorelei notice he had gotten an eyeful of her body, which would likely lead her to tease him which would lead him to blush and stammer and lots of other things he didn't want to do. Instead he partook of her shock.

"Boy, whoever that is can't even spell his own name," he stated.

"That *is* his name, farmboy," Lorelei spoke, with an unusual bit of Meiko-like chill factor. "Our handles are eight letters or less, that's how it works... ...eh, you couldn't have known that. Okay! This is what our Third Date shall be: SHOPPING! Keep your mouth shut and don't embarrass me too much, okay?"

Mallory nodded along, at least familiar with this. "Can I hold your purse?"

"No. Now shush."

Pushing through the door, Lorelei ignored the various laser tracking systems that pointed armed plasma cannons at her head. They were standard security issue for any serious business in this reality. Mallory tried to ignore them and achieved partial success.

Besides, the consumer goods inside the store were far scarier than any simple gun.

Blades. Knives. Swords. Fancy curved sharp things that seemed to serve no practical purpose except to look fancy and curved and sharp. Some hung on hooks on the walls, some dangled from the ceiling (along with helpful yellow sticky notes reading DUCK PLEASE). A few were still stained with blood (with helpful yellow sticky notes reading USED, CHEAP!). All of them looked very, very deadly, providing that you had enough skill to swing them around without lopping off parts of your own anatomy.

The man behind the counter wore skimpy leather goods, much like Lorelei did, although without the same emphasis on various body parts. He was busy reading a datapad loaded with this month's issue of Modern Psycho Depressive Bastard Magazine—at least, until he got an eyeful of who was walking into his shop.

"...LORELEI?" the one who presumably was named QwikSlvr exclaimed. "Lorelei of the Steel Blades Tribe! That CAN'T be you!"

"It's not," Lorelei replied simply, but with a smug smile. "It's just Lorelei now. I left years ago! Man, you never kept up with the forums, did you, Qwik? What're you doing here, anyway? Last I heard you were working with Duke..."

"Ehh... we had a mutual disagreement," Qwik said, setting his datapad down. "Figured it was in our best interests to split the stock and work in separate branches, exotic melee and conventional armaments. Business hasn't been real good here, though... not much call for the REAL l33t weaponry, everybody just wants bigger and bigger guns... hey, you need anything? I know you stick by the double, but a backup weapon maybe? I got some really sw33t snake swords yesterday—uh, who's the n00b?"

"Mallory, don't touch that, I like you having ten fingers," Lorelei tossed off over her shoulder, figuring she had an 80% chance of being correct. (Or a 100% chance, judging by the quiet 'yipe' he emitted after.) "Qwik, this is Mallory Heisenberg. I'm dating him. He cooks things. Mallory, this is an bud of mine from back home, QwikSlvr. We used to frag each other a lot."

"Ah... nice to meet you, sir," Mallory greeted, offering the suspicious shopkeep a smile. "There's a lot of really cool stuff in here, I have to admit! Just like the martial arts shows that Lorelei watches, and... err... is there something on my face?"

"Haven't I seen you somewhere before?" Qwik asked, peering at him in a way that demanded he acknowledge the peering. "I could swear I...... It's YOU?!"

"Uh, it's me!" Mallory exclaimed, in response. "Yes? Me? Err..."

Rather than speak, QwikSlvr immediately thumbed a big red glowing security button, causing a bulletproof plexiglass shield to slam down around the counter area. From behind his protective barrier, he pointed helpfully to the door.

"OUT! Out of my shop, both of you!" he demanded, screaming near the top of his lungs in order to be heard through the inch thick material. "I just rebuilt a month ago, I don't need it burned down by an angry mob! Begone! Vamoose!"

Lorelei frowned a bit. "What, doesn't an old friend at least get an explanat... what is it, Mallory?"

"There's an angry mob outside," Mallory said, barely able to believe his own words as he ducked down and hid behind Lorelei. "I just spotted them outside the window. That street gang you scared off is with them..."

"Really?" she spoke, having the exact opposite reaction any sane person should have (boundless enthusiasm and excitement). "An angry mob? And here I thought this date would be boring! Hmm. We should bail and find a better place to fight, though. Qwik, you got a back door?"

"No!"

The twin blades of blue-hot plasma snapped into being from either end of her double saber, and two flashes of painfully bright light later, there was a hole carved in the back wall of the shop.

"You do now," she added, because you just have to say something like that after doing something like that. "Mal, come on—"

He was through the door first, fear giving him wings.

'Antiparadisia Chamber of Commerce' was another word for 'Whoever controlled the strongest organized crime racket at the time.'

They didn't try to be seedy about it, however. The Chamber itself consisted of a relatively respectable building near the center of town, and even had plush office furniture. It had receptionists who only worked the red light district part-time, rather than full-time. They also had decent coffee, which was worth its weight in human organs in this town.

"So you understand, Miss Mirai, we cannot let this go unpunished," Don Amerello explained, flexing fingers coated with golden rings. "One of the three pillars of our community has been torn out from under us. Very few things will cause the anarchy of this reality to stand united against a threat... this is one of them. We were going to open it to the community at large to hunt the bastard down, but I felt it would be best to be professional about the matter... you agree, yes?"

"Most certainly," Meiko replied, sipping her coffee. "Mmm. Opening it up to the public would result in a chaotic witch hunt... perhaps you'd catch your man, at what cost? Hiring Mirai Consulting to take care of the problem was the best choice. Of course, we won't be a party to whatever punishment you have in mind for him... all we do is catch the suspect."

"That works well for us. For our planned penalty is likely going to take seven months of attention by... other sorts of professionals."

"...right. I will admit however, Don Amerello... I'm a little confused about the victim. What was an old lady doing running a flower shop in this reality, anyway? If you don't mind me asking..."

"Quite all right. Most outsiders wouldn't understand..." the Don spoke, a heavy heart weighing his words. "Miss Mirai... to us, Auntie Mae was not simply a nice old lady totally out of her element. Nobody knows why she chose to establish her business here, but she did, and she treated everyone who she met with the same kindness... an invaluable service in a community such as this. Not even the most hardened killer had the heart to raise a hand to a gentle soul such as her—and the Chamber of Commerce did everything possible to dissuade others from even having the idea of maybe thinking of something unpleasant towards Auntie Mae. I myself visited her every day to purchase a flower, enjoy her tea, and tell her of my problems. She always had an open ear, and aside from suggesting I should be nicer to people and not break their kneecaps as often, accepted me for what I am... and now she's gone. And the punk who did this is going to face the combined wrath of all of Antiparadisia..."

"Yes, I understand," Meiko replied, wanting to get on with things. "Now, what can you tell me about the suspect? Were there any witnesses? Even a rudimentary description would help in our search..."

The Don's three gold teeth sparkled in the overhead fluorescent lighting, his smile quite cold indeed.

"Oh, we know exactly who did it," he said. "All we need you to do is find him. We got lots of guys at the South Side Docks to keep him from escaping, so he is still in Antiparadisia... his name is Mike, and he was Auntie Mae's assistant. A nebbishly little boy who we'd assumed couldn't hurt a fly... but witnesses identified him leaving the scene of the crime wearing a cloak. Not his usual attire, but the face was a dead lock for Mike, and three witnesses gave the same description to our sketch artist. I have a photo here of the punk taken a short time ago... and an artist's rendition of what we're planning to do to him, but I suspect you're not interested in that..."

She reached out for both photos, carefully concealing the second one behind the first.

After exactly one glance, she handed the pictures back.

"I'm sorry, Don Amerello, but we cannot take your case," she spoke with great speed. "I need to be returning to my home now. I apologize for wasting your time but it is of great importance that we be going now."

"You... won't take the case?" he asked, confused. "You came highly recommended—"

"You can have a 20% discount on any future case fees should you choose to use Mirai Consulting at a future date," she spoke without thinking of the financial implications. "Again, you have my apologies. Kisei, we're leaving."

"But—"

The pair snaked their way around office cubicles and were out the door immediately after.

Kisei's eyes flicked back and forth, making sure they weren't followed, hurrying at whatever pace Meiko choose to set. "This is very dangerous, Meiko. They will no doubt be suspicious and place agents on our tail. Was there no option to gracefully bow out of the case?"

"The entire city knows what the suspect looks like," Meiko replied, picking her way through the crowd. "It's not safe here for him. We have to leave Antiparadisia as soon as possible before anyone knows he's here. He better have stayed at the house like I ordered him to..."

"You don't mean...?"

"Mike looks exactly like Mallory. They could've been separated at birth. I can't explain it and I don't have time to look for an explanation—if we don't get Mallory out of here before the locals confuse him for the killer, he could be... he..."

"I suggest we walk faster," Kisei suggested.

They did.

Wooden crates chafe. They also provide poor cover from people shooting at you with lead slug-throwing guns and various energy cannons and things like that. Nevertheless, Mallory rubbed against the heavy abandoned shipping crate, praying it would hold out long enough...

Lorelei didn't bother hiding; she was having too much fun deflecting incoming fire with her double saber and laughing maniacally."This is GREAT!" she exclaimed, after parrying the seventh nearly fatal head shot of the day. "Call of the l33t, baby! C'mon, farmboy, admit it—this is the most exciting thing you've ever lived through!"

"I don't look for excitement! I'm perfectly happy being bored!!" Mallory shouted back over the din. "And I'd very much like to live through it so maybe you shouldn't be encouraging them! Why is it that dates with you keep ending in us running for our lives!?"

"This? This is nothing!" Lorelei replied, flicking an incoming tazer wire back at its origin, promptly electrocuting 11% of the mob. "You should've seen some of the brawls I got into last time I lived here. Whoo!"

"I really think we should stop seeing each other like this, Lorelei! I mean, on the brink of certain death and stuff! And in general! Like I was trying to tell you back in Drome... why am I talking about this now?! We should be running away! I think I have a splinter under my eyelid! I'm going to pass out from fright!"

"Oh, fine, we'll run a bit more," she decided, ducking down behind the crate next to him. "And what's this about breaking up with me? Haven't I done my best to show you a good time? I happen to think we're very compatible, and—"

A torn chunk of wood flew over her shoulder, before being vaporized in midair from a stray energy bolt.

"Running, right," she decided. "I know just the place, assuming it's still standing; there's a warehouse just around the corner! They're great for fights; you can knock over heavy boxes onto people, score sweet railing deaths, and sometimes there's even a machine to make roaring flames for no purpose whatsoever or a conveyer belt leading into a grinding machine! A GRINDING MACHINE and PURPOSELESS FLAMES, Mal! Doesn't that excite you?!"

"Brain... locking... up...!" Mallory warbled.

"On your feet, farmboy, we've got some real chase scene action to get through," she spoke, pulling the limp boy up to his legs and then making a run for it. "And we're not breaking up until the time is right! You'll know why when it happens!"

Kisei's ear twitched.

"Unless rampaging mobs are now a routine occurrence in Antiparadisia, and I am not discounting this possibility," she spoke, "I believe that Mike and/or Mallory have been located. We should make haste—"

"A map."

"What?"

"I should have looked up a map on RealNet," Meiko said, eyes quickly looking from unmarked street to unmarked street. "It changes every day but I could've found a recent one. I have no concept of where we are, much less where the house is..."

Kisei pointed down a particular street with her rifle, which caused would-be stray rampaging mob members to scatter.

"That way," she spoke. "There will be a warehouse dead ahead. A shortcut through it will result in a straight shot to the South Side Docks."

"You're familiar with Antiparadisia?" Meiko asked, breaking into the fastest jog her business formals would allow her to achieve.

"I am innately familiar with it," Kisei spoke, running alongside her employer. "Faster, if you can manage. The crowd is growing louder."

Doors on opposite sides of the warehouse swung open and shut simultaneously.

Much to Lorelei's disappointment, the warehouse had no flame-factory standards, or even crates. It was abandoned, with a hastily spray-painted red X over the doors, marking it for demolition within the week to make room for the ever-expanding population of Antiparadisia.

Much to Meiko's relief, there were no rampaging mob-folk inside the warehouse.

Much to everyone's surprise, it now contained Meiko, Kisei, Lorelei, and Mallory.

"The HELL are you doing here?!" Meiko exclaimed, while Kisei smelted the door shut behind her, using a compressed heat beam from her rifle. "I told you to stay at the house!"

"I wanted to go shopping," Lorelei casually noted, while carving a section of the wall up to fall in front of her door and block it. "How was I to know that it was Pitchforks and Torches Day? Hey, Kiss. How'd the meeting go? Did we get the job? Mallory, I think you should resume breathing. The crowd's not getting in here, we're safe."

"We're not safe," he spoke with alarming clarity as he stepped away from the door... "...I don't know why, but—"

The boy stumbled exactly four and a half steps, tripping over someone.

Tripping over himself.

The other boy was a picture perfect copy of Mallory, with a ragged sweater a crazed look of fear in his eyes (half of which mirrored Mallory's own attributes). Another him. A him who was previously trying to hide behind the door, and now found himself scrabbling to his feet and slowly backing away...

"D-Don't kill me!" he protested, waving his arms defensively. "I didn't do anything! I didn't kill Auntie Mae! You have to believe me, it wasn't me, please!!"

Lorelei, for a change, was flat out stunned. "Uh.... Mal? Why are there two of you here?"

"That would be Mike, I believe," Meiko spoke, stepping up to take control of the situation before it got even more out of hand than it was to begin with. "The Chamber of Commerce wanted us to hunt him down. And I don't know why he looks like Mallory, either. Do you have a twin brother or something, Houseboy?"

(It should be noted that Mallory says nothing for the next few hours, which is a distinct change from his usual strategy of babbling and panicking and running around.)

"Why do you look like... you can't be him...! Stay away from me, stay away!!" Mike howled, backing up against a wall. "He's the one who killed Auntie Mae! I saw him leave the shop myself, he wore a cloak, and he had my face, he had my eyes! Get away from me, you freak—"

"Whoa, whoa, WHOA! Hold on a minute, Mike!" Meiko demanded. "Nobody here killed anyone! Nobody. This is Mallory Heisenberg and I can vouch that he wasn't the one who killed her. ...which means that instead of two of you, there must have been three... Mallory, what are you staring at?"

Wordlessly... Mallory pointed to the ceiling.

Where a man in a cloak stood.

The cloak did not fall downward. It fell upward, which meant that standing on the ceiling looked absolutely natural, if you accepted that gravity was in error. He was smiling upward at them, or rather downward at them on the floor of the warehouse... and as promised, he wore Mallory's face.

Haven't I seen you somewhere before? a silent memory echoed in Mallory's head.

"I'm just as surprised as you are," the cloaked one spoke, in a familiar voice, only... not exactly the same. Softer, yet with confidence you could bend an iron bar around. "It's unprecedented. Two of us? Two of us in the same reality. Well well. Hello, everyone..."

Both bodyguards jumped in front of the pack in a flash, rifle raised, saber at the ready. The smart thing to do was to shoot first and listen to speeches from people defying the laws of physics later.

No sooner than Kisei's boots and Lorelei's soft-soled shoes touched the ground in front of the group, than they found themselves falling. Falling sideways, towards opposite walls of the warehouse, thanks to the same twist of gravity which kept their target rooted upright.

Kisei twisted in the air, lining up a shot and cracking it off in 0.2 seconds. The bright red heat beam fired straight and true towards the cloaked man's left eye... then it bent ninety degrees to the left, ninety to the right, pause, ninety to the right, ninety to the left. An effective bracket around his head, harmlessly melting a spot on the ceiling behind him at the same moment Kisei's body impacted painfully against the wall, head first.

Meanwhile, Lorelei curled up, and bounced off her wall with leg muscles that never went out of shape despite weeks on the couch. She soared upwards in an eye-twisting effect of gravity, intent on taking off his head with her blade...

The blue plasma of her saber flared, warped, wobbled, and twisted around her own body instead. Her scream was one of agonized pain, silenced only when she fell back to her side of the warehouse, and slid down to the floor.

Next, Meiko, Mike and Mallory had a moment to breathe. None of them could. Then Mike took off running.

He didn't have any particular place to run to; both doors had been blocked, and the mob was surrounding the building. But fight or flight was the order of the day, and as the cloaked figure knew, they always chose flight...

He lifted one arm, locking eyes on the escaping boy.

Instantly, Mike crumpled to the ground, as if his body became six times heavier... which it did. Then ten times heavier. Then he screamed. Then there were multiple cracks of bone breaking, and he made no more sound, ever again.

With a smile, the man was in two places at once, then one place at once. Standing in front of Meiko and Mallory.

"You're better defended than we usually are," he commented, not feeling particularly threatened. "I'm surprised. We usually don't make many friends. They must care deeply to sacrifice themselves for you... still, one down. One to go. Two for one... ...or three for one, I guess, miss whoever-you-are..."

Mallory's eyes tore away from the cloaked-him for the first time. Just in time to see the look of fear in Meiko's eyes—the same 'I don't want to die' look that Mallory himself had mastered in recent days...

Weight. He started to feel heavy. His knees buckled. Meiko went down first, hard, her voice starting to scream much like Mike did...

The killer smiled at him, a gentle smile, one that said this was all good and this must be.

"Reality shall be determined by the last one standing," he spoke.

One single thought flashed across Mallory's mind: *Meiko*.

He let **go**.

Thankfully the Cloaked Mallory had on his sunglasses, because otherwise the flash of purple light would have blinded him. Even with protection, spots flooded his eyes for a few moments... long enough to warrant a surprised look around, perplexed at how everybody still alive had somehow left the building without a trace. Only Mike's body remained.

That's odd, the cloaked one thought.

When the rampaging mob finally managed to blast their way into the building, they found only Mike, and rejoiced, for justice had somehow been done when they were not looking.

Dice clattered against the board. The little doggie trotted five spaces ahead.

"Urbana... oooh, finally!" Eiko cheered. "Okay, so that's eight hundred points for the deed, and two hundred to build a hotel... minus the tax deduction for investment in civic projects, taking percentage off the top for license renewal, carry the four, and... um..."

She tapped a finger on the board game, kicking her legs a bit as she paused play.

"It's just no fun without other players," she decided.

With a standard youthful sigh of boredom, she got up from the floor, and headed to the kitchen to pilfer some Krap Snacks from Meiko's secret stash. When she returned, there were more players! Although... she could tell immediately that things were Bad and things were Serious. For starters, they were all lying on the floor, and some of them were bleeding.

"O... oneesan?" Eiko asked. "What happened...?"

Meiko groaned, sitting up and shaking her head to try and get the jackhammers in her brain to stop. "Is everybody okay?" she asked, since that's what you ask, ahead of "What the hell just happened?" and "How did we get back home?".

Lorelei was next up, trying to hold back a blue streak of cursing... wincing as the minor burns on her body sent random jabs of pain to her brainstem. "Nothing seriously wounded but my pride," she replied. "What the h... what just happened...?"

"And how did we get back home?" was Kisei's reply, while she wiped a trickle of blood away from her eye from a forehead cut. "What is going on?"

"I don't know and right now I don't care," Meiko said, trying to get back to her feet despite the extra weight of a houseboy clinging to her. "I'm going to get us back to I's Land *pronto*, and... Mallory, it's okay... I'm fine. You can let go now."

With a weak smile of relief, Mallory nodded, and he let go. Of consciousness.

No fear. Green grass beneath his feet. Blue sky above...

Water trickling down a creek. Birds chirping from the trees...

Her smile...

Was she smiling?

No, she was asleep. And now, Mallory was not.

She was sitting at one end of the couch, near where Mallory had been laid out... he swung his legs over, the now-familiar motions of a morning wakeup, going from lying to sitting on his 'bed'. As he sat up, his head rocked with something he didn't even have a mixed metaphor to describe, beyond *pure agony*.

It was nighttime, judging from the lack of sunlight through the windows. It was I's Land, judging from the pale moonlight that filtered into the room. Not the plain black sky of Antiparadisia, but a real, honest-to-goodness moon...

Milk. Right now, he needed milk. He needed milk and he wished his father was here to talk to him, like he had on a restless night many moons ago...

Meiko groaned, the stirring of the couch cushions rousing her. She rubbed her eyes, turning to look at him as he turned to look at her.

One perfect moment of peace and quiet. Just a moment, but when complete, it wasn't shattered; it simply started and then it simply ended.

"You okay?" Meiko asked of him.

"I don't know," he honestly replied.

"...I should have called a doctor, or something," Meiko replied, eyes drifting away guilt creeping into her voice. "But I's Land isn't exactly swarming with them, and I thought it was best if we... lie low a bit. Just sit things out, if that guy..."

Her eyes snapped back to him.

"Do you know who that was?" she asked. "And do you know how we got back here?"

"I don't know," he repeated. "I don't... I have no idea. I don't remember a whole lot, just... eyes, and..."

Meiko shook her head... and stood, dusting off her blazer. "Well, then... there's no sense worrying, is there?" she said, regaining cool without going all the way to ice. "If it can't be explained, it can't be explained. Wondering endlessly before we learn anything new won't change that. So we lay low, and most importantly... we get on with our lives. Right? That's the sensible thing to do..."

"I remember his eyes," Mallory said, having not listened to a thing she said. "And... and it hurt. And he was hurting you, and I had to do something to stop it, and... I couldn't let him hurt you. So I just... I don't know, but I couldn't let him, I had to do something and I don't know what I did and I had to stop him I —"

"Mallory!"

"—yes?"

"Read my lips: There Is No Sense Worrying," she spoke, careful to get every word across. "We'll figure it out when we figure it out. I'm okay now... and you're okay. Everything's going to be fine now. ...I tried to stay awake so I could, er, be awake when you finally woke up, but... I guess I slipped. I was worried about you, you know. But now I don't have to worry. So. ...I'm not making sense, am I?"

"Oh, that's okay," Mallory said, smiling a little. "I'm used to not making sense myself, so I understand when someone's not making any sense and it's okay. ...if that made any sense either..."

"I think," Meiko said, rubbing her eyes, "That right now I absolutely need something... real. Maybe a—"

"Glass of milk?"

"...yes," she affirmed, a little surprised. "How'd you...?"

"Uh, lucky guess. I'll go get two glasses; you have a seat and rest a bit," he said, getting up. "I'll take care of it! Err... unless you'd prefer to get yours yourself rather than have your Houseboy get it, or something..."

Meiko groaned, shaking her head. "Whatever. Forget the Houseboy stuff, okay? I've been... I'll admit it, I've been acting pretty stupid lately. Something like that really puts perspective on life, doesn't it? Just forget it—"

A vision of beauty in a nightgown leaned against a nearby wall, coughing politely to get the couple's collective attention.

"People are trying to sleep upstairs, kinda hard to do through your groans of pain," Lorelei replied... the bandages on her arms a signal that she was in equal pain. "Keep it down to a whisper, okay? Oh, and Mal...?"

"Err...?"

"I don't think it's going to work out. I hate to do this, but I don't see us being a very compatible couple; it's not you, it's me, believe me, so if it's all right with you... can we just be friends?"

Contrary to the universal laws of relationships, Mallory's reaction was one of pure relief, like a man suffering horrible chemical burns on his skin being washed with a neutralizing base component.

"Yes... yes, we can just be friends!" he agreed. "Right. I think that's for the best. Thank you. ...want a glass of milk?"

"Sure. Make mine a double."

"Right!" he replied, without realizing he had no idea what a double milk would look like. He ducked into the kitchen, rooting around for glasses... leaving the girls alone.

Meiko stared at a nearby wall.

"I think you're ready," Lorelei told her, since she knew Meiko was listening. "I think he's ready, too."

Gritting her teeth, Meiko responded without returning the gaze. "No. No. I'm not going to adore the guy just because—"

"Then screw F.P."

"—huh?"

"Forget about destiny. I don't believe in it, either. Who's telling you to marry him tomorrow? Or at all?" Lorelei asked. "All I really wanted you to do was give it a shot. Keep the option open, instead of hiding from it in fear. Because I know you—especially the bits you don't like to admit you have. When you saw that message in F.P., you saw a chance at something you hadn't planned for but deep down needed badly... go for it, Meiko. He's free now; a little jealousy was the ticket to make you see the truth. Now let whatever's gonna happen happen, whatever the whatever may be."

"...I still don't appreciate being jerked around like that," she said honestly.

"I never claimed to be a master psychologist. Sometimes being a bitch is the only weapon I got, yeah? But you'll give him a chance now, right...? I hardly believe someone willing to stay by his bedside would—"

"Yes, yes, I will," she replied. "Okay. You win. ...and you're right."

"Good. Because after tonight... I think he's gonna need all the support he can get. I'm from the school of hard knocks; you're way better at the gentle stuff than I am."

"Better at what stuff?" Mallory asked, carefully carrying three glasses of milk in two hands. "Sorry, I had to get some clean glasses from the store room, I—"

"Well, I'm off to bed!" Lorelei announced. "Gotta rest up big if we're gonna be stuck here a week. Too many pretty boys to date here on I's Land and not enough time! Later, Mal. Later, Mei."

"ER, your milk—"

And thus, his ex-lover returned to bed. Alone.

Just a plain apartment. Nothing unusual about it, at least not to the naked eye; even to the unnaked eye, it was merely loaded down with the finest microsecurity devices that RealWare's R&D labs ever produced.

The owner of the apartment entered without using the door. His cloak was promptly stored in the closet; he'd retrieve it next time he needed to do a little investigating. Which he'd need to do eventually, especially in light of the unusual events of the day... once things settled down. Once he had time.

Because the blinking red light on his RealNet Workstation suggested he would not have free time anytime soon. He sat down in front of the station, keyed in his password, and a video chat window opened automatically.

The woman on the other end of the stream was not pleased.

"Where were you, Multi?" she asked, in her patented 'I'm angry but I'm not going to sound angry or even hint that I am angry' voice. "I've been trying to reach you for hours..."

"My apologies, Ms. Bates..." he spoke, with an accompanying bow of the head. "I was taking care of some personal business."

"Mmm. Well, water under the bridge. Meet me at my personal dock, I have a press conference to attend tonight on Urbana and I'm not going without my head of security."

"At once, ma'am."

The video window closed, replaced by the standard logo of the Reality Prime Intranet.

The one known as Multi turned his swivel chair around slowly, taking in the sights of his unimpressive apartment.

Such a mundane existence, he pondered, a common thought for him. *But soon it will be vivid. Once the competition is out of the way.*

Dear dad.

Very strange things have happened. Nobody is talking about them because nobody knows what happened and it's not very comfortable to think about, and it wouldn't help anything to worry so says Meiko so we are getting back to normal instead. I am focusing on my studying because my test is in one week's time. Maybe if I can be scared by the test I won't be scared about what happened. And I think Meiko cares about me, so that is a good thing at least from this. She was almost hurt but I think I saved her somehow.

I should go study now. Love your son, Mallory.

PS - Please please tell me if I had any twin brothers or anything, I don't think I did but you didn't tell me mom was Nipponese until recently and I'm worried I'm missing something here as well. Mail me asap. Love your son Mallory Heisenberg who is what I am.

Warm knees. Very warm knees. Legs warm too, but the knees especially; they were entrenched deeper under the fluffy quilted apron around the kotatsu.

'Kotatsu' was a new concept to Mallory, being a Nihongo term Eiko hadn't taught him yet. He was rapidly learning to appreciate this unusual twist; it was the hybrid bastard child of a quilt, a table, and a space heater. You stuck your legs underneath the quilted apron around the table, kneeling or stretching them out (kneeling was very big in Nippon, he had learned) and a heater kept you toasty warm. I's Land could get a bit chilly some nights, despite having a near perfect climate, and this was such a night... particularly with the House's power and water hookups having nothing to hook to on the 'docking' beach, and Meiko conserving power by flipping the heating system off.

And so, Mallory's warm knees contentedly rested underneath the surface of the Kotatsu. He had decided to try kneeling, since his mother was Nipponese and he had to learn this sort of thing. Also because he didn't want to risk accidentally kicking Meiko. She was already →← this close to kicking his head clean off his shoulders, after all.

"No, no, no, NO," she chastised, tapping the data pad with a finger on each 'no,' her teeth grinding together. "No! When the backup sync plug-ins fail, you're supposed to reinstall the plug-in manager. This is the third time we've gone over that! Even I remember, and I'm not the one taking the REC Test!"

Mallory squinted at the diagram, which either represented code package dependency in a Reality Engine's software systems or a move mapping strategy card from a championship Ping Pong round. "Uh... but... this time we went over it from another direction? Or something..."

"There's no way to restore the corrupted data! The RealWare recommended method is to take blue cube number seven from your Reality Engineer Developer Kit and reinstall the entire system. In this situation, just rebooting the thing wouldn't work!"

"But that's always worked for me before..."

"The REC Test may be multiple choice, Mallory, but I seriously doubt option D will be 'Drop back fifty yards and punt the engine!'"

"Right right, but in this situation, why wouldn't the auto-repair systems put the plugins back in order?" Mallory asked, scrolling back up a few pages. "I mean, the systems are designed to try to catch themselves before they fail... all it would need is a little nudge, I think... ah! Yes yes, right here in case example #76a! I WAS right!"

Meiko seethed and sputtered an fumed and raged and looked and fidgeted and coughed and looked aside and nodded slowly.

"...right. Like I was saying. I mean... ah, forget it. Forget it!" she groaned, flopping backwards to lie down on her floor. Her hands went up to massage throbbing temples. "This is NOT working. How can I help you study for this test if I don't know anything about Reality Engineering myself?"

"I said I could study it myself, you know..."

Meiko peered at him at an angle from under her hands. "Do you honestly believe you have a chance at the test only 25% of all applicants manage to pass if I leave this to your capable hands?"

"Uh..."

"Honesty, Mal."

"...I'm not honestly sure," he admitted, glancing at the obtuse, obscure and occasionally obfuscated information on the data pad. "But... I have to pass, right? You said so when you hired me, and Eiko wrote it in the contract. 'Must pass the REC Test within a month, or be terminated.' ...that just means fired, not killed, right? It sounds kinda scary..."

Pulling her weary self back up to sitting position, Meiko thumbed to the next page of questions. "For now, this is the best we can do... let's try to get through a few more pages of these before calling it a night. At worst, I'll learn enough about Reality Engineering to take that test instead and... then we can save cash by not paying your salary, I guess..."

"I know I'm not picking this up real fast. Sorry... uh, you know, it's funny, but—"

"I fail to see humor."

"Not funny ha-ha, more funny strange. Strange how I thought I'd pick this up real fast, what with my mother being an engineer herself, and being able to fix the Reality Engine back home each time it crashed... I guess I was pretty silly for thinking that, but... maybe you shouldn't have hired me. I mean, you really need an engineer, not just a cook. I hate being a bother..."

Meiko rolled her eyes and got a seven. "Now you're definitely sounding Nipponese. You haven't been a bother, Mallory. ...you've been pretty helpful, actually. With the I's Land thing, and looking after Eiko, and all your chores and such... and as for the engine, it hasn't crashed once since you got here, so no big whoop that you're not ready to properly fix it yet."

"You know, I was wondering about that... why do you need an engineer if it doesn't crash?"

"Oh, it crashes," Meiko replied, trying to find a soft question to lob at him from the datapad. "Luckily it hasn't crashed lately, but let's not forget when it dropped on your head... we're VERY lucky it didn't appear in the middle of a mountain or something. In fact... here's one. A mid-sized dock rated mobile home with Reality Engine for Mobiles always lands in docks upside down. What do you do?"

The hamster wheel of Mallory's mind squeaked along with furiousity. "I... uh... wait wait, no hints, it's coming to me... err... ah! You... yoooouu... reinstall the operating system!"

Meiko's eyebrows raised in surprise. "Right on the nose. I think that's the first one you've gotten right tonight..."

"I guessed, actually!" Mallory admitted. "It just seems like the solution to half these problems is to completely reinstall the operating system..."

The datapad slid across the surface of the kotatsu, skidding to a halt perfectly aligned in front of Mallory.

"Let's move on a bit," Meiko suggested, stretching her arms over her head and stifling a yawn. She fetched a business magazine from the floor, opening it to the last article she read. "You study the next ten pages, then I'll quiz you. Then we stop for the night. I don't know how well this is working, but... I'll find a better way to do it in the morning, I guess. It's getting late..."

"I'm on this like rice on whites!" Mallory declared, eyes sliding across the jargon like a skier towards a ravine. "Give me this last week of studying, and I'll pass that test faster than you can say, 'Give me this last week of studying and I'll pass that test faster than you can say—'"

"—done!" he declared, setting the pad down and trying to plug a mental cork in his brain to keep the lumpy goop of knowledge from draining out. "Hit me with that quiz, Meiko, I'm re... Meiko?"

Peering around the kotatsu, he spotted Meiko lying on her side, the magazine lying open beside her. Eyes closed, breathing softly in her sleep. Apparently plowing through the thick fields of knowledge and threshing madly with the scythe of understanding took longer than he predicted.

Briefly, very VERY briefly, he considered picking Meiko up and helping her over to her futon. Then he had a temporal flash forward to the kind of pain he'd experience if she woke up to THAT sort of surprise. As a compromise, he tugged the quilt off the futon, and tried to drape it over her as gently as possible...

It felt good.

There was dread over the upcoming test, yes. There was the worry of failing and being forced to leave the home he'd grown so accustomed to in such a short time... and there was the worry of letting her down, most of all. (And on the sidelines, a recent worry over recent events that he was recently trying to forget...) Doom and worry and fear and doubt were to the north and south and east and west of him respectively, that he knew for certain.

But still, it felt good... spending this time with her, even if most of it consisted of her wondering aloud why he was so dense. She was trying her hardest to help him, and he tried his hardest to get the questions right in return. Despite all the screw-ups and the worries, he felt quite pleased with the night's outcome.

Taking his datapad from the table, he quietly left her room, slowly closing the door behind him. Tomorrow would be another day to study; for now they both needed sleep.

"Oyasumi," he whispered before latching the door shut (and hoping he said the right word).

A minute after, Meiko tugged the blanket a little tighter around herself. Even if nobody was there to see, she smiled in her sleep.

06: IHTFP

Of course, the higher you fly, the farther you plunge screaming towards the ground while on fire and spinning out of control after having your craft ventilated by heavy shell fragments and tracer fire.

Their new location was the shelling; what would happen later would act as tracer fire. But mixed military metaphors aside, without further ado, ladies and gentlemen... the shelling.

"We're in Nippon?" Mallory asked, staring in amazement at the buildings outside his window.

As was standard for the boy, first impressions out the kitchen window were the most lasting. The city outside his window was quite impressive indeed. Nippon was not quite Urbana, as it lacked the latter's level of high-pressure intensity—crowded, busy, but somehow more tranquil in a way he couldn't identify. The buildings were a different style as well (wooden sliding doors and whatnot)... and to further distance the place from the Known and Comfortable, neon signs (currently daytime/off) had been plastered all over the place surface-coated with incomprehensible scribbles...

Lorelei was just as disbelieving, but for her own reasons. "I thought we were laying low? And I thought we were strapped for cash?" she asked, ignoring the window. "Parking in the middle of one of the most active Realities out there is not lying low. And the docking fees in Nippon are ridiculous, even before you exchange points for En..."

"I considered the plusses and minuses of this move in detail," Meiko assured. "We're sticking our necks out for good reason. Mallory needs to study for his REC Test... and I'm not a good enough study partner. So I've enrolled him in the finest nighttime cram school in Nippon."

"Cram what?" Mallory asked, glancing away from the window.

"Cram facts into your brain with a shoehorn," Lorelei explained, flatly. "After all, knowing what you're actually doing is secondary to knowing the answers to the REC Test. I've heard of cram schools—they make the jungles of Tribal Alpha feel relaxing and safe. So we're fronting the cash for docking fees AND for a cram school? What's so bad about kicking back in I's Land, enjoying the surf, and letting Mallory study there?"

"Uh... yeah!" he spoke, deciding to speak out with his speaking voice for a change. "I mean, we were doing fine last night... right? I really thought we'd hit a groove or something, and, uh... I'd rather study with you than go to a graham school—"

"This is more efficient. Eiko?"

On cue, Eiko popped up with a small calculator.

"According to annual statistics for the REC Test issued by RealWare Nippon, cram school students achieve a 34% passing rate," she announced, reading off the numbers to five digit decimal precision. "Students who attempt to study on their own only achieve a 25% passing rate. Therefore, by going to cram school, Mallory has a greater chance of passing and staying with us and then we can play more! Yaaay! You're so smart, oneechan—I'm in favor of this plan!"

Lorelei made the 'feh' face of irritated annoyance. "You're in favor? Even considering how much money this will cost?"

"If you sneak money out of the house fund less often to go on expensive dates, we can compensate," Eiko pointed out oh so helpfully.

"This decision is final," Meiko spoke with Authority. "We'll be in Nippon for the duration. I considered having Mallory take Mellow Fellow's taxi back and forth... but we've freeloaded off I's Land and Mellow more than enough. It's not fair to them to mooch. Get used to another week of downtime—we're not taking a job until this test is over. Except for you, Mallory: your job is to study. To help you focus... we'll do most of your chores. Lorelei will do the laundry, Kisei will clean the house, and I'll do the cooking."

A weak, strangled cry escaped Lorelei's throat at the notion. "...I think I'll go find some guy to bum takeout food off of," she announced. "I'll be back tomorrow, Mei... good luck, Mallory. And I don't mean on the test."

Mallory's stomach sank deep enough to get the bends on the way back up. "Uh, Meiko, you really don't have to do that, I can handle studying and cooking—"

"I repeat: No distractions," she repeated. "And that means you can't bug him to play with you, Eiko."

The young Mirai sister's pigtails drooped. "Awwww..." she aww'd. "That's no fun at all. ...but it means more time to play with you, oneechan! We haven't played dolls or video games or stock analysis in a long time. Do you have any scheduled appointments today?"

"I—"

If being an economist fell though, Eiko would have made an excellent pickpocket, as she had Meiko's Future Perfect open before the letter I could fully escape her lips.

"Hooray! F.P. says you're playing with me today!" Eiko announced, waving the pocket organizer around for all to see. When Meiko moved to grab it away, Eiko snagged her arm like a snare trap, bounding away towards the stairs. "Seeya, Mallory-oniichan! Oh, by the way, you have a message on the workstation account. Baibai!"

"...." Mallory replied, as all the girls vacated in various directions.

The happy thoughts he didn't fully realize he was entertaining of study time with Meiko evaporated like steam from a pot of boiling broth.

But where there's shelling, there's tracer fire...

He'd never received a RealNet message before. Figuring it'd be a pick-me-up, he wandered across the living room to the house workstation, went through the keyboard strokes required (Josef always said his mother always said real engineers unplugged their mice), and opened the letter...

Dear Mallory,

I've been enjoying the letters you send home tremendously. Admittedly you're having a more exciting time out there than I had when I left home -- my journey was downright mundane in comparison. Sorry I haven't replied lately, but things have been very busy, harvest season and all.

But what you sent last time, I have to tell you something that might worry you. I'd suggest you sit down, since there's no easy way to say it, and I promised that if you ever happened to ask, I wouldn't lie. I actually thought you would ask beforehand, after I let slip that your mother was from Nippon, and clearly you don't look even half Nipponese, but... you deserve honesty. So this is the honest truth.

You don't have any twin brothers that I know of. However, I'm sorry to say that the truth is that I'm not your biological father.

Shortly after returning from my multidimensional journey with my newly wed wife, we found you in the western corn field. You were a newborn, but had no baby clothes, no possessions, no identification at all. We checked around the village to see if any mothers had lost their child, or even abandoned it -- but nobody was pregnant at the time. There was no possible way someone from our home reality was your mother, but no outsiders were visiting at the time, either.

The Council, of course, wanted to offload this problem as fast as possible by having one of the outside traders deliver you to an orphanage at Urbana. Your mother, however, wouldn't hear anything of it; she had grown attached to you and would not give you up. It was a hard fight, but we worked together and won the right to call you our own -- as if the Council had a say in it, but it was important we make the peace for your sake. After that, your origin was rarely spoken of... but I'm afraid some of the isolation you felt from the other children was related to this. Suspicions never fully faded away from that day, and a small community like ours has a hard time forgetting things.

Mallory, I'm sorry I lied to you. I felt it was for the best, but I also promised when the time came, I'd make amends. Know that I've never seen you as anything other than my true son, and your mother loved you dearly as well. We are your parents in every sense of the word but one.

If you want to come home for a while and talk about this, I'll understand. I can't say I'm sorry enough. But I love you. Please write back soon, either way.

Love, your father, Josef Heisenberg.

PS - I hope you're getting along well with Meiko. She sounds a lot like your mother, really. Be careful about workplace romances, and I wish you the very best.

...read it one more time, just to make sure.

Maybe three times or five. Hard to say.

Slowly, his body began to ache from sitting hunched over. His eyes started to get very dry from being open.

Mallory?

He was...

"Mallory?"

Being talked to. Addressed.

"I know you're keen on studying for this stuff online, but if you don't get out of here soon you'll be late," Meiko was telling him. "Hello? You in there, Mallory?"

"Late?" he asked, picking up on one word.

"It's almost six o'clock, you've got to get to night class," she prompted. "Time is money here. I left a map on the kitchen table; most folks here only know Nipponese, so don't bother asking for directions. Get moving."

Some tiny part of his brain started wiring concepts together:

late to class → less education → being less prepared for test → failing test → letting Meiko down

Circuit completed, signal slammed through the connections until he was standing up and alert.

"R-Right!" he exclaimed. "I have to go study! I must pass my test! I won't let you down!! I will pass my test and I won't let you down so I have to go right now and everything else can just wait!"

"That's... a bit spooky, but okay, whatever," Meiko responded, backing away slowly. "So—"

The front door closed behind him with a slam.

Nothing trumps a bewildered, slightly depressed mood like the kind of complete alienation Nippon gives to gaijin.

Gaijin was a word Eiko had taught him—it meant 'foreigner', but Mallory understood the concept that was lurking behind the word quite well. The same look of mistrust Nipponese folks gave him as he wandered the streets was the look he'd see on the Council's faces whenever outsiders dropped by Grünwald. He thought he was prepared to deal with that, that he could handle being treated like an outcast in this strange world... but after the odd mood his father's letter put him in, the strange looks only made him feel weirder and weirder.

Not really his father's son, but really his son; Mallory didn't doubt for a second how Josef felt about him. He didn't doubt for a second how his mother felt about him. But not his father, not his mother... simply found somewhere with no logical explanation of how he got there...

It took him a full city block of neon light scribble-signs before he realized he took a wrong turn. As Nippon was notoriously free of crime he did not run into a dramatically appropriate Wrong Side of the Tracks Gang; he simply backtracked, turned right instead of left, and continued on.

If he wanted to pass this test, if he wanted to avoid letting Meiko down, he couldn't focus on this mystery... although it was hard not to worry. A nagging hangnail just begging to be tugged at and dealt with, despite knowing it'll just make things worse to gnaw at it... ever since that day he'd been trying to balance between the immediate demands of his life (REC Test) and the distant demands (finding out what the hell was going on)...

But Meiko *told* him not to worry about it. Outright ordered him not to worry about it. And his father wouldn't want him to be upset... so with much effort, like trying to swallow an entire hot dog (volume of meat + insult to chefly honor), he pushed it down as he pushed open the doors to the cram school. He might get metaphorical stomach cramps later, but for now, he had a test to study for. The mysterious workings of the multiverse awaited his mighty comprehension!

"You are not here to learn about the mysterious workings of the multiverse," the instructor instructed, as his assistant desperately worked on getting the RealNet Workstation to boot up the slideshow program. "This course is not designed to teach you Reality Engineering. If you want to learn that, there are four year courses available at most major universities, including Reality Prime's own RealUniversity. You are here instead to learn how to pass the REC Test. The REC Test has been issued four times a year, every year, for nearly two thousand years. Obviously, this means RealWare cannot generate 100% original tests for every quarter. The patterns used have been well documented; we will teach you common problem structures and word traps that give you the edge. Are there any questions?"

Every person in the room wearing a shirt with actual buttons did not raise their hands. Which meant the only person who raised a hand was Mallory.

"Mr. Heisenberg?" the instructor called, after glancing at Mal's 'Hello My Name Is' tag.

"Uh, what if I don't already know Reality Engineering?" he asked. "I mean, I've been studying it for a while now so I know the basics but I'm not sure if it's the same as a four-year course—"

"Then you're likely to fail. Any other questions?"

"Can I have an ink pen?"

Once someone found an actual ink-using pen for his use, while the RealWare RealSlides program was busy crashing for the third time that night, Mallory jotted down a note to himself on his left hand:

STUDY HARDER!!!

The rest of the class notes were jotted on his data pad using a simple plastic stylus, notes about answer patterns and analogy questions and such, but the only note that was really of use to him was the one seeping into his skin.

The passage of time became a non-issue for Mallory after that; his view of the outside world was blocked by his datapad, filled with flowing prose and diagrams about the nature of reality. When he ate breakfast (cold cereal provided by Meiko's loving culinary talents) he frequently bumped his spoon against the edge of the pad.

It's a good thing he was distracted, because the way the house was getting filthier and more cluttered would offend his homemaking sensibilities. Eiko's toys had been scattered around the living room; other than stepping on a stray Bathing Beauty Biiko™When he woke up in the morning, the rest slid gracefully into the blind spot.

As for the women of the house, they fit perfectly into the blind spot as well.

"Let's play, oniichan!" Eiko called out, bounding around him in a circle as he walked from one room to the other while reading about the fold properties of reality generation waves across a liquid surface. "Look, I got a new Attack Lawyer Larry™With Appeals Court / Shark Tank Playset!™We can pretend we're overturning financial edicts from the Urbana Business Council!"

"Can't play, busy studying," he replied, and moved right along.

An hour later, a grumbling Lorelei wandered past him, dripping wet and completely naked.

"Something's wrong with the Onsen-of-the-Month," she complained. "The water's gone freezing cold. Mal, can you run down to Noyori Labs and ask Ryo-san to look into it?"

"Can't deliver message, busy studying," he replied.

"Right And before then, wanna go up to my room and have mad, passionate, screaming, nails-scraping-down-your-back sex for a minimum of eight hours?"

"Can't have sex, busy studying," he absently replied.

"Figured as much."

An hour later, he stopped wandering about the house.

So far he'd managed to at least skim over the screens of his data pad in a glaze of half comprehension... but this tangle of arrows and labels and mechanical diagrams was stumping him. Either it was a reality synchronization system or an ice cream maker. Instinctively, he decided to drop in on his study partner and see what she made of it.

He grasped the doorknob to Meiko's room while still looking at the diagram, and walked right in.

"Meiko, could you look at....... err..."

Not Meiko's room.

Although this room was familiar. It was just as dark in here as the last time he walked in, and was indeed occupied by the same person. One extremely angry military-type woman.

This time, he had caught her writing in some sort of pink notebook. In a hurry, she snapped it shut. "YOU. Again? How did you get in here? WHY did you come in here?!"

"I, err, um, I was just—"

But now Kisei was up and in his face and very very threatening-looking in her calm and icy sort of way that made Mallory feel warm and runny inside and hopefully not warm and runny down his left leg. Kisei took a moment to work a small lock on her pink notebook before she chewed him out.

"I specifically locked all seven locks on my door today," Kisei spoke... after glancing a split second to verify things. "That's five plus the two I installed after the last time you entered my room. Six have been unlocked—and unless I am delusional, the seventh is completely missing from my doorframe. Even if that oddity were overlooked, there is simply no possible way to unlock them from outside my door. I would like to know why you have invaded my privacy again, but before you give me such adequate reasons to cripple you, I would like to know HOW you managed this feat."

"Errmgmghhlll," Mallory whimpered incoherently.

"You don't know, do you?" Kisei asked, deciding to do Mallory's thinking for him. "This is like the miraculous escape we made in Antiparadisia, isn't it? You didn't know what happened then, either. How many bizarre coincidences have worked out in your favor, Mallory Heisenberg?"

of course a reality engine shouldn't be able to fix itself just by kicking it, that's silly, but for some reason it always worked every time→

would have been hit by the falling house, if not for the rare chance of having two hills on either side of him to support the thing, if not for knowing to drop to the ground and avoid being crushed→

mallory raised his paddle and ended up deflecting the ball in an accidentally perfect defensive maneuver that squeaked it over the net, off the table and right past meiko→

lorelei fell into step/sprint beside him, fine, fine, take all the fun outta my evening, how'd you throw your voice like that, anyway→

reality shall be determined by the last one standing, he spoke. one single thought flashed across mallory's mind: Meiko.→

he → let → go →

The speed at which Mallory evaded her wrath and slipped out her door was impressive. He even managed to squeeze in a mumbled apology during the process.

A puzzle, Kisei thought, anger easily leaving her now that the problem was out of sight.

After taking care to close her door and lock the remaining locks, she returned to her writing.

Two days and two nights came and went like this.

They crashed to a halt when Meiko wandered downstairs in her bathrobe one morning to make breakfast, and found a zombie had beaten her to the punch.

Eiko gave her sister her a silent, well known 'Help Me' look, as she pointed to her bowl of Chocolate Frosted Chocolate Choco-Chunks Cereal, which had a fried egg floating in it.

The zombie shuffled its feet along the kitchen floor, making a scraping sound of two-day-old used socks on dirty floor as he moved. He deposited a plate of bacon and pancakes in front of Meiko, which were swimming lazily in a sea of 2% lowfat milk.

"Made... breakfast..." the dried-out husk wheezed.

"Mallory... how long have you been awake?" Meiko asked, slipping into her seat and lifting a strip of fried pork from its calcium-enriched swamp.

Mallory took a good twenty seconds to answer, eyes glancing upwards as he worked the problem over in his head. "Uhhh... about... forty-four hours. Studied. Went to class. Came home. Too busy studying. Can't sleep. Must pass test... the early bird catches... the thing with the... yak to water... something or other. Right. Who wants toast?"

Two freshly baked hamburgers popped out of the toaster.

"I'm scared, oneechan!" Eiko whispered.

Meiko crossed her arms, leaning back in the kitchen chair. "I suspect night school is not working out for you, then? Damn. Well... I didn't want to do this, but..."

"You're talking about 'that', aren't you?" Eiko asked. "That's what I suggested we do in the first place! Cram school is good, but it's more financially sound for Mallory to get help there. You know Ryo-san wouldn't mind!"

"I know, but... I really didn't wanna impose on him TWICE in one month," Meiko said, ignoring the undead creature who was trying to fry a pair of oven mitts. "We already asked him to take care of two fugitives on the lam, adding Reality Engineering tutoring on top of that..."

"We could have even parked the house in his corporate lot for free, you know..."

"Eiko, it's important not to take unfair advantage of generosity. Ryo-san shouldn't have to give up a docking slot and his free time just because we're in a bind, in the same way I's Land shouldn't be forced to take care of us well after we finished our work there. Even if they want to. I mean..."

"Eiko-chan suggests this is the only way we're gonna avoid being bankrupt AND keep Mallory-oniichan around!" her younger sister fiercely recommended. "And if we run out of money and Mallory has to leave Eiko-chan will CRY! So let's just ask Ryo-san to help us. ...okay? Please?"

Meiko bit her lip. "I don't know... I mean, Mallory could pull through okay —"

"We're out of butter," he spoke, while pouring ketchup into the toaster.

One forced eight-hour nap later, and Meiko was marching him through the streets of Nippon towards Noyori Labs.

He'd marched through these streets before. Not these EXACT streets, but they all looked the same to him; neon lights, old brick and wood buildings, people everywhere looking at him funny. And like those times, he had a destination and a purpose and rubbernecked at a bare minimum. Unlike his arrival in Urbana... where stared at everyone and everything, but nobody stared back...

"How do they know?" he wondered aloud.

The one leading him around glanced over her shoulder. "Eh?"

"How can they tell I'm a gaijin?" he asked, pronouncing the word correctly. "I've never figured that out. Eiko told me that gaijin were treated with caution and stuff but never how people knew... back home, it was a small community so any outsiders would be obvious, but..."

Meiko shrugged. "A sixth sense, maybe? Although if you look closely... well, look..."

She paused in her walk, turning to face him... and point at her eyes with both hands. And get up close and tight with Mallory's personal space, causing him to take a step back...

"There's a slight tilt in the eyes if you're Nipponese," she explained, while pointing it out. "It's not much, but it's noticeable if you know what you're looking for. Really really REALLY old artwork has it more stylized, so maybe it was more obvious in ancient days... ...wait, your mother was Nipponese, right? Here I am up close, and I'm just seeing the same watery, wide-eyed globs I've always seen, no tilt at all..."

"Oh... yeah," Mallory said, brought uncomfortably back to one of his many Worries of the Week. He could parry it with a lie or just change topics, but... with her so close...

Meiko scratched her chin, the universal expression of confusion. "I didn't think it blended out THAT much in half-Nipponese—"

"I was an orphan, apparently," Mallory said quickly, to get it out fast.

"—what?"

"Isn't that the place?"

Meiko failed to shift to second gear. "Wha...?"

"Noyori Labs," Mallory spoke, pointing to the sign just twenty feet away... trying to smile, to reassure her. "We're here! East Edo Branch. C'mon, every minute I'm not studying is a minute I'm... not studying! Let's roll!"

"But—"

"I'll show you the message I got later," he said, switching back for a moment. "Until then, don't worry about it... okay? Please? I'm fine. I'm fine, really. It's okay."

"You sure you're okay?"

This drew Mallory's distracted eyes back to the display panel.

"Wha...?"

"Looked like you were drifting off into la-la land again," Ryo-san said, tapping his laser pointer in one hand. "C'mon, Mallory-kun, foooocus. It's getting late, and Meiko will kill me if you lose any more sleep..."

Here and now. Focus...

Here being Noyori Labs, East Edo Branch. The first room was a plush lobby with a receptionist and security guard who didn't want to let them in at first—not until Ryo stormed out of the elevator and greeted them with enough energy and good cheer to make Eiko jealous. The second room was... well, the elevator. Meiko got off on the fourth floor to do some RealNet skimming and chatting with Belle Pasadina, who was still a guest of Ryo's...

And then there was this place. Mallory had never been in a scientific research lab. Apparently, neither had Ryo, as it resembled a cobbled together mishmash of sterile chemical plants, robotics workstations, coffee makers, bookcases, stand-up video game cabinets, dartboards, barcaloungers, and more —all organized around a to-scale fully working model railroad set that simulated the Edo public transportation system.

'Not because I helped upgrade it a year ago, mostly because I like pushing the levers and going ALL ABOARD! at the top of my lungs,' he had explained earlier while showing plenty of teeth.

Mallory had never met a scientist before, and was betting he still hadn't. Other than the requisite white lab coat and name tag (with Ryo mugging and flashing a V for the camera much like Eiko enjoyed doing) he didn't fit the mold. He wore flower-print shorts, sandals, a T-shirt with ramen sauce stains... and hadn't shaved in a day or two. In other words, he looked more or less as unprofessional as he did the day they snuck Belle out through the Onsen-of-the-Month—

"MAL! YO!"

"Wha...?"

"You were spacing again," Ryo explained, waving his hand back and forth an inch away from Mallory's face. "C'mon, at least pretend you're interested in this stuff. I know I'm a pretty lousy sensei but I'd like to think I'm at least an entertaining one..."

"S-Sorry, sor... 'Goh men hah sai,'" he corrected, bowing slightly in his seat to show respect.

"Hey, not bad," Ryo commented, amused by it. "Eiko's been teaching you, then? I doubt Meiko has, she doesn't give much thought to her roots..."

"A little here and there, yeah. Um... so... where were we?"

"I was just explaining about the secondary failsafe systems," Ryo spoke, clicking his laser pointer back on, tracing underneath the floating diagram projection. "Do you remember what checksum bitdepth the Environmental Hazard failsafe uses for verification upon a potential Reality Engine crash...?"

Mallory tapped his stylus on his datapad. "Err.... no no, wait, it's coming to me... it's.... I've got this, I remember it from studying with Meiko, it's.... it's... I...... have no clue. Six? Four?"

"Four thousand and ninety-six," Ryo said, with a sigh of sensei-esque disappointment. "You were off by a nine and a zero. Mal, you haven't gotten a single question right tonight. Look, I may be a reasonably resourceful guy considering where I came from, but I can't claim to be a miracle worker. And it's looking to me like it'll take nothing short of a miracle for you to pass this test... why in blazes did you want to be a Reality Engineer, anyway? You took the job before you met Meiko, so I know that can't be it..."

Mallory defocused again, thinking back. "I... uh, originally it was because of my mother. She was a Reality Engineer, too, so I figured maybe I had the knack and not just the knock, but... but it turns out she's not my real mother."

"You lost me."

"It's nothing," he dismissed. "So, failsafes. ...where were we again?"

"Good question," Ryo said, dragging over a barstool (as his seating around the lab was quite eclectic). "Where WERE we? Where were you before? 'Turns out she's not my real mother' is a whopper of a 'turns out'. It's got you distracted, doesn't it? If I'm gonna stop losing you, well, let's blow some time and talk about it—"

"I don't have time to blow, I have to pass this test! ...if you don't mind," Mallory suffixed, not liking the sharp tone he just took. "It's just a worry. I can worry about it later, right...?"

"It's worrying you now. Spill it. Sensei demands this of you," Ryo spoke. "If you've been living with Lorelei, you should know I can be even more doggedly persistent than she can. Meiko's just as reluctant to share when she's worried, and I have to drag it out of her too. I won't teach you a lick of reality until you tell me the backstory here. So. Not your real mother because...?"

The message was still in the backlogs on the House workstation, but Mallory recalled it word for word. Each word told to the odd interrogator.

Then some more words about him and his dad, Josef, and his past. Why he went on the trip, how he saw it as a tornado, why he didn't want to leave the House, didn't want to let Meiko down... how he went to Antiparadisia, and the person he found there, and everything. Every detail.

It took 12 minutes. Mallory was good at compressing every thought he had in a tight babbled stream. And Ryo was good at analyzing data, so he only asked for repeats twice.

"...and now I really don't know what to think," Mallory said, once he managed to slow down. "I know how Dad feels. I feel the same, but... it's like I have this family somewhere and they're gone. And now I have this family at the House and if I fail, they'll be gone too, and... it's just all so confusing... and... and that's it. I think. That's all I can think of. ...I guess that was distracting, me, yeah, now that I think about it..."

Ryo's smile wasn't gone. It was merely set aside for the moment, as he leaned back in quiet contemplation. His brain contemplated at an overclocked speed, of course, so his reply was near instant.

"I was an orphan too," he noted.

"You...?"

"Meiko and I were at the same orphanage on Seven Lucky Gods Street," he continued, looking vaguely up at the ceiling as memory parsed itself for him. "'course, I'm five years older than her, so we didn't see each other much. They kept the young kids and the old kids apart. But we both had the same dream, so it was only natural that we talked whenever we could. We wanted to get out of there, of course. It wasn't a bad place, to be honest, but it wasn't what we wanted from life... we wanted to pave our own futures. We had plans. Destinies, I guess. I wanted to hone my science to help people wherever I could think to help, she wanted to provide a good home and comfortable future for Eiko. 'Course, success and prosperity and happiness is a bit hard when you're a poor orphan with nothing to claim as your own except your first name..."

His gaze strayed back down, to avoid losing himself. To focus on Mallory and his problem.

"It's a trick we both learned: we turn disadvantage to advantage," he said, his smile returning. "Disadvantage: Roots, or lack thereof. Advantage: We've got nothing to tie us down; we can make our own future, our own family. See, your dad is your dad not because of blood, but because of a bond stronger than that. He said so himself, in different words, I guess. It's a funny coincidence: *everybody* in your house has broken roots of one sort or another, but that makes you cling to each other."

"We... don't ALL get along," Mallory reluctantly noted. "Kisei seems to tolerate me at best, and I still don't understand what Lorelei is thinking... for a while she was dating me. I think."

"Yeah, well, in Lorelei's case, she sometimes literally clings to people," Ryo joked. "You know... sometimes I wish I was out and about with Meiko. Heck, I was going to take her up on the Reality Engineering post, but... there's just too many projects here at my company to track. I don't see transients as being better than sedentaries... I'd love to be a transient, if only I wasn't so settled in..."

"Really? I've been both... I'm not sure which I... well, no. I guess I'm enjoying being a transient more, even if it's infinitely more dangerous. I never really fit in back home... and now I guess I know why."

"You felt different from everyone else?" Ryo asked, curious.

"Kinda... yes. Kinda no. I did fairly well in Grünwald, in my studies, my cooking. My chores were fine. I was a productive worker, but... it was never really enough to help me feel like I fit with the others... and after Dad told me why, and after Antiparadisia, I don't even know what to think about... stuff. Just stuff."

"Meiko told me about what happened."

"She did?" Mallory asked, surprised.

"She tells me a lot of things..." Ryo said... while glancing around his ramshackle laboratory, distracted by a thought. "I didn't wanna drag this up myself, Mallory, but... would you mind if we do a little test?"

"Whaaa?! But I'm already studying for one test! I can't do two—"

"No no, this would only take a minute. I'm just playing off a hunch... someone who came here once a year or two ago and was asking to use my facilities for a very odd test. He looked a lot like you, too..."

my face...

"Did... did he wear sunglasses?" Mallory asked, a tiny wad of dread forming in his stomach. "Or a cloak? Or smile a lot?"

"Uh, no. Why?"

"N-Nothing. Well... What do I do?"

"Chotto matte," Ryo bit off, before hopping to his feet and rummaging around on a table of gadgets. "Hmmm... koko wa... ah, here we go!"

He emerged with an entirely nonthreatening wandlike thingy with a curly thingy around the straight thingy which was glowing in a happy thingy sort of way.

"Just hold still ooooone second..." Ryo spoke, approaching slowly with the thingy...

Mallory started to sweat. "Err, is this going to hur—"

One wave of Ryo's hand later, and the thingy beeped quietly. The glowing bit turned bright green. Safe green.

"Okay, done," his teacher spoke, studying the light curiously.

"Err... done? Done what? What is that?"

"Page 238."

"Eh?"

"It's on page 238 of your datapad," Ryo said, pointing to the datapad still clenched in Mallory's left hand. "This little baby is a harmonic wave scanner. A simple tool used to check if a Reality Engine is out of sync or not, good way to tell if it's about to crash..."

"Right. Right. Green is... good, right?"

"Oh, yes! Green is very good. No crash imminent!"

"That's a relief!" Mallory exclaimed, leaning back in his chair.

"Although technically it should stay white unless waved in front of a Reality Engine."

The pupil's chair continued to lean back until it was leaning against the floor.

"Go figure," Ryo said, ignoring Mallory's topsy turvy crisis. "Not that I wasn't expecting that. See, that guy who wanted to do this test a year ago, it showed green for him too..."

"WHAT?!" Mallory exclaimed, back on his feet and ready to bust out into a full-fledged panic attack.

Ryo finally took note of the boy's Defcon state. "Er... hey... hey, don't panic, okay? Panic is bad for studying! Deep cleansing breaths, deep breaths, go to your happy place—"

"But I'm a Reality Engine! Or... at least I seem like one to that thing! That's not normal! That's very very not normal!" Mallory exclaimed, unable to achieve his happy place. "What am I? What's going on?! Why's it green, why are there so many people who look like me, I'm just a normal guy, I don't WANT to be not-normal...!"

"Not normal isn't always a bad thing," Ryo deflected. "Not normal can be a good thing. But... this is gonna worry the hell out of you, isn't it?"

Mallory responded by hyperventilating.

With great speed, the scientist reached out and pressed a thumb against a shihatsu point on Mallory's body that forced him to tranquility. In an instant, his breathing went from a high-speed dance beat to a mellow earthy cycle.

"S'not healthy to carry on like that, you know," Ryo spoke... calming himself as well. "All this worry will give you ulcers..."

Despite feeling like a puddle of zen goo, Mallory managed to squeak out a nervous tone with his words. "...gotta worry about the test... no way around that. I gotta worry some, Ryo-san..."

"Yeah, you do... don't you. ...all right, Mallory, I'll make a deal with you," Ryo spoke, the final part of a brief decision making process. "You worry about your REC Test. As for this business with Antiparadisia... how about if I worry about it for you?"

"...you lost me."

"I'll look into the matter for you," Ryo continued, with his trademark smile tightly affixed. "Maybe try to find that guy who came in a year ago. This is something a little bigger than you can take on right now, so let me do the research, let me do the worrying—and you just get on with your life. You and Meiko are staying in Nippon for a while, right...?"

"Y... yeah. She didn't want to impose on I's Land any longer..."

"Okay, then! That works perfectly. I'll stay in close contact. Heck, I'll give you docking space, and Meiko is NOT gonna take no for an answer! As for you, put this whole thing out of your head—don't worry about it! I know I have room enough for my worries and Meiko's worries, I think I can manage to worry for all three of us..."

Mallory looked unsure. "Uh... I don't know, Ryo-san... I mean, not that I have the slightest idea what to do about any of this, but... I don't feel right dumping it on you, either—"

A finger with ramen sauce stains tapped against his datapad, cueing up a page.

"238," Ryo noted. "Harmonic wave scanners. Study from there on. And don't panic! I forbid you from doing so, in the same way Meiko isn't allowed to panic. Oh, and don't forget, the test is in two days!"

And with that, he flew like an eagle.

Admittedly an eagle with one crippled wing and 37% of its feathers removed and/or burned off and partial blindness in one eye, but he somehow kept aloft.

Two days of studying slid by at high speed. He memorized everything he could, studied the case examples, tried to break down complicated concepts into little mixed metaphors... whatever he could do to consume the most knowledge at high speed. Two nights of studying with Ryo, who never mentioned Mallory's previous worries again...

Which was what let him fly, really. He was iffy on dumping all responsibility for recent problems on Ryo's head, especially since he was turning out to be one of the friendliest folks Mallory had met since leaving home. Still, being able to think to himself "I don't have to be concerned with it; it's someone else's problem" kept Mallory's head clear, his mind focused, his brain lively, his mental concept active verb.

The first night he stayed up a little too late studying; one brief scolding from Meiko later and he resumed an ordinary sleep schedule. Reality wave patterns and code installation packages danced in his head while he slept...

And finally, the time was upon him. The place was upon him. Not literally.

After a short taxi ride to the RealWare Nippon East Edo Branch and some hallway roaming, Mallory presented his triplicated signed forms to the testing proctor. He followed the helpful maps to his testing room. He assumed his seat. He performed a short meditative concentration exercise that Kisei had taught him the night before...

(...which was a bit odd, given she hadn't spoken to him since the day he barged in on her for a second time, but maybe Meiko had asked her to help...)

...and finally, the REC Test. In a small cubicle by himself, to ensure he didn't cheat off the hundreds of others taking the test today. No paper involved, simply a table-based touch screen, about to come alive with Reality Engineering questions in one minute's time. He tapped his stylus against the table, going over the acronyms and metaphors he'd used as learning aids. (WHAT? Wave Harmony Amplification Tester. HUH? Heuristic Ulterior Helper. I DON'T UNDERSTAND? Integrated Diagnostic Online NewType Uncompressed Negative Data Energy Recorder Standardized Tool And Neo-Debugger.)

He could do this. He could conquer. He would not let Meiko down. He would follow in his... mother's footsteps. He would become a Reality Engineer!

He would not notice the test had already started until his nervous stylus taps accidentally answered three questions for him.

Then he would frantically look for the 'back' button on the table to fix the answers and end up answering two more multiple choice questions with D.

Panic would set in next. In a fit of inspired madness he tried to remember the spot Ryo had poked to calm him down, and accidentally cut off the blood supply to his neck for two minutes.

Finally he got his act together, forced his lungs to return to normal operating procedures, and studied the question before him.

QUESTION 6: Reality Q has had fluctuations in the third demisphere of their nebulous reality bubble border definition file. Symptoms include massive hurricanes in the weather subsystems and the tendency for light to deflect towards the latter fifth of the spectrum, as well as water tasting like copper. If you only had your Heuristic Ulterior Helper on hand and the reality was already in Safe Mode (Variant #548, SubVariant C) which of the following dynamic allocation techniques would be most suitable for stabilizing the reality?

(A) Mixed Memory Allocation
(B) Self Optimizing Neural Net Syntax
(C) Floating Point Asynchronous Data Allocation and Address Bank Switching
(D) None, prepare self emotionally for fatal Nullspace accident

And he drew a blank. A big, fat blank. (If it were just a little skinny blank it would be less intimidating.)

I can guess on this one, he thought. *It can't hurt to guess if I really don't know. There have to be questions in here that I DO know; until I get to them, guessing is all I can do...*

He didn't know the Eeeny Meeny Miney Mo game, so he just closed his eyes and poked the stylus randomly against the table. Answer D blinked twice before the next question popped up.

Which he had to guess on.

As well as the next one.

And the next...

Next...

....

FINAL QUESTION: Taking into account all you know about Reality Engineering and safety protocols, what is the one thing which must never, ever, EVER under any circumstances be done to a Reality Engine?

(A) Install unauthorized third party software
(B) Replace fluid systems with tap water
(C) Allow a non-certified Reality Engineer to access the system
(D) Kick it

Slumped across the desk, eyes glazed over with Pure Doom, Mallory tapped A.

The desk returned to a neutral RealWare logo, with a tiny message stating that his results would be sent to him over RealNet in a few hours. Helpful maps illustrated the way out of the building.

The overhead light of the cubicle clicked off, to conserve power.

Eventually the janitor found him, and after verifying that he was simply catatonically depressed and not in fact deceased, security kindly ushered him to a taxi.

There's a saying in Grünwald. One so critical to the core of their beliefs that even Mallory's scrambled brain couldn't breed it with other metaphors:

"You reap what you sow."

Which isn't always a nasty thing to say; after all, if you plant a good crop with dedication to good farming, you'll reap a wonderful harvest after the growing season. Hard work equals positive results. Lazy slack-ass attitude equals failure.

As Mallory lurched slowly along the sidewalk of the docking yard, he was still wondering why the metaphor broke. He worked hard. Possibly harder than he'd ever worked in his life, and he still failed. Failed everybody, himself, Meiko, the House, his father... he bit off more than he could chew and ended up choking on the sour grapes of wrath.

He'd been going over another set of words in his head as well, the ones he would say to Meiko to tell her the bad news. Those weren't coherent enough yet for practical use, but maybe that was for the best; there wasn't any easy way to say it. And now he was at the front door of the House, and there was no turning back...

Steeling himself to enter for the last time, he waved his house passkey in front of the doorknob, and walked in...

An explosion temporarily blinded him.

"Eiko, you shouldn't set those things off right in his face," Meiko chided softly.

"Gomen ne, oneechan!" Eiko apologized, stepping back a bit before setting off the next confetti-and-streamers pocket firecracker. With a cheerful *pop*! colored paper went flying into the air—joining similar explosions of fun set off by Lorelei and a very reluctant Kisei.

Mallory hadn't prepared words for this, so he simply stared.

"Hooray, oniichan!" Eiko cheered, now waving a pair of rising sun fans. "VICTOLY! CONGRATULATION!"

To make matters more bizarre, Lorelei pushed a beer into the boy's limp hand, and ushered him into the kitchen to join the others. "Yo, Mal, I KNEW you could do it! That's why I made sure not to buy the party goodies until after your test results came in. ...wait, I meant: I didn't know you could do it! So, hey, good job! Eiko, quit the puppy dog eyes, you're not getting a beer..."

"I will admit that I am... mildly impressed with your feat, Mallory Heisenberg," Kisei offered. "I was expecting crushing defeat, given the size of the task before you and your complete lack of previous experience. I credit most of your success to Noyori Ryo's formidable talents, of course—"

Mallory's beer rolled off the table and hit the floor. He stood quickly, and blurted out a half-mix of the words he was preparing.

"Failed! The test, I did!" he spouted. "I mean... I failed the test! So... so you shouldn't be celebrating. I—"

Meiko quirked one eyebrow. "Hel-lo? Were you listening? We got the test results, Mallory. You passed. In fact—"

Rather than being a party of five, it was now a party of six.

Deciding it was probably better to take this shock sitting down, Mallory sat, while staring at the newcomer.

"Sorry, but even executives with six-figure salaries have to use the smallest room," Mr. Tanner explained, after returning from the bathroom. "Congratulations, Mallory Heisenberg. I came personally to report the scores, as is standard procedure for such high marks: you scored a 99% on your test."

"...nine... ty ...nine?" Mallory asked, unbelieving.

"Yes, well... you did get the last question wrong. You're not supposed to kick engines. But otherwise, it's a very impressive score," Tanner continued. "I contacted Meiko with the results and informed her I'd be dropping in to report them to you in person, but it seems I missed you by a minute there... my apologies. Now, to business—"

"TO BUSINESS!" Lorelei shouted, clanking her can against Meiko's.

"...I meant that I had business to conduct."

"Oh. I thought you were proposing a toast..."

"No, actually, I'm here to offer Mallory a job."

The air in the kitchen dropped six degrees and sixty decibels.

Lorelei was the first to break the silence. "That's pretty lousy, man," she commended, keeping her eyes on the corporate type. "Headhunting is one thing, but trying to break in our turf and hire away Mallory is pretty low—"

"Please, hear me out," Tanner asked, holding up both hands in a peaceful gesture. "I'm simply making an offer; whether or not Mallory chooses to change employers is his decision. This is standard procedure for anyone who scores 97% or above on a REC Test. RealWare is always looking for the best and the brightest, and between this and the recipe Mallory crafted last month, we believe he has excellent potential. Now, you'd start with a standard RealWare entry-level salary of 50,000 points a month—"

"Waaah!" Eiko exclaimed. "That's lots and lots!"

"—but the benefits package is quite good, and your salary will increase as you establish yourself," Tanner finished. "I mean no disrespect to you by doing this, Miss Mirai... it's simply company policy to make the offer."

"Uh-huh," Lorelei spoke, letting each U and H drip with suspicion. "Y'know, Mallory already has a contract with Meiko. She's the one who technically makes this decision, and there's no way we're gonna let our beloved Houseboy get cherry picked like—"

"He should take the job."

This coming from the head of the Mirai household.

"...don't look at me like that, I'm serious," she spoke quietly... trying not to breathe any emotion into it, one way or the other. "It's... an excellent offer. The perfect starting point for a career in Reality Engineering. It's more than we could ever afford to pay him, and it's better job experience than playing... live-in grease monkey to a transient home. Mallory has to think about his future, you know, not just us—plan for where he wants to be in life. If he's going to prosper—"

"I'm staying," Mallory said.

"M—"

"I'm staying," he repeated before Meiko repeated herself... and said it with a smile. "It's okay, Meiko. Don't worry; I am thinking of the future that I want. Tanner-san, it's a wonderful offer, but... I already have a job that I love. It's okay that it doesn't pay much—this is where I want to be. Uh, you're welcome to stay and party a bit if you want, but I'm afraid my answer's kinda final..."

Tanner nodded, going through the motions. "The offer is good for the next two days if you want to think it over... although I suspect final means final, yes?"

A nod from the Houseboy Reality Engineer.

"I'm afraid work calls, then," Tanner spoke, closing up his briefcase. "Have an enjoyable evening, Mr. Heisenberg, Miss Mirai. Good evening."

The defeated (but uncaring) suit exited stage right, closing the front door behind him.

"Well well WELL! Now we can really kick this party into high gear!" Lorelei exclaimed, getting back into her groove. "Eiko, cue up some music on the Workstation! Stuff with cheap rights fees, of course. More drinks! Bust out the chips! Who wants to play spin the bottle? Meiko, how about you?"

"Wha?" Meiko asked, still mildly stunned.

"I believe I shall retire to my room, now that my participation in this gathering has been adequately registered." Kisei announced. "Good evening, Mallory Heisenberg. Rest well."

Ignoring the others, Meiko turned to talk quieter to Mallory. "Mal... you're sure about this? I'd let you go if you wanted that job..."

"Oh, no no, it's okay," Mallory said, settling into his chair. "I'm just glad it's all over! And I'm happy here, working with you... this is the most fun I've had in years! And danger, too, but uh... it's the most fun I've had in years! Besides, I just answered questions randomly on the test and I think really bad things would happen if I tried to take a RealWare job with what I actually know. Hey, I know! Who wants me to make some party mix? I know a GREAT recipe for... baked... bagel bits...?"

Meiko's grip on the edge of the table threatened to bend it in half.

"You... answered... RANDOMLY?!" she hissed through gritted teeth.

"...ummm..." Mallory umm'd, wilting slightly under that gaze...

...until Meiko eased up, slumping into her chair. "...randomly. Of course. I shouldn't be surprised... but you passed. I GUESS that's all that matters... ugh. Geez, Mallory—"

"ONEECHAAAAN!"

Eiko waved one arm frantically towards a bright blinking red light coming from around the corner.

"The Reality Engine's crashing!" she exclaimed. "I just sorta bumped into it by accident when I was pulling out the chair at the Workstation and now it's saying it needs service and it's counting down from thirty to one backwards and I don't know what to do!!"

Like a bold heroic something or other... Mallory rose to his feet.

"Stand back," he stated in the most manly voice he could manage (not manly). "I'll handle this."

Meiko bit her lip, unsure. "Mallory..."

"Do you trust me?" he asked, looking to her.

"I... probably shouldn't," Meiko admitted. "It wouldn't make sense to... but, well..."

"Right, right," Mallory said, chuckling a little. "Okay. Here we go!"

Dear dad!

I have (kind of) passed the REC TEST!!!! I am now a Reality Engineer just like Mother was and it feels very very good indeed!

Oh right, I read your mail and okay. I thought about it a lot and a new friend helped me think about it more and I know all the way down to my toes that you are my Father. I may look into who my biology father is too, since I'm curious now, but don't worry any about me being upset. I don't worry either about some of my problems because someone is worrying instead, and now that I have passed my test and I have my job officially and I'm getting along great with Meiko and the others I am feeling great!

Enclosed is some money I think. If it didn't work let me know, I haven't used the point transfer bank thing before.

Bright times look to be ahead. I feel like I'm home. Our house back in Grünwald will always be home too, but this is home as well. Home is wherever you're happy, I guess, not just where you were born. I have truly found paradise!!! or something like that

your son, Mallory.

PS - After two bad experiences with drinking I think I should be sticking to water from now on. I am writing this between large bad headaches the morning after my victory party.

And my foot hurts from kicking something a little too hard.

Alarm clock ringing. Morning.

Fist to clock, clock stops ringing.

Sweep broken plastic parts away from futon with an arm gesture.

Hangover check. Hangover? No. Breakfast? Probably a good idea, especially with Mallory back on kitchen duty. Exercises first, breakfast second. Gotta stay sharp. Sharp and fed, but sharp first, then fed. Fetch training stick from wall mount weapons rack, twirl into place, go through the motions of the kata...

Despite having a personal philosophy about clothing that boiled down to "Less Is More," Lorelei did not, in fact, go through her warm-up routine topless. That would be silly, and uncomfortable. She went through it bottomless instead.

Slowly her brain woke up as the whirling wooden rod whispered through the air. Instinctive motions slid gracefully into voluntary ones as she grew more alert after a full night's rest... her stances sliding from attack to defense to attack in smooth combinations. She struck at invisible enemies in the air, halting the rod an inch inside their imaginary bodies... nodding in satisfaction at each attack.

"Still got it," she decided, as she did every morning. "And always had it."

"Is it safe to enter, or do I risk severe head trauma?" a familiar voice asked from the other side of her door.

Lorelei spin her stick around thrice, before shifting to back-twirls to avoid accidentally whacking her employer. "C'min!"

The door opened carefully, doorknob left unturned; Lorelei didn't care much about privacy, unlike the sniper down the hall.

"We have a job offer to check out today," Meiko explained, leaning in the doorframe. "But I want to warn you now: you may not like it."

"You know me, boss, I'm ready for anything," Lorelei replied, spinning her weapon from hand to hand as she chatted. "Don't stress about it. I'll handle anything you need handled! Or manhandle any men you need manhandled."

"Mhmm. Well, to prevent you from manhandling me when you find out where we are, you should know that I haven't formally accepted the offer yet; we're attending a sit-down meeting after breakfast to get the details. I could use a bodyguard to get to the meeting, but you don't have to participate in this one if you don't want to."

Lorelei flicked her fingers around the staff, and with a snap of the wrist lobbed it in the air. The spinning training weapon made a WHOOSHWHOOSH noise before landing perfectly back in its slot on her weapon rack.

"Now you've got me curious," she said, fetching a towel she kept nearby for morning workout purposes, and wiping down a bit. "What's so nasty out there that I can't face it? You're forgetting that I'm a beer-drinking, man-eating, bar-brawling son of a gun who's also the Ultimate 16 Champion of Tribal Alpha."

"Actually, no. I'm specifically not forgetting that," Meiko said, still looking unsure. "We're leaving shortly. Mallory made toast so we can eat and run... and Lorelei?"

"Yeah, Mei?"

"Put on some clothes before coming downstairs."

"It's nothing Mallory hasn't seen before..."

"We're NOT starting this again, are we?" Meiko asked, despairing. "I thought—"

"I'm kidding, I'm kidding! He's all yours, Meiko, whether you're taking him or not. I just like to play with his head. And YES, I'll put on my work clothes. Give me four minutes and I'll be there."

Three minutes were spent searching her wardrobe for something suitably skimpy yet functionally efficient yet personally statement-making yet stylish yet comfortable. Thirty seconds were spent strapping it on.

Twenty seconds were devoted to wondering what Meiko was being so vague about, and what in the multiverse Lorelei could possibly object to. She made it a mission in life ever since leaving home to sample damn near anything in life she could, after all; aside from maybe taking a job where she had to date a metric ton of man-fat with pimples on his ass, there was nothing she felt she couldn't conquer. No challenge she couldn't crush, no enemy she couldn't reduce to a small quivering lump of pain. 2,034 dead bodies couldn't be wrong, after all...

Ten seconds later she froze in her tracks on seeing the jungles of Tribal Alpha out the kitchen window.

Home.

07: Player Hater

"Wow, it's humid out there!" was Mallory's usual level of observation and enlightenment.

"The climates of Tribal Alpha are divided into four quadrants: forest, jungle, tundra, and desert," Eiko recited from the House's copy of Twoday's Guidebook For Discerning Reality Tourists. "Each zone presents unique challenges for weekend players and established tribes alike! Docking yards are available in each zone, and represent combat-free zones for non-tribe members..."

"So, it's one huge video game?" Mallory asked, curious. "They run around out there and shoot at each other and fight and stuff?"

"Thaaat's right! And the Ladder of Triumph shows how many points each clan or visiting player rack up from kills and enemy flag captures. You can drop in for a weekend of fun, or move in fulltime by joining a clan and participating in a twenty-four-seven-three-hundred-and-sixty-five-day-a-year fragfest like none other! It's so cool; I've seen all sorts of tournaments held here on RealNet Sports! Oneechan, this is GREAT! Can I go play? I have a slingshot! I bet I could score some points—"

"No, you can't play," Meiko spoke without looking up from buttering her toast. "You and Mallory are staying here, and if you push him into letting you leave the house, you'll be in more trouble than I like to put you in."

"O...oneechan?" Eiko asked, surprised. "But it's just a game—"

"If it was just a game, they wouldn't need their own reality for it," Meiko explained. "Even if it was just a game, you know I don't like you playing violent video games. Violent PEOPLE games are much, much worse. Just because nobody really dies here doesn't mean it's harmless..."

"Uh... I was kinda wondering about that," Mallory said, turning away from the window. "How is it that people can attack each other and not actually hurt each other...?"

Eiko flipped to the next page in the GuideBook. "Simple enough—custom reality! One of the few worlds that doesn't conform to RealWare's Uniform Reality Standards 1.0. The Reality Engine here has a special add-on module created by RealWare seven hundred years ago that makes an invisible 'reality warp bubble' around everybody in this reality. When a weapon hit or other potentially injuring action is felt by the bubble, it takes away 'health points' and when you reach zero, you're knocked out for a few minutes and then moved to a random 'respawn point'! The ServOps Center which houses the engine and Ladder of Triumph is completely automated, a marvel of reality engineering! Oniichan, you should've known that, being a certified Reality Engineer and all..."

"You are upset?"

Lorelei almost went for a martial arts takedown when the whisper floated over her shoulder, but stopped herself after glancing back to see who it was.

The silent-moving sniper glanced down to Lorelei's hand, which was dripping slightly on the floor from where her fingernails had buried into her palm.

"...I'd be lying if I said no, and you don't care for lies, yes?" Lorelei asked, trying to stay calm. Cool. Controlled. Nearly failing to.

"Yes," Kisei confirmed quietly.

"Then yes."

"I see. Meiko has told you this mission is optional for you, yes?"

"Yes."

"And...?"

"I want to see what's going on for myself before I turn around and stomp back here in disgust," Lorelei decided after shoving past her reluctance to go out there.

"A suitable decision, I suppose," Kisei replied, before stepping around her to join the others at breakfast.

Her ears closed off to Eiko going on excitedly about the wonders of Tribal Alpha, as she stepped up for toast as well. Without even looking at Meiko, she buttered and ate in silence.

Truth be told, she would have preferred to go back to bed than face this place again. Not that she was afraid to return, no. Certainly not that. It was more a matter of absolute loathing and repulsion. If this was a positive magnet, so was Lorelei, one always driving off the other...

But even at the edges of her closed ears, she could hear the familiar sounds. Footfalls in the grasses. Weapons fire. Orders shouted. Screams...

The call of the l33t.

Come and play...

The twisted wreckage of an AirBike spun from the sky like a wounded bird. A wounded bird on fire and raining red hot metal fragments on the armies below.

In an act of amusing irony, it crashed into the mobile vehicle repair bay, causing a giant fireball to roar into the sky and the soldiers below to scatter like little green plastic army men in a wind tunnel.

"REPAIR OUR VEHICLE STATION!" one of them shouted into his helmet communicator. "REPAIR OUR... oh, sh1—"

Another explosion heralded his demise. Or rather, his 'fragging'... as the completely unmutilated body simply tumbled backwards from the explosion, knocked out cold by remote. A fresh wave of troops rushed forward, firing rockets and railgun shots and grenades and flamethrowers and more as hundreds stormed the gates of the makeshift fortress...

At the edge of the jungle clearing (clear as in 'stomped flat' or 'burned away') stood three uninvolved bystanders: Meiko Mirai, with her bodyguard Lorelei and tactician Kisei. None of them felt compelled to wander into the ongoing brawl.

"Check with me on this," Meiko asked. "If one of those idiots shoots me, I won't actually be hurt, correct? Lorelei? ...Lorelei?"

"I have trained here before," Kisei filled in, while Lorelei maintained a stony silence. "Any visitors are treated just like other players, except that they respawn at the docking yards. You would simply be returned to the house."

"Right. Well. Regardless, I don't feel like being 'killed' today," Meiko decided. "We're staying right here for now. Our client said she'd send a bodyguard contingent to escort us in if there were hostilities at our time of arrival. But if any of these jokers—"

"Duck," Kisei suggested.

The crew hit the deck as a homing rocket failed to home properly, and detonated a section of jungle fifty feet behind them.

"—and if they even SCRATCH the aluminium siding on the House, there's gonna be hell to pay," Meiko spoke through grinding teeth. "Believe me, I wouldn't take this job if we didn't need the money... and if someone doesn't show to escort us in the next five minutes I'm going to accept living on instant ramen for another week. ...Lorelei, if you wanna turn back now, you—"

"I'm not going anywhere," Lorelei replied quickly. "Besides, it's almost over. Three of them got inside the gates; two runners and a carrier. Standard flanking positions, but tight ones, good skill. There was even a second wave going in to back up the first and carry the slack in the event of failure. My guess is that in the next minute—"

A blazing alarm rocked the jungle, a sound that came from everywhere and nowhere simultaneously. Klaxon-style siren... and then a voice, a machine voice of the automated ServOps.

"D3THL0RDZ 0F P41N HAVE CAPTURED THE FLAG. D3THL0RDZ 0F P41N HAVE CAPTURED THE FLAG. "

A whooping cheer went up from the invading army, as a tattered red flag was carried out of the gates, despite the heavy fire from the fortress walls on the now exiting army. A few members of the victory party were pegged neatly by snipers, but it didn't matter; the major points had been scored. Any frags beyond that were trivial.

To drive the point home, the driver of the invader's primary personnel transport got on a loudspeaker for a final taunt.

"W3lc0m3 t0 th3 b0tt0m, d00dz!" he howled in tribal dialect. "W3 0WNZ J0000!!!1!"

"Looks like the fun's over," Meiko decided. "I think we can forgo the escorts now."

The fortress had seen better days. Weeks, too. Bordering on months.

Walking down the corridors, it was clear that all their resources had been turned towards defense—the fine art of keeping people the hell out. Snipers were positioned at every window, at least as many snipers as they could spare; cots and lanterns had been laid out so they could sleep in shifts in the hallway. Stone rubble and twisted metal littered the place, pushed aside to make a clear walking space down each hallway—fragments stripped from the quasi-science-fiction-medieval-castle-fusion architecture of the fortress.

As for the mood of the place, 'gloom' was an understatement. 'Despair' would probably be closer, except that the various uniformed soldiers they passed didn't look ready to give up—it was the kind of desperate despair that made you fight even harder to protect your way of life...

Although the looks Lorelei got were more than formal nods. They were looks of quiet surprise. Of course, the troops had been informed that Mirai Consulting would be arriving today, and exactly WHO Mirai Consulting consisted of... but knowing someone's coming and seeing them in the flesh for the first time in four years, these are distinctly separate things...

Finally the journey ended at a set of double doors, re-fortified after being blown open earlier by the D3THL0RDZ. Men in ragged crimson uniforms worked the opening mechanisms, allowing them entrance... to the Flag Room.

The Flag Room was the true core of any fortress, the single point that must be protected. Fragging the enemy in droves got you points on the ladder, of course, but nothing compared to the capture of an enemy flag. Of course, once captured, it 'respawns' back in the Flag Room ten minutes later—but by then the damage is done, and as the D3THL0RDZ did, you can safely retreat to plan your next raid.

Not that Meiko knew any of this. But Lorelei did. Memories leaking back into the front of her brain, from the parts she had sealed away along with her other childish mistakes...

Sitting at a war council table were the remaining leaders of the tribe. At the head of the table sat the leader of leaders... the master of masters. A hardened warrior whose prowess in battle was only matched by two others... one who could cut through a swath of men and rack up dozens of frags in minutes... a living embodiment of absolute death.

"Hello, hello!" she greeted, with a songbird's sweet voice. Her hands clasped together, shining blue eyes behind bangs attached to flowing blonde hair. "I'm so glad you could make it! Francis, please, some tea for our guests. I'm so sorry, I had hoped to prepare for your arrival more, but we got distracted by some silly little children... would you like any cookies? I baked some this morning for you! Someone, get our friends some chairs, it's so impolite to leave them standing—"

"We're fine, thanks," Meiko replied, taking control of the situation. "As for the tea, we'll pass. Now, Kelli of the Steel Blades Tribe, correct? I hope you understand that we'd like to get to business right away..."

"Of course, of course," Kelli of the Steel Blades Tribe replied, gesturing for three chairs to be added to the table. Once her guests were seated, she got to the heart of the matter. "I apologize for being vague in my job offer, but I thought it best that you see our situation before deciding... as you no doubt are aware, we are in dire straits. It's quite a sad story, and one I'm hoping you can help us out with..."

"From the looks of it, you're not doing real well in the games," Meiko guessed correctly.

"It's not from lack of sk1llz," Kelli noted, subtly smoothing out her red dress under the table, to maintain appearances. "We have ruled the ladder for generations... at or near the top slot at all times. Our warriors have gone on to form their own tribes which were also quite successful. However, the situation has taken a turn for the worse this year. Our enemies, being quite cowardly (and I mean that in the nicest way possible) have decided to band together against us as a single federation of tribes. This is not one of the simple, fragile alliances of the past that we easily overcame... at this point, there are only fifteen tribes left in Tribal Alpha. And fourteen of them are members of this new alliance."

"Ah. So, essentially, the entire world is against you?"

"It's jealousy, plain and simple," the leader spoke, with a breathy sigh. "We've been strong for so long that it's only natural for the weak to want to take us down. I understand, really, I do; our tribe got to this place over the bodies of others. That's the way of Tribal Alpha, but it does mean developing quite a few enemies along the way. But this alliance... it's against everything Tribal Alpha stands for. They do not seek the friendly competition of the hunt. They have no eye for the trophies and the titles, or the thrill of the fight... all they want is to purge us from this world, plain and simple. The alliance is an unfair fight, and if there's one thing that I cannot stand, it's bullying... but I digress. Are you familiar with the 'purge'?"

"I haven't fully read up on the rules of the game," Meiko admitted... glancing sideways to the silent Lorelei. "Lorelei, do you—"

"The Purge separates the l4m3 from the l33t," Lorelei replied curtly. "Once a month, whatever tribe is at the bottom of the ladder is purged. More or less. There are more complicated conditions needed to satisfy it than that alone, but... I wouldn't doubt that fourteen tribes could put even the mighty Steel Blades at the bottom. Anybody who can't climb off the bottom rung in one month's time gets purged... the reality-warp bubbles that keep them from really getting killed is turned off. After that they have to join another tribe, leave Tribal Alpha and never return, or risk the Final Frag..."

"As I said, it's an unfair way to achieve the goal," Kelli spoke up... keeping her eyes on Lorelei as she did so. "If one tribe alone managed to do this to us, I could accept the defeat. It would be honorable. But this mob mentality is spoiling the purity of the—"

"This is bullshit."

A chill filled the already chilled room.

Meiko briefly considered ordering her employee to hold her tongue, and opted not to.

"...I had hoped that your time in self-imposed exile would help you understand, Lorelei," Kelli replied. "I had hoped that when I hired your consulting firm to help us, you would be willing to stand up for us once again. Although I suppose by hiring you, your employer will make you stand for us regardless—"

"Stand up for what, pray tell?" Lorelei asked, mixing her sarcasm into her seriousness and ending up with something far darker and nastier than her usual playful attitude. "For your high score? Your 'honor'? Your l33tness? I had hoped that my time in self-imposed exile would help YOU understand why I left. You know what? I'm all for the Steel Blades getting the axe. Then maybe you idiots could join the rest of us OUT THERE, in reality. Rei-Lei was right. She was right and I was right to leave in the first place, just like I'm leaving now!"

Okay, now you can intercede, Meiko decided.

"Hold up a minute, Lorelei," she spoke, rising to her feet. "Just one minute while I render my decision here. Miss Kelli, Mirai Consulting is not a mercenary outfit. We are not in the habit of fighting wars for people. If you hired us hoping to use Lorelei's skills—excuse me, 'sk1llz'—to dig yourself out of this hole, then I'm afraid I will have to let you down. I won't order her to help, and have in fact already told her she can walk away from this at any time. If we take this job... then I intend to find a non-combat based solution to your problem. I do not believe in the one-option-only scenario."

"I apologize for disagreeing, Miss Mirai, but there IS only one option here," Kelli responded, trying to sound as sweet and polite as possible rather than irritated. "Within a few days, our reality-warps will be deactivated. Unless we fight our way off the bottom rung in that time, something we cannot do alone, we will be no more... because our tribe will fight to the last, for our honor. We will not run from the duty, unlike some..."

"Oh, what a clever hidden barb at yours truly," Lorelei chewed out. "You know, I decided early on I wanted to see what's going on for myself before I turn around and stomp back home in disgust. And I'm going to do that now. I'm going home."

"Lorelei, you ARE home now!"

"You know what I mean, Mother!" Lorelei barked out, before turning and making for the doors at full sprint.

Nervous eyes peered out from behind a tree. The brain they were connected to via optic nerves within was far more nervous than the eyes that they looked through, since eyes can't actually be nervous, but... the holder (beholder?) of the eyes was too nervous to really think coherently.

"Well? Is the coast clear or not?" an annoyed voice behind him asked.

"It's c-clear," the nervous one replied. "I don't see anyone, just the spawn point..."

His companion stepped around him, carrying the bundled up tent. "All right, good. We set up here. You get the cooking fire going; I'll erect the pup tent. We shouldn't be here more than two days."

The nervous one followed into the clearing shortly after that, studying the stone marker buried in the ground curiously. "It's unmarked, though... are you sure this is the place? I mean, what if we're wrong? We could be stuck out here longer. Or we could be attacked! We're really close to Steel Blades territory!"

"Will you relax, n00b?" the other one hissed, while unrolling the tent. "That's what the traps we're gonna set up are for! And as for the spawn point, it's on the Great Map. Generations of our ancestors can't be wrong! The +5/+5 Mythril Railgun of 0wnage respawns right here every 48 hours. All we have to do is stake the place out, defend it against anybody else, and one of the most w1ck3d guns in Tribal Alpha will be ours! A damn fine prize to take back to the Campers Tribe, and a victory for the Alliance! Now get the coffee going, I'm thirsty after all that hiking... NOW what is it?"

The n00b pointed a shaky finger to the trees high above the respawn point. "I... I think I saw someone! Up there!"

"You said it was clear," the elder camper said, fumbling with a pair of binoculars that had gotten tangled up in the neckerchief of his Camper's uniform. He spun the Zoom dial, and looked upward... and dropped down to a whisper. "Right. One player... a woman. Sitting in a branch above. Not looking at us. She could be camping too... pass me the chaingun—no, the crossbow. Gotta be precise, if she gets away she could tell someone we're here..."

"What if she's part of the Alliance, though?" the panicky one asked quietly. "I mean, we have a fourteen out of fifteen chance of friendly fire here... we could get in a lot of trouble!"

"She's not a friend," the elder replied. "Because she's dropping on us right now. Break right."

"What?" the n00b asked, before being neatly cleaved in half.

At least, the flaming blue of Lorelei's plasma blade sliced through the space where the n00b stood—the effect was a little confusing to the eye, as if cutting through a ghost. But the end result was certain, as the younger Camper's body jerked twice, and fell unconscious to the jungle ground.

The elder, which was not nearly as 14m3 as that, rolled right and avoided Lorelei's follow-through attack. He had his +2/+1 Shining Armor Piercing Ice Zipgun out after that, cranking off two wild shots which were parried by the whirling arc of blue fire... before he found the plasma blade positioned right up to his neck, while he was flat on the ground.

"...damn," the Camper said. "You got me, Steel Blade. Not too bad."

He waited for the artificially induced blackness to overtake him. Except it didn't.

"S'matter, don't you want the frag?" he asked, not particularly interested in begging for the life he knew she wouldn't be able to take. "I thought all you Steel Blades were bloodthirsty little psychos..."

The blade twirled once before being powered down.

"Get out of here," Lorelei ordered him.

"Hey, this is my camp site, get your own," the Camper suggested, getting back to his feet. "Either that or fight me for it. That's how it works, isn't it?"

"I'm not in the Steel Blades anymore," Lorelei replied, trying to keep her voice level. "Fine. Camp here. Get your new toy. Just leave me alone."

"An indie fragger? Weekend warrior?" the Camper guessed, trying to make sense of the situation. "Where's your corporate team-building exercise cronies? Or are you just a violence otaku—"

The sound of a silent bullet vanishing in the warp-space around the Camper was, obviously, inaudible. The sound his body made when it hit the ground was not.

And since she had no need to stay stealthy now, her boots made a slight noise when she touched down from her sniping position.

Lorelei watched her, curiously. "What'd you do that for? He was almost interesting."

"Is there a reason I shouldn't have done that?" Kisei asked, with a mild shrug. "It is not as if the end result matters in this place. For that matter, why did you eliminate the other one?"

Lorelei frowned and then furrowed her brow and then looked aside and then softened and then groaned and then slumped and then shook her head in the span of a few seconds. "...I don't know. Just... something in my bones, I guess. It happened all by itself. 'Call of the l33t.'"

"I am familiar with the term, although I don't see any purpose to it outside of a mission structure," Kisei spoke, scanning the surrounding trees for any reinforcements (none). "Speaking of purpose, you had stated your intent to return to the House. When you did not, Meiko suggested I come look for you."

"Yeah... yeah, I know. Sorry. Didn't mean to worry the boss lady, I just... I wanted to think. And I gotta admit, I DO miss the peace and quiet of the jungle. ...relative peace and quiet. And the fighting. I don't know. I guess I'm a hypocrite, but what else is new? ...and I really blew up back there with Mom, huh? Bet Meiko's pissed. Maybe I should've stayed at home..."

"It did not affect the mission one way or another, even if it was an uncontrolled outburst. Meiko is not concerned about it. Although... no, it is of no importance. Come, we should return home."

Letting herself be snagged by the hook, Lorelei allowed herself a grin. "Ohhhh no you don't, Kiss. You don't drop bombs like 'Although, no, never mind' and get away with it. Even the ice queen gets curious sometimes, doesn't she? You're wondering what was really going on back there, weren't you?"

"...perhaps I was, but it does not really matter."

"Too bad, because I feel like telling the sad, sad story anyway," Lorelei said, having a seat on the sleeping bag the Campers had set out. And stealing some of their freshly brewed coffee. "Mmm. C'mon, sit down. The boss won't spank us for coming back a bit late, and the chances of catching me willing to talk about my past are as rare as... well, as rare as you talking about yours, aren't they?"

Kisei considered this a moment... before allowing a moment of weakness, to join Lorelei in sitting down. "Very well. What, exactly, happened between you and your mother?"

"It's not exactly what happened between me and Mommy Dearest," Lorelei corrected. "It's more about a girl I once knew named Rei-Lei."

Rei-Lei was better than her, in all respects of the word except one.

The only advantage Lorelei really had was her lineage. While both came from the same clan, which was supposedly more important than who your mother or father was, Lorelei was the daughter of Kelli and Rei-Lei was born to a couple who hadn't made much of a name for themselves. By contrast, Kelli was an aspiring team leader who had her eye on the leader of leaders role... and with her own fame and success came fame for Lorelei, the child prodigy whom she was preparing for the distant future as a new leader of leaders.

So while Rei-Lei had to use hand-me-down armor from her parents and a simple sword and shield combo (shields being considered fairly lame, as they were somewhat like but not entirely similar to 'Playing Dee') Lorelei got high fashions and the finest weapon crafted by the Steel Blades... a double saber, a twisted blade on either end of a shaft that could be used to attack or parry twice in the same stroke. Lorelei was the shooting star, destined for greatness; Rei-Lei wasn't meant to be anything more than yet another tribe member who gets fragged while patrolling the base...

But whatever blood ran through their veins didn't agree with destiny. Lorelei got her first confirmed frag at age six on a hunt with her mother... Rei-Lei, out on her own after getting lost one day, achieved her first kill at age five. From there on, Lorelei never overtook Rei-Lei on the Ladder of Triumph... Lorelei would score an A on her martial arts, Rei-Lei would score an A+. Lorelei would single-handedly storm the BL00D5KU775 base and capture the flag at age twelve... Rei-Lei would capture three flags in one day from three different tribes with no backup.

Every day she would receive warmth and reassurance from her mother. "Don't worry, Lorelei. You're an outstanding warrior of good stock, with a true passion for the hunt—you'll achieve a title above her one day. I have faith that you will." The sentence sometimes varied, but the meaning was always the same: You'll catch her some day. Mother knows best...

Lorelei did her best to downplay her frustration. Giving in to it and becoming bitter wasn't her style; she wanted to have fun, like any kid. She got along well with her classmates, known as a prankster and a flirt even at a young age (since it seemed to scare the boys, and fear was ideal to strike into the hearts of your enemies), but whenever Rei-Lei was physically in the room... she had to restrain herself. Especially since Rei-Lei loved to talk to her. A typical conversation went as such:

"Lorelei, hello!" the cheerful young warrior would greet her, whenever she happened to catch Lorelei off guard and forgetting to avoid her. "Hey, what did you think of that test on the fifteen sword stances? I'm not sure I got that last one right—"

"Striking Eagle," Lorelei told her, hoping that would end it.

"Really? I wasn't sure, so I figured it looked a bit like the Wild Coyote," Rei-Lei said, walking alongside her classmate. "Sort of a bent left knee, ready to push off with the right leg... you know, sort of a variant? Not that I've seen a coyote before, except on the RealNet streams, but I'd like to see one some day! And, um, listen, if you wanna spar sometime—"

"I'm busy," Lorelei excused, and hurried along...

...because if she DID fight Rei-Lei, she could lose. Final proof of her l4m3ness, despite her mother's pressure, despite her desire to SUCCEED... and that would be the final crushing straw, what with Lorelei's self doubt already built up after years of coming up short. (The test answer was in fact Wild Coyote, for instance...)

For years, it continued without change. Lorelei would hunt by herself, with her team-mates, with the entire tribe... but always with an eye on winning a title, achieving a goal, anything she could hold over Rei-Lei. Rei-Lei, who seemed to achieve everything effortlessly. Rei-Lei, who never mocked her or made fun of her, as much as Lorelei almost wished she would. Rei-Lei, who didn't even seem to understand how amazing she was...

One month before Lorelei's sixteenth birthday, after a particularly smashing social party attended by all her friends and even a few notable political figures within the tribe—with only the finest decorations and entertainment, paid for by Kelli, who had recently been nominated leader of leaders—Lorelei retired to her room to bask in the afterglow of being liked by so many people... and attacked the problem of Rei-Lei with renewed vigor. Specifically, she called up the RealNet terminal in her barracks, loaded the Ladder of Triumph, and ran a search on ANY title or trophy that was as of yet unclaimed by Rei-Lei. No matter how outlandish.

Lo and behold, one existed. It was called the Ultimate 16: number of frags achieved before any warrior born in Tribal Alpha turned sixteen years of age. Currently, Lorelei had 1,976 kills... and Rei-Lei only had 1,845. Rei-Lei had always focused more on achieving her amazing scores via flag captures than via personal kills—a weak point. But the Ultimate 16 record, set by some kid fifty-seven years ago, was 2,032 kills... and Lorelei only had one month to make up the difference...

Which she would do. It would be one title she could hold over her rival's head, one that her mother would praise her for. Her destiny fulfilled, and motherly praise by the bucketful...

A knock at her door distracted her. She had forgotten to lock the door...

And Rei-Lei entered, carrying a wrapped gift.

"Lorelei, hello!" she greeted, as usual. "I'm so sorry I'm late... nobody told me you were having a big party! I guess my invitation got lost or the messenger got fragged... but don't worry, I got you an early birthday gift! It's a small buckler; I saved up for weeks to buy it for you. You don't have any defensive armor, you know, and my shield's gotten me out of more scrapes than... what're you looking at?"

"*Nothing,*" Lorelei emphasized in as many italicized letters as she could manage... but not fast enough, as Rei-Lei peeked around her at the screen.

"Ultimate 16...? I didn't know there was a title for that! Cool! Hey, I've got an idea; wanna compete for it?" Rei-Lei asked, all smiles. "I'm really behind, so I don't know if I could catch up, but... it might be fun! And you could use your new shield; I bet it'll help you a lot!"

Since Lorelei couldn't think up a solid reason not to, she had to concede to the competition. The urge to scream, to yell at Rei-Lei after so many years of trying to be polite and avoid her had built up... but not far enough. Not yet.

The competition was on. Lorelei fought harder than she had ever fought before; she went on no team hunts, nothing that could score points for anybody else. It was her against the world. She tore through tribe after tribe, unconscious warriors strewn in her wake... some fortresses razed completely to the ground. She wasn't after the flags; she was after the kills. Once word got around of a crazy girl who was tearing apart tribes with no desire for the flags, defenses were boosted... which simply gave Lorelei more people up front to kill.

She kept a portable ladder-checker with her at all times. It was tuned to measure her frag count, and that of her rival. The numbers were not good; somehow, Rei-Lei had come up from behind quickly. Lorelei fought tooth and nail but couldn't overcome. The deadline, her sixteenth birthday and the final score of 2,032 crept closer and closer...

Once, Lorelei considered folding. But her mother, who knew of the quest, wouldn't let her.

"This is for your honor, Lorelei," Kelli explained in her I'm Talking Serious voice, which was just as soft as her usual voice but somehow more potent. "This is your chance to catch her. If you give up now, you'll never know if you could do it... you'll be a quitter. Now, I don't like to think that I raised a quitter. Fight with everything you have, and I know you'll do it, and then I'll throw you the grandest birthday party you've ever seen!"

The bodies hit the floor in greater numbers after that. Neck and neck the girls raced, despite never crossing paths; Lorelei made a point not to hunt anywhere Rei-Lei was hunting. No interference, no cherry-picking her rival's targets; this would be a battle won on her own strength. One week from the deadline, one week from the goal...

And Rei-Lei's score stopped increasing.

Lorelei didn't give a second thought to why this would happen. She didn't think if Rei-Lei got hurt or if anything was wrong; all that mattered was burning her name into the Ladder of Triumph. The game was everything. She slept in the jungle like a Camper, never returning home, spending every hour she could stay awake tracking and killing other players. Numbers scaled, higher and higher...

2,032.

For kicks, she killed two more before returning home. 2,034.

The party was phenomenal; Kelli had gone all out, pulling every string, cashing in every favor she had with the elders of the Steel Blades. One of their own had taken one of the legendary titles of Tribal Alpha, and Lorelei became a local hero. Heroine. And such. Gifts, praise, friends looking a bit jealous, cute boys wanting to date her just to be associated with a superstar, people who didn't really care about her pretending to admire her...

And her mother's love, at last. Victory.

But something was eating at her. It took a few days to figure out what it is, and even then, she only got it sorted out after noticing Rei-Lei's score hadn't climbed one single digit since it stopped cold.

For the first time, Lorelei sought out Rei-Lei, rather than the other way around. It took some time to track her down, as she hadn't been home in a while... the two met at last on a rocky cliff overlooking the jungles that the Steel Blades 0wned. And for a change, Lorelei was the first one to speak.

"I won the Ultimate 16, you know," she pointed out... secretly hoping it would hurt the other girl.

Instead, Rei-Lei reacted with distracted indifference. "You did?" she asked, without moving her gaze from the landscape. "Good for you. I'm glad you could achieve it."

"Why'd you stop?" Lorelei asked, trying to sound merely curious instead of desperately curious. "You had a fighting chance. Not as fighting of one as I did, of course, being so totally l33t, but you could've come close... but you stopped. I was tracking your score. What happened?"

Rei-Lei gave a little shrug. "Nothing, I just... left, for a while."

"Left?"

"Offworld. I went to Urbana. A friend on RealNet suggested I needed some 'fresh air'. So I went to Urbana, then to Nocturn... even visited Nippon for a bit... I forgot about the competition. I'm sorry I couldn't play, but... I guess I lost interest..."

"You... lost... interest," Lorelei spoke, trying to restrain herself. "You just stopped. You gave up... before I could find out if I had FINALLY, really, truly beaten you..."

"Oh, is that why you wanted the title? I'm sorry, I thought it was just a friendly thing, like the other times we competed—"

"There as NOTHING friendly about it, dammit!" Lorelei hissed, finally losing it after so many years. "Do you have any concept of how long I've been chasing you? How hard it was to measure up to you and come up short when I was SUPPOSED to be better? How can you just lose interest, like... like it didn't mean anything to you, when it damn well meant something to me? How could you do that to me?!"

Yell back, Lorelei thought. *Yell at me. Mock me. Insult me. Or cry. Or bow and scrape. Or just do something...*

Instead, Rei-Lei studied Lorelei in silence... with those eyes. Eyes that almost took pity on her, a quiet, sad sort of pity that didn't intend to insult.

"I'm sorry," Rei-Lei replied. "But there's more important things in life than this silly game."

"MORE IMPORT—"

"That's what I was finding out, out there," Rei-Lei explained. "Out there, the first frag is the final frag. We all know that, but it's different to really live that way... it makes life mean so much more. There's so much out there that's so wonderful, and so scary, and even the scary stuff is kinda wonderful when you've never really been afraid before... and I made friends, and I had new experiences, and it was all so strange to me... and the game felt so silly in comparison. I'm told that I've done some great things in the game, but out there, none of that mattered to anyone. And after a day or two it didn't really matter to me anymore. I just... forgot about the competition. I'm sorry."

Alien. That's how it felt: completely alien. Lorelei didn't know if she should be enraged, shocked, sad, angry, or what...

"I'm going to leave Tribal Alpha for a while," her "rival" continued. "Do you want to come with me? You've always been a good friend to me, you know, one of the few friends I really had here. I want to show you the things I've found. Maybe then you'd understand—"

Lorelei was never sure why she ran away then. But she did run, and run all the way back home, entering the Steel Blades fortress in tears. Through sobs, she explained what had happened to her mother...

...who was upset at the news as well, in her quiet sort of way. "I had... no idea Rei-Lei was completely without honor," Kelli had concluded. "To cast aside the glory of the hunt, to trivialize it like that... don't doubt your heart, Lorelei. You won that title. If she gave up, then that means you are better than her. She's shown her true colors now; it doesn't matter what her score would have been if she hadn't stopped. You're the finest warrior in the Steel Blades Tribe, and whatever she says about that doesn't matter—"

"It doesn't matter," Lorelei repeated.

"Right. It doesn't—"

"None of it matters," Lorelei spoke, sobs slowing as realization spread across her like a dawn. "I spent weeks fighting and fighting and fighting and... and for what? Numbers on a computer? Some stupid title? I didn't see my friends, I didn't flirt with anyone, I wasn't... I was just fighting all the time..."

"That's what a warrior does, dear. We fight. Our honor—"

"WHAT honor?" Lorelei spat back, pushing away from her mother. "It's not soldiers in a war, this is... this is a GAME, Mother! It's just a game! Nobody really dies, nobody really gets hurt, we just keep going at it and going at it to get bigger points and see who's more l33t! It's not living. I watch the RealNet streams too, you know! There's more out there and I never left because I was so busy trying to rack up glory, and... and for what? She stopped! I never beat her! And she doesn't even CARE that I was trying to beat her, it wasn't important to her, so... so why should it be important to me?!"

And her mother got stern. Truly stern. "Because it's important to me. It's important to your family, this tribe. This is what we do, we fight for glory! I didn't raise a quitter, did I? You've proven yourself, and you'll keep proving yourself, and one day you'll be the leader of leaders—"

"Of a bunch of spoiled game players who aren't even alive! Forget it. Forget it! If she's going to have more than that out of life, then... then I want that too! I want to live out there. I'm leaving. I'm packing and I'm leaving tonight!"

"You're going NOWHERE, young lady," her mother spoke with pure ice. "You're hysterical, and you're in no frame of mind to be making decisions like that. Besides, I won't let you leave. You're too important to the tribe and—"

The dim light of the fortress gleamed off Lorelei's steel double saber. The weapon given to her as the favored daughter.

"I'm leaving," she iterated. "Around you or through you. If you really cared about me you'd let me do this. I'm tired of playing this stupid game... I'm leaving with Rei... I'm leaving with my friend."

"...you would dare fight your own mother?"

"Would you fight your own daughter?"

Tension.

And Lorelei would never know why her mother then stepped aside, without a word. All she saw was her exit, and took it, leaving her weapon behind.

The coffee pot was empty, and the Campers had respawned somewhere far, far away by that point.

"You wouldn't believe how much my life changed after that... and stayed exactly the same, kinda," Lorelei said, after finishing her last cup. "I guess I'm just a walking contradiction... I learned to see the game as being a waste of my time, but here I am carving up Campers for kicks... anyway, after I left, I was still picking fights in bars and generally living free and wild. Old hobbies are hard to break, you know. It felt okay to me, since I wasn't shooting for some meaningless goal, I was just doing my own thang. If anything, it was one of those positive, life-affirming things to brawl for myself instead of for the Ladder of Triumph. Thankfully whenever I got too crazy, Rei-Lei was there to act as a guardian angel and keep me from experiencing the Final Frag... she's the only real friend I had. Thanks to her, I became the jovial, well-adjusted social delinquent you see today instead of the bitter and awkward social delinquent I was before. It took a whole year to adjust properly to life outside —after that, Rei-Lei left to pursue her own interests, and I took on a job bodyguarding for Mirai Consulting in order to pay the bar tabs and do something constructive with my itchy trigger fingers. As they say, although I'm not clear on who 'they' are, that was that."

Kisei, who possessed a keen analytical mind, needed no additional time to reflect and respond. "So, although you are still an impulsive risk-taker with a weak sense of self-preservation, it is superior to your prior state of being a player in a game. I suppose I can understand how this small upgrade would please you so."

"I'm going to take that as a compliment," Lorelei decided, "Since I know that's as high a level of praise as you can manage. And believe me, small upgrade or not, it saved me. If she hadn't... ten yards behind you, target but don't fire."

Kisei went from sitting on the ground to lying flat with her sniper rifled locked and ready in 0.6 seconds.

The target made her presence obvious after that, walking into the clearing with both arms raised. "Obviously, I mean you no harm, Lorelei..."

The coffee pot iced over when the temperature around Lorelei dropped a few significant digits. "Mother," she acknowledged.

"I've come to talk," Kelli said. "Not be shot at. Just talk. If you're willing to listen, of course..."

"I said all I had to say earlier. Don't waste your time and mine. Kisei and I have to get back to the House now—"

"You don't know the whole situation, Lorelei. You wouldn't be so dismissive of this problem if you knew the truth. All I ask is five minutes... is that too much, my daughter...?"

The D-word. Lorelei flinched... and nodded to Kisei, a silent signal. The sniper quietly stood, shouldered her sniper rifle, and walked off into the jungle.

"You've got four minutes and fifty two seconds," Lorelei said. "Start now."

A bit more relaxed, Kelli downshifted to her usual soft voice. "I understand you've come to a... philosophical disagreement with the hunt," her mother selected from any number of more accurate terms. "I will admit I'm a bit disappointed... but why do you think I stepped aside and let you go those years ago, Lorelei?"

For this, the younger hunter didn't have a snappy response. "...I still don't know. But I'll bite. Why?"

"Love. Simple as that. I love you, and no matter what road you choose in life, I'll support you. Even if I disagree with the road you chose... I knew then when you dared to raise a weapon to me that you were passionate about your choice. How could I deny you that? What kind of a mother would I be if I tried to force you to stay?"

"Flowery. I'm not sure I believe it, but it's flowery—"

"Do you still love me?"

Lorelei gritted her teeth. "Mom..."

"If I haven't completely lost you, daughter... then you'll want to help us," Kelli spoke. "Because the situation is much worse than you're thinking. This is not just a matter of tribal war, it's something much more personal to you... you left before I could tell you, but... the Alliance was formed by someone you know very well. Rei-Lei is responsible for this."

At that, she laughed out loud. "Rei-Lei. Rei. LEI. Oh, mom, come ON. She —"

"When did you see her last, Lorelei? Two years ago, perhaps a bit more? I know that because she came back to Tribal Alpha soon after," her mother continued. "Once she arrived, she formally left the Steel Blades to form her own tribe: the 'Final Strike'. They quickly began drawing allies, and one year later, the Alliance was formalized. They crushed tribe after tribe, pushing enemies to the bottom of the ladder and chasing them out of Tribal Alpha... frightening times, Lorelei. We were aggressive and proud, yes, but these new ones fought like demons. Like zealots following their leader..."

"This is a real yarn you're spinning, mom. Rei-Lei would never take part in the games again."

"Just like you would never take part again?" Kelli asked. "The jungle talks. It says you fragged a Camper today. If you could slip back in, hearing the call of the l33t, what makes you think she couldn't revert to her ways? This is the same warrior who achieved dozens of titles and trophies, more than you ever did... why would her fighting again be so inconceivable? A person can change a lot in a short amount of time... as you have proven, I believe."

"All right, I'll play this game. Let's assume she's actually running this show, even if I don't believe it," Lorelei hypothesized. "And let's assume that she's somehow turned into a psycho. So what? The end result's the same; you're gonna get purged, and I'm not fighting your war for you. Once it's all over, you either join them, or you leave here. I've left here, it's quite a nice experience. Might do you some good—oh, but wait, you're planning to die honorably, aren't you? Think you can really live up to that? I doubt all the Steel Blades are willing to play lemming, even if you are..."

"We also have word that the Final Strike plans to kill us once the grace period is over."

"...what?"

"Even if you don't believe me about Rei-Lei, and even if we decide not to die with dignity, chances are high that we'll never survive long enough to run," Kelli explained calmly. "All they have to do is surround the docking yards, and we'll have no means of escaping this reality. I can't emphasize this enough, Lorelei: we are the hunted here, not the hunters. Believe what you want, but know this—if this situation does not end, if one way or another our warp-bubbles are deactivated, the losses may be great. Yes, I myself intend to die honorably against these aggressors, and perhaps others do not, but in this state of chaos there will be blood one way or another... and it will be something you could have prevented."

"And... and now you're guilt-tripping me. That's low, Mom. Real low..."

"All I'm doing is telling you the facts. The Steel Blades are weak, Lorelei. Our numbers have dwindled, and the constant Dee has exhausted us. You know that while I'm skilled, I alone am not enough to make up the score difference to save us... the only one who can get us out of this hole is the one who earned so many frags in such a short time. The winner of the Ultimate 16..."

"I'm... I'm NOT fighting for you!" Lorelei repeated, frustration mounting... and her will starting to weaken. "I can't say that any more ways than... and... even if you were going to die, it... dammit, Mother, this is not a comfy position you're putting me in here! Yes, yes, I don't want you to die. We have bad blood here but... okay. Yes. I love you. Happy? But don't bring me back into this, Mom..."

"It's your choice," Kelli spoke. "Just as it was when you left. I support your decision either way... but you have to be aware of the consequences. If you do nothing, who knows how this will end? If you fight for us... just this one time... then we'll have another month to fight, regain our standing, or even find alternatives. Lorelei... I know this is hard for you. But I beg you, please... do this for us. For your TRUE family..."

From a leather holster on her back, Kelli produced a weapon... a twisted pair of blades, flawless shining steel. It had been forged years ago, but had been kept in pristine condition.

"Your blade," she said, holding it with both hands, holding it out to her daughter. "I kept it all these years. It's time for you to take up the hunt again, hopefully forever, but even if it's just this once you'll have done the honorable thing."

Lorelei's anger and fire died down considerably, memories flooding back of her days with that cold blade. "...Mom... I don't know... this whole thing is so damned confusing. I hate being confused..."

"There's a cluster of Alliance fortresses half a mile east from here... knowing you, raiding the outer ones will give you enough points. Go for quick kills and flag captures, full offense. There's a respawn point nearby if you slip; I know you've been fragged ninety-nine times and swore you'd never lose again, but be realistic when you fight. It's our way to play the rules of death to our advantage. Above all, avoid the central base; that's where Rei-Lei is, and it's the most guarded. Speed is of the essence, not the challenge of cracking a strong base... Lorelei, this is all I ask. Once more into the breach, for your family. Will you do it...?"

The young hunter did not take up her old weapon.

Instead, she twirled her more modern plasma saber to the ready, both ends flaring with a blue fire that burned like the ice in her voice.

"Fine. I'll get involved," she confirmed. "But only because this situation is too fuxx0red to ignore while hoping for the best... if ANYTHING you're saying is true, then there's a chance someone could die. I know for certain Meiko wouldn't want that, and... I wouldn't, either. But I'll do this *my* way. I want no backup. I don't want you interfering. If I have to dive back into the fray once more I'll dive on my own terms. And then I'm leaving. Agreed?"

With an honest look of relief, mother offered daughter a smile. "That's all I ask of you, Lorelei. And... hopefully when you finish, we can talk, and patch things up...? But I leave it to you. Remember; strike hard and fast at the perimeter. Trust my strategy on this one and you'll have proven your worth to the Steel Blades..."

"Whatever."

Without another word, she turned and marched eastward into the jungle. She didn't need a compass, or even to look up at the sky; this was her stomping ground. This was Steel Blades territory, and the years hadn't erased it fully from her memory...

Which is why she knew she was being watched without actually seeing her watcher. The shape of the jungle felt wrong at one point.

"Well?" Lorelei asked, speaking up.

"Well what?" the voice from the trees asked.

"Weren't you going back to your room to scribble in that book of yours?" Lorelei asked. "Or to report to the boss?"

Kisei emerged from nearly nowhere. No stealth technology, simply m4d h1d1ng sk1llz.

"I meant no offense in regards to overhearing your conversation," she replied. "My apologies. However, I was thinking I would accompany you."

"Really. Aaaand, what interest do you have in this?"

"None. The squabbles of outsiders are not my concern," Kisei said simply. "Nevertheless, as Meiko Mirai's retainer, this is now a mission goal for me. The chance to train a bit, even if within the boundaries of a meaningless game, would also be welcome."

"You really think Meiko would approve of this, then? Us rolling maverick style without checking in and getting our marching orders? I was figuring you'd turn me in, not join me, frankly..."

It took Kisei a moment and a half to admit it. "It is highly unlikely Meiko Mirai would approve. She would prefer negotiation. Likely we will be punished for taking solitary action, but I have my own reasons for this act which I choose not to disclose at this time."

"Huh. You're breaking character quite a bit today, Kisei. I'm impressed. Fine, why not—tag along if you like. They might want a piece of your hide too, frankly; we'll likely not be welcome after we bagged two Campers, so expect a lynching party, not a welcoming party... but above all, don't drag me down with that slow-loading rifle of yours. I don't hide in shadows like a l4m3r Camper, Miss Sniper. "

"You do what you do, and I will do what I will do," Kisei replied, almost but not quite precisely cracking a smile. "That is all the coordination we need."

"Heh. Deal. This could actually be a bit of fun... you know I like to fight. Call of the l33t, I guess. Oh, and in case you overheard Mommy's strategy too, there's going to be a little change in plans..."

Quiet is not good for a guard. Quiet means that you're currently knee-deep in the long stretch of time between loud moments; loud you could deal with, since it was in your face and obvious and demanded reaction. Quiet meant trying to avoid falling asleep waiting for the action.

One of the two guards outside the central fortress of the Alliance was already asleep; the other stayed alert, but did it in a very bored sort of way. He had been working for the Final Strike Tribe for months now, and while the initial fury of suppression was enjoyable (even if it wasn't supposed to be) this quiet time was getting on his nerves. Here there was a huge clearing flattened in front of the central fort, with perimeter forts to take down any incoming armies, and he had to play door guard against a battered Steel Blades force that likely would never come...

Then he saw the might of the invading squadron. Or rather, the single woman carrying a Steel Blades-style double saber who was calmly and casually strolling on up to the gates. Interesting...

It took her three minutes of crossing the open field to get there. On arrival, she jogged to a halt, and studied him head to toe.

"Steel Blade?" he asked. "And from the looks of it, the one who bagged Rick and Nelson of the Campers an hour ago. Word got around about that little stunt, you know, but nobody expected you to show your face again..."

"Ah, yes, the rumor mill," Lorelei spoke, fond memories returning. "I had forgotten that it moves at the speed of frag... well, this makes my job a little harder. But not much... any chance of me peacefully walking in and rapping with the fragger in charge over a couple of beers?"

"No. Let's get on with this," the guard spoke, drawing his rifle. "I'd been hoping I'd see some action before the final campaign was all over... now, where's the rest of your running buddies?"

Puffing out her ample chest, Lorelei spoke with pride. "I am an *army of one!*"

Both the sleeping guard and the wide awake guard dropped to the ground unconscious after their warp bubbles ate a pair of sniper rounds.

"...okay, maybe an army of two," Lorelei admitted after the fact.

With a whirl of her blades, a hole was neatly carved in the central fortress of the Final Strike Tribe, and she was ready to get down to business the hard way. Why did they always pick the hard way?

This is a nice base, Lorelei thought while absently fighting off seven men at once. The walls were perfect for bounding off of for backflip attacks, the ceiling was just the right height for the leaping spin slashes. Whoever constructed it really knew a thing or two about action-packed hand-to-hand martial arts sequences—this was a place you fought in not just to kill the other guy, but to do it in STYLE.

Like the network of pipes built into the ceiling—perfect for getting a handhold on and doing a flipping spin kick that takes down three guys at once. Or the tile floors, the way they had just enough traction for a good footing, but also were smooth enough to do a sliding dash along. The three guys who would be missing their legs if not for the warp bubbles probably would agree that the just-right level of floor buffing gave Lorelei's attack a little extra 'Wow!' factor.

Of course, it was also designed well to provide places to snipe. Lorelei could tell because every now and then, some guy who she had neglected to knock into next week would try to get the jump on her—and be pegged instantly by the silent 'pang' of a sniper round. Not that Kisei was ever visible; she simply moved from spot to spot with absolute silence and flawless stealth. Lorelei didn't mind losing the spotlight too much, since she was a little rusty at taking on an entire army at once, and whatever slack she didn't pick up Kisei was putting away with ruthless efficiency.

After her 32nd frag, Lorelei was truly enjoying herself. (She didn't mind fighting this way; it wasn't for some silly ladder goal, it was just for fun. If anything, it was cleaner fun, since other than some hurt feelings all the guys she cut to ribbons would be A-OK.) The deeper she got into the compound, the cooler the scenery got. There were stairway railings for the bodies to be knocked over. There were warning klaxons and spinning red alarm lights to give the place the right ambiance. And the pièce de résistance, the finishing touch... large machines that seemed to hold no purpose whatsoever except to spout great roaring flames! PURPOSELESS FLAMES!

She was almost disappointed when she got the flag room to confront the boss character. That meant it was almost over. It also meant she had to stop fighting, once she found out who the boss was.

"You know, I really didn't believe her," Lorelei admitted, staying in a defensive stance while squaring off with the only one left to guard the flag. "I had to see with my own eyes. Sorry about the mess, but I'll admit, this place kicks incredible amounts of ass... my compliments, Rei-Lei. Hold back, Kiss, she's mine..."

Sword and shield. Her best friend for one full year, and the misdirected years before that...

Of course, Rei-Lei didn't look happy to be reunited like this.

"I'm not happy to be reunited like this," she admitted. "When I heard that you were back, I was hoping it wouldn't come to this..."

"Come to what, exactly? Me cutting you down before you have a chance to stomp my tribe... and my mother... into foamy red oblivion?" Lorelei asked, ready to attack.... but not attacking. "Or us sitting down and talking about this like the friends I'm hoping we still are, so I can get a better picture of what's going on here?"

Rei-Lei's sword dipped a bit. "Talk...? But... you just cut through all my defenses—"

"Your minions put out the Unwelcome Mat, what did you expect me to do? And you know damn well none of that matters. You taught me as much that this game was meaningless. So, I had a little fun on the way in—are you taking the 'honor of the hunt' seriously enough to really be upset about that? Call it a test I set up for you: if you're angry, and you want to strike me down to avenge your... excuse me... 'fallen brothers', then I guess Mommy was right about you. What's it gonna be, Rei?"

A dangerous pause locked the action in freeze frame, before...

The body tumbled over the side, limbs flailing wildly as it plunged towards certain death.

"Get down, get down! Incoming fire!" the squad leader shouted, dropping low but keeping his machine gun high. "Eat this, you psycho bitch!"

The Evil Super Spy Vixen McViolent™ wagged a finger, hand on one hip in a dominatrix sort of way. "Eiko-chan, you know I don't like you using that sort of language... and where did you get this doll, anyway...?"

Muscles Manslaughter™ pouted, letting his scale replica green plastic M-60 go quiet. "But oneesama, I'm just trying to 'keep it real'! Real soldiers curse a lot. Isn't that right, Mallory?"

From the bottom of the sofa-cliff, Kensuke™ deadly replied, "Uh, I really don't know anything about that sort of thing, so uh, I'll go with Meiko on this one..."

"I'm hooooome! And I bring bounty from the hunt!"

The trio of doll-playing pretend-warmongers looked up at the extremely tardy ex-Steel Blader walking through the front door like she owned the place which in fact she did not. And Kisei entered, too.

"What kept you?" Meiko asked, letting it become public knowledge that she was irritated. "Please tell me you simply wanted some time by yourself, and you were not actually doing something that I'm going to regret..."

"I wanted some time by myself, and I did something that you're not going to regret," Lorelei announced, curling a 'come-hither' finger to Meiko as she strolled into the kitchen. "Check this out, guys, I think I've found the solution to this little situation..."

The Housefolk gathered around the table... while Lorelei rolled out a battered, dusty old document. It was once laid down in white ink on dark blue paper by a machine printer, but now it was faded and blurry.

"Ladies and gentlemen, I give you: The ServOps Center," Lorelei explained. "One fully automated, computer-controlled nerve center for the entire reality. In charge of reality generation, warp bubble control, weapon dump and food dump respawns... and long time ago, someone built this thing to keep the gears turning forever. Why? Who knows? But thankfully for us, they wrote down an exact schematic of the building, including labelling each of the many wonderful devices. And THIS blob here, if I'm not mistaken, controls the Ladder of Triumph. Why fight a war for the Steel Blades when we can slip in, monkey with the machine, and put an end to this without a single non-drop of blood non-spilled?"

"You're proposing we hack the scoreboard?" Meiko asked. "I see. That would work."

Lorelei nudged the quiet Kisei with an elbow. "I TOLD you she'd go for it..."

"I didn't say I'm going for it, I said it would work," the bosslady noted. "In fact, I'm not going for it. Where did you get this blueprint, Lorelei? I doubt you simply picked it up somewhere."

"I did too pick it up somewhere!"

"Where, exactly?"

"In a Final Strike Tribe flag room guarded by two hundred guys, of course," Lorelei said, with some pride. "Kisei and I took 'em out en route. We were quite l33t indeed."

Groaning, Meiko rolled her eyes to give Kisei a sideways glare. "I thought you were going to find her and keep her OUT of trouble, Kisei..."

Oddly enough (for her, at least) Kisei paused a moment before replying. "I have ensured she did nothing to embarrass you or sabotage your efforts, Miss Mirai. Please forgive my leniency in judgement of her actions, but I felt as long as I accompanied her, I could simply hit her with a stun round and bring her home if she put your operations at actual risk."

Lorelei stared a bit, as well. "So THAT'S why you agreed...? Damn, Kiss, I've underestimated you..."

"I must also admit... the... methodology she's employing right now is questionable to me, but... ...Miss Mirai. In the past, you have suggested I turn to Tachi's teachings when I have doubt about the ethics of an issue. I assure you, today I am doing just that. If you have faith in that judgement, then you should not worry yourself about this plan."

"Right, right, don't worry," Lorelei spoke, trying to get things back on subject before they got messy. "See, I did some investigation of my own, to get down to what's really going on around here... it seems they were planning to use it for their own purposes to stop the Steel Blades once and for all. Unfortunately, they lacked a key we have, so they took Plan B: Bludgeoning the Blades into non-existence... but at any rate, figuring this was worth its weight in gold, I took their map and skipped back here to present you with it. Shazam! What's not to go for? It's the kind of quick and clean job you like to take, isn't it?"

"This is not quick, nor is it clean," Meiko spoke. "For starters, this is breaking and entering in addition to tampering with a secured system. That might go above and beyond the call of duty for this mission; I'm not sure I'd want to incur a legal risk, even against an ancient, purely automated—"

"C'MON, Meiko. This is the way to do it! The way to do it your way. All I need are two things... and one is the go-ahead from you. I'll plan the operation and execute it, you don't even have to step outside the House."

"...and the other thing?"

Lorelei scratched her head. She knew this would be the hard sell point. "Well... it's like this. The Final Strike couldn't act on this without a key to get in. We've got that key. Since the system is completely automated, the only people with authorization to enter at any time are fix-it guys who keep the thing from crashing... in other words... certified Reality Engineers."

Everybody looked at Mallory, who was busy trying to put Kensuke's plastic arm back in its plastic socket.

"Uh... what?" he asked, feeling like a big, juicy steak in front of a crack squadron of antivegetarians.

The one-eyed security camera bore a hole through Mallory's head. Or at least it felt like that to him, as he broke out into cold sweats and stammered his way through the prepared speech (badly).

"I-I'm performing a su-surprise... a... an inspection!!" he declared, holding up the Officially Certified RealWare Reality Engineer Identification Card that Mr. Tanner left for him the other night. "As an officiallyregisteredrealityengineer I... I'm going to make sure you won't break down and go boom!"

The computerized voice circuits beeped and blooped. "Error: 'Go Boom' unrecognized phrase. Inspection period established for bi-weekly Thursdays from first of every Urbana Standard Calendar Year. State reason for schedule non-adherence."

"Look, compute THIS, okay?" Lorelei asked, glancing sideways to make sure they were still alone out here. "If you were capable of tuning your Reality Engine yourself, you wouldn't need an engineer. That means if you were capable of sensing an impending system crash yourself before it hits and you gotta call in an emergency... you wouldn't need surprise inspections. But you can't, so you don't, so we're here, so let us in already. Comprendo?"

"Error: 'Comprendo' unrecognized—"

"Do... you... understand?" Lorelei spoke clearly and distinctly (and slowly).

The stainless steel door slid open slowly, hundred-year-old mechanisms whining and grinding as the portal to heaven made way for two impostors.

"Please remember to leave copy receipt and work order in standard memory cube format after finishing work, Reality Engineer," the computer spoke, before the camera resumed its normal left to right security panning.

Mallory's shoulders drooped, the tension no longer keeping him rigidly upright. "...thought... we were doomed for a second there..."

"Shush, and c'mon," Lorelei urged. "We've gotta work fast here..."

Into the door they went, down the halls according to the ancient map. Corridors of computer banks and bits of machinery... clearly designed by humans, as control panels stood at waist height, but with caked-on layers of dust and grime that belied years of disuse. The lights provided enough illumination to find their way, even if the flickering could grow maddening to anybody not legally blind...

This is it, Lorelei thought. *The reason behind it all...* and inside, it was just a big, shiny toy game. A toy game that granted its players little cookies to keep them playing, gave them tools to play with, and never, ever stopped playing. If there was a meaning behind it, a reason it all got started, whoever built the place didn't leave any clues behind.

She largely ignored Mallory's jittery nerves, following the path burned into her memory, not even needing to look down at the map. Within a minute, they were at the heart of the heart of Tribal Alpha... the ServOps Control Room.

"O... okay, here we are," Mallory spoke, taking the map and trying to sound authoritative. (It was HIS credentials that got them here, after all.) He walked from distinctly separate machine to distinctly separate machine, identifying them off the map as none bore distinctive labels. "'Food Negotiation Unit...'"

"Even hunters gotta eat," Lorelei pointed out. "No animals here to hunt for food other than human animals. The system buys food over RealNet and has merchants bring it in; I've seen 'em dock now and then. And that's not what we're looking for, so let's move on, mmkay?"

"Right, right. Um... Weapon Negotiation Unit... Respawn Point Reality Tunneler... ah, there's the Reality Engine, okay... and that makes that the Warp Bubble Generator... and... here!"

Mallory tapped a fancy looking box, with a series of numbers lit up above it in a holographic display. The Ladder of Triumph... normally viewable from fortress workstations with fancy graphics and tribe logos and shiny 3-D trophies. But once those were boiled away, it was really just numbers in a box...

"All right, now... how do we change the scores to make the Steel Blades rule again?" Mallory asked. "You told Meiko you had an idea how to do that, but I don't see any keyboard or buttons or anything..."

"Right, right... well... technically, yes, I know how to change the scores."

"Oh, good. How do we do it?"

The dimly lit room flared with blue light, as the plasma fields snapped into being at either end of a double saber... and the blades slashed diagonally through the Ladder of Triumph.

Mallory screamed and jumped away, as the machine kicked up sparks from exposed wires, emitted a series of screeching electronic tones... and died. The hologram flickered out, random numbers skittering through the air before they all reset to a hard zero and gave up the ghost.

"I didn't tell Meiko WHAT I was gonna change the scores to. 'No score for anybody' feels very appropriate to me. To me, and to Rei-Lei," Lorelei explained... with a smile across her lips, one that had been a long time in the making. Twenty years of her life, to be precise.

"WHAAA?!" Mallory yelled. "Lorelei, what did you DO?! Meiko's gonna kill us! She—"

"The Reality Engine's not linked up to this thing in any mission critical sort of way, right?" Lorelei asked, calmly striding over to a machine and tapping it with her finger. "You've got a sixth sense about this stuff, yes? Tell me. Now. Yes or no. Will knocking this offline crash Tribal Alpha?"

So deep into panic that he was oddly calm, Mallory shook his head numbly. "...it won't crash, no..."

Lorelei's smile jacked up an extra inch.

"Goody."

In one spinning blow, she took the Warp Bubble Generator out forever.

Future generations of the original tribes would look up to their parents and their grandparents, after a long day at school, and ask: Where were you when it changed?

Answers would vary, of course. Nobody was fighting; the Steel Blades were holed up in their fortress, the Alliance were waiting to hear the results of their new agent's mission. Some would be eating, or sleeping, or simply sitting around... but they all heard the same thing, a warning klaxon across the entire reality and the voice of the ServOp Center. Instead of declaring who had captured the flag this time, it had a very different message to convey.

"WARNING. END ALL HOSTILITIES NOW. Reality Warp Bubble Generator has been deactivated. All frags after this point will be 100% fatal. Repeat: End all hostilities now. Please contact Dr. Aaron Bates for routine service. Thank you."

And that would be the last thing the ServOp Center voice would ever say.

After that, all the tribes that had gathered in the Jungle Quadrant for the Campaign to End All Campaigns (as it would be called in history books) made the trek to the ServOp Center at great speed. This was something that concerned them all; everyone who could get there in time did so. And this is what they saw:

The one who was called Lorelei (the Prodigal Daughter of Tribal Alpha, the Vengeance of the Tribes) with some nameless, uninteresting-looking boy emerging from the ServOp Center, smoke billowing out of the door behind them. A contingent of three that had come with the Prodigal Daughter arrived shortly after; and then Rei-Lei of the Final Strike, then Kelli of the Steel Blades...

"Lorelei..." Meiko spoke, trying to restrain her anger. "You had... BETTER... have a good reason for lying to me today."

"Eh? Lie? I never lied," Lorelei said, almost smug in her confidence. "I said I'd find a peaceful end to the problem. And I did! Okay, so I destroyed the entire machine Tribal Alpha's been yoked to for hundreds of years, but it's a peaceful end, yes?"

If Meiko was upset, Kelli was absolutely livid with rage. "You... YOU... MY DAUGHTER, you've killed us all!!" she accused. "Frags are no longer safe! People will die! I thought you didn't want any blood spilled? We discussed this! We had an agreement!"

"I had an agreement to get you out of this problem, and I did, Mom. I think in time you'll understand why. I can see you're a little too upset to talk about this rationally, so if you'll excuse me, I'm going home to have a victory drinking binge—"

"We are exposed to them! They'll kill us all—"

That broke Lorelei's good cheer... as she snapped into a snarling, angry mood. "Mom, QUIT BULLSHITTING ME! I didn't believe you for one minute, and it's a good thing I didn't. Meiko, Kelli's snowed you completely. The Alliance weren't trying to crush the Steel Blades out of jealousy, or dominance, or anything like that. They were trying to get rid of the only ones left on Tribal Alpha who didn't want to declare a reality-wide TRUCE! Rei-Lei? Tag in here, I'm not in the mood to explain anything..."

Rei-Lei approached Meiko quickly, ignoring Kelli's silent mumbles of absolute loathing. "For the last two years, I've been spreading the concept of shutting down the ServOp Center and turning Tribal Alpha in a 'normal' reality," she explained, speaking quickly. "I was surprised at how many tribes agreed with me, were tired of the games and wanted to live a peaceful life at last. A few smaller, newer tribes disagreed, and we had to suppress them using the purges—chasing them out of Tribal Alpha, letting them leave peacefully. It was a Campaign to End All Campaigns; once all who believed in peace were all that was left, we'd disarm and live different lives. But the Steel Blades refused—"

"She wanted to destroy our honorable way of life! Everything we've fought for would be meaningless!" Kelli protested.

"It was meaningless to begin with!" Rei-Lei fired back. "All those titles and trophies and accomplishments were pointless! Everybody in Tribal Alpha except YOU and some young punks who just liked to kill with impunity wanted out. We want to live our lives for ourselves! Even the D3THL0RDZ of all people felt that way. Why couldn't you have accepted that? It didn't have to go this far—"

The setting sunlight glinted off steel... the steel double saber Lorelei had abandoned long ago, now in her mother's hands.

"I'm not going to accept that... that everything I've ever believed in was a stupid game! It had to mean something!" Kelli spoke... as people cleared out in a circle around her, none of them wanting to actually DIE. "If I take you down, then I can rul3 this world once again... as the Steel Blades should! We are L33T, don't you understand?! We're... we bow to no one, and I don't care that the warp bubbles are off, I'll cut your backstabbing heart out, and..."

Rei-Lei spread her arms out, holding no weapon. Not even her shield. "If you're going to kill me... if you CAN kill someone, really murder someone, do it. See how much honor you find in that! Every person you ever 'killed' never meant anything more than a point on the ladder, Kelli. And if you kill me it won't get you a frag point either, it'll just put blood on your hands. The bubbles are gone forever! This is what Tribal Alpha WANTS. And killing me won't stop that, either—"

A blind rage is just the thing for clouding over any doubt you have. The kind of cloud you can do anything in. Like murder someone.

Kelli ran forward, bringing her blade back for a long slash at the one she hated so much, letting out a war cry as she went, not stopping herself, not wanting to think about it—

And was stopped by Lorelei, her glowing blade blocking the strike flawlessly.

"Mom. Calm. Down," she hissed, using all her strength to hold her mother back. "Calm down or someone's gonna be hurt, hurt for REAL. And you're not getting to her 'backstabbing heart' unless you go through MY backstabbing heart first—"

Kelli gritted her teeth, trying to push down harder. "Lorelei, step... aside...! Or—"

"Or you'll kill me? I thought you loved me, Mom. Or were you lying then too? Here's something that ain't a lie: I love you. You've used me and misunderstood me and made me so mad I can't see straight, but I still love you. Now calm down... and think..."

The steel saber rattled a bit as Kelli's hands shook... and then it landed on the soft ground with a thump.

Lorelei deactivated her weapon... putting her arms around the proud woman who was now sobbing quietly into her daughter's shoulder.

The ex-hunters went home. It was over.

Reality is infinite. Life is finite. I've always wondered which is more frightening, the infinite or the finite—the overwhelming amount of things there are to experience, or the fact that you cannot experience them all during your lifetime. Both are horrifying notions once you truly begin to open your mind to them. They are inescapable traps of truth.

However, a logic can be used to soothe the existential pains. If reality is infinite and life is finite, simply live your life without boundaries and take in as much as you can. Never fall into the safety net of the redundant, the mundane, the predictable. Mankind has done this for thousands of years, and have grown stagnant and pale as a result—with no boundaries left to push, they have given up the joy of exploration.

A polite man I met once taught me this, and even if his philosophies did not wholly match mine, I believe in the ideal of life inside reality, reality inside life. It is a teaching that led me away from my stagnant clan's roots, into my new beloved family, and ultimately will lead me to my end. Which is just and proper, in the way of things.

death is as meaningless as the spark of life,
and both are things of great import.

neither can be taken lightly or seriously,
and both are as intangible as the air.

he has instructed me thus.

my quest is a fool's errand which will end poorly.
but it must be done, if his life was to have any meaning.

08: Poetry of War

Fresh air snapped into existence the moment the Engine soft-booted.

Kisei took in a deep lungful of that air... and regretted it immediately. Even if the Engine was no longer in Suspend mode, the air had slowly grown stagnant and horrid over the years. Hadn't the dolls maintained cleaning duties, as she programmed them to? Perhaps they had broken down? On top of everything else, she did not need that hassle... but it was minor in comparison.

Pushing open the wooden gates to the compound, she walked onto the soft grasses she hadn't tread upon in years. The feel of them beneath her soft boots was familiar to the point of sweeping her focus away with nostalgia. Nostalgia was irrelevant, of course, but she allowed herself one moment of reflection...

Home. The secluded, privately owned reality of Tachibana.

Nipponese in style, if not actually attached to the reality of Nippon. The compound, which was all this reality consisted of, was surrounded by a high wooden wall; not that intruders would be repelled by it, not that any world really existed beyond the wall, but such things were traditional. Stepping stones formed a zigzag pattern, also traditional to ward off demons who could only move in straight lines... twisted paths to buildings of the compound, to the koi pond, the fountain. The familiar tock of the wooden fountain filling, emptying against a rock with a clack, filling again...

She was not here to appreciate the scenery. She had an long-standing errand to complete. Doing her best to filter out all the things that called to her, she followed the stones left-right-left, and entered the main building.

The day I came to my realization (infinite reality, finite life) was a day like any other. Which goes a great distance towards explaining how the realization formed... a day like any other. Every day the same. Every mission the same, every victory a repeat, every failure falling flat onto ground covered many times before.

Our clan had operated for thousands of years, since the ancient days lost in the mists of time. And why not lose them, when the years slid by with little to no change? The clan's mission was always the same; maintain the family, serve our clients with secrecy and skill, achieve the goals set before us. Every task, every kill, every service rendered supported the clan's solidity as the finest ninja clan that ever lived.

I say "ninja" even if the meaning of the term has fallen by the wayside. It is an ancient word, and one which has many conflicting meanings; the clan was simply the clan, as things had boiled down to the simplest, easiest formula possible. We move in darkness, we exist in secret, we kill with supreme efficiency. To do otherwise is to bring shame on the clan.

But I digress. Which is not a bad thing, as digressions allow one to explore life, but I would not want to stray too far from my original point.

I was on a mission (same as any other) which took me to a back alley of Nippon. My target had fallen to a dart with ease, and perhaps I was overconfident as I removed my mask in order to enjoy the cool rain of the evening upon my face. As I tossed a tab of genetic erasure chemical onto the body to burn it away, I looked about the alley... and saw that I had been spotted.

Witnesses, of course, are not allowed. Such a failure is to bring shame on the clan, as has been dictated in the rules handed down from generation to generation and so on. The boy would have to die.

Perhaps it was the cool rain which had put me in such a wondrous mood, or the oddly innocent look of the boy... he was a bystander, simply on his way from one place to another when he looked at the wrong thing at the wrong time. The rules said he had to die. The rules said a great many things... but why? I pondered that, as he stared. It wasn't so much a moral compunction against killing him; that sort of ethical crisis would have impaired me on many missions previous if I felt that way. It simply didn't seem fair to rob the young man of his chance to enjoy life.

"Hello there," I called to him in his native language, without malice. "A lovely evening, yes? Hmm. You're wondering what the pile of chemical components behind me was, aren't you?"

"N-No," he said, realizing he was caught seeing something he shouldn't. Children are trained to understand adult displeasure, even when masked (which I was doing).

What I was about to do was against the rules, established for thousands of years, nailing us down to a pattern of life which had worked time and time again. There was no reason to stray from the path... except to truly *stray*. Which I felt perhaps it was time to do.

"My name is Tachi, and I'm an assassin," I told him. "What's your name, young man?"

"M-My name is Ryo," he replied. "Ryo Noyori."

And that is how I met the one who would help me found my new clan.

There was resistance, of course.

"It's your prerogative to not tell me why," Meiko had spoke, through on her finest business voice. "As per your contract, no questions will be officially asked..."

"I appreciate your professionalism in this manner," Kisei had replied.

"...but unofficially, I really want to know why, Kisei. This is so sudden, I mean... why do you want to leave? I know it's not exactly the most exciting work in the world for someone with your training, but I didn't think you were unhappy with it. Or is it something else? I can shuffle your duties to something you like more, if that's what you need..."

"I am appreciative of the work, and satisfied by it. However, I'm afraid I am not at liberty to discuss the matter. As my contract stated, as we agreed to the day you hired me, I have the right to terminate services with twenty-four hours' notice, no questions asked. Please take no offense to my silence on the matter; it would be best if you are unaware of my reasons for this action."

"That's pretty damn ominous, Kisei."

"I apologize for the dramatic overtones, but that is the truth of the matter."

In order to pass the twenty-four hours without further questioning, she retired to her room, locked all six (previously seven) locks and meditated in silence. As good a way to pass the time as any, and free of irrelevant distractions.

There was knocking on the door, of course.

First Lorelei, who was mildly upset upon hearing the news. Kisei had suspected for a long time that Lorelei had a respect for her, perhaps even a friendly level of respect—an attachment Kisei did not need or want, as it was distracting, but one she tolerated... and perhaps encouraged, from time to time, when her discipline slackened.

Next to knock on her door was Mallory, with the dinner she had not eaten. She turned him away with her silence, and thankfully he did not break down her door as he had done twice previous. His voice had tones of worry which she forced herself to ignore.

Once the time period was up, she slipped out under cover of darkness, leaving all her material things behind... all of them, even her book. They didn't matter now. An anonymous taxi (not Mellow Fellow's) delivered her from the House, to Tachibana. To her original home.

Her original home was in a hideous state of disrepair.

Even in the sealed environment of personal reality, even with the Reality Engine in a Suspend mode, the dust had settled thick on every surface. Wooden floors were nearly slippery with it. The grass outside was still green, but a dark and sickly green. The plumbing had gone; she would not be able to shower, which was fine, as she did not need to clean herself for the errand.

This wasn't in her plans. She was hoping that the dolls would have been able to keep the place in decent repair; such shabby surroundings were distasteful. They would suffice, however, which was all that mattered. The presentation of her family home was not important.

sakura in full bloom, spring's rise to power.
a picnic on the open grass, as is traditional.

a pick-and-choose approach to traditions,
that is his way, which is not always mine.

My realization was thus:

The traditions I had followed all my life were stale. They were established in an age long past, a age that never ended and continued to this day. Such an age was a shabby thing, when you saw the infinite possibility that reality brought to us. I had to break away from the cycle and begin to establish myself. To establish my own reality.

Quite literally, too. I left my clan silently and with misleading traces, using all the skills they had taught me. I faked my own death with great care to prevent anyone following me as I left the nest. That was step one.

Step two was to purchase a Reality Engine. RealWare is quite understanding when it comes to discreet reality purchases; small-scale, customizable Reality Engines complete with unlogged repair services were available for the right price. I had taken my life savings with me (money which had no use in my old life, and gathered like dust does in an old house) and it was more than enough to establish Tachibana, designed to my own sensibilities.

The third step would be trickier. I wanted to establish my own clan, but a clan of one was simply silly. I would need others, but hiring muscle was unthinkable. I needed ones who could maintain my ideals, who shared my vision for independence, beauty, and truth in reality... or at least could work without any conflicts with those ideals.

It was Ryo who solved the puzzle for me. I had kept in touch with the boy—formally in order to ensure his silence on the matter of the witnessed act, but by this point we both understood how our friendship worked. The threat of violence was hollow and fake, a simple tool to explain why we continued to communicate with each other... but I digress again.

He was still a young boy, with only the simple education an orphanage could provide to guide him, but he was ambitious. He shared my ideal—he had plans to strike out on his own one day, to establish science that would benefit mankind. And one of his initial ideas proved to be just what I needed.

"The Knowledge Base would be designed by you," he explained, during the meeting I had arranged one quiet summer night. "They would have the capacity needed to run missions, do housework, take care of any routine need you have. They won't be sentient, though; even Love and Hate hasn't gotten that far yet, and other systems like Oscar are pretty primitive. But they'll do what you need them to do, and they'll do until we think of something better!"

He was still iffy on the morality of my work, of course. He made this very clear to me. However, I think he learned to accept my chosen profession because I had splintered away from the mindless sort of death that dominated my early days. I would establish my own code of conduct, my own integrity bred from the best of the Hagakure, from my old clan's patterns, and from new and wild philosophies I had yet to dream of. And through that, I could become more than a simple force of death...

Even if my initial tools were little more than simple dolls of death.

Kisei opened an access panel on the back of the doll's neck, and flicked the off switch. It ceased its mindless dusting, which had already stripped the hallway wall down to the bare brick.

These faceless dolls had gotten stuck somewhere along the way. She had programmed them to run basic housekeeping routines, but the AI had locked into a loop at one point or another... causing the robots to perform the same tasks over and over while neglecting the rest of the program. The end result? A poorly kept home.

The dolls were almost ready to fall apart, as well. The kimonos they wore on their flawlessly white near-parody human forms were ragged and torn. The black wigs, complete with tight buns behind the head, had gotten lopsided and frayed. "Limb dropsie" as they had affectionately termed it struck hard; the old metal joints, well worn after countless missions in the field, had given way and left a few stray arms lying around the house...

Kisei moved from room to room, deactivating any dolls she found. They had done their best, and for that she was appreciative, but perhaps it was time to give them their final rest as well.

they move with a pure mathematical grace,
the motions of the tea ceremony performed in precision.

but eventually the chaos of life sets in,
and one trips over a discarded teacup.

it flails a bit on the ground, tea powder settling on its frame like green snow.

my first smile arose from such antics.

And so, my 'independent contractor' status was firmly established, my 'ninja clan member' status left in the shadows of the past. The dolls killed with great efficiency, and if ever one was lost in the field, it would self-destruct—erasing all traces of its existence. A digital form of seppuku, I suppose, a death with little real meaning given how easy it was to create a new doll. All I required was the basic shell—and I had dozens of empty dolls available—and the Knowledge Base that my friend Ryo had developed. Plug one into the other, and you have a unit suitable for combat...

However, I knew that this would not do in the long run. To have such meaningless weapons was to fall into the patterns of my previous clan. Disposable things... lives and deaths with no consequence, no purpose. I understood that when I asked for Ryo's aid, I knew this would be a stop-gap measure. My final concept was of far more import... but would take time to research, time to perfect...

For this, Ryo could not aid me—he was aiming towards the steel-structured electronic lands of reality engineering, robotics, machines. The dolls. I wanted the only thing truly suitable for the task of taking a life—a living human being.

Thus, I created a daughter.

On the day of her activation (which I declared to be her birth date) she was twelve years in appearance, healthy and strong. In her mind was an organic flash copy of the Knowledge Base that powered the dolls, through a process I developed myself using modified techniques from Ryo's original procedures. When her eyes first opened, she understood the many techniques of taking life and preserving one's own life.

Her first words were, much like the dolls, "State unit designation."

This I had put much thought to.

"Your name is Kisei," I informed her.

"Unit designation input type: numerical only," she replied, her voice a flat monotone. The only tone she knew at the time.

"Yes, well, this is where you separate yourself from the mechanical dolls," I explained. "You will find that if you try to store your designation, despite being non-numerical, it will fit nicely. In fact, you should be able to make your own decisions beyond a pure reactionary level in combat... but I'm getting ahead of myself. Your kimono is over there; clothe, and let's begin. There's so much to do..."

"Define designation," she requested.

Much to my surprise. "Define?" I asked her, delighted that she had taken such action without prompting. Already proving her life force above and beyond the dolls...

"The word 'Kisei' has multiple definitions," she informed, in response to the lilting tone of my words, the questioning tone. "Similar phonics and spellings with variations of meaning. It can mean a vow, an oath or pledge. It can mean a homecoming. It can be something which is rare, or uncommon. It can mean a master player in the game of shogi. It can be the realization of an objective. Or it can mean 'Death'."

"I see, I see. Yes, it is a very ambiguous word; many spellings, many meanings," I said, smiling all the while. "Which definition do you think I intend for you? Guess."

It was a test, of course. A free association test. Which would she favor...?

It took her a half minute to decide.

"I am death," she decided.

"Hmmm, yes, as you said, that's one meaning," I spoke, folding my hands into the sleeves of my kimono. "If you choose to see yourself that way, it's your right. I myself would say... you are represented by all the things you listed."

"I will redefine meaning to map to all meanings," she replied automatically.

"No no, that's not a direct order. You think of yourself however you wish to. It's your right as a living person, Kisei... but, I suppose these are things you'll have to adjust to in time. And we do have time. We have all our lives, until our deaths, to enjoy what life has to offer. Come along. There's much to do."

She didn't have to be here, doing this. The presentation of the house was unimportant. Old duties called to her to straighten out... straighten out her affairs. It was only proper, even if it made no sense to the soldier inside her.

This particular part of her task was the least pleasant. His room had been untouched for longer than any other room in the house, and going back in... should not hurt, not technically. Such things were only illusions. Still, her hand stayed on the slider handle for some time, before moving the paper and wood panel aside...

His room. Spartan, of course, but Spartan with elegance. Unlike her room back at the House, it was decorated. There were flowers (long since dead) in vases, a few statues and other objects of art... and on the back wall, three scrolls which held words of wisdom. These were not the only words he followed, but certainly important ones to him...

the
way
of
the
samurai
is
found
in
death.

To the left, the very core of the Hagakure.

Elegant brushstrokes, hand-made ink and paper. Ancient, but not yellowed or fading, simply proud and strong as it hung on the wall.

Life
is
what
occurs
between
birth
and
death.

In the middle, a saying from his former clan.

His clan had many such sayings. He felt that this was the simplest of them, with the least melodrama attached. It was machine-printed on recycled paper, not bothering to maintain the classic look of brushed strokes.

Let's

share

and

injest

joy

with

To the right, a vertical banner advertisement peeled off a building in Nippon, but printed in poorly spelled foreign words.

'With' what always posed a mystery to Kisei, as the ad pitch had been torn off at that point. He told her it didn't matter what it was 'with,' or rather, one should embrace and ingest joy 'with' everything and nothing in general.

These banners weren't what stayed her hand on the door.

The journal was. It was his journal, with his thoughts and feelings poured out on paper in neat handwriting—but that wasn't the problem. She had left a bookmark in it, a bookmark she swore she would read again on the day of her homecoming. Again, this was an illusory thing which was secondary to her errand... but a promise was a promise. And it would remind her of why she had returned.

She bowed once as a sign of respect to the room in general, much as she would the family dojo, then silently padded over to the work table. The dolls at least had kept it dusted, the book free from rot which would have eaten at the paper...

Perhaps to delay the inevitable, opened it to a random page near her bookmark, and began to read. The bookmark itself would come in time.

I was expecting an uphill battle with Kisei, and she did not disappoint.

I spent one month testing and refining her combat skills. 'Out of the box' she was skilled in various techniques of killing, stealth, combat tactics, target evaluation, and so on. The Knowledge Base saw to that; initially she was little more than one of my dolls which happened to be made of flesh... and capable of more structured speech and comprehension than the limited input/output voices of the dolls.

One day, I decided to present her with the greatest challenge she had yet to face. She stared at my gift with the dull look of incomprehension the dolls would have when presented with data outside their boundaries.

"What do you see in your hands, Kisei?" I asked her.

"It is a book," she described. "The cover is pink. It has a rudimentary latching mechanism which provides an inadequate level of security. The pages inside the book are blank, and made of recycled paper."

"Correct in all respects. I give this book to you with the express desire that you fill its pages."

"What do you wish for me to write inside this book, Father?"

(Getting her to refer to me as 'father' was a trivial task, as her mind simply mapped the word onto my image. Getting her to understand the concept of 'father' and all the emotional implications would have to come later.)

"Poetry. I want you to write poetry in your new book," I explained to her. "You can study the various poetry books and scrolls I have in the library if you want to understand the basic structures, but this exercise will refine your creativity. Write poetry about anything you feel—your happiness, your sadness. Write about what you see around you—poetry of beauty, poetry of horror, and perhaps the most delicate balance the art can reach for... poetry of war."

"Father. Query."

"Yes?" I asked, knowing what the question would be.

"This activity is irrelevant. Why have you assigned the task to me, when time can be more efficiently spent training and developing new combat techniques?"

"Hmmm. You know, I had been waiting for this query, but I hadn't settled on a single answer to give you. I shall improvise. Kisei, what is death?"

"The cessation of biological life processes."

"True, but there is a great deal of philosophy behind it as well. Meaning, Kisei. Death has meaning, despite being meaningless. It's an issue wrought with paradoxes and confusion, and that's quite normal and suitable. I'd like you to read my philosophy books as well; you have plenty of time to do this alongside your normal training. And alongside the new training we'll be undertaking... training in painting and song, as well as physical activities like dancing and games. Have I told you about Ping Pong yet?"

Kisei still didn't quite understand, looking from her new book to me and back and forth. "Are these things relevant, Father?"

"If you are going to take life, you have to understand every aspect of the act, including ones that will seem irrelevant at first," I explained. "Now, come along. We have so much to do... an infinite amount of things, to be honest..."

"Achieving an infinite amount of goals is impossible."

"Ah," I said. "Now we're getting somewhere."

see my first poem.
it is in haiku style.
father will approve.

It is the end of the year, and I am evaluating Kisei's progress.

As predicted, it was an uphill battle, and one which is still not complete. It took a great deal of exposure to art, culture and philosophy before she started making evaluations based on aesthetics and opinion. These are things humans are capable of, and as she was not a simple robotic doll, she simply had to 'discover' the capability within her.

She did not awake to true sentience on a single day. There was not a single moment of realization, at least, none I am aware of; instead, I simply observed her gradual change. Usually when she actively disagreed with me on something. Perhaps she was simply trying to hide her new feelings, to avoid appearing strange to her father?

A good example came when we were having a picnic during the first day of spring. The Sakura blossoms planted throughout Tachibana had emerged, with pink petals swirling in the air... a breathtakingly beautiful sight, one I had designed to be thus.

Perhaps the atmosphere of quiet contemplation is what made her speak up, speak out of turn. She had been crafting a poem—she was writing one a day at that point, simple things, but gradually growing more complex and beautiful as the days went by—when she looked up, at the trees, then at me.

"Why are your views so fractured, Father?" she asked.

It threw me a moment—the pleasure at such a strange question, that is. "Oh? Why do you say they are fractured?"

"You do not adhere to one particular way," Kisei spoke. "The Hagakure teaches: It is bad when one thing becomes two. One should not look for anything else in the way of the samurai. It is the same for anything else which is called 'a way'. If one understands things in this manner, he should be able to hear about all ways, and be more and more in accord with his own."

"I see. And how do you interpret that?"

"It is a simple statement: there is nothing outside of the way of the samurai, the teachings of the Hagakure," she explained. "Therefore other philosophes are not required. All that is required is the way—indivisible and whole. But you pick and choose from many philosophies, including the way, to craft your own way..."

"And that's why it works, Kisei. It is a way. It is simply... my way, I suppose," I replied. "I have inspected other ways, including the Hagakure. The way of my old clan, as well. I swirled them all into my way, which makes my way whole and unique, and I require nothing outside it. And besides... have you ever considered that the Hagakure could be incorrect?"

"Incorrect?" she asked, allowing some of her newly formed emotion to creep into the word—disgust. "It is the way, yes?"

"I hate to use a cliché, but... if the way told you to jump off a cliff, would you do it?"

"If honor demanded I take my life, yes."

I sighed, shaking my head. "Kisei... you have to make your own decisions. You must be true to your own sense of integrity, not blindly adhering to the words printed thousands of years ago. Sometimes they are not applicable to here, not applicable to now. Not applicable to *you*. And it is up to you to decide when they do apply—you could agree with them, yes, but it the agreement must be a decision, not a default. Do you understand?"

Kisei took some time to think through the puzzles I had presented her with, which was well and good. They were paradoxes that one could grapple with for a lifetime.

"I understand," she said at last, even if the words were not 100% firm.

"Excellent."

"This also means I might decide your way is not applicable to me," she warned, much to my surprise... and joy.

"Ah," I said. "Now we are getting somewhere."

She wrote a poem on the spot. I read it over her shoulder, and approved very much.

To willingly question her maker... that was all the proof I needed. She was now truly alive, truly my daughter. I had achieved the final realization of my dream. My lovely, wonderful dream... Kisei.

There were two kinds of pain. One involved a trauma to the flesh of a person, and would heal given the proper conditions and precautions.

The other kind, the kind Kisei felt so very rarely, did not heal so easily. And reading a journal entry like that simply pulled open old wounds...

The bookmark. No distractions. No irrelevancies. Get on with it.

She flipped past a number of pages... to a simple white page, torn from her own pink poetry book and stuck between Tachi's pages at a right angle. The page did not have poetry on it. In the spirit of his writings, it was simply... what happened, and how she felt about it. The only time she ever wrote in that style, words that hurt too much to press against her beautiful poems, words she had to tear out and leave behind, just like she left her poems behind at the Mirai home, casting them off, so she could...

READ, her mind blared at her, trying to work around the swirling thoughts that distracted her. And she read.

It is my fault.

It was a week in which we had no assignments. I was painting a portrait of some flowers. I was focusing on my art, as he wanted me to try to express how the flowers made me feel without using accurate colors. It was a training exercise, he said, because he knows I feel better when it is a training exercise instead of wasted time.

But I was not seeing it as wasted time. I had begun to enjoy the sideline activities that he suggested I do. I was beginning to do them unbidden. It started with writing my poems and then moved on to writing song, creating paintings, and crafting models. Each time it made him smile and

I was painting flowers and thinking of what other things I would do that day and not thinking of

He entered the room and I turned to greet him using the smile I had been practicing and he smiled at me and IT IS MY FAULT

The dart struck perfectly, embedding its tip into a major artery on his neck. Based on my previous experience using similar techniques I can state with firm belief that he was dead before he hit the floor.

The assassin had been hiding in the family art studio for approximately two hours and I had never seen her, as I was thinking more about the painting than I was about proper compound defenses and my alertness to potential dangers.

I immediately attacked the hidden assassin, drawing her out of the shadows of the room and incapacitating her using my paintbrush. I demanded to know why she had done this and who had hired her.

She bit down on a capsule in her mouth and died with foam pouring out of her lips and onto my hands before I could locate an antidote and administer it, taking the information with her to the grave.

I believe that the reason I sat still in the room without taking action after that point was due to a form of emotional shock which I am ashamed I was afflicted with. I also was afflicted with a great deal of crying. When it passed my mind was working properly and could assess the situation in proper detail.

I could not blame the assassin. If I had been keeping alert and ready for combat this wouldn't have happened; that is where blame lies. The assassin was simply a tool of death. She was a tool much like I was a tool, a professional, hired by a client. Her methods were sound and flawless, right up to claiming her own life rather than reveal her client's name, rather than dishonor herself.

I could not help but admire her dedication. The sheer elegance of that death was a level I could only hope to achieve. And because I did not achieve it, he was dead.

With the help of the dolls, I buried Tachi and the assassin in back to back graves behind the compound. It felt proper.

Then I instructed them to dig one for myself off to the side, for later use.

I will become Ronin. I will track down the client who ordered my father's death. I will take revenge. I will then return home, and reclaim my honor after today's horrible failure with my life. I insert this page as the final page in his journal to be a reminder of my errand, my task, my final important duty.

She closed the book of his life, much as her own would close soon.

The journey had taken far longer than she ever had anticipated. The investigation into who purchased death for Tachi was an endless series of red herrings, dead ends, false leads. She had lived in Antiparadisia for a year and a half, fighting for her own life and taking odd jobs through her father's supplier, Duke of Duke's Munitions... all while investigating. The investigation to nowhere.

His old clan was not responsible. They had a myriad of their own problems to deal with, and were not imaginative enough to wait as long as they did to give him some happiness before ending it all. They would not have hired outside help, either; the assassin had no identifying styles or characteristics that fit their teachings, and Tachi often noted that their teachings hadn't changed in centuries.

Ryo Noyori was not responsible. Kisei had investigated him thoroughly upon reading about the witness-incident in Tachi's journal. He was under a death threat, and never fully approved of her father's work, but nothing in his character suggested he would do this—especially after contributing to the dolls and Kisei's own creation.

No new leads turned up. All previous leads closed off. The errand was looking hopeless, and the fight to survive day to day had become her primary mission. When a classified ad appeared seeking a tactical expert for live-in Transient-style consulting, she took the ad immediately. In her contract, she stated she must be able to leave with twenty-four hours' notice, no questions asked. That way, if her continuing investigation—now given a Reality Engine's legs—turned up the culprit, she could leave immediately to take her final revenge...

And throughout her tenure with Mirai Consulting, nothing turned up. Nothing at all.

Until now.

Until yesterday...

A routine thing, taking Mellow Fellow's taxi to Arboria. She had to resupply her MRE ration stocks. While Mallory Heisenberg's cooking was more than adequate (and had she not turned her back on her childhood foolishness, she would say it was highly enjoyable) she wanted the ability to eat in her room and meditate without the awkwardness of interacting with others...

216

"I don't want to get your hopes up," Duke began while ringing up the sale. "But I think I found the guy who had Tachi whacked."

Having experienced exactly 739 false leads to date, Kisei did not get her hopes up, nor would she have shown hope. She simply asked what proof he had. And he had proof.

There, in a video file taken from the hidden camera that recorded all customers who came and left, was a RealWare business executive picking up some mainstream military otaku magazines. And bragging about a new hovertank he had bought after his stock split. Bragging about how he got to a job that pays fifty times more than Duke would ever see in his lifetime by 'Alternative Means'.

Like hiring assassins.

"Really?" Duke had asked, keeping the conversation going. "Ever meet an indie worker from Tachibana? Some great services from that place before they shut down..."

"Tell me about it. Tachi and his robots did the best work I'd ever seen. Shame I had to shut them down the hard way, but hey, business is business," the executive added, with an irritatingly smug look. "Keep that in mind if you ever think of letting these words out of this room."

He was the one.

Kisei's mind pulled back to the present. To the piece of paper in her father's book... and the piece of paper in her hands. The home address of Tachi's true killer.

Enough reading. Enough housekeeping. The errand was now all.

Kisei gave the room a final bow, and then marched down the hall to the weapons cache. It was sealed with a custom reality envelope, coded to a key only she knew—her birthday.

Inside were knives. Guns. Rifles. Ammo. Bombs. Even large vehicles of war...

But she picked a knife, and only a knife. Perhaps her traditional sniper rifle would be a more appropriate weapon—clean and perfect, like the dart that began her duty. But a knife would be more poetic, and she could allow herself the shame of inefficient, emotion-fuelled killing this one last time.

> *blood from the neck, via a left to right stroke*
> *has an intense power behind it. the heartbeat of life.*
>
> *the heart desperately wishes to keep beating,*
> *and thus forces the blood out of the body,*
> *producing an opposing result than intended.*
>
> *in this way, we are all sad and contradictory.*
> *there is a negative form of beauty in that truth.*

In order to travel from reality to reality, one needs an engine-equipped building. A taxi hut, public bus, a small house, a mobile hotel room, an office block... whatever is most appropriate to your pocketbook and your needs. Then there are issues of passport processing, docking, clearance, ongoing dock fees, various inter-reality treaties regarding traffic and commerce, and so on, and so forth. You don't go from A to Z without hitting B through Y.

Unless you have an illegal, unlicensed stealth insertion pod with a Micro-Engine (pirated from RealWare's technology labs) that can slip undetected past even the strongest Reality Engine locking and docking mechanisms. Which Kisei did. It was parked next to the koi pond.

It took her a half hour to corroborate the address given to her with the known maps of the miscreant's home reality, and another half hour to find a good landing spot where she would not be noticed (a broom closet on the tenth floor of the apartment building). Actual travel was instantaneous.

Seventeen alarm systems were tripped by her arrival, and then immediately silenced by the jamming mechanisms inside the pod. Kisei was a bit surprised; considering she was about to break into a heavily secured housing compound deep in the heart of RealWare itself, she was predicting a minimum of twenty alarm systems.

Reality Prime was by far the toughest place to crack for someone of her profession. Given the sheer amount of enemies RealWare had drawn (usually known as 'customers') they spared no expense to keep their home reality under 25,914,192 locks-and-keys. Since RealWare was the richest corporate entity in the multiverse by at least four significant figures, that meant an exceptionally large budget for exceptionally good security...

Fortunately, Kisei was exceptionally good at slipping around exceptionally good security.

Besides, failure was not an option; a death at the hands of RealWare's private security forces would be the least honorable end she could meet. She would not fail him twice.

She wore her traditional uniform and cape, but had her hair nicely tucked away and re-colored, and a face mask of black cloth she could see through as if it were glass. Not that it mattered if anyone saw her face—other than getting away clean in order to truly finish her errand, she didn't care about long-term consequences. Still, she was not trained to be sloppy, and the mask was a matter of honor rather than prudence.

Time to go to work.

Kisei slipped from her pod, closing the hatch behind herself. She would not use the door; instead, she opened a rectangular hole in the outer wall with a handheld cutter. She took care not to cut any electrical systems; anything from a blackout to a tiny glitch would be detectable.

Pulling herself through the hole she had made exactly large enough to slip through, she began to scale the side of the building using adhesive gloves. Tools of the trade, nothing special there. Her cloak helped her blend into the side of the building; the night-time sky would help as well, with the moon (a great shining RealWare logo) on the other side of the building and casting her side in shadow. Kisei climbed six floors, careful to avoid any windows... and stopped in front of her target's home apartment.

The window glass was melted away, which was safer and quieter than cutting. Silently, Kisei slipped into the darkened apartment... then scaled a nearby wall, crawling along the ceiling. Just like the assassin who claimed Tachi did, waiting above eye level, waiting for the right moment to strike with infinite patience...

Waiting.

Twenty-four and a half minutes. Nothing unusual about that. She would only worry if it took him a half hour longer than the estimated arrival time.

At twenty-nine minutes and sixteen seconds, the target was acquired. In the front door, keys tossed on an end table, door closed, heading to the wet bar for a little post-overtime martini...

Kisei dropped from the ceiling like a snowflake, and tackled him to the floor with an immobilizing pin with a minimum of fuss. The blade was held to his neck immediately after, and...

For years, she argued with herself whether or not she would ask this. It was risky to take any 'extra' actions other than the bare minimum needed to get the job done. Of course, if she followed that doctrine, she'd have sniped him from a mile away and been done with it...

"Why?" she hissed, behind her dark mask. Why had this cutthroat businessman, this heartless man, her enemy, the one she had been hunting for years, the one she swore to kill, the one who had to die, the dark shadow who laughed in her nightmares and mocked her inadequacies, the—

—the one who had apparently urinated in his pants, judging from the trickling sound on the carpet and the warm feeling against Kisei's leg. And was now sweating profusely and whimpering...

The crystal drama she had built in her mind ever since that day started to gather fractal imperfections. Little cracks that got bigger...

"P-P-Please, don't...!" he whined in a surprisingly high-pitched voice. "Pleasepleaseplease—"

"WHY?" she hissed, trying to get back on track. "You ordered the assassination of the one known as Tachi, years ago. Why did you do it? Tell me! I have to know!"

"Pleaseplease—"

She drew a tiny red line on his neck, a hint of her frustration.

"I-It was cheaper!!" he blurted out.

She had her answer, he could die now. ...except that the answer wasn't particularly satisfying. Or comprehensible.

"'Cheaper'?" she asked, egging him on.

"I, I, I hired him to kill my boss years ago...!" the man began, fear giving his voice just enough strength to continue. "But, but I couldn't pay him, and he said okay, I could pay later, but I still couldn't pay, and he kept reminding me, and I was worried he'd come for me, and I found some young girl who was just starting out, and she was cheaper to hire than it would be to pay his bill so I had her kill him so I'd be okay and that's all and that's it I swear please don't kill me! I'm just middle management and I didn't even get my boss's job like I thought I would and I feel horrible about the whole thing and it's been gnawing away at me for years and oh god I know I deserve this but please please pleasepleaseplease—"

With a howl of frustration, Kisei raised her knife, and plunged it downward...

Into the floor.

"Pathetic," she summarized, keeping him pinned. "A complete waste, an honorless dog! This is what I have been hunting?!"

"R-Right, I'm nothing!" he agreed, hoping this meant he'd live. "I'm nothing at all! It's not worth killing me! I—"

A hand clamped over his mouth, so Kisei could concentrate in peace.

It didn't matter why, she thought. He did it. He had to die. This was what she was seeking for years, and he had to pay, even if he was a weasel rather than a fox. Honor demanded it, right?

But now whatever grand dream Kisei had been harboring of taking down the monster who was responsible for her pain had fluttered away, as dreams often do upon waking. All she was left with was a scrawny waste of oxygen, wracked with guilt, and smelling like a lavatory. Killing it might be kind.

Kisei pulled her knife from the floor.

"Not tonight," she decided.

"Oh, thank you thank—"

"A Wednesday," she decided. "It will be a Wednesday. Perhaps next Wednesday, or a Wednesday twenty years from now. Perhaps me, perhaps someone I simply select to take care of things for me. I will allow you more time to reflect on the wrongs you have committed, so that your soul is prepared before your life is ended. Is that not fair?"

"F-F... faaaai...?"

"And if you seek me out, hoping to avoid your fate... be careful what you seek, because I will find you first," she stated. "Have a good life."

In the span of two blinks, she was gone.

RealWare Private Security kicked the door open two blinks later.

"Clear!" men with guns shouted, as they stormed into the room, responding to the 18th alarm Kisei had not nullified. Not that it mattered now... she was gone, leaving behind only a cockroach squirming with fear over the concept of a life spent dreading one day a week...

A young man swept into the room behind the forces, glancing around. "I suppose it's too much to hope that you got a good look at the intruder?" he asked, absolutely calm.

The enemy of Tachi babbled quietly to himself. "W... Wed... weds..."

He could have probably tracked down the intruder, the head of security thought. But to do that would be to reveal his unique talents right in the middle of his home reality... which could have implications.

And really, it didn't matter to him. He had larger concerns. Multiverse-large ones.

"Good work, boys," Multi proclaimed, patting a man-with-gun on the shoulder. "I'll write up the report saying we successfully chased off the criminal before any damage was done. You'll receive a stock bonus."

darkness falls, day to night.
moonlight spills on the koi pond.
every sunbeam long since dead.

the light which emerges the next morning is not rebirth,
it is replacement.
to believe otherwise is wishful thinking.

It would have been

It would have been

perfect.

The vengeful daughter, taking the life of the one who wronged her family. A masterful battle against a mysterious foe... except that it wasn't perfect. It was flawed. She couldn't bring herself to do it, not out of weakness, but out of disgust. Just as she did not truly hate the assassin, she could not truly hate the weak man who put the wheels in motion. He had sinned, he had wronged her, but what was he? A nothing. A mistake. Meaningless to her pain. She wouldn't even seek him out on a Wednesday as promised; the threat alone would give the man a lifetime of paranoia, night terrors and suffering beyond the swift release of death...

So what was this, then? She had gone through the motions for the end of her errand. The killing was... done, as it were; now she was to take her own life in the rite of Seppuku, as bushido demanded... the ritual must be obeyed. It was the Way.

All the ritualistic components were ready. She wore a white kimono, the color of death and purity. She had prepared a wooden tray with the proper items: A cup of sake (to be downed in two mouthfuls, the proper amount to show respect and contemplation). A tanto knife, made for one purpose and one purpose only. And finally, a piece of paper, with ink and brush, to compose the traditional poem of one's own death...

And none of it felt right. Not that this would stop her. She had come too far, dedicated herself too strongly to this cause to stop now. Any wrongness she felt was likely due to the dishonor of not following through on her goals. Yes, that had to be it. The sooner she proceeded, the sooner she could have the relief of her end to quell this awkward, ill-fitting life...

She raised the cup to her lips. For her father, one swallow. For herself, another. Then the poem, then the knife. Poem first. Brush dipped in ink, paper ready. To write on. A poem. She had to write one.

It was not a good time to have writer's block.

Poetry came so easily to her in the past. See a thing, and the words rise unbidden. Why would this be so difficult? Her brush hovered over the paper, three black drops falling to it, but no words falling with them. Perhaps she should have composed ahead of... no, it had to be composed at the time of the ritual. It was to encapsulate the last moments of one's life.

Normally such poems of death came in waka style, thirty-one syllables, five lines, 5-7-5-7-7... but all she could think of, the only words that felt true to her at that moment in time, were

at least it is over now.

Pushing through, she let the brush drop from one hand while taking up the knife with the other. She undid the belt of her kimono, letting it hang open, and took firmer grip of the tanto's handle. Placing it where it was supposed to go. Where all the precepts and teachings from ancient books told her it was supposed to go.

Right and wrong did not matter. Only the way. Only what she had been taught. It had to be. She had to do it. Any moment now. She would do it. It would be so. She would reclaim her honor this way. That's how it was supposed to work.

NOW, her mind blared at her, as she pressed the knife in

pulled away by another pair of hands.

"Hey, HEY, whoa, WHOAWHOAHWHOA—" he babbled, trying to pull the knife from her—and succeeding, as she let go in surprise. He fell backwards, nearly impaling himself, face white as a sheet.

The ancient ways said nothing about what to do in this situation, leaving Kisei a bit... puzzled.

"You gotta be more careful than that when using knives, you know!" Mallory Heisenberg exclaimed, setting the knife back down on the tray. "Take it from a guy who nearly lopped off all his fingers making noodles... what're you doing out here, anyway, having a picnic? I called and I called from the front gate but nobody answered so I let myself in, and AHH I'm sorry I didn't know your shirt was open I saw nothing I SWEAR—"

"What... WHAT are you doing here?" Kisei asked, too shocked to really be properly angry.

"St... stuff!" Mallory exclaimed, getting back to his feet... and grabbing the cardboard box he had dropped off the ground. "Your stuff! You left a bunch of stuff behind at the house. ...and locked the door behind you, which is why we couldn't get it here sooner, we had to break in, and you didn't leave a forwarding address so we had to check with Ryo, and Meiko was kinda busy meeting with a new potential client so she sent me over here in a taxi to get you your stuff back and, um, well, here it is. In this box. Right here."

...this is still salvageable, Kisei decided, mind racing to cope with this awkwardness. "Yes. Right. Thank you, Mallory Heisenberg. You may go now."

"Right, right. So. Um. ...are you coming back?" he asked. "Everybody was kinda upset when you said you were leaving, even Lorelei—"

"You may go now," she repeated, hoping he'd take the hint.

"Rightrightright. Okay. And, uh... one other thing, um. Look, I didn't mean anything by it, but it was just lying there, and... uh... here."

From his back pocket, he produced a small pink book.

Cold dread filled Kisei's spine. "My... did you..."

"A little. Only a little! Just... uh... most of it," Mallory admitted. "Ryo had lost your address and it took a while to find, and like I said this was just lying there open in your room, and uh... I got curious, so... I just read a little. Not a lot—"

Kisei snatched the book back fast enough to give Mallory paper cuts... then as she realized she had grabbed something she left behind on purpose, her grip weakened a bit on the cover.

"...it's not as if it matters," she said to herself.

"Eh?"

"They are trifling things," she spoke, not knowing why she was bothering to explain to him. "Irrelevancies. Meaningless words jotted down on paper to... fill the quiet hours. Distractions from my duty. I was better off without such things..."

"But they're really good."

"—what?"

"I mean, um, I'm really no literary critic, but I liked them," Mallory admitted. "A lot of them were pretty morbid, but... some talked about the sun, or the seasons, and things like that. And I am a farmboy, you know, that sort of stuff is near and dear to my heart. So I could really relate to it. And life and death, and... well, it was really interesting stuff. I hadn't looked at things like that before. I hadn't thought you were a writer, either! Are you published anywhere? I heard writers make a lot of money! Or... was it no money? I forgot..."

"...you are only the second person to read my words," Kisei informed him, holding her book closer to herself.

"Really?" Mallory asked, surprised. "Wow! Um, sorry I sorta stole a look, but... I feel kinda honored, then. The other one was your dad, right? You wrote a lot about him. He seemed like a really nice guy..."

"Yes... yes, he was. He was a really nice guy," she said, choosing to use his words. "But he is gone. I have... things to do, relating to that."

"Ohhh... oh, um, I'm sorry," he apologized. "I... think I passed his grave on the way over here. You left the House to visit him, didn't you?"

"In a way, yes..."

"I do that once a year, with my dad. For my mom, I mean. She's buried in Sleep Hill back home," he explained. "I know she can't hear us since she's dead, but... well, it feels kinda like some of your poems feel. Kinda sad, but good at the same time. ...I know you want me to go and I'm talking your ear off, I know, but I wanted to tell you that. I really liked that. I was sort of working up to it, see. ...thanks."

"The... writing moved you?" Kisei asked, confused. "Father always encouraged me to write, even if I eventually saw it as a needless distraction from my purpose..."

"It's pretty good for a needless distraction," Mallory said, with a smile.

The smile...

The same sort of soft, thankful smile that her father wore upon looking at her works. Her poems, her paintings, her sculpture, sometimes even the arguments she had with him brought about that smile...

"...uh... anyway, that's all," Mallory concluded. "I'll go now, so you can have your picnic or whatever in peace..."

His knees belt slightly, as the cardboard box was pushed back into his arms.

"Carry this back to the taxi," Kisei commanded him, resuming her normal flat tones of order.

Mallory peered over the top of the box at her. "Carry...? You don't want it?"

"Take it back to the House for me," she requested. "Put it back in my room. And tell Meiko I shall return tomorrow morning. I must pay my respects to my father, then finish caretaking for the estate. After that... I shall come home."

That night, sleeping in the bed I slept in throughout my childhood, I dreamt...

"Was I wrong?" my child-voice asked.

"There was no right or wrong," he replied, so high above me. "It simply was your way. You're free to make your own choices. Reality is infinite; life is finite. As long as you live your life to the fullest, you cannot do 'wrong'. Even if the results of that life are not what you expected, it will serve its purpose. Even when we stray from the way, the way comes back to us. The question is, what will become of you now?"

"I... I will try to find my way back," I told him. "I lost my way when you left me. I tossed aside everything that you hoped I could become..."

"What you will become... will be a blend of what you were, and what you are. You will be a you that is more you. And that is all you need to be to make me proud, my beloved daughter."

In silence, we sat amongst the Sakura blossoms on a fine spring day, and reflected on this.

"It makes sense to me," he continued. "The Final Rising Death Slam isn't unbeatable! I mean, look at his shot records; he's finished off a buncha guys with it, yeah, but there was that match two years ago against the guy from Aquarius, whatsisname... the guy..."

"That was a fluke caused by the moving netting under the Ping Pong variant ruleset #7," his friend replied. "If they were going with a more... like... NORMAL variant then that wouldn't have happened! The Final Rising Death Slam RULES! It r0xx0rz your sock0rz!"

"That's s0xx0rz!" his friend barked back. "You can't even get l33tspeak right, how can you know anything about Ping Pong? Stupidhead."

"Oh, yeah, like YOU'VE ever been to Tribal Alpha! And they don't even shoot each other anymore, so who cares?"

"So why do you care?"

"Why do YOU care?"

"I asked you first."

"I asked you second."

"So?"

"So what?"

"Make me!"

"Make you *what*?"

"I know you are, but what am I?"

"A loser!" his friend taunted. "And if I got you into a Ping Pong match with variant #7, I'd crush you with the God's Hand Strike my oniichan taught me, so step off! Otherwise—"

"Did you know that the P-Cup Tournament of Champions makes VideoNippon an estimated 200 billion en a year?"

Both boys turned to look sharply at the interloper.

"It's the only stable element in the Nipponese economy for the last century," Eiko continued quickly. "The amount of money pulled in from the multiversal broadcasting rights, when compounded against ticket sales and the normal expenditures involved in such a gala live event, are enough to fund VideoNippon's activities for the remainder of the fiscal year. On that foundation they launch new shows that they use to try and expand the profit margins to allow for some breathing room, but pattern analysis shows that only during times when the 'en' trades well against the 'point' does the programming succeed enough to draw ratings and buy rates that can match even ten percent of the P-Cup tournament's profit! Despite this, I can say with assurance that VideoNippon's stock (traded under the symbol VNP on the Urbana Stock Exchange) is a solid buy, because it consistently performs at a flat rate during times of fiscal crisis! ...Pretty cool, huh?"

Eiko put on her most hopeful smile while the boys put on looks reserved for sneaky adults.

"You're weird," the anti-Death Slam advocate decided, which the pro-Death Slam advocate agreed to with a nod. Both boys picked up their schoolbags and left the playground. Leaving Eiko alone.

Much as she had been during her entire afternoon of play.

Slowly, she walked towards the entrance of the playground, where Mallory was waiting and reading a cookbook.

"I wanna go home," she told him in a small voice.

Mallory peeked over the top of his book, a bit surprised at the announcement. "Home?" he asked. "Er... already? But aren't you having fun playing with the other kids and stuff?"

"No. I wanna go home now."

The boy cast a nervous glance at the wristwatch Meiko had given him in a futile attempt to teach him an organized approach to life planning and duty scheduling. "Ah... I... guess we can go now. Right. Been long enough. Okay! Let's go. C'mon..."

He tucked the cookbook under one arm, took Eiko's hand with the other, and led her across the street to the Noyori Labs Docking Yard. Even simply playing across the street required active adult supervision, according to Meiko...

Because she was just a little kid. Eiko looked at her sneakers as she marched the short distance back home. Just a little kid that the other kids saw as a weirdo, a geek, an *adult*...

What she most wanted to do right now was go upstairs, cuddle under her blanket, and watch MoneyLine in silence.

Instead she was treated to the noise of party crackers going off and confetti filling the air upon entering the house.

"Surprise!" the ladies of the House announced in sync. "Happy 12th birthday, Eiko!"

Oh.

Wai.

09: Birth-Date

They had really gone all out this year. Granted, much of the party supplies were unused extras from Mallory's REC Test celebration, but a new HAPPY BIRTHDAY EIKO banner had been strung up, her favorite kind of cake had been baked by Mallory (lemon cake, coconut icing), and the image of Kisei in her uniform and a pointy party hat trying to sing Happy Birthday was worth all the hassle of putting on her best smile.

It's quite hard to feel awful while at one's birthday party, Eiko was finding, as she wanted to avoid dwelling on her unsuccessful afternoon of play. The cake tasted great, everybody was in good spirits... and she was getting presents! Being an avid student of the consumer retail business markets, she understood the importance of exchanging points for commodities in order to keep the money flowing. And they were neat gifts, too!

From Kisei, she got a tea ceremony set, and a booklet describing the ritual.

"As I know you are currently studying Nippon's history in your sister's home tutoring courses, I believe this cultural artifact is appropriate," was her carefully designed explanation. "This tea set used to belong to me when I was your age... part of my own studies. I hand-lettered the booklet myself using brush stroke calligraphy."

From Mallory-oniichan, she got a Qwik-Bake Oven Set.

"You stick little cakes in this slot here, and the light bulb inside cooks them!" he explained enthusiastically. "You can make cake, cookies, pies, um... cake... and cookies and pies! And it's guaranteed to not be a fire hazard 95% of the time. Uh... can I play with it when you're done?"

From Lorelei, she got a strange looking stretchy pink cloth thing with straps in the back and two cups in the front.

"Lorelei!" her sister shouted.

"What?" she asked. "Mine started sprouting at her age! You don't want her waking up one morning with 'em popping out, catching her totally unprepared, do you?"

Finally, from her sister, the biggest and most expensive present of all... a My First RealNet Workstation, from RealWare. It was pink and covered with little flower stickers, but inside that plastic casing was an honest-to-goodness workstation, just like the communal one in the living room.

"I know you have a Video Network Set, but this can do a whole lot more than that," she explained. "You can get real-time stock market updates, go to fan nodes for your favorite video streams, publish your own home node... just promise me you won't download lots of music or videos; the digital rights rental fees are pretty high."

She thanked her extended family profusely for the gifts, then there was much laughter, smiles, seconds on the cake...

And finally, herself, alone in her room, surrounded by her new prizes and her old prizes and all that stuff.

That's when the smile faded. A party is one thing, but quiet times are another thing... and all the neat toys in the world couldn't make up for being lonely.

Mallory had offered to play with her (mostly so he could play with the oven) but she kinda wanted to be alone. She didn't really feel like a non-lonely sort at the moment so lonely made sense, which didn't make sense but would have to do. So she told them all she was tired from all the partying, and went up to her room to sit in front of her new workstation and watch the stock tickers go by...

RealWare was up five points in heavy trading on announcing that Reality Engines would be available in three new eye-pleasing colors. Of course, their stock was so high compared to every other company on the UST that you couldn't watch their ticker alongside the others; the line graph scale would be totally out of whack. This is why she poked around the stock application on My First Workstation until she could get overlapping windows—one with RealWare, one with a combination of Noyori Labs, VideoNippon, and Krap Foods Inc...

Most kids watched cartoons, she watched line graphs. The very notion of it made her sigh in a dramatic sign of discontent, as she grabbed one of her many Biiko™ dolls, to comb her luxurious blonde hair.

According to the commercials produced by Edo Heavy Industry Toy Concern (updated quarterly), Biiko™ didn't follow the stock market at all. She spent her days driving pink land-cars, travelling in her Beach House to exotic realities, putting on exciting swimwear and dating Kensuke.™ She had a fun, exciting life and everybody liked her... and weirdly, she was an adult. It didn't make any sense that an adult would do all that stuff, if she was a kid who was more like an adult and not like Biiko,™ and... and... and none of it made any sense at all!

In a fit of frustration, she shut down her Workstation, tossed Biiko™ aside, and ran over to flop on her bed. She'd thought about it enough, felt bad enough about it, so... she'd just take a nap. Something to clear her head...

An hour later, she woke to a knock on the door.

"Eiko-chan? Eiko-chan, can you come downstairs?" her oneechan asked through the door. "We've got a new client. I might need you to help with the contract."

Eiko slumped along down the stairs, tired eyes sticking to the floor as she went. Off to the kitchen, the traditional place of hammering out business deals at the ping pong / dinner table...

"Thank you for waiting," Meiko spoke, resuming her seat. "This is my sister, Eiko. She'll be handling contract negotiation. Don't worry about her age, she's quite capable in this area... Eiko?"

"Ah, hello," she greeted, focusing on the clients, trying to force herself to wake up faster. "Yes, I handle all the contracts for Mirai Consulting! So... can you give me the details of the job?"

The clients were nothing out of the ordinary; a Nipponese couple (made sense, considering they were in Nippon at the moment) of reasonably high social standing. The man had an expensive suit, current quarter fashion—his wife had on a similarly expensive and trendy suit of her own. Both gave her the 'Aww, isn't she cute?' smile she had come to expect from clients, too.

"As I understand it, your sister refers to it as a 'standard thief-tracking package'?" the husband said, glancing to Meiko for confirmation. "It seems a full third of our family fortune has vanished overnight... we'd like Mirai Consulting to find the one responsible. We have reason to believe it was a RealNet-based financial break-in, since we keep very little liquid points on hand in scorecards. The banks were of no help, since according to them, the money was withdrawn legitimately—which makes no sense, but... we're hoping your company can be of help."

"Standard thief-tracking package..." Eiko repeated, hopping off her chair and going for the drawer where they keep the legal documents (the one next to the steak knives). She flipped through to the T's, pulled out a standard contract, and returned with a pen. Made a few minor alterations to cover extra RealNet tracking and possible use of external sources, as Mirai Consulting had no RealNet hacking experts, standard legalese, boilerplate, so on and so forth... and slid the finished document over to the clients.

"We take half the fee up front, and half on successful completion of the job," Eiko recited. "We boast a great success record, but in the event that we are unable to find your stolen money, we'll refund the unused portion of the up-front fee after deducting basic costs. Since we're already docked in Nippon, I've deducted our standard fee for docking, but if travel away from Nippon is incurred it may be filed under normal operating expenses instead. Please take the time to read through the document and if you have any questions, let me know..."

While the husband read through line after line of legalese... the wife gave Eiko a warm smile of appreciation. "You're quite a talented young lady," she commented. "Your sister must be very proud of you, just like we're proud of our little Ken-kun..."

"Ken-kun?" Eiko repeated, nudged out of her familiar contract groove by this.

"Yes, he's over there watching video streams... Ken-kun! Come and say hi to Eiko Mirai!"

...and the one who walked into the kitchen also wore expensive, trendy clothes. They were just many sizes smaller, which made sense, as he was many sizes smaller as well.

He stood there uncomfortably, rocking on his feet. "'lo," he greeted quietly.

"Ken-kun, your manners," his mother chided quietly.

"...hello, Mirai-san," he spoke, trying again and adding a little bow in with it. He quickly turned and scampered back to the couch, without trying to make it look like he was fleeing...

Eiko peered around her sister, watching him go. If a big cartoon question mark could blink on and off over her head, it would.

"Oneechan, do you need me for anything else?" she asked.

"I think we can take it from here, Eiko," she replied. "So, as the contract states..."

Eiko slipped out of her chair, slipped around her sister... and crept into the living room curiously. The boy sat back on the couch, legs dangling a bit in front of him as his eyes stayed fixed to the screen... to the line graphs zipping by while a monotone announcer explained the significance of the new color offerings from RealWare.

It wasn't a stealthy approach, but he didn't notice her until she went out of her way to clear her throat.

"Ummmmm..." she started. "How old are you...?"

"Uh... I think I'm 12," he replied.

"Ano? You think...?"

"Mom and Dad faked my birth certificate so I could apply for a good school early," he admitted. "Uh, if you wanna watch something else, that's okay—"

"No no, it's fine! I... was keeping track of the markets upstairs a while back, too," Eiko admitted in turn.

"You watch the financial news?" he asked, honestly quite surprised.

"Well... yeah!" she said, with a tiny bit of hopeful pride. She bounced over, and sat on the couch next to him. "I'm hoping to be an economist when I grow up... a stock broker or a contract negotiator. How about you?"

"Oh, I don't wanna be an economist. That's just want Mom and Dad want me to be."

Eiko bit her lip. He didn't actually like finance? Was he going to think she was weird for liking it? Was—

"I kinda like money, but... I really wanna be a lawyer," he spoke, with the little hesitation one would apply to a deep secret. "You know, defending the innocent, prosecuting the guilty... maybe moving on to a legislative role to decide what laws are good laws and what laws are bad... stuff like that. Although I'll probably play the stock market more once... once I get better at it. Do you do any trading?"

"No, Meiko-oneechan says I'm not ready to do any trading..." Eiko said, with a pout. "I don't see why not. I know more about money than ANY kid my age! Uh... no offense..."

"None taken! Gum?"

He was holding out a little cube of purple-flavored bubblegum.

"...thanks," Eiko said, accepting it carefully... and with a smile. "I love bubblegum! Hey, um... Ken-kun?"

"It's Kensuke."

"Kensuke?!?" she asked, shocked.

"Uh, no, just Kensuke. No trademark. At least, none I know of..."

"Ken-kun!"

Both kids turned to the voice, as various parents and sisters stood in the House foyer.

"Ken-kun, it's time to go," his mother spoke, while slinging her purse over one shoulder. "Come on now, we need to get home before your tutor arrives..."

Kensuke slipped off the couch, adjusting his suit to avoid wrinkling it. "Coming..."

"H-Hey!" Eiko called, to get his attention. "Um... do you live nearby? Do you wanna drop by tomorrow and watch 'Money Matters'? Or 'Important Court Drama,' that'd be okay too..."

"Drop by...?" he asked, a bit shocked at the offer. "You really want me to drop by? Uh... Mom, can I? I'd be home well before my tutoring time... please?"

"Hmmm... I don't see why not," his mother replied. "The Mirais seem to be an upstanding family, for transients... very well. Now come along."

Two minutes later, Eiko was sitting on the couch, happily chewing her bubblegum while the financial outlook for the fiscal quarter looked bright indeed.

"And that is why my surprise last minute evidence shows that the defendant is really the victim of the plaintiff!" the middle-aged lawyer who still truly believes in the good of the system declared. "As you can see from the conflicting testimony of the witness who nobody suspected of anything despite being the first person we interviewed, the reversal of truth which is apparent in the actions which were undertaken becomes readily apparent. I call for a mistrial!"

"Curses!" the overacting shifty lawyer who only cares about money and has an irritating accent that the audience immediately dislikes muttered under his breath. "Quick, men! To the hydrofoils!"

Secret agents burst in through the windows while firing machine guns, while the Evil Genetically Engineered Super Prosecutor Warlord Lawyers beat a hasty retreat.

"Won't someone PLEASE think of the children!?" someone randomly screamed.

The judge considered this in quiet and very meaningful contemplation which you are supposed to pay attention to. "Yes... but at what cost?" he mused. "Case dismissed."

THE END

...Eiko stared at the Video Network Set, while the credits for Psychotic Paralegal #1 through Psychotic Paralegal #8 scrolled by.

"I had no idea being a lawyer was so incredibly dangerous!" she exclaimed.

"Uhmm... I think they're exaggerating," Kensuke guessed... even if he was a little spooked as well. "I mean. Really. I've read some courtroom transcripts and gunfights don't break out THAT often... uh. But it was pretty cool, wasn't it?"

"YEAH!" Eiko agreed, bouncing a bit in her seat. "I mean, the bit with the thing with that guy who had that other thing? Wow! What a plot twist! And the kung fu was great!"

"So... it's okay that we watched this instead of Money Matters? You're not mad at me?"

"Huh?" she asked, pausing in her bouncing. "'course not! I had fun. I can watch Money Matters anytime, so don't worry!"

"Oh, um, I'm not worrying," Kensuke deflected. "I just... well, I guess I'm not used to having friends. ...that sounds really sad, doesn't it?"

"No, no, not at all! Really. Uh. You kinda remind me of Mallory... you know, the guy who made us orange smoothies? He wasn't used to having friends either when he first got here. But you get used to it! I think. ...uh, what do you wanna do now? Do you have to go home?"

"Not for another hour or two," Kensuke said, glancing at his personal wristwatch miniorganizer. "My tutor scheduled a little later today because the feng shui of his sock drawer was disharmonious. So... what do you want to do? I mean, what do you usually do after Money Matters?"

"Usually? I try to grab Mallory-oniichan or Meiko-oneechan and go play dolls."

Kensuke adopted a look of puzzled confusion. "Dolls? Um... I don't think boys play with dolls. It's a sissy girly thing to do. I'd get beat up."

"...oh."

"But I do play with action figures sometimes!" he added, spotting the legal loophole. "It's kind of the same, except there's more guns and more stuff blows up."

"Oh! Um... wanna play action figures, then...?"

Gunfire erupted over the bunker, a hail of screaming hot lead that threatened to rend flesh from bone. The grinding noise of bullets sinking into

Kevlar laced sandbags was deafening, but somehow the commander managed to scream his orders over the fog of war...

"We've got one last chance, men!" Muscles Manslaughter™ howled, while tapping out embers from the last cigar of his life. "I don't expect all of you to survive this final rush... but those who do will go down in eternity as heroes! Gentlemen, this is our finest hour. Smile upon death, your only true friend... now, let's take THAT PILLOW! On the count of three! Strength and honor! ONE... TWO—"

"Sir!" a stuffed monkey shouted, waving his felt arms frantically. "They've ceased fire! Someone's approaching!"

"What?! Give me that periscope!" Muscles Manslaughter™ shouted back, pushing the monkey aside and grabbing the plastic flexi straw. "...it's one lone soldier, waving a white sticky note? Is he surrendering, or just insane...?"

The voice from the other side of the rolled up socks called out quietly. "I'm unarmed! I've come to discuss terms of surrender! If you'll allow me to enter, we can settle this like civilized people!"

The commander looked confused. "I'm Muscles Manslaughter,™ I'm not supposed to be civilized! I shoot first and then shoot the questions later!"

"But as you can see, our Blokks™ ChibiFigs™ have you surrounded," lone soldier Kensuke™ noted. "If you don't surrender, there'll be a great loss of life. I think we can come to mutually satisfying terms that will allow for the creation of a stuffed animal state alongside the Blokks™ state, if we compromise on the location of various borders and allow for give and take. I have some documents prepared which contain five different proposals which my higher-ups have already approved, so if any of them meet your requirements, we can end this war amicably."

"I think we should hear him out," Crazie Monkie™ whispered to his commander. "We've already lost Konbanwa Neko™ and Froggy the Talking Educational Amphibian.™"

Muscles Manslaughter™ considered this, while grinding his massive underbite against his overbite. "...it's true. You're right! With the proper protocols observed and a mutual level of respect, our two conflicting parties can find middle ground. I'd like Attack Lawyer Larry™ to review your documents and then after a seven-day period during which I'll bring an executive summary to our ruling parliament of stuffed animals, we'll contact you. Until then a cease fire is in effect and our forces will withdraw from the Beanbag Mountains. Agreed?"

"We have come to terms!" Kensuke™ agreed, smiling brightly.

"WAI! And the day is saved!" Eiko agreed. "Boy, that was a LOT of fun!"

"I haven't really played action figures like THAT before," the real Kensuke said, fiddling with his namesake doll. "But that's a lot better than shooting and death and stuff..."

Eiko started gathering up the toys, since she preferred her room to be neat after a play session. "How do you usually play them?" she asked. "Is it a boy thing, or something...?"

"I don't usually play with action figures, period," Kensuke exclaimed, shifting to sit cross-legged while Eiko cleaned up. "I don't have anyone to play with. Dad's too busy with work, and he just sort of looks awkward and confused whenever we try to do father / son stuff... and I don't have many friends, like I said. ...I don't think guys my age play with action figures anymore, technically. Although that was plenty of fun, don't get me wrong!"

Eiko paused in her post-play activity... glancing at the Biiko™ in her hand. "Uh... I don't know if girls my age play dolls, either," she admitted. "But I've always played with them, and I didn't really see any reason to stop... it's not weird, right? I mean, any weirder than... um... well. Other kids think I'm pretty weird, that's all..."

"You too?"

"It wasn't always like that, though," Eiko noted, sitting Biiko™ down next to her My First Workstation. "When I was younger at the orphanage I tried to like the same toys and bands and video streams the other girls did. And it went okay, I mean, I think I had some friends... but when I really got interested in my oneechan's textbooks and collecting 'en' coins, they started thinking I was weird. They made fun of me liking boring grownup stuff..."

"I don't see what's so weird about it," Kensuke said, honestly. "So what if we study economics or play with dolls or whatever? It doesn't mean we're adults, either. It's... okay. I thought about this a lot, actually. Lemme explain. I used to think is that the sports the other boys were so into were a strange hobby. Not playing sports, but, like... obsessively thinking about sports all the time! Some guys I meet are really into ping pong, for instance—they collect ping pong cards, they memorize statistics for the star players, they can quote matches that happened twenty years ago move for move..."

"That's some memory for numbers! Are they good at math like we are?"

"Sometimes. Sometimes they're just good at ping pong statistics... but it's like, why do they think we're weird for the things we like, when I thought they were weird for the things they like? It just didn't seem fair, until I figured it out."

"Figured what out?"

"It's all just... stuff. Fun and games. It's all fun in the end, it's just different people think different things are fun," Kensuke explained, leaning back a bit. "There's no 'weird' or 'too adult' about it. I decided, well... as long as you're *having fun* with something, you're still a kid. We'll have to do this stuff as a real job later, and judging from my dad's chronic ulcers, adulthood's no fun at all. So... I wanna have fun with what I think is fun as long as I can... and maybe if I do, it won't be less fun for me later. I'll always be a kid at heart even when I'm old enough to drink! I don't care if I'm six, twelve, twenty-four, forty-eight—as long as I'm having fun it's all good. That's my goal. ...I mean... you know what I mean, right?"

The Biiko™doll fell over from its loose sitting position, nudging the My First Workstation Mouse...

...and the glowing white enlightenment of the screen shone through the darkness of the screen saver, illuminating Eiko's face, reflecting in her wide open eyes.

"...I hadn't thought of it like that," she said, quietly. "I thought I was just weird, since everybody said so, but... but that really makes sense. That really, really makes sense..."

"Uh... yeah, it does, doesn't it?" Kensuke said, smiling a little with pride. "I thought up that myself. It's a great thought thing. So... neither of us should worry about that stuff. And it's good I met you! I haven't met anyone my age who understood that—"

A soft knocking at the door interrupted the grand philosophical discussion, as Meiko entered the chamber of deep thoughts and plushies.

"Kensuke, your parents are here to pick you up," Meiko informed. "It seems your tutor decided to go without socks today, so he's ready for you. Time to go."

"Awwww...." Eiko awww'd, with a pout.

Kensuke got off the floor, dusting off his sport coat. "It's okay, I don't have any tutoring tomorrow," he said. "We can play longer if you like—hey! I know, I know! My dad can get us passes to the premiere of Muscles Manslaughter vs. the Reality Pirates! You wanna go?"

Eiko's face lit up like a bright shiny object. "Really?! Yeah! I'd love to go!"

"Okay! It's a date!" Kensuke replied, grinning big before skipping out of the room.

...Meiko's brain tripped over the word, backtracked, and tried to parse it again. Then her gaze settled on her giggly-happy little sister. Who was just asked out on a date by a boy.

"This is gonna be so cool!" Eiko warbled. "I'll have to withdraw some points from my account to cover refreshment costs and expenditures... um... oneechan? What's wrong?"

"Eiko, can I see you in my off—in my room, please?" Meiko asked politely.

"...uh... uhoh."

It was not entirely unlike a tense contract negotiation situation. Both parties had goals which were nebulous and hazy, to be defined through the give and take of the process. They sat at opposite sides of the kotatsu... tension thick in the air. Thick like the gravy on Mallory's famous Grünwaldian Turkeyshoot Feast.

Currently there was a pause in negotiations, while Meiko consulted a parental movie appropriate-ness node on RealNet. Little thermometer-like grades were given for the relative morality of the film under discussion. If they were real thermometers, the patient would likely be dead due to his internal body temperature surpassing the boiling point of lead.

But that could wait, prior to a more immediate line of questioning the adult ruling party of the first part required of the supplicant party of the second part.

"How would you describe your relationship with Kensuke, Eiko-chan?" Meiko asked, tinging the '-chan' with just enough friendliness to put her opponent at measured ease.

"Rela...? Uh... we're just friends, oneechan," Eiko explained, squirming in her seat. "We like the same stuff, and we play the same games, and stuff. We're friends."

"Do you have a crush on him?"

"N-No, of course not!" Eiko protested, a faint blush showing as is obligatory in such situations. "No way. Besides, there's the whole 'cootie' issue which remains unresolved and could pose a potential obstacle. So we're just friends. You know... like you and Mallory-kun!"

Counterattack. Meiko flinched. Eiko smirked. The tactical angle was promptly changed.

"According to this, Muscles Manslaughter vs. the Reality Pirates is rated 13," Meiko explained, setting her F.P. organizer down and turning it around for Eiko to see. "For reasons of foul language and graphic violence—"

"I know, I know, but I'm more mature than I look!" Eiko protested. "Given my emotional development over the years I feel I'm capable of judging the film in the proper social context rather than relying on dangerous mimicry of the on-screen actions. I believe I have an understanding vis à vis the impact of visualized violence on a culture of impressionable youths. If anything, seeing this movie will help affirm my psychological growth and expose me to elements that I need to cope with as I grow older. Therefore, seeing Muscles Manslaughter vs. the Reality Pirates is not only safe for me, but... I'd go so far as to say it's IMPERATIVE that I see this film! For the sake of my health. Wouldn't you agree...?"

Meiko stared flatly at her sister, arms crossed.

"You added a few points of proof since the last time you gave me that routine," she pointed out.

"...um... I did more research on the subject?" Eiko tried. "Oneechan, please please PLEASE can I go? I really wanna see this movie and it's the only time

I've ever had a friend ask me to see a movie and I really wanna go please please please—"

"I'll let you go."

"—pleasepleasepl—"

"Eiko!"

"Nani?"

"I'll let you see the movie," Meiko repeated.

"...WAI! VICTOLY!" Eiko cheered, flashing a *double* V for Victoly.

"But you're going with a chaperone."

"...oh."

The negotiation complete, Meiko sat back and thought fast. She couldn't go herself; she was in the middle of an investigation job for a client. But the others would be free. So, she could always send...

> "Whoa!" Kensuke whispered out loud. "That was a really gory death just now! Yuck! Hey, what was that 'thud' noise?"
>
> "Oh, that was just Mallory-kun whimpering and passing out behind us," Eiko replied. "More popcorn?"

...no. Instead, she'd send...

> "...so you see, after they start kissing, the shirts come off and then it's the man's duty to fumble a bit at the bra clasp before the woman has to take care of it for him," Lorelei explained. "Check out the detail of how the latching mechanism works—"
>
> "Uh, Lorelei-san, aren't we supposed to be two theaters to the left, seeing Muscles Man—"
>
> "Quiet, kid, this is more educational for you. Hey, she's not wearing panties! Eiko, are you taking notes like I asked you to?

NO. Nooo. No. That left...

Meiko smiled quietly.

The male half of the Date with a capital D paced restlessly outside the multiplex, ignoring the long lines forming to get into the movie. He told her 7:30 so they could be seated early. She'd be here by 7:30. No need to worry, even if it was 7:29. No need to...

And there she was, strolling along the sidewalk by herself, looking bright and cheerful.

"Ken-kuuun!" Eiko called out, waving. "Sorry I'm 52 seconds early, but here I am! Is it time to go in yet?"

"Ah... Eiko!" Ken called back, after his mind tripped over the 'Ken-kun' tag. "Yeah, let's go! ...uh... mom told me Meiko was gonna send a chaperone...?"

"Oh, she's around," Eiko replied, walking up to the ticket booth with her date. "But don't worry, you won't see her. She's real sneaky like.... hi! We've got three passes reserved for Muscles Manslaughter vs. the Reality Pirates, under the name Kensuke. Thanks!"

Eiko pocketed one ticket in her overalls, gave the second to Kensuke, and threw the third up in the air. It did not come down.

The lovely couple walked up to the ticket-clipping guy, and into the theatre. Said ticket-clipping guy was surprised to see a third ticket, pre-clipped with a serrated military knife, already dropped into his bin by the time he looked down.

Despite the overwhelming number of people in queue to see the movie, Eiko and Kensuke had their own little private area. This was accomplished by his father buying up the ten surrounding seats, to provide a nice buffer zone around them. So, despite the shadowy figures of other movie goers... Eiko was having fun pretending they were the only people there.

Her fun level was full to bursting. Here she was at the movies with a friend! With someone who liked her and wanted to go places with her! With a bo... with a friend! With popcorn. And Krap Foods Chewy Things.™And a real, honest-to-goodness 13-rated movie!

And with a chaperone, a fact which had not gone unnoticed despite Kisei going unnoticed...

On screen, Muscles Manslaughter, crack commando for RealWare's Special Reality Corps (available for reasonable rates for your internal uprising or government crackdown) was priming the ripcords on his twin repeating 'Fleshgrinder' bladed projectile launchers, while the renegade Open Engine-powered huts of the Reality Pirates popped up all over Urbana. He rocked the loading chambers of both guns, making a satisfying KUCHUNK sound as tiny nuggets of microfiber cutting death locked into place, ready to carve up some Open Reality Movement scum.

"I'm here to kick fu ₹?q and take bubblegum, and I'm all out of babes!" he declared.

Kensuke cocked his head, rubbing at one ear. "Uh... what'd he just say?" he whispered to Eiko.

"I couldn't tell, it's like there was this little burst of noise..."

Unconcerned with the noise, Muscles Manslaughter strolled up to one of the buildings, and kicked in the door with a boot that two ordinary men could put both feet into. "EAT BLAZING MECHANICAL DEATH, you miserable, toesucking, open source ﬁꓕ ₽ ⊗!!"

A spent NoiseCap (available for reasonable rates from Duke's Munitions) dropped into Eiko's popcorn. Just the thing for precisely timed censoring of certain words that her sister didn't want her to hear.

And when the pirates began to experience the business end of the Fleshgrinders, a folding paper screen with a wooden frame dropped neatly into place in front of them, blocking the view completely. A small note was tacked to it with an (un)poisoned dart, reading 'forbidden' in kanji characters.

Eiko groaned, and sank in her seat. "Oneechaaan! This isn't fair... mou. How am I ever gonna be desensitized to violence if Kisei-san won't let me see any?... what're you giggling at?"

The boy tried to stifle his laugh, to avoid annoying the folks two seats off in three of the cardinal directions. "I just think it's kinda funny," he said. "She really went all out to keep you 'safe'. It's funny."

"...s'not that funny," Eiko said, pouting as the unseen carnage and screams flowed around the screen to her ears. Then considered it a bit. "...okay, it's a little funny..."

Once the fight was over, the screen was yanked back up into the air via invisible plastic wire normally used to garrote three-hundred-pound armed guards, and resumed watching the movie in peace.

Twenty minutes later, Eiko leaned forward to grab her Slushie, and found an arm draped around her shoulders when she leaned back.

"Uh... Kensuke?" she asked, stuck in place (and not because of the gummy floor).

"Um, yeah?"

"Is that your arm?"

"...I think so."

"Okay. Just checking."

"Okay."

"Right. Um, I—"

The screen dropped down again before they could see boobies, and the subject was forgotten. Even if Eiko did lean a little to her left after that. Towards Kensuke.

Stop #2 on the Dating Experience (not that it was a date, since he was just her friend) involved ice cream. Anything involving ice cream immediately got Eiko's full and undivided attention, causing her to forget the mild annoyance of an artificially watered-down action movie.

The dessert shop was conveniently located near the theater—just the thing for folks who hadn't gotten enough of overpriced sugar-gum-based beverages and artery-hardening popcorn. There was an all-night medical clinic four doors down from that—just the thing for folks who HAD gotten enough of overpriced sugar-gum-based beverages and artery-hardening popcorn.

Eiko's metabolism could burn sugar at a phenomenal rate, so ice cream was just the ticket for her after a full movie of other snacks. She sat at the cozy little padded booth, kicking her legs and waiting for Kensuke to return...

He slid into the booth next to her (rather than across from her), while carefully passing a triple-decker cone to her. "Strawberry, coffee, and Aquarius mint. With sprinkles," he announced. "Isn't that kind of a strange combination?"

"No stranger than your triple scoop of coffee, coffee and coffee," Eiko pointed out, balancing her cone with practiced ease and taking a few licks at it. "Mmm! Boy, I hope I can get to bed tonight; oneechan says I get a little hyper when I've had too much—"

A blur whisked past her eyes, and her cone was reduced to two scoops. A note fluttered to the table explaining in concise detail the merits of a balanced diet.

"Awwwww!" Eiko pouted. "No fair! ... but at least she didn't get my two favorite flavors! Um... can I propose a toast using ice cream cones, or do we need drinks for that?"

"Glasses are kinda like cones, I don't see why not," Kensuke decided. He raised his up, flexing the elbow in his sport coat. "What're we toasting to?"

"To... to new friends!" Eiko decided, changing her mind. "And many days of having fun together from now on!"

"Hmm... all right! Sounds good here!"

The cones went 'crunch' softly—and Eiko was reduced to one scoop, the topmost one dropping neatly into her lap.

"WAH!" she panicked, jumping a bit and causing it to roll to the floor. "Nooo! Come back, coffee! I... um..."

When she looked up, she saw Kensuke rolling one of his three coffee scoops carefully on top of her cone.

"Uh, don't worry, I didn't lick it yet," he disclaimered. "And... this way we both have two scoops, so it adds up. Right?"

"...yeah, it does," Eiko agreed, smiling brightly. "Arigato, Ken-kun!"

The two shared a laugh, and got down to some serious dessert intake before anything else went splat. It was a bit messy, but there were napkins, and much fun was had by all. The third party even found herself chuckling quietly before realizing and stopping immediately.

They were still laughing as they walked down the street, towards the Noyori Docking Yard.

"...so when the CIO resigned, it set up a chain reaction that exposed the paper-shredding operations the accounting firm had set up," Kensuke continued. "And when the vice president in charge of talent acquisitions found the photo they had left in the Kensington file, he said, 'That's no incriminating evidence—*that's my wife!*'"

"Hee hee hee!" Eiko giggled (since even her uproariously frenzied laughter was cute in nature). "It's funny 'cause it's true!"

"Hey... you know, Important Court Drama: The Movie is premiering next week," Kensuke said, picking his spot to inject the question he'd been wanting to ask all night. "And, um, assuming you had enough fun tonight... do you wanna go to that movie too? I'd pay, of course."

"Are you KIDDING?!"

"Oh. Well, I mean, if you don't—"

"I'd love to go!" Eiko replied. "I mean... wow! Law is more fascinating than I thought, you know? And... and I did have a lot of fun tonight. Really a lot! And I wanna see you again. ...tomorrow, I mean. If you're free, so we can play. Okay?"

"Sure thing!" Kensuke said, cheering up after the wee moment of fear. "I think I can schedule it around my tutoring. Maybe we could see a different movie? Or just watch a video stream, or go out to eat dinner...? Um... what?"

Eiko had paused in her walking, to peer big-eyed at him. Up close. Too much so for comfort.

"Ken-kun... can I ask you a serious question?" she asked. "Maybe a grown-up one...?"

"Uh... yes?" he guessed. "I don't mind. Ask away."

"Was this a date?"

"D-Date?" he parroted, taking a step back. "Uh... did... you want it to be one?"

Eiko was the one to step back, then. Ball in her court, as she poked her index fingers together, looking down, all the standard signs of a shy young girl. "...I... I was hoping it was one," she told, truthfully. "Not at first, of course! But... I had a lot of fun, and it looked like a date, so that meant that I liked dating, and... I liked going on a date with you. So, it IS a date, right?"

"Y-yes! It's a date! ...I was kinda worried it wasn't one, myself. I mean, I'd never asked a girl out before, and I could've gotten it wrong. I didn't do enough research beforehand... I mean... ...uh, we're here."

"We're where?" Eiko asked, confused. "Somewhere specific in our relationship? Is this one of those baseball analogies Lorelei uses?"

"No, I mean we're at your house," he clarified, pointing to the big building neither of them had noticed they were standing in front of.

"Oh! Home! Right! So... I'll see you tomorrow, then?"

"You bet!"

"...um... Kensuke?"

"Yeah?"

"I think you're supposed to kiss me goodnight before you go," Eiko said, felling the odd little *dokidoki* beating in her heart. "If you want to, of course! I'd be okay with not doing that... uh. Kisei-san, it's okay, right? I don't want you dropping Ken-kun with a tranq dart..."

A nervous pause transpired.

A tiny dart embedded in the wall next to the door, with a note attached. 'Acceptable'.

The note unfolded itself automatically, continuing with 'But no impropriety, young man'.

"I really can?" Kensuke asked aloud, to make sure... as he took a step closer. "I wouldn't mind... if you don't, of course... it's very reasonable to skip that step in the dating process since we're both kids and perhaps not emotionally ready for such a development in—"

"Ken-kun?"

"Yeah?"

She leaned forward and kissed him.

It wasn't the kind of kiss that could light Nippon ablaze. It was awkward and innocent... tight lips touching so lightly that the point of contact could possibly be measured at the molecular level. But at least in Eiko's mind, it was like a full 101-piece orchestra blazing into fugue of romantic music...

My first kiss, she thought to herself. *It tastes like... grape?*

That's when the portal of doom (aka 'the front door') swung open with great force.

Eiko's jaw sagged, on seeing the expression Meiko bore.

"...oh, 私は死ん だ," she whispered.

Both kids were pulled into the house by force, and the door slammed shut behind them.

The mood went from cutely romantic to parentally serious in 0.3 seconds.

Meiko, Lorelei, and Kensuke's parents were there, and none of them looked happy. Kensuke's skin drained of color; Eiko poked at the foyer carpeting with her sneaker, looking at the floor.

"Explain yourself, young man," his mother demanded in a 'I'm very disappointed in you' sort of way.

"I can explain, I can explain!" Kensuke blurted out. "It just seemed like the right thing to do at the time...! I'll never kiss another girl, I swear—"

"What?" his mother asked. "No, no! I meant about the money, Kensuke, the money! What did you do with it?! You are in SO much trouble, young man..."

"The evidence," Lorelei declared... holding up a sealed plastic baggie, containing a tiny purple wad of gummy ick. "I found it 'parked' underneath your father's workstation desk. The same workstation used to drain the family cash supply. Your flavor, I believe, Kensuke-san? I'm a passion fruit type, myself..."

"A quick fingerprint and DNA check proved you were using that workstation when you knew you didn't have permission... it would be best if you fess up now," Meiko suggested not unkindly. "Mirai Consulting has solved the case quite definitively, and you're the culprit. It might be easier on you to be honest about what you've done with the money."

"...Ken-kun..." Eiko whispered, a little scared...

...while the boy stepped forward, some strength coming to him as he did so.

"I was day trading on the Urbana Stock Market," he explained simply. "The sort of thing you two want me to do with my life, right? I'm supposed to be a great economist. So I figured I'd see if I was or not by trying to make money on the market, using everything that tutor drills me on each day. And I lost every en and point I tried to invest. I wasn't even trying to, it just happened because I wasn't any good at being my own stockbroker!"

"Kensuke, of course you weren't ready to trade!" his father exclaimed, feeling his ulcer churn inside. "After another ten or twenty years of training and apprenticeship, then you'll be ready to fill my shoes—"

"I don't WANT to fill your shoes, Dad!" the son barked back. "I want to be a lawyer! I'm not any good with big money, and I don't want to spend years getting good with it! I don't wanna be an adult who doesn't have any fun doing what I do, like you! I want to help defend the innocent and prosecute the guilty and make sure laws work for the people. I'm gonna be a lawyer, NOT an economist, and... and I'll do it myself if I have to, but I'm not studying finance anymore! You can't make me do something that's no fun!"

The kindly mother who had come to Mirai Consulting two days ago with a sweet smile and a soft voice was a red-faced fire breathing monster at that point. "Such impudence...! How dare you talk back to your parents? You're going to study finance, and that's fin—"

"He can study law."

It's a rule of the multiverse that when someone casually interrupts with surprising words, everybody has to turn and look at the source and shut up.

"I'll allow it," his father decided. "Clearly the boy is miserable learning finance. ...I see no reason for him to become something he hates. It'd be an uphill struggle for us and wouldn't help him one bit. He deserves to do something with his life that he enjoys... I would have wanted the same chance from my father. And that's final, honey."

"I... I can really be a lawyer?" Kensuke asked, strength fading (as it was no longer needed). "Really?"

"That's... that's SO COOL!" Eiko cheered, giving Ken-kun a big hug. "VICTOLY for Ken-kun! Hip hip—"

"But he's grounded for the next three months," his father added.

"—hooray..."

"If you're going to be serious about being a lawyer, it means being responsible when you break a law," his father spoke gravely... some of the 'impending doom' returning to his voice. "And I specifically told you not to use my workstation, and you know that gambling the family fortune was obviously prohibited. You'll be home for three months... and that means no RealNet, no video streams aside from educational ones, and that especially means no... 'dates'. Now say goodbye, we're going home."

Eiko detangled herself from her would-be boyfriend, eyes wide with shock. "Grounded...? But... but I just met him! It's not f—"

"Eiko... it's okay," Kensuke said... smiling a little to her. "It's only three months."

"But we could leave Nippon by then... and... and that's exactly 2.083333% of my lifespan to date! What'll I do until then?"

Kensuke turned to go, while his parents slipped on their coats. "You know what you'll do. And... we'll always have Manslaughter. Goodbye."

A quick peck to the cheek, and Kensuke was out of her life for not exactly forever, but close enough to lower her mood considerably. The closing of the door was unnecessarily quiet.

Lorelei rested a sympathetic hand on Eiko's shoulder.

"If you don't see him again, well, there'll be others, kid," she offered. "Besides, it's better to have loved and lost than to have loved and had the bastard stab you in the back by sleeping with another woman while you were working hard to put food on the table."

...but Eiko was smiling, despite the few tears in her eyes.

"It's okay, Lorelei-san," she said, brushing away from the hand on her shoulder. "I'll see him again. And... it was fun. It was fun! That's what matters; as long as I'm having fun, I'm still a kid! Oi, Meiko-oneechan... you should take Mallory-kun on a date, they're a lot of fun!"

Mallory peeked in from the hallway. "Uh, did someone call for me...?"

"**N**o," Meiko replied swiftly, putting boldface emphasis on the N. "I'm going to my room to read. Excuse me."

And Eiko Mirai, twelve years young, couldn't help but giggle.

Dear dad,

It has been a bit since I last wrote you! I have been slightly homesick I am thinking, because I keep dreaming of green grass and blue skies (??) and trees and so on. Very happy places. Maybe I am not homeSICK since I do not feel sick, but home calls, yes? But work calls too, and I have work to do, so I will have to postpone a visit! You understand I hope.

Truthfully I haven't been too busy (beyond the normal chore stuff which I swear this house would fall apart if I was not doing it!) but all the people around me have been really really busy. So I'll talk about what they've been doing.

First of all we went to visit Lorelei's mother. They did not get along well, because Lorelei was not happy with the Tribal Alpha way of life (did you ever go there when you were travelling around? it was one huge game, apparently, but not like Ping Pong). I mostly stayed at home playing with Eiko and tidying up. Meiko was sitting around trying to figure out a good and peaceful solution to the problem, and she was really frustrated so I made her a cup of tea. She said she liked it VERY much, and that was pretty good to hear, since I know I'm only soso with tea and I was hoping I could do something to help her feel better. I did not think I could sell the 'bad guys' a recipe this time. You only get away with that kind of miracle once or twice!

But things worked out okay because Lorelei (and Kisei who acted a bit oddly but Meiko decided to let it go since things worked out okay) came up with some sort of plan with some people that made it so people didn't have to fight anymore. Her mother had some trouble accepting and we stayed two days so they could talk and folks could adjust and stuff and because they were still paying for our docking fees. Meiko was not happy that Lorelei did stuff on her own or that Kisei kind of sort of didn't quite act all loyal or something but you know what? I think she (Meiko) was just happy things were okay in the end. But we did not make any money since we did not technically take the job or did not do what was asked or something.

So while waiting for a job then Kisei resigned from her job. It was a great surprise to everybody, I tell you! She hid up in her room awhile and I tried to bring her dinner, but I guess she did not want to see anyone. Meiko was concerned and was going to try to talk her out of it but told me that "she had to be a professional" and that meant adhering to their contract which said Kisei could leave. I disagreed with that since they were friends (at least as close to friends as Kisei would get!) and friends don't let friends make mistakes and Meiko said I Did Not Understand How Things Worked In Reality and called me Houseboy again, so I backed off. So when Meiko decided we should give Kisei her stuff she left behind I volunteered to go and deliver it; I do not think

Meiko wanted to go since she felt she had to respect Kisei's privacy even if she was worried. Meiko worries a lot but doesn't try to show it because she's the boss and the boss should be confident. It has taken me some time to figure it out (and Lorelei nudged me more than once I can tell you!) but I think that is how it is. I showed up in time because Kisei almost had an accident, and I gave her back her stuff and her book of poetry which I thought was really good and I think it cheered her up some, because she came back! and that was that. I think kisei is smiling a little more now but it is hard to tell because you have to catch it out of the corner of your eye.

And we finally got a job! which is good because money is running low, really low because work is hard to find in a career like ours. A couple here in Nippon lost some money and Meiko knows how to find money so she took the job. But the neat thing was that they had a little boy who was Eiko's age and they played and got along great, which is good because despite throwing a terrific party (she did not suspect the surprise at all!!) I am not sure she was having a good day. But she sure was smiling after! And that made Meiko smile. Even if Meiko got a little nervous when it turned out they wanted to go on a Date. I would have chaperoned but Meiko thought Kisei would be better for some reason so I stayed home. Unfortunately when they came back it turned out that the boy had lost the money so he was grounded, and that is sad for Eiko but she seems happy, so whatever works! I know I would be sad if separated from someone I really liked, but maybe it is one of those deep things.

But now we are again between jobs and that is bad, because as I said the money is low. I am sorry I do not have any money to send home this week because I decided to tell Meiko I would forgo my pay so we would be better off. What do I use it for, anyway? I do not shop any! I could finish a few of my collections (they are gathering dust in the closet; I guess now that I am out and about I do not feel that manic urge to gather multiversal stuff! I am in the multiverse so why get stuff? Right) but it would be better to keep the money in the house and I think Meiko was relieved what I did this although she was in Boss Mode and tries to be kinda straightforward and pro in that type so she just gave me a brief thankyou.

I am settling in very well here. I remember I was in fairly cool control of me back home because well it was home and I was used to home, you know? Nothing surprising or strange or scary. But here it was surprising and strange and scary and all three meant I was kind of jumpy! but now I am adjusting and this place is home too, I think. The people are great and I am good friends with them all and Meiko is really terrific. Really terrific. It is sometimes hard to read her for reasons I have mentioned above but I do my best because I like it when she smiles and I know even if I cannot do a whole lot beyond cooking and cleaning and kicking the engine when it crashes (funny it has only crashed once since I got here) I do what I can and I'm glad when I can help her.

This has been a very long letter!! and I will sign off now because it is late. I got your letter last when you were talking about Nipponese pop music mother really liked (n-pop! n-pop! Eiko educated me there) and I am thinking of sampling some on this workstation so I can get at my roots, you know? I am certain I would like it even if I am not your biological son but we have talked about that already, so you know what time it is, yo. (that is slang! Eiko educated me there too)

Peace out!!!!

Your son Mallory!

Keying in the Send-Mail command sequence (because real engineers never touch the mouse), Mallory zipped his letter to home along.

He leaned back in the workstation chair, rubbing at his eyes. It had been a long day of doldrums... a nice, lengthy letter to write was a good way to break the tedium. But now he had a few minutes before his usual bedtime, and nothing to do... nothing that could fit into a few minutes...

"Mallory?"

"Huh?" he asked, leaning back more to glance over his shoulder (and almost toppling backwards in the process) "Meiko? What're you doing up, isn't it kinda late?"

"I was just going through the want ads upstairs, trying to find a possible client," she explained, tilting her head left to unkink her neck. "Do we have any tea prepped? Just a cup before I get some sleep. Or if we don't have any, I guess water'll do—"

"No no, I can make some tea," Mallory said, turning around in his chair... then turning back again. "Uh, I'll be with you in a second, just wanna take care of something..."

Meiko gave a tired little grunt of acknowledgement, and shuffled off to the darkened kitchen... while Mallory pulled up the RealNet MusicShare program Eiko had taught him to use earlier.

He tabbed over to the genre selection box for *N-Pop*... and close to twenty thousand song titles in a bizarre mix of his normal tongue and Nihongo zipped by on screen. It was a blur of funny little scribble-characters and poorly translated words like 'LORVE' and 'HART' and 'COOLLE!'. No bands he recognized, no titles that caught his eye... but that was to be expected, since he'd never heard any N-Pop before.

Figuring it couldn't hurt to have plenty to listen to, he picked *Select All*, then *Download*. Then turned off the monitor and went to fix Meiko a cup of tea.

If the monitor still had power, two windows would be visible. One was titled *'File Download Progress'*. The second was titled *'Digital Rights Management Royalty Fees for Music Rental'*. Both had started at zero. And both were slowly but steadily growing larger...

10: Yu-To-Me

example #1: an honest night's work

The concept was so effective that Meiko had a hard time believing that Mallory thought it up. Of course, it was simple yet effective, which took it down enough pegs to put it at a reasonable level for the boy.

'Since we've been sort of disjointed lately, what with Kisei leaving for a while and Lorelei having her family problems and Eiko being lonely without her new friend,' the justification went, 'Let's all do something together for a change!'

Meiko had started to explain that odds were Kisei would want to stay in her room and Lorelei probably wouldn't want to hamper her daily night life when Kisei popped out of nowhere to agree with Mallory's sentiment and Lorelei announced she was bored of one night stands for a while and Eiko promptly suggested the group activity to undertake... thus, the outing.

"Eiko, you know that real courtrooms aren't like that, right?" Meiko asked, trying to make sure the younger Mirai sister hadn't been skewed by the farce they just witnessed.

"Oh, I know," Eiko explained, skipping along the sidewalks of Edo while being careful not to step on any cracks. "Kensuke told me all about how courts work and stuff. But Important Court Drama: The Movie was really, really cool! Ne, Lorelei, didn't you think the speedboat chase with the guy in the bear costume was neat?"

Lorelei gave a shrug, nonplussed about the whole affair. "I don't see the point of high-speed motorized vehicles, myself. It's not like there's any reality out there big enough to need one to go that fast. I guess it's just a male compensation thing... speaking of which, I thought the love scene with the prosecutor and the defendant was pretty sweet."

"Love scene?"

"The one Meiko was covering your eyes for."

"Ewww, the one with all the gross wet noises and sticky sounds?" Eiko said, with a cute pout of distaste. "I wouldn't have watched that anyway... how about you, Mallory-oniichan?"

Mallory, who had been watching for police out of the corner if his eye ever since being subjected to a plot about someone being given the death penalty for jaywalking, nearly jumped out of three fourths of his skin when addressed. "Waah?! Ah... yeah, it was... gripping! I mean, wow... justice back home is nowhere NEAR as complicated as that! Of course, we have to deal with the

Village Council being jerks, but... uh. Well, it's different, is all. Kisei? What did you think...?"

Lorelei gave a little chuckle. "Probably not enough assassinations, right, Kiss—"

"The framing device of the Dutch Tilt was overused, turning the shot composition into a flawed work of excess," Kisei smoothly replied. "I found the fluttering paper metaphor to be underutilized by comparison—the visual imagery of the paperwork flowing out of the fifth-story office window with the soft music reminded me a great deal of the sakura blossoms in the spring, and thus evoked an image of beauty and serenity amidst an urban wasteland. However, this one trait was not enough to salvage a script which utilized cliché like a fifty-pound sledge and stereotypes as a tool for plotline simplification."

Mallory was too busy staring to avoid jaywalking, but his instincts jerked him back before he could commit what was supposedly a capital crime. The others had similar reactions.

...to which Kisei cleared her throat politely, and looked aside in embarrassment so mild that it was nearly unreadable. "I... have been attempting to regain my appreciation for the arts," she explained quietly. "My apologies if my assessment is overly complicated..."

"It's... it's really great, Kisei!" Mallory spoke up with, wanting to be encouraging. "I mean, not that I really understood a lot of it, but you put a lot of thought into it and that's great, and... uh... stuff! Yes!"

"I too would say... stuff, yes," Lorelei spoke, possibly the most confused one of the group. "You okay there, Kisei? Not running a fever or anything?"

"I am in adequate health, considering I have been sitting in an uncomfortable seat in an unsanitary theater for the last two hours," the assassin replied, shifting back to her usual flat tone.

Meiko added a little spring to her step. Just a little. "I hear you, Kisei. If we could afford the digital rights rental fees to watch it at home, we'd watch movies that way instead. We can barely afford the RealNet access we already have... public theaters will have to do. ...I think we should go see a movie again soon. This was a good team-building exercise."

"It was fun, too!" Eiko noted. "Fun fun fun fun fun! And... anooo... oneechan?"

"Yes?"

"Where's our home?"

The five residents of the House found themselves staring at an empty docking space, where the House used to be.

Empty, save for the tiny red paper reading: IMPOUNDED.

Fun and games were officially over. It was now Panic Time.

Of course, for Meiko, panic had to be undertaken in an orderly and professional manner. She did not pace in circles, pull at her hair, or any of the usual activities associated with a state of mind-numbing stress. A loud voice, however, was a component in her modification to the process. Particularly when she found out exactly why the House was impounded.

"EIGHTEEN... THOUSAND... seven hundred... and thirty-four N-Pop songs?!" Meiko repeated, staring at Ryo's personal RealNet Workstation screen in horror.

"Uh... well, I wasn't sure which ones I'd like," Mallory lamely defended. "So I figured I'd just download them all..."

Now would be a good time to describe how the rest of the gang was dealing with panic.

- Lorelei was scrunched down into one of the many beanbag chairs around Ryo Noyori's Office / Playroom, arms folded, making sure to silently express a mixture of disdain for the Farmboy's mistake and worry for what's become of their home.

- Eiko was waving her arms madly and panicking, but that was because Ryo's secretary had given her a candy bar in hopes it'd cheer her up, and the sugar was pumping through her veins like molten lava.

- Kisei was quietly reading a 'Model Monorail Monthly' magazine she found lying on Ryo's desk.

- Mallory had found 64 different ways to apologize with big puppy dog eyes and various types of stammers.

- And Ryo was actually quite impressed with the severity of the disaster.

"You know, I'm a heavy media downloader and even I have never racked up this much of a bill," Ryo was calmly stating, reading the numbers over and over to himself. "No wonder they impounded the house. After the first one thousand downloads, the rights fees drained the House points account, and they didn't have a choice but to impound the most expensive property in your estate. Which was your estate. But that's not the most amazing part!"

"What... part... is more amazing?" Meiko asked, looming with Evil Death over the oblivious geek.

"According to my NetWatchdog sniffer program I got off an Open Source Movement node, your workstation's not done downloading," Ryo explained. "So while the house is sitting in the impound lot it's racking up even MORE debt. We can't get in through the onsen, they were smart enough to turn off the door. If you don't get it out of hock and turn off the workstation before... let's see... five in the morning, you'll get a six-figure negative number on your account. Wow, when you guys get in trouble, you don't... err... kid around...? Meiko? Meiko, put down the chair, please..."

"H-Hold it, hold it!" Mallory interjected, despite the immediate threat to his person this spawned. "Wait, we can deal with this! All we need to do is get a job! We're a troubleshooting firm, right? We get a job that pays... uh... LOTS of money and can be finished by tomorrow, and then we can pay off the debt and we're back in black and Bob's your uncle while pulling the other one which has bells on! ...right? A job? That'll work, right, Meiko?"

"A... job," Meiko repeated, slowly lowering the chair, but still seething internally. "Mallory. I've been looking for a job for DAYS. There are none available right now. The chances of finding one which can pay that much in that little time without dipping into the dark side of the law is nil to none."

"Look, there's really no need for hassle here, guys," Ryo assured, now that Mallory had volunteered to absorb her wrath. "I told you earlier, this is chump change for Noyori Labs. I can pay—"

Meiko let the chair drop.

"No," she replied.

"But—"

"No."

"Meiko, I'm just saying—"

"NO."

Ryo buckled like a belt under the firm glare of Meiko. With a sigh, he let his shoulders sag, and admitted to the second option.

"...then you'll need a job," he agreed. "Mallory's right. It's the only way. My first suggestion would be me paying you to do something like stuff promotional envelopes for an hour, but—no, Meiko, I'm not suggesting that, be cool. ...I do know of someone who needs workers tonight. And will pay a lot. And yes, it's legal. But I told him you guys would never go for it."

"Arrange a meeting, Ryo. I'll decide what we go for and don't go for," Meiko said, assuming her full Boss Voice. "I am willing to relax my standards a bit during times of fiscal crisis. A. Bit. Call your friend and Eiko and I will meet with him here at the lab. If you'll excuse me... I'm going to go freshen up. Excuse me."

She marched purposefully out of the lab at high speed, before anything else could be said. The door shut behind her hard enough to knock the crushed velvet painting of a penguin off Ryo's wall.

Lorelei groaned, and rolled her eyes Ryo-wards. "You really shoulda known better than that, Ryo..."

"I know, I know..." Ryo replied, shrinking into his lab coat a bit. "I just figured... worth a try, yeah? Hmm. Confused, Mallory?"

"Uh, a little," Mallory admitted. "But just a little. I think... Meiko doesn't like charity, I mean. That's why she wouldn't take money from you. It's the work ethic thing, right?"

"Sort of," Ryo quasi-confirmed. "The girls here know, but you're new with the troupe... considering the cash flow that's usually not going into that House, didn't you ever wonder how it is Meiko bought such an expensive thing? A fully equipped building with a Reality Engine for Mobiles isn't cheap..."

"You loaned her money for it?"

"Start-up fees," Ryo fully-confirmed. "Both of us wanted to make it on our own. Orphans don't have much in life beyond what they can make for themselves. I was older, so I got the head start... and I gave her a leg up when she decided what she wanted to do. But that's the only time she's ever accepted money from me, and since she hasn't been able to pay it back yet, that just doubles the problem."

"Oneechan's being a baka," Eiko retorted, sulking in a beanbag (as her sugar high had worn off, and was now in crash mode). "Ryo's almost family. There's no reason to not accept the money! And I don't see what kind of job we can do that'll pay that much that soon, unless it's something naughty!"

"Eiko's got a point," Lorelei agreed. "Mind filling us in on what the job is, Ryo? So we know if we have to head for the hills before Meiko finds out...?"

The night-time streets of Edo hold a very special promise.

They glow like gems, neon forests of flash and sparkle. Holograms float in the air, enticing images of youth, wealth, love, power, fun... the cries of traditional barkers echo the same message. Come inside, come inside. We can give you what you think you're looking for. It's a long road between the corporate monoliths of the business district and the quiet, sleepy apartment buildings of the residential district... why not take a short stopover in between? Something to take the edge off another soul-grinding day of work? Something to recapture some magic you thought you lost long ago, if only for a little while...?

Then a little while turns into minutes, turns into hours. Sucked into the web, fed a stream of things you think you want, money flowing from your scorecard like a waterfall to pay for the honor of this wonderful time... until you find yourself staggering back home, away from the trap, poorer and not much wiser from the experience.

They also have really great domestic beer.

"Domestic beer! Domestic sake!" Mallory cried out, banging a little mallet against a wooden drum as he shifted in his scratchy barker's robe uncomfortably. "Err... hot girls! Good times! You, sir, come inside for a bit? We just got a fresh supply of daiquiris from Aquarius, the best in the multiverse! No? Uh, okay then, bye."

The soft *click* of a stiletto heeled shoe on pavement signalled Lorelei's irritation. "Mallory... you don't go 'No? Okay then, bye' when they refuse. It's called the 'hard sell' for a reason—you've got to try harder to get them in here, or we'll never make the money back you lost."

"I'm new at this, okaaaaaaa..." he trailed off, remembering too late that he was trying to avoid looking at Lorelei. After all, she was dressed for the job—which meant wearing a tight red dress that was illegal in six realities, with full makeup and the best hairdo she could wrangle on short notice.

"You see, that's why we've got you out here playing barker instead of mixing drinks inside the cabaret," Lorelei explained, using one finger to tilt Mallory's chin upwards. "If YOU walked into a building loaded with pretty girls trying to seduce middle-aged men into buying expensive drinks, your brains would explode. Speaking of pretty girls, where's... ...good gravy, that CAN'T be..."

"Can't...?" Mallory asked, turning 180 and witnessing an entirely different vision of loveliness.

She had really gone all out... hair twisted up into an interesting bun that felt mature without being TOO mature, held in place with two long pins criss-crossed. A shawl was draped behind her shoulders, hooked around each arm—a gauzy olive green garment, more for decoration than warmth. The dress? Low-cut, but still modest, but still very assertive in the right areas. She wore flats for comfort, walking silently as she approached...

"Uh... I... errr..." someone other than Mallory (see: Lorelei) said for a change. "...where did you FIND that dress?"

"It was in storage at my family home," Kisei spoke, failing to twirl to show it off as such things were unimportant. "I requested Mellow Fellow's services to make a brief stop there and retrieve it. I am fortunate that it still fits me. ...Father believed in being prepared for any social occasion, hence the availability... why are you staring at me? Is the fashion style out of mode? Will I be unable to serve in my duties this evening due to aesthetic difficulties?"

"It's... it's pretty damn impressive, Kiss," Lorelei admitted, rubbing a hand behind her head in a very Mallory-esque fashion. (The real Mallory was too busy scraping the pavement with his jaw to comment.) "Okay, then... let's get to work. The goal here is to get passers-by to go into the place and buy drinks. I don't know how good you're gonna be at that, but—"

Kisei reached sideways, grasping a passing businessman by his necktie without a second glance. She pulled him close, glaring pure ice into his eyes...

"You will enter this establishment and purchase many expensive drinks," she ordered.

"yes'm," the man replied, before disappearing in a flash to go do as instructed.

"...interesting. I believe this job will be easier than I had anticipated," Kisei decided.

Meiko marched through the crowded main floor, trying to ignore the world around her in favor of the voices trickling into her ear via her microphone / headset.

"I don't care if we're running out of Benten, find more," she commanded, weaving around a group of drunken businessmen celebrating a successful corporate merger. "Go to a convenience store if you have to. We've got a group at table six that is going to run out in a few minutes, and that's the only brand they want.... yes, I know. I think we can afford it, with the money coming in... right. Get to it."

A flick of her thumb across her earlobe, and she switched channels.

"Onizuka? There's a pair of guys starting to get loud and rowdy at table seven," she said, standing on her toes to see over the crowd. "I don't like the looks of it. Keep watch over it and be ready to eject. Lorelei's busy working some poor slob at table two, or I'd have her handle it... good. Now—"

"Miss Mirai?"

"One second," she spoke, holding up a finger to silence the man. "Now, I need you to keep an eye on table eight while you're at it; that guy is going past his limit and could get to be a problem. If you need another spotter, find Mallory; he should be inside, we've done enough barking and it's getting near midnight. Okay. Gotta talk to the boss, excuse me..."

Another flick, and her communicator shut down.

"What do you need, Nakago-san?" she asked.

"Nothing, nothing," the middle-aged businessman spoke, upbeat in tone compared to the panic he was experiencing when they first met. "Your team is doing quite well! I don't know where we'd be if you hadn't taken the job, what with key parts of my staff quitting earlier today... it would have been a disaster to have such an understaffed crew on the cabaret's first night!"

"Glad to be of service," she half-lied, adding a formal bow to punctuate it. "You're fortunate you still have your bouncer and bartenders; I don't think we could have covered all those bases..." ...even if that would have been preferable, she failed to add.

"You're doing more than enough, and I'll be happy to pay the money you need at closing time," Nakago-san said. "I felt I should take a moment to commend your work. I'll be in my office if needed."

"Hai, Nakago-san. Thank you," she replied, adding a second bow as the man walked off.

Meiko switched her staff communicator back on... and was thankful to hear no urgent chatter. A rare moment of peace during the busy opening night. She took a seat at the nearest unoccupied table, feet quite sore from walking around in her business best all night, and slipped off her shoes for the moment...

But she couldn't bring herself to really focus on WHERE she was, beyond sitting at a table and taking a break. The reality of it was just too disheartening.

Fortunately for her, a rare ray of light showed through the clouds in the form of Mallory.

"Uh, Meiko?" he said, likewise trying not to focus on the surroundings (for entirely different, male-oriented reasons). "We may have a bit of a problem... the guys Kisei's working on are buying drinks mostly because they're afraid of her."

"Whatever it takes to get the sales," Meiko replied, not caring.

"Well, I know that's the goal, I just figured maybe... uh... it wasn't what we were shooting for. I mean, it's a social club, right?"

"Gosh, that's a nice word for it. That's what you see?" Meiko replied, looking up and around. "I see a bunch of pathetic drunken businessmen, desperate for some kind of attention from anything female, drowning their sorrows in beer. I can't believe we had to take this job... and Eiko in this environment...!"

"Oh, I don't know, looks to me like she's doing fine," Mallory spoke, glancing around a crowd...

...to where Eiko was working the register, tallying bills.

"Okay, that'll be 78,000 en!" she replied, cheerful as can be.

Her customer, however, was not quite cheerful. "Whaaa...? But... but it was just four drinks...!"

"One glass of Finest Super Proper Nipponese White Wine,™ one bottle of Old Grandfather's Venerable Whiskey,™ one Krap Foods, Inc. Twisted Bubblegum Surprise and a domestic beer," Eiko rattled off, running down the slip. "That totals up to 78,000 en. Payment, please!"

"That's ridiculous! I'm not paying—"

A dark shadow engulfed his cowering form.

"Is there a problem?" the softly feminine-garbed midnight assassin known as Kisei asked.

"noma'am," the customer replied, forking over many, many coins to the gleefully capitalistic child.

"...I think she's doing okay," Mallory spoke, turning back to Meiko. "She seems to be having a lot of fun! Maybe she doesn't get to keep the money, but handling it and counting it and taking care of it is right up her alley via the pig in the poke with new tricks!"

"My complaint isn't with her role in this, it's with... with THIS," Meiko clarified. "What kind of image does this present to Eiko about a woman's place

256

in the world? That we should be dressing fancy and hanging on guys, trying to make them happy? Or we should let ourselves be pawed by pervert lushes?"

"That's kind of harsh, don't you think?"

"It's reality," Meiko spoke, slumping down in her chair.

"But it's... I mean... well, here," he said, grabbing her hand. "C'mon! I wanna show you something!"

"Wh—hey!"

Meiko barely had a moment to slip her shoes back on before being dragged away, through the throngs of the crowd, towards the stage...

...where Lorelei was belting out some N-pop song very, very badly with a young business intern in his twenties.

She wore his tie around her head like a bandanna, and was swaying to and fro with him, one arm around his shoulders. Every now and then they would completely bungle a word on the karaoke display screen—Lorelei due to not really speaking the language, the man due to being completely inebriated—and both would laugh their heads off, and stumble over syllables trying to catch up. The crowd let out a whoop of laughter each time, more the 'laughing with' rather than 'laughing at' sort.

"Okay, okay... look," Mallory insisted, stepping behind Meiko so she could see. "What do you see?"

"I see some drunk completely mangling 'Smile For the Future' by Ishi Kazuya," Meiko responded, truthfully. "And Lorelei playing along with him."

"Right, right, but the context is what you're missing," Mallory spoke, stepping back around her. "I've been running all over the place doing errands and mixing drinks and getting people to come in, so I've had a chance to really study this place—"

"I've been doing the same thing, Mallory."

"But have you been paying attention to the people?"

"Of course, I'm trying to spot potential trouble spots and—"

"No, no, no, the PEOPLE," Mallory insisted. "Like... that guy. I got him to come in after talking to him a minute about where he was going. He apparently got scolded at work for being late on a project, and was just gonna go home since he had nothing better to do. So I got Lorelei to bring him inside, and, well... she's been sticking by him most of the night, talking, exchanging jokes —"

"Yes, it's her job to seduce the soul-crushed business folk, Mallory. That's the whole point."

"But does he look soul-crushed now?" he asked, gesturing towards the ongoing horror on stage. "He looks a whole lot better now than when he came in, I can tell you. Maybe we're just trying to make money here, but... these people are here trying to lift their spirits. And that should be job number one! I think Lorelei actually understands that, even if she's been joking about squeezing guys for all they're worth tonight. I say, what good is a social club if it's not putting its heart in the right place? Otherwise, it'd be kind of an un-social club. An antisocial club? Uh, something like that..."

Meiko stared at him, unbelieving. "You can't be... no, wait, I almost forgot. I'm talking to Mallory Heisenberg. You ARE serious."

"Serious as serious does," Mallory spoke with confidence, crossing his arms in a very Meiko-like confident way.

"You know that the world doesn't always operate the way you'd like it to, yes? I doubt all the cabarets in Nippon are idealistic havens of cheesy positive vibes and friendship."

"Well... maybe not, no. But tonight, this one CAN be, right?" he asked. "I think having us here helps. Eiko's cheerful, I'm doing my best to really enjoy myself, Lorelei's in seventh heaven on cloud nine... maybe Kisei's having some trouble with the concept, but it's a start. So... uh... in a VERY roundabout way, I'm just saying, don't worry about Eiko. I think the environment's not all that bad for her."

Meiko's resolution backed up a few steps. "It's... not THAT bad, no," she decided. "I mean... could be worse, right? Could be a strip club or an opium den or something—"

"That's the spirit!!" Mallory cheered, patting her on the shoulder. "So, in the spirit of team pride and the work ethic of our Nipponese roots—"

"Aren't you adopted?"

"—let's make tonight number 1 super special!" he finished, holding up a V for 'Victoly'.

"That's stupid," Meiko didn't say.

"You're scaring me," she also did not say.

Instead... much to her own surprise, she was laughing.

"Huh? What?" Mallory asked, wiggling his 'V' fingers. "Isn't that the right attitude? Should I—"

"It's fine, it's fine!" she insisted, trying to shake off her chuckles. "Jeez. Mallory, you are hands down the most naive, clueless... and you know... it's actually kind of—"

A squawk in her ear distracted her.

"...Kisei just dislocated someone's shoulder after being groped," she announced. "I think I better go deal with this..."

"Hai, hai," Mallory nihongoed. "And remember: lifting the human spirit is job number one!"

"Getting our House out of the clink is job number one," she corrected. "But... I'll see what I can do about that spirit raising thing while I'm at it. 'scuze."

As she walked off to deal with yet another in a series of tiny evening crises, she couldn't stop herself from smiling.

The last of the lot were out the door at 3am, smiles plastered across their woozy faces. Chairs were upturned, stacked neatly on tables. The music had long since quieted down, karaoke simmering away until its heat had dissipated.

At a lone table in the center of the club, Meiko sat with Nakago-san, collecting the pay. Enough en coins to exceed her carrying capacity were stacked up on the tablecloth, being shifted from piles into baggies.

"This really is a bit much, Nakago-san..." Meiko found herself saying. "I think we could get our House back without—"

"It's worth it, it's worth it. My business would have sunk if opening night crashed and burned," he replied. "And even beyond that... your staff did wonderfully. I was never expecting so much customer satisfaction! I'd say Heisenberg-san's cheer and your sister's delight were quite infectious. I even almost caught Onizuka-san smiling, and he hasn't done that since The Incident..."

An example of those 'cheesy positive vibes' Meiko had discussed earlier wandered / staggered up to the table, in the form of Lorelei and her singing partner.

"Heeeyyy," she wheezed, leaning heavily on him with him leaning on her and the two somehow forming a single center of gravity in the process. "I'm gonna... go... shomewhere else. With Ishida-kuuun. So. Don't expect me home. Right."

"Have fun, Lorelei, we're clear here," she spoke, dismissing with a wave.

Next up on the buddy-system parade: Eiko and Kisei, for similar reasons.

Kisei straightened up once in the immediate presence of her employer. "I..." she begun, before getting lost mentally for a moment. "I... believe I have ingested too many alcoholic beverages this evening. Eiko has volunteered to... something... escort. Yes, escort me home. Wait. We don't have a home. I am seeing a logic hole..."

"Ooof," Eiko whined, supporting a lot of Kisei's weight as she teetered to the side. "I'm gonna lead her back to Ryo-san's lab, oneechan. It'll be okay. Even drunk I bet she could beat ten guys with one arm tied behind her back! Come get us in the morning once you get the house back, okay?"

Taking a few coins from the stack, Meiko passed them to her younger sister. "Take a cab instead of walking, please," she requested. "In case Kisei falls asleep on her feet."

"Got it, oneechan! C'mon, Kisei-san, let's go."

"Please explain why there are four of you, Eiko Mirai..." Kisei mumbled, as the two shuffled out of the picture.

3:24am. Plenty of time, with plenty of money.

If stress was an unwelcome addition to Meiko's life, relief was a very welcome addition. The kind of sweet relief that comes from knowing that your problems are solved, and solved beyond the minimum of solvability. A weighty bag in her purse confirmed the future—the House would be safe, and they'd actually have a bit of profit from tonight's mayhem. Whatever anger and panic she felt earlier was almost a distant memory, sinking fast below the horizon as she left it behind...

Of course, relief can be just as much of a distraction as panic, which is why she didn't notice Mallory until she had walked past him.

He was busy mopping up a bit of the mess left behind by a particularly satisfied customer, who had chosen to return his beer on the sidewalk rather than take it home with him. The odor of the mess only struck Meiko at the moment she noticed he was doing this.

"Mallory, we're done," she reminded him. "You don't have to play wage slave anymore, you know..."

"I know," Mallory spoke, mopping away with abandon. "But I'd hate to leave a mess like this for Nakago-san's next wave of staff to deal with the next day..."

"Huh. I'd figured you went back to Ryo's, anyway..."

"What? No way, I'm going with you to get the House back," he explained, rinsing out the mop via a yank of his bucket's handle. "I mean... this is all my fault. If I went back to sleep while you're off dealing with the towing company, it'd be kinda selfish of me. ...ummmm..."

"Ummmm?"

"I'm kinda surprised you're not, uh, more angry at me," he said, unsure if saying it was a good idea in the first place. "I mean, sure, you were pretty upset when you found out, but... and maybe it was just you focusing on work instead of on what happened, but... I mean, I'd understand if—"

"Whatever."

"Whatever?"

"Whatever," Meiko repeated. "We came out of this better than we went into. And... I guess you wouldn't have known about the rights management fees, so I can hardly blame you. And besides, look at you now... you're mopping up the contents of... what is that, anyway, urine or vomit? I can't even tell."

"I think it's both..."

"Anyway, you're above and beyond the call of duty," Meiko continued, while keeping her eyes off the puddle of unidentifiable yuck. "Most guys I know would try to duck out of responsibility, avoid doing anything to correct matters. Go and sleep it off, like you said. Except you've been working your ass off all night, without losing your trademark smile. So... whatever. I don't feel angry. Do you think I should I still be angry?"

"Er, no? Yes? I don't know. I'm not exactly a good judge of these things..."

"Then I'll choose not to be angry," she decided. "I'm too tired to be angry, even if I wanted to be."

Thirty minutes later, they had settled affairs at the impound yard, and the house was towed back to its docking station.

Meiko slept on the living room couch throughout the entire process. 'I'll just lie down a minute to stretch my legs' was the last thing she said before she caved to exhaustion.

After retrieving Meiko's blanket from her cot upstairs, tucking her in, and sending Ryo a quick RealNet message to explain that they'd be at the House for the night, Mallory made himself a crude bed of pillows and went to sleep on the floor nearby.

example #2: visiting day

It was a particular Tuesday (particularly the next week) when Mallory found himself in an unusual situation.

The day started out quite normally. They had just finished a job—a small one, needing only Lorelei and Kisei to leave the house for a while. The money wasn't great, but that plus the leftovers from Cabaret Night were enough to keep them comfortably in the black.

That morning, Meiko arrived for breakfast wearing black and not looking comfortable.

She looked decidedly out of place compared to the rest of the House occupants. Eiko was cheerfully downing a bowl of unsugared corn pops, wearing her favorite overalls; Lorelei was lounging in daily casuals, having her usual quickie of toast and coffee before running off to do whatever it is she did now and then when she wasn't sitting around watching flicks. Kisei simply read the newspaper in her usual uniform.

"That's a new look for you, isn't it?" Mallory asked, trying to sound chipper and encouraging since Meiko seemed to like compliments like that even if she tried not to show that she liked them.

Today it backfired. Not violently, but more like a firecracker that crackled wildly, only to go 'pff' at the end.

"It's visiting day," Meiko said simply, accepting her morning cup of coffee from him. "Eiko, did you forget again...?"

"Forg—oooh, umm... yeah, I did," Eiko admitted, looking a bit sheepish as she slid out of her chair. "I'll go change... unless we're going later in the day? I really would like to get in the morning business reports first, if that's okay with —"

"We always go in the morning, Eiko, you know that. Lorelei...?"

Lorelei peered over the top of her coffee cup... and despite sounding smooth and casual in her words, she held for a very non-smooth moment before speaking. "Can't. Prior engagements. You know how it is. But hey, it's okay, right, I mean—"

"It's okay, Lorelei," Meiko replied, reassuring. "I understand. Kisei?"

Kisei turned to the next page in her freshly printed RealWare Daily PrintNews.™"I have prepared," she spoke quietly.

"All right, we'll go when Eiko gets back."

Quiet moment.

Lorelei departed.

Kisei read.

"Umm..."

Both women looked up at Mallory. Not sharply, or even in surprise, they simply looked up.

"Who are you visiting?" he asked.

There was nothing gloomy about the location, other than the nature of what it was.

Otherwise, all signs would point to good tidings and cheer. The sky was a bright green, not a cloud in sight. The sun shone brightly, casting its predesignated rays down to allow for just the right amount of shadow and light. The temperature was a calm 24°C. Even the methodical brushing strokes of the caretaker, keeping walkways free of leaves, were gentle to the ear and nearly hypnotic...

Still, moods are infectious, and the stillness and chill of Meiko's mood infected Mallory with precision. He kept to the back of the small gathering, not saying a word, as Meiko talked with the gravestone marker.

"The guy behind me is Mallory," Meiko continued softly, despite her intended listener not being able to hear according to all conventional multiversal wisdom. "He's working for me now... and taking good care of us. You'd be happy to see how clean the house has been since he showed up, and yes, I'm eating right again. Money is still a problem, but I promised I'd make a good future for our family, and I'm certain I'll succeed. And... and what else, umm..."

Eiko rocked from foot to foot, uncomfortable in her formal clothes. "Oneechan..."

With a silent sigh, Meiko gave her younger sister a silent nod. "It's okay, Eiko. You can head home now if you want. But say a quick prayer for Mother and Father first."

The younger Mirai sister bowed her head towards the grave for a short while, saying nothing, then hurriedly moved off.

"I should be moving along as well," Kisei spoke, while planting a few incense sticks in a bowl at the grave. "I wish you well in your day of annual mourning, Meiko Mirai. I will be visiting my home as well, to pay respects to my father. I believe it to be fitting, as we are indirectly family... unless, of course, you have assignment that requires me to be on duty—"

"I wouldn't make you take an assignment today, Kisei. But thank you for the offer. I'll see you back at the house tonight."

And then there were two.

As was usually the case in situations like this, Mallory was the first to break the silence.

"If it's okay, uh... can I pay my respects too?" he asked. "I mean, I don't know a whole lot about Shinto yet, so I don't know if I'm allowed or if even asking would be some sort of offense—"

"I'm not very religious," Meiko replied, before Mallory started feeling perfunctory guilt. "And... I wouldn't know if it was allowed or not. Or whatever. Do what you feel you have to do."

"Right, right. Ah... ahem," he began, with a clearing of the throat. "Hello, Mr. and Mrs. Mirai! ... no, too cheerful. Hello, Mirai-sans. Like Meiko said, I'm her new houseboy—"

"I think you count as a family friend now, Mallory. You don't have to call yourself houseboy here."

"—right right. New family friend. And... and like she said, I'm taking good care of them," he continued. "So you don't have to worry about anything, leave it to me! ... too cheerful, too cheerful... I, uh... I'm very happy to be helping out Meiko. And, um... I'm glad I could be here today to meet you, even if you can't hear me because you're dead. Except from what little I know about this stuff, you can hear, because we believe you can. I think. You know, my mother was Shinto too, and I think some of that rubbed off on Dad, because we visited her grave now and then too when most people don't bother since it's just a lump of rock over a corpse—"

"Mallory!!"

"—aaah, which is to say, is what non-believers think, not like us!" Mallory corrected in a panic. "And, and—"

A hand rested on his shoulder.

"...sorry. I shouldn't have snapped," Meiko apologized, dropping her voice back to 'quiet'. "It's okay, you're new at this. And it's not like it matters, it's just an old tradition in Nippon... ...I don't know what to do here, either. Sometimes I wonder why I come out every year to 'talk' to them..."

Mallory turned to face her. "It's because their spirits are still with us, right...?"

"How should I know?" she spoke... a tiny element of frustration with the world sneaking in as she did. "All I know is what I see. I'd LIKE to believe that they're at peace, and I can talk to them, but... I don't know. Do you know about Confusionism, Mallory?"

"Is that the religion with all the sayings they print on cookies and t-shirts and things?"

"No... it's actually a recent religion. Well, within the last few hundred years," Meiko explained... after spotting a nearby bench, and having a seat to rest her tired feet. "Very modern. It was trendy for a while because it explained the entire multiverse and everything in it in a way that made sense and defied the rational demand for 'proof'. Do you know why?"

"Because it said it was okay to be confused by everything?"

...Meiko stared at him. "You heard of it before?"

"Uh, no, but from the name, I mean... it just sort of popped into my head," he said, taking the seat next to her and leaning forward a bit, resting hands on knees. "Confusion. I get confused all the time by life outside my home reality. I've adjusted to a lot, but it's like I'll never stop learning... never run out of stuff to be confused by, too. So... that means that since I'll always be confused, like being confused about whether dead people can hear me, then it's okay to be confused."

"You SURE you never heard it before?"

"Positive! It's just something that clicks with a guy like me, I guess..."

"And a girl like me."

"Eh? But you're—"

"Shinto?" she filled in. "Mostly. I follow a few rites. I had a small shrine to my parents for a while, until a bad engine crash knocked stuff all over the house, and the candles started a fire... I didn't want to put the shrine back up after that. Not just because of the hazard, it just... I don't know how to feel about this stuff, Mallory. How to think about it. What any of it means! Sometimes I think maybe I'm a Confusionist at heart..."

"But you're always so confident," Mallory noted, getting confused himself. "Whenever we have a job to do, whenever anything goes wrong, you rise to the occasion and take control. Even if sometimes I can tell you're just faking it to not look bad—"

"What?!" Meiko replied, defenses rising. "What do you mean by that?"

"—I mean, not that you're not a cool customer or anything! I just... sometimes it looks like..."

He trailed off, as Meiko took a deep breath, forcing herself to calm. A gesture he'd seen many times in her previous.

"...I didn't think it was that obvious," she spoke soon after. "I do my best, and I want to be a responsible sort of leader for the company and... mother-figure for Eiko, I guess, sometimes. But sometimes... like today, for instance, I just don't know what to do. What I should be doing. Tradition says I should come out here, and visit my parents. I just don't know if it's actually comforting or not. Notice how Eiko took off as soon as she could?"

"Uh, I had noticed, yeah..."

"She never really knew Mother and Father. She was two when it happened; I was nine. So she grew up completely in that orphanage, and eventually forgot them... I was the only family she had. Eiko doesn't really feel one way or another about our parents... it's like they're storybook characters. One of these days, maybe I'll just let her stay home on visiting day. It's what she really wants to do. ...or is that right? Should I bring her here anyway? That's what I'm talking about, I just can't tell what I should do and what I shouldn't... am I making any sense here, Mallory?"

"Almost."

Meiko groaned. "Terrific. Almost making sense. Maybe this whole thing's a waste of time, I don't—"

"What does your heart say?"

"...what?"

"Um, that's what my dad always told me," Mallory continued. "Whenever I got really mixed up and I said something like 'What should I do?' he'd always say 'What does your heart say?'. Because usually it knows better. And when it's wrong, at least you can say... hey, I did what I felt was true to me, even if it was wrong. Right?"

"More farmboy philosophy," she commented dryly. "They fed you too much sugar over there, didn't they? 'What does your heart say?' I mean, it sounds like something printed on a greeting card—"

"But that doesn't make it wrong!" Mallory defended, getting to his feet... not an angry defense, but a passionate one. "Okay, yeah, it sounds like a cheesy line in a movie, but... that doesn't cancel it out. I've always done my best to follow my heart when I just can't think straight. You remember when you told me to stay outside and hold your purse while you went shopping for toys? Because you were so mad at me? My head told me to stay put and avoid a beating. But... I guess my heart said you needed someone. So I took option two, and... I mean, that day ended pretty well, right? So sometimes something cheesy really does work."

Since his target audience remained speechless, either waiting in anticipation or crunching that particular speech or both, he continued.

"Maybe Confusionism has it wrong," Mallory said. "Or wrong AND right. Because okay, some things in life you'll never know. We'll never know if there's a soul that you can talk to or anything like that. But standing around wildly wondering and being confused means you're not getting anywhere. So, just listen to your heart. It doesn't make sense but it does give you an answer that you can call yours, right? So... today. Visiting your parents, talking things over with them. What does your heart say about that?"

"How in Nippon do you expect me to listen to an organ in my chest? Or is the answer 'dokidoki'?"

"Meiko... work with me here. I'm serious."

"I don't KNOW what my heart says, okay?!" Meiko blurted, getting to her feet. "It's not something I routinely listen to! I'm a sensible person. A sensible person shouldn't care about two lumps of rotting organic matter in the ground! This is reality, okay? Not your idealistic fantasy land! And just because every time I remember them I remember how much they loved me and I just want to feel that again—"

"THERE!"

"—what?"

"Right there. You did it!" Mallory poke... poking her lightly in the chest for emphasis. "Listened to your heart. That's the first time you really mentioned how you feel about this. That's what I'm talking about. If that's why you come out here each year, then... if it feels good... it does feel good, right?"

Meiko nearly stumbled backwards into the bench, her world taking a minor tumble. "What...? I... I guess, I mean... I do try to think about them each year when I come out here..."

"And remembering them makes you feel good," Mallory completed. "So under all the confusion and sensible stuff, you've got your answer. Sounds like a good one to me! I mean... I feel the same way. When I go visit my mother. I never knew her, but I know her from my father's words, and... those stories feel good to remember. So go with that. Don't think too hard about it and just go with your heart. ...okay? Forget about ghosts and organs and all that and *just go with it.*"

She stood for a long time on top of that idea. Mallory let her think about it, knowing that he took a while to really swallow a big idea himself.

The sweeping of leaves and brooms in the distance kept the scene from absolute silence. Her next words were almost totally unrelated.

"I didn't think a guy like you existed in reality, Mallory."

"I like to make up my own reality as I go along," Mallory returned, with a smile. He stepped around her, to resume his seat on the bench. "So... while you're here, you wanna talk about your parents? Maybe some stories? Stories always help me remember people, since my memory's usually like a cheese grater..."

With a tiny laugh, Meiko joined him on the bench. And began to remember. Whenever she felt the need to cry, Mallory provided a kitchen napkin from a stash he'd pocketed on his way out the door that morning.

example #3: some enchanted evening

On the first buzzing of her alarm clock, Meiko woke.

The morning routine was routine by this point... yawn, sit up, stretch a bit, check F.P. for today's schedule, get dressed, go downstairs, eat breakfast lovingly prepared by Mallory, and then... whatever the day held for her, really. Whatever F.P. listed.

So.

Yawn. Covered, a nice deep yawn belying her exhaustion from staying up all night trying to find jobs on RealNet.

Sit up. Simple enough, despite being groggy.

Stretch a bit. She didn't do any specific yoga-stretching or other fancy stuff, just the basic arms-at-various-angles kind of stretching. She reached for the closed pocket organizer by her futon next.

Check F.P.

That morning, in between getting dressed and checking F.P. was a period of emotional befuddlement, as in bright glowing letters on the tiny organizer's screen, the following words taunted her:

8:00 pm. Dinner with Mallory Heisenberg at Ma Maison in Jukensu Prefecture *(Future Perfect has auto-reserved a table for two for your convenience.)*

9:00 pm. Movies with Mallory Heisenberg. Showing: "Tsukiakari to Sakura." *(Future Perfect has auto-purchased two tickets for your convenience.)*

11:00 pm. Special Midnight Grand Opening of the Edo Tower Aquarium. *(Future Perfect has auto-obtained event passes for your convenience.)*

12:00 am. Kiss Mallory Heisenberg.

1:00 am. Sleep.

Sometimes, F.P. could be annoyingly specific. Or frighteningly so. Or reassuringly so, which is half the reason she owned it—something to ease her worries about her future... even if it compounded her worries from time to time, particularly when it completely failed to list something important, or only vaguely listed something. Such as:

1:16 pm. Hire Mallory Heisenberg, your true love.

Which did appear on her screen that fateful day for four whole seconds before she snapped it shut and hired him on the spot.

Exactly how F.P. worked its wonders was a mystery to her... and a mystery to its creator, as well.

> "I'm not really sure why it works, it just does," Ryo had explained to her two years ago, when he handed her the red prototype, companion to his own blue prototype and a green one he'd intended for someone else. "I was just tinkering around with some loose ideas one day, some open source reality engine technology, some blood samples I'd gotten off a guy who wandered into my lab one day demanding weird tests... you know, sequenced harmonics in liquid generating reality waves... and lo and behold, I got something that almost but not quite totally predicts the future. Who knew? Not me."

> "Does this thing really predict the future?" Meiko had asked, unsure of the plastic widget.

> Ryo did his characteristic hand-rubbing-behind-the-head thing. "I'm not really sure," he admitted. "Sometimes I can totally defy it, like the day it told me to eat tuna fish for lunch. Sometimes when I try, the same thing happens anyway. Usually it schedules things I was going to do anyway, or presents me with neat ideas I wouldn't have thought of but have no problem going along with. So... think of it as a general guideline for the future. Maybe a self-fulfilling prophecy? Does it forge its own reality around you? Who knows? It's way too weird to mass-produce commercially, but since I know you worry about the future, I thought you'd like one..."

She'd been skeptical at first... but came to lean on it for support more and more. It was a way of knowing what lay ahead, so she didn't have to worry. She could see the bright future she wanted for herself, and F.P. laid out the steps to get there. It hadn't really let her down yet, maybe a few wobbly bits and inconsistencies, but never anything disastrous...

...and it had predicted Mallory.

Not that she believed in something as corny as 'true love'.

...and it had predicted what added up to a romantic evening with him.

She could defy it. It's usually possible to do so. Even if usually she just went along with it...

And if she did manage to defy her fate, it would mean F.P. was wrong about other things. Which was both reassuring and oddly frightening to her.

But in the end, the routine dominated once more. She'd checked F.P. She got dressed, went downstairs, ate her breakfast, and informed Mallory that they were eating out that night. Nothing out of the ordinary, nothing out of her control.

Reactions:

"Huh? Why do you want to go out to eat? Isn't that really expensive?"
"I think it'd be a nice change of pace. You've been cooking for us for a long time now, it's high time someone else cooked for you. And believe me, you don't want to taste MY cooking."
"I guess we can, if you like... what sort of place is it? Is it formal? I don't have anything to wear..."
"So go buy something, okay? Unless you really don't wanna go—"
"No no, I do! It'll be fun! Okay... umm... maybe I can get Lorelei to help me go shopping, she knows more about—"
"Not her. Please. I fear what she might do with you as her fashion template."

"You're taking him out on a DATE? Meiko, you temptress, you!"
"I didn't say it was a date..."
"Riiight. Well! I can say I'm happy all my hard work has paid off. Although... can't say you sound real enthusiastic."
"It's just dinner and a movie, Lorelei, it's not some grand gala event."
"So why not skip it?"
"F.P. already made reservations..."
"Cancel 'em."
"And waste them?"
"Are you going just because it's easy, or because you want to go? Or is it both, since you wanted to but couldn't find an easy excuse?"

"Why me, mon? I mean, I don't know ANYTHING 'bout formal wear..."
"I know, but Lorelei would probably have me wearing something... uh... unsuitable, Kisei doesn't know anything about this stuff but she did have a really nice dress on the other day, Eiko would probably scam me out of more money than I can really pay, and... and you're one of the only friends I have outside of the House. And you're a guy, so you know guy stuff, right?"
"Mallory, mon, I don't know nothin' 'bout the threads of Babylonia but what I see on RealNet."
"Mellow-san, my other option is Duke, and he'd have me wear military fatigues to dinner. And I guess I could go home and ask Dad, but... just... it doesn't feel right..."
"You don' wanna go home?"
"I want to go home at a special time, you know? For something more meaningful than asking 'Dad, I have no fashion sense, can you help me?'. That'd just be weird. I was saving up my first visit for something better than this..."

"All right, well... hey, who'm I to turn down a friend in need? The Fellow be takin' you around shopping Mellow Style, then! If I can't find the threads 'o Babylonia, maybe I can get you some nice I's Lander stylin' goin' on..."

"I wish you well in your dating rituals tonight, Meiko Mirai. I would suggest a more formal matchmaking ceremony or perhaps a tea ceremony, but I do not believe Mallory Heisenberg would have the required composure for either. Regardless, you have my best wishes on the evening of your commitment and I have faith in your union's strength."
"...uh..."

"Who, me? Mallory, have you seen my wardrobe? I hang out in a lab coat all day. What do I know about formal wear?"
"Ryo, you're my only hope! You should have seen the getup Mellow Fellow picked out for me... well... actually, I have it in this bag here, take a look."
"AUGH! My eyes, they burn like fire! Close the bag, close it..."
"I didn't want him to feel bad, so I just sort of nodded and smiled a lot... and figured you're my last chance. Ryo-san, I beg you, help me! This is important to me, I don't want to screw things up!"
"Okay, okay! No need to panic, Mallory. It's just a date, we can handle this. ...Mallory?"
"...dd... d... daaaa...?"
"She didn't say it was a date? It sure sounds like one. What did you think it was, then? Mal...? Okay, okay, breathe into the bag. Deep breaths. One, two..."

"WAAAAAI! Oneechan's on a da-ate! Oneechan's on a da-ate—"
"Eiko, it's NOT like that...!"
"Then why are you wearing your best dress, hmmmmm? And that purse, you only take that out for speeeecial occasions... it's so terrific, you're really gonna kiss your true love tonight!"
"WH—"
"I peeked at your organizer again. Teehee!"
"EIKO! I told you not to do that!"
"So are you gonna do it? Kiss him at midnight? Oh, a fated kiss, a dramatic thing, so beautiful and lovely...!"
"I... I don't know. It's just a stupid prediction. You know F.P. can be sometimes be pretty wild..."
"But you still could! It doesn't matter if F.P. really predicted it or not, or if it's destiny or not, you COULD kiss him if you want to anyway. Like if you never read your organizer and just decided to do it, you'd never know if it was a fortune telling or not! Soooo... do you want to, huh, do you do you do you huh?"
"Well..."

dingdong

As circumstances would have it, the traditional method of the man arriving at the door of the woman to escort her out for their lovely evening instantiated that night. (Mostly because it took Ryo a few hours of shopping and Mallory quite a bit of time to get changed into his new clothes.)

"Do you have ANY idea what time it is? We're going to be uhhhhhhhhh..." Meiko started and trailed off, after opening the door.

If she knew that what Mellow Fellow picked out was even worse, perhaps it would've been a relief. As is, there was no denying it... Mallory Heisenberg was sporting a fine light blue tuxedo tonight, suitable for either a lounge singer or a game show host. It was the kind of outfit that clothing designers create just for snicker value when they see it modelled on a live body.

"Uh, did I get the tie wrong?" he asked, fitting with the bow tie and the slightly too tight collar. "Ryo didn't know if ties had sizes or not so we just grabbed one at random, and uhhhhhhhhhhh..."

This time, the awkward staring moment had turned 180°, as Mallory took in the vision of composed beauty that was Meiko Mirai. A simple black dress that fit her quite well, with a white coat to compliment the chilly evening weather... and the purse which cost quite of a bit of her Quarterly fashion budget, a simple design that somehow fit into any ensemble with 100% perfection. The earrings and makeup were nice touches as well.

So, one stared at the other in horror, the other at the other in shock, and it took a few moments to get everything settled.

"We... should be getting to dinner now, right?" Mallory spoke, breaking the silence. "It's almost eight..."

"Right. Right, dinner," she added, stepping out of the House. "Let's go."

Sushi. The very name evokes images of colorfully designed, artistic arrangements of gourmet dining. And massive amounts of money being poured down the drain.

Despite having a decidedly gaijin name, Ma Maison had built a reputation as one of the finest sushi-driven restaurants in all of Edo. It was nearly a lost art, the ability to arrange dead, raw fish in eye-pleasing, mouth-watering combinations... the fishing industries of Nippon were controlled by the same companies that released the engineered creatures into the 'oceans,' controlling breeding and dispersal to ensure a fine crop all year long. (Huge nets had to be erected near the fuzzy borders of the Reality Engine's sphere; otherwise, fish would swim off to what was presumably Nullspace.) Needless to say, all this science, all this skill and talent... it comes at a cost.

For a change, Meiko wasn't the one complaining about fiscal matters.

"It just seems kinda iffy," Mallory continued, tugging at the collar of his Blue-Sky-of-Death-colored tuxedo. He glanced around the restaurant, still overwhelmed with the elegance / expensivegance of it all. "I mean... I could have cooked us both dinner for a lot less than this costs..."

"Mallory, I'm not trying to be thrifty tonight, okay?" his apparent date responded, with mild frustration simmering over a low flame. "That's not the point here. We made good money with the last few quickie jobs, and that cabaret fling... so we don't have to worry about the occasional splurge. Just try to relax and enjoy it, okay? Take it from me, I've had sushi three times before, and it's something a chef like you will really get a kick out of."

"Oh, I know, I've been researching traditional Nipponese recipes. Don't get me wrong, I'm looking forward to it! I guess... I'm just surprised, is all. I didn't think you'd want to splurge, even if... I mean, uh, to put it another way, aren't you usually businesslike and stuff? Being my boss, and all, it doesn't seem like a thing you'd do to waste money like this—"

"Hey, I'm not your boss tonight! And I'm not ALWAYS businesslike, I just... I've had to be that way a lot lately," she half lied. "But it doesn't mean it's the only thing I know. I'm a normal person too! I've got wants and needs and desires and all that, and... and tonight's different. Period. Got it?"

"Yes ma'am."

"Yes MEIKO," she corrected... silently cursing his stubbornness and her own for shaping him this way. "...this is the wrong foot to start off on. Let's forget the whole 'boss lady' and 'farmboy' thing, and just be Meiko and Mallory. I KNOW it's possible..."

"Meiko and Mallory..." he repeated, since his brain worked better when it hooked up with his mouth.

"Right. That's all I want. Don't worry about offending me. Don't worry about pleasing me. Just don't worry at ALL. ...I blame myself."

"Err, blame? For what?"

"For not listening to Lorelei sooner, and trying to keep things safe for too damn long..." she admitted, despite how unusual it felt to be saying that aloud.

"Huh?"

"Forget it. I think I'm babbling at this point. Just be yourself, okay? And forget about how much the chow is costing your boss."

The idea was studied from a few more angles, before Mallory nodded his head once, swallowing it like a fine piece of succulent foodstuff.

"I'll be right back," he decided, nudging his chair out, and getting to his feet.

"Bathroom? The sushi will be here in a few minutes, so don't take too long," she warned.

While he was gone, Meiko busied herself with her organizer, and kicked herself repeatedly in a mental fashion.

She knew it was possible. Whatever wall she had deliberately built up between them—the glorious wall of professional detachment, that wall had fallen flat like a bad cardboard cut-out now and then. Such as when he was helping her buy a toy for Eiko, when he was explaining his Philosophy of Cabarets, and on visiting day...

But all those times had been spontaneous. Strange circumstances which plied themselves to moments where it was possible to be something other than the wacky, clumsy farmboy and his domineering cold boss. Maybe tonight was a mistake... had she read far more assurance into F.P.'s prediction than was really there? Trying to force things, grabbing for something they'd only stumbled over by accident before...

Meiko didn't consider herself an expert on relationships, having never really had one before. (Ryo didn't count. Probably.) Still, even she could see that a couple that only gets those nice tender moments that make it all worthwhile when the stars align in funny combinations was not a couple destined for the kind of romance you only read about in cheap eBooks.

Maybe F.P. was wrong. Maybe Lorelei's crazed romantic scheming was misplaced. Maybe she was better off being the boss, where things worked smoothly more often than not...

Interrupting her dire thoughts, the waiter arrived, with a full platter of sushi.

And with Mallory, who broke away from the water's side to resume his seat.

"Thanks, Tai," her date spoke, giving the waiter a thumbs up. "I'll take it from here..."

Meiko caught herself staring a bit, and dropped to a lower voice as the waiter departed. "You knew the waiter...?"

"Uh, not until tonight, no," he clarified. "But it turns out that like I was hoping, there was a Grünwaldian in the kitchen! We're in nearly every restaurant worth its salt, after all. So... he loaned me an apron, and I figured... it's me, you know? Gotta do what I'd do! What do you think?"

"Of what...?"

"The sushi, of course!" he spoke, doing the standard game show host sweeping arm gesture over a pile of fabulous prizes. "I've been studying, remember? We worked together on some recipes I was tinkering with over the last two weeks, and made a five-flavor sushi platter, Heisenberg Style! I call it: Homestyle Sushi!"

Meiko adjusted her stare to drop a few degrees, settling on the platter. There were indeed five columns of sushi rolls, each with its own color, each looking just as professionally arranged as she knew really good sushi should be...

"I better explain a bit about it before you dig in, 'cause it helps to eat it in the right order," Mallory continued, grabbing his chopsticks to use as a pointing device. "The pink rolls on the far left are the sweetest, liveliest ones, so you can either eat them first or later; sort of a desert. Next to it, the dark green ones, those are a bit cold right now and flat in taste... but if you eat them later on, after they've warmed up, I think you'll find a subtle flavor to them which is quite traditional and tasty."

"I see..." she prompted, pondering the platter. "And the bright red ones?"

"Oh, those are REALLY spicy, so you might want to avoid adding wasabi or anything. And they go best with lots of sake. Sort of a taste that cries out 'Eat me raw—!' Err, you okay? You're coughing..."

"Fine, fine! And... these last two ones...?"

"Those are my favorite," he noted, with a smile. "These brown ones, I added some light cinnamon and coffee flavor... a more mature taste, you know? But once you get past that outer layer with the spices, it has a tender, sweet core that just melts in your mouth, and makes you feel better about things. And the ones next to those... well... they're a weaker taste, and a bit more watery, I'll admit. But that's okay, because it means that it'll get along with the other flavors just fine, and really enhance them as a result. So it's good to eat one of those with any of the others. ...umm... you got all that? I know I should've written up a chart or something, but I was expecting to spring this on you as a surprise one night when I could actually afford—"

"You know what you've done here, right?" Meiko asked... a tiny smile aimed in his direction. "You just made a metaphorical platter of sushi that represents everybody in the House."

"I did?" he asked, surprised. "That's odd... I was shooting for a direct sort of representation, not a metaphorical one... or is that what you meant? I forget, what's the difference between the two? I mean, if what I wanted was to make one type of sushi for everybody, that means it's got implied meaning in flavor, so I guess it could be metaphorical—"

"Mallory?"

"Yeah?"

"I love it," she said, smile widening. "Now shut up and let's eat."

With an identical smile, Mallory twirled his chopsticks at the ready, and plucked a "Meiko-Roll" from the platter. "Eeta daky massyoo!" he declared...

...and the roll slipped neatly from his grasp, to go 'plop' on the wooden cutting board.

"...uh, I forgot to study the whole 'chopstick' thing, since I was too busy studying sushi," he admitted. "I... ah?"

The retrieved roll hovered in front of his mouth, held expertly in place by Meiko's chopsticks.

"Say 'ah' again," she prompted, trying to keep from laughing out loud.

"I am wanting to have you possess the understanding of my feeling of intent. Can you not see the burning spirit that is of the internal of me?"

"Knowing of the feelings you am to be having I have an overflowing jar of support, but the third in the pairing of identities are being improper."

"What you say?"

"If the owning of the thing is very much stimulating onto you lady, until you see this best thing is underneath your vision!"

"But it's the realization of my aspiration! The sensibility is without the central honour. I must banish the negativity to the land of wind and ghosts! The act of stopping me is not something of undertaking, so let's create together!"

"ON TOP OF WATERMELON!"

"I almost followed it until then," Mallory continued, walking by tank after tank of fish (quite live and swimmy-like, instead of dead and compressed into expensive rolls). "I kinda gave up after that. But really, thanks for lending me F.P... even if Ryo's Nihongo translator was a bit flaky..."

"I should've just bought tickets to some other movie," Meiko complained, hands in the pockets of her overcoat. "Something in a language you could understand..."

"Oh, hey, don't get me wrong, I enjoyed it! And after I turned off the translator, I just sorta... tried to read it, you know? From HOW people were saying things and what they did. Stop me if I'm wrong: It was a story about this girl who loves these two boys, and at first they were both really nice and everything but then one of them started going nuts with jealousy, and then there was the thing about foreclosing on the oyster farm—the guy in the suit, right?—and in the end they got the money from a pearl which was like the one in her grandmother's brooch which they did a swaperoo with in the end and everybody lived happily ever after. Right?"

"Uh... no, Mallory, the pearl was actually her grandmother's, and they ended up being bankrupt anyway and she committed lover's suicide. That was the part where you were in the bathroom."

"....oh. Well... I like my version better," he decided.

Mallory cocked his ear to the noises around him after that. The light bubbling of the tanks, the chatter of various slightly important Nipponese persons... expensive shoes on carpet designed to suffer the abuses of a thousand school field trips... and even the faint sound of the wind outside Edo Tower, as they were hundreds of feet up.

"It's weird having fish this high," he noted aloud. "I've never seen living fish before, though... we mostly focus on ground crops back home. And you're saying they don't eat these ones?"

"Most of these fish are just kept around for aquariums. They don't have a functional use," Meiko explained. "Some are released into the wild, just to make the oceans pretty, sometimes to keep the ecosystem balanced... it seems like a lot of effort for something that doesn't matter. They could just program the Reality Engine to balance itself instead, but... well, Nippon's very traditional. This is how things were done in ancient days. A weird blend of ancient and modern..."

"And people come to aquariums to look at the pretty fish, right?"

"And for romantic scenes, yeah."

Mallory halted.

"Eh?"

"Ah... I mean, it's sort of a common thing in videos and stuff," Meiko explained. "In Nippon. A bit like how Edo Tower is the focal point for lots of important things in shows—and in shoujo-style shows, an aquarium's important. You know, two people who could be lovers come to an aquarium, it's all peaceful and natural and quiet, and.... oh. ...I can't believe I didn't think of that until now..."

"Not that you should believe anything in video streams, right?" Mallory said, trying to reassure the spot where he saw Meiko falter. "It's not like everybody who goes to one of these places is some dramatic, fated-to-be-together couple—"

Meiko turned to him, looking serious and nervous and unsettled and calm and serious all at the same time. "Mallory, what time is it?"

"I don't wear a watch!" Mallory protested, waving his bare wrists a bit. "Uh, why? Do we have to go back now?"

With a flick, Meiko had her organizer open...

The time is now: **11:57pm.**
Future Appointments: **12:00 am.** Kiss Mallory Heisenberg.

The stroke of midnight, in Edo Tower, in an aquarium, after a night of romance...

Naturally.

And now she had to find out what the future actually had in store for her. She'd been putting off thinking about it all night, after the great dinner, the strange movie, even exploring the aquarium and talking about fish... an enjoyable evening. Enough to make her forget about the whole point of contention she still held over it. Forget right up to the most important point.

Enough to make her forget to keep Mallory from peeking over her shoulder.

Both turned as red as the striped koi pond fish that fluttered along behind them.

"Uh... uh... is... is that what this is about? I mean, you know, the thing, the place, errr... that?" Mallory asked, pointing with a shaky finger to F.P. "Look, uh, Meiko, listen, I don't want you to feel uncomfortable and I know that you're not really, er, which is to say that I... I don't know what I'm saying, all right, but—"

"It's been wrong before!" Meiko insisted, snapping F.P. closed. "Really! Mallory, don't panic, okay? It's... not really a big deal—"

"But it is! I mean! The thing! The place! That!" Mallory panicked. "And what Eiko told me, how she peeked in it and it said about me that—"

"She TOLD you?!"

"I just laughed it off but I have been thinking about it and I don't know and I really was actually trying to avoid thinking about it and if I knew that this was like that and stuff then I wouldn't have made you go along or did I? I can't remember but the point is that I think maybe we should go home before things get you know kind of strange and even if I really care about you I don't want you to feel—"

"MALLORY!"

"Yes?!"

"...shhh. Just... shhh," she said, putting a finger to his lips. "I've got an idea. It's so obvious, too... just... wait. Wait a moment."

Mallory stared at her in blank shock. "Wfft?"

"Yes. Wait."

Many seconds ticked by. A few fish swam up to the glass, curious at what was going on outside, in a fishy sort of way.

A few aquarium-goers wandered by, discussing the state of the economy in Nihongo.

Time passed.

Mallory's sweat started to wrinkle his safety-mode blue tie, while Meiko remained cool and controlled, keeping the finger there, counting quietly to herself...

Until she lifted the finger away.

And replaced it with her lips.

It wasn't the kind of kiss that could set an empire on fire. Neither of them had any experience at deep, romantic kisses. But it had an honesty to it, a reality to it, a sense of simple truth...

And when it was done, Meiko opened her organizer, giving it a quick peek.

The time is now: **12:03 am.**
Missed Appointments: **12:00 am.** Kiss Mallory Heisenberg.
Future Appointments: **1:00 am.** Sleep.

...and Meiko smiled, snapping the organizer shut again.

"I guess I missed the great midnight kiss," she told the stunned Heisenberg. "F.P. WAS wrong. I chose my own future. A future which involved kissing you, yeah... just not when I was told to do it. Sometimes I don't like being told what to do."

Mallory licked his lips without realizing. "Ah... very clever!" he agreed, voice still a bit shaky. "Sooo...... um..."

"Hmmmm?" Meiko asked, slipping the organizer into her purse, almost teasing in tone as she responded.

"Sooo, err... so... what... does that mean, exactly?"

"It means I made up my mind, by myself. I had a wonderful evening, Mallory. It was everything I could've asked for and then some... and... I think I really do love you. Not because I was fated, I just... you're the most wonderful guy I've ever met, and I'm glad you're with me. I guess... it just took me a long time to even try to accept that."

"You... you mean you really... you, uh... you love me—?"

"I think I do," she said, amused with herself at the admission. "I really think I do. ...it feels so much better to say that now, after trying to avoid it and disagree with it so long... I didn't think it'd be this easy... I'm so calm now. It's strange... ah, you okay there, Mallory?"

"What? Yes. Ah. Yes. I think so?" he guessed. "I just... I mean, I wasn't expecting, to be frank, and... not... sure what to say..."

"Ah... you don't HAVE to say anything, really," Meiko spoke, despite inner hopes. She began to walk along, with or without him. "I guess it was a lot to drop on you, huh? I just really had to get that off my chest, I mean... we can go now if—"

"But I should say something!" he protested, stepping in front of her, blocking her way. "That's how it works! But... but how can I say something like that? It's such an important thing to say, and I don't understand how I feel, but then again I have a hard time understanding how I feel about a lot of things, and just because I care about you and I want you to be happy and anything I can do to make you happy I'd do in a heartbeat because you deserve happiness in life when usually you're so busy taking on the problems of other people and I don't just mean clients so I'm glad I'm with you so I can be there and help because you're a wonderful person and I'd be happy to spend the rest of my life with such a wonderful person like you because you make me feel good inside and without that I really don't know where I'd be and I don't just mean out of a job I mean how I'd feel even though I have trouble figuring out how I feel I really feel strongly about that and I had a great time tonight and I wish it could last forEEEeeeEEeeee...ee...."

"Mallory! Breathe!"

The pale-faced fashion victim spent the new few moments hyperventilating.

Meiko leaned down a bit, to put a hand on his shoulder for support while his body recovered. "Mallory, you're gonna have a heart attack at an early age if you keep that up. What do you mean, you don't know how you feel? Nobody goes on and on like that with so much conviction if they don't know how they feel..."

"Baaah... buuuuh... but... is... is that love?" he asked, with sincerity. "I shouldn't say something so important unless it's really true!"

"It sounds like love to me. Of course, I'm no expert, and it took me this long to figure things out myself, so..."

"Then... if that's love, then... I love you too," Mallory spoke / realized, much to his surprise at his complete lack of surprise about it. "But... I didn't think you'd... I wanted to keep it safe, since you were trying to avoid it and I didn't want to make you feel weird and... but... I mean, I really care about you, and I want you to be happy, and... er... I love you. I'm really bad at speaking stuff, you know that, so sorry if it's awkward—"

"I don't mind awkward. It's kind of cute. And... thanks. For everything."

The fish swam away, having seen the big moment and having kelp to deal with on the other side of the tank.

"Ah... so... what happens now?" Mallory asked, a sense of calm returning slowly but surely. "I mean, in the movies, they just walk off into the sunset and that's that... or they commit lover's suicide. Actually, come to think of it, we ARE on top of a tower that's suitable for jump—err, not that I'm suggesting... you know what I mean. Right?"

"I know, Mallory. Hmm. What now? I'm... not really sure myself, actually. I'm just as new at this as you are."

"Right. So...?"

"I think we go home now," Meiko suggested, with a shrug. "It's getting late, you know? We go home, go to sleep, you wake up early and make me some coffee and we get on with things like we always do. Just... different. We'll see when we get there, I suppose."

"I can do coffee," Mallory agreed, latching onto that... but smiling through his jittery nerves. He held one arm out, hooked slightly. "So, ah... shall we?"

"Why, certainly," Meiko agreed, taking his arm (and his smile) and falling into step.

It was well after sunset, so they couldn't walk off into one, but an elevator did just as well.

As the couple departed the Edo Tower parking lot, two eyes watched them leave. Two eyes identical to the two eyes of one of the lovers...

Exactly identical. The eyes, and the face. The expression was all that differed; instead of Mallory's dazed and happy features, this one was cold and calculating, a hunter stalking prey...

The figure stalked silently, creeping from bush to bush, gaze locked on his target as they hailed a taxi and got on with their lives. When they had left, he rose, a shadow from the shadows...

The stalker took two steps forward, slipped on a discarded soda can, and crashed head first into the nearest brick wall. Out cold in an instant.

A dog wandered by and whizzed on him fifteen minutes later.

As he slept in a puddle of nastiness, one thought bounced around his unconscious mind: *Ryo had BETTER be right about this guy.*

Love.

A new thing to Mallory, except that he'd felt it all along. All it took was a few dozen nudges from Lorelei, the right situation, and the puzzle pieces had locked into place to reveal that what looked like a 2,000-piece jumbled mess (rated ages 18 and up) was actually a picture of two cute and fuzzy kittens. Or something.

(Even in his dreams his words were a disorganized mess.)

So, his dream was filled with love. Love, and comfort. A happy feeling where he was safe...

No fear. Green grass beneath his feet. Blue sky above...

He'd had this dream before, right? Or parts of it. Most parts of it.

Water trickling down a creek. Birds chirping from the trees...

Yes, the next part, he'd definitely had the next part at least. Only tonight it was bright and shining like a star in the sky:

Her smile...

The pavement.

The pavement?

Mallory's eye flicked open in an instant, feeling that cold and clammy artificial surface beneath his hands. His pajamas scraped against the ground, as he quickly got to his feet, quickly wobbled around a bit, and quickly stopped wobbling in a quick amount of time.

Was this still part of his dream? It had to be, since at last check he had gone to sleep on the couch in the living room, which was not, at last check, made of asphalt. This was a back alley of Edo. He could see the colored glow of neon signs in the distance, but nobody else around—

No. Someone else.

"Haven't I seen you somewhere before?" the figure in shadow spoke, eye to eye with Mallory, as they were the same height.

Fear went through Mallory's spine, and his hair stood on end—largely because gravity had suddenly decided it didn't like him anymore.

In a panic, he tumbled upwards, as if the sky was the ground and the ground was the sky without actually being the other way around. His arms flailed around wildly, half in panic, half to get a handhold on something, anything—a fire escape. Yes, a fire escape would be perfect to grab onto, and there would be one in a city alley, based on what he knew about Urbana and places like it...

His hand connected with the cold iron, and he grasped it until the falling sensation stopped, and he simply dangled fifteen feet over certain broken ankleage. He hauled himself over the side, so he could hang onto the structure with more certainty—THEN he began to panic about who had just attacked him.

"It's you! It's you, isn't it?!" he shouted down at his assailant. "The one who attacked us in Antiparadisia—!"

"What? Of course not. Do you see purple-tinted glasses on me?" his own voice floated up from below. "I was just testing you. And given that you just yanked a fire escape into existence, it looks like Ryo was right about you..."

Mallory kept his grip, trying to adjust his eyes to see into the depths of the shadow (even if he was just expecting to see himself). "Well... if not him, then who are you, and what are you doing in my dream?! I could see HIM being in my nightmares, I mean, he's been there before, but if you're me and I'm you but you're not him then WHO ARE YOU!? Mike's ghost?!"

"Eh? Who's Mike?"

"Dead!"

"Oh. That'd explain why he's a ghost, then..."

"WHO—"

"Who am I? Heh," the doppelganger spoke, his smile the only thing visible in the light, white teeth more easily seen through darkness. He advanced towards Mallory, glaring upwards at him the whole time... "Are you sure you want to know? Are you ready for the answers, Mallory Heisenberg? I'm the shadow that defines the shape. I'm the one who stands outside reality. I'm the renegade of the status quo. An enigma wrapped in a question inside a mystery... but... YOU can call me—"

The 'squelch' noise and the meaty THWACK of head against pavement suggested that the mysterious figure had slipped in a puddle and knocked himself unconscious before he could complete his dramatic introduction.

Somewhere in the distance, a train passed by.

Just to make sure, Mallory pinched himself, hoping that he wouldn't dream himself feeling pain when his dream-self pinched himself, thus making the whole exercise moot. He felt pain at the pinch and chose to see this as a sign of being awake.

Now he just had to figure out how to get down, because for some reason, this fire escape had no actual ladders.

A not so tiny part of him really, really wished he was just dreaming.

11: mystery m

"You just LEFT him there?"

"What else was I going to do, drag him across Edo?" Mallory asked. "I nearly killed myself getting down from there! I ripped my pajama bottoms on those garbage cans, then I had to figure out how to hail a cab in the middle of the night in the bad part of Edo without knowing any Nihongo except stuff from shoujo video streams, and... and yes, I left him there! Besides, he was all shadowy and mysterious and stuff. He could've been dangerous!"

"This guy knocked himself out on the middle of a cheesily written prepared speech. I'd call that pitiful, not dangerous," Meiko said, unimpressed. Of course, he had woken her up hours before daybreak, and her mood wasn't interested in getting interested. "Anyway, the House is locked down, we've got a security system, and failing that Lorelei and Kisei can make short work of anybody stupid enough to break in here. At worst we can pop the house off to another one of Ryo's corporate docks in Urbana at a moment's notice."

"But he got me out of the house even without getting into the house and stuff!" Mallory noted, pointing to the pile of bricks roughly equal to one (1) Mallory in mass piled up on his couch sleeping blanket. "What good will any of that do against someone who can do something like that and stuff?"

"I've thought of that as well," Meiko spoke, sliding a small blinking widget to him. "Tracking device. Keep it on you when you sleep tonight. If it leaves the house, my F.P. will signal and I'll have Kisei and Lorelei find you. He's not going to pull the same stunt twice. There's no need to worry now, Mallory. ...you're sure it wasn't that guy from Antiparadisia, right?"

"It wasn't him," Mallory said, with enough confidence. "I don't think I'd still be alive if it was him. He said he was 'testing' me... and... and that Ryo sent him! He mentioned Ryo!"

"Okay, so we call Ryo in the morning and get this matter cleared up. No big deal."

"No big deal?! This could be about... about me, and the whole thing with me that we can't explain, and—"

"Mallory!"

"What?!"

"It's four in the morning," Meiko reminded him. "Keep it down, Eiko needs her rest. Look... I know you're worried. But let's be practical here, okay? This guy is probably still crumpled on the pavement, being urinated on by stray dogs or something like that. If he does wake up, we're going to be ready for him. As for you, you need to get some sleep. Then... in the morning, we'll both go see Ryo together."

"Together...?" he asked, confused as his memory tripped over a problem spot. "But... don't you have to meet a client?"

"...I can cancel the meeting," Meiko spoke, trying to emphasize the No Big Deal Factor. "It's not like I've accepted a contract yet, it was just a job pitch."

"But the money—"

"We're still riding off a narrow profit margin, and that's better than our usual financial state. I think we can afford to turn down one... and if following this really leads to some answers, it could get involving for all of us. I wouldn't want to wrangle a job AND this at the same time. Finding out the truth is important to you, yes?"

"Of course!"

"Then it's important to me," she said, locking down the confidence in her voice. "This is my new 'job' for the time being. And as your 'boss', I hereby order you to bed, houseboy. I want you rested and ready for work the next morning. Or I'll dock your pay."

For a change, he didn't have to ask "Err, are you joking?". He simply smiled, and nodded along. "Right, 'boss lady.' I just hope I CAN get to sleep... I'm all excited and nervous and scared and anticipating and stuff!"

"Drink some milk, it always works for me. And don't worry, all right? In the morning, we'll get all the answers you want from Ryo!"

"You've got me," Ryo said, with a shrug inside his baggy, stained lab coat. "I've got no idea who he is."

Mallory sagged inside and out, despite being well forcibly well rested.

"Okay, maybe you don't know WHO he is, but you have to have some idea of WHAT he is," Meiko continued, pestering the scientist when Mallory wouldn't. "You gave Mallory some pretty skimpy details... that's not like you."

"All I have is skimpy details, I swear!" Ryo protested, cowering under the intense scruntiny of a woman he stood multiple inches over. "I'm sure it's not a big deal. I mean, okay, he plucked Mallory out of his room and they had sort of a reality-based brawl, but... okay, that SOUNDS like a big deal but it's really not a huge thing to worry about, right? Don't you two have to be looking for jobs? I... Meiko, you don't have to resort to the Evil Cold Stare, okay?"

"What? Oh. Sorry," Meiko apologies, backing down a bit. "Instincts. ...but if you're holding back on us, you deserve it! And I have this feeling you are—"

"It's okay, Meiko."

Both old friends turned to look at the new friend. Relatively new friend.

"I mean... we shouldn't bother Ryo with this if he doesn't know anything, right?" Mallory said, trying to be the assuring voice of reason. "No sense in it. So... we should just go. He's got important sciencey stuff to do—"

Meiko waved her hand, cutting him off. "Mallory, you want to know the truth behind all this, don't you? I know this is really gnawing at you inside..."

"Well, uh—"

"And I ALSO know something you don't—that Ryo has a dirty little habit of being selfless to the point of being overprotective. ...or something like that. And I suspect, given that he told you he'd 'Worry for you so you don't have to worry' way back when you were studying for the REC Test, that he has good REASON to worry. Because he knows more than he's letting on. And because he knows I will hate him forever and ever if he doesn't speak up!"

Ryo actually laughed out loud at that one. "Meiko-chan! Come on, we're not kids any more, that silly threat won't—"

"Wanna try me?"

"Well, no, not really, but—"

"Ryo-kun... I know you think you're protecting Mallory," Meiko spoke, returning to her less 'YOU VILL OBEY' sort of speech methodology. "But... I think it'd be better for all of us if you fess up. Even if it's scary. If you want an undeniable logical reason, then... my home's at unknown risk thanks to all of this. Eiko's in danger and so am I, and yes, so is Mallory. You don't like me worrying about things, right? Give me a reason NOT to worry, or a reason to worry for good reason so I can worry about what I'm supposed to be worrying about instead of a needless worry! ...and now I'm packing sentences fragments together like Mallory. See how worried I am?"

She wasn't worried last night, Mallory thought to himself, listening quietly. *Actually, she was acting a lot like Ryo did when I first told him...*

Whatever her words were or how wobbly they came out, they did the job. Ryo had a seat on a nearby lab stool, caving in completely. "...I honestly don't have many details," he spoke, without the good-buddy cheerful front. "What I told Mallory was true. This guy came barging in, no appointment. He knew I had a harmonic wave scanner, and that I had no RealWare ties, which is why he didn't go to some REC-certified engine shop to get the test done... I didn't understand why he wanted it done, but I figured the sooner I got this crazy kid out of my office, the better. ...and I was curious, I'll admit. We took the blood sample—this is before they optimized the wands so you didn't have to extract an Engine's water—and the light turned green. The kid shouted something like 'I KNEW it!' and stormed out, upset. And that's it."

"That's it...?" Meiko egged him on.

"...well, that's all I told Mallory, but there's a little bit more to it than that," Ryo admitted. "This is gonna take a while to explain, and... look, up front, I want to say this is just my crackpot theory and there's honestly no reason to go into a panic about—"

"RYO—"

"Okay! Okay, okay. The kid was gone... but I still had the blood sample," Ryo continued. "Meiko, do you remember when I gave you your F.P.? I mentioned I got the idea from some blood tests, but I didn't totally understand how the thing worked..."

Meiko's hand instinctively slipped into her purse, touching the red plastic case of her personal organizer. "I... think I remember something like that. I didn't think much of it at the time..."

"It was his blood," Ryo admitted. "And the strangest thing about the sample was exactly what the wand proved—it had the same harmonic properties as the water inside a Reality Engine. It could generate reality waves. ...theoretically. I hooked it up to three organizer prototypes I was tinkering with, did some tweaks, mumbo jumbo, and... well, they started filling in my calendar dates. I was hesitant to give the red prototype to you, but that was the night you came over and we had that talk..."

Mallory spoke up for the first time, with new concern. "Talk...?"

"I'd... been having a bad day," Meiko explained. "Business wasn't going well, we were so far into debt that I was afraid I'd have to sell the house... including the debt to Ryo for the home loan—"

"Meiko, I said you never really had to pay that b—"

"I was having a bad day, and... I needed to see a friend. So I came here. And we were talking about the future..."

"More like crying on my shoulder about the future, act—"

"TALKING about the future," Meiko corrected, forcing history to comply with her whim. "And he said he had something that could act as a wobbly guide to the future... it wasn't always accurate, but it'd take some of the worry out of my life..."

"'Future Perfect'. ...Future Imperfect was less marketable," Ryo noted. "I never actually marketed it, I didn't have enough of the blood sample to make more than three. And I don't like selling technology that I don't understand myself, of course. Although mine's done quite well by me, and I know you're happy with yours—"

"We're getting off track, Ryo."

"We are? ...okay, yeah, we are. I studied the blood sample some more, trying to figure out why it had harmonic properties," he continued. "And... okay, here's where we get to the crackpot theory, since this is theoretically impossible. I tried injecting some of the sample into a Reality Engine, replacing the treated water that's normally inside an engine. I figured, what could it hurt? At worst it wouldn't be enough fluid to do anything, or the engine would just crash and vanish into nothingness like it would if I squirted in any random fluid. I initialized the program and sent it into Nullspace so it could establish a new from-scratch reality..."

The other two leaned in close, as it's traditional to do when reaching the punchline of a good ghost story.

"...actually, it did vanish, just like I figured," Ryo admitted. "Scratch one Reality Engine. I could've poured grape juice into it and gotten the same effect."

"That's it?" Meiko asked, unbelieving. "You had us all worked up for nothing?"

"Except for the log data I collected which showed it expanded to a reality of infinite size for an infinitely small amount of time before exploding into an infinite amount of subatomic particles which instantly ceased to exist in the emptiness of Nullspace, yes."

Mallory jumped to conclusions and landed squarely on the 100 pt. mark.

"I'M GONNA EXPLODE?!" he screamed.

"See, this is why I didn't tell him in the first place," Ryo calmly pointed out while Mallory began to hyperventilate. "Science can be spooky stuff, you know?"

"You're not too spooked," Meiko noted, staying calm. "Which means it's not as dire as it sounds. Since you've been playing Mr. Exposition for the last few minutes, care to go a few more...?"

Ryo finished locking Mallory into a shihatsu grip, turning off the boy's panic like a switch. "Right, right," he wheezed, while hauling Mallory onto a lab stool and propping him against a table. He settled down in his own seat to continue. "My crackpot theory. When stimulated properly, the fluid can generate limited reality... like Future Perfect does. Whether it's shaping the future or detecting it I don't know, but it's definitely some variant of a reality effect. And when stimulated TOO much, well... the power is limitless, but the physical nature of it is NOT limitless. That's why the thing burned out and blew up when pushed too hard. And may I note that an engine pushes VERY hard—I can't think of anything Mallory could do that'd hit those levels. Even the... 'tricks' he's been accidentally doing don't come close to that peak."

"I'mmnot gonna splode?" the now calmed Mallory asked, words slurring together like runny tofu.

"You're not gonna explode," Ryo confirmed with a cute little smile. "Relax, Mallory! Look, all of this is basically meaningless to you—and largely meaningless to me. I have no idea how you got this way, or how that guy got this way, or why you look alike, or... well, anything! The only thing I kept from you was that, well, whatever this is, it's pretty impressive stuff. Theoretically limitless. Not that you're planning to turn into a caped crusading super hero with amazing superpowers, right?"

"I, uh... I really wasn't planning on it, no," Mallory said, while his brain pondered exactly how insane the concept was.

"Right. That's why I didn't think it was important. You're an ordinary guy living an ordinary life! Just because you've got a few quirks doesn't mean you have to feel weird, or that you even have to use 'em! I mean, Meiko here can put her legs behind her head, but you don't see her doing that on a daily basi—ow ow ow ow ow..."

"He has a point," Meiko agreed, while pulling Ryo's earlobe off. "Not sure I agree with it, but it's a valid point. Other than today and that one day in Antiparadisia, this hasn't really been an issue, has it? Your whole life's been a series of days where this isn't an issue. We COULD always leave it be... what do you think, Mallory? I'll go with you on this."

"I... I really don't think I can do that," Mallory admitted. "I'm not planning on being a super hero, no, but... if I'm gonna be an ordinary guy I can't have this hanging over my head like the... what's it called... the Dagger of Democracy? Poleaxe of Potemkin? Something like that."

"Are you absolutely sure?" Meiko asked, letting go of Ryo's agonized head feature.

With words that were unusually decisive for the boy, Mallory said: "Yeah."

"All right, then... we'll look into it. Just like I promised last night," she agreed. "Ryo, see if you can find this crazy guy again. Mal... WE are going to want to have a talk with him. And please, stop trying to protect us from stuff like this, okay? ...after what we went through in Antiparadisia, I think we'll be less emotionally fragile if we KNEW the truth instead of hiding from it."

The walk back home was a quiet one.

Quiet was bad. Mallory quietly wished for the usual in-house chaos... Eiko playing, Lorelei making tawdry jokes, Meiko admonishing her for them, Kisei... in her room quiet as a mouse, actually, but other than that something very non-quiet. And he'd be busy in the kitchen or collecting the laundry that tended to pile up anywhere and everywhere... that would have felt right. It would be something he could easily deal with. Something that would keep his blood pressure down and his spirits up...

Instead, he was rubbing a sore spot on his neck where Ryo had pressure-pointed his panicky self. Again. Just like he had the last time he had to deal with this mess, way back when he was studying for the REC Test... panic, panic, mayhem, panic, hyperventilation... worry and worry and panic.

While Mallory did spend a large slice of his mental timeshare with his neurons misfiring in socially awkward ways, it was not a favored state to exist within. He got along for years with only small levels of panic back home. He got along for days at a time when his life wasn't being actively threatened without panic in his new home. But this, and that, from Antiparadisia, to this and now, and the thing, with the guy, the one who looked like him, how it kept him on edge and confused and worried and wishing for the quiet days of, oh, twenty hours past, especially twenty hours past when he was with Meiko in the aquarium and everything was okay even if he was momentarily panicked but that went away and was replaced by this total feeling of peace and joy and—

"Mallory!"

"Er, what?" he asked, unfortunately breaking out of the bright memory in the process. "What?"

"You were zoning out there... just wanted to make sure you were okay," Meiko spoke. "You've had this rabbit-in-headlights look all day. This is really bewildering for you, isn't it?"

"That's one word for it. Or 'perplexing' or 'befuddling' or 'bizarre' or 'inexplicable' or—"

"I'm having my own problems coming to grips with it, actually," Meiko admitted, while taking F.P. from her purse and idly pushing buttons on it. "I nearly lost it back there with Ryo. I don't like losing it."

"I, uh... I was kind of wondering about that," Mallory said, surprised that she'd bring it up voluntarily. "You sounded so confident last night..."

"Hey, someone has to take charge here, yes? That's me, the boss lady. The problem solver. So even if I'm upset about this, I have to have confidence and control or we'll just stumble around aimlessly. You can't handle it, after all."

"Hey, wait a second—"

"I don't mean that to be insulting, Mallory," she clarified. "I just mean this really hits too close to home for you—you need an objective third party. ...as objective as I can get, since you and I, well... and of course, you have trouble dealing with crisis. I doubt you had much of it back on the farm. I, on the other hand, have been living on the edge of crisis, poverty, and job stress for quite a few years. I'm used to it. That's why I'm not alarmed that we're being followed."

"FOL—"

"Eyes front, voice normal, converse just like we've been conversing," Meiko spoke as ordinarily as possible. "It's a blessing in disguise; I was actually hoping this might happen. I hit F.P.'s panic button a minute ago, so Kisei should be tailing us soon. We'll be okay, I promise. And if we're going to get any answers we don't want to spook this guy off... but after he assaulted you, I don't feel like playing his game, so I just changed the rules. Now. Don't turn around to check, but—was the guy last night wearing a trenchcoat? Fake leather?"

"Y-Yeah," Mallory said, walking along a bit stiffly at her side. "Meiko, you sure about this...?"

"This is what I do for a living, Mallory," Meiko said... with a tiny smile, as she looked down at F.P.'s screen. "I solve problems for other people. If I can't solve them for people I truly care about, then... okay, Kisei's in sniping position. Here we go..."

"Wait, wait—she's not gonna shoot him, is sh—"

A light 'piff' noise zipped by Mallory's ear, and the sound of someone behind them dropping followed posthaste.

"Tranq shot, of course," Meiko replied, closing F.P. "Now, let's scoop this guy up and get home before anybody starts looking at us funny. It's time we stopped panicking and started sorting this mess out once and for all."

Tensions ran high in the interrogation chamber. The air was thick with oregano.

This was because the prisoner currently tied to the Interrogation Chair was a highly volatile, dangerous unknown factor who had kidnapped Mallory the previous night and assaulted him. And because Lorelei had suggested, with many smirks and winks, that a pasta dish heavy in oregano with a side of oysters might be a meal Meiko would really really like Mallory to make for her so he had purchased far too many bags of the stuff on his last shopping run.

The man sitting in front of the herbs and spices didn't look too dangerous, but it wasn't from lack of trying.

He wore a scary leather trenchcoat typically reserved for chaotic neutral anti-heroes, the sort that flaps around nicely when you're performing zero-gravity kung fu and hugs the shadows properly when prowling in dark alleys of a criminal underworld. On him, however, it was simply a badly fitting and overly large garment which was yanked off a bargain rack and bore all the tailoring hallmarks of unskilled mass production labor. He wore steel-toed boots, which would be menacing and masculine if not for the fact that they were so heavy he gave away his presence tailing Mallory due to the 'thump, clank' they made on pavement. He was wearing sinister-looking jet black sunglasses when he hit the ground, but the cheap plastic frames remained on the ground where he fell, shattered in three places.

Finally, he had Mallory's physique, which was to say he had none. No rippling abs and muscular arms designed to snap the necks of people who disrespect him in seedy underworld bars, no well-defined cheekbones to get a perfect diagonal cut on during the battle with his sworn enemy in the last reel of the movie. A scrawny body in a wanna-be evil ensemble added up nicely to a very pathetic figure.

Nevertheless, Lorelei had her energy blade at the ready and Kisei had a rifle trained on him as if he could snap and unleash a whirlwind of death and mayhem at a moment's notice. Eiko had been sent to Ryo's place to play with his model monorail, just in case something did go wrong, and the House's reality engine had been put into Sleep Mode to prevent any possible accidents. Preparations were made to the point of paranoia.

And finally, the moment of truth.

"Wake him up," Meiko said, taking one step back (and bumping into a cowering Mallory in the process).

Kisei squeezed the trigger on her rifle, to shoot a tiny chemical dart into the boy's arm that would counteract the drugs—the same chemical used on Belle Pasadina, to keep him paralyzed but snap him back to consciousness. She then slotted a fresh, full-strength tranq dart into the chamber of her rifle in one smooth arm motion. Just in case.

Much like the boy himself, his emergence to the waking world was not particularly impressive.

"Guurrgh," was his grand opening statement, accompanied by a bit of drool from the corner of his mouth. One eye cracked open, peering around, before his body decided it really wanted to go back to sleep.

1.2 seconds later and his brain told his body now was not the time to slack off and he was wide awake with a very alarmed expression.

"You'll never take me alive! Or dead!" he declared, his muscles really wanting to struggle against the ropes but completely failing to.

"We're not going to kill you," Meiko replied. "Now, we—"

A brief flash of purple light flooded the dry goods store room, reality rearranged itself with care, and Lorelei was now tied to the chair while the mysterious young man stood where she previously stood, ready to bolt out of there.

Unfortunately he hadn't thought ahead too far, because instead of running towards glorious, wonderful freedom, his chemically paralyzed body simply crumpled to the floor like a sack of oregano.

Meiko stood over him, looking mildly annoyed as Mallory snuck around to untie Lorelei. "Do you mind not doing that again? Thanks," she spoke. "We hid a tracking device on you while you were out, anyway. The best you could do is swap yourself somewhere far away, and lie there for a while until we find you again. You don't get the paralysis cure until we get some answers— provide them and you go free. Fair?"

"Pff... pfeh!" the Mallory-alike tried to spit, unable to do so due to using up all his spit drooling while asleep. "You're meddling with powers of which you have no comprehension, woman! The very nature of reality is my plaything, to shape at will! I am the shadow that defines the shape! I am—"

"Going nowhere until you cooperate," Meiko interrupted. "I've gotten secrets out of tougher nuts than you. Nuttier nuts, too. And I've got all day to try."

"Bah! Do your worst!" he taunted from his awkward little position on the floor. "I won't say a word to you! Beyond these words I'm saying now, I mean! Ha! You won't break me!"

"We—"

"Wait, wait, this isn't going anywhere," Mallory interjected, while his brain tried to tell his mouth that he was scared of this guy and should probably be simpering a bit more even if the other bit of his brain wanted to look strong in front of Meiko especially after acting like a simpering, panicky guy all day long. "If you won't talk to her, you'll talk to me, right? You tried to talk to me last night, until you fell over and knocked yourself out..."

"I... I did NOT fall over!" the boy protested. "It was... a clever machination! Wheels within wheels, of which you know nothing! Ha ha!"

"But that's the problem, I don't know anything! I mean, anything about this. About you, about my power!" Mallory continued, nerves battling inside him as Meiko stepped back and watched him take charge. "We brought you here so you could explain what's going on with me! You said you were testing me last night—testing me for what? Okay, you kinda attacked me but that's okay, as long as you tell me why I am how I am so I don't keep freaking out over it!!"

...when he realized he'd used one exclamation mark too many, Mallory finally dropped from his rush of adrenaline and cowered a little. But just a little.

An uneasy silence followed. Which was better than further maniacal ranting, all things considered.

"I was going to tell you about this stuff anyway, I just got interrupted," the boy finally admitted, in a less dramatic tone. "I sought you out specifically to tell you all about this stuff, if you didn't know already. But I had to make sure you weren't just HIM in disguise, and that you were ready to find out. You're not him and you're ready. So give me back my arms and legs and I'll talk—but ONLY with you. Not with them. This is 'Us' business only!"

Meiko stepped up again, commandeering the situation. "No deal," she stated flatly. "You've already proven you're dangerous. What makes you think I'd leave you completely unrestrained and alone with Mallory? I know a thing or two about risk assessment, and—"

"I'll do it," Mallory spoke up.

"No, you won't. Mallory, trust me on this, we've handled dangerous people plenty of times in our line of work, and—"

"And I need answers!" Mallory replied, moving between Meiko and the prisoner. "It's risky, I know, but what else can we do? I don't wanna beat it out of him or anything like that! And if we don't work WITH him he could just escape and then I'll miss my chance at finding out... no, no, no. I gotta do it, even if it means doing it alone... right?"

Meiko opened her mouth to protest again...

And saw Mallory wink.

"...I guess there's no other choice, then," Meiko agreed. "Kisei, give the boy the counter drug and let them go. But if Mallory has one scratch on his head when he gets back—or if he DOESN'T come back—I'm going to hunt you down, buster. Don't forget that. Kisei?"

Kisei kept her rifle, as it was during the entire discourse, trained on the fallen form. "I am not questioning your orders and I do not mean disrespect, Meiko Mirai, but I would like to voice my disapproval of this plan..."

From the other side of the room, Lorelei nodded in assent. "It blows," she summarized in a way only Lorelei could.

"Opinions noted, girls," Meiko acknowledged. "Kisei, give him the counter drug."

An inaudble 'pff' sounded, and the boy slowly pulled himself up to his feet. He shrugged into his poorly fitting trenchcoat, trying to regain what little cool and macho composure he could... and cast one last angry glare at Meiko, before putting an arm around Mallory and vanishing in a blast of purple light.

A large pile of newspaper bundles freshly swapped from some street vendor dropped to the floor in their place, roughly equal in mass to the two boys. Silent seconds followed, as the spots on their eyes from the flash faded.

"...he's getting clever," Meiko finally spoke, with a note of satisfaction in her voice.

"Mallory? Clever?" Lorelei asked, suspicious. "How do you figure?"

"He remembered he was carrying a tracking device," the boss lady explained, opening up F.P. and loading her tracking program. "Even if this guy shrugs off the one we put on him, we can find him. And that means Kisei can stalk them, and watch over him to make sure nothing goes wrong while he's getting his answers. It's a perfect plan—that guy doesn't seem like the sort to figure out the loophole, either. Kisei, could you..."

The gap in space where Kisei stood spoke volumes of her depature, having already anticipated the plan and in the process of closing in on her target.

"Not bad... not bad at all," Lorelei admitted with a smirk. "You two are really establishing a rapport, aren't ya? I knew getting you two together was the right idea. What was the tipoff?"

"He winked at me," Meiko said, letting the tease slide. "Our houseboy's definitely getting to be a real covert ops team player."

"What's wrong with your eye?" the other boy asked, peering at Mallory oddly as they walked down a random Edo back alley.

"I think I got some dust in it," Mallory replied, rubbing at his eye. "So... where are we going?"

"Somewhere you can pay me back for the information I'm going to give you," the other Mallory sort-of explained. "Before you freak out again, I just want you to talk to some people. But that can wait; we've got a bit of a walk ahead of us to get there. I've dampened the sound around us a little to keep others from hearing us, so feel free to ask any questions you've got. Apparently you're bursting at the seams with them, after all..."

"You did what?" Mallory asked, straining an ear to hear the usual ambient noise of Edo... and finding it was indeed a bit muffled. "Wow, that's a neat trick! Like your place-swapping thingy and... okay, questions, questions...

wow, I really don't know where to begin... ah! Wait, I do, I'll start at the beginning! So... where are we from? REALLY from?"

"Don't know, exactly."

"And who are our real parents?"

"Don't know that either."

"...and why do we have these powers?"

"Don't know for certain."

Mallory stopped in his tracks, brain slightly derailed.

"Err... what DO you know, then?" he asked. "I thought you said you knew the truth..."

The boy also paused, and turned to face his twin with a slightly annoyed look. "I have speculations, okay? Answers, but not truth. None of us know anything for certain. All I can do is tell you what I think is the way things are for whatever reason."

"Uhh... okay, so... what are the reasons why things are the way they are independent of the reason why they are as they happen to be?" Mallory tried again.

"Ah," his duplicate said, scratching his chin dramatically. "That's complicated."

Internally, Mallory hoped he wasn't as annoying as this other him was proving to be.

"For starters, I'd better properly introduce myself," the annoying twin said, whipping a fresh pair of sunglasses out of his trenchcoat and slipping them on in a quasi-cool manner. "I am the one with no true name, the wanderer between worlds. The lurking truth behind the fiction of your world! But you can call me... 'M'."

"Em...? Em and what? Em-'n-em? Em Smith?"

"No, M. One letter," he of one letter which was M replied. "I grew up in the hard, unforgiving jungle of Suburbana, a drifter with no family moving from foster home to foster home, without a true name to attach to my person! Therefore I have adopted the moniker of M, to EMphasize my Mysterious nature!"

"...right," Mallory replied. "So... my questions...?"

"Oh, right, right. Okay, well, I have no idea where we're really from and can't even begin to speculate," M explained, shooting down one question in a disappointing puff of matchstick-sized flames. "I also don't know who our parents are. But I have successfully speculated about our mysterious origins! It took some heavy covert research at Reality Prime, home of RealWare—the documents concerning our strange and unusual situation are heavily classified. But not classified to the all-seeing eye of M! Those filthy corporate spooks cannot hide from the searing light of the Truth!"

"Wow! It's really that big of a secret?!" Mallory asked, easily impressed.

"Indeed! I had to pay some guy all of fifteen points to raid their QA file cabinets for me!" M stated with pride. "It was filed under 'Product Failure Reports'. JUST AS I HAD SUSPECTED! You see, the MAN (by which I mean Gillian Bates) doesn't WANT us to know about various ways in which Reality Engines can critically fail. They keep their bug reports under tight security! I mean, the cabinet needed a key to open and everything, according to what Floyd the janitor told me. And the horrible truth was within!"

"Right! And... the horrible truth was...?"

With a sweeping gesture, M pulled a highly battered data pad out of the inner pocket of his coat, holding it out for Mallory to accept with a graceful flick of the wrist. "The truth is in here, my brother. You see, I vaguely recalled a school newspaper clipping from my youth in which a Reality Engine accident resulted in triplets. And my dim but sharp memory led me to raiding this file, which reveals the full story! It seems that sometimes, during a highly unlikely set of environmental circumstances, for no reason RealWare can explain... an engine failure when transitioning between realities with a pregnant woman onboard can result in instant delivery of the child. Or, as the story proves, CHILDREN! Yes, three identical children, right down to fingerprints and DNA. An impossibility? I do not believe in impossibilities!"

"Well, it can't be impossible if it happened to someone else," Mallory said, thumbing through the dense, boring corporate notes. "It's only logical."

"Uh, right. But nevertheless! A very rare scenario!" M added, trying to recover some mystique to it. "In that situation, two of the children appeared at the destination, but the father and the other child were translocated to some distant reality. And that is likely how we originated! There was an accident with a Reality Engine, and copies of us... of ourself... what's the grammatically correct way of saying that?"

"Of we?" Mallory guessed incorrectly.

"Copies of we were strewn throughout the multiverse!!" M finished with gusto. "As for our parents, it's unknown. They could have been moved somewhere else. Maybe they arrived at their destination with one of us. Maybe they ended up in NullSpace. We may never know... HOWEVER! That is the Truth of our origin!"

"I thought you said you didn't know the tru—"

"As for our powers, well... it's quite obvious, once you know of our origins," M continued, folding his arms and leaning against a wall in a casually confident sort of way (and nearly falling over since the wall was farther away than he had realized). "Reality Engines operated by generating reality waves from harmonic vibrations of water. What's the human body? 90% water! ...I think. Maybe it was 80%. BUT THE POINT IS! Somehow, in this reality accident which copied us around the multiverse, we MERGED with the Reality Engine's water! That is why when Ryo tested my blood, it identified it as engine water! And thus, using this unique trait, we can manipulate reality around us!"

"Wow! I mean... wow! That's really amazing!" Mallory agreed, buying into the drama. "If it's true, I mean. It does make... a little bit of sense from what little I actually understand about Reality Engines. I think."

M tried to loom in front of Mallory. "And now... you know. The grim, twisted tale of our collective past! Orphaned across the multiverse, with the very blood of gods in our veins, adrift and lost and alone and lost!"

"Uh... it hasn't been all that bad for me, actually. I had a mostly happy childhood and I've got a good career now. I was a little lost but I think things worked out okay for me in the end..."

And his copy visibly deflated. "Why is it that I'm the only one with a tormented, angsty past?" he complained, voice rising back to normal tones after wobbling around the Ominous pitch scale. "I don't get it. Every one of us I've met had a good family life and made friends and stuff! This sucks."

"Uh... I'm sorry?" Mallory offered, patting M on the shoulder in a way which was hopefully comforting. "But hey... you know me, now! If I can't be friends with myself, even another myself, who can I be friends with? Heck, you could find others of us and BOOM, more friends!"

M shrugged the hand off, growling above his breath and resuming his long march through the back alleys of the city. "Don't remind me, please. In fact, that's related to how you're going to pay me back for this information..."

"Huh?"

Rounding the corner, the pair stopped at a community bingo hall.

M opened the door, ushering a puzzled Mallory inside. "You're going to pay me by convincing them I'm not insane," he said. "C'mon. Hope you can get over the initial shock, I need you to back me up in there..."

When the door closed behind him, the sign hanging in the window reading 'Meeting Thursdays and Fridays, 1:00PM: Our Support Group' swung gently back and forth.

In the beginning... there was Mallory.

Then Mallory met Mike. For a minute.

Then both of them met Multi. Three total.

Now M had shown up, and that was four.

And now...

Now there were SEVEN. Seven who all looked exactly like him.

"I know, I know! I mean, Kaori is WAY cooler than Kazuya," number five went on and on. "I don't see how she got voted off the show first. She had the makings of a PERFECT N-pop idol! I swear, the entire season just went downhill after that—it's not like the last two seasons, when we had Akemi and Kaede..."

"Right, Kaede! I'd forgotten about her!" number six chirped away with. "Like, oh my GOD that was such a cute red dress she had in the final episode, you remember that? I almost cried when they didn't give her the contract. It was so sad, after that video clip tribute to her poor departed mother—you know, where she said she'd become the greatest N-pop idol ever when her mother was on her deathbed? Those media executives made a bad decision turning her down after that! Don't you agree, Mallory?"

"................" Mallory agreed. Or maybe didn't agree. It was hard to tell, as the thick hazy cloud of Culture Shock had descended upon his world view.

"Hey, you okay there, Mallory?" number five (name: Melvin, occupation: Stage magician, likes: Hot dogs, dislikes: Bean soup) asked, waving a hand in front of Mallory's eyes.

"Oh, you can blame M for this," number six (name: Megumi, occupation: Waitress, likes: Parasols, dislikes: Bicycle messengers) explained, folding her arms and giving the extremely disgruntled mystery M a harsh look. "Really now, M, you should've, like... explained what Our Support Group was really like before you dumped it on him. The poor boy's so confused now! Mallory-kun, it's okay, really—we're just ordinary people, like you! Only... REALLY like you. Okay...?"

M tapped his foot irritably on the floor, slumping back in his wooden chair (the one in front of the 'It's Okay To Not Be Unique!' slogan on the chalkboard). "You know, I've always wondered... why am I the only SANE one of us? Just my luck, the new one of us I drag in has a mind like a glass trap. Or something. If—"

"Why am I a girl?" Mallory asked, breaking his silence in an awkward way, addressing Megumi. "Me. You. Other. Her. She. Uh. Why?"

"Ohhh, you DO speak! Hwei!" Megumi squealed, balling her hands under her chin. "I was really worried M broke your brain! Ah... as for your question, umm... it's kinda complicated... I mean, uh..." Balled hands went to fingers poik-poiking in front of her face, as a shy blush spread over her cheeks.

Melvin stepped in (without leaving his chair). "Now now, it's okay—we're all us here, aren't we?" he reminded them. "If anybody can understand and accept us, it's us! Mallory, it's like this... Megumi's family supposedly has a family curse. So to avoid it hitting her generation, they gave her a girl's name and dress her in girl's clothing. It makes sense, if you think about it!"

"No, it DOESN'T," M complained in the background.

"Listen, we're all good folks here," Melvin continued, putting an arm around Mallory's dazed shoulders. (Not that the shoulders themselves were dazed, that would be a new high score even for him.) "I think you'll find we're more alike than disalike. Err, or rather, more disalike than alike. Whichever you'd prefer. The point is, I'm glad you could join us today, and I'm sure that together, all five of us can draw strength from each other in the future!"

Megumi pumped a cute little fist in the air. "Go Us!" she cheered.

"Go Us!" Melvin repeated, cheer being an infectious disease.

"Zzzzzzz," number seven snored (name: Matsuri, occupation: Night watchman, likes: Sleeping, dislikes: Having a night job).

Caught up in a wave of good tidings rolling in during low tide, Mallory weakly raised a fist too. "Uh... Go Us?" he tried. "But... but wait, I don't understand. How did you find each other? I mean, aren't we spread all over the place...?"

M spoke up immediately, before Melvin could continue his nurturing support. "I'm the one who found them. Tracking down others was no picnic, believe me. I was under the impression that together, we could figure out what to do about the guy with the purple glasses, not sit around sharing our feelings and singing folk music and having bake sales..."

"Are you still going on about that spooky guy with the purple glasses?" Megumi asked, barely managing to not hide her snickering cute girly contempt. "M, like... come ON, now! None of us have seen this supposedly dangerous guy. You're just being paranoid again! You know, like the time you told us that RealWare was buying children to use as slave labor. Mallory, don't listen to this guy—everything's some grand conspiracy!"

"Uh, actually... RealWare was trying to buy away the children of I's Land to be janitors and stuff for them," Mallory corrected. "I was there for that one, but saved the day with a magic bowl of soup!"

The others of themselves gave Mallory the kind of 'Okay, riiiight, sure, we believe you' look they normally reserved for M.

"Anyway... we should get on with new business now that we've introduced Mallory to the group," Melvin spoke, changing subjects. "I'm glad that Matsuri could join us this time, even if he's clearly had a long night. Let's all thank Matsuri."

"Arigato, Matsuri-kun!" Megumi cheered.

"Zzzzzz," Matsuri replied.

"I wanted to bring up my previous suggestion that we move bowling to Thursday nights, instead of Fridays," Melvin continued. "I have a few more club gigs coming up which are going to land on Fridays, and I'd hate to miss out on one of the most enjoyable times we share together. Megumi, how's your work schedule looking?"

"Ooooh, not good," she spoke with a pout. "Thursdays I have double shift since, like, Eiko can't make it because of that celebrity tag-team game show, you know the one where you drink out of a cow? Right. Well, I'm like, Thursday is bad for me. Wednesday, maybe? Matsuri has off Wednesday nights!"

Melvin had his electronic organizer out, and was tapping on the screen with a stylus. "Wednesdays are good for me. Okay! We go bowling on Wednesdays from now on! Ah, is that okay with you, M? I know you don't like to go bowling, but I feel we need inclusive agreement on things like this... Mallory, how are you for Wednesday nights?"

M's aggravation level topped out to super-combo-powering levels, as he got to his feet with such force of will that his chair flew back eight feet and severely dented the bingo calling board. "Bowling?!" he shouted back. "Why the hell would I worry about what night BOWLING falls on when I've got my life to worry about? Your lives, too! The guy with purple glasses EXISTS, and he nearly killed Mallory! That's why I brought him here, not to bowl with you cretins but to prove that I'm not crazy and that we are all in serious danger! Why won't you people believe me?! I'm trying to keep you alive and all you care about is making buddy-buddy-nice-nice with each other! It's not too late to work together and do something about this!"

Melvin sighed, shaking his head "M, M, M—"

"Don't you start, Mr. Pull A Rabbit Out Of Your Pants," M warned. "You're the worst offender. Megumi I can understand, since she hasn't found a drop of her power—"

"I don't WANT any stupid powers!" Megumi protested. "I want to be a perfectly ordinary, normal young boy in a dress!"

"—but you, YOU at least have some conscious control over your ability," M continued. "And what do you do with it? Cheap tricks and illusions! You don't even have enough dexterity to pluck a coin from behind someone's ear, so you zap one there with your power! You're a cheat, not a magician!"

"And what else should I be doing with it, M?" Melvin asked, his normal cheer starting to sink to levels of unpleasantness at the confrontation. "What do you do with it? You show off. You try to bully people and make yourself look powerful, all while pretending there's some shadow conspiracy trying to get to you! At least I'm doing something productive with my ability—okay, maybe I'm not that good with card tricks the old-fashioned way, but so what? If this is a gift for our own use like you keep saying it is, then I should use it how I want. I just don't want to use it to be like YOU. And at least I don't rant, stutter or use endless mixed metaphors!"

"Leave your speech therapist out of this! I—"

"Stop, stop!" Megumi cried out, covering her ears. "You're all being too mean to each other! And you'll wake up Matsuri if you keep yelling. Now, we're supposed to support each other, that's why we're here! Not to tear each other down like this. I think we all need to just sit down, count to five and breathe. Then we can go into our caves and find our power animals—"

"Nuts to your stupid penguin, I'm talking about important things and stuff and things here!" M continued. "And who says I'm bullying and showboating? I'm defending myself here! Instead of hugging and singing and trying to find your inner badger just to feel safe against the world, you could be getting stronger! I mean... I mean...! Megumi, you haven't even TRIED to tap your power yet!"

"And I don't want to, meanie!" Megumi barked back. "I'm just me, not some sort of... some sort of superpowered weirdo *freak*!"

A chill silence flooded the room like iced tea, as the verboten 'F' word was dropped into Our Support Group.

Megumi's jaw lowered and raised a few times, horrified at her own words. "I, I... I'm sorry... Melvin, I didn't mean to imply you were a... I mean..."

"Megumi, it's okay, it's okay," Melvin said, patting her on the shoulder to reassure. "I understand. We all understand. Sometimes it's hard to cope with being what we are. You don't have to look for your power if you don't want to, we support your personal decision and will be with you every step of the way... guys, I think it's time for a group hug here. We've all said hurtful words and the best way to proceed is to heal rather than harm. Right? ...M? Group hug?"

"I'd sooner hug a... a... a thing which I wouldn't want to hug," M tried to insult.

Melvin sighed, shaking his head in disappointment. "I think you'd better go, M. Maybe we'll have better luck communicating with you after a few days' time out between meetings. Make sure you tell your friend about the meeting schedule, okay? He seemed like he really needed our help."

M shrugged into his trenchcoat, turning to Mallory's chair. "Tell him yourself, he's sitting..."

Somewhere else.

"Somewhere else" being not very far away at all, fortunately. Mallory was sitting against the wall just outside the community bingo hall... looking over the low rooftops of the Nippon skyline, as the sun sank.

He was joined a minute or four later by his recent companion.

"You bailing on me?" M asked, emerging from the building. "Because of them? Look, if they don't want to believe, so what? We know the truth. And we know that there's something out there we need to be ready to fight—"

Mallory waved a hand to silence the other him, while looking away. "M, just... just give me a minute. It's a lot to take in at once. I mean... ...I hate this, you know."

"Eh?"

"Being dazed and confused," he explained. "Ever since I left home I've been like this. It hasn't been as bad lately, not since I've settled into the House and really grown to know... and care for the people there. But today it was like it was all back to the way it was back when it was really confusing and stuff. ...and stuff. So just give me a minute, that's it. One minute."

A bit puzzled, M leaned against the brick wall, watching himself and mentally counting down sixty seconds.

Sixty-four seconds later, Mallory got to his feet. "...they've got the right idea, you know," he spoke. "Supporting each other. It sounds nice... being able to have friends with the same problems you have. I wish I could have met them before..."

"Mallory, they're... I don't want to say delusional, but... deluded, maybe? Something like that. They don't WANT to see the bigger picture—"

"And why would they?" Mallory asked, introspection on full throttle at this point, the words coming without thinking about them in endless loops that mix and mangle them. "If I didn't know better, I wouldn't want to know better. It's... it's hard being like this. So completely different, but you don't know WHY you're different or even HOW different you are because you can't control it... and that someone out there hates you just because of who you are... it's more than one guy who just wants to be happy in life should have to deal with. It's more than I can deal with. At least... I've got Meiko. Meiko and everybody else. All they have in there is each other. And all you have is... err..."

"This is the big friendship speech, isn't it?" M recognized, giving Mallory a bit of a glare. "You watch a whole lot of media streams, Mallory. It's all very rosy and nice and pretty but in the end, all you can rely on is yourself. That's what I've learned over the years. I can't rely on them worth a damn because they don't care. Do you honestly think that they're better off turning a blind eye to what you and I know is waiting for them...?"

"No... no, I don't mean that," Mallory spoke, sagging a bit into himself. "I mean... you're partly right here, just like they're partly right. It's better to know than not know, even if it sucks to know. You know?"

"I know. So... what're you gonna do, then? It's my way or their way. Or you can go back to your happy home and ignore all this. Make up your mind, because I'm beginning to wonder if I was wasting my time trying to get through to—"

"I need to learn how to use my powers," Mallory spoke, since he'd made the decision well beforehand.

M's frown of disdain inverted into an evil looking grin of pleasure. "NOW we're talking! See, that's what I'm going on about, we've gotta get this guy before he gets us. Every man for himself! So—"

"I'm not doing it for me."

"Eh?"

"I told you they had the right idea," Mallory explained, stepping away from the wall, ready to move on. "They're supporting each other. I have people I care for who need that support too. So... next time he threatens her... I HAVE to be ready. I don't have a choice. ...but I'll admit, I'm kinda scared at the idea of facing him again and I hope he just leaves me alone and goes away or something..."

"I'm not afraid," M said, quietly. "I won't be afraid. I wasn't afraid the other two times I faced him. I'm strong, I'm powerful and he's not going to scare me again."

"Right, right," Mallory replied, letting the slip slide. "So... where do we start? And, uh, can we start tomorrow? Because Meiko's probably really worried about me by now and I've gotta go home."

'So I'm gonna spend some time with this M guy and see if I can learn more about what I am,' Mallory had explained. 'I'll still make sure the House is properly fed and cleaned and supplied, don't worry; I think I can fit it in with my other chores! Everything'll be A-OK-FINE-#1!'

Kisei's report had echoed the same, albeit in a more factual sort of way. Mallory had met with a gathering of unimpressive Mallory-alikes, and was now undergoing daily training with M whenever he wasn't busy fluffing pillows or dusting the Reality Engine or making waffles for Eiko. This went on for four days...

...while Meiko sat around the House. Her room, to be specific. Mindlessly tapping at her personal workstation.

Occasionally, she'd browse some business magazines. But once you've read fifty-seven articles on creative downsizing techniques to optimize your staff, you've read them all. Except that you haven't, it only FEELS that way, which is a lousy feeling to add on top of your normal isolation and boredom.

Sometimes she'd check in on Eiko, who was enduring the boring days by playing games like 'Important Courtroom Drama Online' via RealNet with Kensuke, who had managed to hack himself some net access despite being grounded. Which meant no time for her oneechan.

The third day, she found herself actually sorting her dress shoes. She decided to break her tedium by doing something impulsive, and left the House to go get some ice cream, except the ice cream shop had been replaced by a multireality ice cream conglomerate currently undergoing labor disputes and the picket line turned her back.

On the fourth day, just when the tedium was about to break her, Lorelei returned from one of the many small jobs they had been taking to make ends meet while lounging around Nippon. Meiko was almost thankful for the company, until A) she found out how the job went, and B) Lorelei found out how her life was going.

But A first.

"MELTED?!" Meiko repeated, just to make sure she had heard the word correctly.

"Jeez, it's not like it was MY fault," Lorelei protested, lounging on Meiko's futon and adjusting the bandage on her left arm. "They shouldn't have put the barrels there in the first place. What kind of idiot keeps that sort of thing in that sort of place without some kind of warning sign? Anyway, only three of the five buildings were reduced to component molecules, so I don't see what the big deal is. It's not like we were contracted to protect the superstructure, just the shipment. And the shipment is technically there, just in gelatinous form, so... no problem, right?"

Meiko sagged in her chair. "Ugh. This is going to be ugly, ugly... I'll send some messages, try to smooth things out—"

"Actually, the whole place is sort of a smooth lake of butter already—"

"That's not what I mean! Dammit, Lorelei, I... ooooh! Forget it. Just forget it. Never mind." Meiko rubbed her temples, trying to will the pain away. "You can go now. I'll deal with this later."

"Okay, what crawled up your ass today?" Lorelei asked, finishing with bandage adjustments for the time being. "I mean, chewing me out, okay. I can see that. But you're a lot twitchier about it today. S'matter?"

"Nothing's the matter. ...and you can tell I'm lying, right?"

"I was about to say as much," she continued, sitting more square on the futon, to face Meiko directly. "And you also know I'm going to hound you about it and speculate wildly and generally get under your skin until you tell the truth, so you can save us both a lot of hassle by fessing up here and now. So. S'matter?"

"I'm just... bored," Meiko decided.

"And?"

"And what?"

"And what, what?" Lorelei continued. "Bored? So? We've had plenty of downtime between jobs before. You're not exactly the action girl heroine around here either, so even ON a job, you do plenty of sitting around the House. Why would boredom be a problem now?"

"Boredom and stress? I don't know. Does it matter? And... it's been quiet around here. Kisei's out shadowing Mallory all the time, and Eiko's been playing with her friend..."

"It's been quiet around here before, too. Try again. What's different now rather than before?"

"Nothing..." Meiko tried, glancing aside.

Lorelei waggled a no-no finger. "Hounding, speculating, under your skiiiin..."

"Mallory's not around," the other woman admitted. "There. You happy? He's been busy hanging around with those other hims. I don't want to intrude, and he seems to be really determined to learn more about himself, so... he's off with them."

"CUDDLE TIME!"

The 'thud' which never happened was Meiko almost falling out of her chair in surprise but not actually doing so. "...eeeh!?" she replied, one eye slightly larger than the other.

"Cuddle time! That's what's wrong. You aren't getting any cuddle time!" Lorelei diagnosed. "Isn't it obvious? I mean, you declare your love what blooms eternal with the passion of a thousand hearts for the boy—"

"—I wouldn't go THAT far—"

"—and what happens? He dumps you in favor of his guy buddies, leaving you all alone in the house with nothing to do but sigh wistfully and compulsively mastrubate to fill the empty void in your heart."

"And I DEFINITELY wouldn't go THAT far!" Meiko continued to protest, to no avail.

"I bet you haven't even given him a kiss since that first one," Lorelei declared, enjoying the teasing as much as she enjoyed the psychological aid provided. "This is the time for you two to explore the new depths of your relationship—and explore each other's bodies—but where is he? Drinking beer and leering at women in some seedy bingo hall!"

"He said that Megumi was just a crossdresser!"

"Oh god, it's worse than I imagined!" she exclaimed in mock-shock.

"LORELEI!"

"Okay, okay, I'm done. Sorry, I couldn't resist. But be honest now..." Lorelei warned, sliding back to a more serious attitude. "That's the problem, isn't it? You miss the goofball. You wish he was here, with you."

Meiko was about to protest again, before registering that the previous question was no longer a blatant effort to tease her. "...yeah. I guess that's it. I haven't seen much of him lately, just a smile and a hello now and then when he pops in to make meals or do the laundry..."

"That settles it, then," Lorelei decided... getting to her feet, ready to make a bold declaration. "It's time for you to take decisive action. Command him, as his boss who writes the paychecks and owns his soul, that he must take you out on a date!"

"I can't—!"

"Why? Come on, throw your weight around a little! Or is your submissive

Nipponese wifey genetic pattern showing its ugly head...?"

"I can't because this is important to him!" Meiko shouted back. "Look... look. Okay. I'd like to have him here, yes. But... you didn't see how he reacted to all this, Lorelei. He's trying to figure out who and what he is! It's the most important thing to him. What right do I have to jump in there and wave my arms and say 'Pay attention to me! Me!'? That'd be... it'd be damned selfish, is what it'd be. And I don't want to be selfish."

"I wouldn't call it selfish to want to be with the one you love," Lorelei relied, switching out of teasing mode again. "Sometimes it's important to have that kind of selfishness. Otherwise... you could lose him."

Uneasy silence.

"You... you don't really think...?" Meiko asked, voice small.

"No, actually, I see that boy slathering after you like a little puppy until the day you die," Lorelei replied. "He's loyal and loving and too stupid to know there are other women out there. It just felt more dramatic to say 'Otherwise... you could lose him.' Sorry. But my point stands—you can only sacrifice so much before you go stir-crazy from loneliness. So, what you're going to have to do is this... you open that door, you track that boy down and you say, 'Hello Mallory, I'd like you to go out with me tonight—'"

A brief knock sounded at the door, before it opened and Mallory stepped in.

"Hello, Meiko!" he greeted, with a cheerful grin. "I'd like you to go out with me tonight. Okay?"

"..." "..." both girls said respectively.

"Ah... is that bad?" Mallory asked, scratching his head. "Err, sorry if I'm interrupting something, but I just figured maybe you were bored sitting around the place and would want to—"

"Yes, I'd love to go!" Meiko blurted out, getting to her feet in a hurry. "Ah, just give me a bit to pick something to wear..."

"Oh, okay. So, it's okay...? I'm not pulling you away from anything important, am I?"

"Not at all, not at all!" Meiko said, experiencing an unusual level of cheerful compliance. "Um, how formal is the place we're going to?"

"Oh, not formal at all! And hey, Lorelei, want to come with us?"

Lorelei studied the boy for a moment. "You want a threesome? Well, it's a bit kinky, but why not? I—"

"Actually, if you're coming, we'll need someone else too," Mallory said, scracthing his chin next while Meiko stared on in confusion. "If Kisei was around, I'd suggest she join us—"

"I am not going to do anything untoward," Kisei warned, appearing from the shadows of the hallway.

"Oh no, nothing untoward," Mallory explained. "Just good clean fun! And you even get to rent new shoes to do it!"

Ten pins flew apart as if hit with a concussion grenade.

"STO-RAIKU!" Eiko cheered, marking a big fat X on her scorecard. "Another ten points for Team M!"

Grumblings arose from from Team Melvin, as team captain Melvin glared down the gloating M as Meiko strode nonchalantly to her seat.

So far, Team M had been completely annihilating Team Melvin. Mallory was a drag on the score, as he had yet to unlock the manifold mystery of avoiding the gutter—but with Lorelei on the team, Meiko picking up the slack and M getting the occasional lucky strike, they were able to jump ahead in fits and bursts.

Team Melvin, consisting of the stage magician (who was merely an adequate bowler) and Megumi (who was in the neighborhood of Mallory's skill level) and Matsuri (who had to be awakened whenever his turn was up) simply couldn't keep pace with them. And as for the cold-blooded, infinitely skilled assassin in the cloak...

FRAME 9	Mat	Mal	Meg	Mei	Kis	Lor	Mel	M
Score	2	0	1	X	3			

...she picked up three pins on her next turn.

"Ooooh, don't worry, Kisei, you'll do better eventually!" Eiko cheered on, from her position as official scorekeeper. "It may take a few dozen games, though. Meiko was the bowling champion of the orphanage, so you don't have anything to be ashamed of when she crushes you completely!"

"...thank you, Eiko," Kisei replied, barely showing any sort of frustration whatsoever except for that little tiny bit that Lorelei picked at like a splinter, flashing her newly established bowling rival the occasional mad grin.

"Now now, this is just a friendly game!" Mallory reminded them all. "We've all had a stressful week one way or the other, and we're here to unwind and have fun! Right, Meiko?"

"Eh? Ah, yeah, right," Meiko said, distracted. "Let's have some fun. Ah, Lorelei, I think you're up next..."

Loreli glanced over from her position, reclining across two of the hard plastic seats with a can of juice in one hand and the other with an arm around the sleepy Matsuri. "So soon? Oh well, if I gotta..." she said with a mock sigh of regret, detangling herself and adjusting her fingerless bowling gloves. Her orange- and yellow-striped ball, the same color as her hair, was plucked effortlessly from the ball return... and with fluid grace, she sauntered casually up to the line...

FRAME 9	Mat	Mal	Meg	Mei	Kis	Lor	Mel	M
Score	*2*	*0*	*1*	*X*	*3*	*X*		

"All RIGHT!" Lorelei cheered, pumping a fist in the air and doing a hip-wiggle touchdown dance that distracted most of the men in the room who were not named Mallory (for he was used to such things). "What can I say, folks? I 0WNZ0R1Z3 bowling!"

"...what does... zerownzeezerorunzccthree mean?" Melvin asked, nudging his stoic bowling teammate with a prompting elbow, a bit perplexed.

"It is of no importance," Kisei replied, not as smoothly as she would have liked.

"Awww, Kiss, don't tell me you're jealous of my m4d5k1llz," Lorelei teased, leaning forward (and indirectly giving the poor stage magician a good look down her cutoff navel-exposing bowling shirt in the process). "Just because you were too busy learning sharpshooting to practice in the lanes like I used to doesn't mean you're INFERIOR, or anything..."

"There is no particular glory to be found in such a pointless competition," her tormentee responded. "I am only here to partake in ordinary House camaraderie, not to achieve a measure of meaningless victory."

"Ah, so you ARE seeking camaraderie lately!" Lorelei confirmed, with a huffy exhale of triumph. "I was wondering about that, ever since we went to the movies—"

"MEEEELVIN-SAAAN!" Eiko called out, eager to get on with tallying up these fun numbers. "You're up next! Lorelei, I'll institute a delay-of-game penalty, reducing your score by 23% if you don't sit down! ...hee hee, it's FUN being the judge..."

With a pout, Lorelei plunked down in her prior seat(s), resuming her enjoyment of company that was too tired to put up much of a fight. "Spoilsport," she mumbled to Eiko.

And so, the next competitor rose. Summoning what pride he had left after the continuous nine frames of being absolutely routed by his enemy, Melvin reached for his purple bowling ball, and walked to the line with confidence...

"...almost over, isn't it?" M called after him. "Hope you can get a strike, Mr. Presto Chango, or you guys are going down the tuuuubes..."

It was one very simple dig at him. By itself, it wouldn't have done a thing, harmless as a fly. But when you added that fly to the buzzing horde that had been hovering around Melvin all day, through nine continual frames of teasing and prodding...

...Melvin decided to swat those flies.

Without much of a swing, he lobbed his ball wildly down the lane. It was headed right for the gutter... until with something between a sneer and a smirk, and a snap of his fingers, physics bent to his will like an iron bar made of papier mâché.

FRAME 9	Mat	Mal	Meg	Mei	Kis	Lor	Mel	M
Score	2	0	1	X	3	X	X	

"Abracadabra," he mumbled under his breath.

M shot to his feet like a slingshot. "That's CHEATING!" he accused. "I thought we agreed not to use any powers, dammit!"

"Who, me?" Melvin asked, pushing his hands into the pockets of his traditional magician's vest (never leave home without it). "Why don't you ask our official judge if I was cheating...? Eiko-chan? What do you say?"

Eiko glanced back to the pair. "Huh?" she asked, a little dazed. "Oh, sorry... I was distracted by this really cute stuffed animal that was hovering over there just a second ago..."

"She didn't see a thing, so my score stands. Q.E.D.," the master of illusions declared.

"Yeah, well... it ain't standing for long," M declared, grabbing his jet black ball and pressing on towards the lane, shouldering Melvin out of the way. "In fact... let's see how it stands up to THIS!"

With a crack of purple light, more flash than he really needed but exactly as much as his anger desired, his ball flew down the lane at subsonic speeds. It never even touched the glazed hardwood, before...

FRAME 9	Mat	Mal	Meg	Mei	Kis	Lor	Mel	M
Score	2	5	1	X	3	X	X	XIII

Even with three of the pins shattered on impact, there was no mistaking the final score. All eyes of the bowling participants turned on the scene in sleepy ignorance / confusion / horror / distraction / silent contemplation / amusement / anger / satisfaction, respectively—with an additional bit of adorable bewilderment from the official judge.

"Uh... I think that's thirteen pins," Eiko replied. "I don't know how they got there, but... that's a score of 13 for M, so his team wins. Right?"

"That's right! We win!" M repeated, shooting an 'Eat THAT!' look at his rival. "What's the matter, Melvin? You're the one who started this with your carny tricks! If you can't take the heat, get ... out of the... lanes?"

The participant in this little game weren't the only ones watching in confusion and awe. In fact, everybody around them, in the surrounding lanes and the concession stand and even a few near the arcade were watching.

"...I think it's time to go," Lorelei decided, getting up. "You know, for a secret society, you guys completely suck at keeping things a secret. I'm going out for a drink. ...want to come, Kiss?"

"I have other duties," Kisei announced. "But I concur with your suggestion that we depart. Quickly."

M growled under his breath... and promptly passed the blame like a hockey puck. "Dammit, Melvin, you HAD to start something, didn't you...? Mallory! Come with me. Let's get back to our training. Somewhere else."

"Uh, but—"

"Come on!"

It didn't take long for the small gathering to disperse. Mostly.

"Oneechan...?"

Meiko finally looked up, seeing her adorable little sister's questioning eyes up close and personal.

"We better go," Eiko insisted, tugging at her oneechan's hand. "Come on!"

"...I guess he had other things he wanted to do instead..."

"Nani?"

"Nothing," Meiko spoke, getting up. "...let's go home."

Creation spun from his fingertips.

The powers of gods were his to command—creation, destruction, transformation, translocation. Nothing was beyond his reach, and nothing escaped his sight. His mind felt connected to everything and anything and nothingness itself...

But mostly nothingness. In fact, all nothinginess. Because he wasn't able to create anything, destroy anything, transform anything, translocate anything and everything escape his sight. But the nothingness, that he had down, as he squinted so hard his vision blurred while nothing whatsoever happened to the cardboard box. It squatted at the end of the alley, taunting Mallory into doing something, anything to it...

"Uh, Mallory—"

"I've almost got it!!" Mallory declared, hoping that saying it would make it so. It did not.

"Maybe cardboard's too much for you right now," M suggested. "When I first started practicing I couldn't do heavy stuff either..."

With a slump of the shoulders, the drained Mallory leaned against the alley wall. "It's not the weight... I just can't do anything," he said. "I keep trying to focus like you've been teaching me, imagine it moving somewhere else, projecting myself making the thing happen and seeing the before and after and centering myself and humming and chanting 'I think I can, I think I can' mantra and nothing's happening..."

"I don't get it. You already had your breakthrough," M noted, scratching his slightly unshaven chin. "Both Melvin and I, once we had our breakthrough and used our powers for the first time, that was it. We had them. Sure, we had to practice and refine 'em and learn our own tricks but it's not like we were blocked as bad as YOU are..."

"Are you sure it just takes one use? I mean, what if it's because I've only been using them unconciously? ...or is it subconsciously?"

"No, the first time I did it, I threw a desk at someone who was bullying me at school. But I wasn't actively TRYING to throw the desk, it just sort of happened. A lot like what's happened to you so far—it pops up when you need it."

"That's it, then!" Mallory declared, gaining a tiny shred of optimistic glee. He hunted on the ground with his eyes and then his hands for what he sought... "It pops up when I need it, so what you do is... I know! Take this rock here, and throw it at me!"

M took the rock, glancing at it uncertainly. "Uh... you sure?"

"Yes I am, and don't call me Shirley!"

"I didn't call you—"

"I'll have to turn my back, so I can't see it coming," Mallory decided, rotating 178 degrees. "Okay. Surprise me!"

When Mallory woke up, Melvin already had an ice pack generously donated by the ramen stand around the corner, which the bruised boy accepted gratefully.

"...maybe I'll never be able to use it," Mallory pondered gloomily, his shred of optimistic glee having been knocked out of his head by a speeding rock a few minutes prior. "Not unless it happens completely by surprise, which means... I can't train myself to use it."

"It's a possibility. I won't pretend I understand everything about Us," his companion noted, kneeling down to maintain eye level. "I'd hate to think all our training sessions have been a waste of time, though... or that you'd be unready when he finds you again. I've pretty much given up on the others, but you I had hopes for..."

"Hey hey, don't write me off yet! I'm still willing to try. I have to learn this. I HAVE to."

"For your girlfriend, right. You said that. You know, you can do more with these powers than that, as much as I'm an advocate of self-defense. I mean... we've got POWERS! And with great power comes—"

"—great responsibility?"

"I was going to say great side benefits, like not needing to worry about mundane things like food, sleep, travel and so on. All the boring worries of life can be handled by powers! For instance, I can sometimes make food out of thin air, and if not, it's a small matter of relocating some to me—"

"Theft?!" Mallory explained, 70% of him more upset at the idea of stealing food someone else put their heart into preparing than the 30% that was just upset about stealing. "M, that's awful!"

"No, it's appropriation," M justified. "Look, Mallory, we're not like normal people, okay? We're above that. If there's one thing I really want you to understand through our training, it's that we're *special*. I won't claim we're some sort of gods, that'd be really stupid... but we'd also have to be stupid not to take advantage of our advantages! Even Melvin uses it for his stage shows, as lame as that is, so he can make a living. And clearly he had some fun today at the bowling alley with his powers—if he wasn't such a jerk about it too, I'd be applauding that! Or Megumi, for example... if she would just open up to it instead of acting like it's some horrible childhood secret she has to suppress, she'd understand too..."

Mallory glanced down. "I understand how Megumi feels, sometimes. It's not like this is all positives, M..."

"It's enough positives to make a difference, though! It's greater than the sum of its parts and stuff. Too many positives NOT to use them when and where we want just because of the negatives! You, for instance—you want to protect the ones you care about, yeah? So how is that any different from me swiping a sandwich now and then? It's survival, in the end. Survival through what makes us special, Mallory! What's so bad about that? So why not go beyond basic survival and really enjoy yourself, too?"

"I don't care about being special!" Mallory barked back, some rare fire entering his being. "The only reason I'm studying my powers at all is so I can keep her safe! I told you that. So I'm not going to use it like... like HE uses it!"

The night air got chillier.

"...you really see me acting like him, then?" M asked, half defensively bitter and half totally spooked at the accusation.

"N... not as such," Mallory retracted quickly. "Just... it feels like it, you know? The whole do what you want and damn the torpedoes stance. Like, he's killing us, because he can, because he's special. And he... he *cheats*. He cheats reality just to get his way. I don't want to be a cheat, I don't care about being special, I just want to do what I have to do. ...I think there has to be some reason behind all this, beyond just granting us the power to have a good time. Something we all have in common..."

"The only thing we have in common is our whacko birth situaiton, I told you that. The theoretical reality accident that split us up."

"Okay, but where did we come from? No, I know you don't know that," Mallory replied. "But that has to figure into this somewhere. ...do you ever have dreams?"

His counterpart glanced nervously aside, at the nighttime traffic of Edo. "...no," he chose to reply. "Not really, no."

"I've had dreams now and then of this place... I mean, dreaming of a place is no big deal but this one was really weird. Because it had a blue sky—"

"—and green grass?"

Mallory focused the whole of his self on M after that. "And green grass," he confirmed. "Blue sky above, green grass beneath your feet. And there's water, from a stream. And there's birds, and trees..."

"They're singing," M replied, lost in his own memory for a fleeting moment. "I've never heard birds singing, except on video streams. Any sort of ecosystem involving animal life forms is a luxury item usually only spared for expensive designer realities. I've never been to any of those. Have you?"

"There were trees and rivers on Grünwald, but no birds. So why were we both dreaming of birds? And... and there's this girl there. She's smiling..."

"Oh. Well, that breaks that," M decided, snapping out of it and ready to dismiss the dream immediately. "No chicks in my dream. Just lots of cheesy nature ambiance. Mallory, it's just a coincidence—"

"Like a fire escape being right where I need one to be?" Mallory replied, still serious even if his companion wanted to escape seriousness. "How about locks vanishing off Kisei's door when I wanted to go in, or someone talking about a house on fire when Lorelei and I had to escape? How many coincidences are REALLY coincidences?"

"Okay, so that means you projected your dream at me just like your other weird random power incidents, or something. Don't think that everything is a vast conspiracy, okay? ...even if it is. My point is, we're both tired, it's late, we're getting nowhere with the training so maybe you should head home and get some rest."

Mallory got back to his feet, not realizing exactly how heavy his body felt until he tried to lift it. "...I'm tired, yeah. And... oh, uh, Meiko... she's probably worried sick..."

"You want to try training again tomorrow, after the group meeting? Zero progress just means nowhere to go but up..."

"...I'm not sure. I'll decide tomorrow. I want to do this, but... I don't know. My head hurts."

"Probably because I threw a rock at it," M noted.

"Yeah, there's that, too."

Nighttime at the House is quite a different beast from Daytime at the House.

Daytime at the House consists of the occasional group meal, Mallory running around tidying up, Eiko getting underfoot as she spreads her playspace to consume more and more rooms, Lorelei playing either couch potato or pest or both, and Meiko either holed up in her room working on job offers or chattering away with her employees about some issue or another. In short, even if that is long, it's a busy and noisy House.

At night, it's the polar opposite—a quiet and sedate House. Eiko sleeps very soundly, Lorelei (when she's there) tends to crash after a pub crawl or a healthy workout session or both, Kisei keeps to herself, Mallory snoozes on the couch and Meiko either works, sleeps, or sneaks downstairs for some milk. The few times two conscious people do bump into each other—usually Meiko and Mallory—it's a quiet, simple conversation about simple things rather than the hectic day to day business of the day.

Tonight was going to be very different from that and at the same time very similar... a quiet conversation that was anything but simple. Milk would not be involved, despite Mallory's desire to revert to such simple things.

It began simple enough, with Mallory arriving quite late indeed, surprised to find Meiko waiting for him, sitting on his couch / sleeping space and thumbing through a business magazine.

"Ah... hey," he greeted, quietly latching the door shut behind him. "Can't sleep? Need a midnight snack?"

"No, I'm okay," she said, setting the magazine aside for now... and trying to find the best entry point into what she had planned, and despite having mulled the possibilities for hours, the best she could come up with was: "Ah, have a seat next to me?"

Mildly (but only mildly) puzzled, Mallory did as told, settling down on the couch next to her.

The awkwardness would have been adorable, had anybody been around to observe it.

"Mal—" "Mei—"

"You first." "No no, you."

(This was also adorable.)

"Uh... this is about me not spending much time at home lately, right?" Mallory asked. "I've really been meaning to spend more time, but with the training and all I haven't found a lot of chances to—"

"Thank you."

"—eh?"

"I had no honest idea how to approach it, so thank you for jumping the gun and asking," Meiko answered, relieved. "I mean, how do you say something like 'I want you to spend more time with me' without sounding like the typical selfish and posessive girlfriend I'd really rather not be? Just because Lorelei says I need 'cuddle time' doesn't mean I have any right to deprive you of your own life outside this House even if I am your boss, so... ...I'm sounding a bit like you, aren't I?"

"Errr, what? Huh?"

"Going on and on without really having any idea where I'm going to," Meiko explained, in a Mallorean sort of way.

"Uh... I get where you're going," Mallory replied, trying to detangle what others usually have to detangle for him. "I mean, I understand, you'd like me to be around. I'd like to be around! Nothing wrong or weird or selfish about that. But... with great responsibility comes great power, or something. I've learned that! Or something like that. So I have to keep training. Even if my training isn't going very well. Or going at all. Anywhere at all. I have to keep trying!"

"Why is that, anyway?"

"Err... why? Why what?"

"If you don't mind me asking... I'm curious. Why are you working so hard to train your powers?" Meiko asked, turning a bit to face him. "I hate to be blunt about this, but it's the only way I know, and I've been curious. Now that I have you in one place for a few minutes, I have to ask—I mean, I haven't seen you hammer away at something this hard since your REC Test studying. But that was because your job depended on it. Why this? Originally we were tailing this guy and working with him so you could learn the truth, but... you learned the truth already. Do you also have some sort of desire to use this power of yours?"

"...maybe?" Mallory guessed. "I mean, I don't WANT to. I'm not... not really that special, I'm just me. But I have to learn how to use them. That's just the way it is. No way about it, no ifs, ands or buts and I have to teach an old dog how to make a silk purse out of a pig in a poke if I'm going to protect you. It's not like I WANT to be away from the House to—"

"Protect me?"

Mallory caught on to what he just transmitted, with a 2300ms lag.

"Ah... you know, as in... protect," he said, trying to find a gentle way to put it. "From... that guy. You know."

"Mallory... THAT'S why you've been training?" Meiko asked, dead serious. "You're thinking of taking on your copy from Antiparadisia?"

"It's not like I want to!" he protested. "But if he finds us... if he finds us and I can't stop him, who else can? Lorelei and Kisei couldn't stop him! I can't let him hurt you. Or me! Or anyone!"

Meiko sat back, looking straight ahead... digesting that. "So... that's why."

"Uh... kind of, yes. You did ask, so..."

"...okay, I need to clear this up right now," Meiko said... turning back to her boyfriend, and adopting a slight boss poise. Just a slight one. "Mallory, it's not your job to play knight in shining armor. I'm not expecting you to defend me, even against him."

"But—"

"Wait until I finish, please," she requested, putting one finger to his lips. "In Antiparadisia... he got the drop on us. I'll admit to that; we got trounced and for good reason. But what did I tell you when I agreed to help you find out the truth about yourself? I told you I'm a problem solver. Mallory, this is what I do for a living, and if I can't do it for the ones I love... I don't have any right to do it at all. If I'm at risk—my whole family, this whole house, you and me—then I'm going to have a hand in defending myself. I'm not expecting you to do it all, nor do I want you to do it all."

"But they—"

"They couldn't fight him, yes. Not at the time. We know what to expect now, however... and I seriously doubt, knowing those two the way I do, that Lorelei and Kisei are going to just sit back and accept that they're ineffective against him. Those two don't lose a fight that easily and not start dreaming up ways to win the next round... and neither do I. We're going to face him together, all of us, if it comes down to it. I'm hoping that it won't, but... we'll do everything we can."

"..."

"Uh, you can ask questions now," she noted. "Sorry, I just really had to get that out."

"...so... you don't think I should train anymore?" Mallory asked, confused.

"You can if you really want to, Mallory. I'm not going to stop you. I won't be the type who demands you stay home, or live your life some particular way," she explained. "I'm just saying... don't think this is all resting on your shoulders, that you have to beat yourself up trying to save us all. We're all supporting you as much as you support us. That's how I run my business... and I'd like to think that by this point, we'd do it even without contracts. I can't really speak for the others, but... that's how I see it. So... what do you want to do? What's most important to you?"

"...voted off the show! It's, like... justice finally comes to 'Nippon no Aidoru'!" Megumi bubbled onward. "Kazuya shouldn't have made it past the first two elimination rounds when my heroine Kaori got bumped off early. That's just so great, it's like I was right the whole time and nobody believed me but me!"

"It's important to believe in yourself," Melvin recited. "Anything that gives you affirmation of your life is a good thing. You know, Megumi, you may want to try out for that show next season—I bet you could go far, if you believe in yourself!"

"Are you NUTS?!" M protested, leaning forward to jump into the conversation he had no interest in moments ago. "A televised appearance by one of Us? That's just like dangling the carrot out for HIM to come along and beat us with the stick over! We've got to keep a lower profile than that, Mr. Magic Bowling Fingers."

"I'm not the one who created more pins than actually existed, Mr. Mystery Man Wannabe."

"If you hadn't—"

"Uh, guys?"

"—started using your powers I wouldn't have had to use mine! And—what is it, Mallory?"

"I gotta go," Mallory explained, getting up from his chair. "I promised Meiko I'd take her out to the movies tonight, so I have to leave a bit early..."

"Early? What? We've got more training to do!" M reminded him.

"We can do it some other time, can't we? I'm sorry, M, but... I want to make time for my life, too. And for her. So... I gotta go. When's the next meeting— Tuesday, right? We can train after that one."

"Well... if you want," M agreed, watching his counterpart as he headed for the door. "Are you sure this is what you want, Mal...?"

"Yeah... I am. I really am," Mallory said, with a smile. "I'll see you all later! Thanks for the meeting."

The door closed behind him, and the meeting resumed falling into bickering and pop culture and other Usian activities without Mallory.

It would have been nice, if the meeting remained so uneventful.

"...which is why we're going to have to start thinking of fundraising activities," Melvin concluded, after his presentation to the group. "If we want to do more group activity, we'll need more money. With Mallory on board I feel this we're gaining terrific momentum—really getting a critical mass of Us together, you know? Enough so we can make group outings worthwhile, instead of just two people, and two sometimes-theres."

"I'm not a group person," M reminded, bitterly.

"With a growing group, your apathy won't be a problem," Melvin jabbed. "In fact—"

A quiet knock sounded at the community bingo hall door.

"Ah, good! I was getting worried!" Melvin exclaimed, full of pride as he answered the door. "Guys, I'd like to introduce you to a new friend... I've been communicating with him on RealNet for a few days now, and figured it was time to bring him into the fold..."

The smiling boy who looked just like them walked in with confidence and good cheer.

"Hello, sorry I'm late," he apologized, with a little formal bow. "Work was really quite intense today back at my day job, so I couldn't pull myself away in time... ah, Melvin-san, your friend in the trenchcoat looks very pale. Is there a problem...?"

M jumped from his chair, pressing against the wall with fright he knew would be fatal to have, but he couldn't get rid of. "Melvin... Mel, you... YOU IDIOT! That's HIM! THAT'S THE ONE!"

"What?" Melvin asked, confused. "You... oh, good grief, M. You don't mean the one in the purple glasses you keep going on about? Do you see purple glasses on this guy? Honestly, you can be so—"

The flames that engulfed the sleeping Matsuri were bright and brief and very fatal.

"...you really shouldn't trust strangers you meet on RealNet, Melvin," Multi spoke, slipping his glasses back on.

A stack of newspapers appeared where M stood.

Then the newspapers were immediately replaced with a horrified M, who only had a moment to not react before being clocked over the head with the chair he previously sat on.

Melvin tried to defend himself, but the burst of playing cards and shiny coins and rabbits he produced from his highly focused powers did nothing.

As for Megumi, she could do nothing as the smiling, kindly boy advanced on her.

"I... I don't have any powers!!" she protested, cowering in a corner of the bingo hall. "None, none! I'm not a threat to you, I swear, I SWEAR!"

"No powers...?" Multi asked, surprised. "You haven't found them? That's such a shame! You have such potential—I can sense it in you. What if I said you could turn yourself into the girl you always wanted to be? All you have to do is focus on it. Focus everything you have on the one thing you really want..."

"...p...please leave me alone..."

"I said, **FOCUS**," Multi commanded, the sound of his voice completely overpowering to the nervous crossdresser. When given an order like that, when you're desperate, you'd do anything to survive... including cooperate.

Silent purple light briefly flashed in the corner of the hall, giving Multi a momentary pink aura.

"There... you see? That wasn't so hard," Multi soothed, resting a comforting hand on the now purely female's shoulder. "That's all I want from the Multiverse... for people to truly reach for the limitless possibilities. Not to limit themselves. To become glorious... just as you have now."

"I... I'm a girl?" Megumi asked, her voice higher and more natural. A mild hysteric good mood hit her. "I'm a girl! I'm a girl, I'm a girl at last! I'm—"

She slumped to the floor three painful seconds later.

"I'm so happy you could reach your true self," Multi told her body. "I'll remember your fine example in the wonderful future to come... hmm..."

Only one left, as M slowly struggled to his feet, his head filled with warm cotton from the chairshot concussion.

"One, two, three, four..." Multi counted, approaching M with great patience. "I count four. But I remember from one of Melvin's mails that you now had five in your fold. According to my years of work, that would be the last five that exist, other than myself. Where is he...? Where is the one I've seen before, the one who escaped me...? His name. His address. The names of the girls who are with him. My leads at Antiparadisia went dry; I'm afraid I was a bit too ... extensive with them. So instead, you're going to tell me everything I need to know..."

M snarled, trying to pull power into his hands, to shape a wave of reality itself at his enemy. "Go stick your head in a pig, you—"

The wave snapped back on him, driving him against the wall. Multi only had to use one finger to pin him there after that.

"I'll keep you alive long enough for you to tell me," he explained. "I've finished my work for that corporate slavedriver Gillian Bates for the day, so I have hours and hours before I have to report back to Reality Prime. Hours and hours to make you talk..."

Despite the pressure, despite the pain, despite the feeling that all of reality was being turned against him and he could do nothing... one thought was crystal clear to M. That Multi was right. He'd talk.

Which meant he only had one option.

With a scream of defiance, M filled himself with power. He drew reality waves from all over Nippon to himself, letting it flood... and overload.

The explosion caused the wall he was pushed against to cease to exist. As did Multi's right hand.

It had been a pleasant evening's stroll across Edo, until Mallory was swept off his feet by an assassin moving at three times his maximum running speed.

He didn't even have time to ask what was going on or panic before he found himself in the kitchen of the House, deposited there by Kisei. Moments later Lorelei arrived from her own remote call, and Eiko climbed down from her bedroom to find out what all the noise was about...

"Good, you got him," Meiko told Kisei, as calm and still as an iced-over pond, as she crossed the House to take a seat at the RealNet Workstation near the Engine. "We're leaving Nippon immediately. Everybody get ready for transitioning, I'm going to find us a dock as far away from here as possible as fast as possible..."

"Whaaaa... what's going on?" Mallory asked, as soon as he could regain his breath... and caught the note out of the corner of his eye. A simple piece of paper, with some hastily written words on it...

"That appeared on the kitchen table three minutes ago," Meiko noted.

He's found us here. Everybody at the bingo hall is gone.

I can't help you. Get out now. - M

Restless.

It's not just a reality, it's a reality of mind. Or a state of mind. Or both. It's difficult to think about which it is, given the mind-numbing boredom of the place. It's best not to even try; working up the mental effort through the haze of downpouring rain and crushing depression could entail personal injury.

People go here when they want to shut out the rest of the multiverse. Here, you can get away from it all, which means by definition that nothing ever happens here. The most excitement Restless had seen in a while was when Meiko and her crack team of troubleshooters-for-hire temporarily kidnapped a soap opera programmer on the lam here, weeks ago.

Now the House had returned. And stayed. For two weeks. Of staying put. And doing nothing.

Some activity was going on inside, but it wasn't anything worthy of anyone's interest. Lorelei was sitting on one side of the couch, re-coloring her toenails after deciding that maybe silver wasn't as good on her as cherry red after deciding yesterday that cherry red was boring and she needed a change of pace. The day before that she was busy pondering a change of hair color before deciding to keep things the way they are. Even the lively, can't-keep-me-down spirit of the House's resident party girl had been reduced to monotonous self-tuning.

On the other side of the couch, Mallory sat twiddling his thumbs while Meiko watched BusinessDay on the RealNet feeds. He paid half his attention to her, half to the droning voice of the announcer reading off today's corporate mergers and RealWare profit futures, and half on Lorelei's toenail activity. The extra half of attention was due to Mallory being so bored that he forgot you cannot have three halves of one attention.

Sitting on the floor in front of the couch was the youngest of the house, Eiko Mirai. She paid a proper half of attention to the business news and the other proper half to her dolls, which she listlessly nudged around on the floor, unable to work up enough imagination to do anything of interest with them. It was the sort of glum little aura of childhood funk that would make you go 'Awwww...' and want to give her one of those encouraging greeting cards with kittens hanging from branches.

To round out the House roster, Kisei was in her room doing who knows what, but it was likely very uninteresting indeed.

Matters continued to be uninteresting for seven minutes, until Lorelei finally cracked.

"Okay, this blows," she announced, in mid-toenail. "Meiko—"

"No," Meiko replied, without moving her eyes from the screen.

"But—"

"No, you can't leave. We're staying put."

Lorelei sat back, folding her arms in petuant grumpydom. "Hmph. I bet if MALLORY said he wanted to go out, you'd let him..."

"ESPECIALLY not him," Meiko emphasized. "Lorelei, we're staying put for a good reason and you know it, Eiko knows it, Mallory knows it. Right, Mallory?"

"Uh... right," Mallory agreed, with a token amount of reluctance. "But... uh... I, uh... I kinda agree with Lorelei, too. Couldn't we just go out a little...?"

"Mallory—"

"Sorry for interrupting but I really think it'd be a good idea if we all stopped being under voluntary house arrest and stuff," Mallory apologized for interrupting. "It's been a while since we got that note from M and nothing's happened, right? I mean... we've been hiding and not a peep. So... well, we can't stay hiding forever, sooo..."

"So lift the lockdown and let us live our lives," Lorelei alliterated. "C'mon, Meiko! Mal's right, are you seriously thinking we'll play ostrich forever? We gotta get OUT! You're gonna stunt Eiko's emotional growth if all she has is her home schooling lessons and her toys, cooped up in here all day."

"Waaah, she's right!" Eiko exclaimed, bonking her dolls against her head. "I can feel my fragile psyche warping right now! It hurts, oneechan! It hurts!"

Meiko rolled her eyes. "Eiko, quit that or no dessert tonight. ...I wasn't honestly expecting us to hide forever, Lorelei. I just wanted to make sure the heat was off... Okay. Let me put it this way—I hired you as a bodyguard, to help defend us in bad situations. So, make a tactical bodyguard decision. Would you say we're in the clear?"

"Me? A professional tactical soldier whatsit? I'm more the type to shout 'HIYAH!' and cut them off at the knees—"

"You're also the one who wants to go out, so I figure you can decide if you're ready to put your skin on the line in the process," Meiko explained smoothly. "So... what's your professional opinion?"

Lorelei squinted a bit, trying to think hard about something when her instincts were more blunt. "All right. Okay... so... we got a note from M about that guy. He's on to us. But he hasn't FOUND us. He doesn't strike me as a very cunning sort, considering he acted all surprised to find us in Antiparadisia and according to Ryo, he didn't seek out where we were parked before leaving Nippon. Which means... he's got no clue where we are and it's perfectly safe for us to go out drinking and hitting on guys and getting into fights! So yes, let me out, dammit!"

"Yeah, let me out, dammit!" Eiko echoed cheerfully.

"Eiko, language," Meiko chided. "All right, I'm lifting the ban. I'll allow some QUIET, limited trips outside. And you all have to carry trackers, like the one Mallory has. Understood?"

Eiko's dolls went flying as she bounced to her feet with the energy of a spring that's been tightly coiled for two weeks. "HWEI! Freedom!! I know just where I go, and Mallory-oniichan, you're coming with me! Lemme go get your stuff and we'll be gone in a flash!" She bounced her way in leaps and strides to Mallory's storage closet, flinging open the door and rooting around...

"EIKO!" Meiko called, trying to get the energetic one's attention. "Wait, wait! Where are you going?—maybe the ban's lifted but Mallory's not going to some place like Urbana where he'd be easily spotted—"

"Not a problem!" Eiko replied, emerging with a bulky backpack. "There's a collector's convention right here in Restless, I saw an ad for it yesterday! I've got a great idea! Come on, oniichan, let's go let's go let's goooo!"

"W—" was as far as Mallory got before being sucked from the house by the whirlwind of childhood mania. The door slammed shut behind the two of them.

"Eiko, wait, you need a tracker..." Meiko trailed off, realizing the moment had come and gone. "...well, if Mallory's with her, I guess his will do for both of them—"

"Meiko Mirai."

"Wh—!?" Meiko didn't manage to say, snapping her focus back in front of her... and forcing calm quickly. "...Kisei. When did you get here? I didn't hear you come downstairs..."

"As the ban has been lifted... I request a mission," the stoic-looking ex-assassin spoke.

"A mission...?"

"Yes. I would like to request one. Any one will do."

Waving her confusion away with a mental hand, Meiko flipped open F.P. to consult her files. "I actually did have a potential offer called in directly yesterday, but... it's in Urbana, and I didn't think it would be appropriate to draw that much attention..."

With absolute seriousness, Kisei measured and cut her words precisely. "I will endeavor not to put the house at risk, Meiko Mirai. You can count on me. I will prove that to you as I support your efforts and ideals."

"...right," Meiko replied, not sure what to make of that. "Why the sudden interest...?"

"...I have my reasons. I need to reacquire my focus," she responded, less solid than before now that she was put to question. "Meiko Mirai... I rarely make requests of you and I apologize if the suddenness of this one offends—"

"No, no... it's okay, Kisei. Get your gear together and I'll dig up the details. It's a defensive bodyguarding mission, a simple one-night job."

"That would be very acceptable. Thank you," Kisei spoke, adding a small formal bow to the end of her sentence...

...and giving Lorelei a tiny, tiny look just to confirm that yes, Kisei was aware of the strange expression being thrown in her direction and she would offer no specific reply in return. Then, she was gone.

Meiko sat back. Waited for Kisei's return. And glanced to her right.

"...you were all gung ho about lifting the ban. Shouldn't you be running for the hills too?" Meiko asked.

"Me? Hey, I'm doing my nails, I'm not going anywhere yet," Lorelei answered, adding a few more brushstrokes of cherry red for emphasis. "Besides... daytime, you know. Not my thing. Night's where the action is. How about you? Going anywhere special, or waiting for your lover dear to get back first? I have noticed you've been cuddling a bit more... maybe keeping the ban in place so you can have him around and all to yourself...?"

"Oh, please," Meiko groaned, roll of the eyes, and so on as she opend her personal organizer. "I'm not that that childish. Hmm. I might as well head out for some lunch once Kisei's underway, since our 'houseboy' is probably going to be gone for the day... I'm sure F.P. saw ahead and made me reservations..."

"Your boyfriend's blood makes for a handy day planner, huh?"

"...gross, Lorelei."

Smirking it off as she was prone to do, Lorelei focused on her foot handiwork once more. And thought about things, a bit. Just what WOULD she do tonight...? It was obvious, actually: she'd probably get blitzed, meet a handsome stranger, dance a bit and go home. As usual.

As usual... same old same old, like cherry red.

She stopped before doing the last nail, frowning at the thought.

12: Four Simple Things

[1] mint in box

Restless.

It's not just a reality, it's a state of existence. Or of mind. Or something. It has hotels and motels mostly, the occasional restaurant so people could eat something other than plain room service, and a system of public transportation to get people from hotels to restaurants and vice versa.

People on these buses sit still and read their newspapers or data pads or whatever form of information display they have available. They do not talk energetically and bounce up and down in their seat unless their name happens to be Eiko Mirai.

"I got the idea when I was looking through your stuff without asking permission!" she explained without worry of reprisal, holding open the backpack full of packratted junk. "You've got so much neat stuff in there, cool toys and more—why don't you play with it?"

"Uh... honestly, I'd forgotten I'd stashed it all in that closet," Mallory explained, looking at his prized collection as if it was someone else's. "I used to collect this stuff back when I was in Grünwald... you know, own a piece of the multiverse, make it feel like I was really out there, but... I guess I lost track of it once I was actually IN the multiverse..."

"But it's such cool stuff! Like these 'Angst Boy' holographic comics—Pow! Bam! Zap! 'My soul is stretched over the abyss like taut chicken wire!' It's really neato," Eiko said, thumbing through an issue, past the photos of the owner's prized baseball and right to the bloodshed. "Oneechan would never let me buy cool stuff like this. Can I have them?"

"Uh... I'd rather not invoke your sister's wrath..."

"She wouldn't be all wrathy to you, she loves you! You can get away with anything. That's so cool!"

"But it's not even a complete run of the comic," Mallory protested. "I'm still missing issues 65, 34, and 3. It's no good unless it's complete..."

"Ahhh, but that's why I'm taking you with me!" Eiko said, waving a finger in Mallory's face. "We're going to a collector's convention that's in town. Then we can finish up these collections of yours! I'll negotiate you some good deals and we'll have a complete run of comics, of your Love & Hate glasses, and these cards—"

"Cards? Cards!" Mallory remembered, quickly digging through the backpack for them... "My 8-Bit Commandos! '256 digits of power'! Captain Muscular, Rattlemaster, Android Pi, Super Nippon, Pixie Splendid...! I'd totally forgotten about them; have you seen these? They're amazing!"

"They're just funny-looking super heroes on cards..." Eiko said, paying more attention to Angst Boy tearing open some bad guy from sternum to rectum.

"Yeah, but when you line them up edge to edge... hang on, let me pick out two good ones..." he continued, rooting around for another card. "When you put them together, they—"

The two cards interfaced along microscopic connections, and the tiny muscular super hero on the left flexed his pecs. 'My might is extremely mighty! How can you compare to such might?' he boasted... and the more lanky scientist on his right shrugged in his lab coat. 'The muscle that is the brain will triumph over brawn every time,' he replied.

"—they do that!" he finished. "You can combine any two cards and get a different response depending on which cards you use—even which one's on the left and which one's on the right! So, let me think, two hundred and fifty-six cards so it's like... two hundred thousand something possible interactions! And that's not even counting the 'alternate universe' set they released later, doubling the size, making for like FIVE hundred thousand interactions! I think."

"...really?" she replied, interest starting to shift from splatter to the sheer insanity of such a concept. "That's a lot...! Five hundred and twelve cards, though? How many do you have...?"

"Uh... almost all of them," Mallory said, slotting the two cards back into their respective decks. "The trader who I got them from had all of the cards except one. I'm missing The Treehugger from the Alternate Universe deck; he's the opposing card to Mr. Nuke... but that's because The Treehugger's REALLY rare. There were only sixteen of them ever made. There's no chance we could find it, even at some sort of collector's convention."

"Really, no chance...?" Eiko asked, getting a germ of an idea in her adorable little head. "Not a chance at all?"

"Uh, no. No chance."

"I LIKE those odds!"

Mallory hadn't been this overwhelmed since first stepping foot in Urbana, fresh from Mellow Fellow's taxi. Loud, smelly, packed with sights and sights upon sights...

Row after row of rickety card tables, decorated with junk from a thousand realities. Trading cards. Comics. Toys with some pieces missing. Dolls never removed from their boxes. T-shirts, posters, disks with old videos on them, bootleg music, games, puzzles, things, stuff, objects, trinkets, doodads, whatsimajiggers...

Row after row of people in a variety of colorful t-shirts, proudly declaring their fandom for something or another. Packed in tight like sardines, fighting for elbow room to peruse the wares on display, sometimes fighting with elbow strikes over a rare deal. Old people, young people, fat people, thin people, mostly fat people, men, women, mostly men, fans, crazy fans, crazier fans, PEOPLE...

Above it all, above the gigantic hotel room, a banner hung. WELCOME TO CONCON IV.

The parts of him that didn't want to run screaming back to the House where he was comfortable and safe were quite thrilled at the prospect of what lied ahead. What ratio those various parts existed in shifted from second to second, although any whiffs of unwashed fanboys that fluttered by generally shifted towards fleeing.

"Wow! ...eeee. Wow! Uh. Ooeeer. Wow! Um. ...wow," Mallory decided in the end. "This is amazing...! I didn't think such a thing existed! Except maybe in my darkest nightmares! Eiko, do you really think we can get that card in this mess... ... Eiko? EIKO—"

"PINPON!" a furry creature chirped, popping into his view.

"Wagh!" Mallory exclaimed, striking a defensive karate pose and nearly falling over.

"It's me, silly!" Eiko giggled, behind her whiskers. She flexed her brown furry ears a little. "Like it? I got cute little ears and a tail and things at an anime booth over there. Today, I'm the cunning fox, ready to trick people into giving us that Treehugger card! Don't worry, Mallory! Eiko-kitsune is on the job!"

After the shock passed, the pure adorableness of it consumed Mallory whole. He found himself patting the moppet on the head and making goofy smiley faces at her. "That's so 'kowaii', Eiko!"

"KAWAII," she corrected him. "Now, to business! I may be a cunning fox, but we're going to need a native guide in order to find our prey! So, I made a new friend. Hideaki-kun! Over here, over here!"

Following Eiko's beckoning paw, a wide Nipponese man with a shirt bearing a young girl in a school uniform with eyes as large as industrial-grade tires waddled towards them. He extended a meaty paw to grasp Mallory's hand and shake, the various wall scrolls in his backpack rattling around as his bulk shifted.

"Konnichi wa!" Hideaki greeted his new friends. "Eiko here tells me you believe that Mei-mei's character design was far superior in the SECOND series directed by Ano-san than the inferior first series directed by Ohto-san. Right...?"

"Uh... yes?" Mallory replied, spotting Eiko sneaking him a thumbs-up from behind the fanboy. "Oh, yes, definitely! Far superior. She was... uh... much more kawaii in the second series!"

"Right, right! I keep telling people that and they just won't listen! Philistines, all of them," Hideaki minorly ranted. "Well! You're into trading cards, right? You're in luck, 'cause I know where you can get the BEST deals on trading cards. You into Sorcery: The Collecting? Or maybe Fighting Monster Fighters? Or perhaps Sailor Nothing?"

"No no, I'm into 8-Bit Commandos," Mallory explained.

"...oh, those," the fan said, wrinkling his nose in distaste. "Well, okay, I don't think I can help you find those. Not much call for such gaijin silliness. No offense, mind you."

"None taken, none taken..."

"Let's get moving, the crowds will get thicker once the lunch hour is over," Hideaki recommended, rotating himself towards the card section. "We'll need to clear the way. You wouldn't happen to have a bludgeoning weapon, would you? Truncheon? Morningstar +2?"

"Pluswhat? No, I don't... is that going to be a problem?"

"Eh, I can get us through. MOVE IT! Comin' though!" he boomed, starting to part the sea of collectors like a slowly moving freight train.

"Right, right. Eiko, better hold my hand so you don't get loswhoaa—"

"Onward we go, a journey into the west!" Eiko called forth, raising one hand and pointing from her perch on Mallory's shoulders, while the boy wobbled around a little. "Let's go, let's go! On the oniichan express!"

"...ugh... ooh... right... 'kay," Mallory replied, steadying himself. And smiling.

Because despite the bad craziness, the odor, the confusion, the bewildering assault on his senses and his sensibility... he was having fun. Finally let loose from her prison, Eiko's good cheer would not be denied, and tended to soak its way into all around her.

Bounding along behind the rolling boulder ahead of him, Mallory skipped about, as Eiko's tail twitched behind her.

Box after box after box in stacks upon stacks, which were only growing as the merchant continued to stack boxes on box stacks with a stacking-sort of motion.

"See, the problem with the GunRunner is that the plastic prongs on the front that represent the Ocean Wave Gun keep breaking off," he continued, not noticing the dull looks of drowsiness in his victim's eyes. "Considering you could set your watch by the Ocean Wave firing sequence in each episode, it's an important piece to have. Losing it lowers the value of the entire model! So what I do is I use a molecular adhesive—it's expensive, but the value it adds to the collectible offsets perfectly. I'm hoping to offload all fifty of these at this convention but if not, I guess I can dump them at OgenkiCon in Nippon next month..."

"Uh-huh," the normally sociable and pleasant Mallory mumbled out. "But about the card I want...?"

"Ohhh, right," the rotund merchant said, getting back on track after wandering several miles from it. He reached underneath his rickety card table and the paper tablecloth, withdrawing a battered rubberware box. Inside were miscellaneous 8-Bit Commandos cards, each lovingly sealed in temporary clear aluminum foil. "I've got a bunch of singles here, got 'em off some guy who really wanted my life-size inflatable Amiko doll... I don't have much need for them, so if the one you want is in there, I'll be willing to trade."

Eiko quickly stood on her tip toes, glad to be doing something other than sleeping on her feet, and rooted through the box... immediately frowning. "Awwww! They're all copies of the same card—some big purple thing with eggbeaters for hands..."

"Oh! Mr. Hard Boiled?" Mallory asked, pulling a card from the box himself. "These are pretty rare! But I already have one... uh, do you know where I could find other people with cards like these, sir?"

"The guy I got it from is at this con, actually. I saw him at the Sailor Fuku Forever Fan Circle table," the merchant said, squinting to try to find it amidst a sea of several hundred tables. "It's... uh..."

Like a faithful dog, Hideaki the Native Guide stepped in to save the day. "That way," he said, pointing straight and true to Row 4, Aisle L. "They've got a link to a site that has a link to our Kowaii Kaiju Circle. ...but you might want Eiko to stay behind."

"Eh? Why?"

Fandom is, at the core, neither good or bad. It simply *is*.

It is a way of bonding together strangers into friends, friends into closer friends. Through shared adoration of a particular cultural aspect, trust can be forged and secret tokens exchanged that allow the circle to feel as if they share something private from the rest of the world. This inward consumption of media, always appreciated in a unique way even if a similar grouping exists elsewhere, is the enabler of socialization through mutual cultural kinship.

Through that kinship, you can enrich your life by indulging in creative expressions of your fandom-love—creating unauthorized offshoot works, improving your art and writing skill by aping another's style. Such acts can even branch out into your own original work, so inspired by the material that you seek to achieve the same emotional high you get when basking in the glow of the parent intellectual property. Such expressions, shared amoung friends, can be a positive healing force as you integrate your own hopes and dreams and fears and phobias, working through issues and exploring the notion of 'self' as you explore your fandom. Truly, fandom can be a force of constructive goodness.

Or it can be an excuse for perverts to flock to a singal focal point, as it was with the Sailor Fuku Forever Fan Circle.

Eiko stayed quite hidden behind Mallory, only peeking out now and then to confirm the very weird looks the little kitsune girl was getting from the sweaty, bulbous twentysomethings behind the card table.

"Uh... so... I'm looking for this card," Mallory started, trying to get this over with. "8-Bit Commandos... the vehicle model salesman said you might have it...?"

"8-Bit? Yeah, I collect those," the least pleasant one of the bunch stated. "I started out when I got Pretty Polly, then I found Little Miss Can't Be Wrong... sorta expanded from there, figured what the heck? But when I went to our local doujinshi convention and found I didn't have enough money to complete my run of 'Uniform Cutie' I decided enough was enough."

"Right, right. Uh. I'm looking for 'The Treehugger,'" he continued, shuffling a bit to the right to continue blocking the view of some of the fan circle members leaning to their left to look around him. "Do you have that one?"

"Dunno... lemme check," the fan said, fetching a cardboard box from his backpack and leafing through some badly-kept cards with worn edges. "'course, even if I'm not interested in these anymore, it's not gonna be free. We prefer to trade, so I'll think of some—"

"*Give us the child!!*" a feral member of the circle wheezed, hands grasping at the air in front of him and drool collecting on his lower lip. Fortunately one of the more sensible (by a ±3% margin of error) members restrained him, but it was enough to send Eiko zipping across the aisle to hide under someone else's table.

"...you'll have to forgive Kaiken, he ran out of pills an hour ago," the leader spoke. "And... I'm out of The Treehugger, if I ever had any of 'em. Sorry. Hey, can I interest you in our quarterly leaflet publication? It's sort of like a bird watcher's guide, only it's all about great spots to—"

"Uh, no. Do you know anyone else who might have 8-Bit cards?" he wisely interrupted.

"I'm in my happy place, I'm in my happy place..." Eiko chanted, still a little pale as Mallory interrogated the next dealer.

"But like, who REALLY collects those things anymore? They're so ten years ago, so *retro*," the girl in the cardboard power armor replied, careful not to knock over her stack of plastic figures as she shifted about in the costume. "I don't do retro. I live in the NOW. Only the newest, hottest stuff! Anything more than six months gets traded or junked, I mean, why would anybody keep old crap around? My dad's all like 'you should respect artifacts of shared cultural heritage as they are worthy of rememberance' but I'm all like, what-EVAR, you know? Who cares about stuff from a year ago or ten years or a thousand years?"

"Oh, I don't know, I think it's good to read about the past," Mallory spoke up, recalling distant memories of schooling back home. "I mean, if you don't learn about where you came from and how you got where you are, it's like you won't learn from the history that repeats itself—"

"You must be a country boy."

"Eeh? How'd you know?"

"Because only country boys from backward realities care about that," she chided. "Modern folks on the go don't care. Country people and maybe folks in that Nippon place, but that's it, you know? It's like that RealWare motto, 'Technology for Living in Today!' Living in today's all that matters. It's not like yesterday was any different from today, after all. Tomorrow'll be the same too. So why should it matter?"

"Doesn't that mean that, err... you just negated your whole argument that only keeping new things matters since it'd mean new things are the same as old things or things not yet new but soon to be new?"

The costumed girl squinted her eyes a little, trying to jump through the mental hoops afire set before her.

"Do you want my cards or not?" she asked, some part of her deciding it was best to ignore the question. She tossed her dusty card storage folder on the table, as if throwing down the three-ring gauntlet.

Eiko stepped up, and did a high-speed flip through the contents. "Nope, nope, nope, nope, nope... nopenopenope. No Treehugger in here, Mallory-kun..."

With a sigh, Mallory asked the question he realized he'd be asking quite a bit today. "Do you know anybody else who collects these...?"

"Only one. How about that guy selling those models with the Ocean Wave Gun on 'em?"

"We already checked with him..."

"Then you're out of luck," she said, retrieving her folder. "Now can ya move it along? I've got swappers lining up behind you waiting..."

"S-sorry, sorry," Mallory apologized, bowing out of the crowd.

What had begin in a frenzy of good cheer and energy had wound down to a puddle of gloom and absolute despair. Or as close to one as you could get when dealing with a realistically minor problem such as locating a trading card. It was not the end of the world, after all, even if the perspective was warped.

"Look, I really need to get going," Hideaki explained, as Mallory sat in a little slump of depression on a bench at the edge of the showroom. "I've got my own trading to get done today, and it's getting late..."

"Yeah... I guess it's a wash out," the country boy spoke. "Thanks for trying, Hideaki..."

As their native guide wandered off into the crowd, Eiko paced in a little oval in front of her taller charge. "It's not fair," she pouted, kitsune tail flicking behind her in frustration. "You deserve nice things like that card, and I want to get one for you! But I don't know enough about this sort of stuff to really help... and if nobody knows where we could look, where do we look...?"

"It's okay, Eiko. Really! I mean, it's just a card..."

"It's not a card! It's the final step of completing your collection!" she corrected, pointing a dramatic finger skyward and clenching a little first with her other hand. "Once you start something like this, you can't give up! You have to fight, and fight! For everlasting peace!"

"Uh—"

"There's one last thing we can try," she decided, bopping that fist into her other hand, nodding with determination. "I wasn't gonna suggest it, since...

330

uh... I wasn't sure how you'd feel about it, what with everything and stuff, but... it's worth a shot, right? Right...?"

She knelt down on the concrete floor of the showroom, pulling a map from Mallory's old backpack of collectable goodies. Unfolding it, she spread it out at Mallory's feet.

"This is a complete map of every table and every dealer," she explained. "One of them has to have the Treehugger. We don't know which one... but... if you use your power, you can find it!"

Mallory leaned forward, looking down at the map. "Uh... Eiko..."

"You can do neat things with your power, I know you can!" she said. "Nobody in the house really talks about it but I know and see all, for I am Eiko! And I know that you can just, I don't know, close your eyes and poke your finger at the map and that'll be where your card is! You said when we started out that there was no chance at finding it, but I LIKE those odds since they're really your kind of odds! Because... you're lucky. ...right? It works like that, right?"

> Covering his eyes with one hand, making a pointy-finger with the other, he waved his finger around randomly, reaching forward... and eventually poking the glass of the workstation screen.
>
> Peeking between two fingers, he read the entry he had hopefully selected via mystical spiritual powers beyond his comprehension.
>
> "Live-in REALITY ENGINEER wanted..."

"...it... doesn't work like that," he said, pushing the memory aside. "Eiko, I've tried, I can't just use my weird power whenever I want to. I can't do it. I've tried..."

"But you have to! Or else the con will be over, and your card will leave with it! It's your only chance at doing something you have no chance of doing," she pleaded. "Pleeease, Mallory-oniichan...? Just try it once, for me...?"

It's very hard to say 'no' to an adorable little girl with big round pleading eyes and her hands together as if praying to some distant savior.

With a sigh, Mallory nodded his head. "Okay..."

He closed his eyes, and reached down...

It was a miracle!

Who knew it was even possible? A million-to-one chance, the ultimate longshot, the last ditch effort which nobody really expected to succeed, and...

It didn't.

"Cards?" the dealer asked, confused. "I only sell t-shirts here, not cards. Don't you see the big sign marked 'CLOTHING, 1/2 OFF'? What made you think I'd have trading cards?"

Eiko bit her lip, as they walked away from the longshot last ditch chance. "I thought... I thought you could make it happen..."

"I'm sorry, Eiko," he consoled, resting a hand on her shoulder. "It's like I said—I can't just do it when I want to."

"What if we had it be some sort of accident? Like, I spill a drink, you slip and fall and whatever table on the map your index lands on—"

"That'd still be me wanting to make it happen. It'd be cheating—it didn't work when I asked M to throw a rock at me, either. You just can't engineer a coincidence..."

"But... but that's stupid! What good is a neat power if you can't actually USE it except by a complete accident?" she asked, getting a wee bit mad. "Ooooh...! This is annoying. But if it won't work, then... Mallory... do you really wanna give up? We could keep looking—!"

"There's no reason to, Eiko. It's getting late, and we should go home soon. Your sister'll be worried sick—"

"She always worries. That's her job," Eiko noted, but without cynicism. "It's okay, really, she means well so I stay out of trouble to keep her stress levels down. Or at least, any trouble she finds out about, which works the same way!"

"Oh. That's... very nice of you. ...I think..."

"Right. If we're leaving, can I go get some Important Courtroom Drama action figures first?" she asked, pointing a thumb behind herself to a nearby row of tables. "I saw some back there and I have a bit of allowance, so I figured I'd get a Stacy Stenographer to add to my playset..."

He peered around the less-teeming-as-the-day-went-on crowds, to make sure the ICD dealer was within spotting distance. "Okay, but don't take too long. We should get moving."

"I won't take long!" Eiko cheered, getting some of her high spirit back as her kitsune ears twitched. "Be right baaack!"

Benches were a-plenty on the nearby fringes of the room, so Mallory selected one within sight distance of Eiko, and rested his aching legs. He set the battered backpack next to him, one arm around it as his head rolled back and worries overtook his mind. They'd been doing that quite a bit since he found out about his so-called "power..."

He couldn't use it for anything useful. It had saved his bacon now and then (food metaphors feel good) but if he ever knowingly tried to use it to get his ham out of hock, the udder would instantly go dry. It was as useful as an old dog teaching a new trick to a pig in a poke.

Despite being utterly useless, they were the source of much of his misery. Someone hunting him down just because of the power... days of trying to train it, ending in dismal failure... living on the run, putting the people he cared for in danger. What was the big bonus to having a power like that? It had no upside whatsoever, just very nasty downsides... all because he couldn't actually USE IT...

Seeking a distraction, he jammed his hand into the backpack, fiddling around in his card storage box. Exploring all the card combinations, with their little animations, was always a nice way to kill time in a useless way. Why was his power useless? Why? Draw two cards, sit back, put them together...

The Questioning Questor, card #34, from the Bi-monthly Quisition Qomic. Angst Boy, Card #198, from his self-titled monthly series. Edge to edge, 34 on the left, 198 on the right, link them, the one second pause to load the data, the animations...

"Why do you angst so much, Angst Boy?" Questioning Questor asked, scratching his chin.

"You think I ever wanted to be a freak? I never asked for this, and I wish I didn't have these powers!" Angst Boy angsted, slumping his shoulders. "I wish they'd go away!"

Both thin rectangles tumbled to Mallory's lap, his hands still upraised as if holding ghosts of cards that were once there.

If you hate your powers and can't accept them, of course they aren't going to work, a combination of cards and stray ideas previously kept un-thought echoed inside his head. *You don't want them, so you won't REALLY let yourself use them...*

His eyes turned downward, to the now-static cards lying there.

So, if I WANT these cards to be in my hands instead of in my lap, if I really WANT them...

No, that won't work. You could just pick them up. You'd rather do that. You'd rather do that than do what you don't want to do...

Something thundered in Mallory's ears once, twice. Three times, before he recognized it as his heartbeat. Another loud nose came from his throat, as he swallowed.

That's the way it has to be, now that I know the truth—I have to need something. Absolutely need something. Something so strong that I can't avoid using it, I can't deny and wish it would go away. That's why it only works sometimes. I had to protect Meiko, I had to get everybody home before he killed her, killed them, I couldn't not do that, I had to—

"ONIICHAN!"

"Had to—whaaa?" he thought aloud, focus snapping in an instant, fading away just as quickly as it had formed. "What? Who? Eiko...? What?"

"You okay? You were really weird-looking just now..."

"I was just... I was thinking about something, I think—"

He found himself face-to-face with The Treehugger.

"Eiko-chan comes through for you, Mallory!" Eiko announced. "I hereby declare VICTOLY in the search for the card! It was so weird, I was asking about the stenographer figure, and we were talking about Important Courtroom Drama, and I mentioned how I was here originally looking for this card, and he said 'Oh, do you mean this card?' and he said I could have it for nothing because I was so cute although that's not really a good exchange to keep a free market society afloat I decided what the heck and took him up on it and here you go!!"

Disbelieving, Mallory poked at the card representing a cheerful bead-wearing hippie woman a few times. It was solid enough.

"The last card...? We got it? We got it! ALRIGHT!" he shouted, springing to his feet (while Eiko fetched the two cards which promptly fell from his lap.) "Great work, Eiko! Thank you, thank you! It was crazy to think we could find it, but... I guess it was crazy like a fox!"

"Pinpon!" she agreed, ears twitching. "Okay! Let's get home, and we can see what this card does when put up next to the other cards. Um, how many combinations is that again...?"

"Uh... let's see, there's 256 normal cards, and 256 Alternate Universe ones... different sayings if it's on the left or the right..." he thought, trying to tally up large numbers in a medium-sized mind. "So... uh... a thousand or so."

"We'd better get started soon, then," Eiko decided. "The bus will get us back home. Let's go! And, ummm... oniichan?"

"Yeah?"

"What were you thinking about just now?"

"Oh, it's nothing," Mallory said, carefully packing away the (now) three loose cards.

Of course, he hadn't forgot. He just didn't want to think about it right now. Nothing to spoil this suddenly very nice mood. Nothing could spoil it now, not the endless rain of Restless, not the long bus ride, nothing. He'd completed an important puzzle, after all.

Maybe even two of them.

[2] r.s.v.i.p.

Meiko never liked rain.

Rain seemed to accompany her on all her bleaker days. It was there at her parents' funeral, first and foremost—after that it popped up now and then, whenever a business contract would fall through, whenever the bills would start stacking up, whenever she felt alone despite living in a house with three others (and now four). If given the choice between docking the house at a Reality with very little, very prescheduled rain or a place which allowed for the more fashionable random weather, she'd pick a dry climate every time. A nice sunny day, the kind of sunshine that can make even an impossible situation feel like she could deal with it...

Then there was the part of her that felt it was simply silly to put so much emotional weight on the weather. What did it matter if it was raining or not? It was all just a function of a Reality Engine, not some mystical synergy between her mood and the world around her. She had put such childish flights of fancy behind her long ago... when she decided to grow up as fast as she could in order to provide a real home for herself and Eiko...

Shaking her head to clear it, Meiko tried to focus on the here and now. Here, walking down a sidewalk of Restless with her tasteful grey umbrella. Now, lunchtime, as her stomach whined away hoping to be dealt with ASAP. Not the right time or place to let stray thoughts like that float around; she had business to attend to. That's better, much better. Walk along, heading for the restaurant, something you can focus on...

F.P. had indeed scheduled up a seat at a nice restaurant for her. Nothing too expensive, but nothing cheap either; the sort of place where you usually have to book a day in advance but not trendy enough to need to book a year in advance. Just right for her, classy surroundings that fit your budget. She'd been meaning to take Mallory out to a restaurant again, after having such a good time on their first official date—it counted as an official date through retroactive continuity, as she ignored her initial claims of non-datehood which were No Longer Applicable after what happened at 12:03 AM. ...it would've been nice to bring him to this restaurant, if Eiko hadn't gotten to him first. Although technically Meiko had Mallory all to herself for the past week, talking, watching video streams, enjoying homecooked meals, spending time together...

Another distracting memory, as she nearly ran into someone leaving the Ma Maison Restaurant. Collapsing her umbrella and her current thoughts to a handy carrying size, she pushed through the door.

The restaurant was packed. Businessfolk of every phylum and subspecies were present, enjoying a good meal before setting off for afternoon seminars. Meiko pulled out F.P., glancing at her scheduler again and finding no information about what table she was supposed to head to... but that was easily dealt with.

She approached the Maître d', waving a hand to get his attention over the crowd.

"Excuse me, ah... do you have a table reserved under 'Mirai'?" she asked. "Meiko Mirai. My organizer called ahead to make the arrangements...?"

The bored looking fellow in a tuxedo glanced up boredly at her. "Mirai? Mir... M, M, M..." he mumbled to himself, thumbing through the data screen embedded in his podium. "No Mirai, sorry. I—oh, wait, I see. Yes, we have a table for you; it was reserved under the name of your companion. This way, please..."

Companion?

A tiny bit of oddball dread siezed Meiko. Had Mallory reserved them a table? But the travel ban was still on at the time he'd have had to place the reservation, unless... unless he worked with Lorelei to convince her to lift it, intending for this to be a surprise! Which meant it was wrecked, because Eiko had dragged him off and as usual, the houseboy didn't give a whimper of protest. Still, it was a romantic thought for the boy who usually had to achieve his romance through lucky coincidence...

That would've been a cute if slightly disappointing story suitable for a good flick on the video streams, if not for the fact that it was wholly wrong and Meiko's lunchdate was already waiting for her at the table.

The other woman flipped her green pocket organizer closed—but Meiko caught the tiny Noyori Labs logo embossed under the keys before the latch clicked.

"Ah, you're my companion, then?" Gillian Bates, CEO of RealWare Inc. asked, with a bright smile. "Have a seat, have a seat! I was just about to order salads."

People like Gillian Bates do exist. It's hard to know that for certain—REALLY know it, down to the core, because you never see them in person. They exist in a vague, fuzzy sense, as names in a press release or images on the evening news. Rather a lot like elected political officials, their only contact with you is minimal and abstracted through at least sixteen layers of votes, assistants, paperwork, and sheer socioeconomic distance.

When you're expecting a bit of pasta by yourself on an ordinary rainy day and suddenly you find yourself face-to-face with someone who didn't previously exist in your practical reality, it can throw you for a loop. If this were a business meeting, something where matters of great economic weight were being discussed, Meiko would've been calm and confident. As is, having floated in from the rain amidst a cloud of conflicting emotions and memories, she was completely off balance while her companion was not.

"It really is a handy little gadget, isn't it?" Gillian commented with a musical, sing-song little voice that sounded great when fed into a cluster of about 42 different microphones at a press conference. "Ryo mentioned that only three prototypes were made, and I was always wondering where the third one went... I like the clamshell case on yours better. Red's a very powerful color, even if my green shell is the traditional color of money. Yours speaks of passion for your business, mine simply says I have too much loose change to spend on toys... not that Ryo would have dreamt of charging me for it. I keep trying to woo him over to RealWare, he's quite a genius you know, but he's content with keeping relations friendly and friendly alone... ...I'm not boring you, am I?"

"Boring? What? No, no," Meiko said, remembering that her fork was still speared through a few bits of salad. "Sorry, I just... I had a lot on my mind today. And this is obviously a bit of a surprise..."

"All things happen for a reason, I believe. Who knows why we've been brought together?" Gillian asked hypothetically, as she folded her fingers in front of herself. "I for one am thrilled to get out of the ivory tower for a change."

"The ivory what?"

"It's an old saying, dear," the young woman noted. "Like 'cabin fever'. You know... being cooped up in one place? Cooped is a bit of an old word, too..."

"No, I understand... feeling a bit trapped and restless, right?"

"Very much so. Appropriate that I found myself taking a corporate condo over to Restless, then. I imagine you must not have similar problems, what with owning your own business you take on the road with you..."

"We've... been staying in one place for a while, actually," Meiko replied, trying to pick through her initial shock enough to avoid saying something dangerous. "Business reasons. We've been in Restless for a week now. My employees were feeling a bit of 'cabin fever' too, so I decided they could head out today for some R&R..."

"Oh, that's a good idea. Motivating your troops is always difficult during harsh economic climates, and physical ones as well! All this rain, I'm not sure how you can stand it, it'd drive me batty... as does being cooped up. Would you believe this is the first purely social meeting I've had with another human being in weeks? Just too much to do back at the office, and you can hardly call a board meeting a social event... it's so hard to simply connect with people on a purely personal level when you practically live at the office..."

Seeing her opportunity to take some control of the conversation, Meiko interjected with a charming smile and a personal anecdote. "Actually, I find it easiest to connect personally at the office. Since my office goes with me, and my... boyfriend works with us, I can socialize all I like there. In fact, this week I've had some real quality time with him despite needing to stay inside... maybe because of it..."

...too close for comfort there, Meiko realized, trailing off. But too late— Gillian was the sort to latch onto the tiniest little detail, and she pounced.

"What could ever require you to stay in such an awful reality, though?" she asked, curious as a cat. "Most people leave Restless once their business here is concluded. You said you do troubleshooting, correct? I was under the impression from what I've read that freelancers rarely take a job which lasts so long if they can avoid it... the docking fees would just start stacking up, and Restless isn't THAT inexpensive a place to stay—"

"Ah, excuse me..."

The waitress. A perfect dodge, as Meiko picked up her menu, ready to place her order. "I'll have the pasta of the day, please, and a coffee... Mrs. Bates?"

"Please, please, call me Gillian. Mrs. Bates is too formal," she chided, before simply pointing to two items on her menu for the benefit of the waitress. "And it's definitely MISS Bates."

"Ah, sorry..."

"I know I have to maintain the Bates legacy, but traditional marriage simply isn't for me," Gillian spoke, to Meiko's relief as topics shifted. "Fortunately for the ridiculously rich, there are other options..."

"Options...?" Meiko egged on, to put distance between herself and their reasons for staying.

"I already said I had difficulty meeting people socially; going through the entire courtship process just to pass on the Gates lineage is a bit of an impossibility. I would so love to raise a family, mind you... a daughter, specifically, who I can raise to properly guide RealWare into the future. But until the time comes when I find the right DNA to make it happen, I'll have to wait."

"The right man, you mean."

"The right DNA," she corrected. "From someone with the proper traits and values and characteristics I approve of. Eugenics, see. It's all very complicated and I can't claim to be an expert on the subject, but if anybody would have access to such technology it'd be the richest corporation in history, yes...? Hmm. An odd look you're giving me, there."

"Oh, s-sorry—"

"Quite all right, quite all right. I'm used to it. I suppose living in the ivory tower makes me a little eccentric, but the rich are harmless eccentrics by definition," she joked with a chuckle (or at least, a joke to her). "Ask Ryo sometime, the technology was pioneered through a test case made by an old friend of his... but I digress. Have you any plans to have a child with your boyfriend, Ms. Mirai?"

"......uh.... not right now," Meiko spoke, having completely lost control of the conversation again. ('I wonder if this is what Mallory feels like all the time?' she wondered.) In an effort to get a grip again, she decided to take a bolder step... leaning forward a little. "Ms... ...Gillian. Can I ask you a question?"

"Of course, dear."

"Why are you telling me all this? Like you said, it's a bit eccentric. How do you know I won't run for the nearest gossip video stream and tell all about your social worries and family planning?"

"Simple. I don't," Gillian noted... her smile sliding to a more serious expression, for the time being. "But you don't seem the type to do that sort of thing. Or are you?"

"No, of course not... but I could be lying when I say that."

"But you aren't lying, are you? Meiko, as you no doubt know... to succeed in business, you MUST be able to size up the person across the table from you quickly. It's all a grand game of psychology, expensive clothes, and legalese— but psychology first and foremost. I feel confident enough in my own insight that I feel I can trust you. So... can I trust you?"

"Yes... of course," Meiko spoke honestly. "I don't break contracts, even informal unspoken ones. I won't betray your trust—I was just curious as to why you were trusting me, that's all."

"Well, then. I'm glad that's settled," Gillian said, back to smiles and cheer. "And now that I've told you my life, let's hear more about yours. Quid pro quo and all that. So, this boyfriend of yours..."

The pasta was quite good; steamed just right, juicy and tender without being too soft, a combination that rivalled what Mallory had served two days prior for dinner. And while Meiko could taste it and enjoy eating it, she had to preserve a tiny amount of tension—the little paranoia which said 'Don't tell her everything'...

Despite that fear, she found herself opening up quite a bit about how she felt, what she was thinking. Nothing that could tie into the danger they were in, but more than she would have to a total stranger.

"At this point, I'm just hoping I'm getting it right," she continued. "I've never done the romance thing before. Not even the usual failed attempts at it in your wild youth that are supposed to happen—I purposefully didn't have a wild youth. I'm not even in my twenties and there just wasn't enough room for that sort of stuff, even if Lorelei managed to cram a hell of a lot of it into a few years... so... I don't know. I hope I'm getting it right. Fortunately Mallory's never done this before so if either of us are making mistakes, the other won't realize... I'm just going by instinct, like I always have."

"Instincts which have worked out quite well," Gillian reinforced, her pasta long since eaten as she dined in rapt attention to Meiko's words. "There's nothing wrong with trying to take on an adult lifestyle at your age. I've had to do the same thing. It's working for you, yes? Playing by instinct?"

"Well, it has so far. I'm just not so sure when it comes to romance..."

"If you're only blind in one area, then you're already more successful than most who take our path, Meiko. You run a stable business despite the difficulties the transient lifestyle imposes, and you've done it all in a remarkably small span of time early in life. You should be proud."

"I am proud of what I've done! I just hope I didn't cripple my ability to do this sort of thing in the process, since... ...what am I saying?"

"What are you saying?" Gillian echoed, in one of those zen-wisdom sorts of ways rather than a mocking-ha-ha sort of way.

"I'm dumping all these things on you and your name isn't Ryo," she said aloud. "It's bizarre..."

"Does it matter why you're doing it? Clearly you want to share, or else you wouldn't be sharing. I may be charismatic and persuasive but I can't force someone to do something they absolutely don't want to do. ...would you like more businesslike advice about it, however?"

"I know, I shouldn't be readily offering up leverage to someone else. Goes against my debating instinct."

"Actually, I was going to suggest you talk to Mallory about this," Gillian noted. "Ryo's a sweetheart but he's not your boyfriend... Mallory is. You should confide in him. Call it an economic decision; you get more for your investment if you keep your emotional share in one fund."

"...that's a mixed metaphor worthy of Mallory."

"I study a lot of etymology in my spare time, so I tend to juggle words old and new. My point is that rather than divulging to a stranger—not that I find your relationship issues the least bit boring, dear, they're a refreshing change from board meetings—or divulging to an old friend, perhaps you have a better source closer to home..."

"Yeah... yeah, I know. I've talked to him about it briefly, now and then... but not really in depth..."

"No time like the present. Although we still have dessert to go through before you head home, so if you'd like to discuss something a little less personal...? I'm game for anything you feel comfortable with."

Meiko thought a moment.

"Business," she decided.

"Avoiding the personal, then..."

"No... no, it's not that. I don't mind telling you all that, even if it was a bit weird. ...but how often can someone claim to have a chance to sit Gillian Bates down for a talk? I'd be a fool to pass up the chance to talk about RealWare. To get a few answers."

"Seizing an opportunity, then," Gillian replied, enjoying the idea. "Very well; I'm in the hot seat and it's your dime."

"It's my what...?"

"It means ask away, dear. So, to business!"

Cheesecake. By far, Meiko's favorite thing ever to indulge in. A good cup of coffee was a close second, but cheesecake always won out when going head-to-head with the java—a fact she never told Mallory, for fear that he'd enthusiastically make her cheesecake every day, until she inflated like a balloon...

"It simply won't persevere," Gillian explained, between bites of her own cheesecake. "The Open Reality Movement is far too fragmented, too idealistic. Did you know there are fourteen different builds of the Open Engine, fourteen different splinter groups working on it? The one headed by Xyzzy, founder of the ORM, is only in the majority by a tiny fraction. Only two groups are bothering to shoot for a commercial end product, and what venture capitalist would throw their money behind a losing horse? Funding a competitor to RealWare is a sure-fire way to go bankrupt. That's not a threat, either, it's a simple fact established by hundreds of years on the stock markets."

"But—for the sake of argument—what if they consolidated?" Meiko asked. "Or if one build won in the end, and was marketed. You'd have a legitimate competitor, one which costs far less. Wouldn't the Open Engine outsell the RealWare Engine based on that alone?"

"It's not just cost, it's support. You know, Meiko, we have defeated a competitor like this before..."

"You have?"

"Eight hundred years ago, thieves stole a thousand blank engines and added their own hacks to sever their links to RealWare," Gillian explained. "Odds are you aren't aware of this; who bothers with history anymore? But those engines were sold at next to nothing, and were bought up in droves by daring reality pioneers... and two years later, they were gone. How? Strong-arming and aggressive PR. It didn't take much, really, since all we had to do was point out the lack of official support, blacklist a few REC-certified individuals who offered unofficial support to what was clearly an illegal product, and then offer amnesty to the thieves to 'upgrade' to a full engine. Problem solved, and in the end, all money comes to us."

"But that's different this time, isn't it? They've legitimately reverse-engineered your engines—"

"There's a bit of contention about that, but considering there's nobody available to sue nor an appropriate court to do it in, I'll concede the point..."

"And that means you can't stop them," Meiko concluded. "Open Reality is an idea, a bit of knowledge. Even if the groups working on it now don't get a product out the door that can compete commercially, the knowledge of how to build an alternative to RealWare will always be out there. How can you fight that?"

"The same way, of course. Strong-arming and aggressive PR. Flood the market with the things it least desires: fear, uncertainty, and doubt. Why take the gamble on Open Reality when RealWare has offered a stable product for thousands of years?"

"There's a bit of contention about how stable your product is, you know."

"Touché," Gillian noted. "But nevertheless, the weapons are there and we will use them. In business, any weapon in your arsenal is valid... except one. ...which my father never understood..."

"What...?"

"No... no," the CEO spoke, closing her views for the first time that day. "No, I won't go in that direction. Trust you I may, but some things I can't entrust regardless. My apologies. As for killing an IDEA... I'm confident. You underestimate the power of our monopoly, Meiko. The nature of it... it's like a rock. The rock of ages."

"You're saying RealWare is eternal, then? Invincible?"

"Oh, history crashes against it now and then," Gillian conceded. "But history settles back into a level sea in the end. RealWare is indeed eternal... that is, unless a true tsunami arises one day. That is the right word, correct? Tsunami?"

"A tidal wave...?"

"Yes... something so powerful, so alien, so sudden that even against our strongest defenses we cannot stand the storm. A true force capable of change, a dynamic entity which can pull the multiverse out of stagnation..."

"Stagnating?" Meiko asked, mildly puzzled by the shift from economics to philosophy. "Come on, Gillian, the multiverse seems lively enough to me..."

"Oh yes, very lively," Gillian agreed flatly. "Lively as it has been for centuries. Exactly as lively as it ever will be. Do you know the theory of evolution, Meiko?"

"Ah... I'm not immediately famil—"

"No, and why would you be? That's half of the problem right there! ...however. I shouldn't speak so strongly of such things; it's not for me to decide the future. My role is to defend my eternal castle to the absolute best of my ability until a true paradigm shift is capable of unseating me."

"That's... sort of optimistic and pessimistic at the same time, isn't it?"

"Oh yes," Gillian agreed, smiling a slightly mad smile. "Isn't it? Ah, but now we're out of cake, and out of time..."

Meiko glanced down at her empty plate. She didn't even remember eating the rest of her cake, but the satisfied feeling in her stomach suggested otherwise.

"Ah... we should exchange business cards before we leave," Meiko suggested. "It's traditional, after all..."

Nodding in agreement, Gillian opened her green F.P. and pressed a single button. A quiet chittering noise inside the plastic device sounded, and a business card was slowly printed out.

Meiko nearly dropped it in surprise when she accepted the flat paper rectangle. The moment her skin came in contact with it, a tiny hologram of Gillian Bates had appeared in the air over the fine print—a 100% realistic hologram, solid and animated, beyond the cheap technology used in toys like 8-Bit Commandos. The sort of technology that only the richest company in the world had, and usually kept to itself...

"How...?" she asked, curious.

"Trivial enough. I've had my F.P. modified quite a bit to suit my needs... that's one of the enhancements, a specialized business card printer," Gillian replied, slightly smug. "Like it? The paper is 'bone'. It has a watermark. And your card...?"

With a bit of shame, Meiko produced a slightly rumbled paper card with her name and RealNet address in large type. It did not glow, nor produce any amazing high-tech visuals.

"Tch... no no, that won't do at all," Gillian said, refusing to take the card... but not out of disgust, more with the air of one who saw opportunity. "Mmm... how would you like to have a card like mine? It's simple enough, I can have one of my engineers modify your F.P. to add a card printer. It's the same prototype mine is, I can assure you it would work..."

"I don't know..." Meiko said, unsure despite eyeing the RealWare card in her hand with envy. "How expensive would it be?"

"Expen...? Oh! Free, of course! I have more than enough money, Meiko. It's the least I can do for someone who's provided me so much lovely social contact! Let me get a photo of you to encode into the card... stand up, please. And step away from the table a bit."

Thankfully she had thought ahead enough to put on her next best businesswear, as she rose from the table and struck a poise of confidence and professionalism. The tiny yet intense flash of light from the green F.P. nearly blinded her, however.

"There, there..." her companion said, nodding in approval at the small image of Meiko appearing on her organizer's screen. "And one more sample to take—put your finger on this square here, next to the printer..."

"Huh? Why—"

Meiko jerked her hand back quickly, as if touching something very hot. She turned her finger around to see a tiny drop of blood forming...

"Biometric data security," Gillian explained, with a deep smile. "A nice feature, isn't it? It'll ensure nobody impersonates you with your new cards, and you'll be able to sign documents with DRM far better than a fingerprint!"

"Oh... all right," she agreed, shaking her finger a bit to get feeling back into it. "I'd best be going now... it's been an enjoyable lunch, Ms. Bates."

Gillian took Meiko's hand to shake it, but kissed the back of it instead.

"Charmed," she spoke as her goodbye, stepping around the confused woman and out the door of the restaurant. Business had concluded.

Once on the street, with her umbrella open, Gillian studied the stream of data flying across her F.P.'s screen more than she studied the passers-by on the sidewalk. Next to Meiko's picture, a long, long cluster of letters scrolled by; mostly G, A, T and C.

It had been a good day indeed, Gillian decided. A lovely social day.

[3] another night

Restless.

She was used to restless nights; always keeping one ear open, even while sleeping, in case of enemy attack. Waking up to patrol the grounds. Being ready to jump into action at a moment's notice, twenty-four hours a day, light or dark... never quite getting a full night's sleep, not until they were high enough in the food chain to earn better quarters and less routine duties...

But these people... they were awake volunarily. Not to play 'Dee', not to keep an eye out, but because they genuinely wanted to be right here, right now. In the heat of the moment. In the thick of things. A crowd of bodies moving, but not in a fight to the quasi-death, but in a celebration of LIFE...

The beat. The haze. The lights. The SOUNDS...

"...it's not really that big of a deal," her companion explained, trying to speak over the level of the music. "I mean, you've been to parties before. Your mom threw some real galas when she was trying to impress the higher ups... so what's so special about this?"

She stared at the girl to her left in awe. "You can't feel it?" she asked... slowly moving a hand through the air. "The intensity of it? I thought I knew what it'd be like, from the RealNet streams, but... but this is the real thing! A club, a real honest-to-goodness dance club! Music and drinks and partying and boys and maybe the occasional bar brawl, although I haven't seen one yet I'm sure there'll be one—"

"Lorelei, don't forget—"

"I know, I know, okay? But... you mean to tell me you can't feel this? It's amazing! It's everything I was hoping it'd be!"

"I was never much of a social butterfly, remember? I didn't have tons of boyfriends like you did, I didn't go to many parties..."

"But you're in one now! A party the likes of which we've never seen before...! Come on, get in the groove, it's hip and cool! ...those are the right words, right? It was an old flick on the stream I saw, but maybe it didn't go out of style..."

Her instincts told her two opponents were approaching from behind. She had to actively resist the urge to activate her double saber and take them out. That wasn't the right thing to do anymore...

"Hey, ladies!" one of the men called over, turning the charm to 11 (which meant it effectively wrapped around to 1 on a ten-number rotating dial, thus failing miserably). "You two look like you could use some company..."

Lorelei turned to give her opp—her prey—her... she'd need a better term for this, definitely... anyway, she looked at him. "Wow, they sure do grow 'em big out here in the multiverse," she commented more or less to herself.

Her companion shook her head... sliding off her bar stool in the process. "I think I'd better leave you alone with your new boy toy, Lore—"

"I'm with her," Lorelei noted, grabbing her companion's arm to stop her. "Not that you two aren't good company, but it's a girl thing, you know? Off you go, scoot, scoot. Good boys."

There were some funny looks, of course... before the pair decided to move along, spotting some more likely candidates at the end of the bar. Lorelei ignored their departure, flashing a grin in the other direction.

"You okay, Lorelei...?"

"I'm hanging out with you tonight, remember?" Lorelei noted. "The idea of you wandering off to play wallflower like you usually do... no way, no how. You said you'd show me how to live, how to REALLY be alive, right? Well, I'm doing the same for you. BARTENDER! Beers! And ignore our fake IDs, please! ...c'mon, have a seat. We're young and hot and we're finally free to LIVE our lives!"

"Well... okay," the other girl said, resuming her seat... and returning the smile. "You've got a point. We're free, we're alive, and we can enjoy our time! Uh... but you're going to have to teach me how to... you know, handle this sort of stuff. I'm not good with boys, for instance..."

"If you'd return their looks now and then, Rei-Lei, you'd do just fine," Lorelei noted. "You're a cutie yourself, you've just been too busy brawling away in Tribal Alpha to pay attention to that. And I've spent far too much of my life wasting away there with you... so let's drink together to the freedom of the night life!"

The freedom of the night life...

A magical art she'd perfected for years and years, even after they went their seperate ways. Every aspect of it just tickled her pink inside—or more accurately, a hot cherry red. You could go out every night of your life (not that she realistically had time or energy to do so) and not get bored... there was always a new bar, a new song, a new dress, or a new person to spend the night with. She was never bored...

At least, that was the theory. Why she had that stray thought this morning, that same-old, same-old phrase that skipped across her consciousness like a pebble across a pond... a mystery. It didn't make sense. She had been reviewing the elements of a good night jaunt ever since then, trying to figure out what about it could possibly be boring.

The prep phase, that wasn't boring. Granted she hadn't bought a new outfit in a while, so it was a matter of picking from her tried and true standbys; but picking out a good dress, mixing and matching a few accessories, getting just the right LOOK was always a fun time. Meiko dressed for success, trying to look like the all-powerful professional in control of the boardroom... Lorelei dressed to kill. Albeit in a different way than she had long ago.

Tonight's number was yellow. Cherry red was possibly what was boring her, given it was the color of toenail polish she was using when the pebble-thought hit her. So a strapless yellow number, matching shoes, a nice shawl (a bit like the one Kisei wore on the cabaret night, Lorelei had rather liked it) and a short white jacket to go over it for a bit of a retro feel. One look in the mirror was enough to confirm the 'Oh, yeah' factor. Definitely one of her better picks.

If not the prep, then what...?

Walking the city streets at night was certainly enjoyable. She'd taken a cab to Nippon—not Mellow Fellow; he was a dear but last time she tried to go somewhere with him, he was so giggly and spaced out that they had landed on top of a sloped restaurant roof in Suburbana instead of the endless clubscape of Nocturn. This cabbie took her right where she wanted to be... the streets of the Ibiza district, Edo, Nippon.

Neon lights hanging in the darkness, faceless masses of the young and seeking... a thousand and one popular songs floating out of a thousand and one glowing doorways. The occasional drunk singing away happily, the giggles of the girls who were either waiting for their boyfriends or looking for one with the right amount of points... the aura of it all, the tangible feel of the hot night was always a joy for her. She grew up in the jungles of Tribal Alpha, true, but she knew the moment she first set foot in a nocturnal urban jungle that THIS was her true home.

But if not the streets, then what...?

She had picked a club at random. All it had to be was some place she'd never visited; in this case, one of those hybrid karaoke, dancing, and pool-hall places that tried to cater to every market demographic they could. A wild atmosphere of people who might not usually mix, folks of every cut and creed; businessmen, schoolgirls with fake IDs (much like her old one, natch), street women, the down and outs, the deviants, the diehard club-crawlers. Good people. Good atmosphere.

Good drinks, too; she asked for a Blade Dancer's Bourbon and lo and behold, the bartender actually knew how to make that obscure Tribal Alpha specialty. She'd found a rare place indeed, somewhere she could really mix it up; if she got bored sitting around the bar, she could go hustle people at the pool tables, or terrify the innocents with her off-key singing. Every aspect just screamed "Come, have fun!" and Lorelei was eager to do just that.

But if not the club itself, then what...?

Dressing up, going out, picking a place, having a drink... all present and accounted for. As she sat on her stool, swirling her first drink of the night around in its glass, she pondered all long past and all up to now. She still loved her lifestyle. It had done her well.

So why was she so bored? Why had she only now realized that the only times she'd felt genuinely alive out here were that one crazy night 'dating' Mallory, and... hmm. That one night...

"Usually when someone's just sitting there, swirling around a drink and staring into space, it means one of two things..."

Lorelei turned her head towards the voice, continuing to swirl.

"It means either you're an alcoholic, or you're just quite lonely," the devastatingly handsome man on her left said, smiling warmly. "If the first, I'm a social worker and I can recommend a few groups... if the latter, I'm a bit lonely myself, so why not some group therapy of our own?"

"A respectable civil servant? Mother would be happy for me," Lorelei joked. "As for your observation... sorry, I've got a filtering implant for that and any bugs I might pick up after a night of partying. Picked it up three years ago in Antiparadisia. No, I'm afraid I'm just lost in really deep thoughts, that's all..."

"Deep thoughts? Any you'd care to share—perhaps over another drink? And I've heard that dancing's terrific for taking your mind off your worries..."

A good find indeed, she thought. Good muscle tone, nice cheekbones. A stylish 'hook' he can easily use when picking up girls, to be both charming and nice-guy thoughtful, providing a shoulder to lean on... and likely a body to lean against after...

It wouldn't be too different from other nights she'd gone seeking a good time. She certainly could do worse. Why not? Maybe it was just what—

When the would-be therapist leaned back a bit to wave for the bartender, Lorelei spotted the figure sitting by his lonesome at the far end of the bar.

"On second thought, I'm afraid I don't have the hundred points for an hour on your couch," she noted, getting to her feet. "Nothing personal, you understand—but I'm afraid something's come up."

"What...?"

"Good luck out there, okay? I'm sure you'll find someone vulnerable enough," Lorelei commented, walking right by the confused doctor... and to the far superior choice for her evening.

Her instinctive stealthy approach meant he didn't even see her coming until she was all over him. An arm around the shoulders, a kiss on the cheek, and THEN he looked up sharply...

"Heya, handsome!" Lorelei greeted, squeezing him a bit. "Remember me? A few weeks ago, at the grand opening of that cabaret? I had your tie around my head and we were belting out songs while belting down drinks?"

The hapless young businessman's jaw sagged a bit. "Lorelei...?"

"That's me! And you're Ishida, yeah?" she identified, without needing a moment to recall. "I had quite a few to drink that night, but I remembered your name! How could I forget the most satisfying night I've had in weeks? I tell you, I'm damn lucky to meet you tonight—I've been having the weirdest day, can't quite put my finger on it, but I know for a FACT that you and I can break out of that rut and have a good time! So, buy you a drink? Sapporo beer... right? ... Ishida? You okay?"

Boys with a slightly intimidated expression were quite common for Lorelei. She had a rather strong presence, after all. So she continued on.

"Hey now, I know you're happy to see me and all, but no need to explode with joy over it," she sarcastically poked (and literally poked, a finger to his side as she was hip to hip with him). "So, care for a sequel? Maybe this time I'll be able to remember some of it, too. I know people say sequels are never as good as the original, but I bet you and me could break that rule... ...right? Hey, work with me... or... am I interrupting anything? You weren't waiting for someone, were you?"

"Err, no—"

"Then it's settled! Let's party!"

"I'm gay!"

"Bartender! Make my date here a good Blade Dancer's Bwhaaaaaa...?"

He had to repeat himself twice.

An untouched Sapporo beer sat next to the equally untouched Blade Dancer's Bourbon, as Ishida finished his story.

"You couldn't remember how to get back to your place, so I figured I should let you crash at mine," he explained. "I led you there, you sat down on the couch mumbling something about the night still being young, and fell asleep. I made sure to get you a blanket so you wouldn't get cold, but... that's it."

Lorelei's stare hadn't ceased. "You're kidding me."

"It's the honest truth, cross my heart," Ishida spoke, making the motion with two fingers on his hand. "That's it. We had a good time singing karaoke, had a few really good drinks—even if they were kind of on the expensive side—and you fell asleep on my couch. We didn't, you know... do anything. Like I said, I'm not even interested in women like that."

Lorelei crossed her legs and propped her chin in her hand and started Hard Thinking.

"Err... if you have a problem with my being gay, you know—"

"No no, that's not it," she quickly said. "Not it at all. I mean, hey, who hasn't had their little experimental moments...? No, what I'm confused about is why I distinctly remember that night as being so... satisfying."

"Satisfying how?"

"That's what's odd. I don't know. I just remember feeling quite happy the next day, like I'd had the night of my life. The kind of feeling I used to have a lot when hitting the streets at night, but... lately I guess it hasn't felt that way. I hadn't even noticed until today..."

"All we did was sing."

"I know, I know. And I'm not THAT good of a singer, either... something's not clicking here. ...what were you doing in a cabaret full of girls trying to paw men, anyway?"

"Oh, believe me, I wouldn't have gone in there normally," Ishida explained, a little embarassed. "But... remember I was telling you about the problems I was having with my boss and the uptown office block project we're working on?"

"Yeah... I remember that," Lorelei said, recalling. "You said that you were just going to go home and sleep, and I suggested a little beer and karaoke would wash away your worries..."

"It's the karaoke, see. I'm a bit of an addict. I love to sing! And frankly... the few bars in Edo that try cater to folks like me, they've either got no karaoke or a lousy music selection," he said in distaste. "Always awful retro stuff, or 'special interest' oriented tunes. I like the current hits I hear on the radio; I'm a general interest sort of guy, you know? So if it means going to 'general interest' bars to get my fix, hey, what can you do? But it's no big deal, I'm a people person, I can get along with anyone."

"Yeah, me too. Social butterfly. But all we did was sing, and drink, and have a good time...?"

"I take it you haven't been having a lot of fun lately out here?" Ishida asked, curious. "Hmmm... maybe...—ah, listen, if I'm keeping you from finding some guy—"

"Ohhh, no. I'm staying with you tonight," she decided. "I want to find out why something as simple as wailing out the top forty and boozing left me on cloud nine. So like I said before... it's sequel time. You came here because it has karaoke, right? Well, let's go blow our lungs out! Interested? Two's company, after all..."

Ishida paused, before answering.

"Okay, but on one condition," he issued. "Let's avoid getting drunk this time. I want you to remember what made that night special. I think I have a good idea what it might've been, judging from what you told me that night..."

"What? What'd I tell you? Speak, speak!"

"Nooo... I think it'd be better if you figure it out yourself," Ishida said, starting to smile. "This could be fun. Count me in. I've been meaning to try out 'Rainy Day Sunday' by Izumi and Itami, you know... but it's a duet. Care to horribly mangle some Nihongo with me in front of a microphone...?"

---

standing lonely in rain fall down
umbrella unfortunate time of hour

love finding underneath roof
where has bear gone to?

lonely day time unshiny place
frying pan super second moment—

"Get off the stage already!" a heckler from the audience called. "You've been up there a half an hour!"

Of course, nobody FROM Nippon would be so rude as to shout like that. Which was largely how Lorelei and Ishida had dominated the mike from the last thirty minutes, since nobody wanted to challenge them—but the greasy, annoying businessman in the front row already on his third round of Benten beer wasn't quite as polite...

Lorelei, however, didn't miss a beat as the poorly translated love song rolled on. She simply adjusted the lyrics a little.

"Loudmouthed bastard in front roowww, so unfortunate...!" she sang perfectly in tune, even if the bouncy red ball on the video screen wasn't bouncing on those exact words. "Smelling of beer cheap and bad col-OOOGNe, silence golden some tiiiiime, you bet...!"

Adding a little bounce to her hips as she performed for the shocked crowd of soul-crushed businessmen, Lorelei rocked on stage, enjoying the way the drunk turned red and then purple with anger. This was a familiar song, indeed... and the final verse was her favorite, because it usually involved splintered furniture and chaos and—

Ishida's hand clamped on her wrist before she could draw the handle of her double saber from her purse.

"Awww, I can't have a little fun? I'd be quick, I promise," Lorelei whispered to him.

"But you weren't fighting that night," Ishida noted. "You told me that night that you liked a good bar room brawl, but you didn't get into one. That's not why you had fun. And I don't think you want to end your experiment-night in jail, right...?"

"You're assuming they'd catch me, dear."

"Lorelei—"

"Fine, fine," she agreed, letting the handle drop, and taking a bow as the karaoke song rolled to a halt. "Let's adjourn, then..."

The pair left the stage, to the sound of light applause from the gathered persons. Whether it was because the obnoxious foreigner had finally left or because they genuinely appreciated her musical talent remained obfuscated behind a haze of proper social attitudes.

"You know, it's a shame you stopped me," Lorelei commented, as the resumed seating near the stage, next to their unattended (non-alcoholic) beverages. "I haven't had a chance to bust loose in a while, all cooped up at home. It's unhealthy to keep things bottled up like that. You know what they say, you can take the girl out of the fight, but you can't take the fight out of the girl..."

Ishida sipped at his lemonade. "Who said that...?"

"I did," Lorelei said. "It was my usual excuse when Rei-Lei had to bail me out after I rendered thousands of points of property damage to some unsuspecting schmuck's bar. And now I've got those competitive juices flowing and nothing to do with 'em! How about we go to some biker dive? Less classy than this, but more wild—"

"You weren't fighting that night, Lorelei..."

"So I wasn't fighting, I wasn't doing something else that starts with F, and now I'm not drinking," she summarized. "And you're SURE I had a good time on that mysterious evening? I'm having a hard time understanding why... you have an idea why, yes? You said I told you something, when I was drunk..."

"Well... yes, but... it's just one of those things you have to experience," Ishida explained. "Because if I told you NOW, you'd just laugh it off. It's no good unless you understand why, and the only way you can understand is to find out for yourself."

"I'm not the sort for a mystery, you know... the suspense and frustration are digging into me here."

"All right, all right... let's find something to do, then," Ishida suggested, thinking. "You said your competitive juices were flowing, right? Rather than a fistfight... how about another kind of fight? It'd be in keeping with what I'm trying to show you, I promise..."

Another bar. Another adventure...

Although it took four hours total to compete this adventure, the time slid by in a whirlwind of excitement. The minute details would be easily forgotten in the fray, but Lorelei wouldn't forget the memorable moments...

The Karaoke Competition made for a nice compromise between Ishida's hobbies and Lorelei's habits. Here, she could duke it out on the field of battle while he had a rocking good time... although with a twist he hadn't been expecting.

"I could've sworn the flyer said the duet competition was tonight," he apologized, as they reviewed the signs at the signup desk. "Maybe I got the name of the bar wrong, or something..."

"Hey hey, singles competition is fine," Lorelei replied, cracking her knuckles, grinning in anticipation. "You against me, mano-a-womano. Maybe I won't be fighting with blades and blasters, but it's still a fight!"

"Lorelei—"

"A FRIENDLY fight," she noted. "Don't worry. I'm not unfamiliar with the idea of friendly rivalry, even if it took a few years to really set in. Let's just do our best and let the chips fall where they may—and may the best woman win. I've got room in my room for another trophy! So... how's it work?"

"From what I remember... you can pick any song, in Nihongo or not. They've got a costuming room back there so you can dress up for your performance, and the judges weigh in on your overall style and singing..."

Act after act went on before them. Good ones, too; pop acts, rock acts, rap acts. Some foreigners, some locals; the little competition Ishida had suggested was actually quite popular, it seemed. Neither of them had a chance, facing up against this kind of stiff competition... which suited Lorelei just fine. She'd faced worse odds than this, and putting a trophy on the line made it all the sweeter. Wailing away some awful song in front of a bunch of drinkers was amusing and all, but nothing tasted quite like the thrill of the hunt...

Ishida went first, somewhere in the first third of the show.

He had taken advantage of the costume room in the back, walking out in a slightly puffy and loose white shirt. Very much the poet archetype, with his hair fluffed out and the top two buttons undone to give it a casual sensuality... tight slacks, a contradiction in terms, rounded out the presentation of a quite handsome young man who normally hid away in ordinary clothes.

The song he sang was one of love. It was pop, pure pop—smooth and easy, designed to make the ladies swoon, especially when coupled with a 'bishounen' such as himself. Indeed, Lorelei observed a fair amount of swooning in the audience as he performed, and she had to admit to at least a one-fifth swoon herself, despite knowing the truth...

"It was neutral, see," he'd explain to her afterwards. "It's a love song, but it's absolutely gender neutral. There isn't a trace of a 'he' or a 'she' in there, just a 'you' and 'me'. I think that's why I like it so much; I try to sing it only on special occasions..."

She could appreciate that. This was a special occasion. It took a while to sink in, but once she really got into the acts being presented and the atmosphere of good clean fun, she could feel that vibe coming from her fellow competitors. A night for fun, a night for song, a night just for enjoying the night...

Her performance came up during the second third of the show. Ishida had tried to make a prediction well before she hit the stage.

"Let me guess; something dripping with sensuality, and likely you'll switch to a more revealing dress once you hit the costume room," was his soothsayer's fortune.

And because something felt different tonight, something intangible and pleasant, she decided to be different as well.

The costume she wore actually covered more skin than the dress she wore when she walked into the place. Jeans were involved, for starters; also a tank top, a vest, a feather boa, fingerless gloves. It wasn't femme fatale, it was fatal femme; pure punk...

And she didn't sing something oozing with saxophone and smoky piano. She rocked out. Energetic and wild, an anthem of the wild youth she used to be, a little something that was popular on Tribal Alpha back in her day. The closest it got to sensual romance was when she invited the audience to 'kiss this' as part of the third chorus, while flashing the finger. It was a song of rebellion and attitude and affirmation of self.

Although she switched back to her slinky yellow dress before resuming her seat in the audience, she kept that fire inside long after her performance. The smile it brought to her face never left—even when they heard the announcement from the judges.

Out of the twenty-five performances they'd seen that night, there were two winners. It was a tie. Against all odds, even against the odds that they were against previous, Lorelei and Ishida had both ended up victors.

The judges had suggested a 'sudden death singoff,' which might have appealed to her, but she found herself suggesting something else.

"We'll take the tie," she told them. And they ended up carrying off the single trophy together.

"So why'd you do that?" Ishida had asked, after they left the building. "I thought you liked to be number one in contests like that..."

"Maybe I'm just getting older," Lorelei explained, with a smirk. "Utter domination doesn't matter as much, as long as I had a ball doing it. I don't have to score teh 0wnage in everything... I can settle for half-0wnage."

Despite the heavy trophy wearing down her arms as they walked back to Ishida's apartment, Lorelei's spirits stayed nice and high. Conversation was both light and deep, as they walked down the dark-yet-safe streets of Edo...

"So you were just manipulating her," Ishida summarized. "Trying to spur her into jealousy and thus into Mallory's arms?"

"More or less," she explained. "It was amusing. And a good object lesson for her! Overall I'd call it a job well done on my behalf..."

"Were you ever serious, though? About being with him..."

"Well... he's a great guy," she admitted. "Honestly a great guy. The kind you don't find even if you look for a thousand years... and I guess I indulged a little more than I thought I would... but he's not mine, and I don't think he ever was. I didn't want to fall into that delusion, so I simply didn't. No problem at all."

"Don't you get lonely, though...?"

"...maybe," she also admitted, without thinking hard about how much she was opening up to him. "It's hard to tell through the haze of drinking and partying and fighting, naturally. But modern romance, the flowers and the dating and the courtship and the wedding bells... eh. It's really not my game, I know that for sure. I can't settle down, I can't get all lovey-dovey like Meiko and Mallory are trying to be. But what else is there to do with a Saturday night?"

Ishida kept a careful eye on her, as she continued. "What about what you did tonight?"

"What, singing?"

"No... going out on the town with a friend."

Lorelei almost dropped the trophy. But didn't. She also almost ground her stroll to an abrupt halt. And did.

"Eh?" she intelligently responded.

"Well... look at it like this. You'd call us friends now, right?"

"Oh... well, of course..."

"How's this sound to you, then: next weekend, we'll go out again! If you're not on assignment, we could see a movie or go shopping... right?"

"...that's it, isn't it?" Lorelei realized. "What you wanted me to see tonight, what you couldn't just say... damn. You're almost as manipulative as I am."

"I wasn't really trying to be manipulative, I just thought it'd help... and I had an alternate theory, too, based on what you told me. So I wasn't sure, figured I'd have to prove it... Uh. Sorry for being so mysterious..."

"Hey hey, it's okay. I get the idea," she said, smiling to him. "It's so silly I wouldn't have accepted it at face value... friendship, right? The reason I had such a great night when I first met you—"

"—is because we could just have a nice, friendly night together," Ishida filled in. "Exactly. That's what you told me when you were drunk—that you were thrilled I was gay, because it meant you weren't expected to do the usual. You could just relax and enjoy yourself with someone close to you instead of trying to hook up with a stranger, get drunk, or anything like that. It was like the time you spent with her..."

"Rei-Lei," she confirmed. "Heh. Well, I can be a pretty wise woman sometimes... if only I could remember that wisdom after the hangover. It's true —every night I can peel myself away from the house, and hook up with random schmucks looking for a little temporary companionship. But it's always the same, even if it's never the same person... it's same-old, same-old. It wasn't doing it for me anymore. I didn't really feel satisfied... not like I did with Rei-Lei."

"The only friend you ever had," Ishida noted. "You told me that, too. I figured the 'friend' was the key, unless—"

"Oh! Oh, hey, you know, I felt it the time I 'dated' Mallory, too!" Lorelei recalled. "I wasn't honestly trying to get anywhere with him, so I could just kick back and have some fun with the boy. Of all the affairs I've had in recent times, that's the only one I remember... damn. It's so simple, I could kick myself... especially since he's now Meiko's property, and that means I've only got one friend I can exercise this new theory with. That's you, buddy."

"You really don't have any other friends right now? I know you told me that when you were drunk, but I figured it was an exaggeration..."

"Well, I'm a mobile girl, you know?" she pointed out. "We're all over the place. I was never looking for anything that lasts because I knew it wouldn't. After Rei-Lei split to follow her own life, that was it. Other than my co-workers, there's nobody I can really consider a..."

"A...?" he egged on.

"Just a stray thought," she dismissed. "Hmm... Ishida, I think I'm callin' it a night. I had a blast and we've got to do it again sometime. Keep the trophy... I'm heading home for a long soak and a bit of thinking."

Ishida accepted the heavy trophy, hefting it a bit to adjust balance since he wasn't quite as strong as her. "All right. Uh... Lorelei, are you okay? You look kind of distant..."

"Oh, I'm great," she assured him, with a grin. "One of the best nights of my life. Just... got some thinking to do. I'll see you 'round..."

Humming her old, favorite rock song to herself, Lorelei pondered something as she wandered home. After all, for all the fighting, for all the bickering, for all the disagreements... she DID have one person she hadn't really thought of as a friend until now...

[4] honor and duty

Her duty was clear.

Exercising that duty was left to her own judgment. As she had monitored his progress, she noted the steady pattern; arrival, departure. He would be safe on his route home and would not need oversight. However, the intel opportunity here at this run-down bingo hall would be quite valuable if the one known as M ever turned on them.

For the past two meetings of their support group, she had stayed behind a few minutes after Mallory's departure, observing and noting anything she could about their powers and their personalities. All of them could be potential enemies or potential allies in a conflict, and these observations would prove invaluable if such a time came.

When the one known as Melvin introduced a new person to the support group, she took extreme notice from her hidden spot in the rafters of the bingo hall.

When she saw his purple-rimmed glasses, and he began killing them, she knew what had to be done.

Silently, she ejected the tranquilizer round from her sniper rifle. A simple bullet was slipped into its place. A simple instrument of killing, like the bullets she had fired countless times in her past, bullets that claimed countless lives. It was all part of her purpose. Taking the life of her enemy now would be no different...

Her finger did not squeeze the trigger, despite having the enemy within her sights. One tap behind the ear and it would be over...

Her finger did not squeeze the trigger, even as M screamed and exploded, taking the enemy's hand with him.

It did not squeeze the trigger after the stranger had vanished. There was no point then. She had missed the shot.

"Meiko Mirai."

Her instinctive stealth worked against her, as her employer turned in surprise towards her voice. "Wh—!?" Meiko blurted, before resuming her businesslike poise as best she could. (To put Meiko in such a position was not forgivable. To make her lose face in front of her employees was a mistake. To make a mistake in her name was—) "Kisei. When did you get here? I didn't hear you come downstairs..."

"As the ban has been lifted... I request a mission," Kisei spoke, measuring her words twice before speaking them.

"A mission...?"

"Yes. I would like to request one. Any one will do."

Her employer consulted F.P., as expected. "I actually did have a potential offer called in directly yesterday, but... it's in Urbana, and I didn't think it would be appropriate to draw that much attention..."

"I will endeavor not to put the house at risk, Meiko Mirai. You can count on me," Kisei spoke, desperate to put faith behind her words. "I will prove that to you as I support your efforts and ideals."

"...right. Why the sudden interest...?"

(To lie to your employer is an unforgivable act. To obfuscate is an unfortunate must in a situation such as this.)

"I have my reasons. I need to reacquire my focus," Kisei decided to say, telling half of the truth. "Meiko Mirai... I rarely make requests of you and I apologize if the suddenness of this one offends—"

"No, no... it's okay, Kisei. Get your gear together and I'll dig up the details..."

She made certain to leave the metal bullets out of her gear pack. She wouldn't make that mistake twice.

This journal can be very effective for working out my various problems. Father knew it would be instrumental in my development, growing into the human condition as I was. However, it has failed me in this matter.

I have had two weeks to fill multiple pages with my thoughts about what transpired on that night, and I still have not reached a satisfactory conclusion. Of course, matters of honor are rarely simple to resolve; it took me years to make my ultimate decision regarding what to do about my father's murder. I have chosen his path instead of the strict and self-destructive one I followed before... but even taking a flexible path in this case would not allievate the problem.

I had my enemy in my sights, and I did not take his life because to do so would be a dishonor... even if it meant he would continue to plague our existence, and likely attack us again. I have not yet formulated an adequate defense against that attack, and therefore it has a strong chance of success. In essence, by trying to uphold my employer's ideals, I may have condemned her to an early grave... and I cannot bring myself to tell her directly that I have done this.

Perhaps it would help to transcribe my memory of our first encounter.

I took the position of tactical expert and covert operations specialist with Mirai Consulting to aid my quest for my father's killer. A mobile Transient business would provide excellent cover and give me means to access other realities cheaply. I was quite surprised to find out that Meiko Mirai knew of me before I even showed up for my job interview, but I did not let her know it.

"You came highly recommended by Ryo, when I mentioned who was applying for this job," Meiko had told me. "He said he couldn't think of a better person for the role. But he also told me that previous to this point, you were an assassin for hire... which wasn't on your résumé."

"I did not feel it was applicable to the job in question, and thus irrelevant," I explained. (I had not lied to her; I simply felt it would not be appropriate to bring the matter up.)

"It's very relevant," Meiko warned, clearly sounding displeased. "I need someone familiar with combat tactics, covert espionage, technical defensive measures... things which would be helpful on troubleshooting missions, things to keep us safe while we're undergoing missions. But I don't need a killer."

"If my employer doesn't require my services as an assassin, I do not have to use them," I suggested. "It's simply another talent I have, and not mandatory. I did not expect to be asked to kill in the first place; I believe my other skills will be sufficent to serve your needs..."

"Good. Because one condition of hiring you is that you are not to take a life again while under my employ," she stated. "I put the same condition on Lorelei's contract—although for someone from Tribal Alpha, she's got a pretty good perspective on the value of human life... so. Ryo recommends you, you have the skills I need, and as long as you can adhere to that guideline I'm willing to give this a try. Acceptable?"

"I... must humbly request one condition in addition," I added, knowing what needed to be done. "I must be allowed to resign with twenty-four hours' notice, at any time. No questions asked."

Meiko looked unsure, as she should be. "Two weeks' notice is standard, Kisei..."

"I apologize for the burden this places on you, but I may have... family business arise," I noted. "If that day comes, I will need to leave with great speed. I will endeavor to avoid doing this during a critical time, but... I must make this request. If it negates my hiring, I will understand..."

It did not negate the hiring. Although she had misgivings, Meiko hired me, based on Ryo Noyori's faith in me.

I strove to validate that faith every day. I carried out assigned tasks with maximum efficency and skill. I worked with Duke of Duke's Munitions to adapt my rifle for non-lethal ammo types... tranquilizer rounds, beam weapons, and the like. I also employed rounds of mass destruction, but only for times when demolition or forced entry was required.

To date, I have not taken a single life while on Meiko's staff. I have kept my honor, and upheld my duty as outlined by my employer. Even in the brief time where I resigned to hunt my father's killer, no longer bound to her contract, I did not take his life...

But when my enemy, the Mallory-person who had attacked us in Antiparadisia was within my sights and prone to the swift strike of a true killing round, I did not pull the trigger. Because in doing so, I would break my contract and dishonor myself.

In doing this, I may have damned Meiko, Mallory, Lorelei, Eiko, and myself to a future death.

Was it a matter of fear? I cannot conceive that. I have killed before, hundreds of times. I was trained to do this. But if I have not killed in years since, perhaps my emotional center has indeed shifted... or my ethical center. Is this morality? Is this a matter of logic? Is it simply honor? No laws, no codes of life conduct seem to cover this situation properly... not even the code that my father lived and died by.

The flexible path my father followed would have suggested that taking this dishonor was an acceptable thing. Leniency in the face of strict discipline enabled you to do what was needed, even if it was illogical, even if it was 'wrong' on several levels. That leniency allowed me to live to see this day, as I decided I did not need to take my life for my failure to protect Father. But that leniency would have also suggested it was right to go ahead and kill the man.

Perhaps that leniency was right. Perhaps I have made a mistake. But in doing so, would I have alienated myself from those who live in this house? Lorelei, who lived for the thrill of the hunt and 'killed' thousands, has not taken a life despite her clear passion for battle. Meiko has never taken a job which required any of us to kill. By claiming a life, I would become seperated from them—akin to the video stream outlaw hero who saves a town from evil, but then must leave, as his tainted lifestyle of violence has no place in a growing community of life...

...and now I am repeating earlier journal entries, without progress. Much as I pointed out at the start of this entry.

I must take action.

I will wait until the ban on departure is lifted (a ban I helped put in place by not ending this threat). When that time comes, I will request a mission. And I will adhere to my employer's ideals. I will not let Meiko down—through my action or inaction. I must prove her faith in me is still justified.

It was possibly the least defensible place in the entire building.

The walls were glass, all four of them; as a perfect crystal cage, stylish it may be, it succeeded in trapping those within from free movement while simultaneously exposing them to any and all dangers surrounding. At least it was the top floor of the building; up here there would be little outside beyond a few cubicles... which, of course, were perfect for taking cover during a running firefight...

The occupant was the other half of the problem. A very unpleasant individual, who wasn't pleased with anything Kisei did and felt the need to express that displeasure at every available opportunity.

"I thought I made it very clear to that Mirai woman," he repeated for the third time while irritably tapping a pen on paper. "The death threat said I would be dying at one in the MORNING. Not one in the afternoon! Why are you here so early? I have work to do!"

"My apologies, sir," Kisei spoke with a small bow of repentance, because she wanted to be absolutely professional today. "But tactically, we can't assume the one hired to kill you will strike at the time he has predeclared.

Relying on drama in this situation could lead to mission failure; therefore I must guard you for the duration of the day as well as the night."

"I have WORK to do during 'the duration of the day,' you know," he continued. "And I can't do work with you looming around! At the very least you can go wait by the door instead of here by my desk, yes?"

"If the client wishes me to stay by the door, I will. However, I should note that I will be less effective in my reaction time to threats by four seconds if—"

"DOOR!"

So Kisei stood by the door.

The curator refilled his coffee mug from a grimy, well-used pot. Time passed.

"Could you not look in this direction, please?" he asked.

So Kisei looked away.

"Could you not loom so much, please? Even from over there, I can feel you looming!"

"I can assure the client that I am making efforts not to loom—"

"I can't do this. Forget it. Just get out," the curator insisted, pointing to the door with his pen. "I will not have the tranquility of my office violated by some paramilitary commando! Even if it is one I hired myself. Go lay tripwire mines at the exits or something, but whatever you do, do it ELSEWHERE. Thank you."

"Sir—"

"ELSEWHERE!"

Rather than lay tripwire mines at every exit, which would have been dishonorable AND overkill, she set up simple motion sensors at every exit. This took one hour.

She also patched into the security camera system of the museum, feeding the video streams into a multi-function pocket monitor she had brought with her. She didn't expect a skilled assassin to come within sight of any camera, but it was something to do, and it took another hour.

But eventually, she ran out of preparations to make. The musem already had decent security, and Kisei's enhancements raised the bar to more than adequate levels. All she could do now was wait for the killer to strike, which supposedly would be transpiring at one in the morning. The rest of the time she could sit and meditate, or...

Or browse the artwork.

A value judgement was required. Focusing on her duty was the entire point of this exercise, to prove beyond a shadow of a doubt that she could support her employer's efforts with maximum effectiveness. But with maximum effectiveness already achieved through her preliminary work, she was left idle —and would it be dishonorable to enjoy the museum's cultural artifacts on the company dime...?

After all, she had decided in recent times to walk the path of her father once more. His path consisted of appreciating life, rather than sitting and waiting for it to go by in between missions, as she had been doing for years. To walk that path, she MUST appreciate the artwork. It was the only honorable thing to do. Unless honor didn't enter into it...

With a head full of conflicting ideals, and no clear answer on how to proceed, she made an opinionated judgement call rather than one of pure logic. Much as her father would, when given two equal opportunities. She would appreciate the artwork until her duty called that evening.

Decision made, she threw herself into the task with the same intensity she gave her official duties. But this wasn't a cold, mechanical undertaking—it could not be, in order to be truly an art appreciation. Painting by painting, sculpture by sculpture... she'd move from one to the next, trying to explore how each piece made her FEEL. Artwork was not simply pleasing to the eye or aesthetically clever, it was an expression of the artist's soul. Without giving it a full contemplation, from the eye to the mind to the heart to the soul, she could not uphold the artist's honor. This was her father's wisdom.

These hours passed much more quickly than the motion tracker and security camera hours. Slowly, her mood of conflict and confusion faded... the issues of recent days pushed aside for now, her whole filled only with art. With the falling leaves of autumn oil paintings, with the subtle facial expressions of portraits, with the ivory purity of a fine sculpture... she embraced the rare feeling of truly losing yourself in a creative vision. The sensation she sometimes felt when writing her poetry, even in the dark years where she would let time slip away in the cold dark of her room...

Painting to painting, sculpture to sculpture...

To a man.

Perhaps because she was fully entrenched in an art-appreciation mindset, the first thing she did was evaluate his aesthetics. Handsome features, with a strange mix of feminine graces and masculine traits; eyes with a soft expression as they slid over the oil paintings, eyes that truly read the world around them instead of looking for the next means of fulfilling one's needs, eyes of a deep green like the jade of an ancient empire...

If he had noticed her stare and returned it, if he had looked puzzled or disturbed to her, she might have turned around and pretended she wasn't looking. She might have walked away.

"Breathtaking, isn't it?" he asked, not looking in her direction, too wrapped in the painting of a cherry blossom field in spring.

Her appreciative stare shifted by reflex to the painting, and continued to evaluate.

"Every petal was crafted by one stroke of the brush," she explained, tracing the subtle texture with a finger (but not directly touching the painting, as that would be insulting to the artist and destructive to the art). "Thousands of cherry blossom petals, and every one was painted in a single gesture. None of them rushed, every one given the same tender care. Aside from the rest of the work's value, this alone makes it unique..."

He finally looked at her; but it was a side glance, out of the corner of his eye. Nothing that would disrupt the spell of the moment. "Are you familiar with the man's other works...? There are a few in the gallery on the third floor. He moved from nature scenes to portraits in the second half of his life. Some say his latter work was more sophisticated and mature, but I always enjoyed his love of nature's simple beauty more..."

"I... have been to the third floor," Kisei said, remembering the motion detectors she planted there—and the memory breaking her trance. "I have not visited that gallery yet, however. Perhaps I will; thank you for your suggestion. Excuse me."

"You're going now?" he asked. "Wait, I'll come with you... let me get my bag first, I left it by the benches—"

"You wish to come with me?"

"I'd love to discuss his work further," he explained. "Especially with one who understands art. Unless... you'd prefer to go alone?"

Yes, I would, Kisei thought. She had enough things on her mind today to add conversation with a complete stranger on top of it all...

Which is why it made absolutely no sense when she agreed to go with him.

For hours, they walked the museum. They explored, they examined the art... they spent time together so intense, so rich that Kisei felt she was running even as she walked, trying to keep up with what was happening to her...

His name was Gabriel, and he was a freelance photographer. A transient, much like herself; moving from reality to reality in his own cottage—which doubled as a dark room and development lab.

"The word 'photograph' derives from the ancient process of using light-sensitive chemical reactions to produce the picture," he explained to her, as the two sat at the museum's cafe, to take a rest break. (His heavy duffel bag, source of his momentary arm strain, was stored under the table.) "Even though modern cameras can capture directly to an image file which can be manipulated with ease, I've always appreciated the ancient ways of doing things. I don't think you can really consider a screen image 'art', when the process to make it involves so very little effort or thought..."

He talked a great deal, but it wasn't his fault. Kisei found herself not talking very much at all. She'd listen, she'd nod her head, she'd interject when he hit a subject she was knowledgable about... but mostly, she'd listen. His voice, his words, his poise as he discussed art with her... it was like appreciating a sculpture. Her mind was simply soaking it in, trying to contemplate it...

But coming to no answers, unfortunately. She wasn't sure why she'd let him accompany her. It served no purpose, and only served to wreck the silent, simple journey she was undertaking. Granted, when they approached a work of art, having his insight helped add to and refine her own... and even when not directly confronting the artwork, the empty time he'd fill with his words was almost art in and of itself... but why? Why break her solitude for someone she barely knew? (Even if 'barely knew' was more and more false as he talked away...)

She was about to call a halt to this strange experiment when he started asking her questions, rather than supplying answers to ones she had chosen not to voice herself.

"I really should apologize, I've probably been talking your ear off," he started. "I have a habit of doing that to avoid quiet moments. It's a personal flaw, I know. So, you know what I do for a living; what do you do?"

"Me...?" Kisei asked, mentally cursing herself for such an obvious, hypothetical prompting.

"Well, of course you... unless there's someone behind you?" he asked, pretending to lean around her, looking for a third party. "If you'd prefer not to talk, that's all right; I've been getting this feeling that you prefer not to..."

"...I am a troubleshooter," she responded, after a moment. "Freelance, much like yourself. I work for a firm which handles problems."

"Really? What kind of problems? Your uniform seems a bit, ah, military..."

"Sometimes military, but simply... problems in general," she explained, feeling self-conscious about her attire for the first time in years. "What I wear is simply an homage to my past, I suppose... it's not mandated by my employer. Although I have certain standards to adhere to, I am not honor-bound to a particular dress code."

"Honor-bound to a dress code? So if she asked you to wear a paper hat and rubber waders, you would?"

"If honor demanded it, of course," she asked, puzzled at why such a thing would be called into question at all. "However, my employer is... generally quite lenient on matters. And strict on others. ...it is complicated, and probably of no interest to you."

"No no, it's quite interesting. And it's only fair, since I've unloaded half of my life on you..."

"So... this exchange of personal details must be reciprocated?" she asked, trying to puzzle through social customs she was not entirely familiar with.

"I wouldn't call it a matter of honor or anything like that," he noted, holding up his hands disarmingly. "It's okay. It's up to you. Just like I said, if you prefer not to..."

"It is not preference, I am simply... not used to such things. I admit to this, it has been many years since my social training..."

"Social training?"

"I had a very... we shall say 'unusual' upbringing," she decided to say. "Only recently have I begun to try and... hmm. This is complicated to explain... to you or to myself, for that matter. Let us just say I am socially awkward, and leave it at that."

Gabriel tapped his fingers on the cafe table. "If you want my advice... and as you've been receptive to anything else I've said, I might as well go ahead and offer it... 'leaving it at that' is the source of your problem. Not wanting to go in-depth, not wanting to share. But at the same time, you must want to share on some level, or you'd have told me (quite politely, I suspect) to take a hike hours ago..."

"I admit to being confused on that issue," she said, trying to be honest and open now that the challenge was laid down. "Although I would have been perfectly comfortable with browsing the museum alone, I decided to allow you to follow me. And I have listened to you. And yes, I have spoken up at this moment when you decided to press me... so..."

"So...?" he prompted, leaning forward.

The prompt went unrewarded, as Kisei's brow furrowed. Conflict arose again, conflict like her honor clash, conflict as she'd had to deal with over and over recently...

"Tea. You could use a cup of tea," Gabriel decided. "It's perfect for soothing the nerves. We'll have tea, and talk, and I think you'll find—"

"No."

"No?"

"I'm afraid... I cannot," Kisei said, rising from her chair. "I am appreciative of what you are trying to do. Perhaps I have been in my shell for so long that coming out is difficult, but... this doesn't feel right."

"Let's explore that, then!" he suggested, trying to keep things rolling. "Why doesn't it feel right?"

"First of all, I do not know you. I know OF you, quite intensely after our brief but rich time together—but... I do not feel right discussing 'in depth' with you. This is too sudden... not yet, not now..."

"Perhaps another day?" Gabriel asked. "I wouldn't mind seeing you again. There's a wonderful museum in Nippon which I've been meaning to visit, if you get some time off and you're still interested after—"

"There is a second reason," Kisei interrupted. "And I cannot work around that. This is a matter of honor and duty, Gabriel. Not here, not yet. Not like this. I must go now and prepare for tonight..."

"Second reason? What do you mean? Kisei—"

Before the situation could grow more unpleasant for either of them, Kisei left. She did not run; she walked quickly. Very quickly, out of the cafe and to the spiral stairs up to the curator's office... back to her duty.

The conflict inside her raged on, but she knew that this was the right decision. More important matters had to be settled before she dared to work through that aspect of this puzzle...

She was truthful to him—although her actions could be read as dodging an uncomfortable emotion, there was more to her decision than that. This was a matter of honor and duty.

For the remaining time, she sat on a bench outside the glass walls of the curator's office, and meditated. Exactly as she had planned to do before getting involved in the art, and getting involved with him. Time sped along quickly, passing her by just as the museum patrons did...

Eventually the flow of patrons slowed to a trickle, and stopped. Closing time came and went. Light from external windows darkened. Midnight came, and went...

The assassin wouldn't strike until one in the morning. While it would be more intelligent to declare one time and strike at another, to catch your prey unaware, this particular killer would not do that. Beyond honor, there was a need there which Kisei could predict—a need to settle affairs.

At precisely 12:59am, Kisei walked into the curator's office. She loaded a tranquilizer round in her rifle, stopped at his desk, and turned to face the one who dropped from the ceiling in front of her.

Perhaps it was the calm, assured way in which she stood that made him pause. Perhaps it was the look, which said: I know. So even as the curator was in a coffee-fueled panic frenzy in the background, she filtered it out—focusing only on the assassin, as he slowly pulled off his mask.

"How did you know...?" he asked.

"When you asked if my employer had a dress code, you used 'she'," Kisei explained, keeping her rifle trained on him. "I never told you I was employed by a woman."

"You stayed with me after that," Gabriel noted, not bothering to raise the silencer-equipped pistol he held. "Why was that? Were you trying to learn more about your enemy?"

"That is the question I wanted to ask you. But I couldn't ask you until now; it wasn't the right place, it wasn't the right time. You persisted in talking to me, potentially blowing your cover, wanting to get 'in depth' with me... was it simply to learn more about your enemy? Or was it something more...?"

"It was something more," he confirmed, honesty at gunpoint as well as chosen honesty. "It was because you wouldn't talk to me. I could tell there was something there, and it intrigued me... I had to know more. I wanted to help you... that's all. It stopped being about investigating my enemy twenty seconds into it all."

"You said you wanted to go to a museum in Nippon, but you knew things would come to this," she continued, being the asker of questions instead of the source of answers for a change. "Why did you ask me to do that...? The one you knew was your enemy?"

"We're both professionals. We seperate our work from our personal lives," he said. "We could enjoy the artwork, we could enjoy time together, and still do what we had to do. Right...? I hope I'm right, Kisei. Because I can honestly say that I wasn't expecting to feel this way about you..."

"Even with as little social skills as I have, I know that moving this quickly in a potential relationship is untoward, Gabriel."

"I'm an intense person," he admitted. "I see something and I go after it with every fiber of my being. I apologize for moving a bit too quickly, but when I saw something that intrigued me so deeply... well, I had to do it. Perhaps that's what drew me to the work, that need to seize the moment..."

"I... am not certain I am ready for that sort of thing, Gabriel. But aside from that, if as you request, we are to be professional aside from personal—"

She squeezed the trigger. A tiny yellow dart embedded itself in Gabriel's neck.

"Then I must execute my professional duty before we can consider the personal desire," she concluded, lowering her weapon.

It would have been poetic, if he slowly fell, and she turned him in to the authorities. This one who seemed to care for her from first sight...

It would have been art.

Instead, he did not fall. He didn't even get drowsy.

"Immunity," he explained, raising his pistol to take aim at her, even as he pulled the useless dart from his neck. "I have implants that render me immune to most common knockout drugs and stun weapons. If you want to defend your client, you'll have to use deadly force, Kisei... because that's what I'm afraid I have to use to go through you."

Kisei's rifle wavered. She didn't have any steel bullets, not this time.

...but there was the explosive round she normally reserved for locked doors...

"I wish it hadn't come to this," Gabriel said, looking regretfully down the barrel of his gun at her. "I won't kill you while you're helpless, however. If you have a real round, I'll let you chamber it. Although... from what I researched about Mirai Consulting, they don't use deadly force, correct?"

"...as a matter of honor..." Kisei mumbled, hand twitching as she wanted to go for that explosive...

"A matter of honor," he recognized. "I saw a conflict behind your eyes all day. That's what it is, isn't it? A former assassin told not to kill... can you use that force against me? I don't want to have to kill you if you can't even defend yourself, but if I must..."

She spared the tiny, tiny fraction of a second it took to look at the reflection off the glass office walls. Just to make sure.

Kisei took a deep breath, and let it out with a sad sigh.

"As much as I wish to have resolution on that conflict... I regret that I will not be able to find the answer this evening," she said, lowering her rifle.

"Why is that, then?" Gabriel asked, keeping his pistol raised.

"Because in our self-involved moment, both of us have lost track of my client," Kisei explained. "And if you'll notice the open office door, and the strewn papers outside... you'll understand why."

Gabriel lowered his weapon. He knew Kisei wouldn't trick him, purposefully make him let his guard down. Both of them tracked the curator's progress together...

...where he fled the office in a panic while they were so wrapped up in exchanging words...

...where he lost his folder of paperwork, and one shoe...

...and where he tripped over a railing, plunging five stories down the central spiral staircase of the museum. Judging from the fact that he was still down there and not running away at high speed, it was safe to assume he wouldn't be moving under his own power ever again.

Gabriel scratched his temple with the tip of his gun, confused.

"Well, now... where exactly does that put us?" he asked.

"As distasteful as the stalemate is, I believe we have both fufilled our duty," Kisei explained, the logic of it falling into place. "My client is dead, even if it wasn't by your hand; your client will be satisfied. I protected him from you even if I couldn't protect him from his own stupidity; my employer will be satisfied."

"It's... a bit droll, isn't it?" Gabriel said, looking frustrated. "That completely destroys the tension we had earlier..."

"Of that, I am thankful. If that tension had persisted... I might have made a grave mistake."

"You would have shot me...?"

"I might have chosen poorly. And since I'm still not certain how to resolve my dilemma, any choice could have been poor," she clairified. Stepping away from the railing, she slung her rifle to her back. "I believe this is where we part ways, Gabriel..."

"Then... will you see me again?" he asked. "Personally, not professionally. I meant what I said, Kisei... and I know you want to open up to someone. I can sense it inside you—"

"You might be correct. Perhaps that is the next step in my father's path, to find myself again through others... but for now, it will not be with you," she said. "You are impatient, Gabriel. Intense and passionate. I am not. Perhaps another day..."

"I... can learn to wait. I'd do that for you, Kisei."

"If you truly mean the things you profess, then you will be able to wait," she agreed. "Farewell."

She had told one lie that day.

The tension inside her wasn't truly broken by the untimely and vaguely comedic death of her client. As she entered the house once more, she could still feel that tension wound up inside her... the sort that would cause problems with her sleep patterns, even this late at night. If she intended to face the next day with a clear head (which she would have to do, if she wanted to face Meiko and explain the debaucle), she would need to unwind.

After tiptoeing past the sleeping Mallory, after depositing her working gear and uniform in her room, she entered the one place she rarely visited—the Onsen-of-the-Month Club door.

With a towel snug around her body, she was fully prepared to let the warm water wash her cares away. It was the recommended method Lorelei always espoused, and thus had to be worth something...

Which also explained why Lorelei had beaten her to the punch.

"Pardon, I had assumed the onsen would be empty this late at night," Kisei explained, stopping at the door between the antechamber and the onsen proper. "I will retire to my chambers and not interrupt your meditation—"

"I'm soaking, not meditating, Kiss," Lorelei clarified, leaning back in the water and sipping from a tiny sake cup. She had, as usual, forsaken any covering towel. "It's not like you interrupted me scrawling down poetic ramblings..."

"I see. Either way, I shall—"

"I was just thinking, really," Lorelei continued, setting her sake cup down. "Pondering the day. Nothing huge."

...slowly, Kisei lowered herself into the water next to her housemate.

"I have been 'pondering' my day as well," she responded. "It has been an unusual one for me."

"You, have an unusual day? This I MUST hear! Tell, tell! Tell or I'll force it out of you—"

"There will be no need for that, Lorelei."

Because Kisei wanted to tell her.

She started out with the chance encounter with Multi. The indecision, the honor conflict, missing her shot.

She talked about the week she spent holed up in her room, turning it over and over, trying to find resolution and failing. She talked about her fears that she would have dishonored herself, her employer, perhaps even her father regardless of what decision she'd have made. How her personal diary was of little use, just the same words written over and over without any real progress...

And how she met someone very strange today, a man so keenly interested in her and interested in trying to help her. Someone who made her talk when she'd rather be quiet, assuming she really did wish to be quiet, which she was no longer certain of, especially since—

"—I am sitting here discussing these matters with you," she concluded. "Which is not something I would normally do. I trust you appreciate the level of trust I am confiding in you. I feel it is only appropriate, considering the trust you have confided in me from time to time."

"...who, me? What?" Lorelei asked, admittedly a bit dazed by the onslaught of Kisei Talking Aloud, which was a rare thing indeed.

"I recall the time you were unsure of how to proceed on Tribal Alpha, for example," Kisei exampled. "You were willing to explore that ethical puzzle with me. And in turn, I aided you in your quest to bring resolution to that reality. Which was slightly against Meiko's orders, although I feel in the end they supported her ideals... and I was satisfied with being an enabler of your own ideals."

"A what of my what?"

"I was happy to help," she summarized.

Lorelei leaned back in the water, taking it all in. She scratched one hand behind her head. "Damn, I... damn, Kiss. This is a hell of a lot you're laying on me."

"If you would prefer I do not speak of such things—"

"No no, it's okay, this is good," she said, getting into the swing of things. "All right. Well... so you figure you need to open up more, right? Hell, I could've told you that. Why do you think I keep goading you, pointing out when you act like some kind of robot—"

"—genetic root-human clone, actually, not an android."

"What?

"Go on."

"...ah... anyway, I keep teasing you for a reason, you know," Lorelei continued. "Just like I teased Mallory and Meiko back when both of them were acting like little kids, trying to ignore what was between them. Maybe it's not the most direct way of dealing with things, but hey, sometimes even I like to be indirect... point is, I'd LOVE to see you open up more. I'm all for it."

"And why would you love to see that?"

"Why? Well... jeez, Kiss, you're a friend, you know?" Lorelei said, figuring it was obvious. "I poke and I prod and I make fun of you now and then but that's just what I do. Sure, you frustrate the hell out of me sometimes, but lately you've gotten a lot better and keep getting better! So... what was my point again? Sorry, I'm a little drunk..."

"I believe I got your point prior to the moment when your rambling grew incoherent," Kisei teased in her dry sort of way.

"Right! That's the spirit!" Lorelei said, putting an arm around her shoulders. "All right, now. In the spirit of opening up, I order you to have a drink. And I'm gonna solve your little to-kill-or-not-to-kill dilemma in a way that's extremely stylish and simple and will have you kicking yourself repeatedly!"

Kisei poured herself a drink, while raising the One Questioning Eyebrow she traditionally gave Lorelei at times like this. "I have my doubts about your ability to do that, but I welcome the attempt..."

"Right! Oh, this is just gonna blow you away, I know it," Lorelei said, pumping a fist in glee. "Here's the answer. You ready?"

"Of course."

"Ask Meiko."

The pause indicated Kisei was waiting for her to continue. She held her sake cup steady, not wanting to sip until an appropriate time...

"No no, that's it," Lorelei responded to the implied hypothetical query. "Ask Meiko. I mean, the problem is you want to be honorable and obey Meiko's edicts, right? Okay, so you walk up to her, and you say 'What if Multi, the guy who we know wants us all dead and has been actively hunting us down and just wiped out a ton of Mallory's friends, happens to walk in front of my rifle and I happen to have a bullet ready?'"

"She... would instruct me not to kill, as she has in the past—"

"I think you're confusing her GENERAL ideals with PRACTICAL reality," Lorelei said—tipping Kisei's sake up upwards, so she could finally take that drink she was holding. "Look, right now, we're all in hot water. And I don't mean literally, okay? I mean Meiko might be willing to compromise her ideals in favor of not getting horribly killed by a psychotic freak. I bet you that when you ask her tomorrow, she'll agree with me—probably after making some faces and using words like 'begrudgingly' and stuff, but she knows what the score is. And once you have it clarified, well, you're not going to have to worry about what's honorable. You'll just... know."

Kisei opened her mouth to disagree, and closed it when she realized she didn't.

"...why had that not occured to me before?" she asked herself aloud.

"Well, duh. You weren't talking to anyone that week, remember? Not Meiko, not anyone. So busy sitting in your little hole trying to figure it out yourself, not askin' anyone for help..."

"Yes... yes, that would explain it. ...I thank you, Lorelei. This solution is indeed, as you previously declared, 'stylish and simple'. I will refrain from kicking myself, however, as it would serve no purpose."

"Right, then! Now, I will extract my payment for this advice..." Lorelei replied, looking sinister.

"Payment...?"

"See, I'VE been pondering my day too. And while I don't feel like going into intensive detail right now, I can tell you what I decided at the end of it all: I've really gotta party down with my friends more. I was figuring Meiko would be more receptive, despite being attached to Mallory at the hip... but now here you are, getting all cozy with me, so why not? In payment for my sagely wisdoms, you're hitting the town with me tomorrow night!"

"Ah. You are proposing that we engage freely in the nocturnal social activity."

"Bingo!" Lorelei cheered, setting the sake bottle down for now—she'd had enough, not wanting to get completely drunk. "It's settled. Tomrorow, we wear hot and slinky outfits and go club-crawling until we can't see straight!"

"I am not interested in sexually provocative dress or overindulgence of alcohol, Lorelei."

"Okay, okay, I admit that was hoping for too much. But what about the 'we' part...? What do you think?"

Kisei considered the offer briefly. "Assuming I am not assigned a mission by my employer at the time... I suppose I would be available for such an endeavor. Although it is not exactly my 'thing', I will warn you. I may not enjoy it and would require that we end it at any time."

"Ohhh, take it from a seasoned pro, you'll have some fun! Here's your chance to see that there's more to life than a dark and badly furnished little room with sixteen locks on the door! We'll start small, you know, little jazz club here, then a coffee bistro open mike poetry night there, and after a few dozen outings maybe I can finally get you laid and you can learn to relax a little!"

"That will not be required."

"Eh?"

"I am not entirely without experience in the matters of which you are a self-proclaimed expert."

'Slack-jawed' summarized Lorelei's expression perfectly.

"You—?"

Rising from the water, Kisei held her towel in place with one hand, wringing out her hair with the other. "Good evening to you, Lorelei. I believe I will retire to my room now."

"Hey, wait! WAIT! What do you mean, not entirely not having experience of things which I'm proclaimed and so on?"

"I was under the impression that it is dishonorable to discuss such private matters—"

"You're not leaving until you give me all the juicy details!" Lorelei demanded, grabbing Kisei's towel and pulling.

An awkward tumble, a splash, and the battle was on.

[.] one last thing to do...

Technically, you couldn't call it comfort food—not legally. Krap Foods, Inc. had the term trademarked for their handy line of ice cream fudge cheesecake ripple sundaes. Still, the other girls in Meiko's orphanage had always called it comfort food, so comfort food it was.

A little milk and cookies were just the ticket for the young girl grown to be a young woman who was trying her best to be a mover and a shaker in the adult business world while maintaining her sanity and/or emotional stability. Unfortunately, when she quietly padded downstairs that night, she found someone else was already grinding his way through her stash of chocolate chip and 2% lowfat.

Like a kid caught with his hand in the jar which it actually was caught in for a non-metaphoric change, Mallory sheepishly offered the approaching Meiko the cookie he was retrieving. "Uh... sorry, but I woke up when I heard Kisei come home, then I got hungry and Eiko already ate the last of our snacks while we were playing with my cards so I kinda improvised and I forgot this was your jar until I was already through a couple of them, there's one or two left, though—"

"No no, it's okay," Meiko said, joining him to sit on the couch. "Go ahead. ...I'm actually glad you're awake, that's probably healthier for me... you have a minute to talk? Or were you going to go back to sleep right after...?"

"Mhrmm?" he asked, mouth filled with crumbs. (Waste not, want not.)

"Are you... you know... okay with how we're progressing here? Romantically, I mean."

"Err... progressing? What do you mean...?"

"Look, I don't know how to say this without sounding stupid," she warned. "But Gillian suggested I talk about it with you and I put it off all day, so... are you happy with where we are? We've spent some time together over the last two weeks, but nothing really, you know... really ROMANTIC, exactly... ...okay, what's with that look of relief?"

"Ah... heh, um... I was kinda going to ask you the same thing," he said, with the trademark hand rubbing behind his head that Meiko had once found irritating but now inexplicably found adorable. "Ask you, um, once I got around to it. Eventually, you know. Since I've never really had a girlfriend before—err, is that too kids-stuff? 'Girlfriend'? Should I be using 'lover' or 'life partner' or something—"

"So you're just as up a creek right now as I am, then," she concluded, sinking back into the couch in frustration.

"Up a what?"

"Up a creek. With no paddle."

"...oh! Meaning you can't go anywhere because... hey, that's a good one! I'll have to remember it."

"Wha? You, the master of mangling metaphors, never heard—wait, I'm getting sidetracked. MY POINT is that we're both really new at this. So... are you happy with where we are now? Am I doing anything wrong?"

Mallory finished off his milk, setting the empty glass and empty cookie jar on the coffee table. (It was always easier to think with a few calories in you, his father sagely advised.) "Well, considering everything and stuff... I think... we should do whatever we want without worrying about what kind of progress is involved in the doing of the thing that we're up to. 'cause that doesn't really matter as long as we're happy, right? So, um... yeah! I'm happy being with you. But, uh..."

"Yes? What? Anything I can do?"

"Can I kiss you again? Because, um, I really did like it that first time."

"First...? Wait, haven't we—? Not even once since the aquarium?" she asked, rapidly searching her memory and coming up with a big fat zero. "I could've sworn we had... I mean, I've been spending almost all my time with you!"

"Right, right, but we haven't kissed SINCE then," Mallory pointed out. "We've had a lot of fun, don't get me wrong, but we were always watching video streams or you were reading the news while I cleaned or we were baking muffins together like today and I swear the blueberries weren't really all THAT inedible, you did fine—"

Before the boy could finish summarizing their entire relationship to date, Meiko decided to grant that second kiss.

It turned out pretty well, so she moved right to the third one.

Somewhere along the way, she was surprised to find her fingers fumbling at the buttons to her pajama top...

The next few moments were very interesting.

One moment...

It was called 'Urbana Standard Time,' but she knew it was a Bates who originally handed down the standard centuries ago. The PR department had apparently decided that calling it 'RealWare Standard Time' would be too egotistical, and opted not to call a spade a spade.

So, around two in the morning Urbana Standard Time, Gillian Bates was sipping coffee and humming a jovial little corporate jingle. There wasn't much point in sleeping, not when she had so much work to do—work both professional and personal, as she offloaded her organizer's files to her mainframe...

Ahhh, she thought, reviewing the holographic photo which popped up on her viewer. *A fine memory to have this night...*

"Who is that...?"

"Oh, just someone I met today in Restless," Gillian replied, running a finger along the tiny image. "Meiko Mirai, of Mirai Consulting; a tiny independent business firm, not worth buying out. But she's quite a remarkable woman, isn't she? Intelligent, ethical, handsome, a good conversationalist... don't worry, Multi, she's not a threat to my personal secur..."

He wasn't there when she turned around.

Hmmm. That's curious, she mused. *He didn't even use the door.*

One moment...

From the way he was braced against the back of the couch, he saw the purple flash of light over her shoulder well before she did. But both of them felt it, the inrush of air, the *wrong* presence in the room...

Her arms tightened around him, as his own fear tightened inside his heart at the sight.

"Reality shall be determined by the last one standing," Multi recited with a smile, as the room temperature around the pair rose eighty degrees.

There was screaming, but Mallory wasn't listening; instead, he was repeating one phrase to himself, over and over. *I need to do it to save her, I need to do it to save her...*

And then there was nothing, save for a burned-out hole in the middle of the couch.

After the romping and teasing went nowhere, and after Lorelei gave up (but pledged to discover the truth at a later date) both of them fetched towels and headed back into the house.

Or rather, tried.

"I don't get it. Is the thing stuck?" Lorelei asked, as Kisei again attempted to slide the simple wood-and-paper framed door open.

"That is not possible, according to the operations manual..." Kisei replied, having memorized said document the day after being hired. (Always know every exit in and out of a building innately, especially ones which used experimental cross-reality technologies.) But just to be certain, and to hopefully allay her concerns, she pulled on the door handle with every ounce of strength she had in one focused burst...

....and the door snapped off its sliding hinges, revealing nothing save for a brick wall. Not a reality link back to the house.

"Oh, joy," Lorelei groaned. "So here we are, stuck in Noyori Lab's onsen-a-verse with a broken door and nothing but two towels. I swear, I'm gonna—"

"The only way the mechanism could have failed in this manner is if the door on the other side was completely destroyed," Kisei spoke, stepping away from the brick wall, and fetching a nearby bathhouse mop as a makeshift weapon. "Otherwise, it would have responded with an error message. Something has happened back at the house. It would not be inadvisable to assume it is under attack by a certain hostile party."

"What? Kisei, you can't mean—"

"Do you know where Ryo's back door is?" she asked. "I know he has access to all of the onsens for technical support reasons, but it may be our only means to leave this place now."

"—of course," Lorelei replied... fetching a mop of her own, more familiar with double-ended weapons. "But I really, really hope you're wrong..."

Multi was quite pleased with himself, as he stood outside the burning wreckage of Mirai Consulting's mobile home. The dock's fire-prevention systems had contained the blaze, but just as he burned his last remaining rival, the burst was intense enough to utterly destroy the structure in a single moment.

Normally he would have shunned such a flashy display of power, since maintaining a low profile was essential... but with the death of the only one who could have stopped him, why bother restraining himself? It was almost time to put the wheels in motion, and there was no sense in skulking about now.

Of course, there was one loose end...

He glanced down at the sleeping child in his arms.

As the only survivor of the explosion which wiped out her family, no doubt she wouldn't be happy when she woke up. But there was no reason to kill this one; after all, she posed no threat, and children WERE the future. The future was of monument importance to Multi. It was the reason he did what he had to do.

Humming a corporate jingle to himself, he walked through reality, heading for home.

"For quality reality products and technical support, there's only one real choice, RealWare..." he sang.

Hrm.

He'd have to change that, of course. But there was time now. There was time for everything that needed to be done.

Floating...

He was floating. That much he was certain of.

Whether or not he was alive, that was very much in question. Mallory, like most in the multiverse, was not particularly religious. He had no easy answers to what was beyond the thread of life—for all he knew, this could be it. If he heard someone talking to his grave much like Meiko talked to her parents, he'd know for certain, but until then the best he could say was that he was floating.

Experimentally, he raised one arm. It moved, he could feel it move through something wet and thick. The sensation across his skin was burning hot, but a good kind of burn—the sort of burn that, while hurting, lets you know it's a hurt that's better for you in the end. He had no idea why that was, it just felt that way...

Meiko.

That thought slammed down his nervous system like a stack of heavy Reality Engineering manuals. He sat bolt upright—

And rose from whatever liquid he was immersed in, coughing and wheezing as his lungs tried to adjust to breathing air again. His eyes stung, fingers madly wiping away whatever it was, his naked body clamoring over the edge of the (tub?) to get to his feet, to escape, to find Meiko...

The walls were wooden. That was odd, considering the strange crystal structure he'd just climbed out of, with its black immersive liquid. Strange lights danced around the room, or perhaps just dancing in his eyes which were not quite fully adjusted to the situation; he couldn't tell.

One familiar element—his baja sweatshirt and pants, folded neatly on a wooden table nearby. They were burned in places, tattered and nasty, but the yin-yang was still there. He grabbed his clothes and yanked them on, absolutely needing something familiar in this sea of unsettling sights. For some reason, the liquid he was soaking in had evaporated before he got the first leg into his pants...

Out the door, or what was probably a door and not just a beaded curtain of some kind, he had to assume it was a door. He had to assume this was a hallway, despite the oblong shape it took on. More dancing lights adorned the walls, some in the shape of familiar letters but not assembled into words he could read... was he dreaming? He'd heard you couldn't read in a dream. That would explain it, if it was true.

Meiko.

He stumbled down the hallway, hand groping along the hardwood wall, trying to find another door. Even the one he had walked through before had somehow vanished back into the woodwork. Which was impossible.

At least the people rapidly approaching him didn't look impossibly weird. They wore strange white tunics, almost like robes, and were speaking in complete gibberish but at least they were people. Ordinary people. Whom he couldn't understand.

"Where is she?" he asked, blinking furiously, vision a bit blurry without his glasses. (Where were they? He just noticed he didn't have them. They weren't with his clothes.) "Where's Meiko? Meiko Mirai? Please...!"

"Sarhpi, cahy tel dah," a robe-wearing man said, raising his arms in what was presumably a calming manner as they closed on him. "Tu requirl ster..."

Mallory leaned heavily against a wall, trying to press as much of his body against it and away from the people—and fell through what he could only assume, again, was a door and not a beaded curtain of some kind.

Quickly scrabbling to his feet, he noticed two things: One, Meiko's room was much nicer and had a window. Two, the sky outside that window was blue, and the grassy fields were green...

"You need to get back in your tank, Mallory."

He whirled to face a new man, one with a receding hairline, and green robes instead of white.

"You are experiencing some 'culture shock' right now," the man said, carefully pronouncing every word so as not to make a mistake. "That's normal. But your skin isn't done... healing?... yes, healing from the burns. Another hour, and your friend has another three hour, then you'll both be okay and I'll explain everything. This is a promise..."

A multitude of questions rose in Mallory's throat, pouring out with need. "Who are you? Where am I? What's happened?" he asked, asking and asking even if he didn't expect quick answers. "What is going on?! Is Meiko going to be all right...?"

"She'll be fine. You'll both be fine," he said, trying to be reassuring. "Please, just return to your room for now..."

Before Mallory could emit more questions, he felt a tiny prick from behind, and began to rapidly fall asleep. The white-robed man behind him was there to catch him.

The one in green robes breathed a sigh of relief, as Mallory slipped away. "Thank God," he said, wiping sweat from his brow. "What on Earth he-was thinking, getting out of a ri'gn tank early? Let's get him back in, now... ah, heipi mau tu bi, alle..."

This doesn't make any sense, the unconscious Mallory told himself.

Except that it makes perfect sense, the subconscious Mallory told himself. *And you know it.*

13: A Quiet Apocalypse

As the third quarter sales figures were read off, Gillian Bates was wholly focused on the task at hand—swirling her coffee cup around on a diagonal axis with one finger without spilling a drop. It took fine motor control to accomplish this, but she was quite good with her hands... given most of her time was spent tapping away at a workstation, she'd have be.

None of the other CxO's (CIO, CFO, COO, etc.) took notice of this idle activity of their CEO. Or rather, perhaps they did, but they were maintaining the polite fiction and ignoring it. Such a blatantly un-mission-statement-y attitude would earn any other employee a dressing down, but considering the special place the Bates family held within RealWare for the last two aeons, she was allowed a bit of leeway...

And it WAS a dreadfully boring presentation. Profits were stable, of course. They had always been stable. They never really went up too high or down too low—even in times of multiversal recession or recovery, RealWare was a rock. The rock of ages. Nothing could ever unseat it...

The double doors were not flung open. Multi simply pushed them open as anyone else entering the board room might. The fact that there was absolutely nothing dramatic about his entrance, no sense of importance or urgency, drew Gillian's attention away from her beverage mug in an instant. (But she did not let it spill.)

"Yes, Multi?" she asked, before one of her lackeys could ask it. "Is there a security issue at the moment? We are in the middle of something I am told is frightfully important..."

He paused. Clear indication that he had rehearsed this, and knowing Multi as she did, he would likely make a huge speech of some kind. Before he could begin, she made a zipping motion in the air—familiar shorthand between employer and employee, proof of the closeness they had worked with previous.

"You know I'm not particularly interested in the fluff when it's time to get to business, Multi," she reminded him. "Let's summarize. You're here to announce an intention, so you might as well out and announce it."

(Caught him off guard. Typical of him, she thought.)

"I... am here to take over operations of the company," he said, trying to get back into the flow. "I doubt you will believe me, but this is for the best for all concerned across the multiverse. The time is right for—"

Gillian tapped a button on her intercom.

"Security? Gillian Bates. Chief of Security Multi is now fired," she told the grey plastic box. "Please send in... let's see... four officers to remove him from this reality. Consider him armed and dangerous. Gentlemen, if you would please duck underneath the table for the time being to prevent possibility of injury...?"

Her lackeys, of course, sat there with a dumbfounded expression and did nothing. They weren't very good at dealing with such rapid change. Writing them off for the moment, Gillian sat back and waited for the test results...

The first one dispatched wasn't done in a particularly flashy manner. He simply fell sideways, impacting against the far wall as if dropped from an equal height. The problem was that he landed upside down, and thus slid down directly onto his head when gravity resumed normal operations. (Gillian hoped he wasn't too badly injured; a demonstration or not, there was no need to waste valuable workers.) The next two were slammed into each other once, twice... five feet over Multi's head, no less. The final one, that's the one he went all out on—the screams and cracking sounds indicated bones deciding they needed to be broken at the moment instead of whole. He dropped on the spot in the least pleasant-looking position the human body was capable of.

Throughout the process, her former chief of security hadn't broken a sweat. He hadn't broken his cool; he knew he had regained the upper hand, easily sliding back into a position of power. No matter how Gillian had thrown him off his game initially, he was back in contention.

"You didn't have to go that far," Gillian scolded mildly. "All I wanted was a simple demonstration of your capabilities..."

"Now you have me curious," he admitted, walking across the room to stand before her, with no fear whatsoever behind those purple glasses of his. "How long have you known...?"

Gillian steepled her fingers, leaning back in her ergonomic office chair which cost more than Multi's yearly salary. "Ever since you were hired. Or rather, I knew there was SOMETHING unusual about you ever since you were hired. You were quiet, but occasionally too sloppy, Multi. There were occasional fluctuations in our reality engine... each timed with some strange event, some oddity that our programmers couldn't account for in Reality Prime's customized engine coding. You were practicing, weren't you? Honing this unusual skill of yours?"

"You always told me to make the most of myself, Gillian," he reminded. "You sent me to security training seminars. You bought me equipment. You let me hone quite a few skills... and gave me the leeway to hone one of my own, yes."

"I'll get to that in a minute. The second oddity was your personal business jaunts... here, there, and everywhere. Antiparadisia, Nippon, all sorts of unusual locales..."

"Did you send a spy after me?" he asked. "Or perhaps an audio-visual kink...?"

"I couldn't risk it. Not after I trained you so heavily in countermeasures to fight that sort of thing. But I did log your arrivals and departures... your predeclared ones, and the ones where I checked up on you and you didn't happen to be around despite our systems showing you as never having left. It was especially sloppy to vanish on me last night, for instance..."

"I didn't need to worry about subtlety anymore. The first phase of my work is done, after all," he said with some pride. "The competition is eliminated. None remain to interfere in phase two."

"And you don't consider me to be interference, do you...?"

"You've seen a fraction of what I'm capable of," he warned, not in a threatening sense but in a pleading one. "I wouldn't suggest further resistance. We've worked together quite well so far, and I'd hate to harm you..."

"But you'll have to, won't you?" she asked, rising from her chair to meet him eye to eye. "I'm the figurehead. I'm the one who's the undisputed queen of this particular empire, the one who's just as crafty as you, and—I don't intend this as a boast—the one who is much more clever than you. I am a risk to you."

"Clever? I wouldn't say—"

"It's a fact, not a boast," she said, this time more threatening than pleading in her warning. "You're sloppy, Multi. You have great aspirations, it seems, but you've never been able to execute them flawlessly, have you? I can tell from your expression that you HAVE felt frustration at your own errors. Power has gotten you this far, and I suspect power will get you even farther since as you say none can stand against you... but that talent won't help you against me. Having someone like me around only means leaving a strong option open for your downfall. No, if you want to do what you intend to do—and I'm likely not off the mark when I guess that it involves domination of the multiverse through RealWare—you need to kill me. There's no room at the top for two, is there?"

"...reality shall be determined by the last one standing," he recited, his personal mantra.

"Quite right. Otherwise, I'd suggest we work together on your endeavor. I nurtured you, I sponsored you, I waited to see what you would become... I wouldn't want that to go to waste. But you're not going to be able to do this with me, so a waste of some sort is inevitable. You know what you have to do," Gillian told him... and waited.

It didn't take long for her young prodigy to make up his mind. He raised his hand, and she could feel the purple in the air...

She raised her hand to stop him. Instinctively, he did so...

"There's only one problem," she said quickly. "I don't intend to die here. Gentlemen of the board, excuse me—I am stepping out for a while."

In a flash of purple light—originating from the pocket of her business blazer, where her F.P. was tucked away and her hand had been secretly reaching for it—Gillian Bates vanished from the face of Reality Prime on her own terms.

Despite being absent, her words echoed in Mutli's ears. *I can tell from your expression that you HAVE felt frustration at your own errors...*

On impulse, he turned to face the Chief Information Officer, and crumpled his body into a six-inch-wide sphere of flesh within the span of three agonizing, scream-filled seconds.

"From now on you all obey me without question," he nearly growled. "You are not the future, with your generation's backwards stubbornness, but I can tolerate your existence for now. As long as you remain useful and keep this company's mundane day-to-day business afloat, I'll ignore the fact that you continue to breathe. But if you treat me the way she just did, if you even THINK of talking down to me, you will learn the hard way why I am the one in control. Am I understood?"

Terrified faces stared back at him.

"I said, *am I understood?*" he repeated, anger mounting...

Before he had to make another example, there was nodding and agreement and consensus.

Multi left the board room in a much fouler mood than he had going in. Nothing went according to plan except for the most important part... the takeover of RealWare. That was all that was really important to him; any words spoken or actions taken should be trivial in comparison to the actual results. But if so, why was he so angry...?

Victory was his. He could feel it in his grasp; he had crushed all the others, he had at least banished the former shepherd of reality. She would die in time for her disrespectful attitude. He would move to phase two, he would complete the great work, he would be praised for his benevolence and his wisdom... yes. Everything would be well. The big picture mattered most; the future mattered most. The rest he could dismiss from his mind immediately.

Besides, where could she turn to for help in a multiverse owned and controlled by HIS company, RealWare?

The sky was the color of a coredump. Clouds of hexidecimal floated freely, indicating today's system operations status for anybody who needed a quick reference. And in a reality filled with hardcore programmers, engineers and reality hackers, such information was far more important than a daily stock quote or a corporate logo as other realities might have in their skies...

In fact, one wandering programmer was too busy checking on a recent error report hanging over his head to notice the purple flash before him. But he did see the 'enemy' standing in front of him when he looked down, holding her hands in the air.

"I come in peace," Gillian Bates said smoothly, with a tiny smile. "Take me to your leader. Hmm... I've always wanted to share tea with the head of the Open Reality Movement; I suppose I'll have to thank Multi for giving me the opportunity..."

Wooden rafters. Now, those he was familiar with. A soft bed underneath him felt nicely familiar too... and the faint scent of the Great Outdoors, with trees full of sap and birds that sing...

I'm home, he thought.

"You are awakened?"

Except that wasn't his father's voice.

Mallory sat upright quickly and unlike other times when he had been rendered chemically or physically unconscious, he DIDN'T immediately wish he hadn't sat upright quickly. On the contrary, his head was clear, he felt fit and fine, and his sharp focus helped him identify the man sitting at his bedside as specifically not being his father.

Now that he could look at him without a haze of panic, the man felt immediately familiar in that kindly old man sort of way. He was quite healthy for his age, neither underweight or overweight, and had no male pattern baldness to speak of in his silvery locks. In fact, they were tied neatly into a ponytail at the nape of his neck. He closed an ancient-looking yellow and black book as he turned to address Mallory...

"Before you again-run, let me say your friend is fine and she will join us in under two hours," he said up front. "My name is Leeham, and you are Mallory —it was written on the tag in your jacket, yes? You are both safe now. You were burned very badly but I got you to this place, a... a..."

"Hospital?" Mallory guessed, catching on quickly as the man struggled now and then to find the right word.

"I guess that's it. I was never as good at your language as they were," Leeham said, looking slightly upset at his own ignorance. "Hos-pit-al. 'Hyptal'. It makes sense, yes..."

"This doesn't look like any hospital I know of," Mallory said, glancing around what could conceivably have been his bedroom back on Grünwald. "In fact it's one of the only wooden buildings I've seen outside of my home reality and Nippon..."

"I assure you it is in fact a hyp—a hospital. You've seen many things you probably don't recognize, right? Why would one more make a difference?"

"Where am I?" Mallory asked, earlier questions starting to return to the forefront. "What exactly is going on? Last thing I remember, we were... attacked, and yeah, I think there was fire... and you said you had answers! I need to know what's going on! And we have to get home, Eiko and the others —"

"Patience, patience. All will be clear—"

"Is there any particular reason you can't tell me right now?"

"What?"

"Because I know on the video streams they always hold off on the big revelations until the last possible minute but I really think you owe me better than that," Mallory said, trying to be assertive. "Especially since my home was under attack right before I left! So unless there's an important reason I really, really would like to know where I am and how... no, wait, I can answer how I got here I think, but WHERE here is, and how soon I can get back to Restless. Okay?"

"You... ah..." the old man said, trying to follow that stream of babble. "Please, I am not good with the language... talk slower. What is this Restless...? It's a 'reality,' isn't it?"

"Of... course it's a reality," Mallory said, staring at the man as if he'd asked if water was wet. "And we have to get back the moment Meiko wakes up. Can you get me a RealNet terminal, maybe? At least I can get word to Ryo to make sure everything's okay at home. ...and hopefully it's not too late..."

"You can't go back to the multiverse."

"What? I thought this was a hospital, not a prison!"

"No no, I mean... it is impossible. Physically-impossible," he clarified. "For the time being you are here and you cannot leave not because I am wishing-restraining you but because there is no... 'mobile building' you can use, and there is no 'RealNet terminal'. We do not have these things anywhere for you to use."

"That's not possible. Even realities who really, really, really value their privacy like Grünwald have terminals somewhere..."

"Yes, well, we do not," the man said, growing a bit frustrated. "And the reason we do not relates to the story which I intend to tell you. As for why I did not want to tell you right now, I was GOING to wait until your friend was awake, and we were at my home in comfort. That way I would not have to tell the story twice..."

"So tell me now, and I'll tell her later. I promise I'll do my best to remember it and tell it right," Mallory added, even if the man didn't know about his tendency to achieve massive communication breakdowns.

"There is also a matter of the 'culture shock', which I explained—"

"I left home a few months ago and I still haven't fully gotten over the first few culture shocks. I've just gotten used to being confused a lot—like you said before, I don't think one more is really going to make a difference. Now... why can't I leave here?"

"...in the Bard's words, 'as you like it,'" Leeham said, with a sigh. He carefully opened his yellow and black book. "Fortunately the story is brief, as this small book is the only accurate text on that era we had ever uncovered. So, I will read to you from the Notes of Cliff... about what our ancestors termed the Quiet Apocalypse."

It was a dream room. Everything a young girl could possibly want—hundreds of toys, expensive games, complete collections of dolls both common and rare, windows with beautiful views over the greenery of Reality Prime's main campus...

None of that made Eiko happy. Especially after one of the guards let slip that her house had been destroyed and all inside it were dead.

She'd cried for hours after they left her here and locked the door; then she tried to break the windows, but they weren't breakable. The dolls were breakable but some part of her didn't want to break them, since it would really be a waste of perfectly well-invested money in recreational toys. So instead she'd take a few of the board games that were too childish for her and bash them against the wall, leaving little scuff marks on the paint but otherwise doing no damage whatsoever...

Once she couldn't cry any more she plotted escape. Because that's what her oneechan would have done, she'd have been smart and thought about it and tried to thwart her captors. But surrounded by nothing but kid's stuff, locked in with a door she couldn't open or break down and windows she couldn't force, there was very little plotting she could do. There was an air vent in the ceiling, and she'd seen people sneak in and out of buildings countless times through air vents in video streams, but she lacked fancy grappling hooks that would get her up there as well as tools to remove what looked like a very secure grate...

She was busy trying to fashion some kind of climbing gear using only doll hair when the door opened. She made a break for it, running for the door but hit an invisible wall...

"Please, there's no need for that," Multi said, gently lifting Eiko into the air with his talent, and setting her on the bed. And holding her there, just in case. "I'm here to bring you a gift..."

"I want to go HOME," Eiko protested.

"This is your home now," he said, while motioning for the guards to wheel in a small desk and RealNet Terminal. "I understand that the transition will be hard on you. It's going to be hard on everybody; the future can be a frightening thing, I know. But I promise to you that I'll do my best to ease you into the future, just as I will everyone else. And as a token of my sincerity, I'm giving you a workstation... of course, I can't allow you to freely communicate with just anyone, but you can watch any of the RealNet streams and—"

"I want to GO HOME! I don't care about any stupid terminal. You're the bad man who attacked us before, aren't you? Well, my oneechan and my oniichan can't be dead! You're wrong! Oniichan would've protected her..."

"...I see the guards have been a bit loose, and will need to be punished," Multi said, sadly. "I didn't want the revelation to come to you that way, Eiko. You and all the other children of reality are very important to me, and it's important that I earn your trust no matter what I have had to do in the past. You especially, as one of the first, will be of great importance..."

"I won't do anything you tell me to do at all, so nyah," Eiko said, folding her arms. "And you can't make me."

"Actually, I could... but I don't want to. That's not how you start a proper relationship. Which is why I need you as... my spokeschild, I suppose. My liason to the others here in Reality Prime. You've heard of the Preferred Partners Program, correct...? I think you helped negotiate a treaty with I's Land regarding it."

"That's the stupid thing where you get realities to give you their children so you don't shut down their engines."

"I wouldn't use those words, especially not now," Multi said with distaste. "True, the program was little more than a cheap workforce cultivation system before. But now it can be so much more! I've checked with our personnel department and we have about three hundred workers here little older than you. Why should they be doing menial jobs none of the high and mighty RealWare elite cared to do? I want them to help me with MY great work instead. We're going to pave the road to the future, Eiko! A future which will truly belong to the next generation, the ones without the preconcieved notions of what reality 'should' be which have poisoned the multiverse with mundanity. With the imagination and boundless innocence of your peers, we'll—"

"I won't do anything you tell me to at all," Eiko repeated. "I don't care what you're doing or what your crazy talk about the future is all about. You sound like a bad episode of Important Courtroom Drama!"

"...I didn't want to phrase it like this, but you have to work with me instead of against me if you want to regain your freedoms," Multi said, feeling frustration rise for the second time that day. "Obviously I don't want to keep you in this room forever, but until I'm sure you're not going to cause me problems, you'll be staying here. So think about that before deciding what you will and will not do. Now... you can use this terminal to keep yourself entertained, if the toys aren't to your satisfaction. I'll check in on you at dinnertime. Do you want anything special? I can get you food from anywhere in the multiverse. Nipponese, maybe?"

"I'll take a full thirty-two piece sushi platter with caviar and a filet mignon and gourmet chocolate milk with a crazy straw," Eiko quickly ordered.

Multi actually paused to scratch behind his head. "That doesn't sound entirely like the sort of meal a girl your age would want..."

"If you're gonna keep me here like a stupid baka, I'm gonna get what I want, and I want the most expensive dinner I can think of!" Eiko barked back, keen on showing her defiance by exploiting his kind offer. "And... you said I can watch video streams on that terminal?"

"Of course. Anything you want. We have every premium channel, every video-on-demand service—"

"I want to talk to my friends, too."

"That I can't allow," Multi said, reasserting himself.

"Why?" Eiko asked. "Who could I call? You said yourself you killed my family!"

...and Multi actually hesitated. Eiko could see it in his eyes; he wasn't fully sure about something... and the guards hadn't said anything about Lorelei or Kisei, did they...?

"...it's a matter of trust, Eiko," he chose to answer with. "You have to earn my trust if you want the freedom to communicate, and later on, freedom to leave this room. Until then I can't simply give you full access to RealNet, now can I?"

"Then let me talk to my friend Kensuke," she said quickly, seeing her ray of hope. "His address is Kensuke@Onegai. It's a kid's site, messaging for kids. He's my age and he's not anybody special. He'd be safe to talk to, right? You'd monitor what I was saying anyway, right? Right?"

"Eiko—"

"He's gonna be a lawyer when he grows up," she continued, pressing him. "He wants to help people and he never stops reading books or learning things! He's just the sort of person you'd want in this future of yours—and if... if you convince me you're doing a good thing then I could convince him. You'd like that, right?"

I've got him, she thought. *I've got the baka by the things Lorelei keeps trying to talk about before oneechan stops her.*

"I... suppose it couldn't hurt," he decided. "I'll have my people do a background check on your friend first, of course. Standard security protocol. Agreed?"

"Agreed!" Eiko said, giving the awful man a big, cheerful thumbs up.

"Good, good," he said, smiling at last, feeling like things were going well for a change. "In the meantime, I have things to do... I suggest tuning into Reality Prime's corporate feed at three o'clock. Well... tune into ANY feed, really. I'm planning to override all of them. I've got a very important speech to make."

Groggy. Unpleasantly so.

Meiko rarely drank alcohol. A little sake when business called for it, or to celebrate, but nothing beyond that. Some of the girls at the orphanage would always be sneaking out to sample the Adult World in all its vices, but not Meiko; she had her plan, after all. She was already in the Adult World, in a lot of respects...

Memories of the past swirled up to memories of the present, as she rose from the bed. She was wearing some sort of cross between a tunic and a gown, in brown cloth... not her pajamas, which she had already taken half off before—

That snapped her into the moment, for certain. Where WAS she? A bedroom of some sort, a house with a funny shape, everything made of wood...

And Mallory, standing at a balcony, overlooking what seemed to be the upper portions of a vast forest. He turned when he heard her sheets rustle.

"Oh, hey," he said, a bit subdued. "Leeham's gone down to ground level to get some food from the market. This is his place. He said we should just let you sleep, since you were more burned than me and probably had to recover more..."

"Mallory, what's going on...?" Meiko asked, climbing out of bed and moving to join him...

...and seeing something she had never conceived of in all her multiversal travels.

A city in the trees. Each one half-carved, half-built into the natural landscape. There were structures all over the place, each with balconies similar to the one she stood at, some with ornately designed windows... and from what she saw when she dared to look down, not a single asphalt road, no ground vehicles, nothing that looked even vaguely familiar. Still, despite the alien landscape, it was so peaceful and radiant that she couldn't help but feel a sense of calm here...

"What a... nicely designed reality," she admitted, taken aback by the sight.

"It's not a reality," Mallory said. "And we're trapped here. We can't get back home. I think I'd better tell you the story Leeham told me... I don't have his little book but I don't think I'm gonna forget it anytime soon..."

"Story...? Mallory, we've got to get back to the house! We left Eiko there when you... when you saved us..."

"There aren't any mobile houses here, Meiko. No RealNet, either," he said, walking back into the treetop apartment proper and having a seat on a wooden chair. "Assuming he wasn't lying to me, and I really don't think he was... we're not even IN the multiverse anymore. We're somewhere else totally. According to Leeham, it's called 'Earth'."

"Earf?"

"No, Earth. THHH," Mallory thh'd. "It's supposedly a giant ball of dirt hanging in the middle of an open space orbiting a giant ball of gas but I think he's probably wrong about that. Anyway... look, do you trust me when I say we can't actually leave this reality and I'm about to tell you why?"

"I'll draw my own conclusions about the not-leaving part, but I trust you enough to listen to what's probably a long history lesson while Eiko's in peril," she said while sitting on the bed across from him, "Because I know you wouldn't do that without a damn good reason. Right?"

"Right. Okay. Let's see, how'd he start... oh, right. Roughly two thousand years ago, everything was going really, really bad..."

They called it a "Quiet Apocalypse."

Everybody was expecting that if the world WAS going to end, it'd end in some firey nuclear cataclysm or some vast sweeping plague which claimed all life, or maybe even robots coming alive and killing their masters. Something huge. Something that you could really sink your teeth into.

Instead, the "end" came in fits and bursts, with a little bit of everything. First, innocently enough, a computer virus infected every machine on the "Internet" which was running a particular popular kind of software. But unlike other viruses, this one infected through a previously unknown vulnerability and then waited in silence, undetected and polite to other resources on the system...

Several months later, it struck hard, wiping out data all over the world. Not every computer was destroyed in the process, but plenty were—enough to throw the global economy into wild, disoriented lurches up and down the financial scales.

Just as that happened, limited nuclear war broke out between two nations with long-standing grudges. Everybody assumed these weapons would be the end of everything, but only seven of them were used before saner heads finally prevailed. Still, the damage was done, and the resulting mess left in the environment—both political and physical—wasn't helping matters as the world tried to recover from the virus-induced economic woes.

The next phase hit when a virus began to spread. Nobody knew how it started; some suspected mutation from the tiny nuclear war, some suspected government conspiracy, or maybe computer failure at some bioweapons research lab. It wasn't doomsday, but it slowly ate into the population, with no cure in sight. Entire countries were quarantined with little effect, with some people seeming to be immune for no reason at all, with others dying quickly after exposure...

With the vital information networks in turmoil, nations threatening war every day, money markets plummeting and living humans dropping dead... matters were quite clear. Earth was sliding towards doom with steady speed. Every end scenario was playing out at once, none of them really hogging the spotlight, but doing their part to keep things chaotic and deadly for all involved.

Somewhere in the mess, a single technology patent was filed.

Months later, at the nadir of human civilization when nations were openly at war, the poor were starving more than usual and the future was a bleak landscape of endless misery, RealWare arrived.

Using a strange invention by Alfred Bates the First, this corporation promised to save humanity from the dying Earth. They would establish wholly new worlds outside the scope of known reality, where the environment could be controlled, where nobody would have to go hungry, and pioneers would pave the road towards a renaissance, a rebirth of human civilization... somewhere far, far away from here.

There were doubters, of course. But when reports came back from the early adopters that this was no hoax, that the worlds created were pure and safe and ready for settlement, settlers came in droves. The rich at first, but soon the poor as well, as the pricing structures for migration were adjusted. RealWare worked with various national governments, assuring them they would do their best for humanity at large, and all would be welcome in these brave new worlds...

The public, seeing everything fall apart around them, sang praise of RealWare. Nobody else had this technology of theirs; some tried to copy it, but failed. Others somehow... vanished, in mid-research. All the while, waiting lists were filling immedaitely for migration, as entire nations emptied into the newly established multiverse. The affluent and the skilled had their golden tickets but all were in theory welcome... and for five months, RealWare's doors stayed open.

Then they decided they had enough people, and closed those doors. All mobile structures were pulled into the newly independent multiverse, all connections from their RealNet to Earth's networks were severed, and not a single widget of reality technology was left behind on that doomed ball of dirt. RealWare had pulled up stakes and left town.

Earth, as a whole, was livid. They had broken their promise! These new realities were supposed to be salvation for all, not just 'enough' according to RealWare's whims. Rage filled the population, rage and doom as they were the ones left behind. The current leading nation immediately declared war on RealWare, declaring it to be a rogue state harboring terrorism—one presidential election later and they changed their tune, pleading for RealWare to come back and make peace for the sake of all. Neither the warmongers nor peacemongers got anywhere with their aims, since there was no longer any way to reach RealWare or any of the realities in its network.

The multiverse and the universe were now wholly seperate, and never again the two would meet.

"But that's when folks in this real... on this 'planet' started to unify," Mallory continued. "From what Leeham told me, it was like RealWare leaving was a huge kick in the pants... but a kick that made them realize they had to save their own home since now, RealWare wasn't gonna do it for them. Some nations unified, others faded out, the ones that survived enacted new controlling laws to clean up the environment, control the population and so on... basically they got their act together. And now they're really, really advanced compared to the reality we know, which RealWare was apparently keeping as controlled and low-tech as they could... that's why they were able to heal our burns, which would've been fatal otherwise."

"Which I can be thankful for," Meiko said. "As for what I say about the rest of their woes... it's completely not my problem. Okay, so there WAS a 'first reality', and RealWare backstabbed them. Got it. This is utterly fascinating, Mallory, but it's not our problem. We've got more personal issues to deal with, like making sure my sister and my employees are alive and well."

"But that's what I'm saying, I'm saying we might never know," Mallory replied. "We're stranded here! RealWare didn't leave behind anything when they left, no mobiles, nothing. We can't get back! I've... I've brought us to a dead end! I didn't mean to, I was just trying to save you..."

"Without which we'd definitely be dead, so don't kick yourself out of guilt," she ordered. "And yes, we can too leave this place."

"No, we can't."

"Yes, we CAN! Think, Mallory! How did this Leeham guy know you weren't from Earth?"

"He... he must have seen us teleport in. Right?"

"Circumstantial. He knew from the very first minute who you were and what you were and where we're from. And how could he know that if all he had to work from was a school book from days of yore? ...Leeham, if that's you, I know you're waiting downstairs. I heard you come in."

On cue, the old man ascended up from the bottom level of the treetop home. "The wood is a bit rotten," he admitted bitterly. "I need to have it replaced soon..."

"Now do the honor of answering my question," she said. "How did you know we came from the multiverse?"

With a heaving sigh, Leeham gave in.

"You could have been happy here, once I taught you the language your words had eventually evolved into," he said. "I would've welcomed you in. I could grow an extension to the house, I would have my family around me again... if circumstances were different. But I know better than to argue it now. If I had told him the whole truth, well... chances are, Mallory is just as stubborn as his mother was."

If there were a precident, it was long lost in the centuries of forgotten multiversal history.

As far as anyone alive knew, it had never been done before. The idea of overriding every single live RealNet stream everywhere in the multiverse—as well as stream-on-demand services for prerecorded video—was unthinkable. It interrupted the news, it interrupted sports, it even interrupted Love & Hate...

Some people across the multiverse took one look at the face which now adorned their RealNet displays, and thought, "Haven't I seen that guy somewhere before...?"

"I am speaking to you from Reality Prime, home of RealWare," he began. "RealWare, your friend and companion throughout all of history. Always commanded by a member of the Bates family—until now. There has been a changing of the guard. Along with this change, other changes will come... and I felt it was only fair to give you some idea of what to expect. This concerns all of us, everywhere.

"We are about to embark on a brilliant future, all of us. Until now, you have lived in realities which were mundane... pedestrian. Dull. Gravity always moves the same way, there is always air to breathe, there is always a sun and sometimes a moon but otherwise your skies are flat, unappealing colors... essentially you have all lived in the same cookie cutter pattern of Reality. And why? Because RealWare saved their finest creations for the rich, for those who would hide them away from you and indulge in them.

"No longer. My name is Multi, and you may have seen me or someone who looks like me before—but now I am the only one left. I'm going to start changing the realities you know around you, bettering them, improving on the original designs. I have an eye towards guiding us all into a superior age, one where mankind's imagination is truly unleashed... and I think you'll find that over the years, as your children are raised in this wonderful tomorrow, they'll thank you for the cooperation you will be showing me today—"

Eiko turned it off. She'd heard it before. In fact, she didn't think it was possible to be more long-winded and dramatic than he had already been, yet he managed it somehow.

She guessed he had watched a lot of video streams; he was acting just like the hero in some big adventure. He really believed in what he was saying, too, which scared her even more—at least she knew the characters on the screen were just actors and it was all just a big fun story, like playing dolls. He was gonna play dolls too, but with real people...

Scheme. Plan. Get out. She had to be clever and smart and crafty just like her oneechan would be.

Eiko powered on the RealNet terminal.

Just like he'd said, it was really, really restricted. RealWare owned RealNet and could do what it wanted with it; if they didn't want you going somewhere, there wasn't much you could do. Normally this just meant you had to pay extra to visit certain nodes, or you could institute parental controls so your kids couldn't do things you don't like (and you could monitor everything they did do to make sure you still liked it)... but from inside RealWare, under Multi's instructions, it meant this lump of plastic was barely a workstation at all.

But when she tried to log into Onegai, it worked. Of course, huge portions of the node were locked off, essentially she could only message her friends— or rather 'friend' since the restrictions were blocking all her contracts save for Kensuke@Onegai. Which would be enough.

She opened the message composer, praying he still had figured out a way around his parent's rather harsh grounding, and wrote.

"Dear Kensuke, I'm not at my house anymore but I'm okay..."

...he might censor that part, but that wasn't important; if anything it'd raise his suspicions even more. Especially since he knew what Mallory looked like, and now he'd probably seen Multi's broadcast and thought "WTF?", whatever that actually stood for.

"I'm really bored here. I've got a lot of toys and stuff but I lost the My First RealNet Workstation my sister gave me for my birthday which had all my files on it, and I can't get them reauthorized for this one. Can you do me a favor? I really wanna see that episode of Important Courtroom Drama where the interreality superspy in the clown suit was framed for loitering. You know it's my favorite, right? We had so much fun watching that one! There's a copy in the archives here but I wanna watch it with the commercials that were airing when we watched it that day, so I can remember what it was like. Send it to me right away pls. Hugsnkissed! Eiko-chan!"

Hoping she hadn't pushed her luck, she pressed Send with keyboard commands, just like her oniichan had taught her (just like his okaasama had done long ago).

Now, she just had to wait, and hope he got the message. Because they were talking about how the superspy was going along with the frame job just because they had his daughter hostage, and there was this bit where a secret message was smuggled into his dressing room in a cream pie...

She couldn't get a pie over RealNet, but a video file, that she could get. And with any luck it'd have more than clowns and funny commercials.

Alive. It was all alive, and so very, very real...

There were trees on Grünwald, of course. Great trees, tall and proud, with leaves of green and bark of brown and wood of grain and such... and they were generally all alike. Forests of similar trees, arranged in an organized manner for later harvesting. All part of the standard Reality Engine coding package for agricultural realities, staple RealWare programming...

But this, this place was truly alive and wild. Trees grew anywhere they wanted, to any shape and any height they pleased. They grew because they planted themselves through some natural cycle, according to Leeham—an ecology that sustained itself perfectly, even after humanity put a serious dent in it thousands of years ago. In the Realities, a self-balancing ecology didn't come cheaply and usually needed a tweak or two to keep it going... and most folks didn't care one way or another as long as they got their power and their RealNet and their buildings. Trees were decorative and animals were a nuisance...

Animals! He had already seen several birds, many kinds of squirrels as they hiked through the woods. Grünwald had animals—mostly domesticated ones. Wild ones presented a danger to the stability of a reality, RealWare explained. They were available if you wanted them, although they were hard to breed and quite expensive since Reality Engines could only handle life-from-nothing if it was simple life, like plants...

"I didn't think anything like this was possible..." Mallory mused aloud.

"RealWare was never interested in this sort of thing," Leeham commented bitterly, picking up instantly Mallory's unspoken realizations. "If they were, they'd have stayed behind and helped us fix what was wrong. No, instead they decided a controlled reality was the right way to live... one that could be abused as much as you like, without the messy consequences. The sort of mentality that got us into this mess..."

"Things aren't perfect in the multiverse either," Meiko said, gingerly picking her way through the patchy, grassy ground—the hiking shoes Leeham had offered her were too big, so she had to walk carefully. "Engines crash all the time. RealWare has never gotten things fully stable; instead they just make sure the crashes are safe enough to endure until you can reboot or reinstall..."

"Typical of the mentality," Leeham grumbled. "It's easier to change things around a little than get to the root of the problem and fix that. Easier to add a band-aid to a wound, to treat the symptoms and not the disease—"

"As much fun as bantering philosophy is, I'd really like to know where we're going," Meiko said. "'I'll explain when we get there' isn't going to cut it, Leeham. Mallory and I have a serious problem here and if you have a means of getting us home..."

"Don't be hasty, now," Leeham warned, as the group crossed a small creek. "Multiversal folk are always so hasty. Eager to move on, to abandon the past, to press through without thinking too much about why and how—"

"And how do you know about multiversal folk? Have you been there? You have a vehicle, don't you...? That's how you know our language and even a bit about what's out there..."

"What's that huge thing up ahead...?" Mallory asked, pointing to a sizeable lump covered in vines and leaves...

"That, my dear boy, is where we're going," Leeham said, stepping up to the thing... and pulling away a few tangles of overgrown forest, the wild trees deciding to pile up on top of the thing...

When it was clear, a perfectly ordinary front door was visible, complete with a carved wooden sign reading HOME SWEET HOME, in a language perfectly familiar to Mallory.

"A house," Meiko deduced. "So you were in the multiverse once. And you used this to go there. So... why didn't you tell Mallory? You knew we wanted to leave, and you had the means..."

...and an entirely new sensation took over Mallory's whole of self.

It was something strange and alien, but very comforting. Very soothing. He turned in place, studying his surroundings. The grass, the creek, the blue sky high above, the house...

'Realization' was a bit of a stranger to him. But that's what he was experiencing. Culture shock had passed, and in its place, no fear...

No fear. Green grass beneath his feet. Blue sky above...

Water trickling down a creek. Birds chirping from the trees...

Her smile...

Was she smiling?

No, actually, she was frowning.

This wasn't the way he wanted to bring her here. In his dreams, she was happy to be by his side in this place. It was supposed to be a wonderful, joyous moment... not this. But that could wait, because after months of strange dreams about this place, he knew exactly where he was.

"I'm home," Mallory realized.

When Leeham offered nothing, merely looking away with shame, Mallory turned to face him and finish the unspoken revelation.

"You and my mother both went to the Multiverse," he continued. "You found this house somehow, and got it going... and curiosity drove you. You knew the past, you knew what was out there and you had to see... and you explored it together. While she was pregnant with me."

"Wha?" Meiko said, as it was her turn to play the confused one. "Mallory? Come on now, that's not poss—"

"It's true."

Leeham finally raised his eyes, to look at his son directly.

"We were archaeologists," he explained. "On one of our digs in this forest, we came across this house... something which we knew couldn't be a relic of OUR past. The engine we found inside fascinated her. She did everything she could to make it work, for two years she tinkered on it... and I helped her. Once it was running, we threw caution to the wind and activated it..."

"And that's when it happened?" Mallory asked.

"No, we made several trips, actually," Leeham said... a tiny twinkle returning to his eye that could be called mischevious. "We kept our explorations secret, of course. We had no idea how the more restrictive government of this world would react to us discovering the 'traitors' in the Multiverse. But explore we did. We studied your language, your ways, how your culture had dropped into stagnation... it was all so amazing, Mallory! She was drawn into it, and I was drawn with her... we had to learn more. We would journey back and forth so often... and... and then, she..."

"The engine failed," his son answered. "It's just like M found out in his research—I must have... vanished from my mother, and ended up in the Multiverse when the accident happened."

"She didn't live much longer after that," Leeham said, bitterness returning, showing his age again after the moment of youthful memory. "The trauma was too great. We'd lost you, I'd lost her... and for a time, I hated this thing that caused it all, this relic of the treasonous past. I HATED it... but how can you focus hate on a thing? Especially the thing that we put so much love into repairing. No, it was silly, and I realized that after a time. But this didn't mean I had to use it again, either... after all, why go back to that place? There wasn't any point. Not without her..."

He gave the HOME SWEET HOME sign on the door a brief glare. It returned a wooden expression.

"So, I let the forest take the house and never again used the engine," Leeham said, finishing his story. "My tenure as explorer was officially over. I tried to return to my archaeology work on Earth, but my heart wasn't in it. I... faded, I suppose. ...but now here you are! The doctors took a blood sample when I found you, they matched you as my son and didn't think anything odd about it... but Mallory, please, imagine how overjoyed I was! You weren't lost, and somehow, some way, you'd returned to me...!"

"And when I said I wanted to leave, decided not to tell me about this house. You want us to stay."

"It's a second chance, my boy!" Leeham pleaded, approaching his son across the grassy ground. "Maybe God's smiling on me today... the thought that I'd have a family again never even occured to me, and out of the bright blue you came! I... I know you likely have a father on the other side. But please, even if I've only known you a short time, I can feel a connection. You can't leave now! Please...!"

Mallory looked away... his brain had absorbed so much that day, he had to process it. But he didn't fumble, he didn't stammer. He didn't pull the baffled farmboy routine—when he did speak, he spoke from his heart.

"I'd like to get to know you better," he told Leeham. "I really would. Ever since Dad... my dad Josef told me I was adopted I've wondered... but... Leeham, Dad, I can't do this now. I'm sorry, I can't. I've got a family over there that needs me—Eiko, and Kisei and Lorelei, they're all in trouble. I have a life there and things I need to take care of. But I'm not saying I'll abandon you! I just need to go now. I'll... I will come back. I promise you. Okay?"

"Your family..." Leeham repeated, the word having great weight with him. Enough to sag his shoulders, as he realized—much to his original prediction— that Mallory would indeed be as stubborn as his mother.

"I won't abandon you. I promise. I just have to take care of this," Mallory said, quickly reaching out to give his dazed father a hug... it felt natural to him, there was no hesitation. "I can't say I'll live here, but I won't vanish from your life. Meiko and I.... ...Meiko?"

She leaned out of the open doorway.

"The engine's broken," she announced. "I checked, the displays are inactive and it won't reboot. ...sorry, I just didn't want to interrupt you two..."

"It's... it's all right," Leeham said, letting go of his son. "But... it's been years since I abandoned the house. The engine might... not restart. It could be too badly damaged—"

"This looks like a job for an REC-certified Reality Engineer!" Mallory declared, striding into the mobile home, past the two of them. "Leave it to me!"

He paid no attention to his surroundings, except to note: Nicely furnished. Cozy. A fixer-upper. The engine was right where he figured it'd be, the same sort of niche Meiko's engine occupied.

Right, then. THIS he could do!

Rearing back, he delivered a mighty kick to the side of the engine.

A large, metal bit of it fell off. And his big toe hurt. Nothing else happened.

"Mallory!" Leeham exclaimed, horrified. "What are you doing!? Don't kick the blasted thing!"

"No no, wait, I can do this," he said, putting up his hands. "I just have to focus. Have to focus. Right..."

Focus, just like he focused when he teleported here. Focus on something you absolutely have to do, something you need to do, regardless of fear over what you are, something that *must be done...*

Eiko's in danger. They're all in danger. I have to do this. I have to do this for Meiko...

His foot swung straight and true.

Now his little toe was hurting.

He was about to try again when Meiko stuck her leg in the way to stop him.

"This isn't a reality," she said. "It doesn't have an engine. It just *exists*. ...so, your power might not work on Earth."

"I don't know what you're talking about, but I do know kicking it isn't going to work!" Leeham exclaimed. "It took her two years to get it running. I don't even know how it works, she was the engineering-minded one..."

Even in this world, my mother was a Reality Engineer, Mallory randomly mused.

"All right, then..." he said, pushing up the sleeves of his baja sweatshirt. "We'll do this the old-fashioned way, then. I'll just fix the thing."

"Fix it?" Meiko asked. "Mallory, you've never actually tinkered with an engine before. You just gave it the technical tap, so to speak..."

"But I'm a certified engineer," he said. "I'm YOUR certified engineer, the one you hired just for situations like this! It's my job. And I have to have remembered SOMETHING from all that studying, right? I couldn't have passed the test on pure luck... I think... look, I can do this, all right? I'll fix it. I'll sit here and I'll work on it as long as it takes to fix it! I'll fix it, then we'll go get Eiko and everything will be fine! Trust me, Meiko, I know what I'm doing! ...uh, Leeham, do you have wrenches and hammers? I think I may need those for... stuff. And things."

Such a simple room... it'd be easy to overlook it, assuming it to be yet another technology-filled oblong space, just like thousands of others in the well secured network control center. A large room, fifty feet by fifty feet by fifty feet, with displays and control panels along every wall. Just another drop in the bucket of Reality Prime...

But this simple place was his rightful inheritance, his true prize.

He was fighting the others just for this room. Not that they knew it, of course; it was the secret he had guarded feverishly, eager to eliminate the competition before they knew what they were actually competing for... and with the last of them gone, with the woman who put him in a position of power gone as well, it was finally *his*.

The RealNet Core.

"Every single Reality Engine is connected via RealNet back to RealWare," he continued to explain to his young charge, ignoring her impetuous mood. (The guards would grab her if she tried to run, so she didn't bother. At least she was a practical girl, Multi thought.) He added a sweeping arm gesture to the rows and rows of holographic displays, each with detailed information on the run-time of various realities... "Urbana, Nippon, SubUrbana, Restless, Nocturn, Antiparadisia, and so on... thousands of them are connected here. After all, how else could RealWare automatically push software patches to these engines? The core handles all updating, all billing, all remote access to—"

"I wanna go back to my room," Eiko complained. "I'm waiting for a message from my friend. I don't care about some stupid RealNet stuff!"

"But this is very important," Multi tried to explain. "This is how I'm going to lead the Multiverse into the future I promised you, Eiko. This is why I joined RealWare; I knew if I had access to the core of the network, the monoculture of RealWare would give me the power I needed. Let me explain... you know I can manipulate reality, yes...?"

He held out his hand, bending the light in the room slightly to form dancing colors in his palm. He hoped the beautiful gesture would impress the girl, but she remained staunchly annoyed.

"So you can do magic tricks," she agreed.

"But it's much more than magic tricks," he said, flicking his wrist to end the light show. "You see this hand? I made it myself. A very bad man tried to kill me by drawing power into himself and overloading, so he could take me with him—but he only took my arm. And I made myself a new one! I simply willed it to happen, through my innate connection to generated reality. Engines can create life, engines can govern physics—through them I can modify the body, I can modify physics, I can do anything I need to. And through the RealNet core, I can touch engines so very far away, and enact changes by remote, with my power amplified a thousand times!"

"So you can do magic tricks from far away," Eiko decided.

Multi sighed, letting his perfectly ordinary created hand drop to his side. "You don't understand the scope of this. Let me show you something wonderful, then... an idea I had planned for years, waiting for this day to come so I could finally enact it..."

He sat in his swivel-chair, turning to face the displays before him. Keying in a sequence, remote cameras he'd placed there just for this demonstration revealed a series of glass domes, deep underwater...

"This is the resort reality known as Aquarius," he explained. "A very strange reality. Unlike others, it's completely underwater; the families that vacation there visit air-filled domes, taking in the splendor of the customized ocean through glass walls. It's really quite fascinating, and it's close to the ideal of aesthetic I want for the whole Multiverse... but not close enough. Do you know why, Eiko?"

"Do I care why, Eiko?" she mimiced back at him.

"It doesn't make sense, that's why. Air-breathing people, living under water? Wouldn't it be so much easier if we simply... changed things a little...?"

With a flair for the dramatic, he held his hands to the console... closed his eyes, and focused.

His self reached out across the links. Flickering micro-engines, moving data instead of moving buildings, linking him to any Reality he liked. Linking him to the engine in Aquarius, a thing he could tangibly feel, as he changed the ripples in its pure water core...

All Eiko saw was the domes of Aquarius cracking, one by one, and eventually shattering. Water pouring in as thousands of tourists panicked, the sudden doom coming from all sides...

"Wait, wait!" she protested, trying to reach for him—and being restrained by the guards at her side. "What are you doing?! You're gonna kill them!"

"Noo..." Multi said, eyes still closed, still focusing his power. "Keep watching. Keep watching, Eiko, and see the beautiful future I want to make for you..."

...and bodies floated in the water, so many of them...

...and they moved. They moved in a way Eiko had never seen before. Because instead of legs, now they had tails. Just like mer-people from her early fairy tale books...

The people of Aquarius, floating in the water which was now their home, found themselves instantly comfortable with swimming about. Some were still in shock, but others found themselves swimming in little loops, fascinated by this bizarre turn of events. They breathed the water and found they had no difficulty living outside of the protective domes...

"Beautiful..." Multi said, opening his eyes at last. "So very beautiful. Reality can be glorious, Eiko, glorious and wonderful! Why do we persist in living mundane lives in mundane places? We could experience whole new levels of existence, we could let our imaginations run free and wild, creating like gods—"

But now Eiko was screaming.

Confused, Multi turned back to the screen. To the twitching, gasping people of Aquarius, whose bodies were reverting.

It took a full minute for them to stop moving.

"That... that wasn't supposed to happen," Multi said, with a small amount of horror in his voice. "I didn't want that to happen. I—"

His chair wheeled backwards after Eiko pulled away from the guards, pouncing on Multi and flailing at him with her tiny fists. He put up his hands instinctively to protect himself, before the heavily armed men finally pulled her away.

"You're a MONSTER!" she accused, as they were dragging her away. "A horrible, horrible monster! You killed my oneechan and you killed all those people, and you... you should die! You should die for what you've done! I HATE YOU! I HATE—"

The closing door cut off her words, as the guards hauled her back to her room. Multi suspected the next word would have been 'you'.

That wasn't supposed to happen. He had the power now, he had the control. He was going to change the future...

His artificial hand throbbed in pain, much as it had periodically since he crafted it. He clenched his good arm over it, glaring at the screen as the dead floated in place...

It wasn't his fault. He did what had to be done—how could he have made a mistake? He knew he was capable of doing this. He was ready! Why was his power failing him? It wasn't his fault. He couldn't have faulted. He had to be the shepherd with a firm hand on the crook, the one who could save everyone, the one they could have confidence in as a benevolent helper...

It must have been their fault, he decided. The people of Aquarius. They resisted and that's why the change didn't keep; his control over his powers was absolute. But the people, those people weren't ready for the future. They wouldn't have endured long anyway, so this wasn't a setback.

He would continue his plan. Perhaps a few more disasters would occur, but that would just have to be an acceptable level of loss. If every Reality had to burn in order for him to create the true future, then so be it.

For two days, they toiled at the job. It wasn't easy; Mallory tried his best not to look like he had forgotten ninety percent of what he never learned about Reality Engines, but he wasn't going to bluff his way through something so important. For Leeham's part, he could translate the old notebooks they had found—schematics and repair notes penned in his mother's hand, long ago. But he insisted that he wasn't a scientist, and he couldn't truly comprehend the things she talked about, even if he could translate the pure words.

Both poked at the engine in collective incompetence for hours a day. Meiko would take over Mallory's usual duties, namely making the boys lunch and fixing them tea using the mobile home's kitchen... when she grew too restless from sitting around, she'd also work at tidying up the place.

"It's not a bad house, really," she said, as she ran the bizarre Earth equivalent of a vacuum cleaner over the stairs—which was quiet enough for her to speak at a normal volume. Its rollers picked up the dust perfectly, cleansing the fabric in a single pass. "It's a bit like our house, Mallory... maybe it was an earlier model? I like the woodwork all over the place, the trim and molding... it's very quaint. Ours is spartan in comparison..."

"We were expecting something entirely made of plastics and metals," Leeham said, looking up from the piles of notebooks surrounding him on the carpet, as he sat cross-legged while sorting them. "The Multiverse was so technology-driven, we had assumed that any mobile-building they used would be blatantly artificial compared to the naturalist bent Earth culture took on... but it seems we were the 'futuristic' ones, in comparison. This house is very similar to a mid-twentieth-century design... no no, Mallory, that's the 'A'-

coupling."

"This is an A?" he asked, poking at the scribbled glyph on the paper. "I had no idea our language changed so much...!"

"Ah, no, she just didn't have very good handwriting," Leeham admitted. "Half of the translation involves me recognizing her script..."

His look became distant, as he trailed off.

"Ah... you know... I never knew my mother," Mallory said, trying to approach the subject carefully. "I mean, my adoptive mother. It's funny, she was a reality engineer too! But... she died when I was very young. My father, er, my adoptive father—"

"You can call him your father, Mallory. I don't mind," Leeham replied. "Don't feel uncomfortable on my account. I suppose... it's just something we'll have to get used to. But go ahead, please."

"Er, I don't really have anything to go ahead with, I was just making conversation. ...um. He's a farmer, you know! That's like archaeology, right? I mean, you both... um... dig. And stuff."

"I believe I would like to meet him..." his father-of-some-style said. "I would like to say... he's raised a fine boy. I couldn't have hoped for anything better."

"Ah... thank you, er... Dad. Thank you."

"But then again, you had our genes, didn't you?" Leeham joked, giving the boy a smile. "How could you possibly go wrong with those in your system, eh?"

"Yeah, I guess that... I, uh..."

...the one who sent them here had those genes, too. And look how HE turned out...

"Son?"

That shouldn't be possible. All of those who he was had different upbringings, but even M—the bitterest of them all—had saved them in the end. Why was that one so different? He had to be different, after all. There was no way Mallory could be capable of anything like that...

"Mallory?"

"What? Oh... oh, sorry, just... let's get to work," he said, fetching his sonic screwdriver. "A-coupling. We're almost there, I just know it! And... then we can settle everything. I just know it."

Multi drummed his fingers on the fine oak table in a manner most annoyed.

This was Gillian's chair. He made sure to use hers, to sit right where she sat. He'd already crushed one of them and that meant they would obey him.

Everything was supposed to be going smoothly...

"The, ah, official complaint from Restless concerns their weather," one of the CxO's continued. "Or rather, that you stopped the rain—"

"Of course I stopped the rain," he replied. "It didn't make any sense. Why would anybody WANT to live in a reality where it's always raining? I even gave them a permanent rainbow in their sky. Why exactly are they complaining about that?"

"It's not the rainbow, sir, it's the rain. The drainage system and the water supply of Restless have been tuned for decades under the assumption that there would be a constant deluge—without it, their infrastructure's in turmoil. There are water shortages. I've asked our humanitarian aid branches to send them water, of course—"

"If they need water, I'll provide them with water. The southwest quadrant is sparsely populated, yes? Order them to relocate away from it. I'll create them an ocean the likes of which will rival the seas of Nippon!"

"Er... you're going to destroy twenty-five percent of Restless?"

"This isn't destruction, this is creation! I'm trying to create something beautiful. Why can't anybody understand that?"

"Sir, ahh... if I may speak...?" the Chief Operations Officer said, raising his hand like a child in a crowded classroom.

"Of course," Multi said, sitting back in Gillian's chair. "I value your input, all of you. I've said that."

"What we have here is a problem of public perceptions," the executive explained. "While some of the changes you've been making are minor annoyances—no doubt part of a plan of such, er, beauty and perfection that we simply can't see the big picture yet—what you did with, ah, Aquarius... it has people concerned. Some are seeing it as an aggressive act. An act of war. In fact, I have an official request from Nippon suggesting that a treaty of non-aggression is in order—"

"I'm not at war with them! I'm trying to help them!" Multi protested. "Everything I do, I'm doing for them. Are they that foolish that they want to resist the future? It's this mentality that's kept the Multiverse in stagnation for aeons! I'm sorry, but if they can't accept this, then... then that's unfortunate. But the changes will continue. The NEXT generation will understand... yes, they will. I know they will..."

(None of his yes-men replied, figuring that last part was Multi talking to himself. You didn't want to point out that the dangerous psychopath was mumbling to himself, unless you wanted to become a supercompressed ball of human tissue. They were toadies, but they learned fast.)

"...very well. So. Not everybody is happy with the path that I have set for them," he concluded. "I will learn to accept that. And we will continue. I would like to bring up a new issue—Antiparadisia. Why have they not evacuated like I ordered?"

"I was going to get to that next, actually..." The COO replied, shuffling through the files on his desktop-mounted hologram display. "I passed word along that Antiparadisia was to be shut down in two days' time, as you instructed... including your message about how such a vile haven of anarchy had no place in the future. They sent back an official reply this morning..."

Silence settled across the table, as the COO's throat bobbled nervously.

"And...?" Multi prompted.

"To summarize, they rejected your edict."

"I'd prefer if you didn't summarize. What exactly was their response?"

"...understanding that this is me conveying the official documentation I recieved this morning and not expressing any personal sentiment towards you of any sort," the COO prefaced... he raised one middle finger, extended. "They requested that I show this gesture to you and suggest that you 'sit and spin,' sir. ... —don'tkillme!"

The COO braced for what never came. Instead, Multi let his rage loose on the table, which snapped into four pieces. The Chief Financial Officer's leg was broken in the process.

"More throwbacks of the past..." Multi whispered dangerously. "Gentlemen. Excuse me. I see that need to deal with them directly."

Risking personal trauma, the COO felt the need to speak up. "S-Sir, please, another aggressive act—"

"This is a cleansing," the new CEO of RealWare replied, getting to his feet. "Trust me when I say that the only pure soul in Antiparadisia died a long time ago. I should know—I killed her myself. Anything else that walks and breathes in that place is nothing but trash, and I'll deal with that trash accordingly..."

He marched from the board room, ignoring any pleading or protest. His guards accompanied him to the network control center—he'd been doing a lot of crossing from there to the security control center to the executive building and back and forth. Three key locales, but this was the most important of all. He had a personal bodyguard just for his time spent in this building, where he was strongest yet most vulnerable... here, his will be DONE.

Confidently, he strode into the nondescript fifty-by-fifty-by-fifty room, and keyed in a sequence to access Antiparadisia's Reality Engine. And with a flicker of thought, he destroyed it.

...or didn't.

In fact, he couldn't even connect to it. The universal link that he should have to all RealWare engines wasn't even present—the gateways across RealNet to Antiparadisia slammed shut like lead weights, and no matter how he battered at it with his will, they wouldn't budge...

"Sir... sir!"

He resisted the urge to unleash upon the voice approaching him. It would be a waste, and further proof that he wasn't in perfect control of himself...

"I... I was trying to explain, sir," the COO said, wheezing and gasping for breath. "Antiparadisia... they aren't using a RealWare engine anymore. They cancelled their contract and switched to an Open Engine two weeks ago... they're not connected to the core anymore!"

"That... that should not matter," Multi said, frowning deeper than he had all week. "It's all RealNet. It's all engines. Who makes them shouldn't matter..."

"It's the, it's the encryption, sir! The Open Reality Movement, they've... they piggyback off RealNet illegally. Because we own RealNet, so they have no legitimate means online, see—"

"Then break their encryption! I don't see how Gillian Bates would have allowed them to use company resources like that—"

"We've tried, sir. We're still trying. But so far the Open Reality Movement just hacks the protocols every time we make a change. It's like a race, see... every time we lock them out they find a way back in."

"I see. Well. I suppose I could go there in person and deal with this..."

"Sir, ah, that's not a good idea," the COO said. "It's like I said... they see you as an aggressive force. You'd be at risk—"

"I think you'll find I can defend myself with some skill."

"But against ALL of Antiparadisia? They hate you there, and you know what they're like! Anarchists, madmen, killers! Even with that bodyguard you've had hanging around the network control center, you couldn't possibly... I mean... not that I'm questioning you sir, I'm just trying to serve your interests, see..."

"Fine. Fine! I'll leave them be. For now," Multi warned. "Along with the other Open Reality worlds. They aren't much of a bother right now. But... I want more resources allocated to cracking into them. I want access to those worlds. ...Gillian should have never let them stand up to her like this. It would have been so much easier to create the future without these rebels hanging around..."

"I told her the same thing, sir!" the COO said, seeing an opportunity to suck up. "We shouldn't have let them compete in the marketplace, sir! Her father knew how to deal with that sort of trash..."

"Agreed. But... we don't have to go that far, not yet. I don't want to waste potential resources, you understand. ...you know, if only I could turn them in my favor—wait, yes, of course! They've been fighting the stagnation, haven't they? Trying to do NEW things with reality, trying to free it from the shackles of history... yes. Yes, a movement which wants to create a bright future couild be a powerful ally. But... I have to focus on winning over the others first.

Them, I can deal with them later... I can still be in control, I'll still have perfect control..."

(With his new boss talking to himself again, the COO slinked out the way he came in. No need to interrupt when the madman was on a roll, after all.)

The three of them crowded around the display. Blue illumination lit up their faces in the darkness; the boys had been working well into the night when they finally made a breakthrough.

The engine had power. It had power, and it was operational—fortunately for them it wasn't utterly wrecked, it simply needed some wires replaced and some bolts tightened. Once reconnected to the alternative power source Leeham and his wife had installed years ago, it was up and humming like a harmonica.

Except for one problem.

"There's no water," Mallory concluded.

"We've got a perfectly operable kitchen sink over there," Meiko countered.

"Which isn't going to work, because it has to be a specially treated sort of water," Leeham continued. "From what we could tell, it took a large amount of specially treated but otherwise pure water, plus the software that sent vibrations through it for the engine to function. But when we found the house, the engine had plenty of water..."

"There wasn't a crack in the engine. It couldn't evaporate. There's no way it could have lost its water..." Mallory said, groaning as he slumped against a wall. "But somehow, it did. There's no way we can get this thing moving without water, and I don't know how you make that kind of water... I can't remember. I've tried..."

"We could pour ordinary pure water into it and hope?" Meiko suggested. "I mean, I don't know jack about reality engineering, but that's gotta do SOMETHING, right? Maybe it'd be enough to get us home, at least..."

Leeham shook his head. "You could have an accident. This engine, it is very old; you know what it did in the past... no. It's not worth the risk."

"Excuse me, but I'll decide what amount of risk I'm willing to endure," Meiko retorted. "My sister is back there! My friends and co-workers... and I'm not going to abandon them. If we have a shot, even if it's slim, we take it. This 'planet' of yours is lovely, Leeham, but I'm not staying here if we have any chance of going back. Right, Mallory?"

Both of them turned to Mallory, who was too busy thinking to pay attention. His brain had trouble multitasking, after all.

"What? Oh, ah, we gotta go back, Dad. You know that, it's like I said. ...but we're going to need water, Meiko. The kind of water that... would register on one of those wand-thingies Ryo used..."

"Wand-thingy...?—wait. Wait, no, Mallory, you CAN'T mean—"

"It's all we have, Meiko. It's our best shot."

"We're NOT going to use your blood to power this thing!" Meiko exclaimed. "Have you seen the size of the water reservoir in the engine? To fill that, you'd have to... it'd be too risky, and—"

"And my blood's the only liquid we have that resonates just like the water in a Reality Engine! In fact, I'd guess that the reason I have my powers is because... Leeham, you never used the engine again after the accident, right?"

"No... no, I didn't," he said, a little bewildered. "You think this is somehow connected to these abilities you spoke of while we were working...?"

"The water from the engine... it's a part of me now," Mallory said, putting a hand over his heart, over the little ying-yang on his sweatshirt. "That's how I got the powers! That water didn't evaporate or leak out, it somehow merged with me when I got lost! And... and we've gotta put it back if we're gonna be able to leave this place..."

"If so... then there is no need to risk your life in the process," Leeham said, figuring things out as he went along. "Transfusion. You have the same blood type as I do, Mallory; the doctors confirmed it, remember? When they identified you as my genetic son. I'll go back to the hospital and finagle some equipment... and then you can fill the engine and be reasonably healthy after."

"Right! Now we're cooking with three parts oil and one part butter!" Mallory exclaimed. "There's no time to lose—Leeham! Go to the hospital and get... blood-moving stuff! Meiko! Get some orange juice and cookies and things together from the food stocks, I'm going to need calories, I think! Me! Get the engine's reservoir open and ready for a transfer! Let's move, people! Move move move!"

And move they did. Mallory tended to his own end of things, getting the water chamber prepared, putting the engine into sleep mode to keep it from prematurely activating...

"Mallory?" Meiko called out, from the kitchen.

"Yeah?"

"You know... if you do this, your powers might get weaker. You might even lose them..."

"I don't care," he said, speaking with the kind of honesty that only comes from pure distraction as he fiddled with the engine. "If this gets us home, then I don't care what it takes. I'd do anything for you, Meiko. I'd protect you with my life if I had to... do we have any sugar cookies? Those would work best, I think..."

"Y... yeah, we have some," she said, fumbling with the sealed container of cookies. She took her time to cross the house, watching Mallory all the way as he futzed about... watching the determined expression on his face.

That's unconditional love, she thought. *He didn't even have to think about it, he was ready to die if he had to. He'd stay by me, he'd never let anything happen to me as long as he lives... he'd never leave me...*

And at that point, she truly realized that she never wanted to leave him, either.

Unfair. It wasn't fair!

He'd edited her message! He knew it. He knew she'd use some kind of code, that she'd try to get Kensuke a message of some kind. When the reply finally came, but didn't include a copy of the Important Courtroom Drama episode she asked for, she checked her out-box—and found that what really got sent wasn't what she typed.

"Dear Kensuke, I'm not at my house anymore but I'm okay. I'm really bored here. I've got a lot of toys and stuff but I lost the My First RealNet Workstation my sister gave me for my birthday. But I'm happy and being treated well, and everything's great! Hugsnkissed! Eiko-chan!"

It was enough to make her want to throw pillows around the room, so she did while yelling and stamping her feet.

MULTI NO BAKAMONO!

('Bakemono' = Monster. 'Baka' = Idiot. She liked calling Multi that, in her own private little thoughts.)

Kensuke's reply was a bit confused, mostly asking if she was really okay, and asking her to write back. And now she couldn't, because each time she tried, the Workstation locked her out. Multi wasn't going to let her communicate again, not after she pulled that stunt...

Dinner that night, although prohibitively expensive and tasty, was a sour affair in her mouth. Now she really was alone; the only shot she had at communicating was gone. The only consolation she had was more toys and dolls than she'd ever be able to afford herself, and her premium RealNet video streams...

Desperately needing distraction, she tuned into tonight's broadcast of Important Courtroom Drama. New episodes were gonna start tonight, anyway; she didn't want to miss them.

The plot was typical of the show, involving eighty-four doublecrosses and dramatic evidence reveals in mid-trial.

And then the last witness was called to the stand.

The baliff (who was new to the show this season, last time it was this old lady and now it was this seven-foot-tall bald guy) boomed his voice across the courtroom. "The court calls—"

Static.

"—Alex Gunthar to the stand!"

Eiko's jaw dropped.

The last time she saw Alex Gunthar, he was a tiny holographic projection being carried around in the bag of his programmer / lover, Belle Pasadina. They were escaping from a video network company that wanted their property back... and here he was, strolling into the Important Courtroom, looking every bit as cocky and handsome as always.

He raised one hand, putting the other on a book of law.

"Do you swear to tell the whole truth and nothing but the truth?" the baliff asked him.

"Actually, no," Alex replied. "Because right now, I'm being hacked directly into the stream being fed to Reality Prime. Which means I'm not actually part of this overproduced trough of dramatic slop, I'm just here to talk to one very special viewer—and hopefully she's watching..."

"I am!!" Eiko called out, scooting forward on the carpet, closer to the screen. "I'm right here!"

"Of course, we can't hear her," Alex continued, ignoring the other actors going through their lines around him. "But we recently got a message from her, and traced it back across RealNet so we'd know exactly what room in what building to send this feed to. And if she's listening... Eiko? We're going to get you out of there. Ryo's here, and Kensuke's here, and Lorelei's here and Kisei's here. We're all safe, and they're going to rescue you as soon as they can, but they might need your help when the time comes..."

"I'll do anything! I promise, just tell me wh—"

"Once we have a plan, we'll get you details through Important Courtroom Drama," Alex continued in his one-sided communiqué. "So tune in each night. ...look, I don't know how to break it to you, kid... but your sister and her boyfriend, they're not here. We don't know where they are. They might be there with you, but we've got no way of knowing; we didn't even know you were alive until you messaged Kensuke. The others weren't sure if I should bring this up, but I figured you'd wanna know. We'll be in touch... Alex out."

Static.

And this week's guest actor replaced Alex on the witness stand, as the show carried on regardless.

Blue sky above. Green grass below. The sound of a creek.

Was she smiling...?

She was calling to him...

He was sleepy. He didn't want to wake up, but he knew he had to; otherwise she might worry that he wasn't going to wake up, and honestly, he was just tired. Anybody would be after having a good portion of their bodily fluids swapped into a machine.

"'mwake, I'm awake..." he mumbled, trying to sit up. "Everything 'kay...?"

"From what I can tell... yes," Leeham replied, detaching a soft cuff from Mallory's arm. There wasn't any needle mark, nothing to show where blood had been siphoned and replaced, but his flesh was definitely a bit sore there. "The engine is making the same sorts of noises I remember back when it worked... we might have done it."

"No time to lose, then..." Mallory said, swinging his legs off the couch. "Let's get back home."

"Mallory, you're still exhausted," Meiko said, pushing him back on the couch gently. "Look, I know you're serious about this... but we've waited this long. We can wait an hour or so for you to get your bearings and rest a bit. All right...?"

"I'd really rather get going, Meiko. I'll be fine, really, don't worry about me..." he said, worming his way around her and getting to his feet—slightly dizzy, but no worse for wear. "Leeham...? Are you coming with us?"

"Me? Pfah, I'm an old man... I'm not ready for some adventure like this," he tried to joke. "I'll stay behind. I'll wait here. ...you said you would be back, after all."

"And I meant it, too. I'll come back once this is all over... maybe take you to see Josef?" Mallory suggested. "Once everything's better again. I promise."

"This might not work, you know. Even with your blood in the machine, it might have another accident..."

"But I have to try—"

"I know, I know," he said... with a smile. "Just as stubborn as your mother, like I said... and, well... just as brave. I'll take my leave now. Go, and do what you have to do. And I know I'll see you again..."

He reached out, and embraced his son. No further words were needed; he departed quietly, his part in this done.

The two who remained walked to the engine, which blinked and hummed and looked ready to go.

"All set...?" Mallory asked, thumb on the control panel. "I'm going to bring us back to the same docking area we left..."

He looked down, finding Meiko squeezing his free hand.

"All set," she agreed. "Let's go."

At first, they weren't sure they landed in the right place. After all, it wasn't raining anymore, and this was supposedly Restless...

Then they saw the destroyed dock, and the remains of their house.

And the men with the rifles and RealWare uniforms, who were guarding it.

Who certainly noticed their arrival, and the two faces looking out the window in horror...

"Go. Go, go!" Meiko prompted, running back to the engine niche. "We've gotta get out of here!"

"But where—?"

She didn't need Future Perfect for this—Ryo had made her memorize the address and repeat it back to him, eighteen times. It was the last resort of last resorts... and it was easier to just use it without explaining all of that to Mallory in a lengthy way which could put them both in danger of being shot.

The house rocked with purple light as the old engine shifted, the entire structure relocating somewhere else entirely...

When Mallory next looked out the window, he was greeted with a sky the color of a coredump. Clouds of letters and numbers floated freely, along with weird techie system status messages. Not that he knew it at the time, but in the reality filled with hardcore programmers, engineers and reality hackers that he had just landed in, such information was far more important than a daily stock quote or a corporate logo as other realities might have in their skies...

Their arrival was noticed immediately, and a greeting party dispatched. Familiar and unfamiliar faces, but a few stood out: Lorelei, Kisei, Gillian...

"Good, you're here," their leader Ryo said, with his trademark casual smile. "We were getting worried. Now, we can really get started..."

'Tidying up' was too cutesy of a word for it. Mallory was a lean, mean cleaning machine. Whatever machismo he could gather unto himself he did, eliminating dust and dirt like a focused filth assassin. He was the Zen master of tidying up—a familiar and comfortable state of daily routine.

He ran the dust-sweeper around the corner of the coffee table, eliminating a dustball kicked up by Eiko's playing—Most Terrible Lizard King™ was doing battle with Peacemaker Pretty Soldier Biiko™ in her lovely pink camouflage with matching pink non-violent stun weapons, and so far the only casualty was the carpeting.

He scooped up the end result of the horrors of plastic war, then rounded the next corner, asking Lorelei to put her legs up—she promptly put them behind her head, which made him do a bit of a double take, but then it was back to the Zen cleansing routine.

Kisei smoothly shifted her legs onto the L-bend in the couch before Mallory even got there, opting for the more sensible route of simply relocating them while giving Lorelei her usual look of mild disdain. As usual, Lorelei bit back with a sarcastic comment which Kisei ignored, as she resumed writing in her journal.

The carpets finished, it was time to break out the feather duster. He ran it over the various framed pictures of Eiko and Meiko from their earlier days, and took special care to clean the one recent group photo they had taken during the Nippon stopover; the only picture of Mallory in the House, and most importantly, the only picture where Mallory and Meiko were together...

On a whim, he walked over to the RealNet Workstation where Meiko was browsing job listings, and dusted her a bit. She flinched and then sneezed when he flicked the duster over her face... and they both shared a laugh, a wonderfully silly and heartfelt laugh.

Just one perfect moment in time, one which Mallory never wanted to end. If he spent the rest of his days like this, with all of them, he'd be the happiest man in the multiverse...

In order to maintain that happiness, he tried his best to ignore the ghost. Dusting Meiko's Workstation screen a bit, he moved on to dusting the engine in the alcove behind her. Then he'd have to head to the kitchen and clean up Meiko's last attempt at proving her worth in the field of cooking, and he could move on to the laundry...

The ghost stood in his way. His expression hadn't changed since he got there—one of anticipation, of prompting. Prompting Mallory to take some sort of action...

"Leave me alone," Mallory said, pushing past him. "I'm happy. Just leave me alone... I couldn't do anything even if I wanted to. Not against him—"

Him. The memory alone broke his trance, and broke his wonderful moment.

Because immediately, he was there. And he didn't wait, he didn't pause, just as before—he simply burned it. All of it. In one horrifying moment everybody he knew and loved was gone in a flash of purple fire. All that remained was himself and himself and himself. Mallory and Mallory and Mallory, Mallory and the ghost M and the killer Multi...

Multi, who was wearing a sweatshirt much like Mallory's, except with the black and the white of its yin-yang reversed.

Mallory awoke in an instant. It was better to wake an hour ahead of schedule than to have nightmare after nightmare.

14: Beyond Blue Skies

The sky outside the house was black, with gray lettering all over. System status indicators, hexadecimal code, and jargon on top of jargon that Mallory (an REC-certified Engineer) couldn't make heads or tails of.

Of all the realities Mallory had been to, this one felt... very, very weird. It was a bizarre mix of spartan and luxurious; a hodge podge of whatever the Open Reality Movement had felt like cobbling together. Shantytowns stood next to storage warehouses stood next to office buildings stood next to bizarre glass and metal buildings with more aesthetic appeal than functional use. Whatever someone felt like creating, they made it; these were reality hackers, the sort who cared more for what's possible than what makes sense.

And hackers there were, plenty of them wearing various slogan-scrawled geek pride t-shirts. "Realware Sucks" was the most common, but various other ORM ideologies (and witty, oh so clever ORM humor which nobody outside of the ORM ever understood) were present as well. The average age of a citizen of Grep, home of the Open Reality Movement, was twenty-five. Not exactly The Beautiful People, mind you, but certainly The Young Ones.

But... they weren't the only ones here. Because off to the left of Mallory's view (the center of which was dominated by a tall Noyori Labs building, which they were docked next to) was a refugee camp.

From the limited explanations Ryo gave them prior to turning in for night, word was spreading quickly that Multi (that was his name, Multi, Mallory never even knew what his other self's name was until now and even having a name other than his own didn't help the nightmares and he didn't want to know and—)—that Multi wasn't changing any Open Engine-based worlds. He'd posted armed guards around all the RealWare engines, trying to keep anybody from changing systems, so that had to mean open realities were safe, right? Right. And so they fled, heading to any open reality they could... with Grep, home of the ORM, being the most well known and popular.

And so, Grep was bursting at the seams with people. It was crowded, even moreso than Nippon. Mallory could hear the hustle and bustle even in the early morning hour, even before he opened the window to get some fresh air in the musty, cozy old house they'd found. Multi had been busy, Ryo explained...

changing things. And destroying some realities in the process.

Killing people.

Which Meiko couldn't care less about, since she was wholly focused on the one person who wasn't there—Eiko. Always practical, always focused... she wanted to start planning a rescue attempt right away, as they had learned from Kensuke that Multi had her captive. But Ryo insisted that the two of them get some sleep, and deal with it in the morning.

Now, it was morning. And knowing Meiko, knowing how she could get when faced with a problem, she—

"Up already? Good, let's get the others."

—wouldn't have slept a wink. Mallory turned to face her, noting the circles under the eyes, the way she flexed her fingers as she tried to bring some life into them after organizing her thoughts on paper all night...

He wasn't going to chide her for disobeying Ryo's orders. It wouldn't accomplish anything, and she certainly wouldn't go sleep a bit on his say-so. He simply nodded silently, and moved to join her. To support her as best he could... despite feeling so useless.

Morning meeting in the conference room of Noyori Labs, Grep Branch. Present and accounted for:

Meiko: looking quite exhausted but doing her best not to show it. She was nursing from the strongest cup of coffee Mallory could make, something black and thick like tar, with enough kick to raise the dead. She'd brought a pile of papers with her, each coated in thick scrawl; without F.P., she'd had to make do with some old, yellowing stationery in her new bedroom.

Ryo: who had immediately chided Meiko about not sleeping and got an earful of it for his efforts. He looked pretty much as he always did, wearing casual clothing underneath his standard lab coat. He wore his usual cheerful smile, the sort that he could use to mask any true worries, in an effort to raise the spirits of those around him.

Lorelei: who was possibly more restless than Meiko, having been stuck on this world for days now, unable to get any action going towards the primary goal of rescuing Eiko. Having lost her massive supply of hot and trendy clothing along with her signature double-bladed saber, she'd resorted to tearing a "Open Reality = Open Future" t-shirt in half to make a nice midriff shirt. She wasn't going to fret and gnash her teeth and pace in circles AND look bad doing it, after all. As for a replacement weapon, she had a stun rod attached to her hand-me-down belt on her hand-me-down jeans, and wasn't happy about it.

Kisei: who was quite calm and serene, unlike the fiery woman with orange hair sitting to her right in the midriff T-shirt. She wore a slogan T-shirt too, the first time Mallory had seen her wearing anything other than her old green military uniform. She'd somehow found a tranquilizer gun on Grep, which she wore slung across her back much like her missing sniper rifle.

Belle Pasadina: wearing a nice sundress and sitting next to a holographic projection of her lover / creation Alex Gunthar. It took Mallory a few minutes to remember who they were, since that particular mission was over long ago. Long ago, back when he was new at all this, before everything started changing in good ways and bad...

Gillian Bates: whom Mallory only recognized from the RealNet news streams he used to watch back home in Grünwald. Of all the people he'd expected to meet in an open reality, she ran dead last, beat out only by the one he was hoping never to meet again who was responsible for all this... and for her part, Gillian wore the same smile Ryo wore. But she probably meant it, sitting calm and confident and cheerful in her place at the table.

And finally there was "**Xyzzy**", legendary leader of the Open Reality Movement, who was an ordinary guy slumped in his chair and trying not to be noticed, an effort he was exceedingly successful at as the group bantered back and forth.

"The problem here is not method, it's opportunity," Meiko was explaining, as she shuffled her paper stack to the maps which Gillian had given her yesterday. "Right now, Multi is likely moving back and forth between these three buildings on the Reality Prime campus... the security center, the network control center, and the executive offices. He never leaves Reality Prime, so if we're going to get Eiko back, we have to do it with him present and accounted for."

"Considering the guy's like a tiny god, that's not gonna be easy," Lorelei said, leaning back in her chair as she studied the documents. "Isn't he, like, omniscient or something? He'd sense us coming a mile away with his crazy super powers."

"Not likely. From what we know about these powers through Mallory and M, that's not part of the package; even M, whose powers were completely unlocked, couldn't do that. The best he can do is change things he's aware of. So... this rescue would have to be stealthy. Kisei?"

"I have entered the campus of Reality Prime numerous times in the past," Kisei replied immediately, anticipating the question. "I am familiar with the grounds and the security involved. But those two of the three buildings have impenetrable security I do not know how to defeat—they use technology RealWare has never placed on the open market where Tachi could purchase and study it. Given their tendency to hoard patents and use them for their own purposes, we can safely assume the systems guarding them are alien to us and thus undefeatable."

"Undef—wait. Two out of three buildings? Why only two?"

"Because the security center is already guarded by hundreds of skilled, fully armed guards," she explained. "Thus they did not need to waste whatever expensive technology they use trying to keep people out of the other two. Anybody who tries to get in will likely be committing suicide."

"Not so."

The group turned to the one with all the inside dirt—the former CEO of RealWare.

"I know those three buildings intimately," Gillian explained, steepling her fingers together as she addressed the troops. "I can teach you the most efficient path through the security center to its core. Once there, a bit of rampant destruction and the security systems on the other two buildings will fall. It's the only way to gain access; your assassin's analysis of our security is quite on the money, Meiko Mirai. The two key buildings of Reality Prime use reality-locking technology the likes of which reality hackers can only dream of. Frightfully expensive and difficult to maintain, which is why we only have it in two places, but quite effective."

"So, then..." Meiko said, pieces falling together in her head, gears turning quickly. "You're saying if someone who's well versed in fighting off hundreds of people at once takes the efficient path to the security core and trashes it, then someone who's well versed in stealthy infiltration could then enter one of the other buildings and rescue Eiko without being blocked."

"It's marvelous the way you think, Meiko," Gillian said, casting a look of what was probably simple admiration in her direction.

Lorelei grinned ear-to-ear, as she cracked her knuckles. "Good thing we know someone who's good at taking on hundreds of enemies at once, then..."

"As well as one who specializes in stealth-based operations," Kisei added, without the grinning or the joint-fluid-popping.

"Hold on, both of you," Meiko said, trying to curb Lorelei's enthusiasm more than Kisei's lack thereof. "It's a good plan, with one very huge flaw—we have no idea where Eiko is. All we have is a network address, which we can't map to a specific room inside Reality Prime without information we can't get access to. She could be in any of these buildings, or none of them at all. Until we can lock down exactly where she is, nobody's going anywhere."

"Actually, the way I see it, all we need to lock down is where Multi is," Lorelei said. "That way, we can go kill him. After that, fetching Eiko is trivial. Right?"

Whatever roll the group was on came crashing to a halt, as conflicted glances were exchanged around the table.

The first to speak up was Ryo, raising his hand for attention like a kid in class. "Ah... isn't that going a bit far? This isn't a war council, it's a rescue council. If we can get Eiko back and get out without incident, wouldn't that be preferable?"

"But Ryo, darling, this is the natural consequence of Multi's actions," Gillian said. "He surely has to know that; you can't do what he's done without repercussions. Simple cause and effect; he kills, so we kill. I have no real interest in this child you're all concerned about, no offense, but I would suggest you take any opportunity you get to eliminate this man."

"But... but what if it doesn't work?" the more flighty and nervous voice of Belle Pasadina spoke. "He'll be enraged! He'll take it out on everybody in the multiverse! It could be even worse than what he's already done. If... if we leave him alone, then maybe you guys could just stay here—"

"I ain't living life on the run anymore!" Lorelei spat back. "We've been fleeing this guy ever since we met him, and there's no way to escape someone like that. You think you'll be safe here? How long until he finds a way into the Open Reality Movement's little hidey holes? I say take his ass out now before we lose the opportunity. Yeah, murder is naughty and evil and wrong, but you know what? Watch me not care. If ever there was a justifiable homicide, this would be it. Call it proactive self-defense if you have to, but it's justifiable!"

"Couldn't we reason with him?" Ryo suggested. "From what Gillian's told us, he's not really a bad guy at heart; he wants to help everybody out, and he's doing what he thinks is right. And heck, if he's anything like Mallory, then that means... err... wait a minute, where's Mallory?"

"You try reasoning with him while he's turning gravity upside down on you, smiling nicely as he crushes you to death," Lorelei countered. "And leave Mallory out of this; we've already discussed that."

The branch of Noyori Labs in Grep was a tiny one, compared to the home branch in Nippon. Just a simple two-story structure; a conference room, a few small labs, and a nice balcony overlooking the chaotic sprawl of Grep... but there was a nice sliding door between the balcony and the conference room, which is what Mallory needed. Something that would give him a moment's peace.

He leaned on the overlook's railing, crossing his arms and tucking them in a bit for warmth. The "weather" report high above said that it would be a little cold today as they were "feeping" the environmental controls; nothing he couldn't deal with, even if his sweatshirt had been through quite a bit lately and was starting to develop some holes...

"What a mess, huh?"

"I think it's kind of neat, actually," Mallory replied without thinking, looking out across the refugee camps and the haphazard urban planning of Grep. "It's like everybody just carved out a little niche to call home and did what they wanted with it. I like that."

"I meant the situation," the one standing next to him said... his arms folded much as Mallory's were, despite his ORM slogan T-shirt not providing the same warmth. His short-cropped brown hair didn't help much, either; it was the sort of haircut you got when you didn't want to bother washing it a lot, when you had better things to do with your time. His eyes looked a little like Meiko's, in that they were run down and tired. "The situation's a complete mess. ...sorry, I didn't really introduce myself back there. My name's Lewis, but my friends call me Xyzzy."

"Zizzy?"

"No, Xyzzy. It's supposedly an old, worn out magic word," he said. "And with all that's been going on, I'm feeling kind of old and worn out myself. Funny thing, feeling grumpy and old at age twenty-eight..."

"Grumpy?" Mallory asked, turning a little to talk directly with the man. "I thought the Open Reality Movement loved having more people come on board? I read a few articles about it when I was studying for my REC test. How you guys have this 'collective' going, where everybody's welcome and they all contribute to the movement in some way..."

"Yeah, but... look out there. Those aren't recruits, they're refugees," Xyzzy said, nodding towards the camp. "It's not for love of freedom that they're here, but for fear of RealWare. Overnight, we went from being a motley crew of misfits and individualists to being the last best hope for humanity against a psychotic overlord. Some of the more cynical ORM'ers would say we already were that, but... this isn't what I wanted. ...you were just as quiet as me in there, you know. Kinda feels like all of this is out of your control, doesn't it?"

"Well... yeah, it does," he admitted. "Meiko's the one who solves problems, not me. I'm just there to support her... it's the best I can do. I can't really do anything else... I wish I could, but..."

"Sorry for bringing it up, but... don't you have powers over reality like he does? Or did I completely misunderstand what they were talking about earlier?"

"Huh? No, no... I mean... sort of. But I couldn't possibly, I mean..." Mallory backpedaled. "No, they won't help. I can't use them when I want. And even if I could, well... no. I can't. Multi's stronger. He's capable of so much more that I can't really do anything against him..."

"Neither can I, unfortunately," Xyzzy said. "Here I am, supposed leader of the ORM, and I can't do jack. I'm not a rebel commander, a warlord, I'm just this programmer who thought things ought to be different and that means I'm useless right now. That's frustrating. I was considering extending some sort of olive branch to the guy, try to work with him—I mean, we're both sort of against RealWare's mode of thinking. I figured I could persuade him to stop running amok, really work with the people instead of forcing these things on them... but I can't do that. All it'd take is one backstab by him and we're toast... and he doesn't strike me as a trustworthy sort. ...I wish Gillian was still in charge there. At least then it was just business."

"But weren't you two enemies?" Mallory asked.

"In some ways... but ideally, I'd prefer to think of it as being rivals. We just had different views on the direction reality should be moving in, but *she* actually let us compete with her with a 'may the best world view win' mentality," Xyzzy said, with a little smile at the thought. "Despite my grudge, I have to admit that it was kind of fun to butt heads with her. Sure, it was a quote-unquote war, but only in the silliest capitalistic sense. Not in an actual bloody body count and struggle for power sense... and even in that quasi-war, I never wanted utter dominance. I didn't see myself dictating reality like Multi is. I just wanted... I guess I just wanted it free from control."

"Which is exactly what he's not doing," Mallory realized.

"Right. It's strange, he's against RealWare's mundane reality style, but he's even nastier with control than Gillian ever was. Before and after this, RealWare controlled reality; they meter it out, they monitor it, they keep it leashed to a single point of control. ...which is how Multi managed to take it over so easily, too. My father and I didn't think things should be that way, we figured everybody should be the master of their own reality. It extends down into everything the Open Reality Movement does... like the buildings. You said it yourself, everybody carved out a niche to call home here in Grep and did what they wanted with it. We just want to be free."

"I'd love to be free right now," Mallory mused. "I keep dreaming about how things were just a little while ago... we'd go to all sorts of amazing places around the multiverse, doing jobs, meeting people... and I'd work to keep the house from falling apart, and they'd work to keep us fed, and everybody was happy..."

"Mallory... what if those days are over?" Xyzzy asked, face darkening. "We've got to consider the possibility. Multi's strong, you said it yourself. What if we can't stop him? What if he destroys what we've been trying to do here, what if he ends up telling everybody how to live forever? I'm just a geek, man, just a nobody-special. I'm not a fighter. I tangle with engineering problems and deal with marketing flacks, I don't fight honest-to-goodness wars. NOBODY here does... so what could we possibly do to stop this?"

"We can destroy him, of course."

That coming from a more feminine voice, which was strolling through the sliding door. The raised voices from before didn't follow her out; the meeting seemed to be over.

"The discussion regarding Multi's fate has unfortunately been delayed," Gillian informed them, as she walked up to the overlook railing. "Meiko decided that since we still had no means to do such a thing, it was too early to discuss if we would do it or not. I believe she is postponing the inevitable, however..."

"A Tribal Alpha fragger and a shinobi aren't going to be enough against your security forces," Xyzzy said with a little contempt. "And if you really wanted him dead, you could've done it a lot earlier, you know..."

"Are you implying that I should have had my trusted head of security assassinated prior to this?"

"You knew he was going to do this one day. You told us as much yourself! So why didn't you stop him? Of all people, I know you're capable of it—"

"Xyzzy, Xyzzy, you lack forward vision. It's always crippled your movement, and that's quite a shame. How was I to know he would go sour? From all indications, he was set to rise in the ranks like a shooting star," she said, leaning backwards on the railing, a perfect picture of casual poise. "You don't know the boy like I did. Did you know he came to us in the Preferred Partners Program?"

"You mean the cradle-robbing program?"

"Just one of any number of faceless orphans some reality pawned off on us for a lease discount," she continued. "They saw no use for him, just another five-year-old mouth to feed. But I saw potential. He was eager to please, so eager to earn the respect of his peers... and so creative! I still have a painting or two he produced in his art classes hanging in my office; I claimed to keep them around just to embarrass him, but really, I was quite proud of the boy. He quickly earned a paying if lowly position, and fought and clawed his way up the corporate ladder... he was just as adept at making social network connections as he was with paint. He knew who to praise, who to befriend... who to stab in the back. I allocated funding for his training, seeing he had an eye for observing people and an aptitude for clever thinking. Perfect for security work. And the powers...! I was aware he had some sort of gift, after we started seeing anomalies in our corporate Reality Engine. Why, if he hadn't gone rogue, he and I could have revolutionized reality as we knew it..."

"But he DID go rogue. And don't pretend you didn't know, because you did know things were going south," Xyzzy accused. "You could have fired him, if not killed him. Done SOMETHING. Didn't you say once in a public debate with me about open reality that you felt any weapon was justifiable in a battle? If your rival couldn't overcome it, they didn't deserve victory..."

"Oh yes, but you see... Multi is still my weapon," she said, with a sort of mad glee. "He's gone rogue, and I'll have to attempt to destroy him, but if he survives my attempt then it means he *is* the paradigm shift I always wanted! His survival will prove his worth, or his destruction will show him to be just another false idol. Sort of like you, Xyzzy, just a false idol... your band of merry misfits are sadly incapable of inducing the change I seek, or you'd have done it now despite my best efforts. Multi is more of a success story than you'll ever be. For all his wanton destruction, he is... change. Change, pure and simple."

"...I always figured you were a bit eccentric, but not completely insane," Xyzzy bit off bitterly. "This is the kind of change you want? I was perfectly happy with the way the multiverse was before, thank you very much. There were more people in it, for instance!"

"I'm disappointed in you, Lewis. For a zealot, you lack zeal. Your father certainly had a great deal of it—"

"You would know! Your father had him killed!"

...and Gillian's smile faded.

"I... am not my father," she said, absolutely serious. "That is the line I will not cross. Yes... he decided to deal with the earliest incarnation of your movement by simply killing everybody involved. How you escaped alive is a mystery... but I never approved of his action. Do you know why?"

"Enlighten me," Xyzzy coldy suggested.

"Because to do that would be just as wrong as killing Multi at an early age. It would be slaughtering the innocent before they had a chance to prove their worth to history. It's a grossly destructive act, a waste, a disgusting thing... I always told you I wanted to defeat you in the marketplace, and I meant it. Because yes, RealWare's 'defense' force could likely sweep through Grep and kill every man, woman and child here... and that would mean you would never be able to prove if you were the paradigm shift. It would mean I was cheating, I was running in fear of your POTENTIAL alone. I would never do that, Lewis. And that means I could not kill Multi until the time was right... which is now. He has shown his quality... now it is time for him to prove that quality by either perishing or surviving the natural consequences of his actions."

"...fine. Since that's as close to an apology as I'll ever get from a Bates... I accept," Xyzzy said, a bit less chilly than before. It was something to chew on, all right. "But... I'm not my father, either. And if that means I've got less zeal, then fine; I've got less zeal. I just wanted peace, not chaos. The freedom to live in peace."

"Ah, but with peace comes stagnation, yes?"

"It's better than changing reality around like he's doing!"

"Like he's doing," she echoed. "That is the difference maker. Not that he's simply changing reality; after all, you're trying to do that yourself, Xyzzy; you and your movement. There's nothing inherently evil about changing your reality to reach your dreams... mmm. Mallory—tell me..."

Mallory snapped out of his trance, as he sat there quietly ingesting all that he was hearing. "Er, what? Yes?"

"Which appeals to you more... peace in stagnation, or risking change?" she asked him. "Let's say you had the power to change reality as you saw fit— which, ironically, you do in fact have. Are you content to sit back and hope for the best, to wish for peaceful days of comfort and similarity? Or would you reach for what you REALLY want, and try to change things to achieve your dreams? Peace or change, safety or risk? Decide."

On the spot, Mallory felt their eyes boring through his skull. It was six or seven questions wrapped up into one larger issue which he still hadn't come to grips with...

"I don't know," he said honestly. "I really don't know. ...I'm gonna go now. Excuse me."

He turned and opened the sliding door, headed quickly back into the building, away from the uncomfortable situation.

"...would you ease off on him?" Xyzzy asked his rival, quietly. "He's not really part of this. He's just this guy."

"On the contrary, I believe that he could be the most important player in the day's drama," Gillian disagreed. "It all depends on whether he's willing to play a part, or if he'll watch from the side."

Lorelei applied five times as much force as was required to trigger the door opening mechanism. The doors swished open with a satisfyingly science-fictiony door noise—courtesy of some fanboy who built this shelter for Grep months ago.

"I can't believe I even had to argue that," Lorelei continued ranting, as she had ever since leaving the conference room. "Whacking the guy should go without saying! He wants us dead, the least we can do is to do him in return, right? You agree with me, right?"

"For the fifth time, I am in concordance with your views," Kisei repeated from before, adjusting only the number via incrementation. She entered their small personal room, having a seat on her bunk bed. "I have done risk analysis, and it was a very simple analysis to make. He wishes us dead, and has shown tenacity in chasing us; the safest route is to eliminate the problem."

"And Meiko... what was her problem? She barely spoke up! All she had to say was 'It's too early to decide that.' What kind of answer is that? I was figuring she'd be all for this! I told you as much back at the onsen!"

"She is correct in her reasoning, however. Since methods of rescue and assassination both require determining a solid location for Eiko or Multi, we cannot finalize plans for either until—"

"Could you talk a little less formally for a change, please? I'm trying to work up a nice frothy rage here and your stoic attitude is helping a little too much."

"I mean no disrespect by my words, Lorelei..."

"Well... I'm going to kill him, at least," Lorelei decided, walking back and forth in front of the seated Kisei, full of restless energy. "One way or another. If she won't authorize it, I'll do it en route to getting Eiko back. While I'm in the neighborhood, like."

"In direct disobedience of her orders...?"

"You might follow the ancient honorable code of the warrior, but I'm more of the kick ass and ask ethical questions later variety. She can fire me if she likes, but I'm doing this for her own safety! ...you're not going to stand in my way, right? Come on, you AGREE with me about this! Don't tell me you're—"

"Lorelei!"

"What?!"

"...patience," Kisei suggested, lowering her voice, trying to inject some calm. "Patience. There are variables here. Meiko is right; it's too early to say one way or the other. Don't make assumptions about the future. Only... prepare for all eventualities equally. Then once a course of action is decided, you will be ready. Becoming agitated is not going to help you in the here and now, or when the time does come to act."

"So you're suggesting I just sit here and wait, then?" Lorelei asked.

"On the contrary, I am suggesting we prepare for all eventualities... including one which involves deadly use of force. Because at the moment, neither of us has the force we require, do we?"

"Well... my saber's gone, if that's what you mean. Trashed with the house. Your cache of scarily versatile munitions went up in smoke too..."

"Then in order to be ready at a moment's notice, we must prepare ourselves," Kisei decided, rising to her feet. "I have meditated upon how best to dispatch Multi, if the time came to do so. I believe I may have the answer. And since you are keen on taking action, perhaps you can... tag along?"

The problem wasn't how to rescue Eiko. The problem was how to know where she was, so she could then be rescued.

The problem was one of communication. Right now, they had an unconfirmed, one-way communication link. Through Belle's knowledge of her old RealNet studio systems, they could send her the tampered video stream... assuming she was watching it.

The problem was one of confirmation. Confirmation, through communication. Some way for Eiko to respond, so they could tell her exactly where to be, so she could escape... which they couldn't do, because they weren't even sure of where she was.

The problem wasn't how to rescue Eiko. The problem was to how to know where she was...

With a scowl, Meiko crumpled up the paper she was working on, and lobbed it towards the old wicker wastebasket. It missed by a mile, but even if she scored the three pointer it would've bounced off the overflowing mountain of trash anyway.

She couldn't appreciate the lovely study / bedroom she'd selected for herself. She couldn't appreciate the fine wooden molding, the splendid wallpaper, the absolutely fabulous antique oak desk she was working on. All these things in her newly inherited replacement home were quite wonderful and all but she had bigger things to worry about. Home could start being home once she had her sister back in her arms...

Meiko didn't even look up from her writing when the tea set was placed on her desk.

"Technically speaking, the human body can go without water for longer than you have," Ryo Noyori said, sitting on the edge of the desk next to the tea. "But if you're seriously gonna stay awake all the time, you're not going to be able to go without caffeine for that long. So drink up, mmm?"

"Yeah, tea," she agreed, grabbing a cup and draining it completely without bothering to savor the fine taste. Which was for the best, considering Ryo wasn't the multiverse's finest tea brewer.

"Meiko, you've got to stop beating yourself up over this. Not sleeping helps nobody. Everybody's already putting their heads on this problem, they can do without yours for eight hours—"

"Don't ride my ass right now, Ryo, I'm trying to think," she warned, crumpling the sheet she was working on. "I've had plenty of days to spend relaxing and taking it easy in the past. A couple spent pushing myself hard won't kill me."

"But you're not alone here, that's my point. We've got experts in different fields, we've got a lot of brain power to put towards the problem, right? Can't you trust in them...?"

"I do trust in them, actually," she said, finally looking away from her writing. "And it's going to take all of us to do this. But I can't NOT work on it, Ryo. Come on! You know me better than that! I'm the professional problem solver. I take control and I lead the charge whenever there's an issue. I couldn't sit back even if I wanted to, I'd go nuts trying not to think about the problem at hand..."

Ryo laughed softly. "Yeah, that's true... that's my Mei-chan! But come on, can't you let Ryo-kun worry for you instead? I've done it before, you know—"

"Stop."

"Stop what?"

"Just... stop. Don't say that," Meiko replied... quite serious. "Don't play it off, don't laugh it off. And absolutely do not worry for me on this. ...don't worry for me anymore. You were worrying for us when we found out about Mallory, and it didn't make things any easier on us, it just meant we got to sit back and sing la-la-la while stuff happened we weren't paying attention to! No.

I'm a big girl now, Ryo. Let me worry about my problems myself."

Ryo scratched his head, trying to think of a good way he could crack a joke, use a disarming smile, anything from his usual bag of tricks... but that stern look from Meiko, stern not in a 'Meiko's adorable stern glare' sort of way, stopped him dead each time.

"I'm... sorry," he said. "Sorry. Ah. I forget, sometimes. I'm sort of used to..."

"There's no need to apologize, Ryo. ...I'm not angry at you. I'm more angry at myself than anything else... look, just let me work on this for now. All right?"

"All right. How are things going with Mallory, then?"

Meiko's gears of thought skipped a few teeth at the topic shift.

"What?" she asked. "Well... fine, I guess. ...they WERE going fine. Until everything blew up, of course..."

"Good, good," Ryo said, reassuming his usual smile. "I'm glad you have someone, Meiko. Especially if you don't want me worrying for you anymore... well. I'd better get back to the lab, then. Follow my own lines of inquiry, and all..."

"Wait. Why ask that? I mean, yes, it's polite and conversational to ask about my love life, but—"

"It's nothing, it's nothing!" he protested, hopping off from his sitting position on the desk, straightening out his lab coat. "Don't worry about it. Really, don't. It's not even relevant anymore; you've already found someone you love. And I'm honestly, genuinely happy for you; it's all I ever wanted you to have. Don't second guess, don't doubt. Just enjoy it. You deserve to be loved..."

Perplexed, Meiko stared at her old friend as he hummed to himself, heading out of her room... or at least mostly out, before pausing at the door.

"Where is Mallory, anyway?" he asked. "I was assuming he would get you some tea himself, but since the kitchen was empty, I helped myself..."

"Ah... I don't know," Meiko admitted. "I've been busy up here. He's been quiet ever since we got here..."

"Eh? And you didn't ask him why?"

"I... kinda figured he needed his space. Like we talked about. And I was using the time to think..."

"Tisk tisk," Ryo tisk-tisk'ed, with a wry grin. "You're a big girl now, right? Right! So, do the big girl thing and talk to him. I'm sure you can help him and he can help you! But do it after drinking your tea; it's going cold. Ta ta!"

"Ryo...?"

He had fully left the room at that point, humming as he walked away.

Food was a safe harbor. You could think better while eating or cooking, Mallory found; so in lieu of going home and cooking (which he wasn't up for at the moment, as it'd mean going back to the fray) he tracked down a cafe.

Not all members of the ORM were hackers. Some simply provided services for the hackers, such as the owners of this cafe. The menu was written in chalk on a board, with frequent changes as the chefs changed their minds or experimented with new dishes; Mallory picked 'Sandwich Surprise' and was surprised indeed to receive a bowl of soup instead. A bowl of soup which, curiously enough, tasted like a sandwich. The distraction of bizarre cooking was quite helpful at the moment, and he took a mental note to get the recipe before leaving—most restaurants in Grep would give you the complete details of their dishes if you asked for them...

He was busy trying to figure out how an unidentifiable yellow thing in his soup tasted better than it looked (and oddly, tasted like ham and cheese) when a familiar figure wandered by the sidewalk cafe.

"Mellow Fellow?" Mallory called out, hoping that he wouldn't be embarrassed when the fellow turned around and turned out not to be very mellow.

And the fellow was not mellow, but he was Mellow Fellow. A Mellow Fellow without his usual smile...

"'ey, Mallory," he greeted, reversing course and pulling up a chair at his table to straddle without being asked. "I heard you were around here. Didn't figure I'd meet ya, though. Doing a lot of supply 'n fugee runs to RealWare-owned worlds... how ya been? Righteous or unrighteous?"

"Sorta both," Mallory admitted, pushing his soupwich aside for the time being. "Are you okay? You don't look so hot..."

"Been pullin' overtime. Lotta things to do; so many want to come here, and this place be needin' a huge amount of supplies... my engine, my wings 'o freedom, they stealthy, see?" he said, making a small flapping motion with his arms. "I don' bother much with protocols, just sneak in, sneak out. Got nicely tuned, upgraded wings. So, ORM called me, said 'Mellow, we need help,' and I say all right. ...'cause it's better than hangin' around I's Land lately."

"I wish I was hanging around I's Land right now, myself..."

"You remember how they were, yeah? When the Babylonia marched in and demanded our young?" Mellow asked. "Same way now. Not their problem, not their business. Just Babylonia. Doesn't affect us at I's Land! Swear, Mallory, they don't look ahead to the real problems comin' round the bend at them... sometimes I worry I's the only one who's lookin'..."

"I can't imagine Multi would do anything to your reality, though. I mean... it's perfect as is. It's a beautiful place, why would he change anything?"

"It's not just I's Land, mon. It's... all's land. Everywhere. Mellow, he thinks cross-reality, yeah? I's worried for everybody. I's feelin' Babylonia closing in, Mallory. Shadows overtakin' everything, even I's Land... freedom killed in wake of the devil's control... had to do something, couldn't just stand around, you know?"

"So... you're running supplies?" Mallory concluded, although it wasn't much of a jump in logic to make. "Doing your part...?"

"Righteous," Mellow agreed, allowing himself a little smile. "It ain't much but it helps, and that's what counts. Everybody here's pullin' together to support each other, no matter what it means. Gotta do the right thing, Mallory. Small or large, gotta do the right thing."

"...Multi thinks he's doing the right thing, too," Mallory said, opening up his thought stream a little to the I's Lander.

"Eh?"

"The guy who's responsible for all this. He really, honestly thinks he's doing the right thing. Gillian told us about him, how he wants to help out and make people happy... he doesn't sound like he should be a bad guy. I mean... he isn't that far from me..."

Mellow leaned back a bit, rocking his chair slightly; it knocked against the table, each time. "That eating at you, Mallory? The whole twin thing...?"

"Oh, no, no! I mean, I'm me, he's him, it's not like I'm having an identity crisis!" Mallory protested. "That's fine, I'm okay. Really..."

"Yeah, but you just said 'e's not that far from you. Just tryin' to do the right thing. Don't downplay havin' a mirror, man. Be a powerful spiritual thing, having an opposite out there. You can't shake somethin' like that off, and as I's a believer in the connectedness of things, I's seein' how it could be affectin' you..."

"I didn't think about it much until yesterday. I just... let Ryo do our worrying, and we put it out of our heads, got on with our lives. We had a total of two minutes together with the guy, after all! And there were the other me's, and they were so wildly different that I didn't feel too weird then, either. But... if he really feels like he's doing his best to support people when he's doing all these awful things... it's creeping me out. We have the same powers, sure, but others had them too. He's got the same thinking, that's the creepy bit! I don't honestly think I'd run around slaughtering people, but... is he really that far removed from me?"

"You ain't the same at all, Mon."

"He's him and I'm me, I know—"

"I ain't just talkin' names or even physical bodies or mentalities," Mellow said. "There be a bigger, singular key difference here, okay? One absolute difference that makes all the difference."

"Yeah...?"

Mellow waited a moment, so the drama would be right for his grand theory to be presented.

"He's control," he stated. "And you're freedom. And that be that."

Mallory scratched his head, soup long forgotten as he considered it. "O... kay. I mean, that's obvious, right?"

"Obvious, but it's still deep, Mon. It's spiritual, you can't deny the power of it. Somethin' in your core which sets you so far apart that he ain't you and you ain't him. See, Multi—'e wants to tell you what you want and then give it to you. Mallory—'e gets others to talk about what they want and then gives it to them. You work with 'em, he works against 'em even if both of you wanna do what's right. But I's got more respect for your righteous ways than the ways o' him. Mal... he's Babylonia, Mon. Now, I's usin' that word to mean a lot, probably confuse you tons, but that's the reality of what Babylonia means to me—*control*. E's the poison o' Babylonia, pure 'n simple, and you're the antidote."

Mallory stared down at the table. "I'm not an antidote, Mellow. I can't do anything against him. He's too strong..."

"Now, that I's not knowin' a lot about... powers and conflicts and mayhems. All I knows is what I see in you," Mellow explained. "I ain't tellin' you to go to war or not to go to war. You do what you gotta do, Mallory. But do it knowin' you're righteous. That's all I's tryin' to say to you..."

He was about to speak up again, until he noticed the pair approaching. He waved to them, but they didn't approach him—they approached Mellow instead.

"We've been looking all over for you," Lorelei said. "C'mon, Kisei and I need a ride to Arboria. Are you available for a ride? We won't be long..."

"Oh, yeah, I's avail," Mellow said, getting up from his chair. "One hour tops though, gotta make a medicine run to Urbana. You ready to go now?"

"Wait, wait!" Mallory spoke up, rising as well. "I'd... uh, I want to come too..."

Lorelei turned, as if noticing him for the first time. "Eh? Why?"

"I guess... I just want to feel useful right now. To do something to support you all..."

"Mallory, we're about to go shopping for heavy weaponry, not cook an omelet," Lorelei said, with a playful smirk. "You could be suited for playing firing range target, but if you really wanna be useful... go talk to Meiko. She's been stewing in her room all day."

...Meiko?

Meiko!

He hadn't even thought of her once in the last hour!

Mumbling apologies and dropping some Grep monetary scrip on the table, he hurried out of there with Intent and Purpose.

Torn asunder by a short, sharp series of religious wars, the once verdant paradise of Arboria lie in smoking ruin. Craters littered the landscape, some radioactive, some on unstable geographic fronts. The air was thick with the choking dust kicked up by dozens of illegal weapons of mass destruction. No sane person would ever want to live on this hellhole, much less run a thriving munitions business on it as Duke had for years...

At least, until now.

Mellow Fellow's Smiling Taxi Service landed in a verdant field of lush grasses and wildflowers. A few butterflies twirled around the mobile shack, dancing in and out of the windows of this strange new addition to their world... the breeze which flowed in with them smelled vaguely of lilacs...

The trio stepped out of the shack, puzzled with the collective equivalent of having solved an eight-hundred-piece jigsaw marked as "Adult" difficulty which, once fully assembled, turned out to be a pair of adorable kittens.

"Mellow... it's not quite 4:20, right?" Lorelei asked. "So you didn't land us in the wrong reality, presumably..."

"This be the armpit of Babylonia, the hellzone of Arboria. My engine, she tells no lie..." Mellow replied. "We is where we is, even if—"

"HEY! OVER HERE!"

In the distance, there was a small campsite erected; survivalist's pup tent and smoke-free cookfire, plenty of surveillance equipment open and ready to be installed. And one very, very enraged former munitions dealer, who was approaching with speed.

"Will you look at this? Just LOOK at this mess!" Duke wailed, gesturing wildly at the pleasant fields of nature's pure beauty. "It's awful! It's a disaster! I'm ruined, I tell you—RUINED! I have half a brain to load up with what I have left and go blow the hell out of Reality Prime—!"

"It seems that Multi has decided to restore Arboria to its former glory," Kisei correctly deduced.

"You're damn right he did! You remember my warehouse, the one full of billions of points of heavy military weaponry? Gone. A few redwoods poked up through the ground under it, set off some of the explosives, the whole thing blew—and grass grew over the crater immediately after. Grass! Lush, green, lovely grass!"

"Grass? Oh, how horrific," Lorelei mocked. "You'll have to hire someone to mow the lawn now..."

Kisei ignored Duke's plight, addressing him on a direct business level. "I require a weapon from you, Duke. One which I know you have in stock at a more secured location than your warehouse... I believe I mentioned I might one day return for it. Has it survived this... natural disaster?"

"Are you deaf, Kisei? I just said that my whole sto... ...wait, you can't mean —"

"I do."

"Tell me you're going to use them to blow that schmuck's head off," Duke said, gleeful instead of spooked by the ominous unspecified weapons. "Not that I wouldn't give them to you otherwise, a promise is a promise, but I'd derive SO much satisfaction knowing they're gonna be put to good use..."

"There is a distinct possibility that they will be used in that manner."

"Right! Well! I'll just be five minutes with my metal detector and an autoshovel," he announced, grabbing a nearby case. "Be right back. Excuse me, ladies..."

"Yeah, you do that, Duke," Lorelei said, waving him off... and then dropping to a whisper. "Kiss? What exactly is Duke about to dig out of the ground? It's gotta be something nasty, if even HE wouldn't sell it openly. You're not going to use a full-fledged nuclear bomb, are you? We just want the freak dead, not all of Reality Prime turned to glowing putty..."

"That would be inefficient," Kisei agreed. "However, it is indeed a banned weapon. One which Tachi obtained with great difficulty, and felt it would be best to store off-site from our home—"

Duke was back in under a minute with a black case.

"Looks like I picked the right site for my camp—it was behind the tent," he said, passing the case over. "You still have the skills to go with those, though, Kisei...? I thought you were strictly a rifle expert nowadays..."

Inside the case were two unassuming-looking pistols. They'd be easy to mistake for ordinary metal-slug-throwing guns, except for the additional bulk of two water-filled purple cartridges on the back, and no obvious ammunition-loading mechanism...

Lorelei's jaw didn't drop, but she did stare quite intently as Kisei took a hold of the guns, one in each hand, and began doing some warmup exercises and gun-kata stances with them...

"Okay... I'll bite," she said, once curiosity had overwhelmed her. "Kisei, how on earth did you get your hands on a pair of Reality Pistols? They've been banned for centuries! ...do they even work?"

"Do they work? Do they WORK?" Duke asked, in the tone one would use if accused of having sex with a housepet. "Lorelei, this is Duke you're dealing with! I don't sell bad goods. I've kept these in good condition, digging them up each year just to make sure the parts were fresh, the micro-engine water stable, and the explosive charge viable. They'll work just fine... assuming Kisei's still got the skills..."

"Let me make sure my memory is accurate. I only read about them in a Tribal Alpha history book, after all... Reality Pistols work by teleporting a tiny explosive charge. There's no real bullet and no actual firing, it doesn't zip through the air, it just appears right where you want it to and then explodes. Correct?"

"Correct!" Duke affirmed, ignoring Kisei as she continued to stretch and warm up, using a variety of guns-akimbo poses to prepare herself. "One explosive round per gun, no more, no less. No reloading in battle possible, since it takes an hour to disassemble and insert a new charge. Highly illegal, since they also tend to destabilize host reality engines when they're overused in battle, but one shot in that freak's head shouldn't hurt anyone... problem is getting the shot into his head."

"It's a gun, Duke. Point and shoot, yes?"

"It's a teleporting charge. You point, yeah, and you shoot—but how far ahead of the muzzle the charge teleports depends entirely on the skill of the marksman," he explained, overjoyed to play the know-it-all. "The trigger's analog. How far you squeeze it determines how far the charge shifts across reality—ranging from one meter to thirty meters depending on the pull distance. Which means you have to have ridiculous amounts of manual dexterity to hit anything, to the point where you can control your trigger finger down to the sub-milimeter... and if you're gonna carry two of them at once, which only makes sense considering they're single-shot weapons, that means being ambidextrous on top of all that—"

"You got anything buried that I can use?" Lorelei asked, on a whim. "Double saber, maybe? Mine's scragged. I'd prefer a force blade, stun and other modes, like I had before... and if you have any other illegal reality-technology gear I could use, load me up. Money is no object! We nicked Ryo's scorecard."

"Well... I dunno, I've only got a few crates of stuff salvaged. I'll see if I've got anything. Wait here."

Lorelei let the military fanboy rummage around, joining Kisei as she focused on her Zen mastery of the weird little guns.

"I don't mean to cast doubt on your madskillz, Kiss, but you sure about these things?" she asked, hoping Kisei wasn't so into the zone that she could no longer hear spoken words. "Sounds like they're hellaciously difficult to control. And if you only get one shot against this guy..."

"Pick a target," Kisei asked, within her sphere of absolute calm.

With a shrug, Lorelei glanced around... and pointed at a random cluster of trees. "All right, hit one of those—"

With grace that cats would be envious of, Kisei twisted herself into a flawless defensive posture to use against attackers, while simultaneously aiming two guns at two different targets that the human eye couldn't actually see.

There wasn't any audible noise from the guns, but two trees—ones positioned behind several rows of other trees, thus impossible to hit with a normal bullet—were sliced in half by tiny explosive charges, splinters flying as they toppled to the ground.

Kisei nodded once in satisfaction, before turning back to Lorelei. "The sniper is silent, but slow," she explained. "The element of surprise is useful, but that alone may not be enough against my enemy. He can stop bullets; bullets are too slow. With these, I will be able to strike my target at the speed of thought."

"...damn," Lorelei summarized her position on the subject, staring in awe at the superhuman feat. "I think I'm love."

Then she looked down, finding two strange objects thrust at her by the scrawny army guy.

"It's all I have," he said. "One force saber similar to your old one, but only single-bladed. And as for illegal reality technology, I've got this shield... it'll project an invulnerable field, but you can only use it in short bursts before the battery drains. Only battery I have, too. Take it or leave it."

Gingerly, Lorelei grasped the blade of the saber—lighting it up, the familiar blue glow comforting while the lumpy circular shield hung loosely on her arm. *She* wasn't the one who used sword and shield, usually...

"Terrific," she said, with distaste. "Instead of berzerking my way through, I'm going to be playing Dee. Rei-Lei would be ROTFLing right now."

Meiko was slumped against her desk, but not asleep. Just dejected.

She was stuck in a pattern; fatigue had eaten into her, and completely wrecked her thought process. She wasn't going to get far like this, constantly hitting the same points over and over in a redundant fashion that was repetitive and unhelpfully redundant. The crumpled up wads of paper had grown to ridiculous sizes, the actual basket no longer visible...

It was time to pack it in.

Except that she was being offered tea again.

"Ah, I didn't realize Ryo already made you some..." Mallory said, after bringing it in. "Oops. Well... you're going to need it so you can stay up, right? So I guess two loads of tea can't hurt..."

She was going to comment on how it was officially time to go to sleep and she'd have to pass on his tea, but was too tired to make an effort at rejecting him when he was just trying to help. So, she decided to apologize for something else...

"I'm sorry—"

"I'm sorry—"

"ER"

"You're—"

"What—"

"Stop," Meiko ordered. "This is another one of those moments where we're both apologizing for something and stampeding over each other to get it out. This time, we're talking turns, and I call dibs on the first one. I want to apologize for hiding out up here and ignoring you ever since we got here."

"Uh... that's funny, I was going to apologize for being such a quiet loner lately..."

"Oh, good, then they're compatible apologies," Meiko said with what cheer she could manage. "No harm, no foul. And if I can add one apology on top of that, I'm sorry, but I have to pass on the tea. I'm throwing in the towel and getting some sleep."

"Right, right," Mallory said, nudging his teaset away from her. "Sorry, I just... well, I wanted to feel useful. But I know that there's not a whole lot else I can do right now, after all, other than..."

She waited patiently for him to finish his sentence before finishing it for him.

"Let's get this out of the way," she suggested. "Maybe it was wrong of me to ask the others not to bring it up, for them to leave you alone... your powers. They might be used against Multi, right?"

"Well... right, except—"

"Except that it's a bad idea, of course. I tried explaining to them that you can't really do it on command, and even if you could... I wouldn't allow it."

"I'm not? Not that I'm complaining, but, uh... why?"

"Because... you stand a strong chance at dying in the process. You're not going to be the one to valiantly sacrifice his life for me, Mallory. I'm not going to allow that kind of drama in my life. I have trained experts on my payroll for a reason, and this is it. So your powers aren't going to be a factor in our rescue. We have to think of something else."

"Of course, yeah, I know, I agree," he dogpiled in concurrence. "Something else. Definitely. ...maybe I can be useful in helping you think through this stuff? An outside perspective can't help, right? Can't hurt! I meant can't hurt..."

"Hey, if you want to sift through my notes while I'm unconscious, feel free," she offered, wearily pulling herself out of the seat she'd been wedged into for the last few hours. "But I've been going over and over this and I can't get anywhere. We've got all these great people, all these great resources... as much as it feels odd to think of people as resources... and no way to combine them to get what we want. Lorelei, Kisei, Ryo, Alex, Belle, Mellow, Xyzzy, Gillian... Open Engines, security buildings, RealNet hacking, weird technologies... it's all a blur right now..."

On a whim, Mallory nudged a precarious pile of notes to see if it would topple. It did. A few notes fell side by side.

"Alex and RealNet hacking," he read off the two notes. "Hacking and Alex, Alex and hacking..."

"I'm going to crash," Meiko announced. "Wake me up if anything important happens. Seriously, please wake me up, don't let me sleep out of pity..."

"Okay. I don't think I'm gonna get real far here alone, though," he said... and then, glancing at the cards, randomly mused to himself. "You know... it's a shame Alex isn't an official member of the Important Courtroom Drama cast. Eiko would probably love to have an official action figure of him... and he's a better hero than I am right now."

Meiko halted her bedward progress.

"Repeat that," she requested. So he did.

Her gears, groaning from metal fatigue, resumed turning...

The Council of Various Interesting Persons reconvened at Noyori Labs an hour later. Meiko had no organized plan, just a series of notes scrawled in her own handwriting (and Mallory's, when her wrist went limp), but she could tell it straight from her brain—her looping thoughts now were obsessively studying it, after all.

"Action figures," she announced. "That's the link we need. Eiko loves to buy action figures from her favorite shows. She has every figure from Important Courtroom Drama except one—Alex Gunthar, the character we hacked into the show. And just as we have access to the video streams, we also have access to the production company's commerce node. Ladies and gentlemen, we are going into the toy business."

"Insert smarmy, uncomprehending comment here," Lorelei added. "But I think I know where you're going with this..."

"We're going to hack their commerce node to insert an Alex Gunthar figure into their toy stocks," Meiko continued. "But this hack will only show if displayed on the same RealNet Workstation we know Eiko is using. From there, she'll be able to purchase the figure... and since we can check if the figure is purchased by someone, that'll act as our communication feedback. If she buys the figure, it means she's seeing our broadcast. She'd be the only person capable of buying it because of her location and the hack."

Lorelei thought about it. "Makes sense, but who says she's going to be able to buy it? The kid likely doesn't have a scorecard of her own..."

"Multi will buy it for her, if she's persistent enough," Gillian added in. "He's eager for acceptance, especially from the children he idealizes. That's why he let her message Kensuke, and in fact that's why he's keeping her alive in general. He'll buy the toy if she tries hard enough."

"And Eiko is quite capable of finagling money out of strangers, much less emotionally vulnerable strangers like Multi," Meiko added to the addition. "So. What we're going to do is give Eiko specific instructions through Alex, and then she'll signal to us via the toy purchase when it's time to act out our half of the plan. If you recall, all we needed was to know exactly where she'll be... and again, we're going to exploit Multi to do it. We need him in one of the two buildings, executive or network control. There's no real reason why a kid would want to go to the executive building... but if Gillian's right, then all Eiko has to do is play along with Multi and ask to help him with his 'great work' which he does from the network control center."

"Which he will do, since the creativity of a child is of utmost importance to him," Gillian said, looking more and more pleased as the plan unfolded. "Sharp thinking, Meiko Mirai. You'd make a fine employee for RealWare..."

"Thank you, but I'm happy with my chosen profession," she said, without missing a beat. "So. Eiko butters Multi up until he agrees to let her work with him on some project—likely non-lethal, Eiko's smart enough to pick a harmless modification to the multiverse for her request. And right before she leaves, she's going to ask for the toy. That'll be the signal that we have to move, because I doubt she'll be able to keep him in the network control center for long. Lorelei smashes her way into the security center to disable the defenses, Kisei sneaks into the NCC, both leave with Eiko in tow. Mission complete. Questions?"

Lorelei was about to speak up—until Kisei put a hand on her arm, silencing her. It was her turn to clear the air.

"Meiko... I would like to request authorization from you to use deadly force against Multi," she said. "I am aware of your feelings on the issue of assassination, but you have heard the arguments in favor of ending this nightmare before it becomes even more of a safety risk than it already is. If you authorize it... I will deal with both the rescue and the elimination in the same mission. ...I will commit seppuku afterwards for my unclean act if you demand it, although I realize this is not likely in line with your thinking."

The knights of the round conference table went silent, waiting for their leader's reply.

For a moment, it seemed as if Meiko had fallen asleep. But her eyes opened soon after; she was merely thinking it over.

"Authorization granted," she stated. "I wish it hadn't come to this. I really do... but we don't have a choice. He's just going to keep chasing us, and ruining our lives, and... as much as I hate to be responsible for singing a death warrant... I'll sign it. But this is SECONDARY to rescuing Eiko. Don't do it if you don't have a clear and absolute opportunity, Kisei. No self-sacrifice. No mistakes. We'll live on the run if we have to rather than lose anyone to this... this monster. Agreed?"

"Agreed. I will go prepare myself for the mission now."

"You might want to wait on that, Kisei. Important Courtroom Drama doesn't air for another couple of hours... and then we need to wait for Eiko to manipulate Multi into joining her in modifying reality. It could be well into tonight. It could be days from now, even."

Lorelei sat back, pondering the plan. "Meiko, it sounds good, but... what if the purchase never happens? What if we're waiting for hours to days to weeks to forever...?"

"Then... I don't know," Meiko admitted, as she got shakily to her feet. "We'll think of something else. I hope. For now, I'm going to my new home, and I'm going to bed..."

Mallory was right there to help her out of the room, wordlessly assisting. The others departed to make their own preparations—and to play the waiting game.

He kicked aside a few stray wads of paper, helping Meiko across the floor of her bedroom. He helped her sit on her bed. He turned out the lights for her.

"I'll be right downstairs on the couch if you need me," he told her. "But get some sleep, all right? Everything's going to be fine. I know it will."

"I hope so, Mallory... I really do," she said, sagging in as she sat in place. "It's all so... iffy. A lot of variables. A lot of questions. And if they can't stop him... if he just keeps coming after us..."

"Kisei and Lorelei have never let us down before. I'm sure everything's gonna be okay..." he said, trying to reassure her... which was a tough job, when he was also feeling nervous about it all. "ER right. So... goodnight, Meiko."

"Mallory..."

"Yes?"

"You don't have to sleep on the couch, you know."

"Huh...?"

Meiko wrapped her arms around herself, looking very small and scared.

"I don't want to be alone tonight," she said. "Please..."

He sat next to her, and offered the best thing he could; a hug. And a kiss.

She kissed him more than he was kissing her, until he kissed her back just as much. The room felt slow and quiet...

"Meiko... you've got to get some rest..." he reminded her, as she lay back on the bed with him.

"I don't care," she said. "It doesn't matter. I need to be with you tonight. I don't want to be alone..."

She won't be, he decided. Not tonight, and never again.

There they were, right as they had predicted. Everything was going according to plan.

Eiko and Multi, in the spacious network control center. Kisei, sneaking in through shadows no eyes could possibly penetrate. Lorelei, getting ready to run in in case anything went wrong...

And it did. Kisei fell from the shadows, dead. Eiko was screaming. Lorelei rushed, and for her efforts she fell dead as well.

Next to die was Eiko. Then Meiko. All the while, Multi was smiling, because he knew it was right and good and what had to be for the sake of everything.

And the ghost, the ghost was always there, shrugged deep into his black trenchcoat, always staring at him. What are you going to do about it? he was saying with those eyes. What are you going to do about it...?

He didn't wake up screaming. He just woke up. He didn't sit bolt upright, he didn't even move; Meiko, sleeping next to him, hadn't stirred a bit.

It wasn't going to work.

He was lying around and not doing anything but wishing, hoping, praying.

Are you content to sit back and hope for the best, to wish for peaceful days of comfort and similarity? Or would you reach for what you REALLY want, and try to change things to achieve your dreams? Peace or change, safety or risk?

The yin-yang of his sweatshirt stared at him from the desk chair which he'd thrown it over.

He's the poison of Babylonia, pure and simple, and you're the antidote.

Meiko slept soundly next to him, so exhausted, but so at peace from being in his arms... so perfect. So right... everything he had dreamt of, everything he wanted right here. But so fragile right now...

What are you going to do about it?

He wasn't useless. He had one very good use, if only he could find it in himself to do it...

That's the way it has to be, now that I know the truth—I have to need something. Absolutely need something. Something so strong that I can't avoid using it, I can't deny and wish it would go away. That's why it only works sometimes.

There wasn't any escaping that now. So... he'd simply make peace with it. He'd do what he had to.

You're not going to be the one to valiantly sacrifice his life for me, Mallory. I'm not going to allow that kind of drama in my life.

He kissed Meiko on her cheek, a simple goodbye, and grabbed his sweatshirt. There wasn't time for an apology...

Sometime later, the door to the room quietly opened.

"Meiko...?" Gillian asked, peering into the room. "Dear, it's time to wake up..."

Groaning at the interruption, she awoke from her sleep, holding the sheets to her body as she sat up. "The toy...?"

"Purchased," Gillian confirmed. "In addition, crayon drawings have started to appear all over Urbana's buildings. Eiko's making her move, and it's one she knew we'd never miss; Lorelei and Kisei have already been dispatched to Reality Prime. Get dressed, and let's go monitor the mission. Where's your counterpart...?"

Blinking to get her eyes used to the darkness, Meiko looked around... but saw nothing.

Flexing her muscles, Lorelei bounced the heavy shield against her forearm a few times. She wasn't used to this fighting style, but she'd be a quick learner. Either that or she'd be dead, so a quick learner it would be...

Kisei, on the other hand, was flowing and natural as she kept a solid grip on her Reality Pistols. For someone who had only used a rifle for the last few years, the new weapons were just as much an extension of her physical body as the old weapon was. Lorelei felt a tiny pang of envy at that, encumbered with her clumsier gear...

When Mellow Fellow's mobile shack shifted, Kisei was at the window, ready to give the signal to move quickly if they were spotted. A few tense moment passed, before she spoke up—which meant they were safe, otherwise she wouldn't bother with words.

"I suggest that you leave shortly after we do, Fellow-san," Kisei suggested. "This may very well be a one-way trip for us, and there is no sense in losing you as well."

"I-and-righteous-I's stayin' put," Mellow said with as much authority as he could muster. "This is a crusade for me, too. You don' worry, your getaway vehicle'll be right where you left it. Get goin'."

Wordlessly, the two slipped out of the hut—wearing black jumpsuits provided by Duke, they blended in perfectly with the night air of Reality Prime. They hugged the edges of the campus, away from the spacious gardens and fountains where they'd stand out like a pair of sore thumbs... instead, the shadows guided them towards the triumvirate of buildings, two out of three of which would be their targets for the evening.

Right before they'd have to part company... even if it risked the mission, Lorelei had to speak up. She spoke in a near-silent whisper, one she'd learned through her years of raids in Tribal Alpha.

"You really think this is a one-way trip?" she sub-vocalized.

"I would prefer not to fail my mission, obviously," Kisei replied in a similar whisper. "But we must be prepared for all possibilities. The hagakure teaches me to meditate upon eventual death, as it could come at any time."

"Yeah, well, I'm gonna do my best to avoid 'eventual' equaling 'today'... but... I gotta ask something before you go. Just in case."

"We do not have much time—"

"What did you mean, when you said you weren't entirely without experience when I talked about getting you laid? Back at the onsen. You never told me, and it's been driving me nuts."

"Ah," Kisei said... and broke into a tiny, tiny smile before responding. "I have never had sexual intercourse, actually. I was lying in a manner of jest and teasing which I felt you would appreciate, given your normal standards for such lighthearted camaraderie."

"...right. We've got to work on your sense of humor. And we WILL have time to do so... especially after that bar-crawl I'm still planning on dragging you to. So get the job done and we'll go dress sexy and have beers in Nippon to celebrate. Deal?"

"As you wish," Kisei agreed.

Both women parted ways, heading to their separate objectives.

And for all Kisei's tracking skills, she couldn't detect the one who followed her, because he didn't want to be detected.

The security control center. Gillian had taught her the most efficient path through it, once which would only involve fighting a dozen people at worst. There would be slinking through air vents, and some detours through storage rooms, et cetera, et cetera.

Which she'd inevitably fail at. Lorelei was not stealthy, and any attempts to be so would probably go wrong—especially lugging around a pair of weapons she wasn't at 100% with. So, she decided hours ago on a little unspoken change in strategy...

In the words of Zerg, fellow member of the Steel Blades Clan, "Just rush that shit down." So she did.

The front door caved easily after a crossing pair of slashes from her blade, and a burst of the pure reality bubble formed by her shield.

The next six armed guards went down hard, stunned into submission with the blade; she'd had to bounce off the walls a few times and there was thankfully a few pillars to hide behind and somersault between.

The next two hallways involved running along the walls and executing non-lethal yet deadly-looking pirouette slashes on the phalanx of guards coming after her—she collapsed a few walls as she went to keep the few stragglers from following her, cut any walls she found to sever security system wiring, and generally hack and slashed the living hell out of everything around her...

All in a day's work, and truth be told, kind of boring. She'd had flag runs in Tribal Alpha that were more brutally exciting than this. And, much as she hated to admit it, the shield was proving infinitely useful; if she timed when she squeezed the activation trigger, she'd barely have to bother dodging gunfire. Playing Dee had a few advantages, which explained how Rei-Lei kept beating the pants off of her.

Her objective was the core room of the security center, the power plant which kept those nasty high-tech defenses alive and kicking. Reaching the room was a simple affair—then she noticed that there were considerably more guards in that room than Gillian had anticipated. As in, one hundred more of them than Gillian had anticipated.

Ah. NOW it was officially fun.

What followed were three of the most blissful moments of Lorelei's existence, a frenzied orgy of mayhem and carnage the likes of which would go down in Tribal Alpha history, if Tribal Alpha cared about that sort of thing anymore. By the end of it, standing atop a pile of unconscious RealWare security personnel... Lorelei felt so satisfied she was concerned she'd have to change her jumpsuit, to avoid it remaining sticky and damp in personal places.

Then she noticed that all the lovely power plant equipment she was simply going to deactivate had taken a lot of damage in the process, and was about to explode, killing everybody including herself, which was bad.

Praying that she'd gained enough skill points at playing Dee to play it on a much larger scale, she jammed the dial on her shield to Maximum and held down the activation trigger...

A full minute later, once the explosions ceased, she relaxed. Despite the room being coated in soot and still on fire in several places, she hadn't lost a single life. Shield battery drained, Lorelei sat on top of her pile of conquests, and took five.

It was all up to Kisei now.

When the steady hum coming from the shielding around the Network Control Center was silenced—and more importantly, the series of explosions and mayhem from the Security Center was silenced—Kisei made her move.

She hugged shadows as if she were betrothed to them. Every skill, every year of training under her father led up to this mission—above all others, she could not fail. Failure meant failing those important to her, and she would sooner die than allow that... but death would mean failure, so she would not die, and she would not fail. It was simple and pure.

According to Gillian's notes, there would be a large antechamber which connected to the actual NCC core room. It would have rafters and shadows. Which meant, much as Kisei silently predicted, it would be a perfect place for a personal bodyguard to strike from.

Even in shadow, a sniper round embedded itself where Kisei was half a second ago. She chose a deeper shadow to hide within, and waited. And waited.

The bodyguard was a professional, but something was causing him to hold back. She knew why once he spoke up.

"I thought those guns were illegal, Kisei," a voice spoke from nowhere; perfectly echoed off the chamber walls, to mask its true origin point.

"Gabriel," she confirmed, using the same voice trick to remain hidden. She couldn't afford to do this, to talk to him. She had to get on with the mission. Time was a factor...

"I'm under contract, Kisei. I will protect the body of one Multi, CEO of RealWare. I'm very sorry it's come to this again..."

She slinked along the walls, heading for the doors. Perhaps she could talk him to distraction, then make her move. Taking on both Multi and Gabriel would be difficult... but she did have two guns. She could make each count.

"I have been authorized to use deadly force by my employer this time, Gabriel," she told him as she moved. "I am no longer restrained. I will kill you if I must to achieve my mission."

"But will you use that force? I know I'm not exactly your lover, Kisei, but I'd like to think you have enough feeling towards me not to execute me. Or are you still being fiercely loyal to your code, as before...?"

"No. This is for more than my code," she said, raising one gun as her ears began to pinpoint her target. "This... is for those I care about."

One step into the light, to draw his fire, to distract him. One smooth motion to pull the—

She wasn't alone. They weren't alone.

She quickly stepped back into shadow, avoiding another sniper round in the process. Who? Who had just walked past her? She felt nothing, saw nothing... but could tell someone was here. Another bodyguard?

Either way, she had missed her moment. Cursing silently, she waited for her next opportunity, and prayed she would not be too late for Eiko...

The ordinary room, the place of power, the core of RealNet. Multi focused on the work, translating the crayon drawings Eiko had made, overlaying them onto the mundane buildings of Urbana...

"Do the giant lizard next! Do it, do it!" she cheerfully commanded, poking at her drawing with one finger. "It'll look so cool on the Urbana Stock Exchange next to the butterflies and the fairies. Oooh, I know, give it dragon wings! That'll be even better—"

The sharp crack of gunfire snapped Multi's focus. (Far away, a large chunk of the Urbana Stock Exchange collapsed as his misdirected focus ripped away from it.) He turned to look at Eiko... and saw worry in her eyes. She knew something...

Quickly, he held her in place with his power, and rose from his chair. "Gabriel! Gabriel, what's going on?!" he shouted out to the antechamber. "Who's...."

He was across the room as well as where he was, and the door had never opened.

"You're not Gabriel," Multi said, too stunned to say anything less obvious.

"No," Mallory confirmed... calm and at peace, as he addressed his opposite. "And I'm not you, either. But I'm close enough, for this..."

Eiko's smile was bigger than it had been in days. "M... Mallory-oniichan —!"

"Don't step closer," Multi warned, raising a hand, ready to gather his power. "Don't step closer, or I'll kill her. You know I'll do it!"

"No, you won't."

The new CEO of RealWare frowned as much as Eiko was smiling, and killed her with a thought.

Except he didn't. Couldn't. Nothing happened. In fact, Eiko had wriggled free of his powered grip, and was already running to go hide behind her beloved oniichan.

Fine, Multi thought, and decided to make both of them explode into flames instead.

That didn't happen either.

"What the...?" he exclaimed, staring at his reformed hand in disbelief. "My power... you've disabled it!? HOW?"

"I didn't disable it, I'm just countering it," Mallory told him... still advancing slowly, as he herded Eiko behind him with one hand. "I'm using my power to make sure the opposite of whatever you're trying to do happens."

Furious, Multi stepped backwards, grasping the console with one hand. RealNet, and Reality Prime's engine flowed into his being—he drew upon power, the kind of greater power he'd use to modify entire realities. Surely THAT would be enough to overcome this ridiculous trick....

But again, when he tried to crush his enemy, turn gravity inside out and pound his flesh into nothing... nothing is exactly what happened. He could feel the countering now, rising in power to match his own, even without an engine to feed on. Mallory Heisenberg was drawing on more of the power than Multi had ever been able to draw upon unaided... impossible. Unthinkable!

"What do you hope to prove by this? You'll hit your limits eventually. My powers are stronger, stronger than any of the others and certainly stronger than yours! I'll defeat this attempt with ease..."

"No, you won't. Because I have to stop you," Mallory repeated... so calm, so focused compared to any other time in the entirety of his life. "I can't really fight you, I can't defeat you; but for Meiko and for everything I love and care about, I can at least stop you. It's all I can do. Eiko, get back against the wall, quick..."

The air visibly thickened, a purple haze which threatened to crush the both of them. Multi didn't care. He built his power higher and higher, desperate to win, to overcome this... he pushed himself harder than ever and every time Mallory stepped forward, unconcerned, not showing the tiniest signs of breaking, it only pushed Multi to go further. He saw through the haze, saw the young child trying to move but being pushed back by it, trying to approach but moving slowly, as if time were flowing like syrup around them...

"You can't keep this up," Multi said, in disbelief. "It doesn't make sense. You could barely do anything before, how are you doing this now...?"

"I just... decided I had to do it," Mallory said, with a shrug and a very Mallory-esque goofy smile. "Just like I had to do what I did before, to protect Meiko. Once I accepted it, it was easy. We're like a yin-yang, Multi; I have to balance you out, not fight you. Yin-yang, poison-antidote, whatever you want to call it. I can stop you, even if nobody else can. You had to kill the others because they could potentially find a way to stop you, right?"

"Re... reality shall be determined by... the last one standing...!"

"Well, we're both standing and neither of us can do anything to the other," Mallory reasoned. "I think I've demonstrated that by now. So... what's the point? Let's both call it quits! Listen, Meiko and the others, everybody in the multiverse only want you dead because you won't stop hurting them! All you have to do is give up, stop doing what you're doing. You don't have to die here!"

"Give up...? Don't you understand? This is the future! It's what has to be done, I can't give up," Multi protested, as the room around them started to fade from view. "I'm in control. I can do this. I can overcome you!"

He drew from reserves he didn't even know he had. He drew from every engine, everywhere. Everything, everywhere. He was tied into the multiverse on the whole—and even that wasn't enough. Something eerily pure about Mallory kept him on the exact same level...

"You can't draw this much power," Multi warned. "You'll... explode. I saw it happen to M. You know it'll happen!"

Mallory looked around himself, at the distant and fading everything of all. "Yeah... I know. Well... if I have to do that, then I have to do that. I'd do anything for her, and you're not going to keep me from protecting her... so if you won't stop, then we're both going to have to die for her. I'm sorry it had to be this way... she's gonna be really mad at me, I think..."

A soundless scream emerged from Multi's self, as the two deadlocked mirrors ceased to exist in conventional reality.

Her ideal of becoming speed was rapidly fading away, as she was forced to hide in shadow and await opportunity. She spent no mental energy on anger at herself for getting trapped in this situation; she had to react at the speed of thought...

There. Purple light from the cracks of the closed doorway. It would provide a distraction to anybody concentrating less than she was, and she was the epitome of concentration...

Three muscles were used; one to raise the gun, one to twist her wrist for positioning, one to squeeze the trigger...

And one to adjust it a few inches to the right. Four muscles, then. The end result would be satisfactory regardless.

Gabriel dropped from the rafters, right from the hiding spot she had predicted he was using. His arm fell a moment afterwards, rifle still in the disembodied hand.

Kisei sprang from the shadows, quick to pounce on his body—she slapped down a wad of immobilization gum to his uninjured arm, as well as one to the bleeding shoulder which had been shattered by her Reality Pistol shot. Sputtering blood, he spoke to her through a woozy smile.

"I'm glad it was you," Gabriel he said. "I'm glad it was you to kill me..."

"You are not dying," she informed him. "I aimed specifically to ensure that; you are not the one I wished to use deadly force against. You will not stop me from my objective now. ...I will send a medical team here once I am done. Stay conscious."

Her "enemy" watched helplessly, as Kisei shoved the doors to the NCC open, tossing away her spent pistol and aiming the other one with intent to kill...

Except that someone had beat her to the job. Multi was enveloped in a light that hurt to look at, one which bent and twisted reality in ways the human mind couldn't fully comprehend... but in the confusion, she could tell that there were two figures rapidly dissolving before her eyes: Multi, and Mallory Heisenberg.

She didn't bother shooting, as by the time she had registered the sight, both were gone.

Instead, she picked up the shocked Eiko, and turned to leave. One way or another, the mission seemed to be complete.

Here is nowhere. Here, you are everywhere.

Nearly every citizen of the multiverse had been here, whether they knew it or not; it existed between things. It was there in the molecules of your coffee cup, it was as distant as your deepest memories. It did not exist despite existing, and the only place mortal eyes had glimpsed it was in the depths of complicated reality mathematics which only seven or eight people currently alive could even start to comprehend.

For lack of a better name, it was Nullspace, and the two of Mallory were ascending through it at uncontrollable speed.

He didn't have a body. He possibly didn't have a mind, but he fought to believe that he did have one. "He" was he, be it Mallory or Multi, this state would apply to either of them. As well as the fear either of them was feeling.

"Stop this..." Multi was begging, even if he wasn't using a physical voice induced by air over vibrating cords of flesh to say the words. "Stop this, please! We can't survive it...!"

"You can stop anytime you want to," Mallory said, fighting through the fear. "But I can't stop until you do. I told you that. Just give up! I don't want to die any more than you do!"

"But it's my dream..."

And in that flash, Mallory knew what his counterpart's dream was. He could feel the passion for it, the desire to achieve a limitless existence where none would be wanting and nothing bad could ever happen. No matter how clumsy Multi was at achieving his goals, no matter what flawed methods he used, what he really wanted was pure and shining and wonderful...

Mallory had to force himself to look away from it.

"You can find another way to have that," he suggested. "It doesn't have to be this way!"

"There is no other way. Reality shall be determined by the last one standing..."

Ascend the corporate ladder. There's no room for second best. Achievers ascend, failures descend. Work for your own glory—

—work with your friends, with your family. It doesn't matter who's best. Together they can do what you want to do...

That perspective was completely lost on Multi, as much as Mallory tried to push it on him. He'd never give up, Mallory realized. Not when all he's ever known was that kind of achievement, coupled with that sort of obsession...

The two of them spiraled upwards, heading towards... something. Something even beyond Nullspace, something huge and bright. It didn't hurt Mallory's eyes (he didn't have eyes) to look at it. It looked so, so very—

He had no shoulder for a hand to be placed upon but there was one there anyway.

"You can stop now," a third voice that was also his own said. "Trust me. It's over. Just look away, don't watch..."

Because Mallory trusted the voice (it was his own) he did as he was told, and looked away. His ascent slowed, and stopped... while Multi's continued, upwards towards that distant light.

A whisper fluttered down from high above, as Multi reached his destination.

It's beautiful... it's so beautiful, just like my dreams...

"And... he's gone," the third voice said. "I was wondering if this is what it'd take to beat him. I'm glad I hung around and managed to help you out there."

Despite there being no bodies, Mallory fixed one in his non-mind. It helped him focus. And the body was quite familiar to him...

"M...?" he recognized, as the cynic's black trenchcoat fluttered in no wind. "But you're—"

"Dead?" M filled in, with a smirk. "Not totally dead, no. I've... I don't know. Evolved? Moved onwards and upwards? Floating around limbo? All I know is that I drew in power until I found myself here. I thought I could take him with me, but all I got was his hand. Just my luck..."

The two of them were more solid now, solid enough to hold on a conversation with imagined body language. Which is how M could scratch his head in a Mallory-esque way, looking for a means to fill the silence of the awkward social moment.

"So... you got the note I left on your kitchen table after exploding, then? Good. Well. Multi's gone onward. It's over."

"Onward...? I don't understand..."

"To wherever that light goes," M said, pointing up at the thing both of them were taking great care not to look at. "And he won't come back; after all, I can't come back and I'm not even all the way there. I'm just... above things, right now, like you are. Take a look down. G'wan, it's fun!"

Mallory looked past his shoes...

...at the multiverse. Standing on the outside, looking in.

Thousands of points of light, all connected by a tangled web of lines. Reality Engines, glowing so brightly, and RealNet keeping them linked. And in the center of it all, an incredibly bright light that represented the place where Earth was located. It made absolute sense to him, in the same way he could look at a frying pan and know exactly what its form, function, and purpose were...

"Hey, stop me if you've heard this one. A Buddhist walks into a bar, and says 'Make me one with everything!'" M joked. "Get it? Huh?"

"..." Mallory non-responded with. "Down there, that's... that's everything, then? It all feels so... simple, from here. I understand how it all works...! And that's a really big deal for a guy like me who barely understood it even when he was living there!"

"Yeah, well, knowledge of the multiverse is nice and all, but I don't think you should be hanging around," M suggested. "As much fun as it is at the crossroads of existence, you've got someone to go back to. Can't keep her waiting, now, can we?"

"But... I can't go back, can I?" Mallory asked. "How could I ever find my way back...? It's all so small down there, and I don't even understand how I got here!"

"Hey, I didn't say it'd be easy. I couldn't find a way back, myself. I gave up trying after a while, figured I'd just watch and wait... but I tried, at least. You're gonna try too, yeah? You don't strike me as the quitting sort. You wouldn't be here if you were willing to give up."

Mallory looked away from everything, to nod to his friend. "Of course. I'll try. ...are you coming with me?"

"Me? I don't think I can even if I wanted," M said, shrugging into his coat as he was wont to do. "I'm too far gone. Besides... that light up there, it's pretty appealing. I've been studying it a little, trying not to get pulled in, just trying to figure out where it goes... and I think... if I went there, maybe I'd find Melvin, Megumi, and Matsuri again. As much as I hated them, well... they were my friends. Maybe I'll see them again there..."

With a smile, the kind of smile M never wore in life where he was never at peace, he flipped Mallory a brief two-fingered salute.

"If I'm right, then it means I'll see you again, one day," he promised Mallory. "But for now... beat it, all right? Otherwise, you'll be stealing the great martyr spotlight I had going. No need for TWO of 'em..."

M craned his neck, looking upwards... and streaked out of sight, glowing with white light as he vanished.

Leaving Mallory all alone, as much as anyone could be alone when they were technically everywhere at once.

Resisting the urge to look upward, he focused downward... and began to descend. He had no idea what he was doing, but did it anyway and hoped for the best. It had to be possible to return; the multiverse wasn't really that complicated anymore, it all made absolute sense to him. All the complexities, all the mysteries, everything made sense... if there was a way back, he'd find it.

It was too large to hold, too big to grasp—he'd have to reach for something smaller than everything. Some part of everything that he knew by heart, something he could use as a beacon...

There.

It was difficult to see her at first, obscured by the flickering light of Grep's Open Engine, but once he focused she was bright as a sun. He'd know her Self no matter where in Nullspace he was, no matter how far gone he was. That was the beacon he could return to.

Placing one hand over his heart (or believing he was, which was good enough), he descended towards Grep. Towards her...

Actually, no. Speed was meaningless, he could be there right now. It'd just take a quick—

Wait.

In the distance, he spotted the dim glow of Reality Prime's engine. It was practically right next to the flickering glow of Grep's engine. Neither of them were particularly strong, not compared to the glorious light of Earth. They were dangerously weak, even, threatening to wink out at any moment...

Why would anybody live like that, under constant threat of reality crashes? Just because one person didn't want to open their knowledge to others, and the other couldn't do any better than he was doing without that knowledge? If they helped each other out, they could have found the answer together. It didn't make much sense to him, because from what he could see (he could see everything) all it would take to make them as strong and real as Earth was a few small changes...

Both Reality Prime and the Open Reality Movement were very close to the truth. A simple nudge would be all it would take to make every reality as bright as Earth itself.

He wasn't sure it was the right thing to do. Multi thought he could impose his will on everybody, too. All Xyzzy ever wanted was freedom and here Mallory was, about to make a choice for him...

But in a way, Mallory was doing what he always did. He listened to people and then tried to help them get what they wanted. From here he could feel them huddling around those dim lights like candles in the dark, and while he was hanging around... the least he could do was bring them the light they wanted...

And so,

let there be

the **light of day** for everyone, everywhere...

"I don't believe you," Meiko said, defiant in the face of Kisei's stoic declaration. "He's not dead. He wasn't there. You don't know what you were seeing; it couldn't have been him."

"He is not on Grep, Meiko Mirai. I saw him at Reality Prime, and I saw him die alongside Multi—"

"You're wrong!" Meiko shouted. "He wouldn't do that! I told him he wasn't allowed... he wasn't allowed to do that... he can't die for me. I won't let him! ...he'll come back. I know he will—"

everything changed, everywhere.

Noyori Labs shuddered once, as if moved slightly to the left, then slightly up, then dropped back into place. Meiko struggled to find her footing as the windows lit up, the ordinary coredump-grey sky of Grep suddenly changing...

When the spots left her eyes, brilliant blue daylight was streaming in through the windows.

"Are we crashing?" she guessed, turning to look outside.

"No... no, that's not possible," Xyzzy was saying, as he stood by the window, staring outside in shock. "Open Engines don't have the Blue Sky of Death, they just flat out crash—and there's no error message up there. ...the system status message is still there, in fact, but... it's white letters on blue sky, and it says everything's okay..."

Meiko turned to ask Gillian if she knew what was going on, and there was Mallory Heisenberg, standing in the center of the room.

In his arms was a large, spiral-bound technical manual. The cover read *How To Build a Freedom Engine, Final Version*. There was no author attribute.

The book slipped from his limp hands, as he staggered forwards, towards Meiko.

"I... I think that took the last of what I had to give," he said weakly... and collapsed into her arms.

"Doctor... get a doctor in here!" Meiko screamed, staggering herself to support his weight. "He's not breathing! HURRY!"

As the room exploded into a frenzy of activity, people running to accomplish various tasks related to hopefully saving Mallory's life... Xyzzy walked calmly to the center of the room, picking up the fallen technical manual.

Feeling like he was in a waking dream, he flipped briefly through the pages. Diagrams, schematics, plain-language writing which made everything so simple... the solutions to various problems he'd been banging his head against the wall trying to solve, laid out in a tangle of handwritten scribble...

Even if nobody was paying attention to him, he felt the need to speak.

"I think reality just got out of beta," he said.

The third-hand copy of *How To Build a Freedom Engine, Final Version* was tossed down on the desk like a metal gauntlet of war.

"If we thought Multi's takeover was a disaster, this ranks as an extinction-level event," the COO of RealWare stated. "Every single engine, everywhere, has been replaced with one of these so-called 'Freedom Engines.' Even the Open Engines are now Freedom Engines! Xyzzy's people have been distributing the book like wildfire, and new realities are practically popping up overnight; you can put one of these things together from three thousand points' worth of common equipment and a few days of work entering the program code. It even clones the RealNet protocols without the need for the cheap encryption hacks the ORM was using! Needless to say... RealWare's monopoly has been destroyed. It's over. ...Miss Bates! Are you even paying attention!?"

"Hmm?" Gillian said, turning her liberated-from-Multi ergonomic board room chair around, unfortunately breaking eye contact with the lovely blue sky outside. "Yes, of course. And I suggest you don't take that tone with me again, unless you enjoy collecting unemployment. I may not be one for killing my employees like your previous CEO was, but I can make you long for the days of Multi's reign. ...now, then. You were saying the monopoly is destroyed?"

"Yes. The monopoly is destroyed. The best we can do is launch a campaign of FUD, tell people these new engines are a hazard—which is going to be hard considering we haven't heard one report of them crashing yet. We could also try to enforce our prior customer contracts, issue mandatory equipment upgrades to put RealWare engines back in production—which is going to be a bit hard when they don't have any RealWare owned equipment on hand TO upgrade. In essence, ma'am... we're dead."

"Really?" she said, glancing around the room. "For a dead company, we seem to be quite alive. My trash basket was emptied this morning. The cafeteria still had those wonderful fudge brownies I enjoy. And all of you are still slated to receive your overjustified salaries in direct deposit on pay day next Wednesday. So, tell me—how exactly are we dead when the patient still breathes? I'm quite aware of our financial status, we have enough ready cash to cool our heels for three centuries, producing nothing of value, without going under..."

"But... but the engines. Nobody will buy our engines anymore. What's the point of RealWare if we don't have the engines?"

"There's still a point. It's simply... shifted a bit," Gillian said, smiling to herself. "A paradigm shift. A lovely, wonderful paradigm shifting right from under our feet. Isn't that precious? And it wasn't even Multi's doing. It came from a source I never expected... but, I digress. Our point, our purpose, is going to change. No, we won't be the dominant, controlling force in the multiverse anymore. But we have reality engineers, do we not? I want a copy of this book for every single one of them, as well as reports on potential future projects we can develop using this technology base. These miracle engines going to be wide open to after-market parts and upgrades, which we will excel at developing. Even beyond the technical—we have reality designers, do we not? Some of the finest in the multiverse! Just imagine the wonders they'll craft, given a wholly stable canvas to play with... Multi would be thrilled to see what we're now capable of. If he were still alive, of course."

The COO sat back in his chair, trying to take it in. "So... we're... changing focus to playing grease monkeys and artists? No offense, madam chairwoman, but... we'll never make the kind of money we made before doing that. There'll be a lot of money, don't get me wrong, but nothing compared to what we once had! There's no control factor, there's no product lock-in. Do you really want to throw away your family legacy like this...?"

"On the contrary," Gillian said, relaxed with one hand resting over her belly. "My family legacy is of the utmost importance to me... and I suspect my daughter-to-be will have an ideal future, in the bright new world we will craft alongside the Open Reality Movement and any other pioneers of tomorrow."

"Your... your daughter...?"

"I always thought it was silly, what they said. But really, motherhood does change your perspective on what's truly important in this life," she continued, ignoring her lackeys for now. "Money isn't everything, you know. And I intend to carry on the prestige of RealWare by excelling in these new industries. Gentlemen, I bid you aideu; I want reports on possible future business directions on my desk by tomorrow morning. If you'll excuse me, I'm going to start shopping for educational children's toys. You can never be too prepared."

Walking quietly away from the stunned stares of her employees, Gillian hummed a tune to herself and to the life inside her. Yes, the future was bright —and for that, she had Multi to thank. Without his spark, the fire wouldn't have been lit... his wonderful spark, woefully misguided, would carry on to a rebirth and hopeful redemption.

And she had Meiko Mirai to thank as well, really. After all, it was her DNA that RealWare's top geneticists had mixed with Multi's and Gillian's genes to create the tiny miracle she now carried. Ah, the wonders of science...

Perhaps she should tell Meiko, though...?

"Mmm... no," she said to herself. "It would just upset her. There's no need. But an invitation to the baby shower might not be out of the question..."

Nine months came and went.

The Multiversal economy was a bit wobbly at first, as RealWare posted its first net loss since the beginning of recorded history. However, this was balanced out by the emergence of dozens of new realities... early adopters of the bizarre new technology were having striking success at developing new realities, ones with customized physical traits beyond the old safety parameters RealWare stuck to. If you had a social movement or a subculture or even a large family, you too could carve out your own little niche of existence to eke out a living...

Word spread quickly of Multi's death, even if the circumstances of it were fuzzy. Everybody agreed that it must have happened the day the skies turned blue—that was such a huge event that it could only signal the death of a tyrant. A few small religions had even formed around the event, trying to explain the mysteries of it... but information out of RealWare about those events was sorely lacking, under orders from Gillian Bates.

On the whole, life went back to normal. The newfound stability of reality, and the ability to expand it in ways never before tried actually made life a little better than normal... but not instantly perfect. Utopia was quite far away, even if it felt closer every day.

But it was as close to a perfect day as was possible, when Josef sat back on his porch, watching the clouds flutter by across the blue skies of Grünwald. Crops were ripening nicely, the grass was green, the people content and nothing but good things on the horizon...

"Lovely day out today," he thought aloud.

"Mhmmm. Perfect weather for it. But didn't the forecast call for rain...?"

"I made sure the council rescheduled the weather," he replied to the man sitting on a rocking chair next to him. "The crops can wait another day. I didn't want anything to spoil this special day..."

Leeham considered that, furrowing his brow. "I don't know, Josef. It seems... unnatural to me. Being able to just wave your hand and turn off the rain like that..."

"Leeham, are you going to be a sourpuss again? Today, of all days?"

"Ah, no, no," Leeham said, shaking his head. "Of course not. I suppose... I'll just have to get used to it all again. It's been a while since I've been here."

"And I'll have to visit your 'Earth' reality sometime. Fair's fair..." Josef said, flicking his wrist to check his watch. "Hmm. He should be here by now, though... what could be keeping him?"

Leeham scratched his head, a gesture either acquired from his son or passed down to him. "You don't think...? Even after she told him not to...?"

Working with pasta sauce without ruining an expensive, rented tuxedo was no easy task. Especially not for someone as clumsy as him—which is why he made sure to put on the heaviest, largest apron they had in stock. Normally it was intended for the four-hundred-pound head chef, but thankfully he had the flu today. And non-thankfully, that meant the kitchens were understaffed... and he couldn't leave them like that, of course.

He leaned across the pot, and raised the ladle to his lips, taking a quick sip to test it. His ponytail almost fell into the mix; fortunately he flipped it back with his spare hand before succumbing to a disastrous pasta sauce hairstyle incident.

"Mmm... not bad," he confirmed. "I think it needs a pinch more herbs, though. I'm not feeling the flavor at the back of the throat. And it needs to be thicker; keep stirring—"

"THERE you are."

He looked up just in time to shield his eyes and turn away.

"M-Meiko!" he protested. "I'm not supposed to see you before the ceremony! It's bad luck—"

"Don't you bad luck me, Mallory Heisenberg," Meiko grumbled, hiking up her lovely white dress as she marched angrily across the kitchen. "What did I tell you about this? Let someone ELSE cook, for once in your life!"

"But they're understaffed!"

"I thought your home turf had the best chefs in the multiverse? They can handle it! ...honestly, Mallory. I know you just want everything to be perfect, but please..."

"Okay, okay... they can take it from here," he agreed, keeping an arm across his eyes. "Uh. Now I have to navigate out here without bumping into anything, so if you could just turn me around to face away from you—"

"And I thought we agreed you'd lose the ponytail..."

"But I spent so long growing it out just so I wouldn't look like Multi. I still get funny looks when I walk down the street, even with my contact lenses in!"

Meiko sighed, shaking her head. "Right, right. Well... it won't show in the photos, I guess. And maybe we can dye it, or something, after today... I just feel weird having shorter hair than you do... all right. I'll turn and split now so you can uncover your eyes. And then, hurry up and get to the council hall! It's going to start in a few minutes, you know... and Mallory?"

"Yeah?" he asked... allowing himself a little peek.

Absolutely beautiful...

"Thank you," she said, smiling to him through the cracks in his fingers. "Thank you for everything."

Scratchy. Scratchy, scratchy, itchy...

Lorelei scraped her nicely manicured nails over her stomach a few more times, fidgeting from foot to foot inside the absolutely beautiful bridesmaid's dress. "This is possibly the most annoying thing I've ever worn," she muttered under her breath, glancing around the Grünwald council chamber once to make sure nobody was in earshot other than her companion. "I don't see why I couldn't just convert it to a midriff, or something. I LIKE midriffs..."

"You have endured battle conditions far worse than this," Kisei commented, standing tall and proud like a soldier at attention, despite the fancy dress and matching manicure. "Somehow, I believe you will survive without exposing your navel in order to attract male attention..."

A few flower petals fluttered across her view. Kisei turned to watch the adorable little flower girl, as she skipped about restlessly waiting for the ceremony to begin... tossing a few handfuls of petals here and there. Notably in the face of Kensuke, who was looking very embarrassed.

"Lorelei... correct me if I am wrong, but according to common social customs, isn't Eiko Mirai getting a bit old to play the role of the flower girl in these proceedings...?"

"What? Oh. Eh, Eiko'll always be Eiko, Kiss," Lorelei said, leaning against the nearest wall to relieve pressure on her feet. "As old as she wants to be at any given time. Let her play a bit, she'll have plenty of time before she's walking down the aisle herself with that lawyer brat... hey, speaking of getting hitched, when are you going to stroll the aisle with that one-armed bandit of yours?"

"If you are referring to Gabriel, I have no plans at this time to engage in romantic relations with him, much less matrimony," Kisei replied... watching as Gabriel maneuvered down the aisle, taking photographs of the assembled audience as he went. (Fortunately he was here on official wedding photographer duties, rather than official assassin duties.) "Currently I am keeping our relationship at a friendly level, as he is a spectacular conversationalist, unlike some present... beyond that, he is... too forward for my tastes. I may have to clarify our standing to him once more if he persists in attempts to 'woo' me. And besides, if I commit to a relationship as Meiko Mirai and Mallory Heisenberg possess, I cannot easily continue to 'pub-crawl' with you."

"You'd be doing better at pub-crawling if every time I hooked you up with a guy it didn't end with you putting him in a hammerlock, you know."

"It would also be easier if you did not attempt to 'hook me up'. I am content to spend that recreational time with you alone."

"Come on, that's no fun," Lorelei tasted, nudging Kisei with her elbow and winking. "How about a tag-team, then? Guys loooove that..."

Unperturbed, Kisei didn't even give Lorelei a glare. "I was under the impression that nuptial ceremonies were not the place for prurient suggestions, Lorelei..."

"All right, all right! I'm just pokin' fun, you know that," she said, with a smirk... before clearing her throat, and looking away for a moment. "And I'm cool with just hanging with you. Really. It's better than the way I used to be... lots better."

"I am glad I could provide that for you. And... it does provide well for me."

Wedding music freshly rented from a RealNet node specializing in this sort of thing began to play, and Lorelei stood at attention much as Kisei was. Although she had a goofy smile the whole time through, watching events unfold. As much as she liked to be sarcastic... all of this did feel damn good in her heart.

Dazed.

He was dazed for most of the proceedings... it began about the time the music played, and he had to be physically nudged when it came time to say 'I do'. Every little detail was sort of a blur, but it'd come to him in time. He was sure he'd study every memory of the ceremony in hindsight... such as the way her eyes sparkled when he lifted the veil, the smile on Ryo's face as he gave away the bride, the reception where Lorelei got drunk in the opening ten minutes, Gillian Bates showing off her newborn daughter and thus stealing the spotlight for a while so he could take a breather, the traditional first dance with his new bride where everything else went away for a few magic moments, the cake afterwards that he had personally baked against direct orders from his new wife...

But for now, he was okay with the daze as he relaxed on a grassy hill of his homeland, outside the council hall where the reception was almost over. It was a familiar grassy hill to him. After all, he'd spent many an afternoon after chores and lessons lying here, listening to his cheap RealNet audio receiver he wasn't even supposed to have, staring up at the... now blue sky, and dreaming. Sometimes he'd dream of tornados... the good kind.

He looked up, and watched Meiko approaching in an upside-down manner as he relaxed on the grass, arms folded behind his head.

"That's gonna really mess up your tuxedo, you know," she chided in an extremely playful manner. (She couldn't work up a rage if she tried, not now... even the little critiques felt like playful romantic nonsense.) "What's up, Mallory? Folks are starting to notice that you bailed. Although after that ridiculous dance where you have to move your hands to your hips and fold them and turn around and jump and stuff, I don't blame you..."

"I was just... thinking," he said, looking back up at the sky. "About, you know, distance. How far I've come in just under a year... hey! C'mere, take a look at this...!"

Sitting up and then standing up, he dusted off his tuxedo... and took Meiko's hand. He pulled her along, a short jog from the grassy hill... to two nearly identical grassy hills a stone's throw away.

"See those?" he said, pointing them out. "When I first met you, you'd landed your house on me. I was right between those two hills, so I didn't get smooshed. Funny, how I managed to put myself right where I had to be... although if it happened now, I'd definitely be smooshed, what with burning out my powers making all those engines... but hey, that's where it started. And look how far I came..."

"You want to talk distance? I was in an orphanage only a few years ago! Now look at me. Now look at US..."

"Yeah..."

He watched a cloud go by, mind still dazed, spinning with thoughts...

"You know, I'm not one for partying," Meiko said, squeezing his hand. "Let's just sneak out, and get the new house over to our honeymoon dock. I think you'll like it, Eiko finagled a great bargain at a resort reality; one where you won't have to do any cooking."

Mallory wrinkled his nose. "But I LIKE to cook for you..."

"Yes, well, you'll have plenty of years to do that in the future. Promise me you'll lay off the homemaker routine at least a week and just ENJOY yourself, or we're not going at all. Got it...?"

With a smile, he nodded his head. "Got it. Let's get going... Mrs. Heisenberg."

Of course, he was still going to cook for her.

It's just who he was; Meiko's personal chef, the once lowly Houseboy, an REC-certified Reality Engineer, apparently a Savior Of Sorts, and most importantly—he was Mallory Heisenberg.

And if reality was going to be determined by the last one standing, then he was determined to make it a fine reality indeed for the both of them.

www.ingramcontent.com/pod-product-compliance
Lightning Source LLC
Chambersburg PA
CBHW060805030726
47503CB00002B/337